GW00356879

WHAT THE BIBLE TEACHES

General Editors
TOM WILSON
KEITH STAPLEY

Contributor

JOHN HEADING

John Heading was born and brought up in Norwich, where he was converted and baptised. He has lived in Cambridge, Woodford Green and Southampton, and now lives in Aberystwyth, Wales, where he is employed at the University College of Wales, having written and edited many mathematical books. He has also written in book form many of the Bible study sessions that he has conducted in the assembly at Aberystwyth; these are commentaries on Chronicles, Daniel, Luke, Acts, 1 Corinthians, 2 Corinthians, Hebrews and Revelation. He has written many magazine articles and series, and has produced a *Dictionary of New Testament Churches*. For many years since 1962, he was co-editor of the magazine *Precious Seed*, and has also edited many of the Precious Seed publications: *Church Doctrine and Practice*, *Treasury of Bible Doctrine*, *Day by Day through the New Testament*, and *Day by Day in the Psalms*. He wrote the commentary on Matthew in the series *What the Bible Teaches*.

WHAT THE BIBLE TEACHES

with
Authorised Version
of
The Bible

IN ELEVEN VOLUMES
COVERING THE NEW TESTAMENT

VOLUME 6

JOHN RITCHIE LTD
KILMARNOCK, SCOTLAND

ISBN 0 946351 12 0

WHAT THE BIBLE TEACHES

40 Beansburn, Kilmarnock, Scotland

Typeset at G.T.P., 411 Hillington Road, Glasgow G52 4BL

Printed at The Bath Press

CONTENTS

ABBREVIATIONS

AV	Authorised Version or King James Version 1611
JND	New Translation by J.N. Darby 1939
LXX	Septuagint Version of Old Testament
Mft	New Translation by James Moffatt 1922
NASB	New American Standard Bible 1960
NEB	New English Bible 1961
Nestle	Nestle (ed.) Novum Testamentum Graece
NIV	New International Version 1973
NT	New Testament
OT	Old Testament
Phps	New Testament in Modern English by J.B. Philips 1962
RSV	Revised Standard Version 1952
RV	Revised Version 1881
TR	Textus Receptus or Received Text
Wey	New Testament in Modern Speech by R.F. Weymouth 1929

PREFACE

They follow the noblest example who seek to open the Scriptures to others, for our Lord Himself did so for those two dejected disciples of Emmaus (Luke 24:32). Whether it is the evangelist "opening and alleging that Christ must needs have suffered and risen from the dead" (Acts 17:3) or the pastor-teacher "expounding ... in all the scriptures the things concerning himself" (Luke 24:27) or stimulating our hope "through the patience and comfort of the scriptures" (Rom 15:4), he serves well in thus giving attendance to the reading of the Scriptures (1 Tim 4:13).

It is of course of equal moment to recognise in the exercise of able men, the continued faithfulness of the risen Head in giving gifts to the Church, in spite of her unfaithfulness. How good to recognise that "the perfecting of the saints ... the work of the ministry ... the edifying of the body of Christ" need not be neglected. Every provision has been made to ensure the well-being of the people of God. And every opportunity should be taken by the minister of Christ and those to whom he ministers to ensure that the saints "grow up into him in all things which is the head, even Christ" (Eph 4:15).

At various times in the post-apostolic period, certain teachers have come to prominence, sometimes because they succumbed to error, sometimes because in faithfulness they paid the ultimate price for the truth they had bought and would not sell. Some generations had Calvin and Luther, others Darby and Kelly, but in every generation God's voice is heard. It is important that we hear His voice today and recognise that He does speak through His servants. The contributors to this series of commentaries are all highly-respected expositors among the churches of God. They labour in the Word in the English-speaking world and have been of blessing to many throughout their years of service.

The doctrinal standpoint of the commentaries is based upon the acceptance of the verbal and plenary inspiration of the Scriptures so that their inerrant and infallible teachings are the only rule of conscience. The impeccability of Christ, His virgin birth, vicarious death and bodily resurrection are indeed precious truths worthy of the christian's defence, and throughout the volumes of this series will be defended. Equally the Rapture will be presented as the Hope of the Church. Before the great Tribulation she will be raptured and God's prophetic programme will continue with Jacob's trouble, the public manifestation of Christ and the Millennium of blessing to a restored Israel and the innumerable

Gentile multitude in a creation released from the bondage of corruption.

May the sound teaching of these commentaries be used by our God to the blessing of His people. May the searching of the Scriptures characterise all who read them.

The diligence of Mr. J.W. Ferguson and Professor J. Heading in proof-reading is gratefully acknowledged. Without such co-operation, the production of this commentary would not have been expedited so readily.

T. WILSON
K. STAPLEY

JOHN

J. Heading

JOHN

Introduction

1. **Introduction**
2. **Survey of John's Gospel**
3. **Outline**
4. **Bibliography**

1. Introductory Remarks

In the author's contribution on the Gospel by Matthew in this series of commentaries in *What the Bible Teaches*, he set out certain important matters dealing with (i) the Greek text and translations, (ii) the interpretation of Scripture, and (iii) the name to be used whenever the Lord Jesus Christ is referred to in a purely historical context. The same principles have been adopted in the present commentary on John's Gospel, but they will not be repeated in detail here. For full details, readers are referred to the opening pages of his commentary on Matthew's Gospel. Additionally, the author devoted over eight pages to the "Religious and Political Background" to Matthew's Gospel. The same treatment is relevant to the present commentary on John's Gospel; it is therefore suggested that readers digest these background pages. Since space considerations preclude their insertion here, only a brief summary will be given in the following paragraphs.

The Greek Text and Translations

The Greek text of the NT that was in use for several centuries was "The Received Text" (*Textus Receptus*; TR). The AV was based on this text. But more recently, other Greek manuscripts have been used by editors to produce what are, to them, better Greek texts, and from these are derived the many modern translations of the NT, many of which hardly appear to take a stand on the pre-eminent status of the Lord Jesus. Thus to the sincere believer they are immediately suspect. The present commentary is based on the AV, not with any blind adherence to a particular Greek text or translation, but using amendments when it is thought proper for the sake of the truth.

The Interpretation of Scripture

Parables, miracles, prophecy and teaching on many matters need interpretation. When Scripture presents its own interpretation an author may only comment, without adding his own interpretation. But when no interpretation is given, suggestions must be made that are consistent with the Scriptures and with the context of the passage. Suggestions cannot be dogmatic and unalterable. In the Synoptic Gospels, this is particularly important when parables are interpreted; in John's Gospel, it is important when the miracles (presented as signs) are considered, for signs contain spiritual meanings.

The Name of the Lord Jesus Used in Historical Statements

Although John's Gospel is the Gospel of the Son, it would not be right to use this title in every paragraph—just as we have not used the title "King" throughout Matthew's Gospel. In keeping with the post-resurrection confession, "It is the Lord" (John 21:7), we shall use the title "the Lord" throughout.

Conversational Style in John's Gospel

There is one peculiar feature in style that contrasts the three Synoptic Gospels on the one hand with John's Gospel on the other. The apostle John loved to record conversations or dialogues. The Lord was nearly always at the centre of these dialogues, while the other parties were either the apostles, other disciples, the priests and Pharisees, or the Roman authorities. Occasionally, there are brief dialogues between men and women with the Lord absent. This conversational style pervades John's Gospel, so much so that it is absent only in chs.15,17, the former being an unbroken discourse of the Lord to the apostles, while the latter is the prayer of the Son to the Father. In our commentary we have sought to stress this stylistic feature as clearly as possible, namely, every speaker is identified at the beginning of the relevant paragraphs by inserts such as "The apostles speak", "Peter speaks", "The Lord speaks".

Religious and Political Background

The roots of all the Gospels are found in the OT. Politically, the Jewish people lost their independence when they were carried away into Babylon. By way of interpretation and direct vision, to Daniel was revealed the four great world kingdom of Babylon, Medo-Persia, Greece and Rome. When the NT opened, Rome was the occupying power in Judaea, administered by a Roman governor or proconsul, Pilate being the governor of particular note in the four Gospels. Jewish religion had its two subdivisions—temple and synagogue, both being prominent in John's Gospel. There was only one temple—that built by Herod in Jerusalem, but there were many synagogues. In the temple, the ceremony of the law was practised (containing all the innovations of the priests), while in the synagogues the teaching of the moral law (as interpreted by the Pharisees and scribes) was taught and practised.

There were various groupings in the religious, political and national spheres of society. The Pharisees adhered scrupulously to the law of Moses, avoiding politics, and hating the Romans. The Lord branded them as hypocrites (Matt 23:13-33). The Sadducees were mainly interested in secular power, rejecting the Pharisees' doctrine, and were entirely materialistic in their philosophy. The scribes and lawyers preserved the law, engaged in teaching and administered the law. The Sanhedrin was the Jewish council of highest authority; membership consisted of the high priests, the Pharisees, Sadducees, and scribes and lawyers. The Herodians were more of a political party supporting the Herods, avoiding any dispute with Rome. The Samaritans occupied the territory between Galilee and Judaea; they derived from the inhabitants of the northern kingdom of Israel after its deportation to Assyria in 2 Kings 17. Hence the land that the Lord frequented in His ministry was fragmented by so many divisions amongst men, politically, religiously, socially and nationally. All this must be taken into account when reading any one of the four Gospels.

Links with the Old Testament

Each of the four Gospels is, in its context, richly linked with the OT. As far as John's Gospel is concerned, we read of the OT personalities: Abraham, Jacob, Moses, David, Elijah and Isaiah. The Gospel of John is also rich in references (spiritually or traditionally) to the OT tabernacle and temple, together with the service associated with these structures. Thus we find the manna, the glory, the Lamb, the house of God and the temple, and various feast days (Passover, tabernacles).

The fact that there are four Gospels speaks of their universality in time and space. Thus there are four seasons: spring, summer, autumn and winter. There are four compass directions: north, south, east and west. In Dan 7 there is reference to the four great world empires, spanning the earth of biblical history, and also the sphere of application of the prophetical message throughout time. In the parable of the sower in Matt 13 there are four kinds of soils, the field being the world. Thus the four Gospels are sufficient to record the ministry of the Lord Jesus, available for men throughout the world and throughout the time of opportunity.

Since the early years of Christianity, the character of the four Gospels has been likened to the faces of the living creatures in Ezek 1:5,6,10, "As for the likeness of their faces, they four had the face of a man, and the face of a lion, on the right side: and they four had the face of an ox on the left side; they four also had the face of an eagle". The face of the lion answers to the Gospel by Matthew, the Lord as King. The face of the ox answers to Mark's Gospel, the Lord as the Servant and Sacrifice. The face of the man answers to Luke's Gospel, the Lord in His perfect Manhood. The face of the eagle answers to John's Gospel; far from being seen in connection with the Lord's earthly work, it answers to the

Lord's heavenly character as the Son. Thus we have the four well known statements:

1. "Behold, thy King" (Zech 9:9) —the Lion, Matthew's Gospel.

2. "Behold, my servant" (Isa 52:13)—the Ox, Mark's Gospel.

3. "Behold the man" (Zech 6:12) —the Man, Luke's Gospel.

4. "Behold your God" (Isa 40:9) —the Eagle, John's Gospel.

There are many direct references and allusions to the OT in John's Gospel (not so many as occur in Matthew's Gospel). We list the majority of these in tabulated form below.

Direct quotations

John 1:23 = Isa 40:3 ....(the voice of John the Baptist)
2:17 = Ps 69:9 ....(the zeal of the Lord's house)
6:31 = Ps 78:24 ....(bread given from heaven)
6:45 = Isa 54:13 ....(all taught of God)
8:17 = Deut 19:15 ....(the testimony of two men)
10:34 = Ps 82:6 ....(I said, Ye are gods)
12:15 = Zech 9:9 ....(the King riding into Jerusalem)
12:38 = Isa 53:1 ....(the manifestation of unbelief)
12:40 = Isa 6:10 ....(they could not believe)
13:18 = Ps 41:9 ....(Judas betraying the Lord)
15:25 = Ps 35:19; 69:4 .....(hatred without a cause)
19:24 = Ps 22:18 ....(dividing the Lord's garments)
19:36 = Exod 12:46;
Num 9:12 ....(a bone of the Lord not broken)
19:37 = Zech 12:10 ....(the One whom they pierced).

Allusions, direct and indirect

John 1:51 = Gen 28:12 ....(angels ascending and descending)
3:14 = Num 21:8 ....(Moses lifting up the serpent in the wilderness)
4:20 = Deut 12:5 ....(the place of worship)
4:37 = Mic 6:15 ....(sowing and reaping)
5:10 = Jer 17:21,27 ....(not lawful on the Sabbath day)
6:14 = Deut 18:15 ....(the Prophet that should come)
6:49 = Exod 16:15 ....(eating manna in the wilderness)
7:22 = Lev 12:3...........(Moses gave circumcision)
7:38 = Isa 44:3 ....(rivers of living water)

7:42 = Ps 89:4; 132:11;
Mic 5:2............(Christ of David and from Bethlehem)
8:5 = Lev 20:10;
Deut 22:21 ....(stoning when guilty of adultery)
12:13 = Ps 118:26 ....(the coming of the King of Israel)
12:34 = 2 Sam 7:13;
Ps 89:29,36; 110:4 (Christ abideth for ever)
17:12 = Ps 109:8...........(none is lost but the son of perdition)
19:28 = Ps 69:21...........(the Lord's thirst on the cross)

Authorship

Theologians have written at great length on the subject of the authorship of the fourth Gospel, since the name of John as author does not explicitly appear in the text itself. The arguments are long and involved, embracing faith and unbelief in the various writers. Traditionally, of course, the apostle John has long been recognised as the author, and there are important arguments, both from external and internal evidence. As far as the internal evidence is concerned, arguments are successively put forward that narrow the name of the author down to John the apostle, who does not mention himself by name, only by the phrase as "the disciple whom Jesus loved". Thus the author must be a christian of Jewish origin. Then he must have been a Palestinian Jew, not living abroad. Then he was actually present during the ministry of the Lord, a witness and also an apostle. Finally, the writer was John, the son of Zebedee, the disciple whom Jesus loved. As is the case with so many books in the OT and NT, there are those who refuse to believe that John was the writer, and once unbelief is operative, all sorts of arguments can be deduced to support a faithless hypothesis.

The Apostle John

With his father Zebedee and brother James, John was a fisherman on the Sea of Galilee. No doubt he was first of all a disciple of John the Baptist; then he was a follower, disciple and apostle of the Lord Jesus. Although so appreciative of the Lord's love, yet he was true to his name, one of "the sons of thunder" (Mark 3:17), for he desired fire to come down from heaven as judgment upon the Samaritans (Luke 9:54). Yet this latter character must have been overcome by the love of Christ, enabling him to be chosen by God to write the fourth Gospel in a style that showed forth divine love in its fulness. He, with Peter and James, was specially selected by the Lord to witness the raising of Jairus' daughter, to witness the transfiguration of the Son on the mountain top, and to be near the Lord in His agony in the garden of Gethsemane. In the record, John appears to have been the only apostle at the cross of the Lord Jesus, and to witness His death. He appears only at the beginning of the Acts, Peter and Paul having the dominant position, as apostles to Jews and Gentiles, throughout most of that book. He is called a "pillar" in Gal 2:9.

What happened next is a matter of tradition, suggestion and speculation. He is thought to have dwelt principally at Jerusalem, until the death of Mary, the mother of the Lord. Before the destruction of Jerusalem in AD 70, and after the death of the apostle Paul, he is thought to have taken up residence in Ephesus, where he died at a great age. He saw the rise of heresy that denied the physical nature of the body of Christ, and having been a witness years before of that perfect and true Humanity, he wrote his Gospel and also the first Epistle of John to counter that heresy, and to present positive truth about the Word made flesh (1:14; 1 John 1:1; 4:2-3).

2. Survey of John's Gospel

The object of the Holy Spirit through John was to develop in believers a deeper faith in the divine nature of the Person of the Son of God who had become flesh. All the signs, historical events, prayers, teaching, discourses and conversations (with His own disciples and with men in the world) were selected so as to provide witness to the Son. John would show that the One who came out was the One who was going to enter in again, with a perfect blend of humanity and Deity manifested in between. This is the Gospel of the solitary Son here below, with a few faithful followers. It presents the tabernacle-temple aspects of the One who was dwelling amongst men. This Gospel presents glory, His hour, the sent One from the Father, the relationship between Son and Father, true faith as distinguished from formal knowledge, and the Jewish feasts.

The One who came unto His own is seen as received by the few and rejected by the many. This is the great feature that we wish to stress in our commentary, and to this end we have divided the twenty-one chapters into five sections:

1. The Reception of the Son (chs.1-4)

2. The Rejection of the Son (chs.5-12)

3. The Reception of the Son (chs.13-17)

4. The Rejection of the Son (chs.18-19)

5. The Reception of the Son (chs.20-21).

This great division of mankind between the few and the many not only marked men in those days, but is also characteristic of men today and in all past years.

Chapter 1 presents the Word and the Light as stepping from the eternal habitation; He is seen both in creation and as dwelling amongst men. His identity is established by many names and titles. The witness of John the Baptist identified the Son after His baptism, and then we have the calling of some of the original disciples.

Chapter 2 presents the first sign, and the first adverse reaction of the Jews to the maintenance of His honour. The turning of water into wine established His glory when His disciples perceived that here was One quite unlike any other man. The temple of His body was infinitely greater than the material greatness of Herod's temple in Jerusalem, and even at this early stage in Jerusalem the Lord's thoughts were upon His crucifixion and resurrection.

Chapter 3 shows the Son as the object of faith for eternal life. The dialogue with Nicodemus, showing at first his ignorance as a Pharisee, then presents the Son as lifted up to secure eternal life, though the results of unbelief are also clearly spelt out. At some stage Nicodemus became a disciple through faith. The chapter closes with John the Baptist's final testimony concerning the Son.

Chapter 4 leads to the description of true worship, contrasting with all that the Jews and Samaritans engaged in. The conversation with the woman at the well leads to the Lord's personal testimony that He was the Messiah. Her own testimony in the city led to the conversion of many. The second sign relates to the healing of the nobleman's son, showing the necessity of exercising faith over and above any evidence of natural sight.

Chapter 5 commences with the third sign, the healing of the lame man on the Sabbath Day. This raises hostility on the part of the Pharisees, particularly as they interpreted the Lord's words as implying His Deity. Then follows a long discourse showing the works of the Son in life and in judgment, together with a list of a variety of voices giving testimony to the Son.

Chapter 6, containing the fourth and fifth signs, shows the Lord providing food and protecting His own. The feeding of the 5 000 gives rise to a lengthy discourse, in which the Lord presents Himself as the Bread of Life. But at the end, this truth proves to be too deep, and even unacceptable to the people, so that only the apostles cleave unto the Lord as the Son of the living God.

Chapter 7 shows the development of opposition and division against Christ. He went up to Jerusalem secretly at the feast of tabernacles, before commencing a public testimony in the temple courts. He corrected the Jews' false understanding about the Sabbath Day, spoke of His coming forth from, and returning to, the Father, and about the Holy Spirit. All this brought division as to His Person, and also amongst the Sanhedrin, when Nicodemus took a stand for the Lord.

Chapter 8 teaches that when there is no condemnation, there is also to be no continuation in sin. The Lord testifies to the Pharisees that He is the Light of the world. He draws a sharp distinction between liberty granted by the Son, and bondage caused by Satan, for the devil was in effect the father of the Pharisees. They attempted to stone the Lord, because of His claim to have seen their father Abraham, and to have existed before him.

Chapter 9 presents the sixth sign. Here we have development from initial blindness to a knowledge of the Son, though the Pharisees remained in sin. The man who was granted his sight passed through a legal investigation by the Pharisees, but they could not shake his initial faith, which was then confirmed by the Lord revealing Himself to him as the Son.

Chapter 10 reveals the Lord as the Good Shepherd. The healed man and this

Shepherd are both on the outside. The Shepherd preserves the sheep by giving Himself, and by taking His life again. The unity of the one flock is stressed, together with the oneness of Father and Son. The Jews seek to stone Him for this "blasphemy", but He escaped out of their hands since His hour was not yet come.

Chapter 11 demonstrates the Son's authority over death. We find the Lord's absence and Lazarus' death; then His presence and compassion. The seventh sign shows the glory of God through the raising of Lazarus. When the Sanhedrin heard of this miracle, they hatched a secret plot to put the Lord to death, else the hearts of all the people would be turned to Him.

Chapter 12 deals with events that anticipated the death of the Son of God. His anointing by Mary related to His burial. His triumphant entry into Jerusalem was not to take the throne of His kingdom, but to take the throne of His cross. Greeks wanted to see Him, but the Lord spoke of the seed dying and of the Son of man being lifted up. Isaiah 53 is quoted to show why there was so much unbelief. The chapter concludes with the fact that His mission was for salvation and not for judgment.

Chapter 13 constitutes preparation for the secrets of the sanctuary. The walk must be practically sanctified for entrance into the sanctuary. Then we read of the identity of the betrayer, together with his final departure from the apostolic group. The Son is seen as glorified, and He talks of love, though divine love cannot overlook the fact that Peter would soon deny his Lord and Master.

Chapter 14 is the first of three chapters presenting the secrets of the sanctuary saintward. The Son speaks of His Father's house to which all believers will be taken. He also speaks of the Father seen in the Son, of the promise of the giving of the Spirit, and of His character and work. After this, the Son with the eleven apostles leaves the upper room for the garden of Gethsemane.

Chapter 15 is an unbroken discourse on fruitfulness. This is achieved only when the Lord's disciples abide in the vine—Himself. This is not the result of independent self-effort, but derives from the divine choice. At the same time, sacrificial love is called for, though the separated position of the disciples may well lead to persecution by those who hate the Lord.

Chapter 16 concludes this discourse. It commences with the enemies of God thinking that they perform His will when they persecute His people. Yet the Holy Spirit is seen as working in men's hearts with convicting power. The Lord promises to see the disciples again in resurrection after their few days of sorrow after His death. The chapter ends with the subject of answers to prayer, and with the Lord's anticipation of leaving the world to return to the Father.

Chapter 17 presents the most intimate secrets of the sanctuary Godward. The Son is in prayer, firstly concerning His eternal relationship with the Father. Then He speaks about His own disciples whom He had kept, praying that they may be kept after His departure. He then prays for every subsequent believer, concerning their mutual love and unity, and that they may behold His glory.

Chapter 18 commences with the Son rejected by Judas, yet with the manifestation of His eternal power in His Name "I am". He then seems to be rejected by Peter in his denial, whose lack of power is seen in his statement "I am not". He is then rejected by the Jewish Sanhedrin. Pilate presents an undignified spectacle as he moves in and out to satisfy the Jews' desire not to be defiled, and to Pilate's dismay the Jews request Barabbas rather than the Lord.

Chapter 19 shows Pilate giving in to the demands of the Jewish leadership. The Son is scourged, mocked as King, and crucified. The touching incident of the mother of the Lord and the apostle John at the cross is recorded, after which John as witness gives clear testimony that the Lord's death was real. Two bold, faithful disciples, members of the Sanhedrin, place the holy body in a sepulchre.

Chapter 20 relates the Son's resurrection manifestations in Jerusalem. There are misunderstandings caused by unbelief, as well as Mary thinking that He was the gardener. Then there are the events in the upper room, first with only ten apostles present and with Thomas absent, and then the second time with Thomas present, leading to his great confession, "My Lord and my God".

Chapter 21 concludes with a resurrection manifestation in Galilee. The eighth sign shows that all service should be accomplished according to His will and in His strength. Peter is then questioned three times concerning the reality of his love for the Lord, after which He predicts Peter's ultimate death by crucifixion, while John joins the ranks of all believers who live as anticipating His promised coming again.

This is the survey of the Gospel that now lies before us. The style of the exposition is such that much has been written in great detail, yet space limitations dictated that some topics could not be treated as fully as they properly merit. Yet we believe that every paragraph can be expanded into a sermon in the minds of those able and gifted in that direction. May all readers come to appreciate more deeply the Person and work of the Son of God who is so prominently recorded in this Gospel.

3. Outline

Chapters 1 to 4

The Son—His Reception

I.	*The Establishment of the Son's Titles and His First Disciples*	1:1-51
	1. The Word in Eternity and in Creation	1:1-5
	2. The Light of the World in the World	1:6-14
	3. The Testimony of John the Baptist	1:15-28
	4. John's Identification of the Son of God	1:29-34
	5. The Calling of the First Disciples	1:35-51
II.	*The Establishment of the Son's Authority over Nature and Traditional Religion*	2:1-25
	1. The First Sign: The Son's Glory in Cana of Galilee	2:1-12
	2. The Son's Temple-Body	2:13-25

III.	*The Establishment of the Son's Authority in Teaching and Testimony*	3:1-36
	1. The Son's Answers to Questions Raised by Nicodemus	3:1-13
	2. The Son as the Revealer of Eternal Life	3:14-21
	3. John the Baptist's Last Testimony Concerning the Son	3:22-36
IV.	*The Establishment by the Son of True Worship*	4:1-54
	1. True Water	4:1-18
	2. True Worship	4:19-26
	3. True Witness	4:27-42
	4. The Second Sign: Faith in the Lord's Word	4:43-54

Chapters 5 to 12

The Son—His Rejection

I.	*The Son of God Rejected*	5:1-47
	1. The Third Sign: Healing on the Sabbath Day	5:1-15
	2. The Father and the Son	5:16-30
	3. Witness to the Son	5:31-47
II.	*The Bread of Life Rejected*	6:1-71
	1. The Fourth Sign: The Feeding of the Five Thousand	6:1-14
	2. The Fifth Sign: The Lord Walking on the Sea	6:15-24
	3. The First Question	6:25-27
	4. The Second Question	6:28-29
	5. The Third Question	6:30-33
	6. The Fourth Question	6:34-40
	7. The Fifth Question	6:41-51
	8. The Sixth Question	6:52-59
	9. The Seventh Question	6:60-67
	10. The Eighth Question	6:68-71
III.	*The Christ Rejected*	7:1-53
	1. Before the Feast of Tabernacles	7:1-10
	2. During the Feast of Tabernacles	7:11-36
	3. At the End of the Feast of Tabernacles	7:37-39
	4. After the Feast of Tabernacles	7:40-53
IV.	*The "I Am" Rejected*	8:1-59
	1. The Woman not Condemned	8:1-11
	2. Double Testimony	8:12-20
	3. Who Art Thou?	8:21-30

	4. "My Father" and "your father"	8:31-47
	5. The Lord before Abraham	8:48-59
V.	*The Light of the World Rejected*	9:1-41
	1. The Sixth Sign: The Blind Man Healed	9:1-7
	2. The Neighbours Question the Man	9:8-12
	3. The Pharisees Question the Man	9:13-17
	4. The Pharisees (Jews) Question the Parents	9:18-23
	5. The Pharisees Question the Man	9:24-34
	6. The Son Questions the Man	9:35-38
	7. The Lord Speaks to the Pharisees	9:39-41
VI.	*The Good Shepherd Rejected*	10:1-42
	1. The First Parable	10:1-6
	2. The Second Parable	10:7-18
	3. The Effect of the Two Parables	10:19-30
	4. The Deity of the Son	10:31-42
VII.	*The Resurrection and the Life Rejected*	11:1-57
	1. Before the Lord Came to Bethany	11:1-16
	2. Martha and Mary Meet the Lord	11:17-37
	3. The Seventh Sign: Life from the Grave	11:38-46
	4. The Sanhedrin Plots against the Lord	11:47-57
VIII.	*The Corn of Wheat Rejected*	12:1-50
	1. The Supper in Bethany	12:1-11
	2. The Lord's Triumphant Entry into Jerusalem	12:12-19
	3. The Lord's Answer to the Greeks' Desire to See Him	12:20-36
	4. Unbelief Illustrated from the Prophecy of Isaiah	12:37-43
	5. Summary of the Lord's Teaching in John's Gospel	12:44-50

Chapters 13-17

The Son—His Reception

I.	*The Upper Room: The Son's Activity*	13:1-38
	1. The Son—to be Called Lord	13:1-17
	2. The Son—to be Betrayed	13:18-30
	3. The Son—to be Glorified	13:31-35
	4. The Son—to be Denied	13:36-38
II.	*The Upper Room—The Son's Teaching about the Comforter*	14:1-31
	1. The Father's House on High	14:1-4
	2. The Question of Thomas	14:5-7
	3. The Statement of Philip	14:8-21
	4. The Question of Judas (not Iscariot)	14:22-31

III. *The Way to Gethsemane: The Son's Teaching about Fruitfulness* 15:1-27
1. The True Vine: its Branches and its Fruit 15:1-8
2. Love, the First Fruit of the Spirit in the Believer 15:9-16
3. Hate, the Fruit of the Flesh in the Unbeliever 15:17-27

IV. *The Way to Gethsemane: The Son's Teaching about His Departure* 16:1-33
1. Aspects of Persecution 16:1-4
2. The Work of the Holy Spirit 16:5-15
3. The Lord's Statements Regarding His Death and Resurrection 16:16-22
4. Prayer in His Name to the Father 16:23-33

V. *The Way to Gethsemane: The Son in the Sanctuary* 17:1-26
1. The Son's Eternal Relationship with the Father 17:1-5
2. Prayer on Behalf of His Disciples Who Would be Left 17:6-19
3. Prayer on Behalf of All Subsequent Converts 17:20-26

Chapters 18-19

The Son—His Rejection

I. *The Betrayal by Judas and the Denial by Peter* 18:1-27
1. The Betrayal of the Lord by Judas 18:1-11
2. The Lord Taken, and Peter's First Denial 18:12-18
3. The Lord before the High Priest, and Peter's Further Denials 18:19-27

II. *The Lord before Pilate* 18:28-19:16
1. Pilate out to the Jews 18:28-32
2. Pilate into the Judgment Hall 18:33-38
3. Pilate out to the Jews 18:38-40
4. Pilate into the Judgment Hall 19:1-3
5. Pilate out to the Jews 19:4-7
6. Pilate into the Judgment Hall 19:8-12
7. Pilate out to the Jews 19:13-16

III. *The Crucifixion of the Lord and His Death* 19:17-42
1. Pilate, the Soldiers and the Cross 19:17-24
2. The Women, and the Lord's Death 19:25-30
3. The Lord's Body Laid in a Sepulchre 19:31-42

Chapters 20-21

The Son—His Reception

I.	*Resurrection Manifestations in Jerusalem*	20:1-31
	1. Mary, Peter and John at the Sepulchre	20:1-10
	2. The Lord with Mary in the Garden	20:11-18
	3. The Lord with the Apostles in the Upper Room	20:19-31
II.	*Resurrection Manifestations in Galilee*	21:1-25
	1. The Eighth Sign: The Lord's Provision in Service	21:1-14
	2. Peter's Love	21:15-17
	3. The Apostles' Future Foretold	21:18-25

4. Bibliography

Bellett, J.G. *The Evangelists: being Meditations upon the Four Gospels*. London: G. Morrish.

Brown, David. *The Four Gospels*. The Banner of Truth Trust, 1969.

Best, K.I. *Bible Study Notes on the Four Gospels*. London: C.A. Hammond.

Bullinger, E.W. *The Companion Bible. Part V. The Gospels*. Oxford University Press.

Darby, J.N. *Notes on the Gospel of John*. London: G. Morrish.

Darby, J.N. *Synopsis of the Books of the Bible. Volume III*. Matthew-John. London: G. Morrish.

Davies, Benjamin. *Harmony of the Four Gospels*. London: The Religious Tract Society, 1879.

Gilmore, W. *The Gospel of the Son of God*. Kilmarnock: J. Ritchie.

Godet, F. *Commentary on the Gospel of St. John* (three volumes). Edinburgh: T & T Clark, 1892.

Grant, F.W. *The Numerical Bible: The Gospels*. Loizeaux, U.S.A., 1904.

Heading, J. *Luke's Life of Christ*. Everyday Publications, Canada, 1981.

Heading, J. *Matthew*, in *What the Bible Teaches*. Kilmarnock: J. Ritchie.

Hendriksen, William. *A Commentary on the Gospel of John*. The Banner of Truth Trust, 1959.

Henry, Matthew. *The Four Gospels*. London: Hodder and Stoughton, 1974.

Hutchinson, John. *Our Lord's Signs in St. John's Gospel*. Edinburgh: T. & T. Clark, 1892.

Jamieson, Robert, Fausset, A.R. and Brown, David. A *Commentary, Critical and Explanatory, on the Old and New Testaments*. London: William Collins.

Kelly, W. *Exposition of the Gospel of St. John*. 1898, 1923.

Kelly, W. *Lectures on the New Testament Doctrine of the Holy Spirit*. London: G. Morrish.

Knox, W.H. *The Gospel of John*. Essex: Bookman, 1957.

Lovering, E.L. *In the Beginning: Selected Studies in Genesis and John*. Everyday Publications, Canada, 1985.

Meyer, F.B. *Gospel of John*. London: Marshall, Morgan & Scott, 1960.
Morgan, G. Campbell. *An Exposition of the Four Gospel Narratives*. London: Oliphants, 1956.
Morgan, G. Campbell. *The Gospel according to John*. London: Marshall, Morgan & Scott, 1933.
Plummer, A. *The Gospel according to St. John*. Cambridge University Press, 1906.
Ridout, S. *The Four Gospels*. Bible Truth Library, U.S.A.
Ryle, J.C. *Expository Thoughts on the Gospels: St. John* (3 volumes). London: William Hunt, 1865, 1869, 1873.
Sykes, R.H. *Friend of the Bridegroom*. Everyday Publications, Canada, 1982.
Tasker, R.V.G. *The Gospel according to St. John, an Introduction and Commentary*. London: The Tyndale Press, 1964.
Vine, W.E. *An Expository Dictionary of New Testament Words*. London: Oliphants, 1940.
Vine, W.E. *John, His Record of Christ*. London: Oliphants, 1957.
Vine, W.E. *Leading Themes of the Gospel of John*. London: Pickering & Inglis, 1924.
Wilson, T. Ernest. *The Farewell Ministry of Christ, John 13-17*. Loizeaux, U.S.A., 1981.

Text and Exposition

CHAPTERS 1-4
THE SON—HIS RECEPTION

I. The Establishment of the Son's Titles and His First Disciples (1:1-51)

1. *The Word in Eternity and in Creation*
1:1-5

v.1 "In the beginning was the Word, and the Word was with God, and the Word was God.
v.2 The same was in the beginning with God.
v.3 All things were made by him; and without him was not any thing made that was made.
v.4 In him was life; and the life was the light of men.
v.5 And the light shineth in darkness; and the darkness comprehended it not."

In the first half of ch.1, we have the history of the Son, unknown by man, stretching from "the beginning" up to the time when He was identified by John the Baptist (vv.33-34). John and his testimony are described in vv.6-36, though between v.8 and v.14 we appear to have the testimony more particularly of the apostle John as author through the Holy Spirit. Certainly v.14, "the Word . . . dwelt among us", was the experience of the apostle John, showing that the statement "the world knew him not" (v.10) did not close the door to faith being exercised in the Lord.

The historical order is: the eternal past (vv.1-2); creation (v.3); Gen 1 (v.4); man morally (v.5); one witness (v.6); the Light and Word on earth (vv.9-11,14). Five classes are seen in these early verses: the Word and the Light (vv.1,7-9); the world (v.10); the one witness (v.7); "his own", the Jews (v.11); "the sons of God" by faith (v.12).

1 When we read of "the beginning" we must always ask, The beginning of what? The context must decide. In Gen 1:1 it was the beginning of God's act of creation. In Mark 1:1, it was the beginning of John's testimony. In Luke 1:2, it was the beginning of the ministry of Zacharias. In 1 John 1:1, the beginning refers to the Son's eternal preincarnate Being, that John proved by his own personal experience of Him physically to have become flesh (to counter a popular heresy of the day that denied this). In John 1:1 also, the beginning represents the state prior to the creation, prior to what we know as time in relation to all existing physical things. It was not an act, but it described an existence without a beginning, and without any creation to bring the Word into existence. There was the eternal "I am" (John 8:58), also put in the past tense in Rev 1:8; 1 John 1:1, "which was", namely, "the was-being One" (*ho ēn*). He was "before the foundation of the world" (1 Pet 1:20), while the Son Himself described His eternal Person as "before the world was" and "before the foundation of the world" (John 17:5,24). In that eternity past, He is described as being "with God"—a separate Personality but as One in the Godhead.

The Greek wording of this verse is used by heretics to deny the absolute divine nature of the Son, that He was (and is) One with the Father. "With God" has the definite article "the" attached, but in "the Word was God" (*theos ēn ho logos*) there is no definite article attached to "God". Hence heretics would translate this as "the Word was a God", thereby denying the absolute Deity of Christ. However, in Matt 1:23, we read "Emmanuel . . . God with us", literally "*the* God with us" since the definite article is present in Greek. And also in John 20:28, Thomas said, "My Lord and my God" (*ho kurios mou kai ho theos mou*), literally "The Lord of me and *the* God of me", namely with the definite article "the" attached to "God". These two examples prove conclusively the absolute Deity of Christ, and reduce the heretics' claims to nothing.

The title "Word" was used only in the writings of John:

1. In his Gospel: "the Word" (1:1,14).

2. In his Epistle: "the Word of life" (1 John 1:1).

3. In Revelation: "The Word of God (Rev 19:13).

In the Scriptures, words from many sources (religious, mythological, political, and from nature) were used by the Spirit of inspiration to express divine truth, else in many cases there would have been no words available. (For example, the mythological word "tartarus" used for "hell" in 2 Pet 2:4.) We must not read too much, if any, of the original meanings into such words, else we may be sidetracked beyond the scriptural meanings of such words. Thus the term "word" (*logos*) was a wellknown Greek term. It was half personified already in Ps 33:6, "By the word of the Lord were the heavens made". The Word was that Person of the Godhead, foreordained from eternity past, and sent into the world when the time was come, to be the expression of God revealed to created beings: ". . . he hath declared him" (John 1:18).

2 To state that this One was "in the beginning with God" is a safeguard inserted to avoid heresy that the Word was created. Both He and God within the Godhead existed in the beginning. This existence was not produced by any initial cause—such is unknown in Scripture, for He had "neither beginning of days" (Heb 7:3). Rather, it was an eternal state.

3 This verse is a double statement—the first a matter fact, and the second another safeguard. The revelation of the Word's work in creation is an extension of what is stated in Gen 1:1-3, a revelation that could not have been made there, where we read of God and the Spirit of God. But in our verse we now read of the Word, thereby showing exactly what is implied by "us" in Gen 1:26, namely the Holy Trinity. This truth is developed in the epistles: "by him were all things created, that are in heaven, and that are in earth" (Col 1:16); "his Son . . . by whom also he made the worlds" (Heb 1:2); "the worlds were framed by the word of God" (11:3), that is, by the divine command.

The second part of v.3 is another way of implying that the Word was not created; if nothing was made without Him, then He is excluded from the totality of what was created. Note also that many pre-creation activities also refer to ourselves, such as "his own purpose and grace, which was given us in Christ Jesus before the world began" (2 Tim 1:9; Titus 1:2).

4 By "life", John was not thinking of biological life, rather of that eternal spiritual life, "This is the true God, and eternal life" (1 John 5:20). See also 11:25; 14:6. The Word as Life and Light possessed these characteristics before the creation; light and life were formed in the creation in Gen 1 because of these higher spiritual realities in the Word. The heavenly pattern gave rise to the earthly pattern. The forces between electric particles (manifested as light) and the forces in molecular biology (manifested as life) were introduced in the beginning. It is the experience of these processes that counts, rather than their explanations; ultimately they cannot be explained, for these processes are rooted in the One who upholds all things now by the word of His power (Heb 1:3); when that power is withheld, then all natural things will be dissipated and will vanish away (Rev 20:11).

This Life on earth radiated Light to men—in addition to the physical light with which all are familiar. It is with this radiation of Light, of course, that John's Gospel is concerned.

5 When light shines in absolute darkness, nothing can be seen except the source of that light. If an object is placed in its path, then it becomes visible unless the object is black, when it remains invisible since a black object reflects no light. Such physical considerations have their spiritual analogues. The moral state of darkness in the human heart is described by Paul in Rom 3:10-18, every statement being quoted from the OT. Yet the apostle added in 2 Cor 4:6, "God, who commanded the light to shine out of darkness, hath shined in our hearts, to give the light of the knowledge of the glory of God in the face of Jesus Christ". But if hearts in darkness remain in unbelief, then there is no response to the true Light. These men could not recognise the Son of God as the Light; for example, when the Lord asked whom men said that He was, various speculations were given indicating complete ignorance in darkness (Matt 16:14).

2. *The Light of the World in the World* 1:6-14

v.6 "There was a man sent from God, whose name *was* John.
v.7 The same came for a witness, to bear witness of the Light, that all *men* through him might believe.
v.8 He was not that Light, but *was sent* to bear witness of that Light.
v.9 *That* was the true Light, which lighteth every man that cometh into the world.
v.10 He was in the world, and the world was made by him, and the world knew him not.
v.11 He came unto his own, and his own received him not.
v.12 But as many as received him, to them gave he power to become the sons of God, *even* to them that believe on his name:
v.13 Which were born, not of blood, nor of the will of the flesh, nor of the will of man, but of God.
v.14 And the Word was made flesh, and dwelt among us, (and we beheld his glory, the glory as of the only begotten of the Father,) full of grace and truth."

6 Vv. 6-8 introduce John the Baptist, though the description of his ministry does not commence until v.15. He was "sent from God", and the Lord Jesus was sent from the Father. But what a difference! In the Lord's case, as the eternally pre-existing One He stepped down to be born of a virgin. In John's case his birth was arranged by God through elderly parents, but his existence commenced only with his conception. John was also sent forth into service, in keeping with the OT prophecy, "Behold, I send my messenger before thy face" (Mal 3:1; Mark 1:2).

7 There is always a divine objective in the service of God's people; they should not invent their own service, neither should they run away from God's choice of service. In particular, John came "for a witness". This side of his service is mainly described in John's Gospel, namely in 1:29-34, where he identified Him as the Lamb of God, as the Son of God, and as the One who would baptise with the Holy Spirit, and in 3:27-36. Other aspects of his divinely given service are: "many of the children of Israel shall he turn to the Lord their God . . . to make ready a people prepared for the Lord" (Luke 1:16-17), and "I indeed baptize you with water unto repentance" (Matt 3:11). In his witness, John identified Christ in the flesh as Lamb, Son and the Light, though later the apostles identified Him in resurrection as Lord and Christ. His witness was "that all men . . . might believe", in keeping with Paul's words in Ephesus about John's ministry, "that they should believe on him which should come after him, that is, on Christ Jesus" (Acts 19:4). The word "all" means all those who came into contact with John during his ministry. Compare this with "all nations" (Mark

13:10; Luke 24:42); "in all Judaea . . . and unto the uttermost part of the earth" (Acts 1:8); "unto all" (Rom 3:22; 1 Tim 2:4). This concept that men might believe is characteristic of John's Gospel—1:50; 2:11; 3:16; 4:39; 5:24; 6:69; 7:38; 8:30; 9:38; 10:38; 11:26 are typical examples all under differing circumstances.

8 The Spirit of inspiration issued this disclaimer, so that there should be no possibility of any misunderstanding or mistake. Though John "was a burning and a shining light" (John 5:35), he definitely was not "that Light". His life and testimony were so distinct that people in expectation "mused in their hearts of John, whether he were the Christ, or not" (Luke 3:15). His strict denial of this supposition appears only in John's Gospel, "I am not the Christ" (1:20; 3:28). During the Lord's lifetime, no one claimed to be Christ, though afterwards many antichrists would make that claim, and certainly they will in the future, when many shall say "I am Christ" and shall deceive many (Matt 24:5), and when the man of sin shall claim to be God (2 Thess 2:4).

9 The Greek text of this verse permits an uncertainty as to its rendering. Texts, margins and footnotes allow the variation. The uncertainty resides in the words "that cometh into the world", the verb *erchomenon* being a present participle. The AV refers this verb to "every man", but JND and the NEB refer it to the true Light. (In the former case, the ending *-on* is masculine accusative; in the latter case, it is neuter nominative since the word for "Light" (*phōs*) is neuter.) We prefer the latter rendering, "He was the true Light which, coming into the world, lightens every man", the context being the manifestation of the Light in the world, not men coming through birth.

The "true Light" should be taken with the "true bread" (John 6:32), the "true vine" (15:1), and "the truth" (14:6). There had been physical manna provided by God in the wilderness, and there was plenty of falseness around, and light could be darkness (Luke 11:35). The "true Light" and the "true bread" are the spiritual counterparts in Christ to the light and bread in the holy place in the tabernacle, while the light of glory and the golden pot of manna were to be found in the Holiest of all.

When light falls on a surface, it shows up its reflective power. Moreover, light is sometimes absorbed, and is re-emitted. In Moses' case, after having been in the glory of God's presence, his face shone; namely he absorbed the glory falling upon him and then re-emitted it (Exod 34:29-35; 2 Cor 3:13). On the other hand, if Light falls upon dark and evil hearts then they could not reflect anything of Christ. This is the open manifestation of the effect of Christ upon men; but the Light would possess the complete spectrum, including, for example, X-rays. Visible light touches upon that which is outward, but X-rays touch upon that which is inward. Thus the Lord had the power of introspection, as in the case of Nathanael (1:47), of men in general (2:25), of the Samaritan woman and her past history (4:18,29); truly, "the Lord looketh on the heart" (1 Sam 16:7; Heb

4:12-13). Moreover, it is internally that the Light has "shined in our hearts" to grant us spiritual knowledge (2 Cor 4:6).

10 The word for "world" (*kosmos*) occurs three times in this verse (it occurs five times in 15:19 and three times in 17:15). A glance at a concordance will show that the word occurs far more times in John's Gospel than anywhere else in the NT. It occurs nineteen times in the Lord's prayer in ch.17. The word stands in contrast to the Son from heaven, for usually the word refers to the world of men, and only occasionally to the physical creation. In the expressions "in the world" and "the world was made by him", no doubt there is an element of the physical, but after that the world of men is implied, "the world knew him not". The Lord stood in complete contrast to this world of men, "ye are of this world; I am not of this world" (8:23). This world of men had no knowledge naturally of this One in their midst; faith in the messages of the various witnesses sent by God was necessary for any man to know Him. Their ignorance was demonstrated, for example, by the names that they applied to Him (Matt 16:14). Even the religious leaders knew no better, for they knew not their own OT Scriptures that spoke of Him.

11 The first "his own" (*ta idia*) is neuter plural, but the second (*hoi idioi*) is masculine plural. This is more restricted than the whole world of men. His own things stood not only for the Jewish people, but also for the whole of the Levitical system of worship and service (Rom 9:4-5). There was very little left that could bring pleasure to God's heart. But His own people did not receive Him (except the very small remnant to whom the truth was made known, such as Zacharias, Elisabeth, Joseph, Mary, the shepherds, Simeon and Anna, none of whom is mentioned in this opening chapter). Even John the Baptist did not know Him, until His Person was revealed to him at the Lord's baptism when the Spirit descended upon Him (John 1:33), for "I knew him not" prior to that event.

12 Yet men are changed only by one way—by receiving Him and by believing on His Name. The verb "believe" (*pisteuō*) is the burden of John's Gospel, occurring far more times than in any other NT book. By contrast, the word "faith" (*pistis*) does not occur in John's Gospel, although it is a very common NT word. In this verse, the word translated "sons" is strictly "children" (*tekna*). (This is also the case in 1 John 3:1, 2.) As a child, one is introduced into the family of God, rendered possible through the death and resurrection of the Son, who in 20:17 for the first time named His Father as "your Father". On the other hand, the status of sonship implies dignity, heirship and the spiritual blessing of being able to use the title Father (Gal 4:5-7).

Believers have "power to become" the children of God. The word "power" (*exousia*) means "authority", rendered indiscriminately as "power" or "authority" throughout the AV. The important thing is that believers "become" children of God; they are not always children of God from their natural birth — unlike the Son who was the Son eternally, One who never became the Son, in contrast to the modern heretical translation of Ps 2:7, "Today I have become your Father", and its equivalents.

13 Since these "children of God" had a beginning, the concept of spiritual birth is introduced; the motivation of this birth had to be distinct from any natural origin. Three negatives are given, the last two being the result of "will". These natural concepts have their own unspiritual counterparts.

1. "Not of blood", not based on national considerations. Paul made reference to men of all nations being joined by a common blood (Acts 17:26), no doubt in the sense that all have been derived from Adam. It was not the privilege of only a select nation (such as the Jews) to give rise to believers as the children of God.

2. Not "of the will of the flesh", namely not through the rites of ceremonial religion. In the Epistle to the Galatians, Paul used the concept of "the flesh" as a contrast to the truth of the Spirit as the commencement of the christian life.

3. Not "of the will of man", namely, not through the energies of humanity and its works, for salvation is "not of works, lest any man should boast" (Eph 2:9; 2 Tim 1:9).

Rather, this new birth is "of God", implying a miraculous transformation at conversion. Later, the Lord expounded this truth to Nicodemus, "That which is born of the flesh is flesh; and that which is born of the Spirit is spirit" (3:6). Peter wrote that being born again is by that which is incorruptible, namely by "the word of God, which liveth and abideth for ever" (1 Pet 1:23).

14 This is the last time that the title "the Word" appears in John's Gospel. The contrast is with v.1, namely, the eternal Word stepped into His own creation as being "made flesh". He would take upon Himself that which He had not had before, being able to feel, see, hear and sense as Man without sin, through a perfectly-holy prepared body and nervous system characteristic of the physical creation and so distinct from eternity, yet never ceasing to be the eternal Word. Truly, "God was manifest in the flesh" (1 Tim 3:16).

In this verse, the Son "became" (*ginomai*) flesh, what He had not been before. Similarly, He became a minister of the circumcision (Rom 15:8), He became a "merciful and faithful high priest" (Heb 2:17), He became the Head of the corner (Matt 21:42), he became the Author of eternal salvation (Heb 5:9), and on the cross He became a curse (Gal 3:13).

By saying that the Word "dwelt among us", John was using "tabernacle" language. The word "dwell" used here is *skēnoō*, meaning "to tabernacle", since the word for the noun "tabernacle" is *skēnē* (often used in the Epistle to the Hebrews). The verb appears only five times in the NT, once here in John's Gospel, and four times in the Revelation (7:15; 12:12; 13:6; 21:3). As the glory of God dwelt in the tabernacle in OT times, so the divine Son dwelt amongst men: "let them make me a sanctuary; that I may dwell among them" (Exod 25:8). The glory was manifested in the tabernacle (40:34-35), and in Solomon's temple (1 Kings 8:10-11). But John saw both the moral glory of the Son, and also the physical glory that radiated from His Person on the mountain top. This glory was not hidden within a material temple, but was perceived by men of faith.

The Word was described by John as "the only begotten of the Father", a description that has been given many explanations by expositors. The modern tendency is to translate *monogenēs* merely as "only" in the sense of unique, and of course this is true. In fact, JND's French version has "son fils unique" in 3:16. But evangelicals feel that something is omitted by using the word "only", since this corresponds to *mono* alone, whereas the addition of "begotten" corresponds to *genēs*. The old theory of "eternal generation" does not appeal to the present author, merely pushing the difficulty back to the eternity past, and not explaining anything.

This word is translated "only" in Luke 7:12; 8:42; 9:38, not referring to the Lord. It is also used in Heb 11:17 referring to Isaac, though Abraham had other offspring; there it means that there was no rival in Abraham's affections, for Gen 22:2 adds "whom thou lovest". It is used of the Lord only by the apostle John (1:14,18; 3:16,18; 1 John 4:9). We admit that often words with an entirely human and physical meaning were pressed into use to describe entirely spiritual concepts; too much of the physical meaning must not be imported into the spiritual meaning, and sometimes nothing at all. The corresponding verb *gennaō* is used of begetting, conceiving, and bringing forth in birth, in an entirely natural sense. This verb is used in Acts 13:33, quoting Ps 2:7, "Thou art my Son, this day have I begotten thee". This is a prophetic psalm, and in the context refers to the Son being brought forth in glory and display at the inauguration of His millennial kingdom. In Acts 13:33, a careful reading of the context shows that Paul was referring to the bringing forth of the Lord Jesus for public ministry after His baptism. Thus we believe that the description "only begotten" refers to the time when the Son was manifested in open display to men, particularly to John the Baptist and the other men named later in John 1. It refers to the Son in time, rather than in eternity. His eternal nature had been described in the opening verses of ch.1, but in v.16 the days of His flesh are under consideration. Readers may have other explanations, but when 3:16 is quoted to the unsaved in gospel preaching, clearly they have no understanding of the word whatsoever.

The Word is described as "full of grace and truth". The Son was full in every characteristic; nothing was minimised and nothing was lacking. All fulness dwells in Him (Col 1:19; 2:9). There had been divine grace and truth in OT times, but minimal when contrasted to that revealed in the Son, for He was the truth.

3. *The Testimony of John the Baptist* 1:15-28

v.15 "John bare witness of him, and cried, saying, This was he of whom I spake, He that cometh after me is preferred before me: for he was before me.
v.16 And of his fulness have all we received, and grace for grace.
v.17 For the law was given by Moses, *but* grace and truth came by Jesus Christ.
v.18 No man hath seen God at any time; the only begotten Son, which is in the bosom of the Father, he hath declared *him*.
v.19 And this is the record of John, when the Jews sent priests and Levites from Jerusalem to ask him, Who art thou?
v.20 And he confessed, and denied not; but confessed, I am not the Christ.
v.21 And they asked him, What then? Art thou Elijah? And he saith, I am not. Art thou that prophet? And he answered, No.
v.22 Then said they unto him, Who art thou? that we may give an answer to them that sent us. What sayest thou of thyself?
v.23 He said, I *am* the voice of one crying in the wilderness, Make straight the way of the Lord, as said the prophet Isaiah.
v.24 And they which were sent were of the Pharisees.
v.25 And they asked him, and said unto him, Why baptizest thou then, if thou be not that Christ, nor Elijah, neither that prophet?
v.26 John answered them, saying, I baptize with water: but there standeth one among you, whom ye know not;
v.27 He it is, who coming after me is preferred before me, whose shoe's latchet I am not worthy to unloose.
v.28 These things were done in Bethabara beyond Jordan, where John was baptizing."

15 *John the Baptist speaks*. In Matt 3, Mark 1 and Luke 3 there is given the testimony of John *before* the Lord's baptism, but here in John's Gospel, John the Baptist speaks *after* the Lord's baptism. In v.15 he recalled what he had spoken before the baptism; at that period, he knew of the Person, but he did not know the Person Himself (vv.31, 33). The One who was "preferred before" refers to position and status, the honour and dignity of the Person of whom John was the forerunner. Additionally, by saying "he was before me" John referred to time, even the pre-incarnate existence of the One to whom John would point. Compare Col 1:17 "he is before all things", though here a different Greek preposition is used (*pro* instead of *prōtos*).

16-17 It appears that vv.16-18 are not the spoken words of John the Baptist, but the written words of the writer, the apostle John, by divine inspiration. One reason is that the word "we" appears in v.16, unlike the Baptist's testimony that employs the singular "I" (vv.15, 20, 23, 26, 30 etc.).

This divine fulness relates to the eternal nature of the Son's Person. For example, in Isa 6:2 only the hem of His garments could be in the temple, while the heaven of heavens could not contain Him, such was His fulness. Yet this fulness could be transferred without the Son suffering any loss of His fulness, for He was an infinite reservoir of fulness. After His death and resurrection, the church is spoken of as His fulness (Eph 1:23). Yet we have received this fulness as the children of God; that which can be transferred to His redeemed has been transferred. Life and love are two such examples; His life and His love are found in His fulness first, yet we have received them; see 14:19; 1 John 4:19.

The expression "grace for grace" may appear difficult to understand. Both JND and the NEB translate this as "grace upon grace". This Greek preposition *anti* also occurs in the phrases, "An eye for an eye" (Matt 5:38); "a tooth for a tooth" (Matt 5:38); "evil for evil" (Rom 12:17; 1 Thess 5:15; 1 Pet 3:9); "railing for railing" (1 Pet 3:9). The preposition means "over against" and hence "in place of". In other words, an eye, a tooth, an evil, a railing replace a previous eye, tooth, evil, railing. Consequently, "grace for grace" means a new grace replacing an old grace. This is confirmed by v.17. The old was "the law given by Moses", but the new was "grace and truth" come by Jesus Christ. There was an old kind of grace associated with the law, but the Lord substituted the new grace of the gospel. For example, "thou hast also found grace in my sight" (Exod 33:12, and elsewhere in this chapter), the Greek word for "grace" in the LXX is *charis*, as in 1:16. The same may be said of "grace is poured into thy lips" (Ps 45:2), and "the Lord will give grace and glory" (Ps 84:11). So Moses knew of God's grace so soon after the giving of the law, and no wonder, for the commandments themselves contained the promise "showing mercy unto thousands of them that love me" (Exod 20:6). Even if this grace were valued by men in the OT, we can be thankful today that we have received the grace that has come through the gospel of Christ. Hence the Son is "counted worthy of more glory than Moses" (Heb 3:3).

18 The apostle John would ensure that there was no conflict of thought between God the Father being invisible, and the Son manifest to human eyes. He would reaffirm the truth of Exod 33:20 (the chapter containing many references to OT grace), "there shall no man see me, and live". Paul stressed this fact, "whom no man hath seen, nor can see" (1 Tim 6:16). Yet the Father has been declared by the Son, and this commences openly in John's Gospel in 5:17-20, where the Father and the Son are presented as working together, with the Son doing what He sees the Father doing. The doctrinal climax of this truth is reached in the Lord's words to Philip, "he that hath seen me hath seen the Father" (14:9).

Using the title "the only begotten Son" again, John added that the Son is in "the bosom of the Father". John used this word *kolpos* (bosom) and *stēthos* (breast) to describe the place where he reclined at the last supper (13:23,25; 21:20), the former meaning essentially a hollow thing, and the latter a firm part.

Of course, "the bosom of the Father" is void of natural implications; it represents spiritually a position of nearness in the love of the Father for the Son and the love of the Son for the Father. This mutual love between the Lord and John was seen in the reclining position at table in the upper room.

19 *Priests and Levites speak.* There were two main questions that the religious leaders asked John:

1. Who was John? His answers appear in vv.20-23;

2. Why did John baptise? His answers appear in vv.26-27, 31.

The religious leaders were expecting someone to come, as evidenced by their further questions in v.21. This is quite unlike formal religious leaders today who are not expecting the Lord to come according to His promise. The grouping "priests and Levites" shows that the arrangements introduced by Moses and David were still being followed, but with a difference. In the OT men of faithfulness engaged in these various aspects of tabernacle and temple service, but in the NT the system was but a vain copy, useless to God and to men, with the leaders being lovers of ritual and ceremony rather than lovers of God; as the Lord said, "in vain they do worship me" (Matt 15:9).

20 *John speaks.* In v.8 we have the Spirit's disclaimer, "He was not that Light", but here we have John's personal disclaimer, negatively in vv.20-21, and positively in v.23. They did not ask him whether he were the Christ, but his answer "I am not the Christ" shows that this was in their minds, for at that time men were expecting Christ, and "mused in their hearts of John, whether he were the Christ" (Luke 3:15). The Baptist's strict denial appears only in John's Gospel. Later, it would be easy for deceivers to claim to be Christ, not in the Lord's lifetime, but throughout the ages, and particularly in the end times, for "many shall come . . . saying, I am Christ; and shall deceive many" (Matt 24:5, 23). Note: as men thought that John might be Christ, so it was thought that Christ might be John (Luke 9:7,19).

21 *Priests and Levites speak.* They remained unconvinced that John was but an ordinary man with an extraordinary calling. They therefore try "Elias", the OT Elijah, as later suggested in Matt 16:14. Indeed Elijah the prophet was promised to be sent before "the coming of the great and dreadful day of the Lord" (Mal 4:5; Matt 17:10). In Matt 17:12, the Lord stated that "Elias is come already, and they knew him not". This means, not that John was Elijah directly, but that John would go "in the spirit and power of Elias . . . to make ready a people, prepared for the Lord" (Luke 1:17).

John the Baptist speaks. His clear negative answer makes it impossible to assert that John was Elijah in person. John was associated with Elijah only in the sense revealed by Gabriel to Zacharias.

Priests and Levites speak. They knew their OT Scriptures according to the letter, so knew that a special Prophet was promised (Deut 18:15,18); God's words would be in His mouth. This Prophet appears several times in John's Gospel, for example, 6:14; 7:40.

John speaks. He would claim no honour that he did not possess. He knew that part of the OT that did apply to him, and that part that did not apply to him.

22 A negative answer was of no value to these men, so they explained the origin of their mission to John. There were those who were over them in the Jewish hierarchic leadership, namely the Pharisees and priests. A subsidiary question is appended, "What sayest thou of thyself" (or "about (*peri*) thyself"), not only Who? but What? Apparently knowing who he was would not be sufficient to explain the nature of this person and work.

23 *John the Baptist speaks.* In Matt 3:3; Mark 1:3; Luke 3:4, the synoptic writers have quoted Isa 40:3 in the third person—Luke 3:4-6 provides the complete quotation from Isa 40:3-5. But here John the Baptist quoted from Isaiah in the first person, "I am the voice". The same phenomenon may be noted in "This is my beloved Son" and "Thou art my beloved Son" (Matt 3:17; Luke 3:22).

John provided no self-identity, though Paul did in Phil 3:5; he was just "a voice", not even "a man" (John 1:6). He was just a voice speaking forth the words, commands and warnings of God. Clearly John knew the OT Scriptures very well, as any preacher must. Even naturally speaking, it was clever to be able to quote words from a roll not marked by verses, but all the NT writers could do this, the result of diligent listening, study and meditation, even if they had not handled and read an actual roll. The quotation from Isa 40 comes from the context containing "iniquity is pardoned" and "the glory of the Lord shall be revealed", characteristic of the Lord's ministry. The thrust of John's ministry was the exhortation, "Make straight the way of the Lord", so as to be morally a people prepared for the presence of Christ; there had to be fruit meet for repentance. Moreover, John's personal life had to match his preaching, else this would be hollow and vain.

24-25 *Priests and Levites speak.* This is the first mention of the Pharisees in this Gospel, the last mention being in 18:3. Their opposition to the Lord grew, mainly on doctrinal grounds, until the climax when they sought His death. It is useful to trace the activity of the Pharisees through the Gospels, using a concordance as an aid. They asked about the origin of John's baptism, as if this was the province only of great men, such as Elijah, Christ or that Prophet, for a special religious class according to their way of thinking. This is the same today in many circles—a priestly class of men restrict the carrying out of baptism to themselves, with no examination of Scripture to see whether these things are so. Some expositors inform us that John's baptism developed from a rite that already existed in his day, as if it were rooted in the history of the nation. However, christians are not asked to believe that, since Scripture tells us nothing about any history of this practice. Rather, it was the divine will that caused John to take up this baptism of repentance; it was God who "sent me to baptize with water" (1:33), and it was the Lord who sent His apostles forth to baptise (Matt 28:19). Today, believers who baptise young converts should also realise that they are called upon by God so to baptise according to the scriptural mode of immersion.

26-27 *John the Baptist speaks*. John answered this second major question by humbling himself in favour of the One unknown in their midst. John was in their position once; "whom ye know not" refers to the Pharisees, "I knew him not" refers to John (v.31). Yet John identified Christ the next day when He was actually present (v.29).

As the writer often says, "Good teaching is worth repeating". It appears that John repeated himself, as the Lord often did. For this reference to his unworthiness to unloose the shoe's latchet of the Lord is also found in Luke 3:16. There, it was said *before* the Lord's own baptism, but in John's Gospel it is recorded as having been spoken *after* the (unrecorded) baptism of the Lord. John felt himself unworthy even to stoop down to the Lord's feet, though in 13:5 the Lord stooped down to wash the apostles' feet. In fact, John felt his humility so much that he believed that he should be baptised by the Lord (Matt 3:14), and his constant perception of himself was that "I must decrease" (3:30).

28 The AV states that Bethabara was the place where these events were taking place — a map will show that this was about fifteen miles south of the Sea of Galilee. But other Greek texts and editors of the Greek text, as well as the RV and JND translations, give "Bethany" instead, not, of course, the Bethany on the eastern slopes of the mount of Olives near Jerusalem, but another place with the same name by the river Jordan. Today its position is unknown.

4. *John's Identification of the Son of God*
1:29-34

v.29 "The next day John seeth Jesus coming unto him, and saith, Behold the Lamb of God, which taketh away the sin of the world.

v.30 This is he of whom I said, After me cometh a man which is preferred before me: for he was before me.

v.31 And I knew him not: but that he should be made manifest to Israel, therefore am I come baptizing with water.

v.32 And John bare record, saying, I saw the Spirit descending from heaven like a dove, and it abode upon him.

v.33 And I knew him not: but he that sent me to baptize with water, the same said unto me, Upon whom thou shalt see the Spirit descending, and remaining on him, the same is he which baptizeth with the Holy Ghost.

v.34 And I saw, and bare record that this is the Son of God."

29 This paragraph will show how John knew that this One (a relative according to the flesh) was the Son of God: this took place at the Lord's baptism when the Spirit descended like a dove. When v.29 opens, this revelation had already taken place; John knew Him not only as the Son of God but also as the Lamb of God.

John the Baptist speaks. It was when the Lord was "coming unto him" that John burst out in public testimony. No response is recorded in the paragraph. Clearly this took place after the temptation of the Lord. Here John testified because of the *work* of the Lamb; in 1:36 he testified because of the *walk* of the Lamb. Before the Lord's baptism, John had known Him as a natural relative, morally perfect, sanctified and a different Man, yet he did not know His Person. He then knew Him as the Son of God because of divine revelation, but we are not told how he knew Him as the Lamb. John knew the OT Scriptures, and he could put "two and two together". John was in the good of the nature of the OT Passover, knowing of the purity demanded of the lamb and its use in deliverance from bondage (Exod 12:5). The perfect Man and the Son of God alone answered to the original Passover. Moreover, he knew the prophecy of Isaiah (40:3-5), so he must have known ch.53 as well, where the perfect Servant is seen as "a lamb" (v.7) to be wounded for transgressions (v.5). Only the Son of God truly fitted this prophecy. By "the sin of the world", John did not mean that everyone would be saved; his preaching of judgment and wrath excluded that thought (Matt 3:10). The availability of salvation is "unto all", but it is only accepted by "all them that believe" (Rom 3:22). The apostle John made the same distinction: propitiation was for the sins of the whole world (1 John 2:2), yet forgiveness and cleansing come through confession and faith (1:9). Note that the word "sin" refers to the root, while "sins" refer to the fruit.

30-31 The Lamb is the fulfilment of what John had declared previously in v.15. No one could be other than humble in contemplating the Lamb of God. Yet here John declared the object of his mission to Israel. This had three main parts:

1. to prepare the way of the Lord, by gaining a prepared people through repentance and baptism,

2. to cause the Son of God to be identified to Israel,

3. to disappear (through violence) from this scene when his mission was ended, so that he, in the minds of the people, should not be a rival to the Lord and His own ministry.

John's baptism in water would lead to a stupendous revelation when the Lord submitted Himself to John's baptism.

32-33 John's testimony took place *after* the Lord's baptism, though he had received a message from God *before* this baptism. John saw something happen that took place at no other baptism — he saw "the Spirit descending from heaven like a dove", and remaining upon Him. Only John could see the Spirit in this form, and only John heard the voice from heaven. The Lord's baptism provided the forum for this event, and John was waiting for it. Others confessed their sin when they were baptised, but here the voice expressed pleasure in His Son. Note that other emblems of the Spirit are used in Scripture, such as:

1. Dove —His gentle and tender ministry.
2. Dew —His refreshing and fruitful ministry.
3. Fire —His penetrating power and testing ministry.
4. Water—His life-giving and productive ministry.
5. Wind —His sovereign and irresistible ministry.
6. Oil —His sanctifying ministry.

In v.33, the word "thou" shows that John alone saw the Spirit descending. And the Spirit came upon that unique One, concerning whom John heard the voice from heaven, "This is my beloved Son, in whom I am well pleased" (Matt 3:17). By this means John knew that this One was the Son of God, and also knew that it was He who would baptise with the Holy Spirit. He had said previously that the One coming after him would baptise with the Holy Spirit (Matt 3:11); now he knew who this would be. Not that the Son had not had the Spirit before—that would have been by measure, and the Son possessed the Spirit not by measure (3:34). Moreover, it was the eternal Spirit who moved in the experience of the Son (Heb 9:14). Rather, the Spirit descended (i) to identify the Son to John, and (ii) to send Him forth in service (Luke 4:1,14, 18).

Of course, the Spirit is also seen as active in other spheres: in relation to the OT people of God (2 Sam 23:2; 1 Pet 1:11; 2 Pet 1:21), to the church (Acts 2:4), to individual believers (1 Cor 6:19), and will be equally active in a future day (Joel 2:28).

34 John did not keep this holy information to himself; his testimony now centred not only on the Lamb, but also on the Son. This mellowed his ministry considerably, when contrasted with the thunder of Luke 3:7-14. Paul, too, testified to the Jews concerning the Son immediately after his conversion (Acts 9:20).

5. *The Calling of the First Disciples* 1:35-51

v.35 "Again the next day after John stood, and two of his disciples;
v.36 And looking upon Jesus as he walked, he saith, Behold the Lamb of God!
v.37 And the two disciples heard him speak, and they followed Jesus.
v.38 Then Jesus turned, and saw them following, and saith unto them, What seek ye? They said unto him, Rabbi, (which is to say, being interpreted, Master,) where dwellest thou?
v.39 He saith unto them, Come and see. They came and saw where he dwelt, and abode with him that day: for it was about the tenth hour.
v.40 One of the two which heard John *speak*, and followed him, was Andrew, Simon Peter's brother.
v.41 He first findeth his own brother Simon, and saith unto him, We have found the Messiah, which is, being interpreted, the Christ.
v.42 And he brought him to Jesus. And when Jesus beheld him, he said, Thou art Simon the son of Jona: thou shalt be called Cephas, which is by interpretation, A stone.
v.43 The day following Jesus would go forth into Galilee, and findeth Philip, and saith unto him, Follow me.
v.44 Now Philip was of Bethsaida, the city of Andrew and Peter.
v.45 Philip findeth Nathanael, and saith unto him, We have found him, of whom Moses in the law, and the prophets, did write, Jesus of Nazareth, the son of Joseph.
v.46 And Nathanael said unto him, Can there any good thing come out of Nazareth? Philip saith unto him, Come and see.
v.47 Jesus saw Nathanael coming to him, and saith of him, Behold an Israelite indeed, in whom is no guile!
v.48 Nathanael saith unto him, Whence knowest thou me? Jesus answered and said unto him, Before that Philip called thee, when thou wast under the fig tree, I saw thee.
v.49 Nathanael answered and saith unto him, Rabbi, thou art the Son of God; thou art the King of Israel.
v.50 Jesus answered and said unto him, Because I said unto thee, I saw thee under the fig tree, believest thou? Thou shalt see greater things than these.
v.51 And he saith unto him, Verily, verily, I say unto you, Hereafter ye shall see heaven open, and the angels of God ascending and descending upon the Son of man."

35-37 The word of truth, as living, now spreads out to gain believers on the Son and Lamb of God. We shall notice the following:

1. Andrew and another (vv.35-39) through John the Baptist;

2. Peter (vv.40-42) through his brother Andrew;

3. Philip (vv.43-44) through the Lord Jesus;

4. Nathanael (vv.45-51) through Philip.

This verse effectively terminates an era, that of "his" disciples (see 3:25; Matt 11:2; Luke 5:33). Thus the apostles never had personal disciples; no believer today is a disciple of another believer, for the Lord calls us "my disciples" (15:8). False discipleship is seen in Acts 20:30.

John the Baptist speaks. The walk of Jesus caused John to exclaim again, "Behold the Lamb of God" — with the intention of gaining disciples for the Lord, to form a chain of testimony that would grow throughout the region. These five simple words (there are five words in the Greek) were sufficient to commence the chain of testimony; as Paul wrote, "I had rather speak five words" (1 Cor 14:19). By this testimony John knew that he would lose his own followers, but this was a small price to pay that the Lord might increase.

Of these two disciples, Andrew was one. The other is not named: it may have been John the writer of the Gospel, since he always referred to himself in an oblique way. The sincerity and convicting power of the preacher were sufficient. Through experience, they had trusted the words of John the Baptist in the past, so now their trust avoided argument (as Nathanael in v.46), enabling them to follow the Lamb immediately.

38-39 *The Lord speaks.* Clearly the Lord went before in a position of preeminence, so He had to turn to see the two disciples following. The act of following Him is not some blind rite, but sincerity draws forth a response from the Lord, for those who seek shall find, and it shall be opened to those who knock. In fact, the Lord would seek the motives of all potential followers, in this case by asking "What seek ye?", as if they were seeking something rather than someone. Mixed motives are found in Luke 9:57-62.

The two disciples speak. By calling Him "Rabbi" (Teacher) they indicated their willingness to learn (for this title means "teacher", *didaskalos*, as the apostle interpreted). (Note: in 3:26, John the Baptist's disciples called him "Rabbi".) It is remarkable that these two men were able to call the Lamb by the title "Master" (Teacher). Had they known Him in an ordinary sense before, perhaps listening to Him, but not knowing who He was? Certainly a readiness to hear is a blessing, for it leads to the removal of ignorance. However, their question "where dwellest thou?" was not concerned with an amplification of His title "Lamb". We know that He dwells in the eternal light, in eternity, on the throne on high, in the Father's heart, in the church, and in the hearts of individual believers.

The Lord speaks. "Come and see" was the first invitation given by the Lord in John's Gospel. "Come unto me" (Matt 11:28) is the more usual invitation, for "Come and see" is unique, in the sense that here the Lord offered hospitality; usually the reverse was the case, when men and women offered Him hospitality, for He had not where to lay His head — for example, He found hospitality in the homes of Mary and Martha, and of Zacchaeus.

So they abode with Him that day — namely that night until the following day (v.43). Effectively, we have here in principle the first local church, for with the

Lord there were Andrew, the other disciple, and Peter who evidently was there that night, in keeping with the Lord's words, "where two or three are gathered together in my name, there am I in the midst of them" (Matt 18:20).

40-42 Andrew, one of John the Baptist's disciples, is named here for the first time, and so is Simon Peter, even before he had been given his special name by the Lord. Naturally, Simon and Andrew had worked together as brethren in one family; later Peter and John would work together spiritually as brethren in the family of God (Acts 3:1).

Andrew speaks. Andrew's testimony was that they had found the Messiah, namely, the Christ. This means "the Anointed One", the Hebrew and Aramaic forms being transliterated into Greek as Messias, though the proper Greek word is Christ (*messias* and *christos*). The OT is full of the promise of the Messiah, and men were expecting His coming (Luke 3:15). But how did Andrew know that the Lamb was also the Messiah? No doubt this was included in John the Baptist's teaching, but how did John know? Either by God speaking to him as in v.33, or he associated the anointing by the Spirit with the anointing necessary for One to be the Messiah (the Anointed One). So Simon knew the Christ by the testimony of his brother; later in Matt 16:15-17 he knew this fact by revelation from the Father.

The Lord speaks. Upon seeing Simon, the Lord implied that He knew him and also his father's name, even before being introduced by Andrew (see v.48). He was given a new name that would suit the purpose for which God would choose him (just as Abram was changed to Abraham; Saul to Paul, and other cases). His new name Cephas is from the Aramaic, its Greek form being *Petros*, meaning a stone. The name is not to be confused with the similar Greek word *petra* meaning a rock, as in Matt 7:24. The realisation of this difference prevents the identification of Peter with the "rock" (*petra*) in Matt 16:18. Peter was going to be small, although impetuous and powerful.

Peter's occupation of fishing and his discipleship can be listed as follows:

1. In John 1:42 the Lord did not say "Follow me" when Andrew drew him away from his fishing to be brought to the Messiah. It is as if He would test the faithfulness of Peter to see if he would follow Him.

2. In Matt 4:18 He found Peter fishing again by the Sea of Galilee. The Lord said, "Follow me", and he would be made a fisher of men. Again, Peter left his fishing, and followed Him.

3. In Luke 5:1-11 Peter had returned to his fishing again. Having caught nothing, and having seen the miraculous catch of fish, he confessed to being a sinful man. So he forsook all and followed Him.

4. In John 13:36 the Lord announced to Peter that he could not follow the

Lord there and then. Stating that he would follow the Lord even unto death, he soon forsook Him and fled, and shortly afterwards denied Him.

5. In John 21:3 after the Lord's resurrection, Peter decided to go fishing in the Sea of Galilee so familiar to him. Only when John said, "It is the Lord" did Peter know who was standing on the shore. In the final conversation that ensued, the Lord predicted Peter's ultimate death by crucifixion, adding "Follow thou me" when Peter asked what would happen to John.

6. In the Acts Peter never returned to fishing again, following the Lord until his decease "as our Lord Jesus Christ hath showed me" (1 Pet 1:14).

43-44 Day follows day in this record, the next day in the series being in 2:1. The previous events must have taken place relatively near the north of the Sea of Galilee, so that a quiet day's walk would bring them to these northern towns. A balance is maintained as to who finds new disciples. In v.37 the two men found the Lord themselves. In v.41 a disciple is used as the agent. But here in v.43 the Lord Himself finds the new disciple.

The Lord speaks. "Follow me" is simple and explicit; would that converts could be gained today by such words. So Philip became the fourth apostle to be called during these days, assuming that John was implied in v.37.

In v.44, a little geography and background are provided. Bethsaida was a town on the north-east coast of the Sea of Galilee, while Capernaum was on the north-west. Peter appears to have had homes in both places.

Apart from being named in the various lists of the apostles (Matt 10:3; Mark 3:18; Luke 6:14; Acts 1:13) Philip appears in four events:

1. his call and early testimony (1:43-48);

2. his testing about obtaining bread (6:5-7);

3. being involved with the Greek's enquiry to see Jesus (12:21-22);

4. his question to be shown the Father (14:8-9).

45 *Philip speaks.* The name Nathanael means "gift of God", and this man is mentioned only here and in 21:2. He is thought to have been one of the apostles, particularly Bartholomew (through circumstantial evidence), whose name is placed next to that of Philip in the lists of the apostles recorded in the three Synoptic Gospels (see above), though not in Acts 1:13. Philip's statement "We have found him" is in everyday language, since strictly Philip had been found by the Lord. Philip had already learnt a lot about the Lord. Spiritually he recognised Him as the One predicted by Moses and the prophets (Luke 24:27, 44). Naturally, he had learnt that His name was Jesus (meaning Saviour), that

He was "of Nazareth" (a despised and lowly place) with no reference to Bethlehem the town of His birth, and that he was "the son of Joseph", with no mention being made of His mother who was still alive.

46 *Nathanael speaks.* He was of an initially mild argumentative character. Without further enlightenment, he held to the traditional assessment of Nazareth, and could see no work of God arising therefrom.

Philip speaks. "Come and see" is an invitation to the formation of faith. By themselves the words of a preacher do not constitute faith; there must be a spiritual movement to the Lord so that the sight of faith may be formed.

47 *The Lord speaks.* Being divine, the Lord had that capacity to assess character. The word "indeed" means "truly" (*alēthōs*). He was therefore a special Israelite, distinct from the majority around him, a man of moral uprightness and a man susceptible to faith. As Paul wrote, "they are not all Israel, which are of Israel" (Rom 9:6). He was a man who valued the covenant, the promises and the OT. Moreover, "no guile" implies that he was open, with no secret cunning devices as Jacob before him had.

48 *Nathanael speaks.* He may have thought that Philip had previously told the Lord about him, so asked the question "Whence knowest thou me?" to clear the matter up.

The Lord speaks. The Lord used the occasion to introduce the miraculous element, knowing that this would induce faith and confession in a true Israelite (in many others, miracles would not produce faith). The word "Before" proved to Nathanael that the Lord did not rely upon human testimony concerning men (note His use of this word in 8:58; 13:19; 14:29). The Lord's statement shows that He knew details of Nathanael's occupation, for all things are open to Him (Heb 4:12-13). The reference to the "fig tree" may well be prophetic, but normally to sit down under one's fig tree implied well-being, safety and prosperity over an extended period of time (1 Kings 4:25 etc.). The fact that the fig tree contains prophetic overtones is seen in Luke 21:29-31.

49 *Nathanael speaks.* Faith was suddenly formed. He linked the miraculous with Philip's statement regarding the OT prophecies. His reply linking "the Son of God" and "the King of Israel" showed that he knew the OT well enough to make this connection. For example, "I set my king upon my holy hill of Zion . . . Thou art my Son" (Ps 2:6-7). This is the first testimony in John's Gospel regarding His Person made directly to the Lord; see 6:69; 11:27; 20:28.

This confession of the Lord as King was accepted, for He would accept such a testimony of Kingship only when uttered in faith. Later, men tried to make Him King by force (6:15) but He could not accept this, since it really arose through unbelief. By contrast, God will have to use force when He introduces His King into the world at the commencement of His millennial reign.

Note the three ascriptions to the Lord's Person in ch.1, and how men would prefer the opposite at His trial and crucifixion:

1. Lamb (v.36). Men will prefer the Passover lambs instead (18:28).

2. Son of God. Men would prefer Barabbas (18:40), meaning "son of father".

3. King of Israel. Men would prefer Caesar in Rome (19:15).

50-51 *The Lord speaks.* This knowledge of character would lead to many wonderful miracles, which in turn would lead to His kingdom in glory. Perhaps Nathanael had been meditating on the OT, for in Micah 4:4 there would be millennial safety under a fig tree. The Lord would lead from Ps 2 to Ps 8, where the "son of man" is seen in overall control of the universe. The title "Son of man" was the Name by which He referred to Himself; it refers to His sufferings, and to the glory that should follow. When He will be on earth in kingdom glory, the angels will maintain a special communication with heaven, marking Him out as unique amongst His subjects in that day; see Gen 28:12.

II. The Establishment of the Son's Authority over Nature and Traditional Religion (2:1-25)

1. *The First Sign: The Son's Glory in Cana of Galilee* 2:1-12

v.1 "And the third day there was a marriage in Cana of Galilee; and the mother of Jesus was there:
v.2 And both Jesus was called, and his disciples, to the marriage.
v.3 And when they wanted wine, the mother of Jesus saith unto him, They have no wine.
v.4 Jesus saith unto her, Woman, what have I to do with thee? Mine hour is not yet come.
v.5 His mother saith unto the servants, Whatsoever he saith unto you, do *it*.
v.6 And there were set there six waterpots of stone, after the manner of the purifying of the Jews, containing two or three firkins apiece.
v.7 Jesus saith unto them, Fill the waterpots with water. And they filled them up to the brim.
v.8 And he saith unto them, Draw out now, and bear unto the governor of the feast. And they bare *it*.
v.9 When the ruler of the feast had tasted the water that was made wine, and knew not whence it was: (but the servants which drew the water knew;) the governor of the feast called the bridegroom,
v.10 And saith unto him, Every man at the beginning doth set forth good wine; and when men have well drunk, then that which is worse: *but* thou hast kept the good wine until now.

v.11 This beginning of miracles did Jesus in Cana of Galilee, and manifested forth his glory; and his disciples believed on him.
v.12 After this he went down to Capernaum, he, and his mother, and his brethren, and his disciples: and they continued there not many days."

In Acts 2:22, Peter spoke of the "*miracles* and wonders and *signs*" that God did by Jesus of Nazareth. It is therefore important to see where the actual words "miracles" and "signs" appear in the four Gospels. There are two distinct Greek words involved, *dunamis* and *sēmeion*. The former means "power" and the latter "sign". In Matthew, Mark and Luke, when referring to the deeds of the Lord Jesus, this first word (*dunamis*) is often translated "mighty works", and we could rightly substitute "miracles"; the word is translated "miracle" only once (Mark 9:39) but not referring to the Lord. *Dunamis* does not appear in John's Gospel. The second word (*sēmeion*) always appears as "sign" or "signs" in Matthew, Mark and Luke, except in Luke 23:8 where "miracle" appears in the AV; neither is the word used in the sense of "miracle", rather of events to which a distinct supernatural meaning must be attached. In John's Gospel, only the word *sēmeion* is used, translated "miracle, miracles" thirteen times, and "sign, signs" four times. But John's objective is to present all the miracles that he records as signs rather than miracles. In other words, the Spirit requires us to look beyond the actual works of power, so as to see distinct spiritual meanings to which the events were pointing. Hence in 2:11 John writes of "the beginning of the signs" that Jesus accomplished.

In ch.1, the Son's Person is made known to the few men who became His disciples. In ch.2, His power, glory and authority are made known, with a reference to His death and resurrection that would be accomplished in three years' time, though this implication was hidden from the wise and the prudent. Two events are recorded.

1. In the first miracle or sign, water was turned into wine (vv.1-12); the actual event constituted the miracle, but as a sign the event looked forward to its repercussions (v.11). These were that His glory (mentioned in 1:14) should be manifested, and that His disciples should believe on Him in an enhanced way.

2. We then have the cleansing of the temple, and "the temple of his body" (v.21). We may say that this event was also a sign, though not stated to be one, and this temple-cleansing was not a miracle. For the Lord used the event to speak figuratively of His death and resurrection, after which the disciples' faith was further enhanced, for then "they believed the scripture, and the word which Jesus had said" (v.22).The object of John's record of the signs was the formation and development of faith, "that Jesus is the Christ, the Son of God" (20:30-31).

In (1), the wine, provided by men, had been exhausted by men. The Lord provided His new version of the wine. In (2), the sacrifices, provided by men, had been thrown out by the Son. He then spoke of the new version of sacrifice — His body to be destroyed in death.

The first sign was also to demonstrate the necessity of change, and that the Son had power to effect that change. He could change things naturally (as in the case of the water), and He could change things spiritually, as in the case of His temple-body raised on the third day (v.19), and as in the case of the new birth (3:4-7). The spiritual change would be from Jewish ritual to joy in the Spirit of God, from temple-formalism to the reality of His body.

1 John stresses that this event took place on "the third day". The commencement of this series of days occurs in 1:19-28, where we read of John's humility and his denial that he was anything other than "the voice of one crying in the wilderness". The first day was "the next day" (1:29, 35), namely John's identification of the Son of God, and his testimony of the Lamb of God that led to the call of the first disciples. The second day was "the day following" (1:43), when further disciples were called. Finally, the third day was the day of this marriage in Cana. We need not be surprised at this, since the sign speaks of newness of life through a divine miracle, necessitating resurrection.

Cana was a village a few miles north of Nazareth; its exact location is uncertain. Capernaum (v.12) was situated about 22 miles north-east of Nazareth, lying on the northern shore of the Sea of Galilee. Cana was the home of Nathanael (21:2). Moreover, it was at Cana that the Lord accomplished a "miracle at a distance", for it was there that He healed the nobleman's son who was sick at Capernaum many miles away (4:46). In John's Gospel, Cana is always known as "Cana of Galilee" (2:1, 11; 4:46; 21:2). Galilee was a province separated from Judaea by Samaria; the first three Gospels largely trace the Lord's ministry in Galilee, while John traces His ministry in Judaea and Jerusalem. It was named a few times in the OT (Josh 20:7; 1 Kings 9:11; Isa 9:1); the prophet Jonah originated from Galilee (2 Kings 14:25). In NT times, this Roman province was governed by Herod the Great, Herod Antipas and Herod Agrippa (Luke 3:1).

2 We have here the presence of the Lord Jesus at a marriage. The bride and bridegroom must have been friends, or even relations, of Mary, since she was present. Joseph's name does not occur, as if he were no longer alive when the Lord commenced His ministry. Mary, as the natural mother of Jesus, appears only as a background character after the Lord's birth; she was present during the initial stages of the crucifixion (John 19:25-27), and she was in the upper room with the disciples after the ascension (Acts 1:14). Clearly the Lord's first disciples had been immediately received into the family circle, since they had been called by the Lord only one or two days previously.

The presence of the Lord is a mark of a true marriage, as distinct from the many hypocritical marriage services that take place so easily in religious circles today, where bride and bridegroom seem to treat God as a kind of infrequent convenience and advantage—this is not the attitude of faith. The marriage feast followed traditional customs: the feast was usually held in the bridegroom's home (Matt 22:1-10), sometimes at night (Matt 25:6); the refusal of an invitation was regarded as an insult (Matt 22:7).

The OT opens with a God-formed union — He was there, and Adam and Eve were the work of His hands. The NT closes with the "Lamb's wife" and the bride (Rev 19:7; 21:2,9). In between, we read of all sorts of strange relationships. In Gen 19, there are two women with the same father and husband! There are two sons with the same father and grandfather! In Rev 17, the religious woman "Mystery, Babylon the Great" will have effectively married the whole world. Needless to say, the Lord is not present under such immoral and idolatrous circumstances. Nor can He be there if any should seek to be espoused to another husband (2 Cor 11:1-4) apart from Himself, or to a sinful world and its pleasures. Christian marriage should be wholly in keeping with the divine purpose for Christ and the church (Eph 5:25).

3 *The mother of Jesus speaks*. A crisis had arisen in the organisation of the wedding feast; it was normally expected that the best wine would be drunk first, followed by wine of lesser quality. However, all had been consumed. Strictly, the crisis was not for Mary to solve. So when the mother of Jesus said to Him, "They have no wine", we may ask whether this was mere casual conversation on Mary's part with no real motive behind the statement, or whether she believed that Jesus could do something to resolve the crisis. After all, more could have been purchased in the market; no doubt this would have been a difficulty had it been night time, but we doubt that because John is very careful to state when an event takes place at night (3:1; 6:16; 13:30). The circumstances were certainly not like the story of Elijah's cruse of oil during a famine; nor like the feeding of the 5 000 in the wilderness where it would have been impossible to buy food. We suspect that the Lord used this somewhat casual statement so as to arrange for the subsequent miracle to show forth His glory. Other expositors believe that Mary knew that the Lord was about to commence His miraculous works, so thought that the crisis could lead to His first miracle at her suggestion.

The word for wine (*oinos*) should be noted. This is the normal word for wine, and is used often in the NT. It is used in the Gospels mainly figuratively in the Lord's teaching, such as putting new wine into old or new bottles (Matt 9:17). In Paul's epistles, the word is used five times in practical contexts (Rom 14:21; Eph 5:18). In Revelation, it is used of God's judgment, or of the excesses of fornication of Mystery Babylon the Great (Rev 14:10; 17:2). On the other hand, the contents of the cup when the Lord first instituted the breaking of bread are described as "the fruit of the vine" (Mark 14:25), and not wine. We shall say more about the relationship between the vine and wine later.

4 *The Lord speaks.* The title "Woman" used by the Lord need not sound surprising. This word *gunē* occurs many times in the NT, usually translated "wife" or "woman", the context determining the rendering that is necessary. Only on a few occasions is the word used as a title: "woman" is found in Matt 15:28; Luke 13:12; 22:57; John 2:4; 4:21; 8:10; 19:26; 20:13,15, and "wife" in 1 Cor 7:16. No doubt in our verse, under similar circumstances today, the title "Mother" would be used in English, though the Lord avoided using any title of physical relationship when speaking to Mary. The thirty years of living with her had ended, and now He would be in the company of His disciples until His death. Similarly, it should be noted that the word *teknon* (child) is often used as a title "son" (Matt 9:2; 21:28; Mark 2:5; Luke 2:48; 15:31, etc.), and *anthrōpos* is used as a title "Man" (Luke 5:20; 12:14; 22:58, 60).

"What have I to do with thee?" translates the four words "*Ti emoi kai soi*", literally "What to me and to thee?" In other words, "We are both guests; as far as the organisers are concerned, they do not expect us to do anything to solve their problem". But the Lord had greater things in mind — not just a miracle, but a sign.

"Mine hour is not yet come" has produced differing explanations from the expositors. Mary, no doubt, was thinking of the present, believing that the Lord could, and would, do something Himself, that the time had come for Him to accomplish His first miracle, for Mary would think of a miracle and not a sign. But the Lord had a greater purpose than that of a miracle — He wanted the event to be a sign, and particularly relating to the future. Since the miracle would be one of change; since the following recorded event would relate to the change in His temple-body from death to resurrection (v.19), and since John consistently uses the "hour" (*hōra*) to refer to His forthcoming death (7:30; 8:20; 12:23, 27; 13:1; 17:1), we believe that the Lord was really referring to His ultimate service, that of sacrifice, when the Spirit would be given after His ascension. The miracle in Cana certainly manifested forth His glory (v.11), but when His hour was come, He looked forward to greater glory, "Father, the hour is come; glorify thy Son" (17:1)—truly, "from glory to glory". The sign then has a deep spiritual meaning.

5-6 *The mother of Jesus speaks.* "Whatsoever he saith unto you, do it" are the last recorded words of Mary. Clearly she expected something to be done, but she did not know what the Lord would and could do; certainly she could not have expected a sign. John records v.6 in his Gospel so that Gentile readers should understand why the waterpots were there; compare Mark 7:3-4 where Mark explained to his Gentile readers certain aspects of Jewish ritual. These six pots would not be placed in any conspicuous place ready for the accomplishment of the miracle; they were placed merely for the convenience of the guests. It is said that a firkin was equal to about eight and a half gallons. Note that the record states that the pots contained "two or three firkins" each, namely the Spirit of inspiration in many places in Scripture provides only approximate figures. Perhaps there were smaller and larger waterpots present. In any case, the total amount of water available would be well over one hundred gallons. No doubt the water was available for cleansing purposes, for the Lord condemned ritual for its own sake, saying to the hypocrites, "This people honoureth me with their lips, but their heart is far from me" (Mark 7:6), and "Woe unto you, scribes and Pharisees, hypocrites" (Matt 23:25-29). Truly only a miracle changes ritual into spiritual; today, the conversion of a dedicated ritualist is a miracle of grace.

7-8 *The Lord speaks.* The Lord gave two commandments, each of which was obeyed. He would not allow any subsequent trick-explanation to be invented, after the manner of unbelievers today; all miracles are "explained away", thereby reducing the Lord's deeds to the level of any competent man. The priests and elders used this method to explain away the empty tomb (Matt 28:13); the feeding of the 5 000 is explained by saying that the lad who brought the loaves and fish was merely an example to others who then produced their own provisions for general distribution. Knowing the propensities of the human heart, the Lord insisted that all the six waterpots were filled with water to the brim, to avoid any suggestion that wine had been hidden in any empty or half-empty pot. Bypassing the consternation of the organisers, the servants had to bear to the governor some of the contents of the pots, known by them to have been water when they filled them. This must have been an act of faith on their part, since it would appear to them that they had to bear water to the governor until they realised that a complete change had come about in the nature of the liquid. In fact, v.9 states that the liquid in the pots was water even at the moment of drawing, so we conclude that the change took place either at the moment of drawing or during the time when it was carried to the governor. We are not told, so we do not speculate with any dogmatism. But it would seem that if any had used the contents of the pots for washing they would have found them still ordinary water. The servants provide us with a lesson: be obedient to the Lord, even if subsequent circumstances are not clear at the time.

9 The name "ruler of the feast" is the same as "governor of the feast"—the name occurs here in this passage three times, but nowhere else in the NT. This man had no idea that a miracle had been accomplished; the servants had a better understanding than a man in a higher position. No doubt an example of things being hidden from the wise and prudent but revealed unto babes (Matt 11:25), and "God hath chosen the weak things of the world to confound the things which are mighty" (1 Cor 1:27). In fact, far from wanting to learn from the servants, the governor wanted to commend the bridegroom. It is interesting to note that the word *numphios* ("bridegroom") always appears parabolically in the Gospels in the Lord's teaching, except here in John 2 where the word must be taken literally.

10 *The governor speaks*. The governor thought that the bridegroom had provided the additional wine, knowing nothing of the power of the Lord present amongst the guests. This is so today; whatever men see around them in nature, the Lord is discounted. Men scoff, implying that the continuity of all things from the creation discards the necessity of believing in God (2 Pet 3:3-5). Peter knew that the people in Jerusalem thought that he personally had the power to heal, refusing to believe that the miracle was the work of "Jesus Christ of Nazareth" (Acts 3:12). How different from the words of the psalmist, "When I consider the heavens, the work of thy fingers" (Ps 8:3); he did not discount the reality of God's power.

Moreover, the new wine was considered by the governor to reverse the normal conventions of men. The best was kept until the last, when men had "well drunk" that which was worse. To a believer, this is not surprising, since the provisions of God always surpass the provisions of man. Men seek to start well, and then degenerate through their own lack of moral and spiritual power. God takes men up at the lowest, and raises them up to the highest; we think of Aaron sunk in the depths of sin through providing idolatry for the people, yet being raised by God to the heights of highpriesthood in Israel; we think of Saul, the chief of sinners, raised to the apostleship of the Gentiles. Yet usually men are not prepared to recognise the value of something new provided by the Lord; they prefer to say, "The old is better" (Luke 5:39).

This miracle is sometimes used to suggest that it is quite in order for believers to drink strong drink. However, the matter is not quite as simple as merely saying, "Well, look at John 2". In the OT, wine is described as having such awful consequences that we must ask, Would the Lord make a beverage having all the potential to lead to such disastrous results? The first thing that Noah did, having built an altar unto the Lord, was to plant a vineyard (Gen 9:20), though there is no record that this kind of husbandry was practised before the flood. The result was that Noah became drunk, leading to Canaan being cursed, leading in turn to all the idolatrous nations named in Gen 10:15-20. Later, Nabal was drunken at a feast, leading to his death the next morning (1 Sam 25:36); Belshazzar's drinking of wine accompanied idolatry, ending with his death and the overthrow of the Babylonian kingdom (Dan 5:4,30); the prophets also have much to say about the effects of strong drink.

God's purpose in the natural sphere of His creation was one of life and growth. In particular, His activity in plant growth ended with the fruit, from which seeds would emerge to yield further plants similar to the original (Gen 1:11-12). Thus in Jer 40:12, the actual gathering of the grapes is stated to involve "wine and summer fruits very much". (The same Greek word is used in the LXX as in John 2.) The decay and fermentation process takes place afterwards, leading really to decomposition of the juice and death. This was not part of the creation of God, but all forms of decay and death came in because of sin and the cursing of the ground. God is still doing His part in nature today, as the Lord upholds all things according to His power. In other words, He is always changing rain water into fruit juice as a living process—what we understand as a natural process. It is this that God wanted in the parable: the fruit of the vineyard (Matt 21:34). Even if the Son were cast out and killed, He would ultimately receive the fruits in their season. Similarly in the Lord's parabolic teaching in John 15, He is the true vine, and we are His branches producing fruit, namely, life as the end process. To go further in the NT, the winepress of the wrath of God speaks of His judgment (Rev 14:19).

In John 2, the Lord miraculously bypassed His own processes in creation instantaneously, a characteristic feature of His miracles. The rain water from a well was turned into wine, but we believe that He stopped at that point where divinely-controlled processes terminate, namely at life itself. The processes of fermentation, hastened usually by chemical reactions devised by men, are the ways of decomposition and death, and we do not believe that the Lord ventured along that pathway. He stopped where men would usually take over, but produced the best tasting juice that men had ever tasted!

The consequences of this are important. He wanted His disciples to be faithful, powerful and sanctified in their lives and service. This accounts for the powerful and effective ministry of John the Baptist; his father was instructed that he "shall drink neither wine nor strong drink; and he shall be filled with the Holy Spirit even from his mother's womb" (Luke 1:15). To be filled with the Spirit is the opposite of partaking of wine as a beverage.

No doubt in the abstract "there is nothing unclean of itself" (Rom 14:14). But believers do not do things merely as unto themselves; rather they consider the effect of their actions upon others, particularly upon younger believers. In fact, all must be done as an act of faith, else judgment may fall (vv.22-23). This is what happened in the assembly in Corinth; some were drunken even at the Lord's Supper, and consequently suffered judgment while in this scene (1 Cor 11:21, 29-32). Paul could foresee a bad example in 1 Tim 3:3, so elders in a local assembly were instructed not to be "given to wine". Paul states the general principle in Rom 14:21; it is good not to drink wine if this act stumbles anyone else, leading to weakness in other believers. Not to follow this general principle is to present a poor weak testimony oneself. In fact, the author believes that this practice is equivalent to having fellowship with the song of the drinkers of strong drink, spoken prophetically by David as the words of the Lord Jesus on the cross (Ps 69:12). Such men are the enemies of the cross of Christ. Moreover, the customary partaking of wine at a traditional toast is really equivalent, historically at least, to pouring out a drink offering to a heathen deity.

11 This turning of the water into wine is declared to be the "beginning of miracles (signs)" performed by the Lord. It showed forth His glory, and certainly refutes the so-called "childhood miracles" that are recorded in ancient manuscripts known as the apocryphal gospels. By contrast, the first plague that

God did through Moses was the turning of the waters of Egypt into blood, speaking of judgment and death (Exod 7:19).

In the OT, the glory of God had been manifested in tabernacle and temple, though this glory had ultimately forsaken the tabernacle (Ps 78:61) and temple (Ezek 11:23). Before this, Isaiah had been privileged to see the glory in and above the temple (Isa 6:1), interpreted by John as being the glory of Christ (John 12:41). But now the divine glory was again manifested on earth in the Person of the Son. This glory was seen in His divine power in miracles, as in this event in Cana and in the miraculous raising of Lazarus (John 11:40). This glory was seen morally in all that the Lord did, as One full of grace and truth (John 1:14). And this glory was seen openly above the brightness of the sun on the mount of transfiguration (Matt 17:2). In glory the Lord ascended (1 Tim 3:16), later to be seen by Paul (as Saul) on the Damascus road. And now we have "the light of the knowledge of the glory of God in the face of Jesus Christ" perceived by faith (2 Cor 4:6). No wonder "his disciples believed on him", for this was a development of a faith that they had already exercised in ch.1. A deeper acquaintance of His divine Person and power was being formed, though later this faith would sometimes be found wanting, "O ye of little faith" (Matt 8:26; 14:31).

12 Thus the Lord remained in Capernaum, until the time came for His journey to Jerusalem for the first passover feast during the years of His public ministry. His believing mother, His unbelieving brethren, and His believing disciples were still with Him, though the links with the former were now tenuous, as far as natural relationships are concerned. In verses such as Matt 2:14, Joseph is named first, followed by "the young child". In Luke 2:41-43, again His parents are named first, followed by "the child Jesus". Again, in John 2:1, "the mother of Jesus" is named first, followed by Jesus in v.2. But now the first sign and miracle has changed this. In our verse 10, "he" is named first, followed by the others. His glory ensures that He has the first place in service and in divine preeminence.

2. *The Son's Temple-Body*
2:13-25

v.13 "And the Jews' passover was at hand, and Jesus went up to Jerusalem,
v.14 And found in the temple those that sold oxen and sheep and doves, and the changers of money sitting:
v.15 And when he had made a scourge of small cords, he drove them all out of the temple, and the sheep , and the oxen; and poured out the changers' money, and overthrew the tables;
v.16 And said unto them that sold doves, Take these things hence; make not my Father's house a house of merchandise.

v.17 And his disciples remembered that it was written, The zeal of thine house hath eaten me up.
v.18 Then answered the Jews and said unto him, What sign shewest thou unto us, seeing that thou doest these things?
v.19 Jesus answered and said unto them, Destroy this temple, and in three days I will raise it up.
v.20 Then said the Jews, Forty and six years was this temple in building, and wilt thou rear it up in three days?
v.21 But he spake of the temple of his body.
v.22 When therefore he was risen from the dead, his disciples remembered that he had said this unto them; and they believed the scripture, and the word which Jesus had said.
v.23 Now when he was in Jerusalem at the passover, in the feast *day*, many believed in his name, when they saw the miracles which he did.
v.24 But Jesus did not commit himself unto them, because he knew all *men*,
v.25 And needed not that any should testify of man: for he knew what was in man."

When one Greek word is unnecessarily translated by two or more different English words (such as the pairs "right, just", "Spirit, Ghost", "to minister, to serve"), and when two different Greek words are translated by one English word (such as "temple", "man", "another"), then the reader of the NT must be on his guard. It is therefore necessary to examine the Greek words behind the one English word "temple" occurring in this passage.

The Greek word *naos* is defined as "a shrine or sanctuary . . . among the Jews the sanctuary of the temple, into which only the priests could lawfully enter" (Vine). This word is used fifteen times of the sanctuary in Jerusalem, once of a future sanctuary there, seven times of the body of the Lord Jesus (of which five were spoken sarcastically by the false witnesses and those at the cross), seven times metaphorically by Paul in his epistles, sixteen times in Revelation (once as a sphere of heavenly blessing, eleven times of the sanctuary in heaven issuing forth judgment on earth, twice of a structure on earth, once of the Lamb, and once of its absence in the millennial city).

The second Greek word is *hieron*, defined as "a sacred place, a temple . . . that in Jerusalem, signifying the entire building with its precincts, or some part thereof, as distinct from the *naos*, the inner sanctuary" (Vine). The word appears 69 times in the Gospels and in the Acts, once used by Paul in connection with a common religious practice in Jerusalem, and once in a heathen sense.

In a few contexts, both *naos* and *hieron* are found. Thus in Luke 1:9, the priest Zacharias "went into the temple of the Lord", the word *naos*, inner shrine, being used, since only priests were allowed to enter the sanctuary. The same word appears in vv.21, 22, where the people on the *outside* marvelled that he had been so long "in the temple", namely, *inside*. Yet after the birth of the Lord, His parents brought Him into the temple (*hieron*), where Simeon saw Him (Luke 2:27), where Anna served constantly (v.37), and where later the Lord was found at the age of twelve (v.46).

Thus in our present passage (John 2:14-15), the Lord found tradesmen "in the temple", making a profit at the expense of those entering to serve God with sacrifices purchased from the profiteers. The word used for "temple" is *hieron*, embracing the actual house, the courts and precincts where the public could enter. Immediately afterwards, the Lord said to His critics, "Destroy this temple (*naos*), and in three days I will raise it up". In their reply, the Jews then used the word *naos*, while John also used this word in his explanation, "he spake of the temple of his body". In other words, the Lord's body was a vessel, a shrine, a Holy of Holies, where the Son resided, as He moved and worked here on earth.

These two words are also used in a heathen setting relating to the idolatrous city of Ephesus. The great temple of Diana in Ephesus is called a *hieron*, but the "silver shrines" being made for Diana are described by the word *naos*. Heathen religious gain was being made by the craftsmen, as is common practice today in certain circles of Christendom (Acts 19:24, 27).

The Lord never entered the *naos*, since He was not of the priestly family of the Levites (Heb 7:13-14). His connections with the *hieron* were:

1. He was taken to the "pinnacle of the temple" (Matt 4:5).

2. "The blind and the lame came to him in the temple" (Matt 21:14).

3. He "departed from the temple" and the disciples showed Him "the buildings of the temple" (Matt 24:1).

4. During the last week, the Lord spent the daytime "teaching in the temple" (Luke 21:37-38).

In the Gospels, the word *naos* is used as follows:

1. The Lord used this word four times in His teaching in Matt 23:16-21.

2. It was the veil of the inner sanctuary (*naos*) that was rent when the Lord died on the cross (Matt 27:51), showing to the ministering priests that the holy of holies was empty, that there was no ark, no throne of God amongst His people as in the OT tabernacle and temple.

3. The strangest reference of all is in Matt 27:5, where Judas "cast down the pieces of silver in the temple (*naos*), and departed". Whether he actually gained access to the separated place, or whether he got one of the priests to cast the money down in the forbidden place, we are not told. Yet the

betrayal money was found in the inner shrine, then to be used for the purchase of "the field of blood" (Acts 1:19).

In the epistles, the word *hieron* is used only once (1 Cor 9:13), referring to the Jewish practice of extracting tithes to maintain priests and Levites. But Paul uses the word *naos* eight times:

1. In 1 Cor 6:19, the body of the believer is called "the temple of the Holy Spirit which is in you", namely, the believer's body should be sanctified and meet for the indwelling presence of the Spirit. Thus Paul exhorts, "glorify God in your body", a reference to the glory of God in the OT tabernacle and temple.

2. In 1 Cor 3:16-17, Paul uses the word *naos* three times to refer to the local assembly: "ye are the temple of God", the gatherings of the Lord's people being the place where the Lord is found with His own.

3. In 2 Cor 6:16, "ye are the temple of the living God" refers to separation, and can apply both to the individual and to the local assembly.

4. In Eph 2:21, the whole building "groweth unto an holy temple in the Lord", referring to the Lord as the "chief corner stone" in what is often termed the universal church.

5. In the end times after the rapture of the church, the anti-Christ is seen sitting "in the temple of God, showing himself that he is God" (2 Thess 2:4), taking over an inner structure that will be built in the future, and vainly copying the glory of the past.

The lack of the word *hieron* in the epistles implies that God has no interest now in material dwellings for His presence (Acts 7:48), while the metaphorical use of *naos* indicates His choice to make His presence known in the bodies of individual believers and in their gatherings in His name.

13 The "feasts of Jehovah" is a very wide subject, there being seven principal feasts introduced by God in Moses' time, with a few others being introduced later by the Jews, such as Purim (Est 9:26-28). Details as given by God through Moses are found in Lev 23; Num 28-29; Deut 16. In order throughout the year, the seven are: the feast of the Passover, of unleavened bread, of firstfruits, of Pentecost, of trumpets, of atonement, and of tabernacles. The first four were spring feasts, while the last three were autumn feasts. They were divine appointments, when men had to meet with God in the place that He would choose. The seven feasts fell into three well-defined groupings: Group 1 comprised the first three, taking place within one week; Group 2 consisted of

Pentecost only, taking place fifty days after the Passover; Group 3 comprised the last three feasts, taking place in the seventh month. They were prophetic in character, needing the NT to unlock their spiritual meanings. The first three speak of the sacrifice and resurrection of Christ, with moral implications for the Lord's people. The fourth feast speaks of Pentecost for the church, and the subseqent church age. The last three speak of the restoration of Israel in the future.

These three groupings were specified to Moses even before the tabernacle was built. In Exod 23:14-17, it was commanded that all males should appear before God at three specific times: at the feast of unleavened bread, at the feast of harvest, and at the feast of ingathering. This is repeated in Deut 16:16, the three occasions (embracing the three groupings) being called: the feast of unleavened bread, the feast of weeks, and the feast of tabernacles. "All thy males" had to meet in "the place which he shall choose". For example, it was the feast of tabernacles that was kept after the temple was dedicated (2 Chron 7:8-10), while in Hezekiah's time, many in the northern kingdom refused to come to Jerusalem for the feast of the Passover (2 Chron 30:5-11).

The parents of Jesus went up to Jerusalem each year at the feast of Passover (Luke 2:41), "the child Jesus" accompanying them at the age of twelve. But when the Lord commenced His ministry, the scene is set by the title of the feast, "the *Jew's* passover". As far as the traditionalists amongst the Jews were concerned it might have seemed the fulfilling of the obligations to keep the Lord's Passover, but the Spirit of inspiration refused to recognise that it was "the Lord's passover" (Exod 12:11) any more. Similarly we read of "a feast of the *Jews*" (John 5:1), and "the *Jews'* feast of tabernacles" (John 7:1). God would not acknowledge man's religion that was but a fictitious copy of His own instructions. The same situation is found in Matt 23:38, "*your* house".

The Passover as carried out in Herod's temple courts was so different from that carried out in Solomon's temple by faithful kings. That is why the Lord was ready to cast out spurious activity. After all, He was the unrecognised "Christ our passover" (1 Cor 5:7), having divine authority to deal with counterfeit religion. There were four Passovers during the Lord's three years' ministry; as He came into Jerusalem on the last occasion to be the true Passover, He again cleansed the temple in a similar manner (Matt 21:12-13). But the Lord had a special desire for the last Passover, "With desire I have desired to eat this passover with you before I suffer" (Luke 22:15), for He knew that this would be the last Passover faithfully accomplished by Himself and His disciples. After that, God would abandon recognising the annual Passover feasts, since Christ, the true Passover, had been sacrificed. Instead, for the church, the Lord's Supper was introduced until He come, the disciples breaking bread on the first day of each week (Acts 20:7; 1 Cor 11:23-26). The Person and work of Christ cast out the old so that the new might come in.

14 Many of the Jews arriving from afar would have no sacrifices, so provision was made for them to purchase "oxen and cattle and doves" in the temple courts, changing their currency at the same time for the purchase. This was not only for the convenience of the purchasers, but for the profit of the traders, no doubt connived at by the priests who would themselves pocket some of the profit. In Deut 14:24-26, God had allowed money to be brought "if the way be too long". So the Lord's anger was demonstrated not against the actual practice, but against the profiteering motives of the merchants. Today, vast profits are made in the commerce of religion, while in the future the merchants will weep at the overthrow of the merchandise of Mystery, Babylon the Great (Rev 18:11-17), for they had been "made rich by her".

15 The Lord had divine authority to expel the traders in religion, although they did not learn the lesson for long. For He did not spend too much time in Jerusalem, and as soon as He had returned to Galilee, the old practices must have commenced again. Divine compassion in the first paragraph of ch.2, and divine love revealed to Nicodemus in ch.3, are placed one on each side of the Lord's righteous anger. Men were prepared to argue with Him here, but in the future, when "the wrath of the Lamb" is manifested (Rev 6:16), men will recognise the source of the wrath, seeking to hide themselves from "the great day of his wrath". No doubt these men were surprised at this unexpected arrival of a Man with such authority in judgment, but this reflects on Mal 3:1-3, where God's Messenger "shall suddenly come to his temple", as a "refiner and purifier of silver", when such men will not be able to "abide the day of his coming". So at his Passover, the Lamb of love was also seen as a Lamb of wrath.

This desecration of the temple courts recalls the desecration of the Sabbath in Neh 13:15-22, where traders inside and outside Jerusalem were prevented from selling their merchandise on the Sabbath. In NT times, those who defile the temple of God (as the local assembly) would be defiled by God, "for the temple of God is holy" (1 Cor 3:17).

16 This cleansing of the temple recalls certain OT cleansings. Thus Hezekiah effected the removal of idolatrous refuse from the place of God's habitation (2 Chron 29:16-18). The refuse was disposed of in the brook Kidron, to ensure that the uncleanness was carried away, not to be used again. Asa burned idols there (2 Chron 15:16), and Josiah cast the dust of the altars there (2 Kings 23:12). In Hezekiah's case, it took eight days to cleanse the interior of the house, and another eight days to cleanse the exterior. Such accumulated idolatry corresponds to the vast amount of unevangelical religion absorbed by many believers in their unconverted days. In Paul's case, he would not rebuild the things that he had destroyed (Gal 2:18). See Neh 13:8-9 for another OT example.

The Lord speaks. He uses the expression "My Father's house", in a sense quite distinct from the same expression in John 14:2. This house in Jerusalem had no divine command for its building (unlike the OT tabernacle and temple where

God dwelt). Herod had this temple built at his own volition, to be an architectural masterpiece. There was no ark within the veil, and God's presence was not implied. We believe that the transformation to God's house *only* occurred when the Lord was actually present; at all other times it was the house *of the Jews*, ripe for destruction (Matt 23:38; 24:2). Today, God does not dwell in temples made with hands (Acts 7:48), for the house is the church of the living God (1 Tim 3:15).

The accusation "an house of merchandise" became "a den of thieves" three years later (Matt 21:12), showing the ongrowing degradation of the human heart. The Lord's description "my house" must be understood only in the light of His presence there at the time.

17 When did the disciples associate this action of the Lord with Ps 69:9, "The zeal of thine house hath eaten me up"? This Psalm shows prophetically the words of the Lord on the cross, and His subsequent triumph. Yet in John 2:22 it was only *after* His death and resurrection that they understood His words, so we would believe that their understanding of Ps 69 only matured when the Holy Spirit was given who would guide them into all truth. Prior to the giving of the Spirit, their understanding even of the plainest teaching by the Lord was very limited or even non-existent; see Matt 16:22; Mark 9:32; Luke 18:34.

The reproaches of men fell upon the Lord because of His zeal for His Father's house, because of the status and position that He gave to the Father throughout John's Gospel. This zeal was a burning desire in His soul to do God's will without any delay. Divine zeal has an important place in the Scriptures. Thus Isaiah encouraged Hezekiah with the thought of a faithful remnant, that "the zeal of the Lord of hosts shall do this" (2 Kings 19:31). Again, the results of the Child being born, with the throne of David being established for ever, are promised because "The zeal of the Lord of hosts will perform this" (Isa 9:7). It was in His zeal that He stated through Ezekiel that His anger would be accomplished (Ezek 5:13). Examples of believers manifesting zeal are found in Col 4:13; Titus 2:14. It is good for a man of faith to emulate God's zeal, as did the priest Phinehas, who "was zealous with *my* zeal among them" (Num 25:11 marg). There are also examples of misplaced zeal by unbelievers, such as Rom 10:2; Phil 3:6, and there is an example of misplaced zeal by believers in Acts 21:20.

18-21 *The Jews speak.* Taken with v.16, these verses continue to show how John's style in recording events was that of a conversationalist. The Jews asked for a sign (the same word *sēmeion* as used for "miracles" in vv.11, 23). This demand was characteristic of the Jews; later Paul wrote that "the Jews require a sign", though all the apostle had to give was "Christ crucified", a stumblingblock to the Jews (1 Cor 1:22-23). The Jews were not satisfied with the Lord's miracles as signs, for later in Matt 16:1 they tempted Him and "desired him that he would show them a sign from heaven". This the Lord would not do, for evidently they wanted some spectacular phenomenon to happen in the heavens. "No sign shall be given" in the sense that they desired, said the Lord; rather all He would provide was the "sign of the prophet Jonas" (Matt 12:39-40; 16:4). To us, this speaks of the Lord's death and resurrection, and similarly in John 2, He would provide a sign metaphorically relating to His death and resurrection. But only believers can see the nature of these signs, for faith comes by hearing the Word, not by outward signs.

The Lord speaks. "Destroy this temple, and in three days I will raise it up" is one of the great statements of the Lord concerning His death, spoken at the beginning of His ministry. In Matthew's Gospel, the first mention of this comes much later (16:21). As we have shown before, the word for "temple" here is *naos*, the inner shrine, a most suitable word to be used for this purpose, when shorn, of course, of all its traditional trappings. Admittedly, the believer's body, after conversion, is the temple of God and His possession (1 Cor 6:19). But the temple that the Lord spoke of was His own body—"that holy thing that shall be born" (Luke 1:35), "the Word... made flesh" (John 1:14), and "God... manifest in the flesh" (1 Tim 3:16). This temple was Deity in Manhood, a new experience for the eternal Son, yet a temple-body carried up to heaven at His ascension.

When the Lord said "Destroy", this would be a deed of the Jews in collaboration with the Romans. The Lord predicted the "three days", as He stated elsewhere (Matt 16:21; Luke 18:33). He also stated that He would raise this temple again. Thus the resurrection of Christ would be a united divine work, that of the Lord Jesus and of God the Father (Acts 2:24, 32; 4:10; 10:40; Eph 1:20).

The Jews speak. Of course unbelieving Jews could never understand a spiritual sign expressed in ordinary human words; they could easily understand the words "destroy, temple, three days, raise up". To them, it did not make sense; already Herod's temple in Jerusalem had taken forty-six years to build (and it would not be complete until just before its destruction in AD 70). Moses' tabernacle took about five months to construct; they knew that many years had been necessary to build Solomon's temple and the new temple after the return from the captivity. Yet here was a Man claiming to be able to rebuild an even greater temple in three days. The rational mind and spiritual truth are poles apart, for "the natural man receiveth not the things of the Spirit of God,... neither can he know them" (1 Cor 3:14).

The verb "I will raise" used by the Lord in v.19, that used by the Jews "wilt thou rear" in v.20, and that used by John "he was risen" in v.22 are all parts of the same Greek verb *egeirō*. In the NT there are two very common verbs used for resurrection; translations usually make no difference between them.

1. The Greek verb *egeirō*. In a physical sense, this is given many renderings in the AV, such as rising from a bed, the rising of false prophets, to raise up children, and to awake (Matt 8:25). In this sense it is used dozens of times

of resurrection, because death is likened to sleep, as in the case of Jairus' daughter: "the maid is not dead, but sleepeth . . . the maid arose" (Matt 9:24-25). The word is used nineteen times in the great chapter on resurrection (1 Cor 15), and dozens of times elsewhere when resurrection is being discussed. However, on only nine occasions is the word "again" appended, for example, "the third day he shall be raised again" (Matt 7:23). But this word "again" does not represent any Greek word. Both the RV and JND do not use the word "again" in connection with resurrection when translating this verb *egeirō*. The Greek word for "again" is *palin*, a word that appears dozens of times in the NT, but only three times of resurrection in quite specialised contexts (John 10:17,18; 16:22).

2. The Greek word *anistēmi*. This verb has essentially two renderings in the AV: to rise up, and to stand up physically. It is used many times of resurrection, being the contrast to lying down in death. However, on fifteen occasions when resurrection is implied, the word "again" is attached in the AV, though not representing any Greek word. For example, "the third day he shall rise again" (Matt 20:19), "Thy brother shall rise again" (John 11:23). Both the RV and JND appear to be inconsistent in their insertion of the word "again" in those verses where it appears in the AV.

The conclusion is that the word "again" should not be used after these two verbs when resurrection is implied, although it sounds so appropriate traditionally to our ears. Of course the Lord was alive *again*; His life being eternally distinct from any semblance of sleep and of lying down, but it is always best not to insert extra words into translations merely to complete the sense when they are not necessary.

22 The disciples were quite different from the unbelieving Jews. The Spirit of God enabled the disciples to remember these things, but only *after* He was risen. But Satan enabled the unbelieving Jews to remember the Lord's words *before* His death. Three years later the Jews had not forgotten. It was Matthew who recorded these events, so John's Gospel (written later) shows where these Jews got their knowledge from. At the Lord's trial before the high priest, two false witnesses claimed that He had said, "I am able to destroy the temple of God, and to build it in three days" (Matt 26:61). Note their deliberate alteration of the Lord's words: He had implied that *the Jews* would destroy the temple, while these false witnesses claimed that *He* would destroy it. The next day, those around the cross reviled Him, saying, "Thou that destroyest the temple, and buildest it in three days, save thyself. If thou be the Son of God, come down from the cross" (Matt 27:40). They thought that the temple was a physical building, so if the One on the cross could build it again miraculously, then in the same way He could come down from the cross. This was but to make a mockery of His sufferings.

There seems to be a reference to this in Acts 6:14, when Stephen was accused, though no doubt he referred to Matt 24:2 when Herod's temple would be destroyed.

This faith exercised by the disciples must refer to their remembrance after His resurrection. The "word" refers to the Lord's description of the sign of the raised temple, showing that knowledge and understanding are necessary for faith to have a sure foundation. But "the scripture" is something additional. Since Ps 69:9 was quoted in v.17, we believe that "the scripture" refers to the OT in its prophetic unfolding of the sacrifice and resurrection of Christ. Certainly this applied to Peter in Acts 2, where he freely quoted from three Psalms that refer to resurrection (Ps 16:8-11; 110:1; 132:11). Peter knew this, for the Lord had only recently unfolded to them "all things... in the psalms... concerning me" (Luke 24:44).

23-25 The passover was the beginning of the feast of unleavened bread, so the Lord spent many days in Jerusalem, performing "many miracles". This makes it clear that the description "the second miracle" (John 4:54) cannot mean that there was only one miracle before, namely the turning of water into wine. Many people believed in His Name when they saw these miracles, but they formed the minority, for totally, believers formed only the "few" and "a little flock". Moreover, this faith was restricted to what they saw; the fulness of His Person was not revealed to them, in the way in which His Person had been so deeply described in John 1 (as the Word, the Light, the Son, the Lamb, the Christ, the King of Israel). But the majority of men knew nothing of this, for His Person was hidden from them. He "knew what was in man", in the hearts of the masses in Jerusalem at that time; all were dead in trespasses and in sins. Being the Word manifest in flesh, He needed no man to explain this fundamental fact to Him. Because of the state of their hearts, He "did not commit himself to them". This word "commit" is the usual word for "believe", namely *pisteuō*. This can mean, "to trust oneself to"; for example, Paul was entrusted with the Gospel (Gal 2:7; 1 Thess 2:4; 1 Tim 1:11; Titus 1:3). Thus the Lord would not entrust Himself (both doctrinally and physically) to men, knowing that hatred would rapidly be formed in their hearts. We can be thankful that He was later able to entrust Himself to loving hands who cared for His material needs, such as those in the home of Mary, Martha and Lazarus in Bethany. But on other occasions He actively did not commit Himself to men—for example, when He had to leave Nazareth and the temple in Jerusalem (Luke 4:30; John 8:59).

III. The Establishment of the Son's Authority in Teaching and Testimony (3:1-36)

1. *The Son's Answers to Questions Raised by Nicodemus* 3:1-13

v.1 "There was a man of the Pharisees, named Nicodemus, a ruler of the Jews:

v.2 The same came to Jesus by night, and said unto him, Rabbi, we know that thou art a teacher come from God: for no man can do these miracles that thou doest, except God be with him.
v.3 Jesus answered and said unto him, Verily, verily, I say unto thee, Except a man be born again, he cannot see the kingdom of God.
v.4 Nicodemus saith unto him, How can a man be born when he is old? Can he enter the second time into his mother's womb, and be born?
v.5 Jesus answered, Verily, verily, I say unto thee, Except a man be born of water and *of* the Spirit, he cannot enter into the kingdom of God.
v.6 That which is born of the flesh is flesh; and that which is born of the Spirit is spirit.
v.7 Marvel not that I said unto thee, Ye must be born again.
v.8 The wind bloweth where it listeth, and thou hearest the sound thereof, but canst not tell whence it cometh, and whither it goeth: so is every one that is born of the Spirit.
v.9 Nicodemus answered and said unto him, How can these things be?
v.10 Jesus answered and said unto him, Art thou a master of Israel, and knowest not these things?
v.11 Verily, verily, I say unto thee, We speak that we do know, and testify that we have seen; and ye receive not our witness.
v.12 If I have told you earthly things, and ye believe not, how shall ye believe, if I tell you *of* heavenly things?
v.13 And no man hath ascended up to heaven, but he that came down from heaven, *even* the Son of man which is in heaven."

1 In chs.3-4, the Son and His message are presented so as to be received; in ch.3, it is to a man, while in ch.4, it is to a woman. The same appears in Acts 16, where first Lydia and then the jailor are saved: "there is neither male not female: for ye are all one in Christ Jesus" (Gal 3:28).

In John 1:24, the Pharisees wanted to know about John's person and teaching; here in ch.3, another Pharisee wanted to know more about the Lord's Person and teaching, while in 5:18 the Jews (evidently the Pharisees) were already prepared to kill the Lord Jesus because of His activities and teaching. The Pharisees were a group of men adhering to their own traditions regarding the law of Moses, in particular their oral tradition that interpreted the written law. The Lord branded them as hypocrites (Matt 23:13-33). Paul (as Saul and unconverted) was the most bigoted of all the Pharisees recorded in the NT, "as touching the law, a Pharisee" (Phil 3:5). As a "ruler" (*archōn*), Nicodemus was a member of the Jewish Sanhedrin, a body of leaders who had wide powers, meeting in Jerusalem as the highest Jewish tribunal. It was composed of Sadducees, Pharisees, scribes and the high priest. Later, in John 7:50-51, we find Nicodemus taking a half-way stand for the Lord, stating that they should not judge the Lord until they had heard Him. But in 19:39-42, now quite openly and boldly, he came with Joseph of Arimathaea to place the body of Jesus in the tomb. We do not believe that he was present when the word "all" is used of the Sanhedrin, when the Lord was considered to be guilty of death (Matt 26:59).

2 Without teaching received through the Spirit, all men are in ignorance and darkness. Academic expertise does not cover up ignorance of the word of God. Even present-day theologians often resemble Nicodemus, but they have no intention of coming to Jesus by night. So this ruler sought Jesus by night because of fear of his own religious sect, who would later have men put out of the synagogue for confessing the Lord (John 9:32; 12:42). See also Jud 6:27. But those who come sincerely, shall find, as the Lord promised (Matt 7:7).

Nicodemus speaks. "Rabbi" is a polite title given to a teacher; Andrew and Nathanael had previously used this title (John 1:38, 49), while later John the Baptist is addressed by this title (3:26). Nicodemus was struck by the Lord's teaching and miracles; strictly, he used the word "signs", evidently feeling that the Lord's works answered to the signs that the Jews were seeking after. To Nicodemus, these signs did not prove the Lord's Deity, they only showed that He was "from God" and that God was "with him". Such a profession is not equivalent to the possession of salvation. The Lord would never reveal Himself to a merely curious mind, such as that shown by Herod (Luke 23:8). But Nicodemus was an honest seeker, no doubt thinking that the Lord was only a prophet (John 4:19; 9:17), though both to the woman at the well and to the man given sight He revealed Himself as Christ and Son of God respectively. For prophets such as Elijah in the OT worked miracles, but they were not divine.

Nicodemus used the description "teacher" (*didaskalos*). Several Greek words are translated "teacher" (a list is given in the author's comments on Matt 26:25 tin the companion volume on Matthew's Gospel). Nicodemus used the most common word; his use of the word "teacher" shows that the Lord must have engaged in teaching the people (no doubt in the temple courts) during the days of the feast. This is how the daytime was occupied during the last week of His ministry on earth (Luke 21:37). In other places, this word *didaskalos* is used many imes as a *title* when men addressed the Lord, such as "Master, say on" (Luke 7:40). The apostles never used this title, using rather "Lord" (*kurios*), Mark 13:1 being an exception, "Master, see what manner of stones and what buildings are here".

3 *The Lord speaks.* This answer does not appear to be immediately connected with Nicodemus' statement. However, the Lord knew what was in the Pharisees' hearts, that they were wondering "when the kingdom of God should come" (Luke 17:20). Their land was under the jurisdiction of Rome, the fourth beast of Dan 7, a nation hated by the Jews. To regain possession of their land would be equivalent to the kingdom of God. Both politically and religiously, their concept of the kingdom of God had no connection with God's thoughts concerning His kingdom. For His kingdom would be characterised by divine rule in the hearts and lives of His people. This kingdom comprised the moral rule and authority of God (Rom 14:17; 1 Cor 6:9-11; Eph 5:5). It was (and is) not with observation (Luke 17:20), though the three apostles were privileged to "see the kingdom of God" (Luke 9:27) when the Lord was transfigured before them. The kingdom will be seen with outward display when the Lord reigns in glory, and will be extended to eternity (1 Cor 15:24). The immediate reference to the kingdom in the Lord's answer is to the moral life of a believer now, though we recognise that this verse is often used in an evangelistic sense as extending to the future. The subject of the future comes later in the Lord's discourse (vv.15-17).

The doctrine of being "born again" is of fundamental importance. The word "again" (*anōthen*) is not the usual word for "again" (*palin*). Strictly, it means "from above", as when the veil was rent from "the top" to the bottom (Matt 27:51). John quotes the word five times, as "He that cometh *from above*" (John 3:31); "except it were given thee *from above*" (19:11). In other words, this birth is entirely distinct from ordinary human reproductive processes, introduced by God in Gen 1:28, "Be fruitful, and multiply". The apostle John had previously written that the sons of God are "born, not of blood, nor of the will of the flesh, nor of the will of man, but of God" (1:13). This second birth is a divine miracle, being accomplished by no man, not even by an evangelist; it is entirely "anew", as the word for "again" is sometimes rendered. The first birth causes a man to sink downwards, but this second birth causes a man to rise upwards; one is earthly, the other is heavenly.

4 *Nicodemus speaks.* This Pharisee had no idea that the Lord was making a spiritual statement, distinct from his political and religious aspirations. His misunderstanding was similar to that recorded in John 2:20. This is always so, "the natural man receiveth not the things of the Spirit of God" (1 Cor 2:14). 'Thus the woman at the well thought that the Lord's reference to "water" was to natural water (4:15); the Jews in Capernaum thought hat His reference to "the bread ... my flesh" was to His actual physical flesh (6:52); the Pharisees thought that His words "whither I go, ye cannot come" referred to His killing Himself (8:21-22). Such carnal interpretations of truth arose because men were 'from beneath ... of this world" (v.23). And so it was with Nicodemus; by suggesting a second physical birth, he was not being argumentative; he displayed spiritual ignorance, yet sought after the truth.

5-6 *The Lord speaks.* This is the second of three times that the Lord says "Verily, verily" (amen, amen) in this discourse. The duplicated form of this word occurs 25 times in John's Gospel, but only the single form appears in the other three Gospels.

Here the Lord amplifies the meaning of "born" in v.3, discarding entirely the natural suggestion of Nicodemus in v.4. The birth for entrance into the kingdom of God is "of water and of the Spirit", or, strictly, "of water and Spirit", for the preposition "of" occurs only once. In other words, the concepts of "water" and "Spirit" are closely connected, and cannot be divided. This answer of the Lord has brought forth more theories and suggested explanations than for most scriptures, though 1 Cor 15:29 "baptized for the dead" is a close parallel!

1. "Water" is taken to refer to natural birth, followed by "Spirit" referring to the second birth. This is crude, having no basis in Scripture.

2. Many expositors, both evangelical and nonevangelical, take "water" to refer to baptism. If the doctrine of the new birth were consistent with the doctrine of baptism, this would be a valid explanation. However, the new birth is the new beginning of the christian experience, but baptism is not a beginning. It is loved by those who visualise Christianity as a series of rites and ceremonies, but to those taught in the Scriptures, baptism is an act of testimony after the beginning, namely after conversion. In any case, the close connection between "water" and "Spirit" negates baptism as an explanation, since John the Baptist draws a sharp contrast between them, a fact that Nicodemus might have known. John baptised with (or, in) water, but the Son would baptise with (or, in) the Holy Spirit (John 1:33). In other words, physical water on the one hand, and the Spirit on the other, are too distinct for them to be linked together in the Lord's statement "of water and Spirit".

3. The Lord would use figures from the OT, with which Nicodemus should have been familiar, as for example later, when He quoted Moses lifting up the serpent in the wilderness (v.14). Through Ezekiel, God described a new moral and spiritual condition for His people after the captivity: "I will sprinkle clean water upon you, and ye shall be clean . . . A new heart also will I give you, and a new spirit will I put within you: and I will take away the stony heart out of your flesh, and I will give you an heart of flesh. And I will put my spirit within you" (Ezek 36:25-27). Here the old is put away, and God introduces the new. The heart is desperately wicked, and none can cure it; rather, cleansing leads to a new heart, and God then places a new Spirit within. It is the same today; we are cleansed through the word of God revealing the value of the blood of Christ, after which it shows a new pathway for the believer. See also John 6:63. The Spirit not only superintends this change, but then enters into the believer's heart. This new life does not reform the old nature, but is additional to it, the old man being reckoned as crucified with Christ.

Thus we are a new creation in Christ (2 Cor 5:17), with all things become new. We are "born again, not of corruptible seed, but of incorruptible, by the word of God, which liveth and abideth for ever" (1 Pet 1:23). We are born of God, and so do not practise sin, "for his seed remaineth in him: and he cannot sin, because he is born of God" (1 John 3:9). See also 1 John 4:7; 5:1, 4. This is a chief characteristic of the life lived by those who are born again.

The Lord stresses that the transmission of likeness is inevitable (v.6). Lasting characteristics are transmitted that cannot be changed. This is so naturally, in the biological and zoological spheres. Herb and tree brought forth "after his kind" (Gen 1:12); Adam begat Seth "in his own likeness, after his image" (5:3). And this is so morally; "by one man sin entered into the world, and death by sin; and so death passed upon all men" (Rom 5:12); "in Adam all die" (1 Cor 15:22); "as we have borne the image of the earthly" (v.49). But the new creation, commencing with the new birth, extends unmarred to eternity.

Those born of the Spirit will display manifestations of the Spirit's presence within. They will display the mind of Christ; they will be engaged with things that are above; they will use the spiritual gifts that the Spirit imparts; they will love the word of God given by inspiration by the Spirit. Such things give character to those born of the Spirit: by their fruits we shall know them, for "every good tree bringeth forth good fruit" (Matt 7:16-20). This new man born from above cannot grieve or quench the Spirit.

7-8 The word *thaumazō* is translated either "to marvel" or "to wonder". Thus the Lord Jesus marvelled both at unbelief and at faith (Mark 6:6; Matt 8:10). The Jews and multitudes often marvelled at His miracles and at His teaching. Evidently, Nicodemus must have given some indication that he marvelled at the Lord's description of the origin of the new birth, but the Lord wanted men to have faith, not to marvel at things that could not be fully understood.

Nothing could be seen of the inner working of the "water and Spirit" that would yield a new life as a result of the new birth. Afterwards, its effects would be seen, of course, but not its origin. Even in those days, men must have been interested in the cause of things—how much more today scientists want to know the underlying causes that cannot be detected by the naked eye, using electron microscopes and vast telescopes to explore the extremely minute, and the extremely distant objects of God's creation. The Lord uses the path of the wind to illustrate this inquisitive nature of man. And very apt the illustration is, for the Greek word for "Spirit" is *pneuma*, which also means "wind". The origin of a particular current of wind, and its destination, could not be detected in those days, though it effects could easily be perceived. The wind would break the cedars (Ps 29:5); the stormy wind would raise up the waves (Ps 107:25); it could rend the mountains and break the rocks (1 Kings 19:11). In Eccl 1:6, the metaphor of the wind is used in a different way: it goes round in circles, with its origin and destination at the same point, implying the vanity of the works of men on earth, as generations come and go.

The work of the Spirit in the new birth is likewise. Whence He comes, and how He works, cannot be explained.

> I know not how the Spirit moves,
> Convincing men of sin;
> Revealing Jesus through the Word.
> Creating faith in Him.

But this is no reason for refusing to accept the truth. "Faith cometh . . . by the word of God" (Rom 10:17), not by sight, nor even by understanding.

9 *Nicodemus speaks.* The man is still perplexed, even though "these things" have their figurative roots in the OT, of which he should have been an expert expositor. But he is more humble than in his previous question in v.4; he does not raise an impossible question as if to argue against the Lord. The only way to obtain an answer to a question as "How can these things be?" is to listen to the words of the Lord. If this is avoided, no answer can be received.

10-12 *The Lord speaks.* The Lord calls Nicodemus by the word "master", namely "teacher", the same word *didaskalos* that Nicodemus used of the Lord. Nicodemus betrays himself as an ignorant teacher, not even knowing the way in which these principles are dealt with in the OT. Even academically, a teacher should be an expert in his own subject, able to contend for his field of expertise. An ignorant teacher is equivalent to the blind leading the blind (Matt 15:14; 22:29).

V.11 provides us with a vital principle of translation: the Lord speaks to "thee", Nicodemus, a *singular* pronoun being used. Yet He speaks about "ye" in vv.11-12, namely, people in the *plural*. This is clear in the AV, yet most modern translations indiscriminately use "you" always, failing to distinguish between the singular and plural in contexts where both appear in the Greek text. This lack of precision, as a deliberate policy on the part of the translators, cannot lead a believer to obtain an exact understanding of Scripture. We will quote a few examples, so that readers can see what is at stake; dozens of examples occur throughout the Bible.

1. Exod 4:15; "thou" refers to Moses, "you" to the children of Israel.

2. Exod 29:42; "thee" refers to Moses, "you" to the children of Israel.

3. Matt 18:9-10; "thine, thee" refer to one disciple, "ye, you" refer to many.

4. Matt 23:37; "thee, thy" refer to Jerusalem as an entity, "ye" to all the people separately.

5. Matt 26:64; "thou" refers to the high priest, "you" to all who will see Him in glory in the coming day.

6. Luke 10:13; "thee" refers to Chorazin, "you" to Chorazin and Bethsaida.

7. Luke 22:31-32; "thee, thy, thou" refer to Peter, "you" to all the apostles.

8. John 1:50-51; "thee, thou" refer to Nathanael, "you, ye" refer to future spectators of the glory of the Son of man.

9. 1 Cor 8:9-12; "thee, thy" refer to individuals, "yours, ye" to all members of a local assembly.

10. 2 Tim 4:22; "thy" refers to Timothy, "you" to all readers of the Epistle.

11. Titus 3:15; "thee" refers to Titus, "you" to the church in Crete.

By saying "we" in v.11, the Lord takes a place amongst the godly teachers in Israel; we suspect that He implied the godly prophets in the OT. They knew, having been taught by God, and He knew, being one with the Father. As far as the Jews as a whole were concerned, they received not this true witness, neither from the Lord amongst them, nor from the OT Scriptures that they possessed as the oracles of God. Truly, "his own received him not" (1:11; 3:32). Without doubt, Nicodemus was not included in this embracive statement, since at some stage he became a courageous man of faith. Neither do we believe that he is included in v.12; this applied to Pharisaical teachers, but not to one to whom the truth was now going to be unfolded. By "earthly things", the Lord is not referring to natural things; rather he refers to spiritual events that take place on earth—the truth of the second birth that He had just described. If this cannot be believed, neither can subsequent things, namely the "heavenly things" to be described in vv.13-21, for here we have the Son in heaven, the Father manifesting His love from heaven, the giving of the Son being a purpose from heaven, and "everlasting life" stretching into heaven.

13 The heavenly truth now to be described could only be given originally from One in, or from, heaven. The prophets of the OT and the apostles of the NT had never had that privilege; the Lord Jesus alone was the revealer of this truth. Afterwards, of course, His servants could pass it on, but only as having learnt it from the Lord. The Lord is not speaking of His own ascension here, to be accomplished after His resurrection. The Lord came down first, and was thus the true authority of this heavenly teaching; later the Holy Spirit would come down, also to be the true authority of truth revealed to the apostles. In the clause "the Son of man which is in heaven", the words "which is" are *ho ōn*, namely "the being One", a title used in Rev 1:4, 8; 4:8; 16:5. In other words, His Person was always One with the Father in heaven, although in Manhood He was on earth in the days of His flesh. He usually employed the title "Son of man" when referring to Himself; it implies His authority then and in the future, though it is not a title used in His relationship with the church and its members (Acts 7:56 and Rev 1:13 being exceptions). The title had its roots in the OT (Ps 8:4; Dan 7:13).

2. *The Son as the Revealer of Eternal Life*
3:14-21

v.14 "And as Moses lifted up the serpent in the wilderness, even so must the Son of man be lifted up:

v.15 That whosoever believeth in him should not perish, but have eternal life.
v.16 For God so loved the world, that he gave his only begotten Son, that whosoever believeth in him should not perish, but have everlasting life.
v.17 For God sent not his Son into the world to condemn the world; but that the world through him might be saved.
v.18 He that believeth on him is not condemned: but he that believeth not is condemned already, because he hath not believed in the name of the only begotten Son of God.
v.19 And this is the condemnation, that light is come into the world, and men loved darkness rather than light, because their deeds were evil.
v.20 For every one that doeth evil hateth the light, neither cometh to the light, lest his deeds should be reproved.
v.21 But he that doeth truth cometh to the light, that his deeds may be made manifest, that they are wrought in God."

14-15 *The Lord continues speaking*. The Lord now introduces a supreme example of the heavenly interpretation of an OT incident. In Num 21:4-9, the complaints of the people against God and Moses brought about judgment; fiery serpents bit the people so that many died. After their confession of sin, Moses had to make a fiery serpent of brass, placing it on a pole, so that all who looked on it should live. Admittedly, this brazen serpent became a religious relic of idolatry, with incense burnt before it; only about 800 years later was this serpent broken by Hezekiah (2 Kings 18:4). This remarkable and unusual miracle towards the end of the wilderness wanderings was a type of the work of the Lord Jesus on the cross. In effect, what was lifted up by Moses was made like the cause of the people's failure, yet retaining the purity and metallic perfection of brass that remained uncontaminated. Similarly, the Son of man "must" be lifted up on the cross. There He was made a curse for us; He was made sin, that which had caused the downfall of men, yet in Himself retaining infinite divine perfection. As Paul wrote, "he hath made him to be sin for us, who knew no sin" (2 Cor 5:21). The Lord said "must", as He also said after the event, "all things must be fulfilled" (Luke 24:44).

The word "up" occurs in many verses relating to the movements of the Lord:

1. Lifted up: John 3:14; 8:28; 12:32 (His cross).

2. Raised up: Acts 2:24; 10:40; 13:34; Rom 8:11 (His resurrection).

3. Taken up: Acts 1:2,9,11,22 (His ascension).

Here we have the divine objective of the cross towards men. It is the counterpart to the children of Israel looking by faith at the serpent lifted up. The work of Christ would be negative and positive: not perishing and having eternal life. "Perish" is the destiny of those who have experienced only the first birth;

"eternal life" is the destiny of those who have also experienced the second birth. For believers, the first destiny has been replaced by the second. Throughout the NT, this word "perish" (*apollumi*) is used of both things and persons; it does not mean that the object or person will disappear completely; rather the thought is that of "ruin, loss, not of being, but of well-being" (Vine). The ultimate implication is that of eternal death. By contrast, life is "eternal" (v.15) and "everlasting" (v.16). Strictly, these two different English words here represent one Greek word, *aiōnios*, meaning "without end". the AV translators have used "eternal" and "everlasting" indiscriminately throughout the NT, using both words even in contexts where *aiōnios* occurs twice, such as Matt 25:46; Acts 13:46-48. The word that properly means "everlasting" (in the sense of continuity without interruption) is *aidios*, appearing only twice (Rom 1:20; Jude 6). So apart from these two cases, the word "everlasting" should always be changed to "eternal" ("without end").

16 This verse presents the core of the gospel message; it interprets v.14 and repeats v.15 as a result of this interpretation. (A child may be encouraged to read the verse many times, with the instruction to find the actual word "gospel" in the verse. The word appears as the initial letter of six words in order through the verse: "God, Only, Son, Perish, Everlasting, or Eternal, Life".)

Giving and loving form the components of the gospel message. Love is not defined in the Scriptures; it is perceived by its effects, as can be seen in 1 Cor 15. In the NT, there are various circles of divine love, that carefully focus on the Person of the Son. Our affections also should be formed by these circles of divine love, and we are exhorted not to love things that are in the world (1 John 2:15). We may note five aspects of divine love, all of which are also associated with giving, for this is a characteristic of love.

1. *The world* (John 3:16)—of course, in an evangelistic sense. The demonstration of this love was that God gave His Son.

2. *The individual* (Gal 2:20) who has been delivered from this present evil age. Paul knew that He "gave himself for me".

3. *The local company or church*. In 2 Thess 2:16, He "hath given us everlasting consolation"; in John 13:1-3, the Lord loved "his own which were in the world", knowing that the Father had given all things into His hands; in Rev 3:19, "as many as I love", to them He will "grant" (the same word, "give") to sit with Him in His throne (v.21).

4. *The church as the body of Christ* (Eph 5:25); He "gave himself for it".

5. *The Father's love for the Son* (John 3:35; 10:17); He "giveth not the Spirit by measure unto him", and "hath given all things into his hand".

For the meaning of the adjective "only begotten" (*monogenēs*), see our notes on 1:14.

17-18 These two verses present the inevitable division amongst men, brought about by the sacrificial work of Christ being presented to them in the gospel message. He came to seek and to save that which was lost, not "to condemn the world". There is a difference between the words "condemn" and "judge", and this is not always clear in the AV. Strictly, the word *krinō* means "judge", referring to the process of a trial, but the word *katakrinō* means "condemn", referring to the passing of the sentence. In vv.17-19, the verb *krinō* occurs three times, and the corresponding noun once, in which case the words should be translated "judge" and "judgment" (RV, JND). The word "condemn" (namely, the passing of a sentence) properly occurs in verses such as "they shall condemn him to death" (Matt 20:18); "Neither do I condemn thee" (John 8:10); "Who is he that condemneth?" (Rom 8:34).

That "the world through him might be saved" shows the availability of eternal life; it is available for all, though v.18 shows that unbelievers do not avail themselves of it. Paul writes of this availability on several occasions: "a ransom for all" (1 Tim 2:4-6); "unto all" (Rom 3:22); "he died for all" (2 Cor 5:15), though he qualifies these last two quotations to show who avail themselves of the life under offer.

In v.18, the difference is one of faith or otherwise. "He that believeth" is a present participle, *ho pisteuōn*, namely the continuous exercise of faith which cannot have an end. By contrast, the one condemned "hath not believed" in the Name. This is *mē pepisteuken*, a verb in the perfect tense, carrying the meaning that an act of unbelief in rejecting the Son in the past has its effects even to the present. The same tense is used for "is condemned", namely "is judged"; the process of judgment commenced when unbelief commenced, and the effect of judgment continues as long as unbelief continues.

19-21 These concluding verses show the nature of the continuous judgment. The Lord as the Light of the world shines upon all. Believers practise what is truth, and are glad that the Light commends such deeds as accomplished in the power of God. But unbelievers hide in dark corners to avoid the Light (and even to escape condemnation, Isa 22:19; Hos 10:8; Luke 23:30; Rev 6:16), to avoid being discovered (as the word "reproved" means), still loving their deeds of darkness, even though this means judgment, condemnation and death. See Luke 12:2-3.

3. *John the Baptist's Last Testimony Concerning the Son* 3:22-36

v.22 "After these things came Jesus and his disciples into the land of Judaea; and there he tarried with them, and baptized.
v.23 And John also was baptizing in Aenon near to Salim, because there was much water there: and they came, and were baptized.

v.24 For John was not yet cast into prison.
v.25 Then there arose a question between *some* of John's disciples and the Jews about purifying.
v.26 And they came unto John, and said unto him, Rabbi, he that was with thee beyond Jordan, to whom thou barest witness, behold, the same baptizeth, and all *men* come to him.
v.27 John answered and said, A man can receive nothing, except it be given him from heaven.
v.28 Ye yourselves bear me witness, that I said, I am not the Christ, but that I am sent before him.
v.29 He that hath the bride is the bridegroom: but the friend of the bridegroom, which standeth and heareth him, rejoiceth greatly because of the bridegroom's voice: this my joy therefore is fulfilled.
v.30 He must increase, but I *must* decrease.
v.31 He that cometh from above is above all: he that is of the earth is earthly, and speaketh of the earth: he that cometh from heaven is above all.
v.32 And what he hath seen and heard, that he testifieth; and no man receiveth his testimony.
v.33 He that hath received his testimony hath set to his seal that God is true.
v.34 For he whom God hath sent speaketh the words of God: for God giveth not the Spirit by measure *unto him*.
v.35 The Father loveth the Son, and hath given all things into his hand.
v.36 He that believeth on the Son hath everlasting life: and he that believeth not the Son shall not see life; but the wrath of God abideth on him."

22-23 The Lord's visits to Jerusalem were always relatively short, and He would move back to Galilee when the feast days were over. This particular return to the north commenced with Jerusalem (John 2:13), Judaea (3:22), Samaria (4:4), and Galilee (4:43), reminding us of His instructions to the apostles that their testimony would move out from Jerusalem, to Judaea, Samaria and to the uttermost part of the earth (Acts 1:8). In John 1:28, John was baptising "in Bethabara beyond Jordan", while later in 3:23 the place was "in Aenon near to Salim". Bethabara was near the mouth of the river Jordan where it joins the Dead Sea, but Aenon is usually understood to have been situated over 40 miles to the north (about 22 miles to the south of the Sea of Galilee).

The statement that "he ... baptised" is remarkable (the verb *ebaptizen* is singular, in the imperfect tense, showing that this was a continuous activity while they tarried there). However, 4:1-2 tells us that although the Lord was baptising, yet He Himself "baptised not" (again the same verb in the imperfect tense). This implies that the Lord was guiding in the baptismal process, yet the actual physical act was done by the apostles. "There was much water there" is a statement that would be quite irrelevant if the traditional mode of sprinkling was being used, but immersion demands "much water", the river Jordan supplying this need. There are many different kinds of baptisms given in the NT.

1. Baptism unto Moses (1 Cor 10:1-2).

2. John's baptism (Matt 3:6; Acts 19:4), a baptism of repentance.

3. The baptism of the Lord Jesus (Matt 3:13-17).

4. Baptism by the Lord's disciples (John 3:22).

5. The baptism of suffering (Matt 20:22-23).

6. Baptism in the Holy Spirit (Matt 3:11; John 1:43; 1 Cor 12:13).

7. Baptism in fire (Matt 3:11-12), namely judgment.

8. Believers' baptism in water (Matt 28:19; Acts 2:41; 10:47; etc.).

The nature of baptism (4) in this list is not explained; men could believe on the Lord, but could not perceive the value of His forthcoming death and resurrection, something so important in believers' baptism today.

24-26 The rest of ch.3 is occupied with the final testimony of John the Baptist before he was cast into prison. The statement should be compared with that in Matt 4:12, "John was cast into prison", showing that this imprisonment commenced after the Lord's temptation and before, at least, one arrival in Galilee. The reason behind John's imprisonment is found in Matt 14:3-4, namely, his faithful declaration of the law of God even to those in highest authority. Another reason is that the continued testimony of John could not be allowed to eclipse that of the Lord Jesus, whose ministry was just commmencing. By saying "I must decrease" (3:30), John appeared to imply that his own service was complete. But his final recorded testimony (vv.27-36) shows a spiritual maturity that completely overshadows his original teaching of judgment (Matt 3:7-12).

The fact that a man, John, could have disciples, gave place to the Lord having His disciples. From henceforth, believers would not be disciples of other believers; men would be disciples of the Lord only, as He often said, "my disciple" (Luke 14:26,27,33), and "my disciples" (John 8:31; 13:35; 15:8).

Evidently the religious teachers among the Jews would contend and argue with John and his disciples, just as later they would argue with the Lord. The contention was about "purifying", though details are not given. No doubt the Jews who rejected water baptism unto repentance were more concerned with their own ritual that used water, such as washing before dinner, cleaning the outside of the cup and plate (Luke 11:38-39), described as "the tradition of the elders" (Mark 7:3-4). Traditionalism and ritualism maintain their cause by contention. Again, the uninitiated Jews may have been arguing about the relevant differences between John's baptism and that practised by the Lord's disciples.

John's disciples speak. Addressing John as "Rabbi", they thought that "all men" were coming to the Lord's baptism, and only few to John's baptism. They seem to manifest a spirit of jealousy, failing to understand the new concepts introduced by the Lord. No doubt "all men" was an exaggeration of their own impression, for the fact was that "no man receiveth his testimony" (v.32). To these disciples, the Lord was a nameless One, "he that was with thee", not the Lamb of God and the Son of God that John had confessed in ch.1. Here was complete ignorance of Christ in spite of these men being disciples of an outspoken godly man, showing the danger that a godly man may present, even a barrier to others' perception of One far greater than himself.

27-28 *John speaks.* It is not really clear whether the words of John the Baptist continue to the end of the chapter, or whether the latter verses are the additional written words by the Spirit of inspiration through John the apostle and author. Here is the true origin of the gain of converts: the ability and opportunity to gain converts is given from heaven. This applied to John, and it applied to the Lord for He brought these features of service down from heaven. Thus just before He gave Himself, He contemplated in John 17 the many things that had been given Him: "power over all flesh", "men which thou gavest me", "the work", "the words", "glory" (vv.2,6,4,8,24). In our case, all spiritual gifts that we possess are from heaven: from God (Rom 12:3), from the risen Lord (Eph 4:7-11), and from the Holy Spirit (1 Cor 12:11).

Additionally, John states that the reason for his present lack of success in gaining new disciples is that "I am not the Christ". Previously, men had "mused . . . whether he were the Christ" (Luke 3:15). He was rightly adamant, "I am not the Christ" (John 1:20), though later Herod thought the opposite, that Christ was John the Baptist risen from the dead (Matt 14:2). In the end times, however, false Christs will be only too ready to claim this status (Matt 24:24; 2 Thess 2:4; 1 John 2:18; Rev 13:11-14).

John always knew that he had been sent (John 1:6,33). All servants of God should realise this. Paul as an apostle had been sent (Acts 13:4; 26:17), and none can preach "except they be sent" (Rom 10:15).

29-30 To explain his position further, John uses the figure of a bridegroom. We do not believe that his knowledge extended to the fact of the calling out of the church to be the bride of Christ; this truth was revealed later, when Paul would present the Corinthians as "a chaste virgin to Christ" (2 Cor 11:2), when he wrote of Christ loving the church in terms of a husband loving his wife (Eph 5:25), and when the church is seen as the Lamb's wife (Rev 19:7). The figure was used in the OT of Israel, "as the bridegroom rejoiceth over the bride, so shall thy God rejoice over thee" (Isa 62:5); no doubt John in his mind was thinking of this quotation. In the context, John refers to the Lord's disciples as the bride. As the friend of the Bridegroom, John could rejoice at the substance of the Lord's teaching, and of course in the fact that the Lord possessed many more disciples than he did. In this sense, John would decrease and the Lord would increase; his authority would decrease while that of the Lord would increase. This is the true spiritual attitude for every believer, to perceive the pre-eminence of the Lord in all things. Of course, those who humble themselves before God will be exalted in due time (1 Pet 5:6), and although John was later beheaded, the Lord exalted His servant, stating that he was "more than a prophet" (Matt 11:9), of all those who had been born, not one was "greater than John the Baptist" (v.11), and the authority behind his baptism was "from heaven" and not "of men" (Matt 21:25).

31 As we have said before, these closing verses may be the Spirit's commentary on John the Baptist's words, extending the idea behind "He must increase". In this verse, we have contrasts between the person and work of John and the Person and work of the Lord. The Lord was the Occupant of heaven, and He came forth from heaven, bringing a heavenly message to men. John perceived himself as "from the earth" (*ek tēs gēs*), and he remained "from the earth" (the word "earthly" is exactly the same phrase as "of the earth" in the AV). Moreover, he spoke "from the earth" (the third time this identical phrase appears in the verse), namely as a man from earth rather than from heaven (nothing to do with "worldly talk or teaching" in a derogatory unspiritual sense). John is contrasting every aspect of his service with that of the Lord.

32-33 The first part of v.32 is similar to v.11; there the Lord identified Himself with faithful teachers in Israel, but here John (or the Spirit) refers the seeing and hearing uniquely to the Lord (not "we" but "he"). The Lord brought down treasure out of heaven, not to cast it before swine, but to present it to His flock. "No man" receiving His testimony refers to all men except the Lord's own people; men believed not on Him because "they could not believe" (John 12:37-39), demonstrated by the quotation "Lord, who hath believed our report?". The "many" received not the Lord's testimony, but only the "few" believed (Matt 7:13-14). See John 6:66.

By receiving the Lord's testimony, a believer "hath set to his seal that God is true", or "hath set his seal to this, that God is true" (RV). Other men are therefore calling God a liar (1 John 5:10). In John 6:27, the Father's seal upon Christ proves that He is the Giver of eternal life; our faith is similar to the sealing of a document to authenticate it—we authenticate the fact that God is true.

(**34-35** Whether men believe or whether men do not believe, neither in any way challenges the fact that the sent One was always speaking the words of God. As the Lord said to the Pharisees, "I speak to the world those things which I have heard of him" (8:26; 12:49,50). To confirm this in another way, John (or the Spirit of inspiration) says, "God giveth not the Spirit by measure unto him". Here is infinite possession and infinite understanding of the divine mind. To us, God distributes "the measure of faith" in the sense that gifts differ according to "the proportion of faith" (Rom 12:3,6); again, in our case the Spirit enables us to understand things that are freely given us from God (1 Cor 2:10-14). But in the Lord's case, He was eternally resident in Deity, always doing everything through "the eternal Spirit", even the offering of Himself without spot to God (Heb 9:14). This goes far beyond Luke 4:18, where the Spirit of the Lord was upon Him, to preach and heal; this refers to His service on Fearth, whereas "not... by measure" refers to His eternal Person. The Spirit coming upon Him at His baptism related to His service on earth, not to His eternal knowledge of the eternal Father. Indeed, "The Father loveth the Son" relates to eternity, "for thou lovest me before the foundation of the world" (17:24). And since a chief character of love is that of giving, how true it is that the ather has given "all things" to the Son; for example, "All things are delivered unto me of the Father" (Matt 11:27). For ourselves, because of love in Rom 5:8, God has freely given us "all things" (Rom 8:32).

36 This last verse is a direct echo of vv.15-18. It reflects upon the difference between the Lord's disciples and the many who would not believe. The "wrath" refers to God's anger in judgment—it is a present anger. In verses such as Matt 3:7 and 1 Thess 1:10, "wrath" is future, and appears to refer more particularly to the judgment prior to the coming millennial kingdom, thus cleansing the earth for the coming King's reign.

IV. The Establishment by the Son of True Worship (4:1-54)

1. *True Water*
4:1-18

v.1 "When therefore the Lord knew how the Pharisees had heard that Jesus made and baptized more disciples than John,
v.2 (Though Jesus himself baptized not, but his disciples,)
v.3 He left Judaea, and departed again into Galilee.
v.4 And he must needs go through Samaria.
v.5 Then cometh he to a city of Samaria, which is called Sychar, near to the parcel of ground that Jacob gave to his son Joseph.
v.6 Now Jacob's well was there. Jesus therefore, being wearied with *his* journey, sat thus on the well: *and* it was about the sixth hour.
v.7 There cometh a woman of Samaria to draw water: Jesus saith unto her, Give me to drink.
v.8 (For his disciples were gone away unto the city to buy meat.)
v.9 Then saith the woman of Samaria unto him, How is it that thou, being a Jew, askest drink of me, which am a woman of Samaria? for the Jews have no dealings with the Samaritans.
v.10 Jesus answered and said unto her, If thou knewest the gift of God, and who it is that saith to thee, Give me to drink; thou wouldest have asked of him, and he would have given thee living water.
v.11 The woman saith unto him, Sir, thou hast nothing to draw with, and the well is deep: from whence then hast thou that living water?

v.12 Art thou greater than our father Jacob, which gave us the well, and drank thereof himself, and his children, and his cattle?
v.13 Jesus answered and said unto her, Whosoever drinketh of this water shall thirst again:
v.14 But whosoever drinketh of the water that I shall give him shall never thirst; but the water that I shall give him shall be in him a well of water springing up into everlasting life.
v.15 The woman saith unto him, Sir, give me this water, that I thirst not, neither come hither to draw.
v.16 Jesus saith unto her, Go, call thy husband, and come hither.
v.17 The woman answered and said, I have no husband. Jesus said unto her, Thou hast well said, I have no husband:
v.18 For thou hast had five husbands; and he whom thou now hast is not thy husband: in that saidst thou truly."

The background to this story of the Samaritan woman at the well is important. In fact, a forbidden marriage in the OT could have disastrous religious consequences after a lapse even of more than 1 000 years.

In passages such as Exod 34:12-17; Deut 7:1-5; Josh 23:12-13, God would not allow marriages between the children of Israel and the nations around; their daughters would turn the men of Israel from the Lord to idolatry. In particular, the leaders in Israel should have set a good example, for others quite naturally would follow their example, whether in things good or bad. In the book of Judges, idolatry was rampant in Israel, and Samson as a Nazarite (Judges 13:5,7) and as a leader should have recognised his divinely-given position of separation. Yet later he loved Delilah a woman of the Philistines (Judges 16:4), and the Lord departed from him (v.20).

In particular, Solomon the king's wife was a daughter of Pharaoh; she could not live in Jerusalem because the ark of the Lord was there (1 Kings 3:1; 2 Chron 8:11). Moreover, Solomon knew the law of God given through Moses, for a king must not "multiply wives to himself, that his heart turn not away" (Deut 17:17). However, towards the end of his life, "Solomon loved many strange women", although God had said "Ye shall not go in to them" (1 Kings 11:1-3); his 700 wives turned away his heart. God's judgment fell. He would rend the kingdom from Solomon and give it to another. Hence after Solomon's death, the northern kingdom was set up under Jeroboam, a king who introduced every kind of idolatry so as to prevent the northern tribes from returning to Jerusalem (1 Kings 12:26-33). The subsequent kings were always idolatrous in one way or another.

About 250 years later, idolatry was so bad that God delivered the nation into the hands of the Assyrians (2 Kings 17:1-23). After this, the land was repopulated by other nations (v.24), "they possessed Samaria, and dwelt in the cities thereof". One of the priests of Israel was then repatriated (v.27), in order to teach the new population his own brand of idolatry. These people became the Samaritans, possessing the Pentateuch and a temple on mount Gerizim, which was a mount of blessing according to Deut 27:12. In fact, the Samaritans insisted that mount Gerizim was the original mount Moriah, and that this was the place which God had chosen to place His Name there (Deut 12:5) rather than mount Zion in Jerusalem.

In the Lord's time, there was always enmity between the Jews and the Samaritans. Since Samaria lay between Judaea to the south and Galilee to the north, with the river Jordan to the east, many Jews would bypass Samaria if they journeyed from one province to the other, crossing and recrossing the river Jordan to avoid Samaritan territory. Thus the Lord used this concept of enmity in His parable of the Good Samaritan (Luke 10:30-35), in which the priest and the Levite passed by on the other side, to avoid the wounded man (inferred to be a Jew). But the Samaritan, far from avoiding the wounded man, gave him every kind of help. Similarly, the woman at the well recognised that "the Jews have no dealings with the Samaritans" (4:9), though the Lord would not act like that, neither would Philip when the gospel entered Samaria (Acts 8:5). But apart from the men of Sychar, the Samaritans would not receive any Jew passing through to go up to Jerusalem, and the tradition of hatred was so engrained in the apostles' hearts that they had no qualms in thinking that fire should come down from heaven to consume them (Luke 9:54).

All this followed from Solomon's sin 1 000 years before, and accounts for the woman's position in the story. Truly, "some men they (sins) follow after" (1 Tim 5:24).

1-6 In John 3:26, John the Baptist's disciples knew that the Lord was gaining more disciples than he; he willingly explained why. But here, the Pharisees knew this fact also, but the Lord did not explain why. Mere traditional religionists have no right to know the reasons behind the works of the Lord—the wise and prudent remain in ignorance, while the truth is revealed to babes (Matt 11:25; 21:16). Thus the Lord left the habitual grounds of the Pharisees, to return to Galilee through Samaria, knowing that salvation would visit the city of Sychar shortly. He therefore came to this place, with memories so rooted in the OT. "The parcel of ground" that Jacob gave to Joseph is found in Gen 33:18-20, purchased by Jacob after his reuniting with Esau. Jacob built an altar there, calling it "El-elohe-Israel" (God the God of Israel). At his death, Jacob recalled that he had given Joseph "one portion above thy brethren" (Gen 48:22); later the bones of Joseph were buried there (Josh 24:32). Yet the sanctity of the place had been forgotten throughout the existence of the idolatrous northern kingdom, and the Samaritan religion displaced "God the God of Israel".

"Jacob's well was there", a well being commonplace in those days, yet the Lord would use this to develop the message of the "living water". In the OT no account occurs of the building of this well, though we read of Abraham and Isaac digging wells (Gen 21:25; 26:22). In fact, the Lord was taking up things traditional and natural, in order to substitute truth and spirituality.

The description "wearied with his journey" shows the perfect humanity of the Lord in the days of His flesh. This physical weariness and His thirst show that these experiences are not connected with sin; they are the portion of all men created and formed from the beginning. The Lord came where we were, and was not miraculously immune from normal experiences that pertain to the body. Note that John records that it was "about the sixth hour". The Spirit of God gives exact numbers on occasions, and only approximate numbers on other occasions, depending upon the knowledge of the writer at the time. Here it was only *about* midday, but in John 2:6 there were *exactly* six waterpots. In this story, there were exactly five husbands (4:18), while there were exactly five loaves and two fish in John 6:9. However, the number of men is stated to "about" 5 000. In John 21:11, the number of fish is given exactly as 153, evidently because someone counted them rather than the Spirit miraculously providing the total.

7-8 *The Lord speaks.* The woman was there at the right time to suit the Lord's purpose, just as Rebekah came to a well at the right time, making God's will known to Abraham's servant (Gen 24:13-20). When others needed food and drink, He provided it, as in John 2:7-9; 6:11, but when He needed drink, He asked another for it. When He was hungry, He would not act miraculously to produce bread from stones at the temptation from Satan; rather He would wait until angels came and ministered to Him in His need (Matt 4:11). However, the Lord knew that He had something to offer the woman, rather than the woman actually providing something for Him; skilfully He developed the conversation to lead to this end.

It is remarkable that all the disciples had gone into the city to buy bread (upon their return they misunderstood the situation entirely). In other words, they left the Son of God alone; in John 3:22, He tarried with them, but here no one would tarry with the Lord. Had some remained with Him, no doubt they would have criticised or prevented the conversation with the Samaritan woman, in keeping with the prejudice that they, as Jews, had towards the Samaritans. Later, on a more solemn occasion, the Lord predicted that "ye . . . shall leave me alone" (John 16:32) on account of their lack of courage.

9 *The woman speaks.* The woman recognised all the enmity existing between Jews and Samaritans, and was perplexed about this lonely Man's request. There is progress in her recognition of the Lord, from "Jew", to "prophet" (v.19), to "Christ" (v.29). This is similar to the progress made by the blind man healed in ch.9; "Jesus" (v.11), "prophet" (v.17), "Son of God" (vv.35-38).

10 *The Lord speaks.* He knew that there was complete ignorance on her part. Had she known that He was the Christ, the Son of God, she would have realised that He had something to offer her had she asked for it—something spiritual rather than natural. A request in prayer is always answered in keeping with the divine will, and certainly this was the divine will in this case. Not having the complete OT, she did not appreciate even the spiritual concept of "living water" as in the verses "me the fountain of living waters" (Jer 2:13), and "living waters shall go out from Jerusalem" (Zech 14:8). Possessing the Pentateuch, no doubt she thought of physical water provided miraculously in the wilderness (Exod 17:6; Num 20:11).

11-12 *The woman speaks.* The title "Sir" is *kurios,* namely "Lord". This is properly a title given to One divine, but it was also a title of ordinary respect, and the context must determine when the title "Lord" is inappropriate. This title "Sir" may also be found in verses such as John 4:49 and 12:21 (when Philip was addressed). In 9:36, the healed blind man said "Lord" before he believed on Him as the Son of God. It is difficult to decide whether this should more appropriately be translated as "Sir"; certainly the NEB uses "Sir" in this verse. The translated title "Lord" used by Martha and Mary (11:21,27,32) appears to be most appropriate.

The woman clearly thought that the Lord referred to the actual physical water in the well as "living water". V.15 suggests that her only desire was to be freed from the burden of drawing and carrying water. In other words, spiritual concepts expressed in metaphorical terms were interpreted entirely in physical terms; we cannot speculate how the woman thought that this unknown Stranger could provide a constant supply of water without using the well. This is more than Jacob could do for himself, his family and his cattle. Hence she asked the question, "Art thou greater than our father Jacob?", as if Jacob were a hero to her. This thought of "greater than" occurs five times in the Gospels (three times in the Lord's words, and twice in others' questions):

1. "In this place is one greater than the temple" (Matt 12:6);

2. "A greater than Jonas is here" (Matt 12:41);

3. "A greater than Solomon is here" (Matt 12:42);

4. "Art thou greater than our father Jacob?" (John 4:12);

5. "Art thou greater than our father Abraham?" (John 8:52).

13-14 *The Lord speaks.* These two verses present a great contrast; v.13 is natural while v.14 is spiritual. The first represents the former state of the woman, while the second represents her latter state. Paul draws the same distinction in 1 Cor 2:11, "For what man knoweth the things of a man, save the spirit of man which is in him? even so the things of God knoweth no man, but the Spirit of God". For the living water refers to the Holy Spirit, as John 7:38-39 makes clear. The Spirit is the greatest possession of a believer, appropriated at the time of his conversion, originally given when the Lord was glorified. Moreover, the ideas behind "never thirst" and "eternal" clearly demonstrate the security of the believer; there can never be a cessation of belief, leading to a losing of salvation and thirsting again. Similarly, the appropriation of the flesh and blood of the Son of man leads to eternal life (John 6:54-58).

15 *The woman speaks.* She still continued to interpret the Lord's words in a materialistic sense. Her desires were self-centred, wishing to avoid thirst and the necessity of coming regularly to the well to draw water. God's gifts to His people do not permit laziness in their daily routine, as Paul wrote, "If any would not work, neither should he eat" (2 Thess 3:10; Eccl 2:24; 3:13; 5:19). This materialistic interpretation of spiritual words is also seen in John 6:52 (by the Jews) and in 6:60 (by His disciples).

16 *The Lord speaks.* Truth that was not comprehended led the Lord to probe more deeply into the conscience of the woman. By asking her to call her husband, the Lord deliberately touched upon a raw spot in the past of her life. Salvation, without having regard to the question of sin, is not a scriptural concept.

17-18 *The woman speaks.* By saying "I have no husband", the woman was keeping something back, not realising at that stage that the Lord knew all things. She had no desire to open her heart fully to this lonely Stranger. The complete confession of her sinful life was necessary before she could know Him as "the Saviour of the world".

The Lord speaks. There is such a thing as speaking the truth while at the same time hiding almost everything. Speaking "the truth, the whole truth, and nothing but the truth" is difficult for most men and women. By saying "I have no husband", the woman may have been telling a lie, if she thought that the present man she had was her husband. The Lord made it quite clear that only the first man had been her husband; the others could not be according to the law contained in her Pentateuch, "Thou shalt not commit adultery" (Exod 20:14). Effectively, the woman was copying Solomon before her—he had 700 wives, while the woman had five husbands. Judgment fell in Solomon's case, while blessing came upon the woman. The proper husband-wife relationship is found in passages such as Eph 5:22-33; Col 3:18-19; 1 Tim 3:2,12. We recall that the Sadducees concocted a trick question about a wife having seven husbands, in this case following the letter of the law (Matt 22:25-26).

2. *True Worship*
4:19-26

v.19 "The woman saith unto him, Sir, I perceive that thou art a prophet.
v.20 Our fathers worshipped in this mountain; and ye say that in Jerusalem is the place where men ought to worship.
v.21 Jesus saith unto her, Woman, believe me, the hour cometh when ye shall neither in this mountain, nor yet at Jerusalem, worship the Father.
v.22 Ye worship ye know not what: we know what we worship: for salvation is of the Jews.
v.23 But the hour cometh, and now is, when the true worshippers shall worship the Father in spirit and in truth: for the Father seeketh such to worship him.

v.24 God *is* a Spirit: and they that worship him must worship *him* in spirit and in truth.
v.25 The woman saith unto him, I know that Messias cometh, which is called Christ: when he is come, he will tell us all things.
v.26 Jesus saith unto her, I that speak unto thee am *he*."

19-20 *The woman speaks.* At last the woman's heart was touched, though not to the point of recognising that the Stranger was One divine. No doubt she was not thinking of a successor to the OT prophets, for these were outside the record of her Pentateuch. Perhaps she thought of Moses' words, "would God that all the Lord's people were prophets" (Num 11:29). But the opening up of her life by this Stranger, showed that He had some power of miraculous discernment. Others also made this limited confession: "a prophet mighty in deed and word" (Luke 24:19); "This is of a truth that prophet" (John 6:14; 7:40); "He is a prophet" (9:17). But how limited an understanding this is of the Son of God!

In v.12, the woman used the words "our father Jacob", because the Samaritans thought that they stemmed from Ephraim and Manasseh (according to the Jewish historian Josephus). In v.20, she used the words "Our fathers", no doubt thinking of the time when an altar was built on mount Gerizim in keeping with Deut 27:4-5 (strictly, the altar had to be built on mount Ebal according to the Hebrew text, but the Samaritan Pentateuch had "Gerizim" substituted in place of "Ebal"). The Samaritans' ancestors had built a temple on Gerizim in Nehemiah's time, but this had been destroyed some 160 years before the event in John 4. Clearly the woman was relying on her love of her traditional religion.

21-24 *The Lord speaks.* The Lord was casting away all traditional religion. These verses deal with the false that was to be discarded (the Samaritan method of worship), with the true that was to be discarded (the Jewish religion given in the OT), and with the true that was being substituted in place of both of these. We may deal with the Lord's replacement doctrine under five heads:

1. *Who worships? The old false.* The Samaritans consisted of the remnant of the northern kingdom of Israel, together with many imported foreigners (2 Kings 17:24-41). They practised a mixture of Jewish ordinances and foreign rites.
   The old true. These were the people of God according to the love that caused Him to choose this people to be a "special people unto himself" (Deut 7:6-8). They would never allow their "adversaries" (the Samaritans) to assist in the building of the temple (Ezra 4:1-3).
   True worshippers. The fact that they would "worship the Father" shows that they were sons after the new birth—"born . . . of God" (John 1:13). They had to have a new spiritual origin in order to engage in this new mode of worship, and by their testimony they would embrace all believers gained in "Judaea, and in Samaria" (Acts 1:8).

2. *Where does one worship? The old false.* The woman pointed to the centre of Samaritan worship when she pointed to "this mountain". The Samaritan Pentateuch, of course, contained no reference to Jerusalem having been chosen by God to be His centre on earth. From Deut 12 onwards, repeated reference is made to "the place which the Lord your God shall choose out of all your tribes to put his name there" (v.5). That this referred to mount Zion could not be seen until the books of 2 Samuel and 1 Chronicles are reached, where Asaph stated that God "chose the tribe of Judah, the mount Zion which he loved" (Ps 78:68). The Samaritans therefore relied upon a verse such as Deut 27:12, where a mountain in Samaria is named. So the woman was completely deceived by ignorance, upbringing, and by the usual affection of the flesh for religious tradition of the past.
The old true. In v.20, the woman provided information on this point, "ye say, that in Jerusalem is the place where men ought to worship". In the OT, during years of faithfulness or of idolatry, the Jews always adhered to Jerusalem. In Ps 132:13, Solomon recalled, "the Lord hath chosen Zion; he hath desired it for his habitation". See Isa 27:13; 64:11; Jer 7:2; Ezek 46:9. When in captivity, the hearts of the Jews were still centred on Zion, "By the rivers of Babylon . . . we wept, when we remembered Zion" (Ps 137:1). See Dan 6:10. The Samaritans would regard any Jewish temple at Jerusalem as savouring of apostasy.
True worshippers. In v.21, the Lord exposed the uselessness of both Samaritan and Jewish systems, "neither in this mountain, nor yet at Jerusalem". He certainly did not condone the existence of Herod's temple, whose ceremony had degenerated to the level of the carnal man. Its future was described as, "there shall not be left here one stone upon another, that shall not be thrown down" (Matt 24:2). Hence true worshippers would no longer be required to resort to a *place* but to a *Person*. The place of worship would be every believing heart (Eph 5:19), and every gathering of believers of whom the Lord said, "where two or three are gathered together in my name, there am I in the midst of them" (Matt 18:20).

3. *Whom does one worship? The old false.* Being divine, the Lord could discern the exact direction of the Samaritan form of worship, "Ye worship ye know not what". The OT revelation of God had only been partially unfolded in the Pentateuch. The limited Samaritan Scriptures could never include the blessed revelation of God as found in the Psalms and in the prophets. Worship must be based upon a full revelation; at the best, the Samaritans had only a half-God, and this is no true God at all.
The old true. The Lord continued, "we know what we worship". By saying "we", He identified Himself as the perfect One with His earthly people, at least with those faithful ones in OT and NT times. For the rest, Rom 9:4-5 shows what the Jews should have known of God, but alas they knew nothing. The pious could be "zealous towards God, as ye all are this day"

(Acts 22:3), but when the Person of Christ is absent from supposed worship, then God Himself is absent also in spite of zealous assertions to the contrary.

True worshippers. "Worship the Father", said the Lord, implying the Father as revealed in His fulness in John's Gospel. In this Gospel, the title is always "the Father" or "my Father" until after the resurrection of Christ, when He changed the title when speaking to Mary to "your Father . . . your God" (20:17). Here the true and lasting relationship to the Father is formed, enabling worshippers to cry, "Abba, Father" (Rom 8:15).

4. *When does one worship? The old false.* The woman proudly declared, "Our fathers worshipp*ed*", a tradition in the past. The Lord replied, "Ye worship", a continuous present experience. In any religion erected by man, the present is determined by the past.

The old true. The woman said, "Jerusalem *is* the place where men *ought* to worship" (two verbs in the present tense). Here we find the present aspects of traditional worship. Both the temple and synagogue services embraced present continuous activity, involving ceremony, sacrifice, and legalistic teaching. But the Lord condemned it all, however correct it might have been when introduced in the OT, "in vain they do worship me, teaching for doctrines the commandments of men" (Matt 15:9).

True worshippers. The Lord swept aside all the Samaritan and Jewish traditions. Instead, He introduced "the hour cometh", that is the hour of His cross, leading to the christian period thereafter. John's is the Gospel of the Lord's *hour*, while Luke's is the Gospel of the *place* of sacrifice (trace the Lord's path to Jerusalem from Luke 9:51 to 19:41, and note how Jerusalem as His goal is constantly mentioned). Moreover, the Lord said, "and now *is*", showing His discerning grace, since even then before His cross He always had a few faithful disciples who were able to worship God through Him.

5. *How does one worship? The old false and true.* Details are not given in the passage, but we have already quoted the Lord's estimation, "in vain they do worship me". The manner of Samaritan worship must have been worse. Formal sacrifices failed to reflect Christ to God, and hence "The Lord hath cast off his altar" (Lam 2:7; Isa 1:11; Mal 1:8). We are thankful for a few exceptions, such as faithful Zacharias (Luke 1:8-11).

True worshippers. The Lord expounded the only true approach in worship: "in spirit and in truth". This is an antitype of the OT worship "in the beauty of holiness" (Ps 96:9 and a few other references). We understand this to refer to one's spiritual dress, our standing allowing us to worship spiritually. Paul claimed to "worship God in the spirit" (Phil 3:3), having no confidence in the flesh. "In spirit" suggests the heart is in contact with

God, instead of the eyes, ears and hands being occupied with material sacrifices and representations; "in truth", the heart is occupied with God's revelation, rather than with the paraphenalia of the Jewish and Samaritan religions. "In spirit and in truth" takes us into the very heart of deity, for "God is a Spirit" and "I am . . . the truth" (John 14:6).

25 *The woman speaks.* Her words show that she trusted in what she had, but this was not enough for salvation, since she had not partaken of the living water as yet. However, such sincerity is a good prelude to the formation of faith. This was so in the case of Cornelius in Acts 10; he was devout, fearing God and giving alms, praying to God always (v.2). This was good material for the gospel, and he was saved after Peter started preaching. The woman quoted Deut 18:15-19, believing that Messiah would be the next Prophet to follow Moses. The Jews were also looking for this Prophet (John 6:14; 7:40), while Peter and Stephen used this promise in Acts 3:22; 7:37.

26 *The Lord speaks.* On very few occasions did the Lord reveal Himself directly as to His Person; here it was as the Christ; in 9:37 it was as the Son of God. Normally, the Father revealed Him as "the Christ, the Son of the living God" (Matt 16:16-17). Strictly, the Lord's words are "*egō eimi, ho lalōn soi*", namely, "I am, the One-speaking to-thee". "I am" is a title of the Lord (Exod 3:14), rather than just a part of the verb "to be". The Lord used this title when speaking to the Pharisees in John 8:24,28,58, and in 18:5,8 when He answered Judas and the officers from the chief priests who had come to arrest Him. The power behind this title caused these men to fall to the ground, but not for long, since the purpose of God had to be fulfilled.

3. *True Witness*
4:27-42

v.27 "And upon this came his disciples, and marvelled that he talked with the woman: yet no man said, What seekest thou? or, Why talkest thou with her?
v.28 The woman then left her waterpot, and went her way into the city, and saith to the men,
v.29 Come, see a man which told me all things that ever I did: is not this the Christ?
v.30 Then they went out of the city, and came unto him.
v.31 In the mean while his disciples prayed him, saying, Master, eat.
v.32 But he said unto them, I have meat to eat that ye know not of.
v.33 Therefore said the disciples one to another, Hath any man brought him *ought* to eat?
v.34 Jesus saith unto them, My meat is to do the will of him that sent me, and to finish his work.
v.35 Say not ye, There are yet four months, and *then* cometh harvest? Behold, I say unto you, Lift up your eyes, and look on the fields; for they are white already to harvest.

v.36 And he that reapeth receiveth wages, and gathereth fruit unto life eternal: that both he that soweth and he that reapeth may rejoice together.
v.37 And herein is that saying true, One soweth, and another reapeth.
v.38 I sent you to reap that whereon ye bestowed no labour: other men laboured, and ye are entered into their labours.
v.39 And many of the Samaritans of that city believed on him for the saying of the woman, which testified, He told me all that ever I did.
v.40 So when the Samaritans were come unto him, they besought him that he would tarry with them: and he abode there two days.
v.41 And many more believed because of his own word;
v.42 And said unto the woman, Now we believe, not because of thy saying: for we have heard *him* ourselves, and know that this is indeed the Christ, the Saviour of the world."

27 Having missed this conversation and self-revelation of the Lord, the disciples returned, entirely occupied with natural thoughts. There is another hint of this attitude in Mark 6:30, where there is too much stress upon "they". Paul was not like this at the end of his first missionary journey; then they spoke of "all that *God* had done" (Acts 14:27). So His disciples "marvelled" that the Lord was talking to a Samaritan woman, so contrary to mutual custom. They may also have marvelled that the woman so quickly left her waterpot to return to the city. In fact, they were silent to start with, the two recorded natural questions remaining unasked. Hesitation in talking with the Lord shows a lack of confidence, as also is found in Mark 9:32 when they "were afraid to ask him" regarding his statement about His death and resurrection.

28-30 The woman temporarily discarded the natural, so as to witness to the spiritual. Having found the Christ, she had to witness of Him to others, as did Andrew and Philip in 1:41,45 and as Paul did in Acts 9:20.

The woman speaks. Whether "all things that ever I did" is an exaggeration based on v.18, or whether the Lord revealed more to the woman than recorded by John, is not stated. Her witness of Christ was not based on the revelation of His Person, but on His ability to unfold her past; she asked them to assess whether this Man was the Christ, rather than stating that she knew this fact by His personal revelation. In spite of her past life, the response was immediate—they came to the Lord. This should be contrasted with the testimony of "just Lot", for he "seemed as one that mocked unto his sons-in-law" (Gen 19:14). Even the testimony of Saul (as recently converted) was not received immediately in the Jerusalem church—his past life discredited him until Barnabas explained how he had been converted (Acts 9:26-27).

31-33 *The disciples speak.* Showing complete ignorance of priorities that God had placed before His people, "man doth not live by bread alone, but by every word that proceedeth out of the mouth of the Lord" (Deut 8:3), and of the fact that the Lord had manifested this truth before Satan (Matt 4:2-4), the disciples said, "Master, eat", addressing Him as "Rabbi". The fact that He had more important food, in the form of doing the Father's will, was beyond their knowledge. If one jumps to conclusions, such conclusions are bound to be natural and not spiritual.

The Lord speaks. By saying "that ye know not of", the Lord showed them their state of ignorance, at the same time being quite prepared to show them the truth in the following verses. Things are hidden from the wise and prudent (Matt 11:25) who "hear not, neither do they understand" (13:13), but His disciples did not fall into that category. It should be pointed out that the word *brōma*, usually translated "meat", refers to solid food as distinct from milk.

The disciples speak. Perpetuating their ignorance, and speaking so that the Lord could not hear them (as they thought), they could not understand the Lord's reference to food, just as the woman could not understand His reference to water. This shows up the vital principle that spiritual realities are expressed in ordinary everyday words, but that these words must be discerned spiritually.

34-38 *The Lord speaks.* This picture-story is rich in spiritual meaning, recalling that the Lord often used agricultural similitudes in His teaching, whether fields, soil, seed, growing plants, harvest, trees, roots, fruit, sheep, shepherds, and so on. His food was twofold: to do the will of the Father, and to finish this work. Job had said long before, "I have esteemed the words of his mouth more than my necessary food" (Job 23:12). Through the psalmist, the Lord had said, "Lo, I come . . . to do thy will, O God" (Heb 10:7; Ps 40:7-8). The will of the Father for the Servant-Son is given a prominent place in John's Gospel (5:30; 6:38). In our present verse, the Lord's food was the will of God concerning the salvation of this woman and the men of the city. Moreover, in His prayer in 17:4 the Son contemplates His work achieved in His lifetime, "I have finished the work which thou gavest me to do" (the Greek verb *eteleiōsa* being in the aorist tense), while His final cry on the cross before His death was "It is finished" (19:30) (namely *tetelestai*, a verb in the perfect tense). We recall Paul's words towards the end of his life, "I have finished my course" (2 Tim 4:7), where the verb (*teteleka*) being in the perfect tense, marks the conclusion of his exercise expressed in Acts 20:24, "that I might finish my course" (*teleiōsai*, the aorist infinitive).

In v.35, speaking metaphorically, the Lord contrasted what He was saying with what the disciples were saying. They could visualise a natural harvest in four months time, but He could see a spiritual harvest ready for the reapers there and then. He had sowed the good seed in the heart of the woman, and she was now sowing it in the hearts of the men of the city. A few minutes or a few hours were all that were necessary for this good seed to grow, men know not how. As the Lord said elsewhere, "The harvest truly is plenteous" (Matt 9:37; Luke 10:2). But it needed faith on the part of men to see this ripe harvest ready for the reapers.

In vv.36-38, the Lord was describing His people's service beyond what was being accomplished at Sychar's well. In the context, the Lord was sowing and the Lord was reaping—the disciples were doing nothing. But in later service, when faith and spiritual power are more in evidence, "other men" labour in sowing if the Lord sends them to that sphere of service, always under the control of the divine Sower. These are evangelists who go forth with the good seed, which is the word of God. But those who follow are the reapers, those who care for the souls of the converts, those who are the pastors and teachers (Eph 4:11). The fact that "One soweth, and another reapeth" reminds us of the great principles of service described by Paul. Service is not left in the hands of one man, for "the body is not one member, but many" (1 Cor 12:14), and it is according to God's pleasure that the members are distributed throughout the body (v.18). All rejoice together in work well done for the Lord, and receive "wages". These are not financial wages, for this would hinder the gospel of Christ which is "without charge" (1 Cor 9:12,18). Rather the converts themselves form the wages in a spiritual sense, "our . . . crown of rejoicing . . . even ye" (1 Thess 2:19). Each individual will "receive his own reward according to his own labour", and "then shall every man have praise of God" (1 Cor 3:8; 4:5).

39-42 The record then reverts to the city of Sychar. The testimony of the woman that the Lord had revealed her past was sufficient to ensure that "many" believed on Him. Scripture does not say "all" believed on Him. In Sodom, no one received Lot's testimony; the evangelists from Jerusalem to the northern kingdom received a hostile reception, though many of some tribes humbled themselves and came to Jerusalem (2 Chron 30:10-11); in Nineveh, "from the greatest even to the least of them" repented at the preaching of Jonah (Jonah 3:5; Matt 12:41); in Athens only a very small minority received Paul's teaching (Acts 17:34); no one in the country of the Gadarenes welcomed the Lord after the miraculous restoration of "Legion" (Luke 8:37). Every case is different, but in Sychar the harvest was ready.

To come to the Lord is the only thing that faith can properly do. A man with newly-formed faith cannot remain where he is. An initial faith needs ministerial nurturing so that this faith can grow. Thus the Lord remained with them for two days, evidently engaging in a teaching ministry. The same occurred after the conversion of Cornelius; Peter and others remained in Caesarea for "certain days" (Acts 10:48), evidently to further the faith of those recently baptised and who had received the Holy Spirit.

The men of Sychar speak. The Lord came to the city, and spoke to others who had not come out to Him. The result was that "many more believed". They confessed that their faith derived not from the woman's own testimony, but from the direct teaching of the Lord Himself. The words of the Lord are all-powerful. He Himself said, "I have given unto them the words which thou gavest me; and they have received them, and have known surely that I came out from thee, and they have believed that thou didst send me" (John 17:8). The

Lord's words enabled them to know that He was "the Christ, the Saviour of the world"—that is to say, not of the Jews only. As John wrote many years later, "the Father sent the Son to be the Saviour of the world" (John 4:14). Another title involving "the world" is "the light of the world" (John 9:5), and similarly "the Judge of all the earth" (Gen 18:25). The universality of His work as Saviour and as Judge is thereby clearly demonstrated. These Samaritans must have become "true worshippers" in the hour that "now is", thereby establishing a pattern that enabled the one Samaritan leper to return to give glory to God (Luke 17:18) because of his faith commended by the Lord.

4. *The Second Sign: Faith in the Lord's Word* 4:43-54

v.43 "Now after two days he departed thence, and went into Galilee.
v.44 For Jesus himself testified that a prophet hath no honour in his own country.
v.45 Then when he was come into Galilee, the Galilaeans received him, having seen all the things that he did at Jerusalem at the feast: for they also went unto the feast.
v.46 So Jesus came again into Cana of Galilee, where he made the water wine. And there was a certain nobleman, whose son was sick at Capernaum.
v.47 When he heard that Jesus was come out of Judaea into Galilee, he went unto him, and besought him that he would come down and heal his son: for he was at the point of death.
v.48 Then said Jesus unto him, Except ye see signs and wonders, ye will not believe.
v.49 The nobleman saith unto him, Sir, come down ere my child die.
v.50 Jesus saith unto him, Go thy way; thy son liveth. And the man believed the word that Jesus had spoken unto him, and he went his way.
v.51 And as he was now going down, his servants met him, and told *him*, saying, Thy son liveth.
v.52 Then enquired he of them the hour when he began to amend. And they said unto him, Yesterday at the seventh hour the fever left him.
v.53 So the father knew that *it was* at the same hour in the which Jesus said unto him, Thy son liveth: and himself believed, and his whole house.
v.54 This is again the second miracle *that* Jesus did, when he was come out of Judaea into Galilee."

43-45 The implication of vv.43-44 is that the Lord would bypass Nazareth; He would rather enter Galilee than remain in "his own country". A map will show what was involved; Nazareth lay in the very south of Galilee, but Capernaum and the cities on the north coast of the Sea of Galilee lay about twenty miles further north-east into Galilee. Nazareth was unkind to its Prophet; He had "no honour in his own country". On one occasion when He had been very outspoken in the synagogue of Nazareth, they had been filled with wrath, and sought to kill Him by casting "him down headlong" from the edge of a hill (Luke 4:28-30). On that occasion, He had said, "No prophet is accepted in his own country" (v.24). On another occasion in Nazareth, He said a similar thing (Matt 13:57).

The Galilean Jews were evidently devout in as far as they had respect to the law of Moses; they had been to Jerusalem for the Passover, since every male was under an obligation to go to Jerusalem three times in a year. These men had seen the miracles (signs) that the Lord had done in Jerusalem (2:23), and hence they were quite prepared to receive Him, so that further signs would be done in their country. But receiving the Lord because of signs is not the kind of faith that the Lord wanted, if indeed signs lead to faith. This, then, leads to the next sign recorded in vv.46-54, designed to show the superiority of faith that is formed by, and exercised in, the words of the Lord. However, this reception of the Lord was not lasting, for later He had to denounce the cities of Chorazin, Bethsaida and Capernaum in Galilee because they would not repent in spite of the fact that "most of his mighty works were done" there (Matt 11:20-24).

46-47 Even if the Lord would have no honour in Nazareth, His fame would be remembered in Cana (a few miles north of Nazareth). The word "nobleman" is a translation of the Greek word *basilikos*, and refers to a courtier, a man in the service of a king. The word is an adjective, and apart from this paragraph in John 4, the word occurs only three other times in the NT: "the king's country" (Acts 12:20), "in royal apparel" (v.21), and "the royal law" (James 2:8). It is likely that this nobleman belonged to Herod's court, and some have suggested that he was Chuza, Herod's steward, whose wife Joanna was among the women who ministered to the Lord (Luke 8:3).

This man's son was sick at Capernaum. The father had heard that this miracle-Worker had arrived in Galilee from Judaea, and his faith was stedfast in believing that the Lord could heal his son. It does not state that this man had been in Jerusalem, and that he had seen the miracles performed by the Lord. Rather, he took note of the testimony of others, so sought out the Lord after He arrived in Cana. He knew nothing of "miracles at a distance", and did not expect such an event; his request "come down" refers to the level of the Sea of Galilee below the heights of the hills around Cana. Similarly, Jerusalem is referred to as "up", while the country around would be described as "down"; see Luke 10:30; 19:28; Acts 18:22; 21:15.

48 *The Lord speaks.* A modern translation, through failing to distinguish between singular and plural on account of a policy to use "you" always, will miss the point here. The Lord did not say "Except thou", but "Except ye", namely He was referring to Jews in general. He is testing the man as one of a nation. No Jew would believe in the testimony of another concerning Christ, unlike many of the men in Sychar previously. Generally the Jews claimed that signs and wonders would produce faith, but the Lord knew that this was indicative of unbelief. Thus the Pharisees said, "Master, we would see a sign from thee" (Matt 12:38; 16:1; Mark 8:11); the Jews said, "What sign showest thou then, that we may see, and believe thee? what dost thou work?" (John 6:30); Paul wrote that "the Jews require a sign" (1 Cor 1:22).

The Jews would not believe, even if they did see signs and wonders, though in the future men will believe a lie when they see Satan's "power and signs and lying wonders" wrought by the son of perdition, the anti-Christ (2 Thess 2:9-11).

49 *The nobleman speaks.* Addressing the Lord as *kurie*, the nobleman repeated his request that the Lord "come down". Here was faith indeed; he really believed that the Lord could and would work a miracle if He came to Capernaum. Such simple childlike faith can be seen throughout the Gospels; thus, "speak the word only" (Matt 8:8); "come and lay thy hand upon her" (9:18); "help me" (15:25).

50 *The Lord speaks.* The Lord always had respect to such simple expressions of faith. Thus in the three cases mentioned above, the conclusions were: "I have not found such great faith, no, not in Israel"; "Jesus arose, and followed him"; "O woman, great is thy faith". In the nobleman's case, the Lord's power exceeded what the man expected. His command, "Go thy way; thy son liveth", demanded the exercise of further faith on his part. The Lord would not go down, but instructed the man to go down instead. The man believed the Lord's own word, as distinct from that of witnesses in Capernaum (the same had occurred in the case of the men in Sychar). In fact, the man believed that this would be a new kind of miracle—the Lord's power acting over a distance of between ten and twenty miles. And we may go further, for converts today are saved by the Lord's power coming upon them from heaven itself.

51-53 *The servants speak.* The news "Thy son liveth" could not have been unexpected by the father on account of his faith, though later the proclamation "he is risen" (Matt 28:7) must have been completely unexpected by the women who had come to the Lord's sepulchre. In the nobleman's case, faith can ask intelligent spiritual questions without expressing any doubt. The man found out that it was neither before nor after the seventh hour that his son was healed.

The seventh hour was a measure of time after noon, corresponding to our 1 p.m. The meeting with the servants took place the next day—the man had journeyed and they had journeyed, meeting perhaps at the half-way point. Why there was this delay, we are not told. Perhaps the man did not hurry, on account of the certainty of his faith. The story should be contrasted with that of Jairus' daughter; the daughter had died, according to news brought to Jairus; there was a delay brought about by the intervening miracle, and the Lord did come to the house—no "miracle at a distance" here; yet Jairus had to have faith before the Lord arrived at the house (Mark 5:22-43). In Capernaum, "himself believed" shows that his faith was enhanced, and his "whole house" believing reminds us of verses such as Acts 11:14; 16:15,32-34.

54 The sign shows the spiritual value of faith placed directly in the Lord's words; "faith cometh by hearing, and hearing by the word of God" (Rom 10:17). The "second" sign refers, of course, to the two signs in Cana, not to the overall miracles that the Lord had performed (John 2:23; 4:45).

CHAPTERS 5-12
THE SON—HIS REJECTION

I. The Son of God Rejected (5:1-47)

1. *The Third Sign: Healing on the Sabbath Day* 5:1-15

v.1 "After this there was a feast of the Jews; and Jesus went up to Jerusalem.
v.2 Now there is at Jerusalem by the sheep *market* a pool, which is called in the Hebrew tongue Bethesda, having five porches.
v.3 In these lay a great multitude of impotent folk, of blind, halt, withered, waiting for the moving of the water.
v.4 For an angel went down at a certain season into the pool, and troubled the water: whosoever then first after the troubling of the water stepped in was made whole of whatsoever disease he had.
v.5 And a certain man was there, which had an infirmity thirty and eight years.
v.6 When Jesus saw him lie, and knew that he had been now a long time *in that case*, he saith unto him, Wilt thou be made whole?
v.7 The impotent man answered him, Sir, I have no man, when the water is troubled, to put me into the pool: but while I am coming, another steppeth down before me.
v.8 Jesus saith unto him, Rise, take up thy bed, and walk.
v.9 And immediately the man was made whole, and took up his bed, and walked: and on the same day was the sabbath.
v.10 The Jews therefore said unto him that was cured, It is the sabbath day: it is not lawful for thee to carry *thy* bed.
v.11 He answered them, He that made me whole, the same said unto me, Take up thy bed, and walk.
v.12 Then asked they him, What man is that which said unto thee, Take up thy bed, and walk?
v.13 And he that was healed wist not who it was: for Jesus had conveyed himself away, a multitude being in *that* place.
v.14 Afterward Jesus findeth him in the temple, and said unto him, Behold, thou art made whole: sin no more, lest a worse thing come unto thee.
v.15 The man departed, and told the Jews that it was Jesus which had made him whole."

In chs.1-2, we have had the formation of faith in the Lord's disciples, His word and the first sign being used to this end. In ch.3, there was the formation of faith in one man, the word of the Lord and the man's knowledge of the signs in Jerusalem being used. In ch.4, we have seen the formation of faith in a woman, in men, and in a man and his house, the word of the Lord being used to achieve this. Now in ch.5, we have the formation of hatred against the Lord, both by reason of His word and by the sign accomplished on the infirm man. This sign and its consequences are recorded because they commence the development of this hatred, a hatred that grows until the Lord's crucifixion. (The reader should check such a growing development of hatred in the other three Gospels, pinpointing the occasions in which are found the first intentions to seek His death.) In ch.5, the miracle (sign) is performed in vv.1-9; then we have the testimony of the man and the evil intention of the Jews in vv.10-18, and finally the uninterrupted discourse of the Lord in vv.19-47.

1 The words "a feast of the Jews" show the deadness of the Jewish religion. Some have suggested that this was the feast of Purim; this was an artificial feast, not commanded originally by God (Est 9:26-28), and a devout Jew was under no obligation to go up to Jerusalem on that occasion. Others suggest that it was the feast of tabernacles, while others suggest that this was the second Passover in the Lord's ministry (the first Passover being in 2:13), accounting for the fact that the Lord went "up to Jerusalem". If this is so, then the third Passover would be in 6:4 (a feast of tabernacles occurring in 7:2), with the last Passover being first mentioned in 11:55. Only the presence of the Son gave God any interest in what was happening in Jerusalem on the feast days. Today, of course, it is "Christ our passover" that really matters (1 Cor 5:7).

2-4 This "sheep market" is really "sheep gate", being represented in Greek by the one adjective *probatikos*, with the word for "gate" (*pulē*) understood. This was one of the north-eastern gates of Jerusalem, being near Herod's temple on mount Moriah. The builders of the wall in Nehemiah's time commenced at the sheep gate and ended at the sheep gate, the description encompassing the city (Neh 3:1,32; 12:39). The pool of Bethesda (meaning "house of mercy") near this sheep gate must be distinguished from the pool of Siloam (John 9:7) situated to the south-east of the city.

In the five porches surrounding this pool lay a multitude of "those without strength" as the verb *astheneō* means; these people had no knowledge of the fact that a divine Healer was in their midst, although most of them must have been there during the Lord's previous miracle-working visit to Jerusalem (2:23).

It must be recognised that the words "waiting for the moving of the water" in v.3 and the whole of v.4 are omitted in many manuscripts from which the so-called modern translations are made. Moreover these words are omitted in the RV (though included in its margin), and in JND's translation they are placed in brackets. The descent of an angel to heal the first one who steps into the moving waters is a strange concept, and quite out of keeping with the way God acts in both OT and NT, and would even appear to be a rival to the Lord Jesus in His divine capacity to heal. Faith is not unintelligent when it has to weigh up such a strange concept whose absence from the text is supported by many manuscripts. In fact, it was an intermittent natural spring whose waters had healing properties. The Jews, who were much concerned with angels, interpreted this phenomenon as angelic in character, since they had no knowledge of any scientific explanation of such healing waters. The man clearly believed this angelic explanation, as can be deduced from his remarks in v.7, though strictly the phenomenon was quite natural, popular superstition having ascribed it to some supernatural agency. Such a gloss was written in the margin of a manuscript not containing these words, as a sort of explanation to later readers who might wonder whatever the Jews were doing and thinking. A subsequent copyist of the text would then incorporate the gloss into the text itself, and that is why it appears in the TR from which the AV is translated.

5 This man had had this infirmity for thirty-eight years (compare this with the forty years of the lame man healed by Peter in Acts 3:7; 4:22 also in Jerusalem). It would appear that this man in the days of his youth had committed some folly that had resulted in his permanent injury (v.14). Thus the man had been incapacitated in Jerusalem when the Lord as a babe had been brought into the city (Luke 2:22), and when He came up to Jerusalem at the age of twelve (2:41-42). He must have been in despair that healing would ever be his, that he was waiting in vain.

6 *The Lord speaks.* The Lord had an intimate knowledge of all things which were "naked and open" unto His eyes (Heb 4:13). We have already noted this divine introspection of the inner heart of men in passages such as 1:47-48; 2:24-25; 4:17-18. We will see this fact later in passages such as "Jesus knew from the beginning who they were that believed not, and who should betray him" (6:64); "Neither hath this man sinned, nor his parents" (9:3). Additionally, the Lord knew facts that were ordinarily hidden from men, such as "Lazarus is dead" (11:14); "Jesus knew that his hour was come" (13:1); "The cock shall not crow, till thou hast denied me thrice" (13:38); "ye shall be scattered" (16:32); "knowing all things that should come upon him" (18:4). Events unknown to us in heart, time and space, are all known to the Lord.

By asking the man, "Wilt thou be made whole?", the Lord was drawing out the heart of the man to Himself; the question reflected on the man's desire rather than on any knowledge and faith that the man might have possessed.

7 *The man speaks.* The impotent man addressed the Lord as *Kurie*—a polite form of address to the Stranger rather than any recognition of His Lordship. Thus the AV "Sir" is the appropriate translation. The answer shows that the man trusted in the Jewish tradition, and after all these years still had no one to help him into the water. He hoped that the Lord would assist him only to the end that he could partake in the superstition; he had no idea that a miracle-Worker was speaking to him. But to partake in blessing from the Lord, one's faith should rise far above the works and superstitions of men, like the leper in

Matt 8:2 who said, "Lord, if thou wilt, thou canst make me whole". However, the exercise of faith depends upon the possession of knowledge, and this the man lacked. Divine mercy was not withheld because of that, else no one could ever be saved from preconversion ignorance.

8-9 *The Lord speaks.* Not knowing the identity of the Stranger, the man would not realise the power behind the Lord's words, "Rise, take up thy bed, and walk". One can hardly say that the man was able to exercise any faith at all under the circumstances. In fact, the man was healed first, and upon feeling this great fact, only afterwards did he take up his bed and walk. In Matt 9:2, it was the faith of the ones who brought a man to be healed; in Acts 3:6 it was Peter's faith that enabled the lame man to be healed; in Acts 14:9 the faith was that of the cripple. In other words, all cases have their peculiar features; there was no such thing as a stereotyped miracle in the NT.

Miracles were characterised by being immediate, complete and lasting. Some claim to be miracle-workers today, often with a great show of their apparent abilities. If such claims are substantiated, then such works are those of the so-called alternative medicine, whose adherents embrace unbelievers as well as believers, showing that their achievements cannot be likened to those of the Lord and His apostles. In v.9, the adverb "immediately" translates the Greek word *eutheōs*, a word that occurs more times in Mark's Gospel than in the other three Gospels. (For example, it appears nine times in ch.1 alone, characterising the busy service of the divine Servant.) In the AV, the word is variously translated as "straightway, immediately, forthwith, anon, as soon as, by and by". The word for "bed" is not the same as the word used in Matt 9:2. There, the word is *klinē*, referring to a couch for carrying the sick. But in John 5, the word is *krabbatos*, referring more particularly to a mattress for the poor. Both words are used in Acts 5:15 in the order in which we have referred to them. However, different translators use different words for these two Greek words.

The day on which this miracle was performed was "the sabbath", a day that the Pharisees had bound up with legalistic requirements quite beyond OT demands, thereby placing burdens upon men that had no divine authority. Certainly, no manna had to be gathered on the sabbath (Exod 16:23-26); no sticks were to be gathered on the sabbath (Num 15:32-36), and no buying and selling were to take place on the sabbath (Neh 13:15-22). As we shall show later, the Lord's work on the sabbath day was one principal matter that the Jews held against the Lord of the sabbath.

10 *The Jews speak.* These men were always on the watch for any kind of activity that contravened their own ideas of the sabbath day. They were there immediately, disregarding the divine power behind the miracle, manifesting the same attitude as did the unbelieving Jews in John 11:46. Their statement "it is not lawful" was not based on the OT, but upon the Pharisaical interpretation of the law. This event was the commencement of the Jews' watching and listening, so as to try to find something with which to condemn the Lord. The basis of their observations was never according to truth, but always according to their own errors, ritual, religion, teaching and interpretation. Throughout the Lord's ministry, this Jewish method led up to Luke 20:20, "they watched him, and sent forth spies . . . that they might take hold of his words".

11-15 *The man speaks.* He recognised that there were two parts in the Stranger's intervention: 1. the healing, 2. the words "Take up thy bed". Similarly in Matt 9:1-7 there were two parts in the Lord's work: 1. forgiveness granted, 2. the words "Arise, and walk". The fact that the man dared to take up his bed on the sabbath indicates that he perceived that this One had authority over the sabbath, and that the Pharisaical law could be disregarded.

The Jews speak. The question "What man is that?" is the beginning of an inquisition, a method used by the Jews to extract information for their own use, seen at its height in John 9 when the healed blind man was questioned.

The man exhibited ignorance of a divine Person, for the Lord had not remained with him. In fact, the Lord was going to find him, rather than let the man find the Lord. The Lord would mingle with the crowd, so that the man should not identify Him—not to escape any danger as vv.18-19 clearly show. Compare this with Luke 4:30, where He passed through the midst of men leaving them helpless, and with John 8:59, where He escaped because His hour was not yet come (some suggest that He made Himself invisible when He left the temple).

In the days of the church, when trouble was overcome by the power of God, those who had been blessed would go to "their own company" (Acts 4:23; 12:12). But during the Lord's lifetime, the man would turn to the best that he knew in his basic ignorance, namely to "the temple" (that is, the *hieron*, being the temple courts in this case). However, One greater than the temple found him there, and identified Himself as the Stranger-Healer. There appears to have been no identification of Himself as "the Christ" (John 4:26) or as "the Son of God" (9:35-37). The man knew Him as "Jesus", and if this went beyond a natural name to a spiritual name (Saviour) in his mind, then he absorbed precious truth.

The Lord speaks. "Sin no more" implies that the man's state had been caused by some sin thirty-eight years before. (Contrast this with Luke 13:2-5; John 9:2-3.) What could be worse than thirty-eight years infirmity? Clearly not another thirty-eight years, for life did not last that long. Perhaps the Lord implied a removal from this life altogether, as "sleep" (1 Cor 11:30-32). See Gal 6:7.

The man speaks (indirectly). The man did not know that the Jews would use this information against the Lord; rather his words were those of testimony not of betrayal. He was under no obligation to remain silent, as in Mark 1:44. The Lord's purpose was that antagonism should build up, in preparation for the deeds of men when His hour came. He had not come "to send peace, but a sword", and unbeknown to men, He was guiding events to that great occasion when He would be crucified (Matt 10:34).

2. *The Father and the Son* 5:16-30

v.16 "And therefore did the Jews persecute Jesus, and sought to slay him, because he had done these things on the sabbath day.
v.17 But Jesus answered them, My Father worketh hitherto, and I work.
v.18 Therefore the Jews sought the more to kill him, because he not only had broken the sabbath, but said also that God was his Father, making himself equal with God.
v.19 Then answered Jesus and said unto them, Verily, verily, I say unto you, The Son can do nothing of himself, but what he seeth the Father do: for what things soever he doeth, these also doeth the Son likewise.
v.20 For the Father loveth the Son, and sheweth him all things that himself doeth: and he will shew him greater works than these, that ye may marvel.
v.21 For as the Father raiseth up the dead, and quickeneth *them*; even so the Son quickeneth whom he will.
v.22 For the Father judgeth no man, but hath committed all judgment unto the Son:
v.23 That all *men* should honour the Son, even as they honour the Father. He that honoureth not the Son honoureth not the Father which hath sent him.
v.24 Verily, verily, I say unto you, He that heareth my word, and believeth on him that sent me, hath everlasting life, and shall not come into condemnation; but is passed from death unto life.
v.25 Verily, verily, I say unto you, The hour is coming, and now is, when the dead shall hear the voice of the Son of God: and they that hear shall live.
v.26 For as the Father hath life in himself; so hath he given to the Son to have life in himself;
v.27 And hath given him authority to execute judgment also, because he is the Son of man.
v.28 Marvel not at this: for the hour is coming, in the which all that are in the graves shall hear his voice,
v.29 And shall come forth; they that have done good, unto the resurrection of life; and they that have done evil, unto the resurrection of damnation.
v.30 I can of mine own self do nothing: as I hear, I judge: and my judgment is just; because I seek not mine own will, but the will of the Father which hath sent me."

16-18 These verses show the basis of the antagonism that the Jews showed against the Lord—leading to persecution and the intention to kill Him. The verbs "to slay" in v.16 and "to kill" in v.18 are the same Greek infinitive *apokteinai*. The two reasons are:

1. He had broken the sabbath day.

2. He made Himself equal with God.

The Lord speaks, v.17. By stating "My Father worketh hitherto, and I work", the Lord touched upon both these points. He did not say "*The* Father", but "My Father", and the Jews knew that this title, coupled with the assertion that the Father and the Son were working together, implied equality within the Godhead. Moreover, the use of the present tense "worketh, work" implied a continuity of work that embraced all the days of the week, including the sabbath.

As far as the sabbath is concerned, God rested on the seventh day (Gen 2:2-3), and this fact was codified in the law (Exod 20:9-11). This rest occurred because the work of creation was complete, but after that God was always working towards and in His creation, as Paul wrote, "by him all things consist" (Col 1:17). That is to say, every particle of matter in the universe is related to every other particle by laws of force, and by this means the universe remains as a cohesive working whole; if God's permanent control were removed, or "dissolved" as Peter wrote (2 Pet 3:11-12), then the earth and heavens would pass away, as will ultimately happen (Rev 20:11). Thus the Lord's work continued on the sabbath—works of love and mercy. But the Jewish leaders showed no mercy, since their hearts were hard and set upon bondage for their fellows. Many times in the four Gospels the Lord interpreted work on the sabbath as based on mercy and necessity. The following texts give reasons why the Lord allowed work on the sabbath day: need (Matt 12:4; Mark 2:26; Luke 6:1-5); obedience (Matt 12:5); heart transcending the mind (Matt 12:7); the Son of man is Lord (Matt 12:8; Mark 2:28; Luke 6:5); compassion and preservation of life (Matt 12:11,12); the necessities of life (Luke 13:15); salvation (Luke 14:1-6); requirements of the law (John 7:22-23), while no explanation was finally given in John 9:14.

As far as the deity of the Son is concerned, it is important that believers should thoroughly grasp the important texts on this subject. Apart from John 5:17-18, these are: Matt 1:23; John 1:1; 10:29,33; 20:28; Rom 9:5; Titus 2:13; Heb 1:8; 1 John 5:20. To claim the Son is less than deity is heresy, answering to "another Jesus, another spirit, another gospel" (2 Cor 11:4). Heretics will always point out that in the Greek of John 1:1 "the Word was with God, and the Word was God" (*ho logos ēn pros ton theon, kai theos ēn ho logos*) there is no definite article before the second name God, and so they translate it "the Word was a God". This false conclusion is negated by John 20:28, where Thomas confessed "My Lord and my God". In the Greek the definite article stands before the name God: "*Ho kurios mou kai ho theos mou*", namely, "The Lord of me and the God of me". Similarly in Matt 1:23, "God with us" translates the Greek "*Meth hēmōn ho theos*" with the definite article before the name of God.

Thus in v.18 the Jews refused to interpret the commandment "Thou shalt have no other gods before me" (Exod 20:3) so as to recognise that the two Persons, Father and Son, exist within the Godhead. This the commandment in no way denied, since the context refers to physical images paraded as gods. In fact, the Jews used the commandments in Exod 20:3-11 as an excuse to attempt to slay Jesus, in spite of the clearest testimony to His Person by His works and doctrine. Similarly today, every reason is invented for rejecting the Lord.

In the following verses, vv.19-47, the Lord dealt with the Jews in two ways:

1. The nature of divine unity is described in many different ways (vv.19-30).

2. The Lord describes many kinds of witnesses to His Person (vv.31-47).

Note that these verses form an uninterrupted discourse, unlike some of the following chapters, where the Jews and others will make constant interruptions. In fact, ch.15 is the next chapter with a discourse without interruption.

Again, note the negative way in which the Lord sometimes accused the Jews: "Ye have not his word" (5:38); "ye have not the love of God" (5:42); "ye have no life in you" (6:53).

Unity In Person. We have already seen that the Lord's words "My Father worketh . . . and I work" imply equality within the Godhead.

19-20 *The Lord speaks. Unity In Action.* The AV translation "The Son can do nothing of himself" should more properly read "The Son can do nothing from (*apo*) himself". The origin of the Son's works is in question; He confessed that His miracles did not originate from Himself, but that there was unity in action with the Father. The Father's love is the basis of this unity in action; in fact, the Father shows and the Son sees, and as a result, miracles are performed. The Lord here promised that "greater works" would be done, above the signs already performed. Resurrection, demonstrating "the working of his mighty power" (Eph 1:19), is the greatest divine work, seen first in Lazarus "whom he raised from the dead" (John 12:1) though he must have died again; then in Christ, seen only by witnesses chosen before by God (Acts 10:41), and who was constituted the firstfruits of them that slept (1 Cor 15:20); and finally in all believers in the future resurrection day at the rapture (1 Thess 4:13-17). But this abounding power is seen even today in all who are quickened (Eph 1:19; 2:1,5).

21 *Unity In Life-Giving.* This power in life-giving is seen as that of the Father and that of the Son, whether it refers to the spiritual life that believers possess upon their conversion, or whether it refers to the physical resurrection yet to come. This is seen in the Lord's prayer to the Father when Lazarus was raised (John 11:41-42), and in the verse just quoted that "he" raised him from the dead (12:1). It is seen in the Lord's words regarding His own resurrection, "I will raise it up" (John 2:19), at the same time His resurrection being declared to be the work of God (Acts 2:24,32). Similarly, it is God who quickens us together with Christ (Eph 2:5), yet it is the Lord who gives unto His sheep eternal life (John 10:28). The duality of action is therefore complete in every aspect of resurrection.

The healed man stood in contrast with all others not healed. In the future; men will be similarly subdivided, so in His discourse the Lord now deals with principles of judgment, whether positively or negatively.

22 *Unity In Agreement Regarding Delegation Of Judgment.* In John's Gospel, the Father is not seen in relationship to men generally, only to believers. It is as God that He is seen in relationship to the world. Thus the Father does not judge men, but since judgment is necessary, this work of judgment has been committed to the Son. Divine love does not dispel this necessity of judgment, though theological and religious leaders would often deceive unbelievers into thinking that this is so. Thus in the period of the church, it is the Lord seen as walking as Judge among the seven golden lampstands (Rev 1-3). In Rev 6:17, the great day of the wrath of the Lamb is described. In 2 Thess 1:7-9, it is the Lord Jesus who is seen "in flaming fire taking vengeance on them that know not God". In Athens, Paul declared that God "will judge the world in righteousness by that man whom he hath ordained" (Acts 17:31). See also verses such as Matt 25:45-46; Luke 19:27, bearing in mind their prophetic contexts. In other words, the Son under various titles is seen as the One who engages in judgment.

23 *Unity In Equal Honour.* The words for "honour" are *timaō* (verb) and *timē* (noun), and those for "glory" are *doxa* (noun) and *doxazō* (verb). The AV translators have on several occasions used "honour" for these last two words, where "glory" is the appropriate translation. This is noticeable in John 5 (but not in the RV). Thus in vv.41,44 (twice), the word is *doxa*, namely "glory", and not "honour" as appears in the AV. But in v.23, the word is *timaō*, properly translated "honour" four times. The thought is that of assessing the value of a person or thing. Thus the word is used in 1 Pet 2:7, "unto you therefore which believe he is *precious*", in 1 Cor 6:20, "ye are bought with a *price*", and even of Judas' betrayal money, "the *price* of him that was valued" (Matt 27:9). Then believers glorify God as a result of having assessed His value, namely, they magnify and extol Him on account of what they know about Him.

In v.23, the Lord made it clear that honour is due to both Persons—the Son and the Father. He stated this positively and then negatively. It is not up to a man to decide that he will honour the One or the Other; it is either both or neither. In religious circles, it is too easy for unbelief to contemplate God but not the Son. Knowledge of One implies knowledge of the Other (John 8:19); hatred of One implies hatred of the Other (15:23); denial of the One implies denial of the Other (1 John 2:23).

24-25 *Unity In Granting Eternal Life.* Both hearing the word of the Son and believing on the Father are presented here as requisites for eternal life. (See Acts 20:21 for a second set of two requisites.) Again, in John 3:16 it is belief in the

Son, and in 17:8 it is the word from the Father. Certainly in our verse we have the eternal security of the believer, because the verb "is passed" in "is passed from death unto life" is in the perfect tense, namely *metabebēken*, implying the lasting effects after the original event.

The fact that the passage from death to life in a believer has already taken place does not deny the resurrection of the body in the future; Paul had to contend with such a doctrine (2 Tim 2:18), for its proponents were overthrowing the faith of some. In fact, in v.25 the subject is spiritual life from spiritual death, while in vv.28-29 the subject is resurrection after physical death. By "The hour is coming" the Lord implied that His sacrifice on the cross would form the true basis of faith, just as in 4:23 it would form the basis of true worship. Nevertheless, in both cases the Lord added "and now is" showing that the opportunity existed even before the cross, since He was with them. In v.25, the spiritually dead shall hear the voice of the Son of God; He attached great importance to this fact. Thus His sheep "shall hear my voice" (John 10:16), and to Pilate, He said, "Every one that is of the truth heareth my voice" (18:37). Moreover, all those in the grave "shall hear his voice" (John 5:28).

26 *Unity In Possession Of Life.* The life of the Son is bound up with the life of the Father. Here, the Father has given life to the Son; He has also given Him the Spirit (John 3:34-35), and glory (17:24). These are the eternal possessions of Deity; there was no time when the Son did not possess these things. By saying that the Father had given life to the Son, no doubt the Lord refers to the fact that in Manhood He did not cease to possess that eternal life. Believers now possess eternal life that stretches into the future, but the Son was the only One in the days of His Manhood on earth who also possessed life that stretched back into the past eternity. In this He was one with the Father.

27-29 *Unity In Authority To Execute Judgment.* We have discussed a similar topic in v.22. The authority to execute judgment has been granted to Him because He became Man. And He judges righteously because of His Person, and because He committed Himself "to him that judgeth righteously" (1 Pet 2:23). The title "Son of man" is the title by which He usually referred to Himself. It originated from the OT, where Ezekiel was often called "son of man" (Ezek 2:1,3,6,8 etc) because he was a prophet of judgment and restoration. Daniel saw the Lord as "the Son of man" coming in the clouds of heaven (Dan 7:13) to eliminate the kingdom of the fourth beast, thereby to establish His own kingdom uniquely and without rivalry. It is as a ready Judge that Stephen saw Him as Son of man (Acts 7:56), and it was as One judging amongst the seven churches that John saw Him as "one like unto the Son of man" (Rev 1:13).

Divine discernment will ensure that all men are raised in their proper order. No mistake can be made. "The hour is coming" refers to the future generally, though Lazarus in the tomb heard the Lord's voice, "Lazarus, come forth" (John 11:43). The resurrection of believers will take place "at the last trump" (1

Cor 15:52), when the dead shall be raised incorruptible. We interpret the trump as the Lord's voice that will be heard, for this is how the Lord's voice twice sounded to John on the isle of Patmos (Rev 1:10; 4:1). Additionally, 1 Thess 4:16 tells us that the Lord will descend with a personal shout of command, with the additional voice of the archangel Michael.

There is no such thing in Scripture as a "general resurrection". As the Lord said in v.29, there is a resurrection unto life and a resurrection unto judgment. There is a "first resurrection" and an implied "second" resurrection at the end of the one thousand years millennial reign of Christ. Believers in the church will be raised at the rapture; those who will have been martyred during the great tribulation after the rapture will be raised when the Lord comes in glory (Rev 20:4), while at the final dissolution of the heaven and earth John saw "the dead, small and great, stand before God" (v.12). The distinction between these categories will be made on the ground of faith (John 3:18; 5:24), and the existence of faith or otherwise will determine the kinds of works—good or evil. Of course, the Lord was not teaching a doctrine that asserts that salvation comes by works; v.29 must be taken in conjunction with those previous verses that speak of faith.

30 *Unity In Assessment*. Justice depends upon the law that is behind a judgment, and also on the integrity of the judge administering that law. Laws and methods of administration differ between countries and between centuries; laws are changed according to prevailing fashions; what is a crime today is not a crime tomorrow. Sins that were intolerable in the Scriptures are legalised today in many countries; men may therefore get away with their practices of such evil for a season, yet not before God. But in our verse we have the absolute standard of Deity. The standard of the Son is that of the Father, and hence the standard of the Son is "just". He seeks not His own will in His standard of assessment of faith, of good works and of evil works. His will is that of the Father who sent Him, as are His works (v.19), His words (7:16) and His witness (v.37).

3. *Witness to the Son*
5:31-47

v.31 "If I bear witness of myself, my witness is not true.
v.32 There is another that beareth witness of me; and I know that the witness which he witnesseth of me is true.
v.33 Ye sent unto John, and he bare witness unto the truth.
v.34 But I receive not testimony from man: but these things I say, that ye might be saved.
v.35 He was a burning and a shining light: and ye were willing for a season to rejoice in his light.
v.36 But I have greater witness than *that* of John: for the works which the Father hath given me to finish, the same works that I do, bear witness of me, that the Father hath sent me.
v.37 And the Father himself, which hath sent me, hath borne witness of me. Ye have neither heard his voice at any time, nor seen his shape.

v.38 And ye have not his word abiding in you: for whom he hath sent, him ye believe not.
v.39 Search the scriptures; for in them ye think ye have eternal life: and they are they which testify of me.
v.40 And ye will not come to me, that ye might have life.
v.41 I receive not honour from men.
v.42 But I know you, that ye have not the love of God in you.
v.43 I am come in my Father's name, and ye receive me not: if another shall come in his own name, him ye will receive.
v.44 How can ye believe, which receive honour one of another, and seek not the honour that *cometh* from God only?
v.45 Do not think that I will accuse you to the Father: there is *one* that accuseth you, *even* Moses, in whom ye trust.
v.46 For had ye believed Moses, ye would have believed me: for he wrote of me.
v.47 But if ye believe not his writings, how shall ye believe my words?"

31 The Lord had made it clear that His ministry was not from and for Himself. He was sent from the Father to teach the words of the Father and to do the works of the Father; He was also appointed as Judge. He was not self-appointed. Yet His previous discourse relating to the unity within the Godhead would not be accepted as having any authority by the Jews who were seeking to slay Him. Hence the Lord now deals with many aspects of the great cloud of witnesses that give testimony to His Person.

The Lord continues speaking. The Witness Of The Son. This can be seen by v.17, "My Father worketh . . . and I work", recognised by the Jews as a testimony concerning Himself, though they would not believe Him. They accepted the declaration of their law, "the testimony of two men is true" (Deut 19:15; John 8:17); hence they would not believe the sole testimony of the Lord. Thus when He said, "If I bear witness of myself, my testimony is not true", He meant that, as a solewitness, the Jews would not accept His testimony as true. To those who knew His Person, His sole testimony was accepted as absolutely true, as when He testified that He was the Christ and the Son.

32 *The Witness Of The Spirit.* By "another that beareth witness of me" we feel that the Lord referred to the Holy Spirit (the Father is referred to in v.37). The word for "another" is *allos*, meaning another of the same kind. This reminds us of "another Comforter" (John 14:16), for "he shall testify of me" (15:26); additionally, He shall guide into all truth concerning the Son (16:13). See also 1 Pet 1:11 for the Spirit's work of testimony in the OT.

33-35 *The Witness Of John The Baptist.* This lower witness is in contrast to the higher witness of the Father, Son and Holy Spirit. The contrast lies in the fact that the Jews sent to John, but they could not send to the Father. Originally, they asked him about himself, "Who art thou?" (John 1:19), but John quickly turned the subject to the Lord as the Lamb and the Son, and his testimony was successful in gaining converts. But a man's testimony was without power if not supported by a superior Witness from heaven. The Lord described John as a "burning and a shining" oil-lamp, a secondary light indeed when contrasted with the light from heaven. As "burning", John had consuming zeal within; as "shining", he manifested truth outwardly. To start with, the Jews liked this, even when he preached words of judgment since they came out to be baptised; but as soon as he identified Christ, some were offended, leading to his imprisonment and death. But generally, men held "John as a prophet" (Matt 21:26).

36 *The Witness Of Works*. It is true that "John did no miracle" (John 10:41), though Herod later thought that this was possible (Matt 14:2). Thus the works that the Lord did provided a greater witness than the testimony of John. The Lord owned that these works had been given Him by the Father to finish, and that they testified of Him. Thus the miracle on the sea enabled Peter to recognise this testimony, and he confessed "thou art the Son of God" (Matt 14:33). See also John 9:33; 10:32. Moreover, the Lord would "finish" every work given to Him; nothing would be left undone or half-done, since there was nothing that He could not do nor complete. See 4:34; 17:4; 19:30.

37-38 *The Witness Of The Father*. The Father's witness was manifested at the baptism of the Son (Matt 3:17), on the mount of transfiguration (Matt 17:5), and in His words from heaven in John 12:28. But such testimony from on high can only be recognised by hearts open to the Father's voice; consequently in speaking to the Jews the Lord gave four negatives:

1. "Ye have neither heard his voice". In Exod 20:19 the people had no desire to hear the voice of God from Sinai, only the voice of Moses. By contrast, Moses heard His voice from off the mercy seat in the tabernacle (Num 7:89).

2. "Nor seen his shape", for no man shall see Him and live (Exod 33:20), as Paul wrote, "whom no man hath seen nor can see" (1 Tim 6:16).

3. "Ye have not his word", for this is only spiritually discerned. As John wrote later, "Whosoever . . . abideth not in the doctrine of Christ, hath not God" (2 John 9). By contrast, young men who are strong have the word of God abiding in them (1 John 2:14).

4. "Him ye believe not". Only faith can transcend these negatives that otherwise dominate in an unsaved man; the witness of the Father then remains unknown.

39 *The Witness Of The Scriptures*. "Search the scriptures" is often translated "Ye search the scriptures" because the verb *ereunate* may be either indicative or imperative. Since the Lord is not issuing instructions to the Jews in the passage, we believe that "Ye search the scriptures" is more in keeping with the context. This must have been a current religious attitude amongst Jews, a mechanical use of the Scriptures with the Person of Christ unknown. The Scriptures can give life only when their true testimony is accepted by faith. Even the apostles understood this only when the Lord opened the law of Moses, the prophets and the psalms, "that they might understand the scriptures" (Luke 24:44-45). Otherwise there is neglect of "so great salvation" (Heb 2:3).

40-44 The word "honour" that appears three times in these verses should be rendered "glory" (*doxa*). The Lord explained why He was not received, and hence why men would not glorify Him by believing.

There was no love for God in their hearts, although this is only possible because "he first loved us" (1 John 4:19). Their love for the world ensured that the love of the Father was not in them (2:15).

Men would not receive Him because He came in His Father's Name. He manifested a humble dependence upon the Father. Rather, men preferred another who would come in his own name. This refers ultimately to the anti-Christ who will claim identity with God (2 Thess 2:4); men will receive him, his doctrine and his works, as believing a lie and not the truth (vv.9-12). They will be satisfied when this wicked one is revealed.

Additionally, men will receive glory from men, and this will detract completely from the fact that glory is due to God alone, and that true glory can come from God alone. Men will glory in each other, a feature that marks society today, when heroes in high society, in the world of sport and entertainment, are raised to positions of preeminence far above their fellows. Even the Corinthians were not immune from this attitude: "let no man glory in men" (1 Cor 3:21) wrote Paul to those who were raising gifted servants of God on to pedestals that thereby displaced Christ, and "Your glorying is not good" (5:6) because of carnal enjoyment of others engaged in moral evil.

45-47 *The Witness Of Moses*. The Lord would not bring fresh charges against the Jews—there were enough already, found in the OT Scriptures that these Jews professed to trust. Moses had written concerning the Lord in a passage such as Deut 18:18 "I will raise them up a Prophet . . . and will put my words in his mouth". Hence if a man believed in Moses, so should he also believe in the Lord; anything else is hypocrisy. Moreover, if a man does not believe in the writings of Moses (concerning the Prophet), then it would be impossible for that man to believe on the Lord. Such a direct assertion is needed today, when some professing believers have doubts concerning some of the writings of Moses—the creation story and the flood, for example.

In conclusion, we may mention a few more witnesses:

The Witness of the People. For example, in John 12:17, the people "bare record" concerning the Lord's work in raising Lazarus. So did the woman at the well, and many who were healed.

The Witness of the Apostle John. "He that saw it bare record" (John 19:35) concerning the spear and the blood. See also John 21:24.

The Witness of Believers. "Ye also shall bear witness" (John 15:27; Acts 1:8).

Thus men are surrounded by a great cloud of witnesses. We should not therefore listen to criticisms of the Scriptures by ignorant men, however learned and academic they may appear to be. We listen to the truth in Christ, plus the testimony of these others that none can justifiably resist.

II. The Bread of Life Rejected (6:1-71)

1. *The Fourth Sign: The Feeding of the Five Thousand* 6:1-14

v.1 "After these things Jesus went over the sea of Galilee, which is *the sea* of Tiberius.
v.2 And a great multitude followed him, because they saw his miracles which he did on them that were diseased.
v.3 And Jesus went up into a mountain, and there he sat with his disciples.
v.4 And the passover, a feast of the Jews, was nigh.
v.5 When Jesus then lifted up *his* eyes, and saw a great company come unto him, he saith unto Philip, Whence shall we buy bread, that these may eat?
v.6 And this he said to prove him: for he himself knew what he would do.
v.7 Philip answered him, Two hundred pennyworth of bread is not sufficient for them, that every one of them may take a little.
v.8 One of his disciples, Andrew, Simon Peter's brother, saith unto him,
v.9 There is a lad here, which hath five barley loaves, and two small fishes: but what are they amongst so many?
v.10 And Jesus said, Make the men sit down. Now there was much grass in the place. So the men sat down, in number about five thousand.
v.11 And Jesus took the loaves; and when he had given thanks, he distributed to the disciples, and the disciples to them that were set down; and likewise of the fishes as much as they would.
v.12 When they were filled, he said unto his disciples, Gather up the fragments that remain, that nothing be lost.
v.13 Therefore they gathered *them* together, and filled twelve baskets with the fragments of the five barley loaves, which remained over and above unto them that had eaten.
v.14 Then those men, when they had seen the miracle that Jesus did, said, This is of a truth that prophet that should come into the world."

1 "After these things" evidently does not mean immediately, since a number of months must have elapsed between the previous feast in 5:1 and the forthcoming Passover in 6:4. This miracle is the only one that is recorded by all four evangelists (Matt 14:13; Mark 6:32; Luke 9:10). Only Luke tells us that the place where the miracle was performed was in "a desert place belonging to the city called Bethsaida", implying that the crossing of the Sea of Galilee took place between the north-western shore and the north-eastern shore, perhaps a crossing of about six miles. Only John informs us that the Sea was also called by the name Tiberias, a name that he also uses in 21:1 after the resurrection. The only verse in which the city of Tiberias is mentioned is 6:23. This city lay on the west coast of the lake, having been named after the Roman emperor Tiberius when it was founded by Herod Antipas in AD 20. It was a Gentile city, though after the destruction of Jerusalem in AD 70 it became the chief city of Jewish learning.

2 No doubt there was a great multitude present on account of preparations being made to go up to Jerusalem for the Passover. They followed the Lord because of their curiosity concerning His miracles (signs) of healing. If this is the only reason for following the Lord, then it can quickly lead downhill spiritually, and to instability; this is what happened in the latter part of the chapter when the Lord derived spiritual teaching and lessons from the miracle.

3 The Lord went up into a mountain to be with His disciples, for the intention was to be with them "privately" (Luke 9:10). Mountain scenes were common in the Lord's experience: the mount of temptation (Matt 4:8); the mount of instruction (Matt 5:1); the mount of provision (John 6:3); the mount of isolation (Matt 14:23; John 6:15); the mount of compassion (Matt 15:29); the mount of transfiguration (Matt 17:1); the mount of prediction (Matt 24:3), and the mount of ascension (Acts 1:12). In the present case, the Lord sat "with" His disciples. There are very noticeable differences in the uses of this word "with". Thus when the breaking of bread was instituted, He sat down "with the twelve" (Matt 26:20), and the twelve apostles sat "with him" (Luke 22:14). The latter refers to the end of the old dispensation when men came where God was (to the tabernacle and temple), but the former to the new dispensation where the Lord comes where His people assemble in His name (Matt 18:20).

4 Once again a recognised feast was called that "of the Jews", showing the level to which Jewish ceremony had sunk. In the book of Exodus, God made provision for His people in various ways. In the night they had to eat the passover roast with fire (12:8). They had to eat unleavened bread for seven days (12:18). In spite of their murmurings, God provided manna each night (16:2,12-15). To lead the people in the wilderness, God came down in the pillar of fire and cloud (13:21). The divine presence was with them in the tabernacle (25:8).

Because of the people's disbelief in Moses' writings, the Lord introduced new replacement features prior to the forthcoming Passover feast. There would be provision for the partaking of the true Passover Lamb (John 6:56). The heavenly manna was the Lord Himself (vv.48-51). The Lord came down to the disciples on the sea (v.19), while afterwards His presence was with them on the ship. The parallels between the historical events in Exodus and these events in John 6 are therefore remarkable.

There are two signs in our passage: the first (vv.5-14) is concerned with inward provision, while the second (vv.15-21) is concerned with outward protection. The result of the first was that men wanted to make Him king (v.15), while the ultimate result of the second was that many went backwards (v.66). This contrast with the prophetical descriptions in Ps 2:6; 110:3, "Yet have I set my king upon my holy hill of Zion"; "Thy people shall be willing in the day of thy power". The discourse that follows these two signs is a broken discourse. It commenced by the lakeside (John 6:25) and ended in a synagogue (v.59), though we are not prepared to attempt to assess where the break occurred. The discourse is divided into sections, each commencing with a question or remark. The first four are introduced by "they"—the people; the next two by the Jews, the seventh by His disciples who shortly afterwards abandoned their discipleship, and the last by Peter in response to a question from the Lord.

5-6 This great company which came "unto him" is contrasted to v.3 where He sat "with his disciples". As we have said before, the Lord was introducing that which was new to His disciples, but the people continued according to the old tradition. The Lord's eyes were first of all upon His disciples around Him; then to see the multitude He had to lift "up his eyes", while finally He "lifted up his eyes to heaven" as He spoke to His Father (John 17:1). Conversely, the Lord instructed His disciples to lift up their eyes to see the harvest (John 4:35), while under all circumstances His people now should learn to look up stedfastly into heaven (Acts 7:55; Ps 121:1).

The Lord speaks. The Lord would show compassion on all those who were not rejecting Him in their hearts (the converse is found in Matt 11:20, where few mighty works were done because the cities would not repent). He would meet their needs physically first, and spiritually afterwards; they loved and appreciated the former, but many were offended at the latter. In both cases the Lord would build upon a foundation: in the first He would build upon the people's knowledge of the book of Exodus. By asking Philip, "Whence shall we buy bread, that these may eat?", the Lord was testing the spirituality and faith of Philip, and he was found wanting. He would show him his shortcomings. Certainly he had an advantage that ordinary men did not possess. In John 1:43-46, when he was first found and called by the Lord, he followed Jesus as the One who had been foretold in the OT. He had seen the miracle of the turning of water into wine, when His disciples had believed on Him. He would have known of divine power recorded in the OT, when Elisha poured oil from the one pot into many (2 Kings 4:1-7; see also 1 Kings 17:12-16). Truly Philip started well, but he slowed up later in his understanding, so much so that the Lord finally had to ask him, "Have I been so long time with you, and yet hast thou not known me, Philip?" (John 14:9).

7 *Philip speaks*. All Philip could do was to engage in some mental arithmetic, and inform the Lord of the result. He expressed his result in terms of the Roman coin, the denarius (Greek, *dēnarion*); Matt 20:1-16 suggests that one denarius was a labourer's daily wage, while the good Samaritan paid two of these coins to the innkeeper (Luke 10:35). Philip's mind worked on the assumption that one person could be partially fed with 200/5000 = one twenty-fifth of a denarius. The Lord did not comment on such pathetic materialistic considerations, but Andrew was not backward in joining in with a further manifestation of unbelief.

8-9 *Andrew speaks*. The fact that he is stated to be "Simon Peter's brother" takes us back to 1:40-41, where Andrew, thrilled with his having found the Messiah, first found Peter before coming to the place where the Lord dwelt. It is remarkable that Peter took no part in the present conversation, since he usually acted as spokesman for the twelve. (At least, his confession concludes the whole event in 6:68-69.) But Andrew was no better than Philip before him; memory and sight, but not faith, dominated his thinking. He had seen water turned into wine—one substance into another, but there had been no previous miracle in which the Lord had created something from hardly anything; faith in the creation must accept this, since "the things which are seen were not made of things which do appear" (Heb 11:3). In other words, his expectations were based only on what the Lord had done before; faith could not appreciate that the Lord was able to do things as yet unexperienced.

By observing that a lad had five loaves and two small fish, Andrew laid the foundation of a theory propagated by present-day theologians who have no faith. Those who reject the concept of miracles in Scripture explain the event by stating that the example of the lad in providing his own loaves and fish thereby encouraged everyone else to part with their own provisions—some less and some more—enabling distribution to be made to all the multitude. Such a theory disregards entirely the fact that the event is stated to be a "miracle" (sign).

10 *The Lord speaks*. God is not a God of disorder and confusion, as Paul wrote later, "Let all things be done decently and in order" (1 Cor 14:40). The Lord would not have His disciples distributing food to the huge multitude in a random manner, as they all milled around Him. Smaller groups for convenience and fellowship over a meal were far more appropriate, and grass was more suitable than stony soil. Such natural considerations are necessary even when a very non-natural miracle was about to be performed. In "Make the men sit down", the word for "man" is *anthrōpos*, meaning human beings in the context. But in "the men sat down", the word for "man" is *anēr*, meaning a male person.

It should be noted that the record states "about" five thousand. Inspiration did not provide exact numbers when such information was unimportant. Thus in v.19, it states "five and twenty or thirty furlongs"—John could not possibly have known the actual distance and he was not enlightened by the Holy Spirit when he wrote his Gospel many years later. Even Luke was uncertain of the Lord's exact age at the commencement of His ministry (Luke 3:23), and he was also uncertain of the exact number of believers in the church as it was first formed in Jerusalem (Acts 2:41; 4:4).

11-12 In Matt 14:19, the record states that the Lord looked "up to heaven"; John's record does not state this, only that He "lifted up his eyes" to look on the company. But the giving of thanks is important in all accounts of the miracle. In this connection, we note that the Lord gave thanks at the tomb of Lazarus (John 11:41); because the truth was hidden "from the wise and prudent" (Matt 11:25); at the institution of the breaking of bread (Luke 22:19); and that Paul gave thanks for food before all on the ship (Acts 27:35). The word for "to give thanks" in our v.11 is *eucharisteō*, used also in Matt 15:36 (the feeding of the 4 000), Luke 22:19 (for the bread), Matt 26:27 (for the cup), and Acts 27:35 (on the ship). A cognate word is "to bless" (*eulogeō*), meaning to speak well of; it is used of the bread in Matt 14:19 and Luke 9:16, of the bread at the institution of the Lord's Supper in Matt 26:26, and of the bread after His resurrection in Luke 24:30. So in the present miracle, since both words are used, the Lord both blessed (with thoughts directed to the food) and gave thanks (with thoughts directed to His Father).

The miracle took place as an act of distribution; it was not a case of a huge mass of new food appearing suddenly. The Lord broke off new pieces from the existing bread, giving these new pieces to His disciples. The distribution process, "he distributed to the disciples, and the disciples to them", is similar to the propagation of truth today. What Timothy had heard from Paul, he had to commit to faithful men who in turn would be able to teach others also (2 Tim 2:2). This is how the distribution must have taken place (see Matt 14:19), though we should point out that the RV and JND, through following other manuscripts, translate the above words simply as "he distributed to them".

With a typical meaning, the fish speak of the initial step of salvation (Luke 5:10), as evangelists and their message are received. Bread speaks of food partaken by believers after conversion, as well as mutual fellowship between believers (1 Cor 10:17).

The Lord speaks. The Lord provided all that was necessary to fill the people; additional kinds of food were quite irrelevant, a lesson today for some who are not solely satisfied with the sincere milk of the Word. He provided the right food (Luke 11:11), and it was with "good measure, pressed down, and shaken together, and running over" (Luke 6:38). This accounts for the fact that there were many fragments left over. These could not be "lost"; of His own disciples the Lord said, "none of them is lost" (John 17:12), implying eternal security.

13 There are two different Greek words for "basket" occurring in the miracles of the feeding of the 5 000 and the 4 000.

1. *Kophinos*. This word occurs six times in the NT—all in the miracle of the feeding of the 5 000. This was a small basket—a "hand-basket", and in the present case one each must have been carried by all the twelve apostles.

2. *Spuris*. This is used four times in Matt 15:32-39, where the feeding of the 4 000 is described. It also appears in Acts 9:25, when Paul was let down the wall in a basket. This was a large basket, capable of carrying a man. In this miracle, each basket seems to correspond to each of the seven loaves, though why such large baskets were available is not stated.

14 *The men speak*. The men knew enough of the OT Scriptures to express their assurance that the miracle (sign) proved that the Lord was "that prophet that should come into the world". (See Deut 18:15,18; Matt 11:3; John 1:21; 7:40). This promised Prophet would be raised from among the children of Israel, and He would be like unto Moses. The people would recall that Moses had been closely associated with the giving of the manna in the wilderness, as the Lord said later, "Moses gave you not that bread from heaven . . . He gave them bread from heaven to eat" (John 6:31-32; Ps 78:24, referring to God; Neh 9:15). But they failed to perceive the millennial aspect of the manifestation of this Prophet, as is also seen in the following verse where they confused the time when the Lord should be manifested as King.

2. *The Fifth Sign: The Lord Walking on the Sea* 6:15-24

v.15 "When Jesus therefore perceived that they would come and take him by force, to make him a king, he departed again into a mountain himself alone.
v.16 And when even was *now* come, his disciples went down unto the sea,
v.17 And entered into a ship, and went over the sea toward Capernaum. And it was now dark, and Jesus was not come to them.
v.18 And the sea arose by reason of a great wind that blew.
v.19 So when they had rowed about five and twenty or thirty furlongs, they see Jesus walking on the sea, and drawing nigh unto the ship: and they were afraid.
v.20 But he saith unto them, It is I; be not afraid.
v.21 Then they willingly received him into the ship: and immediately the ship was at the land whither they went.
v.22 The day following, when the people which stood on the other side of the sea saw that there was none other boat there, save that one whereinto his disciples were entered, and that Jesus went not with his disciples into the boat, but *that* his disciples were gone away alone;
v.23 (Howbeit there came other boats from Tiberias nigh unto the place where they did eat bread, after that the Lord had given thanks:)

v.24 When the people therefore saw that Jesus was not there, neither his disciples, they also took shipping, and came to Capernaum, seeking for Jesus."

15 Just as the people misunderstood the Lord as the Prophet, so they misunderstood Him as King. Certainly He was born "King of the Jews" (Matt 2:2), and the chief priests knew this from Micah 5:2, thereby causing king Herod to act so cruelly so as to preserve his own position (Matt 2:3-18). However, the divine purpose revealed to Mary was that God would give Him the throne of His father David (Luke 1:32). God would not allow men to raise His Holy One to the highest throne on earth; He Himself would set His King upon His holy hill of Zion (Ps 2:6), though later men would crown Him King in mockery (John 19:2-3). So the Lord would remove the opportunity from these men, particularly as His kingdom then was not of this world (John 18:36). Thus He departed to be in isolation, to show by the next sign that He had ultimate authority over the nations.

16-18 John leaves us somewhat surprised that the disciples should want to cross the sea, thereby leaving the Lord alone on a mountain. The promise is that He will never leave nor forsake us (Heb 13:5), but there were other occasions when they left the Lord alone (Matt 26:56). However, in the present event, Matthew has informed us that "Jesus constrained his disciples to get into a boat... while he sent the multitudes away... he went up into a mountain apart to pray" (Matt 14:22-23). So it appears that they hesitated to leave Him alone, and must have departed with heavy hearts. But the Lord had all events under His control.

Evening turned into night, and the crossing to Capernaum involved a distance of several miles. Whether the Lord was with them or not, a storm could arise (cf. Matt 8:24), but under all circumstances He could intervene at the right moment. To see the Lord walking towards them on the sea caused them to be afraid. There is usually in the hearts of men a fear of supernatural events that are beyond natural experience, particularly in the present miracle before the disciples knew that it was the Lord. In fact, they thought that they saw "a spirit" (Matt 14:26), causing them to cry out for fear. The same occurred after His resurrection, when "they were terrified and affrighted, and supposed that they had seen a spirit" (Luke 24:37). Even John later "fell at his feet as dead" (Rev 1:17).

20 *The Lord speaks.* The Lord had no desire that His disciples should remain in ignorance as to who He was, nor that they should remain in fear. His words, "It is I (*egō eimi*); be not afraid", deal with both points. In John 18:6, the same identifying title caused fear in the officers who fell backwards, but here this title brought peace. In Luke 24:39, the words "it is I myself" removed fear from the troubled hearts of the apostles, as on Patmos when John was revived by the announcement, "I am the first and the last" (Rev 1:17).

21 John's record passed over the event that Peter walked on the water to go to the Lord (Matt 14:28-30). Matthew used the word "immediately" to describe the Lord stretching out His hand to catch Peter in the act of sinking through lack of faith. But John used this word "immediately" to describe what happened when the disciples welcomed the Lord into the ship: "immediately the ship was at the land whither they went". In a sense, there were four parts to this miracle:

1. The Lord walking on the water;
2. Peter walking on the water;
3. The wind ceasing (Matt 14:32);
4. Passing over the intervening miles in an instant of time.

Theoretical physicists suggest that under certain unusual circumstances (not on earth!) it would be possible for an object to pass from one point in the universe to another point, without traversing the space between, and requiring no time in which to make the transfer. Such is theory, but in our passage this event was a fact, taking place on earth as well.

In Matt 14:33, the conclusion was that the disciples worshipped Him, saying, "Of a truth thou art the Son of God", but in John 6, Peter made a similar confession at the end of the discourse (v.69). Perhaps we are right in saying that neither of these confessions reaches the height of that given in Matt 16:16, where Peter's knowledge derived directly from revelation from the Father.

The interpretation of this sign is not hard to ascertain, in the light of the context where men wanted to make Him king by force. The sign pointed to what will actually happen. In Isa 57:20-21, the troubled sea is defined to imply the wicked, for whom there is no peace. In Rev 17:1,15, mystery Babylon, the great religious whore of the future, sits upon many waters, defined to be "peoples, and multitudes, and nations, and tongues". In the future period known as "the great tribulation", taking place between the rapture of the church and the coming of the Lord Jesus in glory the saints of that future age will suffer at the hands of the political and religious leaders (Rev 13), corresponding to the apostles in the boat in the storm. Then the Lord Jesus will come to rescue His own, at His second advent in glory. His work will subdue the nations so as to prepare for His reign of peace, and the great tribulation will come to its end when His own people at that time are carried safely over to enter His glorious kingdom. At that time, the Lord will truly be "King of kings" (Rev 19:16) since God will bring forth His Son, giving Him His rightful throne over the nations.

22-24 The movements of the Lord in vv.19-21 were quite unknown to men in the world, just as today men are ignorant of His movements through death, resurrection and ascension back to the Father's presence. In v.22, the people noticed that the disciples and the Lord had arrived in one boat, and that this boat now had left with the disciples, but not with the Lord. Having obtained shelter for the night (Matt 14:15 explains that there were villages around), they assembled again the next morning, no doubt anticipating another free meal (v.26). They could not find the Lord (v.24), so continued their search for Him by crossing the sea to Capernaum using other boats for the purpose. V.23 is inserted in brackets to explain how there came to be enough boats available to convey a large multitude back over the sea. It may appear surprising that three verses are devoted to explain this at length, but the object of the record is to lay bare the people's thinking, so that the Lord could take this up in the first verse of His subsequent discourse (v.26).

Capernaum was the place where the Lord usually resided when He was in Galilee. Originally, He had left Nazareth, to dwell in Capernaum (Matt 4:13), a city that is described as "his own city" (9:1). It was here that He provided that tribute money for Peter (17:24-27). His dwelling in the city caused Him to state that the city was exalted unto heaven, to be brought down to hades (v.23).

3. *The First Question*
6:25-27

v.25 "And when they had found him on the other side of the sea, they said unto him, Rabbi, when camest thou hither?

v.26 Jesus answered them and said, Verily, verily, I say unto you, Ye seek me, not because ye saw the miracles, but because ye did eat of the loaves, and were filled.

v.27 Labour not for the meat which perisheth, but for that meat which endureth unto everlasting life, which the Son of man shall give unto you: for him hath God the Father sealed."

25 *The people speak.* As they asked the question, "when camest thou hither?", the people did not suspect that a miracle had taken place. Some of the Lord's miracles were intended only for the apostles and for a privileged few to see. In fact, some private miracles had deliberately to be kept secret from others, though beneficiaries did not always follow the Lord's request (Mark 1:44-45). In other cases, where the curious desired to see special signs, the Lord would not satisfy their curiosity (Matt 16:1-4).

26-27 *The Lord speaks.* He did not answer the people's question directly; compare this with the more sincere question, "where dwellest thou?", to which the Lord gave a direct answer of invitation (John 1:38-39). In fact, the Lord worked according to the principle that He Himself enunciated: "whosoever hath, to him shall be given . . . whosoever hath not, from him shall be taken away even that he hath" (Matt 13:12). The Lord knew why the people were seeking Him; He knew their hearts (cf. John 1:47; 2:25; 3:20; 4:18; 5:6; 6:61). To them, the sign meant nothing; as they had sat around on the grass, most must have been at a distance from the Lord, so had not seen what had taken place. Neither did they care; they were merely interested in receiving and partaking of free food without having to work for it. This is an entirely carnal attitude towards the Lord and His work, a very low appreciation of a miracle. Moreover, when the Lord said, "Ye seek me", He was referring to their carnal attitude in seeking for more free food; others sought for Him with similar base motives, as in 7:34; 8:21; 18:4,8. Yet others sought Him spiritually, as in 1:38; 13:33.

By saying "Labour not... but for...", the Lord was presenting a proper balance in motivation. It is the same balance as in Matt 6:25-34: take no thought for natural necessities, but seek "first" the kingdom of God. It is a question of priorities; it is a question of laying up treasure in heaven. For example, the rich man in the parable in Luke 12:16-21 stored up the fruits of his labour in vast new barns, but he was "not rich toward God".

Certainly the Lord did not mean, "Don't work at all". Paul wrote later that if any man would not work, then "neither should he eat" (2 Thess 3:10). Instead of partaking of the liberality of others because of one's own laziness, a man should eat his "own bread" (v.12)—that is, bread for which he himself had worked. Paul's own example should be noted (Acts 18:3; 20:34); such productivity would then enable a believer to "support the weak" (1 Thess 5:14). But daily work should never be at the expense of labouring "for that meat which endureth unto everlasting life", a concept that the Lord would explain later. We read of living bread, living water, the living Father, the living way, a living sacrifice and a living Stone. Such food is obtained only from the Son of man; as "sealed" by the Father, He has been marked out uniquely as the One alone who provides this food.

4. *The Second Question*
6:28-29

v.28 "Then said they unto him, What shall we do, that we might work the works of God?

v.29 Jesus answered and said unto them, This is the work of God, that ye believe on him whom he hath sent."

28 *The people speak*. By asking "What shall we do, that we might work the works of God?" they had the thought of doing rather than believing dominant in their hearts. They took the ground of law and not that of faith; they wanted help as to how they might keep the OT law. (Note that the verbs "labour" and "work" are one word in Greek, namely *ergazomai*.) This was the attitude of the rich young ruler (Matt 19:16), and also that of the Philippian jailor (Acts 16:30). It is the attitude that neglects the evangelistic truth, "now the righteousness of God without the law is manifest" (Rom 3:21). In fact, the people used the plural form "works", as if each separate commandment demanded individual attention as a burden in life—but the Lord replied in the singular, "work".

29 *The Lord speaks*. He knew that His answer would puzzle the people, but this is always the effect of spiritual truth on the uninitiated. Only one work is necessary—that of believing on the One who had been sent. This truth, of course, characterises John's Gospel, which was written to bring out this fundamental fact (20:31). The Lord referred to the initial exercise of faith and the subsequent experience of it (the TR has the aorist subjunctive *pisteusēte* the verb "believe" as if it refers to a single act, but other Greek texts have the present subjunctive *pisteuēte*, implying a continuous experience). The Lord was not referring to the subsequent works that follow faith, something very important for believers today. Thus Paul wrote of "faith which worketh" (Gal 5:6); "your work of faith" (1 Thess 1:3); "that they which have believed in God might be careful to maintain good works" (Titus 3:8).

5. *The Third Question*
6:30-33

v.30 "They said therefore unto him, What sign shewest thou then, that we may see, and believe thee? What dost thou work?
v.31 Our fathers did eat manna in the desert; as it is written, He gave them bread from heaven to eat.
v.32 Then Jesus said unto them, Verily, verily, I say unto you, Moses gave you not that bread from heaven; but my Father giveth you the true bread from heaven.
v.33 For the bread of God is he which cometh down from heaven, and giveth life unto the world."

30-31 *The people speak*. Their question shows that the people were not satisfied with the Lord's miracle in feeding them—such an event would not cause faith in an unbeliever or nominal disciple. They adopted the usual Jewish approach: "the Jews require a sign" (1 Cor 1:22). In fact, they required something far more spectacular then any of the Lord's miracles performed thus far. These miracles did not cause faith in the hearts of the Lord's brethren (according to the flesh) (John 7:3,5), nor in the hearts of many others later (John 12:37). The desire for more spectacular miracles in Matt 12:38; 16:1 led the Lord in both cases to refuse to produce such signs, offering only the sign of the prophet Jonah.

In quoting the OT, the people used the words "Our fathers", which must be compared with the Lord's words later, "Your fathers" (vv.49,58). In their quotation, they demonstrated the kind of sign that they desired. The giving of the manna in the book of Exodus was something known to have taken place from heaven—it was something that the Lord had given men to eat (Exod 16:15). To their minds, this was really a sign, unlike the feeding of the 5 000. Their quotation comes from Neh 9:15, "Thou... gavest them bread from heaven for their hunger". A similar thought appears in Ps 78:24, "he... had rained down manna upon them to eat". However, the children of Israel in the wilderness reacted in the same manner as did the people after the feeding of the

5 000, for in Ps 78:32, we read, "For all this they sinned still, and believed not for his wondrous works".

32-33 *The Lord speaks.* In His answer, the Lord touched only briefly upon the OT. Moses indeed did not give bread from heaven (and the people owned this fact); similarly, He added, "my Father giveth you the true bread from heaven". The people did not object to the title "My Father", as the Pharisees had done earlier (John 5:18). Note that the Lord still did not define what was meant by "the true bread". He was leading step-by-step to this great truth. Indeed this new bread "giveth life to the world", and this bread "is he which cometh down from heaven". This is the AV and JND translation of the present participle *ho katabainōn* being masculine in form. But this is not the only translation of this participle, since the previous word for "bread" (*artos*) is also masculine; thus the RV translation is "the bread of God is that which cometh down out of heaven"—referring to an object rather than to a Person. In the logic of the context, we prefer this translation, since the Lord developed the subject step-by-step. It is not until v.35 that the Lord referred to Himself as "the bread of life". Having heard His remark in v.33, the people would still be thinking of something physical rather than of a Person. (Similarly in John 4:15, the Samaritan woman still thought that the "living water" was physical.)

6. *The Fourth Request*
6:34-40

v.34 "Then said they unto him, Lord, evermore give us this bread.
v.35 And Jesus said unto them, I am the bread of life: he that cometh to me shall never hunger; and he that believeth on me shall never thirst.
v.36 But I said unto you, That ye also have seen me, and believe not.
v.37 All that the Father giveth me shall come to me; and him that cometh to me I will in no wise cast out.
v.38 For I came down from heaven, not to do mine own will, but the will of him that sent me.
v.39 And this is the Father's will which hath sent me, that of all which he hath given me I should lose nothing, but should raise it up again at the last day.
v.40 And this is the will of him that sent me, that everyone which seeth the Son, and believeth on him, may have everlasting life: and I will raise him up at the last day."

34 *The people speak.* Their physical interpretation of the Lord's words still persisted. The continuous nature of what comes down in v.33 caused them to ask to receive this bread "evermore". They would not have to work for bread, in the same way as the woman would not have to draw water every day (John 4:15). Such strange deductions show that the natural mind is not in contact with the mind of God. They did not realise that they were asking for Himself!

35 *The Lord speaks.* At this stage of the conversation, the Lord now identified His Person with the bread, although He knew that this revelation would cause the people to cease in their desire to receive the bread and to partake of it. This great title "I am the bread of life" must be taken in conjunction with the other great titles given to, and by, the Lord throughout the Scriptures. The Lord was already there, and the people had come to Him physically, so the added statement "he that cometh to me shall never hunger" is an additional thought, spiritual in its meaning. The partaking is a spiritual act, accomplished by faith. Those who adhere to the perverted doctrine of transubstantiation would insist that a wafer or piece of bread actually becomes the body of Christ, whatever its outward form and shape, and that the physical act of partaking is the actual partaking of His body. By maintaining this perverted doctrine, the religious hierarchy keeps its iron hold over the minds and souls of the millions who willingly submit themselves to their leaders.

The Lord also added something new, the fact that faith in Him would remove thirst for ever. We do not feel that this refers to the living water that the Lord promised in 4:10 when He spoke to the Samaritan woman, for that conversation would be unknown to these Jews in Galilee. Rather, He was preparing the people for further revelation when he would not only speak of His flesh, but also of His blood (6:53-56).

36 However, even before introducing this further concept, the Lord knew that the people were in a state of unbelief. Sight had not given way to faith. In Galilee, the cities would not repent, even though most of His mighty works had been done in them (Matt 11:20-24). Elsewhere, He stated that He had come into the world so that "they which see might be made blind" (John 9:39), adding that this meant that "your sin remaineth". This unbelief now led the people to argue against the Lord's teaching, and it led to their departure from Him in John 6:66, after which they walked with Him no longer.

37 The Lord spoke quite positively—the Father gives, and the Son keeps; but the implication for the people was that the Father had not given them to the Son, and hence that there was nothing for Him to keep (in spite of His compassion upon them when they had been hungry in the desert place). In fact, the Lord was describing salvation as a two-stage process. In His prayer in John 17, He made several references to the fact that the Father had given His people to Him: "I have manifested thy name unto the men which thou gavest me out of the world" (v.6); "I pray for them ... which thou hast given me" (v.9); "keep ... those whom thou hast given me" (v.11); "I will that they also, whom thou hast given me, be with me where I am" (v.24). Additionally, such a possession is so precious to the Lord, that a believer can never be cast out, in spite of His knowledge of all weaknesses and failures. In His prayer, He said, "none of them is lost" (17:12), and John quoted this again in his record in 18:9. Elsewhere, He promised, "neither shall any man pluck them out of my hand" (10:28).

38-40 The eternal security of the believer is bound up with the Lord's words, "I will in no wise cast out". The ultimate reason lies in the Father's will, and in the fact that the Son's will is to do the Father's will. He stated in v.38 that He came down from heaven, with the express intention of doing the Father's will. This had been His motive expressed prophetically through David, "I come . . . I delight to do thy will, O my God" (Ps 40:7-8; Heb 10:7). The Lord had already said similar words to His disciples (John 4:34), and to the Pharisees (5:30), and He would yet say similar words to His Father in the garden of Gethsemane (Matt 26:39).

In vv.39-40, the Lord explained two aspects of the Father's will that were of relevance in the present discourse.

1. That those who see the Son, and believe on Him, should have eternal life.

2. That those who believe on the Son, should be raised by the Son at the last day.

There is a difference between v.39 and v.40. In the former verse, "all which" (*pan ho*), and "it" (*auto*) are neuter, while in the latter verse "every one which" (*pas ho*) and "him" (*auton*) are masculine. The former suggests what is collective, while the latter what is individual. In other words, a believer can never hide himself in a crowd away from the purpose of God.

What the people understood by "at the last day" (*tē eschatē hēmera*) we cannot say; no doubt their minds would be filled with Jewish tradition. But believers today have the totality of revealed Scripture. It is an all-embracive term, including the time when the redeemed will be raised (used by the Lord four times in this discourse, vv.39,40,44,54, and by Martha, 11:24), and also the time of the judgment of the unsaved at the great white throne (John 12:48). Scripture never confuses the first resurrection with the second raising that leads to "the second death" in Rev 20:6; 21:8. Another expression, "the last days", used by Paul in 2 Tim 3:1, refers to the end period of the present church age, times in which we believe we are now living.

7. *The Fifth Question*
6:41-51

v.41 "The Jews then murmured at him, because he said, I am the bread which came down from heaven.

v.42 And they said, Is not this Jesus, the son of Joseph, whose father and mother we know? how is it then that he saith, I came down from heaven?

v.43 Jesus therefore answered and said unto them, Murmur not among youselves.

v.44 No man can come to me, except the Father which hath sent me draw him: and I will raise him up at the last day.

v.45 It is written in the prophets, And they shall be all taught of God.

Every man therefore that hath heard, and hath learned of the Father, cometh unto me.
v.46 Not that any man hath seen the Father, save he which is of God, he hath seen the Father.
v.47 Verily, verily, I say unto you, He that believeth on me hath everlasting life.
v.48 I am that bread of life.
v.49 Your fathers did eat manna in the wilderness, and are dead.
v.50 This is the bread which cometh down from heaven, that a man may eat thereof, and not die.
v.51 I am the living bread which came down from heaven: if any man eat of this bread, he shall live for ever: and the bread that I will give is my flesh, which I will give for the life of the world."

41-42 *The Jews speak.* There is no longer a physical desire for special food, but a murmuring against the Lord's teaching. This is not the same as the blatant opposition shown by the Pharisees to the Lord's teaching in John 5:18. In the present case, there were three stages in the development of the opposition:

1. Concerning His natural family relationships (v.42);

2. Concerning the partaking of His flesh (v.52);

3. Offence at a hard saying, leading to the departure of the so-called disciples (vv.60-61,66).

The desire for bread in v.34 had been annulled upon the realisation that the bread referred to Himself. This answers to Rom 9:32, "they stumbled at that stumblingstone" which had been laid in Zion.

The excuses of the Jews are given in v.42; they engaged in entirely natural reasoning, showing that the spiritual implications of the Lord's words were completely ignored, misunderstood, or not understood. This murmuring was not just a single act, for the two verbs "murmured" (v.41) and "said" (v.42) are in the imperfect tense, showing that the Jews were doing this continuously even as the Lord was speaking to them. They claimed that the birth of Jesus had been like that of any other man—they knew Joseph and His mother, but they knew nothing of the message that Gabriel had brought to Mary (Luke 1:26-38) and that the angel of the Lord had brought to Joseph (Matt 1:20-21). Although the Jews had asked the Lord for a sign, they failed to recognise the sign that had been promised through Isaiah (Isa 7:11-14). Thus they could not understand how a birth (to them, entirely natural) could be described by the Lord's words, "I came down from heaven". To unbelief, this would be impossible. It would imply the eternal existence of the Lord prior to His birth on earth; believers, of course, know that this was so, for "In the beginning was the Word" (John 1:1) and "Before Abraham was, I am" (8:58). In the vain thinking of the Jews, they were somehow supposing that the Lord meant that His physical body had come down from heaven, rather than His Person descending from the Father.

43-44 *The Lord speaks.* Clearly the Lord did not answer the Jews' question. Apart from the words "the Father which hath sent me", the matter was too holy to be placed before unbelievers. In the Lord's statement, a man coming, and a man being raised, repeat His words in vv.37,39. But He added, "except the Father . . . draw him", implying that the Jews had not been drawn by the Father. In other words, a man cannot come unless there is an outside power—the drawing by the Father. This verb "draw" (*helkuō*) appears five times in John's Gospel, three times in a physical sense in drawing a sword or a net (18:10; 21:6,11) and twice in a spiritual sense, "I . . . will draw all men unto me" (12:32). No violence is implied in this act, unlike the verb *surō* where strong force is implied (the former word is changed to the latter in John 21:6,8).

45 In order to provide one example of the way in which the Father draws, the Lord quoted Isa 54:13, "And all thy children shall be taught of the Lord", the context being that of future restoration. There are various ways in which the truth enters into the heart of a man, leading to faith and salvation.

1. Directly by God (Isa 54:13). Referring to the new covenant, God said, "I will put my law in their inward parts, and write it in their hearts".

2. By the Son: "God . . . hath in these last days spoken unto us by his Son" (Heb 1:2).

3. By the Holy Spirit: "he shall teach you all things" (John 14:26).

4. By the written word of God.

5. By His servants and His prophets (Heb 1:1).

6. Through nature, "For the invisible things of him from the creation of the world are clearly seen, being understood by the things that are made, even his eternal power and Godhead" (Rom 1:20).

On account of this quotation, the Lord then added another feature that characterises a man who comes unto Him: "Every man therefore that hath heard, and hath learned of the Father". The words "of the Father" are *para tou patros*; they do not mean that a man learns *about* the Father, but that he has learned *from* the Father. The man really learns of Christ. Hearing and learning of Him ensure that a man comes to Him by faith, else the learning cannot be true learning. Hence any religion that does not lead to Christ cannot be of God.

46 Yet the Lord would always differentiate sharply between Himself and any man who comes to Him by faith. Only "he which is of God" has seen the Father: these words are *ho ōn para tou theou*, namely "from God"; they refer to the Son who had ever seen His Father. No mere man could share this impossible privilege; as God said to Moses, "there shall no man see me, and live" (Exod 33:20), and as Paul wrote, "whom no man hath seen, nor can see" (1 Tim 6:16). Instead, the Lord declared, "he that hath seen me hath seen the Father" (John 14:9).

The Jews, however, had never seen the Father because they had never gazed on the Lord by faith. They merely looked on Him as One born of His parents whom they claimed to have known.

47 Down to v.58, the Lord then dealt with the question of partaking of Himself, by which one would possess eternal life. Throughout, the truth is illustrated by physical symbols and words that have entirely spiritual meanings. To misunderstand these symbols and words is to take carnal ground, which is perhaps even worse than unbelief, for it may include idolatry.

48 The Lord introduced this last part of His interrupted discourse by saying, "I am that bread of life", repeating His statement of v.35. Strictly, in both verses, the words are *ho artos*, meaning "the" bread of life, not "that" as the AV of v.48. Both the RV and JND properly translate v.48 as "*the* bread". The expression "bread of life" suggests that the Lord is not only the Source of life, but that He transfers life to those who believe. Believers partake of life, and they receive life in so doing.

49-50 A great contrast is now introduced, similar to that given in v.27. The Lord spoke of "Your fathers" and "a man", but neither embraced the unbelieving Jews who were listening to Him, for they did not have the OT manna, though in unbelief they did have the true bread from heaven present amongst them. The provision of manna in the wilderness was miraculous, but it did not give life apart from the maintenance of natural physical life. Of those who passed through the wilderness wanderings, we read, "When your fathers . . . saw my works forty years . . . they have not known my ways . . . They shall not enter into my rest" (Heb 3:9-11), leading to "whose carcases fell in the wilderness" (v.17). Even men of faith, such as Moses and Aaron, died at the end of the forty years.

The contrast in v.50 is found in that which "cometh down"—not the body of the Lord Jesus, but His actual Person. To eat of this means to excercise faith in Him, with the result that he shall "not die". This does not refer to the absence of physical death, but to the absence of spiritual death. The serpent said to Eve, "Ye shall not surely die" (Gen 3:4), although God had said "thou shalt surely die" (2:17). God meant both physical and spiritual death, for "sin entered into the world, and death by sin; and so death passed upon all men" (Rom 5:12), "in Adam all die" (1 Cor 15:22). Satan, by his remark, meant that physical death would not occur immediately. But spiritual death is turned into spiritual life—eternal life—by partaking of the living bread. As Peter wrote later, "being born again, not of corruptible seed, but of incorruptible, by the word of God, which liveth and abideth for ever" (1 Pet 1:23).

51 Something new is introduced into this verse; John was very careful to record this in his Gospel. The first part of the verse leads to the second part, since the Lord had already expressed the truth that He was the living bread come down from heaven. In v.32, the Lord stated that it was the Father who gave the true bread from heaven, and we have noted that this refers to His Person. But now in v.51, the Lord Himself is seen as giving bread, defined to be "my flesh". In other words, it is no longer His Person coming down, but what He became when He had come down. John had stated this before, "the Word was made flesh and dwelt among us" (John 1:14), and "as the children are partakers of flesh and blood, he also himself likewise took part of the same" (Heb 2:14). A belief that accepts His Person but refuses to acknowledge that He partook of flesh and blood is no faith at all. In John's old age, this was a prevalent heresy; he stressed the truth in his epistles: "Every spirit that confesseth that Jesus Christ is come in the flesh is of God: and every spirit that confesseth not that Jesus Christ is come in the flesh is not of God: and this is that spirit of antichrist" (1 John 4:2-3); "many deceivers are entered into the world, who confess not that Jesus Christ is come in the flesh" (2 John 7). The Lord Jesus foresaw the existence of this heresy that He did not partake of flesh and blood. The giving that the Lord spoke of here must refer to His sacrifice on the cross, so both His Person and His sacrificial work must be appropriated by faith. We read of this sacrificial giving in many places:

1. "Who gave himself for our sins, that he might deliver us from this present evil world" (Gal 1:4);

2. "Who loved me, and gave himself for me" (Gal 2:20);

3. "Walk in love, as Christ also hath loved us, and hath given himself for us, an offering and a sacrifice to God" (Eph 5:2);

4. "Christ also loved the church, and gave himself for it" (Eph 5:25);

5. "The man Christ Jesus, who gave himself a ransom for all" (1 Tim 2:6);

6. "Who gave himself for us, that he might redeem us from all iniquity (Titus 2:14).

Those who believe this truth have eternal life, and shall never die.

8. *The Sixth Question* 6:52-59

v.52 "The Jews therefore strove among themselves, saying, How can this man give us *his* flesh to eat?
v.53 Then Jesus said unto them, Verily, verily, I say unto you, Except ye eat the flesh of the Son of man, and drink his blood, ye have no life in you.
v.54 Whoso eateth my flesh, and drinketh my blood, hath eternal life; and I will raise him up at the last day.
v.55 For my flesh is meat indeed, and my blood is drink indeed.
v.56 He that eateth my flesh, and drinketh my blood, dwelleth in me, and I in him.
v.57 As the living Father hath sent me, and I live by the Father: so he that eateth me, even he shall live by me.
v.58 This is that bread which came down from heaven: not as your fathers did eat manna, and are dead: he that eateth of this bread shall live for ever.
v.59 These things said he in the synagogue, as he taught in Capernaum."

52 *The Jews speak*. The word for "strove" is *emachonto*, a verb in the imperfect tense, showing that there was a continuity in their action, evidently taking place as the Lord was speaking. This verb *machomai* appears only four times in the NT, as also does the noun *machē*. The verb means to fight, quarrel, dispute, that is to say, amongst themselves, as they sought to ascertain the Lord's meaning from a physical point of view. Truth that is "hard to be understood" leads to improper action on the part of the ignorant (2 Pet 3:16).

53 *The Lord speaks*. In this verse, another new concept is introduced—that of the blood of the Son of man. It is the blood of sacrifice, a particularly suitable subject for the Passover season when the blood of lambs was shed. The reference explains what the Lord meant by the giving of His flesh in v.51. His sacrifice would end in His death, a truth that was unknown to these Jewish unbelievers, even if their leaders were already seeking His death (though not thinking of the sacrificial nature of His death). As the Lord said to John on the isle of Patmos—although He had been the living One, He became dead (Rev 1:18).

Both to eat and to drink mean to appropriate by faith. These two verbs do not imply continuity, for they are in the aorist subjunctive. They imply a once-and-for-all act of appropriation, leading to eternal life. Continuity comes in v.56.

Ritualists love to associate this act with their eucharist (corresponding to the Lord's Supper for believers). But there is no connection between the flesh and blood in this verse with the body and blood (bread and the cup) in the institution of the breaking of bread (Matt 26:26-28). In John 6:53 the thought is that of initial appropriation; it is the principle of turning from unbelief to faith, from death to life, from darkness to life. But the breaking of bread is an act of remembrance and worship every Lord's Day, and is the portion of those who are believers already. The former is a commencement, the latter is a continuance. The former is once-and-for-all, the latter is week-by-week, namely "as often as" (1 Cor 11:26). If the former act of appropriation is not done, the Lord stated that "ye have no life in you", but if the breaking of bread is not engaged in, there is no lack of life, only spiritual weakness is demonstrated.

54-55 "Hath eternal life" stands in contrast with "ye have no life in you". These verses form the final part of the Lord's discourse, so He stressed again the eating of His flesh and the drinking of His blood. He knew that the Jews were still thinking physically, and therefore that they would find great offence in their false understanding of His words. They would think of the OT sacrifices, certain of which could be eaten. But it was absolutely forbidden to partake of blood, "Only ye shall not eat the blood" (Deut 12:16). That is why in Acts 15:20 even the Gentiles had to abstain from blood, so that Jews should not be offended.

In v.54, the verbs "eateth" and "drinketh" are present participles (as in v.56). Whereas in v.53 a once-and-for-all act is implied, here there is a continuance for growth and maturity. This is essentially the difference in John's mind between his Gospel and his first Epistle. The former was written "that ye might believe that Jesus is the Christ, the Son of God; and that believing ye might have life through his name" (20:31), namely it was evangelical in character. But the latter was written "unto you that believe on the name of the Son of God; that ye may know that ye have eternal life" (1 John 5:13), namely it was ministerial in character.

In v.55, the word "indeed" is *alēthōs*, an adverb meaning truly. Other Greek manuscripts have *alēthēs*, an adjective meaning true, real, so some translations read "real food . . . real drink" (NEB). To think heretically of the Lord as a mere apparition is to deny the reality of His flesh and blood.

57 The Lord finally dealt with the character of this new eternal life. He referred first to Himself and then to the believer. The AV preposition "by" in the phrase "by the Father" may lead readers to wonder what it really means. The preposition is *dia*: the RV rendering is "I live because of the Father . . . he also shall live because of me", while JND translates the verse as "I live on account of the Father, he . . . shall live also on account of me". In other words, in His Manhood the Son as the sent One was living on earth because of the purpose of the Father; otherwise He would not be living on earth as the Word having become flesh. Similarly with believers; they live and they shall live because of the purpose of the Son to raise them at the last day. If this resurrection were not to take place, there would be no point in having life now; we would be "of all men most miserable" (1 Cor 15:19).

58 In conclusion, the Lord as the perfect Teacher, and knowing the best way in which to present a subject, ended His message with a summary. All the thoughts in this verse have occurred before in the passage:

1. The bread which came down from heaven (vv.32,33,38,50,51);

2. Your fathers did eat manna, and are dead (vv.32,49);

3. The one eating of this bread shall live for ever (vv.35,40,50,51,53-57).

59 So John added the remark that His discourse ended in the synagogue in Capernaum. It had commenced by the seaside (v.25), and somewhere in between the discourse had changed its venue. We cannot be dogmatic as to where the change took place, but there seems to be a break between verses 34 and 41. Prior to this paragraph, the people spoke, but after this paragraph, the Jews spoke.

The word "synagogue" appears many times in the three Synoptic Gospels, referring to the Lord's ministry in Galilee where the venue for His preaching would often be a synagogue. But in John's Gospel, the word appears only twice (6:59; 18:20), the reason being that John mostly records the Lord's ministry in Jerusalem, and there He used the temple courts as a primary venue for contacting the people with His teaching. In 18:20, the Lord referred both to synagogue and temple, "I ever taught in the synagogue, and in the temple", the former being in Galilee, and the latter in Jerusalem. The Lord had no fellowship with the Jewish practices and teaching in these establishments, since they were so contrary to the divine mind; indeed, He was cast out of the synagogue in Luke 4:29, and out of the temple in John 8:59; 10:39. He used them only as places of contact with people who were willing to listen.

9. *The Seventh Question*
6:60-67

v.60 "Many therefore of his disciples, when they had heard *this*, said, This is an hard saying; who can hear it?
v.61 When Jesus knew in himself that his disciples murmured at it, he said unto them, Doth this offend you?
v.62 *What* and if ye shall see the Son of man ascend up where he was before?
v.63 It is the spirit that quickeneth; the flesh profiteth nothing: the words that I speak unto you, *they* are spirit, and *they* are life.
v.64 But there are some of you that believe not. For Jesus knew from the beginning who they were that believed not, and who should betray him.
v.65 And he said, Therefore said I unto you, that no man can come unto me, except it were given unto him of my Father.
v.66 From that *time* many of his disciples went back, and walked no more with him.
v.67 Then said Jesus unto the twelve, Will ye also go away?"

60 *The disciples speak.* The context must decide who "his disciples" really were. When the Lord said "my disciples" (John 15:8), they were characterised by abiding in Him and bringing forth much fruit. But there were many others, going by the name disciple as learning from Him, but never taking anything into their hearts. In this passage, there were true disciples—His apostles; natural disciples "ever learning, and never able to come to the knowledge of the truth" (2 Tim 3:7); and the critical Jews who listened merely to destroy. In the light of what happened next, we conclude that "his disciples" were amongst the middle class of this list of three possibilities. We see in this class a kind of religious person who will not accept the truth if it does not suit him to do so.

When the people said, "This is a hard *saying*; who can hear it?", they used the word *logos*, meaning word, an expression of thought. It must be distinguished from v.63 where *rhēma* (its plural form) means what is actually uttered in speech. Whereas the AV has "saying", JND translates the clause as "This word is hard". A believer will not find the Lord's word as hard, since such truth is spiritually discerned (1 Cor 2:14), but the unbeliever will find such things to be foolishness. Spiritual truth, when expressed in ordinary words, is hard when such words are interpreted physically, when a physical interpretation gives offence, and when it goes against traditionally conceived ideas. The Lord's parables proved to be hard for the apostles to understand, since they had to ask Him to interpret them (Matt 13:10,36). In their case, the Lord explained fully, but in John 6, the Lord provided the Jews with no explanation of the symbolism behind His teaching. As the Lord said concerning unbelief, "because they seeing see not; and hearing they hear not, neither do they understand" (Matt 13:13). But of faith, He said, "whosoever hath, to him shall be given" (v.12).

61 *The Lord speaks.* The Lord "knew in himself" that these men were murmuring in the background against His teaching. He did not hear them directly, but nothing remains unknown to Him; He is "a discerner of the thoughts and intents of the heart" (Heb 4:12). An example of this divine act of introspection of others is found in Luke 5:22, where "Jesus perceived their thoughts" when the scribes and Pharisees were reasoning amongst themselves. By asking the question, "Doth this offend you?", the Lord sought out the root cause of their opposition. He used the word *skandalizō*, a verb that occurs many times in the Synoptic Gospels, but only twice in John's Gospel (6:61; 16:1). It is always translated "offend" (AV), and means the placing of a snare or stumblingblock before a person. Spiritual truth always has this effect on unbelievers, particularly when cherished interpretations are seemingly being cut out by truth that appears to them to be of an unknown character (Rom 9:32-33).

62-63 These two verses taken together show that the Lord finally dealt with the actual acquisition of faith. A literal translation of v.62 is, "If then ye should see the Son of man ascending up where he was before?". This stands in contrast to the several previous verses where the Lord had spoken of the fact that He had come down from heaven. If the first had not provoked faith, then neither would the second, even if they had been privileged to see the ascension of the Lord (which was not possible, since they were not chosen to witness this glorious event). One coming down could not produce faith (Luke 16:30-31), nor could One supposedly coming down from the cross. A physical witness of the movements of the Lord is not essential to faith, for the Spirit quickens.

V.63 provides the ultimate reason why these men could not understand the Lord's words. There are two great opposites in operation whenever a man hears the words of Christ. We refer to the flesh and the spirit. Thus Paul distinguishes between the spirit of the world and the spirit which is of God (1 Cor 3:12). In Gal 5:19-23, he distinguishes between the works of the flesh and the fruit of the Spirit. An unbeliever can be motivated only by the principle of flesh; however refined and educated he may be, a man of one birth can manifest only that which characterises him naturally. But a believer can be motivated by the Spirit of God, so His understanding, His graces, His works are manifested. Nothing profitable, as assessed by God, can arise from the flesh, but everything pertaining to life arises from the Spirit. Alas, a believer can also manifest the nature of the flesh in unguarded and unspiritual moments. Thus there were those who had begun in the Spirit, and were then seeking to become mature in the energy of the flesh (Gal 3:1-3). Even the apostle Peter manifested both sides of his inner nature; in Matt 16:16 his confession of the Person of Christ derived from an exercise in the spirit, but he then rebuked the Lord, showing an exercise in the flesh (v.22).

In the sentence, "the words that I speak unto you, they are spirit, and they are life", many Greek manuscripts have the perfect tense "I have spoken" (*lelalēka*) instead of the present tense "I speak" (*lalō*); hence the RV and JND use the translation, "the words which I have spoken unto you are spirit and are life". Thus His spoken words entirely transcend all the teachings of the Pharisees and Jewish religious leaders, which could never bring life. Life leads to life, and death leads to death. The Lord's teaching derives from a different source, and always remains on an infinitely higher plane. These remarks are just as important today as in the day when they were first spoken.

64 The Lord looked upon the congregation in the synagogue, and knew that "some" did not believe (extended to "many" in v.66). This effectively repeats what the Lord said in v.36. He did not have to wait until the end of His discourse before knowing from its results who did not believe. He knew "from the beginning" who they were—no doubt from the beginning of the discourse (though of course, His knowledge of the hearts of men was independent of time). Note that the Lord's knowledge extends to two classes of men:

1. "Who they were that believed not"—the Jews and the people generally.

2. "And who should betray him" (in the singular). This refers to Judas (v.71).

The word for "betray" (*paradidōmi*) often is translated to deliver up. The context must decide which word best suits the situation. Thus in vv.64,71, the AV and the RV both use "betray", but JND uses "deliver up" in both verses. In fact, the word "betray", used of Judas, occurs dozens of times in the AV, but JND renders the word by "deliver up". The idea of treachery seems to be absent from the latter word, in English at least.

65 The Lord's last words to these Jews were a restatement of the truth that all men are divided into two classes: those who do come to Him and those who do not; see Acts 28:24. In effect, this is a repetition of thoughts occurring in vv.37,44. To the unbelievers and to the betrayer, it was not given by the Father that they should come to the Son.

66 Men turn their backs on truth that is unpalatable, and this means turning their backs on the One of whom the truth speaks. Such "disciples" are not believers. They had been willing to learn for a season, but such a motivation is not faith if no spiritual fruit is produced, since by their fruits they shall be known (Matt 7:20). Learning *from* Him must be learning *of* Him if this is to be faith. In Luke 4:22,28-29, His "gracious words" led to men being "filled with wrath" and to the casting out of the Lord. In Acts 8:9-24, Simon heard the preaching of the gospel by Philip; he even believed and was baptised. Yet his subsequent wickedness showed that he was still in "the bond of iniquity", unforgiven and about to perish. How different are true believers: to them the words of Christ are so attractive, that they ever walk with Him.

In a parable in Luke 14:16-24, all those who were bidden to a supper "began to make excuse", so they were kept on the outside. But it was even worse in Ezek 8:16, where twenty-five men had their backs to the temple of the Lord, and were engaged in worshipping the sun in the east. Consequently, God departed from them as His glory left the temple for the last time. Similarly in the NT; unbelievers may leave the Lord, and ultimately He will leave them also, for in Matt 24:1 He left the temple for the last time, and never returned. Believers in weakness may leave the Lord temporarily, as when "all the disciples forsook him, and fled" (Matt 26:56), but the Lord does not reciprocate, for He promises "I will never leave thee, nor forsake thee" (Heb 13:5).

67 The Lord would test the reality of the faith of the twelve. They were surrounded by a multitude forsaking the Lord. Would the twelve join the many instead of remaining separate as the few? Would joining the multitude provide an easier life than remaining with the Lord? Being with a minority brings with it a stigma and a reproach. Of course, the Lord knew the answer to His question before He asked it, but He gave Peter the opportunity to make his confession.

10. *The Eighth Question* 6:68-71

v.68 "Then Simon Peter answered him, Lord, to whom shall we go? Thou hast the words of eternal life.
v.69 And we believe and are sure that thou art the Christ, the Son of the living God.
v.70 Jesus answered them, Have not I chosen you twelve, and one of you is a devil?
v.71 He spake of Judas Iscariot *the son* of Simon: for he it was that should betray him, being one of the twelve."

68-69 *Peter speaks.* Peter was always ready to speak, sometimes to blurt out statements in the energy of the flesh (Matt 16:22; 17:4,25; 26:70), and at other times humbly to make statements according to the Spirit of God. The double-sided nature of the tongue is much deplored in James 3:3-12, for this shows what is in the heart.

On this occasion, Peter was entirely spiritual. Others may flock to false apostles, false prophets, false teachers, false evangelists, and even to the anti-Christ of the future. In the OT, a man had only to say "I will be king", then men would follow Absalom, Sheba and Adonijah in their multitudes.

Note the development of the confession of the Person of Christ:

1. "Of a truth thou art the Son of God" (Matt 14:33). This took place in a ship. It arose because of divine power (the Father's works).

2. "We believe and are sure that thou art that Christ, the Son of the living God" (John 6:69). This took place inside or just outside the synagogue. It arose because of the divine preaching (the Father's call).

3. "Thou art the Christ, the Son of the living God" (Matt 16:16). This took place in the borders of Caesarea Philippi. It arose because of the divine Person in their midst (the Father's revelation).

In v.69, there is a variant reading in some Greek manuscripts; thus the RV and JND give the translation "we have believed and known that thou art the holy one of God".

The title "the living God" appears many times in the Scriptures: e.g. in connection with

1. Thirsting (Ps 42:2; 84:2).

2. Divine relationships (Matt 16:16; John 6:69; 2 Cor 3:3).

3. Divine possessions (2 Cor 6:16; 1 Tim 3:15; Heb 12:22).

4. The believer's service (1 Thess 1:9; Heb 9:14).

5. The believer's trust (1 Tim 4:10; 6:17).

6. The unbeliever's departing (Heb 3:12).

7. The unbeliever's judgment (Heb 10:31).

70-71 *The Lord speaks.* The Lord had chosen twelve originally, "he called unto him his disciples: and of them he chose twelve, whom also he named apostles" (Luke 6:13). Judas "which also was the traitor" (v.16) appears last in the list of the twelve. In His prayer, the Lord declared "those that thou gavest me I have kept, and none of them is lost, but the son of perdition; that the scripture might be fulfilled" (John 17:12).

The Lord's words, "one of you is a devil" (*diabolos*: in the Gospels, this is the only time when this word is applied to a man. Otherwise, the more usual word *daimonion* should be translated "demon", although this word is not used in the AV). Clearly, the Lord's accusation had no effect on the apostles; they did not ask, "Is it I?". They did not recognise that anything was wrong until the last supper, and even then, when Judas went out, they thought that he had gone to give something to the poor (John 13:29). Today, believers must discern the intrusion of error, for Paul warned that grievous wolves could even enter a local church to join themselves to the elders, and thus wreck the flock (Acts 20:29).

III. The Christ Rejected (7:1-53)

1. *Before the Feast of Tabernacles*
7:1-10

v.1 "After these things Jesus walked in Galilee: for he would not walk in Jewry, because the Jews sought to kill him.
v.2 Now the Jews' feast of tabernacles was at hand.
v.3 His brethren therefore said unto him, Depart hence, and go into Judaea, that thy disciples also may see the works that thou doest.
v.4 For *there is* no man *that* doeth anything in secret, and he himself seeketh to be known openly. If thou do these things, shew thyself to the world.
v.5 For neither did his brethren believe in him.
v.6 Then Jesus said unto them, My time is not yet come: but your time is always ready.
v.7 The world cannot hate you; but me it hateth, because I testify of it that the works thereof are evil.
v.8 Go ye up unto this feast: I go not up yet unto this feast; for my time is not yet full come.
v.9 When he had said these words unto them, he abode *still* in Galilee.
v.10 But when his brethren were gone up, then went he also up unto the feast, not openly, but as it were in secret."

We have here the next visit of the Lord to Jerusalem, lasting from 7:10 to 10:40. The Lord was not subject to the ordinances of the feasts, for He was the

Fulfiller and Fulfilment of them; nevertheless, so as not to offend the Jews who treated these feasts in a carnal way, He always went up to Jerusalem as far as is recorded. His movements were governed by their spiritual meanings. The Passover would speak of His death; Pentecost of the Spirit given, with the feast of tabernacles speaking of the end time after the harvest (the separation of the wheat) and the vintage (the judgment upon the ungodly). This feast will not, of course, be fulfilled until that coming day, when it will be a time of the open display of the Lord in glory.

In vv.1-9, men tempted Him to go up and show Himself in power; this He would not do, since His time was not yet. In vv.10-13, men in Jerusalem expected Him to be there. In vv.14-36, most men did not recognise Him; His teaching led to a confusion of thought about His Person, something typical of the present day. In vv.37-39, the Spirit was promised after the Lord was glorified. The conclusion in vv.40-53 was that there was further division, brought about by confusion amongst the religious authorities.

1-2 Since the Passover had been near in 6:4, we assume that the Lord went up to Jerusalem. John provides us with no record of His teaching and miracles accomplished there at that time, but it must have led to further enmity, with the Jews seeking again to kill Him. Thus He would not remain "in Jewry"—or rather, He would not "walk" there, namely He would not dwell, teach or do miracles there as the Son of God. "Jewry" is a strange word, occurring again in Luke 23:5, when the Jewish leaders accused Him before Pilate, saying, "He stirreth up the people, teaching throughout all Jewry, beginning from Galilee to this place". The Greek word for "Jewry" is merely *ioudaios*, and when a country is implied in the context it is properly rendered "Judaea" (RV, JND).

The Lord knew the secret plotting of the Jews in Jerusalem, so usually He would give them no opportunity until His hour was come. Job spoke of men who said to God, "Depart from us; for we desire not the knowledge of thy ways" (Job 21:14), and this also marked the Jewish leaders in Jerusalem, whose actions often kept the Lord from Judaea since they so disliked His righteous condemnation of their deeds.

Once again, a feast is called "the Jews' feast", instead of the original title "the feasts of the Lord" (Lev 23:2). Men had carved out their property from what had originally been the province of God. The holy things of God had been (and still are) twisted for the advantage of men. Thus in Ezek 44:6-8, "my sanctuary . . . my house . . . my bread . . . my covenant . . . mine holy things" had been changed by men, so as to be described by God as "for yourselves". Similarly in Ezek 16:14-15, "my comeliness" was changed to "thine own beauty" (the whole context in vv.1-34 should be read).

3-5 *The Lord's brethren speak.* There is no Scriptural reason why these "brethren" should not be the later sons of Joseph and Mary. However, theologians (with prejudiced ideas to uphold and justify) have engaged in much dispute, seeking to demonstrate that Mary had no further children after the birth of her firstborn, the Lord Jesus. Thus from olden times, it has been suggested that "his brethren" refer to near relatives, perhaps sons of Joseph by a previous marriage, perhaps sons of Mary's sister, the wife of Cleopas. But where Scripture is silent, mere speculation quickly leads to strange doctrines. In Matt 13:55-58, we read of these brethren with names "James, Joses, Simon, Judas", and with sisters as well. In Matt 12:47, these brethren stood outside a house desiring to speak with the Lord. In spite of present unbelief, yet in Acts 1:14 we find that they associated with those who continued in prayer and supplication, so at some stage they had been converted. The manifestation of the Lord in resurrection to James must have been connected with this conversion (1 Cor 15:7). James later became a prominent figure in the Jerusalem church (Acts 12:17; 15:13; 21:18; Gal 1:19; 2:9; James 1:1).

In v.4, these brethren had a completely wrong impression (obviously caused by unbelief and prejudice) of the objectives of the Lord. The meaning of v.4 is that they thought that the Lord was seeking to display His own glory openly, and hence they were surprised that He was doing miracles in Galilee "in secret", namely, far from the religious centres in Jerusalem, where they knew that He had disciples. John states explicitly that these brethren did not believe in Him (v.5); they saw His works, but sight did not cause faith to develop. Their taunt "show thyself" has some interesting parallels.

1. It was not "cast thyself down" (Matt 4:6), rather it was He "made himself of no reputation" (Phil 2:7).

2. It was not "show thyself" (John 7:4), rather it was "he humbled himself" (Phil 2:8).

3. It was not "pity thyself" (Matt 16:22 literally), rather it was "the sacrifice of himself" (Heb 9:26).

4. It was not "Save thyself" (Mark 15:30), rather it was He "gave himself" (Gal 2:20).

The fact that His brethren did not believe shows that one can have no confidence in the flesh. Their family privilege is no precursor to faith. Even when on the cross, the Lord would not commit His mother to His brethren, rather it was to the apostle John. When these brethren wanted to talk with Him, He substituted those who do the will of His Father in heaven; such an one would be "my brother". This was spoken before His cross, but after His cross and resurrection He called the disciples "my brethren" on the highest spiritual level (Matt 28:10; John 20:17).

6-9 *The Lord speaks*. In the statement, "My time is not yet come: but your time is alway ready", the word "time" must be distinguished from another word "hour" often used in John's Gospel. As far as the "hour" is concerned, John's

Gospel is the Gospel of the hour, namely, the hour of His sacrifice. On the other hand, Luke's Gospel is the Gospel of the place, tracing the Lord's pathway to Jerusalem as the place of sacrifice. Today, believers must concern themselves with the scriptural time and place of worship. But the Lord's "time" must be interpreted in the context of the feast of tabernacles and of the showing of the Lord in glory at the end of the age, bearing in mind that the Lord would firstly not go up to Jerusalem, and then afterwards He did go up. The Lord was referring to the time of His public display in glory, when all shall see Him. Even today, this has not yet taken place; it is the great endpoint of all prophecy that traces God's purpose for His Son. In other words, the true fulfilment of the feast of tabernacles is still future. By contrast, for the Jews "your time is alway ready", namely the "Jews' feast of tabernacles" was formally observed every year. So the Lord would not immediately go up to Jerusalem, so as to distinguish between His time and their time.

At the same time, the question of hatred entered the situation. This was the outward reason why the Lord would not go up immediately; He was hated because He assessed the world correctly, and openly declared it, that the world hated Him. He amplified this later to His apostles (15:22-24), stating that they hated both Him and His Father. But the world loves its own, those who have the same standards and outlook on matters of mutual concern. Thus the world loves those who hate the Lord, and hates those who love the Lord. As He said in 3:20, men hate the light, because their own deeds are evil, and because they loathe the thought of their deeds being reproved. Consequently, it was safe for any orthodox Jew to go up to the feast; they would be willingly received by the religious leaders.

By saying, "Go ye up unto the feast", the Lord was not condoning formality, rather He was encouraging faithful adherence to the OT law that was still in existence. Such an encouragement should lead men to say, "I was glad when they said unto me, Let us go into the house of the Lord" (Ps 122:1). But then the Lord used the word "yet" twice (*oupō* means "not yet"): "I go not up yet unto this feast; for my time is not yet full come". This means that He fully owned the future implication of the feast for Himself, but the first statement implies that He intended to go up to the feast later, so as to permit no criticism on the part of the Jews.

So the Jews en masse flocked up to a Christless Jerusalem, while the Lord remained for a season in Galilee.

10 All the Jews who went up to Jerusalem went up in large companies, as can be seen from the description in Luke 2:44; no doubt His brethren followed the same custom as they went up to the feast of tabernacles. They left the Lord alone in Galilee, as He had been left alone in Jerusalem in Luke 2:43. However, the Lord later went up to the feast "in secret" and "not openly". He went up as the unknown Christ until He was discovered by means of His teaching. This is typical of the Lord's present work on high. He comes down to His people, unknown to the world, but recognised by faith as believers gather in His Name with His presence in the midst.

2. *During the Feast of Tabernacles*

7:11-36

v.11 "Then the Jews sought him at the feast, and said, Where is he?
v.12 And there was much murmuring among the people concerning him: for some said, He is a good man: others said, Nay; but he deceiveth the people.
v.13 Howbeit no man spake openly of him for fear of the Jews.
v.14 Now about the midst of the feast Jesus went up into the temple, and taught.
v.15 And the Jews marvelled, saying, How knoweth this man letters, having never learned?
v.16 Jesus answered them, and said, My doctrine is not mine, but his that sent me.
v.17 If any man will do his will, he shall know of the doctrine, whether it be of God, or *whether* I speak of myself.
v.18 He that speaketh of himself seeketh his own glory: but he that seeketh his glory that sent him, the same is true, and no unrighteousness is in him.
v.19 Did not Moses give you the law, and *yet* none of you keepeth the law? Why go ye about to kill me?
v.20 The people answered and said, Thou hast a devil: who goeth about to kill thee?
v.21 Jesus answered and said unto them, I have done one work, and ye all marvel.
v.22 Moses therefore gave unto you circumcision; (not because it is of Moses, but of the fathers;) and ye on the sabbath day circumcise a man.
v.23 If a man on the sabbath day receive circumcision, that the law of Moses should not be broken; are ye angry at me, because I have made a man every whit whole on the sabbath day?
v.24 Judge not according to the appearance, but judge righteous judgment.
v.25 Then said some of them of Jerusalem, Is not this he, whom they seek to kill?
v.26 But, lo, he speaketh boldly, and they say nothing unto him. Do the rulers know indeed that this is the very Christ?
v.27 Howbeit we know this man whence he is: but when Christ cometh, no man knoweth whence he is.
v.28 Then cried Jesus in the temple as he taught, saying, Ye both know me, and ye know whence I am: and I am not come of myself, but he that sent me is true, whom ye know not.
v.29 But I know him: for I am from him, and he hath sent me.
v.30 Then they sought to take him: but no man laid hands on him, because his hour was not yet come.
v.31 And many of the people believed on him, and said, When Christ cometh, will he do more miracles than these which this *man* hath done?
v.32 The Pharisees heard that the people murmured such things concerning him; and the Pharisees and the chief priests sent officers to take him.

v.33 Then said Jesus unto them, Yet a little while am I with you, and *then* I go unto him that sent me.
v.34 Ye shall seek me, and shall not find *me*: and where I am, *thither* ye cannot come.
v.35 Then said the Jews among themselves, Whither will he go, that we shall not find him? will he go unto the dispersed among the Gentiles, and teach the Gentiles?
v.36 What *manner* of saying is this that he said, Ye shall seek me, and shall not find *me*: and where I am, *thither* ye cannot come?"

11-13 *The Jews speak.* There were three kinds of questions that the Jews were asking: Where is He? Who is He? What is He doing?

1. In v.11, they expected the Lord to be present, and must have been surprised that He appeared to be absent. They were completely ignorant of the dispensational motives in the Lord's heart. In v.34, the Lord knew that they would seek Him, but men could find Him only when it was the divine will that He should be found. Those who seek shall find (Matt 7:7), but this promise is for the earnest seeker, not for those with vain motives. Thus those who sought His dwelling in John 1:38 were permitted to find.

2. His character and works caused men to speculate upon His Person. They were giving their answers to the question, "What think ye of Christ?". The word for "good" is *agathos*, describing a character that is known by its effects and results. The unsaved can only know this about Christ, so could not use the other word for good, namely *kalos*, implying an intrinsic goodness (for example, in John 10:11, describing the Lord as the "good" Shepherd). Thus the rich ruler called Him "Good (*agathos*) Master" because the outward works of the Lord's character were all that he could see. Hence the Lord was a subject of debate and discussion, as men spoke of His outward moral integrity. Today unholy men will speak of His existence, His deity, His birth, His perfection, His miracles, His death, His resurrection, in an unbelieving philosophical kind of way. As far as His Person was concerned, they wondered whether He was that Prophet, John the Baptist, Elijah, or Jeremiah (Matt 16:14).

3. Other Jews assessed the Lord as deceiving the people. They would claim that His miracles were a kind of trickery, or done in collaboration with Beelzebub (Matt 12:24), and that His teaching was contrary to the OT, however appealing it might be to some. Later in John 7:47, the Pharisees claimed that their officers had been deceived by the Lord, since they found that "Never man spake like this man". After His death, the Pharisees stated to Pilate that the Lord was "that deceiver", because He had said that after three days He would rise again (Matt 27:63).

But even amongst these disputers, there was the "fear of the Jews", namely, of the Pharisees. So no one would speak openly in favour of the Lord. Thus in John 9:22, there was fear that men would be put out of the synagogue if they confessed Christ. The same is stated in 12:42. Joseph of Arimathaea was a secret disciple "for fear of the Jews" (19:38), while the apostles gathered behind shut doors "for fear of the Jews" (20:19). However, all this was swept away for believers when the Holy Spirit was given; in Acts 2, boldness was the order of the day (see Acts 4:13,29), though Peter later succumbed to fear even of Jews who believed (Gal 2:12).

14-15 *The Jews speak.* The feast of tabernacles lasted for eight days (Lev 23:39; Neh 8:18), so the Lord commenced His teaching only after a few days of the feast had passed. As usual, He taught in the temple courts (*hieron*), His practice being to commence early in the morning (Luke 21:38). There is no record that the Lord did miracles in Jerusalem at this feast; there was no open display of His deity. The Jews knew that He was not an officially credited teacher, so they questioned His authority, even though He was obviously equipped to teach. Today, in many religious circles, only those with formal education and having been ordained are recognised as being able to teach, yet they are often completely surpassed by humbler men with a real spiritual ability to preach and teach (these being Spirit-given gifts). By asking, "How knoweth this man letters?", the Jews failed to perceive in Him a divine teacher who needed no education in the schools of men. (The same word *grammata* is used of Paul by Festus in Acts 26:24.) Similar expressions of surprise are found elsewhere, such as "the people were astonished at his doctrine: for he taught them as one having authority, and not as the scribes" (Matt 7:28-29); "Whence hath this man this wisdom?" (Matt 13:54). They refused to recognise the divine origin of His teaching, even though this was clearly made known to them.

16 *The Lord speaks.* This is the answer to the Jews' perplexity, an answer that continues into vv.17-18. The Lord followed up the Jews' question that implied schools, teachers and scholars—a well-taught scholar should ultimately know a subject as well as his teacher. Effectively, the Lord implied a metaphor (and we speak reverently) concerning the eternal school of the divine throne. Throughout eternity, the mind of the Son was identical to the mind of the Father. The Lord's doctrine was the Father's doctrine. He said the same thing in John 8:28, "as my Father hath taught me, I speak these things". This should be the attitude of the Lord's people today in their service—they teach what they are taught from the Scriptures by the Holy Spirit; had this been observed throughout the church age, there would not be the divergencies of Christendom so prevalent at the present time around us.

17 The first word "will" in this verse is the verb *thelō*, meaning to desire; we may translate the sentence as, "If any man desire to practise his will, he shall know of the doctrine". How can the will of God be known? By desiring to practise it. Our understanding of such fundamental phenomena as life and light comes through personal experience of these things; they are not mere cold definitions. Similarly with the knowledge of the will of God and with divine teaching. An academic exposition may be suitable for unbelief, but by itself this does not lead to a heart-knowledge of divine teaching. How can we know that the Lord's teaching was (and is) divine teaching? A faith that works enables us to know "whether it be of God, or whether I speak of myself". Here, the first word "of" is *ek*, namely, *out of*, while the second word "of" is *apo*, namely *from*. The first shows the Source—God Himself; the second would show the teacher as a self-source (as v.18 shows), the self-seeking of personal glory. The same word *apo* is found in John 16:13; the promised Spirit will *not* "speak *from* himself".

18 Any teacher on earth who teaches his own ideas is seeking his own glory and self-advancement. The Lord never could and never did take that attitude. By recognising this fact, we can discern the direction of glory-seeking in those who exalt themselves, or who expect others to exalt them. This is the contrast between Christ and the anti-Christ. The latter "shall come in his own name" (John 5:43), exalting himself above all that is called God (2 Thess 2:4). By contrast, a humble one, seeking the glory of God on high, proves that he is true and righteous. Men of pomp and glory shall descend into hell, while the Lord shall be exalted and sanctified in righteousness (Isa 5:14-16). For the combination of truth and righteousness, see Rev 15:3; 16:7; 19:2.

19 By speaking of Moses' law, the Lord was referring back to v.17, the desire to do God's will and to understand the doctrine. This did not describe the attitude of the Jews. God had given the people the law indirectly through Moses, since they had no desire for God to speak directly to them (Exod 20:19). This law had to be read at the feast of tabernacles (Deut 31:10; Neh 8:14; 9:3), so the Jews could not claim ignorance. Yet the Lord accused them that none kept the law. The reason is obvious: law-keeping was (and is) impossible, though the Jews would not recognise that fact. They boasted in the law, yet dishonoured God by breaking it (Rom 2:17-23). By keeping the law, save in one point, there was complete guilt before God (James 2:10). In particular, the Lord stressed an outstanding sin of the leaders—"Why go ye about to kill me?". This intention was clearly contrary to the commandment, "Thou shalt not kill" (Exod 20:13), an intention that had grown since the event recorded in John 5:16, where men sought to slay Him because of two features of the Lord's teaching and work that they so grossly detested.

20 *The people speak*. No doubt at this stage it was the Pharisees who had the intention of killing the Lord; the state of heart of the common people had not as yet reached that stage. So they resented the Lord compounding them with the leaders, though ultimately they would all reach the same level, since the chief priests would move the people (Mark 15:11). They therefore blasphemously accused the Lord, "Thou hast a demon". The AV translation "devil" is definitely wrong, for that word is *diabolos*, referring to Satan and to none other. Rather, the Jews used the word *daimonion*, meaning "demon", though unfortunately always translated as "devil" in the AV (with the exception of Acts 17:18, where "gods" is used). A demon is an evil spirit, usually seen as occupying a man, and being cast out in many of the Lord's miracles. Elsewhere, He recalled that the people accused John the Baptist of having a demon (Luke 7:33). Through not wishing to recognise the divine power possessed by the Lord, on one occasion the Pharisees declared that it was by Beelzebub, the prince of the demons, that He cast out demons (Matt 12:24), leading to the parables in Matt 13 when the Lord sought to hide the truth from such evil men. These blasphemous accusations continued in John 8:48,52; 10:20.

21-24 *The Lord speaks.* The Lord recognised that the continued intention of the leaders to kill Him stemmed from the miracle that He had performed on the sabbath day in John 5:16; this might have taken place one and a half years previously, so the leaders had long memories. (See Matt 26:61 where men quoted what had taken place three years previously.)

In vv.22-23, the Lord gave another reason why it was legitimate for Him to do miracles on the sabbath day. (We have given a comprehensive list in our comments on John 5:17.) In the law, Moses had stated that a male child had to be circumcised on the eighth day of its life (Lev 12:3), a divinely-given rite that stemmed from God's covenant with Abraham (Gen 17:11; 21:4; Acts 7:8). See Luke 1:59; 2:21 for NT examples of this period of eight days. Thus if this eighth day happened to fall on a sabbath, then the law of circumcision superceded the law of the sabbath; this law of the sabbath was subject to a higher law. At this the Jews would never complain, so they had no cause for complaint when the superior law of mercy and kindness had a priority over their cherished law of the sabbath. Thus it was lawful "to do good ... to save life" on the sabbath (Luke 6:9).

Rather, they should not judge "according to the appearance". Their minds were dull when attitudes were hardened by a built-in cherished tradition. The appearance formed by adherence to the letter should be abandoned by adherence to the spirit behind the word (2 Cor 3:6). This is an application of wisdom, that descended from above in the Person of Christ (Isa 11:2-4), while the wisdom of men was "earthly, sensual, devilish" (James 3:15). One could only interpret the true nature of the sabbath by judging righteous judgment—namely, following the approach of the righteous One in their midst. Anything else was unrighteous, even if it seemed to fit in with the letter of the law. Samuel hardly judged righteous judgment when he falsely discerned Eliab as the Lord's anointed, since he looked on the "outward appearance" rather than on the heart (1 Sam 16:6-7). Similarly, if we judge our own outward works to be satisfactory, then we may be disregarding God's righteous pronouncement upon such works.

25-27 *Men in Jerusalem speak.* These were actual residents in Jerusalem, rather than any of the multitudes who had come up to the feast. They knew that their leaders were intent upon killing the Lord, unlike those in v.20 who seemed not to be aware of this fact. They were perplexed as to why the leaders did not arrange the arrest of this One in the midst (though in their own way these leaders were indeed plotting the capture of the Lord, vv.32,45). In fact, the people thought that this apparent hesitancy implied that they had some superior knowledge, that they knew "indeed, that this is the very Christ". In v.26, the words "indeed" and "very" both stand for the Greek adverb *alēthōs*, though many MSS omit the second occurrence "very". After all, the people were "in expectation" (Luke 3:15) about the appearing of their Messiah. Yet in v.27, these men claimed to have a knowledge even superior to that of their leaders! He had arrived from Galilee, not from Jerusalem. This was sufficient in their minds to show that He was not the Christ. However, their ignorance was pathetic, in that they claimed that no man shall know where Messiah comes from. By this, they overlooked their own OT Scriptures, which made it clear that their Ruler would come from Bethlehem (Mic 5:2) as far as His first advent was concerned. Other Jews knew this fact (John 7:42), so this dabbling with religious knowledge was bound to cause a division sooner or later. Believers know the facts:

1. He came from Bethlehem as far as His natural birth was concerned.

2. He came from Galilee as far as His ministry was concerned.

3. He came from the Father as far as His Person was concerned.

4. He will come from heaven to the mount of Olives at His second advent.

28-30 *The Lord speaks.* The scene has not changed from v.14; the Lord was still in the temple courts engaged in His teaching, with various groups of Jews listening to Him. When He said, "Ye both know me, and ye know whence I am", He referred to the natural knowledge that some (but not all) possessed. Some knew that He was "the Prophet", (v.40); some thought that He was "the Christ", (v.42), though others did not believe this fact, (v.27). Some thought that He originated from Galilee (v.41); some must have known that He had been born in Bethlehem, since Luke, in writing his Gospel, had checked all his sources of information (Luke 1:3), so the facts must have been fairly widespread. Yet on a spiritual plane, these Jews were in complete ignorance. Twice the Lord mentioned here that He was sent from the Father; the Lord knew Him, but they knew Him not.

Some, however, realised what the Lord implied by these remarks, that "he that sent me" referred to the Father; hence the anger of some was aroused so they sought to take Him. Here it was the people who sought to do this, but in vv.32,44, it was the representatives of the leaders. In Ps 2:1-2, we read of both the people and the rulers who were against the Lord's anointed. In both cases, God would not allow the hands of wicked men to touch the Son here below, until they finally "took Jesus, and bound him" (John 18:12). Until His hour came, there was divine restraint upon the hands of men; at that time, no authority had been given from heaven for men to take Him. The Lord was safe under the protection of heaven (Ps 65:7; 91:11; John 8:20). Until His hour was come, there were twelve legions of angels to protect Him—namely, 72 000 angels. And if each angel could deal with 185 000 men (2 Kings 19:35), then these myriads of angels could deal with about thirteen thousand million men at one time. Such was the provision of heaven whereby the Son of God on earth was protected until the end, when protection was withdrawn as the Son entered into death by way of the cross.

31 *The people speak.* When John wrote that "many of the people believed on him", he was not referring to what we call "saving faith". These men would not seek to take Him; they would not seek to blaspheme His Person (as v.20); they accepted His teaching without understanding it; they distanced themselves from the intentions of the priests and Pharisees. But they did not believe that He was the Christ, since they said, "When Christ cometh". No doubt they had the strange ideas about His Person described in Matt 16:14. They therefore thought that the Christ to come would do more signs (not miracles) than the One in their midst. The Lord's "miracles and wonders and signs" (Acts 2:22) failed to demonstrate His true Person to them.

32 The Pharisees would not tolerate the ordinary people theorising about the Person of Christ, as seen in vv.25-27,31,40-43. They could see that such remarks suggested a half-way stage to becoming disciples of the Lord. This is obnoxious to politically-minded unbelievers, and they would seek to control what the people thought. (Today, there is the advantage of independent scriptural thought; this avoids interdenominational proselytism, under which power the thoughts of the masses can easily be controlled.)

No doubt there was an official meeting of the Jewish Sanhedrin, that authorised the officers (*hupēretēs*), evidently this council's bailiffs. In other words, the stage had arrived where the Jewish leaders would not take even the slightest risk that men might be interested in the Lord and His teaching. The lack of success of their mission is seen in v.45. (Note, elsewhere the Pharisees sent unto John in 1:19,24, while later they sent for the apostles in prison in Acts 5:21.)

33-34 *The Lord speaks.* The Lord had said that He had been sent, and that the leaders were plotting His departure through death. He now made it clear that men would have no control over the time of His departure. He would be with them still for "a little while" (*mikron chronon*). This period would last for about six months, between the feast of tabernacles and the following passover. The Lord used a similar expression "a little while" (*mikron*) twice in John 16:16, the first referring to the period of hours between His final ministry and His death on the cross, and the second to the period between His death and resurrection manifestations. In our verse 33, the Lord would return to His Father, after death and resurrection, by means of the ascension. This act of going would be voluntary; men could not cause His ultimate death. It would be He who would give His life (John 10:17-18); no man could take His life from Him, so when He said that men "shall put him to death" (Luke 18:33) He was referring to the physical act of crucifixion.

After loving hands had taken Him down from the cross, unbelieving men would never see Him again (until His second advent in glory when every eye shall see Him). They would seek Him, but while remaining in unbelief they would never come to the ultimate destination above that welcomed Him back. This seeking may be by feigned belief, as in v.31, or it may have been that the leaders really thought that the Lord's body had been stolen from the tomb (Matt 28:13-15), so they would seek for it to avoid the conclusion that He had actually been raised to life again. (See 2 Kings 2:16-18 when men sought Elijah's body.) The expression "thither ye cannot come" appears three times:

1. John 7:34, spoken to the religious men in the temple.

2. John 8:21, spoken to the religious leaders in the temple.

3. John 13:33, spoken to the disciples in the upper room.

35-36 *The Jews speak.* The Jews interpreted the Lord's remarks entirely naturally, that his going implied a physical journey of considerable distance. Note that the word "Gentiles" is not the usual word meaning nations, but it is *Hellēnes*. By "the dispersed", the Jews implied the ten tribes who had long since been scattered after the end of the northern kingdom in 2 Kings 17. By the second use of the word, they also implied non-Israelites, namely Gentiles in Greek-speaking countries. This was the mere speculation of unbelief, though the gospel message did go forth to the nations through Paul's missionary journeys.

Note John's style in recording men's questions that contain the actual statements of the Lord. This phenomenon occurs here, and also in 16:17 where the apostles repeat the Lord's words in their question.

3. *At the End of the Feast of Tabernacles* 7:37-39

v.37 "In the last day, that great *day* of the feast, Jesus stood and cried, saying, If any man thirst, let him come unto me, and drink.
v.38 He that believeth on me, as the scripture hath said, out of his belly shall flow rivers of living water.
v.39 (But this spake he of the Spirit, which they that believe on him should receive: for the Holy Ghost was not yet *given*; because that Jesus was not yet glorified.)"

37-39 *The Lord speaks.* The Lord would no longer address His remarks to the Jews generally; in these verses blessing is directed to the individual, "any man . . . him . . . he that believeth". He often took up everyday events around Him, and used them metaphorically to illustrate deep truth. According to the custom of the day, daily during the first seven days of the feast of tabernacles, the priests brought water from Siloam in a golden vessel, and poured it out upon the altar, as an act of remembrance of water coming out of the rock, and as an act of anticipating spiritual refreshment in the days of Messiah. But on the eighth and last day of the feast, this was not done. Therefore the Lord substituted Himself as the Source of water from which a man could drink. Thirsting was an exercise similar to that of the psalmists of old, when it was said:

1. "My soul thirsteth for God, for the living God" (Ps 42:1-2).

2. "My soul thirsteth for thee, my flesh longeth for thee in a dry and thirsty land, where no water is" (Ps 63:1).

3. "My soul longeth, yea, even fainteth for the courts of the Lord" (Ps 84:2).

4. "Ho, every one that thirsteth, come ye to the waters" (Isa 55:1).

In v.38, the word "belly" is followed by the RV and JND; the word is *koilia*, physically meaning a cavity interior to man, but used metaphorically to denote the inner self. (See Prov 18:8.) In v.39, John explained what the Lord meant, though no doubt he did not know this meaning until the Lord was glorified (see John 2:22). Believers possess the Holy Spirit who dwells within, for the believer's body is "the temple of the Holy Spirit" (1 Cor 6:19-20). This Spirit was similar to the "rivers of living water". Taking the context into consideration, we do not feel that this refers to the Spirit flowing out of a believer to meet the needs of thirsty souls around (though this is true in other contexts, and is why the gifts of the Spirit are given in 1 Cor 12:1-11), but to the Spirit within always increasing in a maturing soul. It is a personal matter, just as the well, providing living water within, and springing up into eternal life (John 8:14), is a personal experience. As Paul wrote, it is God who "ministereth to you the Spirit" (Gal 3:5).

The Spirit had been operative in the OT, and also during the time when the Lord was here, but not in the sense of being promised in John 14-16 after the Lord had gone away to return to the Father. The indwelling Spirit is a feature of the church age; on the day of Pentecost, Peter declared, "Therefore being by the right hand of God exalted, and having received of the Father the promise of the Holy Spirit, he hath shed forth this" (Acts 2:33). It was necessary, therefore, for the Lord to be glorified before the Spirit could be given.

Note in v.39, the Greek word for "Spirit" and "Ghost" is *pneuma*; the AV translators used these two words indiscriminately as possessing the same meaning.

There has been much discussion amongst expositors as to what is meant by "as the scripture hath said" (v.38). This is not the same as "It is written", where we expect to have an exact quotation. Rather, the phrase means that the OT referred to something, perhaps indirectly, typically, metaphorically. Of the many verses suggested, we may mention a few: "Therefore with joy shall ye kdraw water out of the wells of salvation" (Isa 12:3); "there shall be upon every high mountain, and upon every high hill, rivers and streams of water" (Isa 30:25); "in the wilderness shall waters break out, and streams in the desert" (Isa 35:6-7); "I will pour water upon him that is thirsty, and floods upon the dry ground: I will pour my spirit upon thy seed" (Isa 44:3); "every one that thirsteth, come ye to the waters" (Isa 55:1); "thou shalt be lie a watered garden, and like a spring of water" (Isa 58:11). But none of these quotations refers to water flowing from an inner cavity. Rather the most apt verse appears to be Exod 12:6, where water came out of the rock, and the people were able to drink. For there appeared to the people that there was a miraculous cavity in the rock out of which the water flowed to meet their need. See also Num 20:11; Deut 8:15; Ps 114:8.

4. *After the Feast of Tabernacles*
7:40-53

v.40 "Many of the people therefore, when they heard this saying, said, Of a truth this is the Prophet.
v.41 Others said, This is the Christ. But some said, Shall Christ come out of Galilee?
v.42 Hath not the scripture said, That Christ cometh of the seed of David, and out of the town of Bethlehem, where David was?
v.43 So there was a division among the people because of him.
v.44 And some of them would have taken him; but no man laid hands on him.
v.45 Then came the officers to the chief priests and Pharisees; and they said unto them, Why have ye not brought him?
v.46 The officers answered, Never man spake like this man.
v.47 Then answered them the Pharisees, Are ye also deceived?
v.48 Have any of the rulers or of the Pharisees believed on him?
v.49 But this people who knoweth not the law are cursed.
v.50 Nicodemus saith unto them, (he that came to Jesus by night, being one of them,)
v.51 Doth our law judge *any* man, before it hear him, and know what he doeth?
v.52 They answered and said unto him, Art thou also of Galilee? Search, and look: for out of Galilee ariseth no prophet.
v.53 And every man went unto his own house."

40-42 *The people speak.* By the Spirit of inspiration, John appears to be fond of this method of describing the attitude of the people (7:25-27; see Matt

16:14). His object was to demonstrate the principle stated by the Lord in Luke 9:49-51, "I am come to send fire on the earth . . . Suppose ye that I am come to give peace on earth? I tell you, Nay; but rather division". This division is seen in families, amongst the people as in these verses, and amongst the Jewish leaders (John 7:50-53). Thus some people thought that the Lord's teaching showed that He was the promised Prophet (Deut 18:15,18); others (*allos*, of the same kind) thought that He was the promised Christ (in John 1:19-22 the Pharisees asked John the Baptist whether he were the Prophet or the Christ). Clearly, the people did not associate the Prophet with the Christ, and this caused the division. Others who did know that the Lord had been born in Bethlehem were certain that Christ should not come from Galilee (see v.27). They took the point of view adopted by Nathanael before he saw the Lord (John 1:46), "Can there any good thing come out of Nazareth?". To prove their point, the people appealed to the Scriptures (not using an actual quotation). How true they were! but this shows that the truth can become darkness in the minds of unbelievers, when the letter and not the Spirit is in operation, when the holy manna "bred worms, and stank" (Exod 16:20). The people made two points about the coming of Christ:

1. He is the seed of David. This is a NT truth, as seen in Matt 1:1; 22:42 (this last verse being the confession of the people); Luke 1:32; Rom 1:3. It is also an OT truth, the people's confession deriving from their understanding of the OT: 2 Sam 7:12-14,16; Ps 132:11; Isa 9:6-7; 11:1; Jer 23:5.

2. He comes "out of the town of Bethlehem, where David was". This was predicted in the OT (Mic 5:2), a town from which David originated (1 Sam 16:1). And of course it was perfectly fulfilled in the NT regardless of the fact that the home of Joseph and Mary was in Nazareth (Matt 2:1; Luke 2:4).

43-44 In one way or another, the Lord's Person was a stumblingblock to all men in unbelief. This division was caused by various opinions and theories about the Lord, many taken from Scripture, but applied in darkness; this is the origin of the many divisions in Christendom—subjects taken from the Scriptures, but not held according to truth. Similar divisions were reported by John in 9:16; 10:19 (where the word "again" is added, to show that this was a repetitive feature). There was also a division in the Jewish Sanhedrin, for Nicodemus stood out against the other Pharisees (vv.50-51).

As we have pointed out before, there were two classes of people who sought to take the Lord. Firstly, there were ordinary people who objected to His teaching—clearly not those who thought he was the Prophet or the Christ (v.39). And secondly there were the officers sent from the Sanhedrin (vv.32,45). They had no hesitancy in doing this openly in Jerusalem; later at the next Passover, the leaders knew that they would have to take Him secretly, saying, "Not on the feast day, lest there be an uproar among the people" (Matt 26:5). However, there was no possibility of evil hands being placed on the Lord until His hour was come; divine intervention prevented this from happening.

45 *The Sanhedrin speaks.* These officers returned empty-handed, to the consternation of the chief priests and Pharisees. Their plan had misfired, so they attacked the officers with the question, "Why have ye not brought him?". When the roles are reversed, when men have to be brought before God for judgment, there will be no possibility of this not being put into effect.

46 *The officers speak.* These men had been affected, not by the Lord's miracles, but by His teaching—in particular the teaching in vv.33-38. Even the hardest of men can be affected for a season by His teaching, and can therefore be rendered impotent in their designs against Him. In Matt 7:28-29, His teaching caused astonishment, for it was so distinct from the scribes' teaching. In Matt 22:34,46 men were put to silence on account of the authority and logic of His words. In Luke 4:22, men in the synagogue wondered "at the gracious words which proceeded out of his mouth", though shortly afterwards they changed their minds and were filled with wrath.

47-49 *The Pharisees speak.* It was a common feature at that time for the religious leaders to accuse the Lord of being a deceiver. Any man affected by His teaching had been, according to them, deceived. Even some of the people had made this accusation (John 7:12), while after His death, the chief priests and Pharisees made this accusation to Pilate, "we remember that that deceiver said" (Matt 27:63), referring to His declaration that He would rise again. Men hated the Lord before they hated His followers (John 15:18), so they would made a similar accusation against Paul, "as deceivers, and yet true" (2 Cor 6:8).

Their question, "Have any of the rulers . . . believed on him?", was their way of getting the officers to confess that no one in authority had believed on the Lord, so the attitude of these subordinates was unjustified and not following the party line. Strictly, the implication behind the question was wrong, for Nicodemus was a Pharisee, and yet was a disciple, while in John 12:42 we read that many of the chief rulers "believed on him", though they did not make an open confession of this fact. As for the common people who seemed to be attracted by the Lord's teaching, the Pharisees had nothing but contempt for them; they knew not the law, and so were cursed. They were in ignorance, not having received the Rabbinical teaching; by "who knoweth not the law" we presume that they referred to the OT prophecies of a Messiah coming in glory, to their eyes quite different from the lowly Jesus who sought not His own glory and who did not display it to unbelieving eyes. However, the common people attracted by the Lord's teaching knew better than the religious leaders, and this feature is common today, with the base of the world having a far greater spiritual knowledge of Scripture than those who are theologically mighty (1 Cor 1:26-29).

50-51 *Nicodemus speaks.* This man, fearful in John 3:1, and exceptionally bold in 19:39, is seen here in a half-way stage of spiritual development. He appealed to the law in a justifiable way. It was right for a man to be heard before being condemned: "Hear the causes between your brethren, and judge righteously between every man and his brother" (Deut 1:16). The priests and the Pharisees had no intention of abiding by these principles of their law, as is witnessed by the later trial of the Lord before the Sanhedrin. Nicodemus did his best, and the evil day of men was put off for a season, until the arrival of the Lord's hour.

The phrase "one of them" (v.50) is interesting, and recalls membership of other groupings. In our day, "one of" defines a company, loyalty to which denotes loyalty to the Lord:

1. "Onesimus, a faithful and beloved brother, who is one of you" (Col 4:9).

2. "Epaphras, who is one of you, a servant of Christ" (Col 4:12).

This is membership of a local church, where fellowship, service and likemindedness exist and are appreciated. See also Luke 24:22; John 12:2.

52-53 *The Pharisees speak.* In self-defence, they accuse Nicodemus of being a Galilean, and hence a supporter of the Lord as a Galilean. They were wrong in supposing that the Lord originally had come from Galilee, and they were wrong in the knowledge of OT facts. It was not true that no prophet arose from Galilee, for Jonah was of Gath-hepher of Galilee (2 Kings 14:25). As soon as one is wrong in the understanding of the Person of Christ, then everything else goes wrong as well. If one does not hold the Head, then strange doctrines rapidly originate and spread, as in the case of the Colossian church.

There is a vital principle in "And every man went unto his own house. Jesus went unto the mount of Olives". In these words, we find a complete contrast. On the one hand, the members of the Sanhedrin went to their own houses, dissatisfied, unspiritual, with nothing for God. On the other hand, the Lord went to the mount of Olives, and we rightly assume that it was to abide in the home of Mary, Martha and Lazarus in Bethany on the eastern slopes. He had appreciated this home ever since he had been received into it in Luke 10:38. This was a home where love reigned (John 11:5), and where fellowship was prominent (12:1). We believe that the Lord spent His last nights in this home before He was crucified (Luke 21:37). Today, the homes of believers are places where the Lord can dwell, contrasting with homes of unbelievers, described metaphorically in Isa 13:20-22, "their houses shall be full of doleful creatures: and owls shall dwell there . . . and dragons in their pleasant places".

A similar contrast is found in 1 Chron 16:43, "all the people departed every man to his house: and David returned to bless his house". The ark had been established on mount Zion with rejoicing. The people were satisfied with the provisions that they had gained (v.3), but David appears to have been about the only one who was spiritual—he returned "to bless" his house. And this led to his exercise to build a house for the Lord, as distinct from tents (17:1-5), with the Messianic promise being made to him (vv.11-14).

We may also draw attention to Exod 33:7-10. Moses, Joshua and others who sought the Lord went out of the camp to the tabernacle—these were spiritually minded. But the others were content to remain at the doors of their tents, no doubt worshipping, but seeing no point in meeting with the Lord; these were not spiritually minded.

IV. The "I Am" Rejected (8:1-59)

1. *The Woman not Condemned*
8:1-11

v.1 "Jesus went unto the mount of Olives.
v.2 And early in the morning he came again into the temple, and all the people came unto him; and he sat down, and taught them.
v.3 And the scribes and Pharisees brought unto him a woman taken in adultery; and when they had set her in the midst,
v.4 They say unto him, Master, this woman was taken in adultery, in the very act.
v.5 Now Moses in the law commanded us, that such should be stoned: but what sayest thou?
v.6 This they said, tempting him, that they might have to accuse him. But Jesus stooped down, and with *his* finger wrote on the ground, *as though he heard them not*.
v.7 So when they continued asking him, he lifted up himself, and said unto them, He that is without sin among you, let him first cast a stone at her.
v.8 And again he stooped down, and wrote on the ground.
v.9 And they which heard it, being convicted by *their own* conscience, went out one by one, beginning at the eldest, *even* unto the last: and Jesus was left alone, and the woman standing in the midst.
v.10 When Jesus had lifted up himself, and saw none but the woman, he said unto her, Woman, where are those thine accusers? hath no man condemned thee?
v.11 She said, No man, Lord. And Jesus said unto her, Neither do I condemn thee: go, and sin no more."

1 We have already commented on this verse at the end of the previous chapter. It must be admitted that the passage 7:53 to 8:11 is not contained in the so-called oldest Greek manuscripts of the NT, though it is contained in the TR. Neither the AV nor JND makes any reference to this fact, and the passage appears in its usual position without comment. The RV places the passage in brackets, with the marginal note: "Most of the ancient authorities omit John

7:53 to 8:11. Those which contain it vary much from each other". The NEB omits the passage in the usual place, though it is printed as an addition at the end of John's Gospel, with the note, "This passage, which in the most widely received editions of the New Testament is printed in the text of John 7:53 to 8:11 has no fixed place in our ancient witnesses. Some of them do not contain it at all. Some place it after Luke 21:38, others after John 7:36, or 7:52, or 21:24". We would offer the following comments.

1. At the end of ch.7, apart from v.53, the Lord was talking to the people in the temple courts (vv.28-31), while the Pharisees had been gathered in their council (vv.45-52). If the disputed passage is omitted, 8:12 commences with the words "Then spake Jesus again unto them", namely to the Pharisees in the temple (vv.13,20). Thus there is an illogical break in the passage, which does not occur if the disputed passage is present, for in it we find the Pharisees in the temple with the Lord on the following day.

2. In cases of MS uncertainty, the author is always attracted to the work of Ivan Panin, *The New Testament in the Original Greek. The Text Established by Means of Bible Numerics.* Ivan Panin discovered a numerical pattern that pervades every paragraph, sentence and word in the NT. Even if so much as one word is displaced, altered or omitted, the pattern is obliterated throughout the whole of the NT. By this means, Panin was able to demonstrate the status of every disputed paragraph, phrase and word, caused by variations in the hundreds of Greek MSS. As a result of this all-pervading numerical pattern, Panin concluded that the passage John 7:53 to 8:11 actually should be present in the NT, otherwise the whole pattern, evidently the result of divine inspiration, would be destroyed.

2 The Lord has set an example: to rise early in the morning and to engage in service leads to profitable results. Wisdom is necessary when one rises early, else sometimes the result may be "counted a curse to him" (Prov 27:14). In the OT, God Himself set a good example as working through His servants the prophets. In particular, the book of Jeremiah contains more references to rising up early than any other OT book. Thus, "And the Lord hath sent unto you all his servants the prophets, rising early and sending them; but ye have not hearkened" (Jer 25:4). A concordance should be consulted for all similar references.

It was the Lord's practice when in Jerusalem to teach in the temple courts. "All the people came early in the morning to him in the temple, for to hear him" (Luke 21:38), while throughout the daytime, He remained there teaching (v.37). The Lord recalled this practice to the priests prior to His trial (22:53). Even at that late stage in His life here below, "the people were very attentive to hear him" (19:48). Teaching forms a prominent part of the service in a local church; a church without substantial teaching is a hungry and starving church, though its members in spiritual weakness may not discern this fact. That is why the church in Antioch in Syria was so prosperous; it was there that Paul and Barnabas for a whole year "taught much people" (Acts 11:26).

3 The scribes and Pharisees were ready at this early hour to attempt to trick the Lord; they were always on the lookout for some event so that they could criticise the Lord's reaction to it. To take a woman engaged in the "very act" of adultery shows that they had their spies in many quarters. They had the letter of the law on their side; it formed one of the ten commandments (Exod 20:14), and the punishment was clearly stated (Lev 20:10). But they calmly overlooked the fact that there were in the OT far more references to adultery in a metaphorical sense, referring to religious idolatry (Jer 3:8-9, etc). Thus the Pharisees could boast that they were not adulterers (Luke 18:11), though hypocritically they overlooked the fact that the Lord had accused them of being "an adulterous generation" (Matt 12:39; 16:4). In other words, far from putting their own house in order first, the beam remained in their own eye while they occupied themselves with the mote in the woman's eye (Matt 7:1-5).

4-5 *The scribes and Pharisees speak.* They claimed to the Lord that they had uncovered sin, and referring to "Moses in the law", they demanded to know the Lord's decision on the matter, "but what sayest thou?". No doubt they had Deut 22:23-24 in mind, "ye shall stone them with stones that they die", so if the Lord would not agree that this should be done, they were quite willing to stone Him instead (John 8:59). This practice had lapsed, owing to custom, and to the fact that adultery was so common an act. Similarly with work on the sabbath day; the offender would be stoned outside the camp (Num 15:35). They would trick the Lord to reintroduce stoning for adultery, so that they could then stone Him for performing miracles on the sabbath day. They would seek to involve the Lord with the Roman occupying powers, for at that time the Romans would not allow the Jews to put a man to death by stoning, only they, the Romans, could put a man to death by crucifixion (John 18:31).

The sin of adultery is very prevalent today, both physically and spiritually. In many parts of the world, it is legally permitted since divorce is legalised. It has become a matter of simple routine, and the Scriptures are never referred to; the same applies to other matters that are associated with the subject of sex. Paul made it clear that adultery was one of the works of the flesh (Gal 5:19). On a spiritual plane, the apostle's desire was to espouse the Corinthians to one husband, so as to present them as a chaste virgin to Christ (2 Cor 11:2). Yet he had to add, "But I fear", showing that he knew that there could be a deflection to adulterous matters even in christian circles, as men attached themselves to "another Jesus". Purity in the service and fellowship of a local church are of no moment to those who have no desire to take heed to God's mind revealed in the Scriptures.

6 The object of the Pharisees was not to preserve morality amongst the Jews, but rather to tempt and accuse the Lord. In Matt 22:15, they sought how they might entangle the Lord in His talk, but in each case His reply put these evil men to silence. Ultimately their trickery would find two false witnesses willing falsely to quote the Lord's words, "I am able to destroy the temple of God" (Matt 26:61).

In v.6, note that at the end the words "as though he heard them not" are in italics in the AV. Strictly, they do not appear in the Greek text and are omitted in the RV and JND; they were added by the AV translators as if they were necessary to make sense. However, no words are necessary to make sense, though the Lord stooping and writing with His finger on the ground needs interpretation.

Many have been the explanations of the expositors of the Lord's action-parable. The Pharisees wanted the Lord to be a judge in the matter, but He said that He had not come to be the Judge of the world. Rather, the OT Scriptures were the judge of men, and the Lord would make this clear to the Pharisees who at that time were boasting in the law of Moses (v.5). It is stated in Jer 17:13: "all that forsake thee shall be ashamed, and they that depart from me shall be written in the earth, because they have forsaken the Lord, the fountain of living waters". The Lord was therefore indicating the distance between Him and the Pharisees, a fact already demonstrated in John 7:53. They were near with their unsanctified mouth and lips, "but their heart is far from me" (Matt 15:8).

7-8 *The Lord speaks.* The fact that the Pharisees "continued" asking their questions shows that they did not know the meaning of their own OT Scriptures. In effect, they continued in their own condemnation of the woman, thereby boasting in the law, yet dishonouring God when they broke it themselves (Rom 2:23). The Lord had only to say one sublime statement in order to break the deadlock: "He that is without sin among you, let him first cast a stone at her". Having said these words that showed that it was not He who was actually condemning the Pharisees (they would condemn themselves by their subsequent actions, and so would the OT Scriptures), He continued writing on the ground, thereby bringing the OT Scriptures to bear upon their consciences once again.

The Lord's statement, being in the singular, referred to a particular man. No doubt the reference is to Deut 17:7, where we read of the "first" hand to cast a stone, after which the hands of the other people would follow. In this OT passage, the first hand had to be that of a specific witness of the sinner's act worthy of death, but the Lord added "He that is without sin among you" rather than an actual witness. Moreover, He said "among you", so as to exclude Himself. For He was without sin, and even on moral grounds could have cast the first stone. But divine mercy was transcending the punishment demanded by the law. Again, the man to cast the first stone had to be one without a beam or even a mote in his own eye, else he would be a hypocrite.

9 The Lord's words "without sin" are not the same as "not having committed adultery physically"; no doubt many could be described like that (Matt 19:18-20). The Lord went to the heart and conscience of these men, and they recognised their state before the law, if not before God. "If we say that we have no sin, we deceive ourselves" (1 John 1:8); "there is none that doeth good, no, not one" (Ps 14:3; Rom 3:10-12). So the word of God was proved to be powerful, "and sharper than any twoedged sword" (Heb 4:12). The eldest as the most responsible, departed first, followed by all the others. They put themselves on the outside, but it seems that they quickly returned, so as to cast the Lord out with stones in v.59.

The Lord was left alone with the woman—she was standing, but the Lord was stooping to the ground until the Pharisees had departed. In other words, salvation is a personal matter between a sinner and the Lord. In his Gospel, John picked out these personal encounters with the Lord; see 3:1; 4:7; 5:5; 9:1; 11:1; 20:11; 21:15.

10 *The Lord speaks.* If there was no condemnation from the divine side, then there could be no legitimate condemnation from the human side. The Lord addressed her using the same title as He had given to His mother in John 2:4: He gained her confidence immediately. This is the truth brought out by Paul in Rom 8:34, "Who is he that condemneth?", for nothing can "separate us from the love of God, which is in Christ Jesus our Lord".

11 *The woman speaks.* By saying "No man, Lord", she was referring to all the Pharisees who had disappeared temporarily. But she was not thinking evidently of the divine side. This has led to differing translations of the title "Lord", translating the Greek word *kurie*. The AV and RV both use the title "Lord", but JND and the NEB use the alternative rendering "Sir". The context must decide, and until the Lord's final remark we cannot see that this woman had any knowledge of His divine Person.

The Lord speaks. Here was no religious leader, a Pharisee, stating that there was no condemnation. Here was a special Man stating this truth, with the added command, "sin no more" (see 5:14). The woman's knowledge of Him must have increased tremendously at that saying, though how far her faith developed we cannot say. But there was to be no more adultery if there was to be no condemnation. The truth of no condemnation in Rom 8:33-39 is closely associated with Rom 6-7 where Paul taught that justification by faith implies continuing no more in sin, using in these two chapters four different methods of pressing home this important fact.

John chs.8-11 contain matters of principle, applicable to the Jews:

1. Ch.8, adultery, as applied to the Jews (Jer 3:6-10).

2. Ch.9, blindness is happened to Israel (Rom 11:25).

3. Ch.10, "He shall feed his flock like a shepherd" (Isa 40:11).

4. Ch.11, "life from the dead" (Rom 11:15).

2. *Double Testimony*
8:12-20

v.12 "Then spake Jesus again unto them, saying, I am the light of the world: he that followeth me shall not walk in darkness, but shall have the light of life.
v.13 The Pharisees therefore said unto him, Thou bearest record of thyself; thy record is not true.
v.14 Jesus answered and said unto them, Though I bear record of myself, *yet* my record is true: for I know whence I came, and whither I go; but ye cannot tell whence I come, and whither I go.
v.15 Ye judge after the flesh; I judge no man.
v.16 And yet if I judge, my judgment is true: for I am not alone, but I and the Father that sent me.
v.17 It is also written in your law, that the testimony of two men is true.
v.18 I am one that bear witness of myself, and the Father that sent me beareth witness of me.
v.19 Then said they unto him, Where is thy Father? Jesus answered, Ye neither know me, nor my Father: if ye had known me, ye would have known my Father also.
v.20 These words spake Jesus in the treasury, as he taught in the temple: and no man laid hands on him; for his hour was not yet come."

12 The rest of ch.8 is concerned with a very detailed conversation between the Lord and the Pharisees: in v.20, it is stated that He "taught", yet it is really a conversation used by the Lord for teaching purposes. The attitude of the Pharisees was most unpleasant, for every remark and question that they made sought to contradict what the Lord had said. This attitude is what we may call "such contradiction of sinners against himself" (Heb 12:3).

The Lord speaks. He is still in the temple (see 7:28; 8:2,20,59), His usual venue for teaching when in Jerusalem. He announced Himself as the "I am". This is characteristic of the chapter, sometimes being used with another title (vv.12,23), and sometimes as a title in itself (vv.24,28,58).

Two lights were lit at the feast of tabernacles to symbolise the pillars of cloud and fire during the wilderness wanderings. Sweeping that all on one side, the Lord announced Himself as "the light of the world"; only those who followed Him as His disciples could walk in His light. It is important to read 9:5 in this connection, since there He used the same title, adding "As long as I am in the world". This means that He is not the Light of the world now; He had that description only when He was here on earth. For His disciples throughout the subsequent years, He said elsewhere, "Ye are the light of the world" (Matt 5:14), so it would appear wrong to keep singing "The light of the world is Jesus" as referring to the present time. He was, of course, the true Light, while that of His people is derived light.

The subject of light pervades the Scriptures. Spiritual and moral light come first; physical light was created afterwards as a picture of what is spiritual and moral. Thus God is light (1 John 1:5); Christ is the Light (John 8:12); the Lamb is the Light (Rev 21:23); the word of God is light (Ps 119:105); local churches are the light of testimony (Rev 1:12); the Lord's people are lights (Matt 5:14); the gospel is light (2 Cor 4:4); the path of the just is light (Prov 4:18).

13 *The Pharisees speak*. By saying "Thou bearest record of thyself", they were correct, but by adding "thy record is not true", they were false. This may have been correct of many a man, but they failed to appreciate that this One was divine, and that anything He said of Himself was true. In the Acts, we have the self-testimony of Paul on several occasions, and on each occasion the testimony was given in truth without exaggeration (Acts 22:1-21; 26:2-23).

14 *The Lord speaks*. Here the Lord contradicted the assessment of the Pharisees that His witness was not true (the word for the noun "record" in vv.13,14 is *marturia*, namely "witness"). It was true on account of His having come from the Father's presence and that He was returning to His Father's presence, implying that He was divine, quite unlike other men on earth. Hence He knew the truth and He spoke the truth. He said the same thing to His disciples in 16:28; the disciples believed it (v.29) and understood, since truth was revealed to them. But the Pharisees had no revelation; they thought as men and received only the teaching of men. In spite of the fact that the divine Teacher was speaking to them, they remained blind (9:39-41).

15-16 The Pharisees adopted their assessment (which was false) because they judged the Lord's testimony according to the flesh—the principle that is the opposite to a spiritual assessment. For the understanding of the wise is foolishness, and the natural man does not receive the things of the Spirit of God (1 Cor 1:19-20; 2:14). There is, in fact, only a fleshly judgment and a spiritual judgment; there is no half-way position. By saying, "I judge no man", the Lord implied that He, by Himself, alone and independently of the Father, did not assess the reasonings of men.

Rather, there was always a divine dovetailing of discernment and action by Himself and the Father, a truth that is prominent throughout John's Gospel. The Pharisees might have thought that the Lord was alone, but the Lord knew that this was not so—"I and the Father that sent me". Even when all His disciples would leave Him so as to flee, He said the same thing, "yet I am not alone, because the Father is with me" (16:16). This great fact had important repercussions concerning the truth of His testimony.

17-18 To prove the validity of the joint divine testimony of the Father and the Son, the Lord quoted from the OT, from "your law", stressing thereby that this was something that the Pharisees should have known. Deut 19:15 states that "one witness shall not rise up against a man for any iniquity". This principle is also stated in Num 35:30, "one witness shall not testify against any person". Rather, "at the mouth of two witnesses, or at the mouth of three witnesses, shall the matter be established". To make this process as safe as possible, the law firmly stated, "Thou shalt not bear false witness" (Exod 20:16). That is why at the trial of the Lord the priests ultimately found two witnesses by whom the Lord might be accused. But their witness was false, and the witness of one did not agree with that of the other (Matt 26:60; Mark 14:59). But as a principle, the duality of witness goes far beyond that of proving guilt. Samuel stated that the Lord was a witness and that His anointed (Saul) was a witness concerning the integrity of Samuel. In our exposition of John 5:31-47 we have seen this principle enacted many times over. It was because of this that the Lord sent the seventy chosen disciples "two and two before his face" (Luke 10:1). Peter and John were together in Acts 3:1; Paul and Barnabas were sent forth together by the Spirit from Antioch (Acts 13:2-4), while later Paul and Silas went forth on the second missionary journey (15:40). In the matter of finance, two took funds to Jerusalem (11:30), while Titus and "the brother" went to Corinth to deal with the matter of the collection (2 Cor 8:17-21), so as to demonstrate honesty before men.

Thus in our verse 18, there were two witnesses of the Lord's Person—He Himself and the Father. This was sufficient, and stands in contrast to the many witnesses quoted in 5:31-47.

19 *The Pharisees speak.* The Lord had said "the" Father, unlike in 5:17 where He said, "My Father". However, the Pharisees knew what was implied, so asked the question "Where is thy Father?", using the word "thy". No doubt this was a loaded question, though designed in ignorance, as the subsequent questions also demonstrate. In His answer, the Lord used "my" twice in connection with His Father, knowing that this would raise hatred in the hearts of men.

The Lord speaks. The answer to the Pharisees' question must revolve around the knowledge of both the Son and the Father, of the position of both the Son and the Father. The Lord would not separate the two Persons of the Godhead. Knowledge of Him would lead immediately to knowledge of the Father, implying that ignorance of His Person must lead inevitably to ignorance of the Person of the Father. The Lord said the same thing about seeing Him and the Father (14:9), and about hating Him and the Father (15:23); the same applies to a denial of the Son and the Father (1 John 2:23).

20 The Lord was making these remarks "in the treasury", namely the place in the temple courts where people could give their offerings for the service of the house of God (Mark 12:41). Men may be casting in of their abundance, but the Lord valued the woman's heart that sincerely could offer only two mites. Once again there was divine intervention to prevent the Pharisees' hatred causing them to lay hands on Him; the hour of His sacrifice was not yet come. Only when the hour of the fulfilment of "the determinate counsel and foreknowledge of God" had come could men by wicked hands take and crucify Him (Acts 2:23).

3. *Who Art Thou?*
8:21-30

v.21 "Then said Jesus again unto them, I go my way, and ye shall seek me, and shall die in your sins: whither I go, ye cannot come.
v.22 Then said the Jews, Will he kill himself? because he saith, Whither I go, ye cannot come.
v.23 And he said unto them, Ye are from beneath; I am from above: ye are of this world; I am not of this world.
v.24 I said therefore unto you, that ye shall die in your sins: for if ye believe not that I am *he*, ye shall die in your sins.
v.25 Then said they unto him, Who art thou? And Jesus saith unto them, Even *the same* that I said unto you from the beginning.
v.26 I have many things to say and to judge of you: but he that sent me is true; and I speak to the world those things which I have heard of him.
v.27 They understood not that he spake to them of the Father.
v.28 Then said Jesus unto them, When ye have lifted up the Son of man, then shall ye know that I am *he*, and *that* I do nothing of myself; but as my Father hath taught me, I speak these things.
v.29 And he that sent me is with me: the Father hath not left me alone; for I do always those things that please him.
v.30 As he spake these words, many believed on him."

21 *The Lord speaks.* "I go my way" refers to the fact that men could not take Him, and that in reality He Himself would walk along the pathway leading to the cross, without men forcing the issue. He had just spoken about "whither I go" in v.14. Again, in 7:34 He had spoken of men seeking Him; this may be a reference to men seeking eternal life apart from Himself (Matt 19:16), or to the awful circumstances yet future when men shall cry in desperation "Lord, Lord" to no avail (Matt 7:22-23). His way was a sinless way, but theirs was the opposite. He would die as the perfect sacrifice, "without blemish and without spot" (1 Pet 1:19), but they would die with their sins unforgiven, for "sin has reigned unto death" (Rom 5:21). They were on the broad way, and could not come to Him on the narrow way; this seems to be an example where it would be impossible for these men to repent—their final destiny was fixed and unchangeable.

22 *The Jews speak.* "Whither I go, ye cannot come" is similar to statements made by the Lord to the Jews in 7:34, and to Peter in 14:36. In all three cases there was a reaction by those who heard. In 7:35, the Jews invented an explanation, while here they invented another explanation, "Will he kill himself?", apparently in the sense that they themselves would not commit suicide. Judas the traitor would commit suicide later (Matt 27:5), but they had no idea what the voluntary nature of the death of Christ really meant (John 10:17).

23-24 *The Lord speaks*. The Lord here provided three reasons why the Pharisees would die in their sins:

1. "Ye are from beneath", contrasting with the Lord's status, "I am from above". This does not mean that the Pharisees ascended from the pit, as will the smoke and the locusts in a day yet to come (Rev 9:2-3). Rather it speaks of the origin of the character of the Pharisees, as v.44 will make clear. By contrast, the character of the Son derived from heaven, from the Father Himself.

2. "Ye are of this world", contrasting with the Lord who was "not of this world". To be of the world implies that a man's outlook, motives, interests and occupation concern the morality, the pleasures, the politics and the religion of mankind generally, with no heavenly outlook, motivation and occupation. Such men are confederates of the beast out of the sea and the beast out of the earth (Rev 13:1,11). The world had a prominent place in the warnings of the NT, particularly in John's writings. The position of believers has been described by the Lord as "not of the world" (John 17:14,16); twice He added, "even as I am not of the world".

3. "If ye believe not that I am he", namely *egō eimi*. This title shows the eternal nature of the Person of the Son, reminding us of the titles "I am that I am" and "I am" by which God revealed Himself to Moses (Exod 3:14). It is the title of Deity Itself, spanning the two eternities. Of the Son it is written, "thou art the same, and thy years shall not fail" (Heb 1:12); He is "the same yesterday, and to day, and for ever" (13:8); of Himself He said, "I am he that liveth (the past)...I am alive for evermore (the future)" (Rev 1:18). Failure to believe in that Eternal Life means that the unbeliever has no life, so shall die in his sins.

25-26 *The Jews speak*. This title "I am" reminded the Jews too much of the OT title of Jehovah, so they were compelled to ask, "Who art thou?". They ask to make sure, not in the quiet spiritual way in which believers may enquire concerning things difficult to be understood, but in the loud unbecoming manner of unbelief when faced with deep truth.

The Lord speaks. He did not repeat His titles, but called attention to what He had said "from the beginning". Some suggest that this refers to the OT manifestations of divine titles, but in the context we feel that the Lord was referring to the consistency of His testimony over the years in which He had been in contact with the Pharisees in Jerusalem.

In 16:12, the Lord had many things to say to His disciples, but here He had many things to say to the Pharisees. The last things that He would say would be the many woes in Matt 23. There were things to be spoken to "you", namely the Pharisees, and many things to speak to "the world"—to the particular and to the general. All things would be true, however much the Pharisees would criticise Him, since (without mentioning the title of the Father) He had heard all things from Him that had sent Him.

27 As soon as the Lord would mention His Father, unbelief and criticism would raise their ugly head. But only to say "he that sent me" would lead to a manifestation of complete Pharisaical ignorance. To us, having read the chapter many times, the connection is obvious, but the darkened hearts of the Pharisees failed to perceive the connection at a first hearing; they remained blind.

28-29 *The Lord speaks.* Placing the responsibility for His forthcoming crucifixion upon the Pharisees, the Lord then announced that those guilty of this would ultimately know His title and Person "I am". The reference to being "lifted up" occurs in three contexts in John's Gospel:

1. To a seeking individual (3:14).

2. To the rejecting Pharisees (8:28).

3. To the curious Greeks, the apostles and the people (12:32).

The Lord implied that this title "I am" associated Himself with Deity; He did nothing and He taught nothing apart from this relationship; all this would be clarified after His being lifted up. We suggest several ways in which this statement was, and will be, fulfilled.

1. By the knowledge of the Father and the Son that comes through believing the gospel message.

2. By the Jews in the future when, after centuries of unbelief, they come to know the Son as their Messiah.

3. At the judgment of the great white throne (Rev 20:11-15), when these unbelieving Pharisees will at last recognise the Judge whom God has ordained (Acts 17:31).

Although the Father will be known after the cross, yet He was always with the Son prior to the cross. The oneness in Deity did not only exist before He came down from on high, but this same oneness permanently existed during the days of His Manhood on earth, shown by the words "with me" and "not . . . alone". Hence nothing else could be done except to "please him" in word, thought and deed. Thus the Father could announce His pleasure in the Son both to John the Baptist, and to Peter, James and John on the mount of transfiguration. This divine assessment should also apply to believers—that we should please Him as He assesses us according to His standards: "not as pleasing men, but God, which trieth our hearts" (1 Thess 2:4); "working in you that which is wellpleasing in his sight" (Heb 13:21).

30 The verb "spake" is a continuous participle *lalountos*, showing that it was while the Lord was actually speaking that some believed—it does not refer to the end of His remarks. The same can be seen when Peter was preaching in Cornelius' house: while he was speaking (the same Greek participle is used) the Spirit fell upon those who were listening showing that they had believed (Acts 10:44). Several times John used the verb "believe", not in the sense of believing faith unto salvation, but in the sense of acquisition of facts. See John 7:30; 20:8-9. This assertion is proved by v.31, where discipleship is based not so much on this acquisition of facts but on continuing in the Lord's word. Belief that saves is a matter of the heart, not only of the mind.

4. *"My Father" and "your father"*
8:31-47

v.31 "Then said Jesus to those Jews which believed on him, If ye continue in my word, *then* are ye my disciples indeed;
v.32 And ye shall know the truth, and the truth shall make you free.
v.33 They answered him, We be Abraham's seed, and were never in bondage to any man; how sayest thou, Ye shall be made free?
v.34 Jesus answered them, Verily, verily, I say unto you, Whosoever committeth sin is the servant of sin.
v.35 And the servant abideth not in the house for ever: *but* the Son abideth ever.
v.36 If the Son therefore shall make you free, ye shall be free indeed.
v.37 I know that ye are Abraham's seed; but ye seek to kill me, because my word hath no place in you.
v.38 I speak that which I have seen with my Father: and ye do that which ye have seen with your father.
v.39 They answered and said unto him, Abraham is our father. Jesus saith unto them, If ye were Abraham's children, ye would do the works of Abraham.
v.40 But now ye seek to kill me, a man that hath told you the truth, which I have heard of God: this did not Abraham.
v.41 Ye do the deeds of your father. Then said they to him, We be not born of fornication; we have one Father, *even* God.
v.42 Jesus said unto them, If God were your Father, ye would love me: for I proceeded forth and came from God; neither came I of myself, but he sent me.
v.43 Why do ye not understand my speech? *even* because ye cannot hear my word.

v.44 Ye are of *your* father the devil, and the lusts of your father ye will do. He was a murderer from the beginning, and abode not in the truth, because there is no truth in him. When he speaketh a lie, he speaketh of his own: for he is a liar, and the father of it.
v.45 And because I tell *you* the truth, ye believe me not.
v.46 Which of you convinceth me of sin? And if I say the truth, why do ye not believe me?
v.47 He that is of God heareth God's words: ye therefore hear *them* not, because ye are not of God."

31-32 *The Lord speaks.* As we have pointed out, the kind of belief manifested here is not "saving faith" unless accompanied by the exercise of true discipleship. The belief in v.30 has no eternal life associated with it. No doubt the knowledge of facts is good in itself, but it is a stepping stone to better realities. Knowledge of the Son is better than knowledge about the Son. Continuance is a matter of obedience, for there can be no life apart from obedience: "elect... unto obedience" (1 Pet 1:2). Blessing comes, as Paul wrote, "if ye continue in the faith grounded and settled" (Col 1:23), otherwise some "should seem to come short of it" (Heb 4:1), akin to Matt 13:22 where some hear the word and yet become unfruitful. In turn, abiding in the word leads to knowing "the truth" rather than "about the truth"; truth refers ultimately to the One who is "the truth". This is the gain of spiritual experience rather than theological training. And this truth makes one free. This liberty is the power to do what one ought, whereas licence means doing what one likes. Such freedom removes one from bondage, and only those removed from it have eternal life.

33 *The Pharisees speak.* The development of the rest of the chapter causes us to feel that the following conversation is concerned with the hardhearted traditional Pharisees rather than with the Jews of vv.30-31. From Abraham's time onwards, these Pharisees thought that they as a nation were free, never having been in bondage to any man or nation. They overlooked the many years spent in bondage in Egypt in the book of Exodus; they overlooked the many periods of bondage that their nation had suffered in the book of Judges; they overlooked the seventy years captivity in Babylon that they had sustained as recorded by Jeremiah, Ezekiel and Daniel. They even overlooked the fact that they were there and then under the domination of the Romans; they were willing to accept Caesar as king when it pleased them (John 19:15). But most of all they overlooked the fact that the Lord was not talking about national and political bondage; He was speaking about bondage to sin—they were "the servants of sin" (Rom 6:20). However, men will not recognise this form of bondage, for they enjoy sin and have no desire to enter into the freedom that Christ provides.

34-36 *The Lord speaks.* If the Pharisees failed to understand the implication of bondage, the Lord's reply quickly put them right. "Committeth" is the present participle *poiōn*—the one doing or practising sin as a regular and ongoing feature of life. Such, of course, were the Pharisees because of their continual hatred of Himself. The bondage consisted of being a "servant of sin", namely a *doulos*, a bondservant. This is a question of sin reigning (Rom 6:12), of one's members being instruments of unrighteousness unto sin (v.13), of sin having dominion over a man (v.14), of being servants of sin unto death (v.16).

V.35 forms a miniature parable. A servant does not have to remain in the same house for all time. This refers to a man in bondage in a house of sin. He remains there, either until he is converted (made free, liberated), or until he dies physically. This is similar to v.9, where the Pharisees could not remain in the presence of the Lord; they had to depart. But "the Son abideth ever". Recalling that this is a parable, we do not assess this to refer to the Lord Jesus as the Son; the RV translates it as "the son", referring of course to a converted person. He abides in the house of salvation for ever. The context of Gal 4:7 is different, but Paul wrote, "thou art no more a servant, but a son"; bondage (v.3) had turned into the glorious liberty of the children of God. As such, we "stand fast therefore in the liberty wherewith Christ hath made us free" (5:1).

Only the Son liberates a soul that believes, and this is true liberty—"free indeed". There is no other method by which true liberty can be attained. Some thought that He would have given liberty from the Roman bondage of occupation of their country (Luke 24:21), but this will only come about when the Son of man coming in glory will destroy the fourth beast, when the kingdom shall be given to the saints (Dan 7:23-28).

37-38 The Pharisees in v.33 had boasted that they were "Abraham's seed", participating in the liberty that flows therefrom. Of course the Lord confirmed that they were "Abraham's seed" physically, but morally and spiritually their bondage was illustrated by the fact that they were seeking to kill Him (see 7:19). Abraham was a man of faith (Rom 5:3; Gal 3:14; Heb 11:8), but the Pharisees in unbelief were breaking many laws in their dealings with Christ.

However, the contrast was not only between Abraham and the Pharisees, but between the Lord and the Pharisees. The contrast was between "my Father" and "your father". (How different this is from the blessed statement the Lord later made to Mary in John 20:17, "my Father, and your Father".) All His words, deeds and character were identical with those of His Father, while in the case of the Pharisees their deeds derived from their father. Of course, at the start they did not understand that He referred to a different father from that which they supposed—they thought of Abraham, while He was thinking of the devil (v.44). Misunderstanding is a common feature of unbelief!

39 *The Pharisees speak.* By asserting "Abraham is our father", they demonstrated the certainty of boastfulness and ignorance. They little realised that, although many would sit with Abraham in the kingdom of heaven, they would be cast into outer darkness (Matt 8:11-12).

The Lord speaks. His answer, of course, related to spiritual and not natural conditions. Like would produce like, as in the creation; a good tree cannot yield bad fruit, and by their fruits they would be known. So their proposed intention to kill Him proved that they were not Abraham's children, for he had brought forth life (as being Isaac's father), but they hoped to eliminate this final Seed of Abraham amongst them. As Paul wrote in Rom 9:7, "Neither, because they are the seed of Abraham, are they all children", and "They which are the children of the flesh, these are not the children of God" (v.8).

40-41 Here the Lord directed attention to one reason behind the Pharisaical intention to kill Him: He spoke the truth, not only because He could not do otherwise, but because He heard all things from God. In 10:32, their intention to kill Him was on account of His works rather than His words. But the words and works of Abraham stood in complete contrast to those of the Pharisees. His faith led to righteousness being imputed (Rom 4:3), and to resurrection typically (Heb 11:17-19). The Pharisees were so different, and the Lord went to the root of the matter, "Ye do the deeds of your father", referring, of course, to the devil and not to Abraham.

The Pharisees speak. These men finally realised that the Lord was not talking physically about Abraham. By not being "born of fornication", they claimed that they had no idolatrous origins, and that they did not bow down to idolatry; they claimed the God of the OT as their Father. Yet although there had been no direct idolatry amongst the Jews for over 500 years, the nation had been steeped in it, as verses testify such as Ps 78:57-58; Jer 2:27-28; Ezek 16:15; Hos 2:4.

42-43 *The Lord speaks.* The lack of idolatry is not a sufficient basis for being in contact with God as Father. This must be by faith and love, with the realisation that the Lord had come down as the sent One from God, that He had not come down under His sole initiative. This is stressed again and again in this Gospel, yet the Pharisees could never understand it. The Lord stated that the reason for this lack of understanding was that "ye cannot". There was an inevitable impossibility about it. Their assertion that "we see" implied that their sin remained as a barrier to faith and understanding (9:41). The parables were designed to keep the truth from such men: "because they seeing see not; and hearing they hear not, neither do they understand" (Matt 13:13-15; Isa 6:9-10). This is also quoted from Isaiah in John 12:40, showing that an important principle is involved—men in darkness cannot understand or believe.

44 Grace would refrain from such plain speaking until it became necessary. The Lord's people today must be very careful in any condemnatory language that they may use—if such is ever necessary. The Lord knew, of course, the truth behind the accusation, "Ye are of your father the devil", however strong such an accusation may sound to our ears. Paul also used such strong language on the island of Cyprus during his first missionary journey, saying to Elymas the sorcerer, "thou child of the devil" (Acts 13:10). As the Lord said elsewhere, "the tares are the children of the wicked one" (Matt 13:38). No doubt John recalled these words of the Lord Jesus when he wrote later, "In this the children of God are manifest, and the children of the devil" (1 John 3:10). In other words, in the same way as believers are born of God, so were these Pharisees born of Satan. Various characteristics of the devil are described:

1. "The lusts of your father": in other words, the strong Satanic desires. These would be enforced into the minds of his children, causing them to desire to do such things also.

2. "A murderer from the beginning", seeking to destroy the life of men by claiming that Adam and Eve would not die (Gen 3:4). Thus death passed upon all men (Rom 5:12), brought about by Satan. Again, he caused Cain to slay his brother; he caused all the righteous blood to be shed upon the earth (Matt 23:35). The phrase "from the beginning" is used again of Satan by John to describe the devil sinning (1 John 3:8).

3. He "abode not in the truth". This may refer to the state of Satan prior to and after his fall, "Thou wast perfect in thy ways from the day that thou wast created, till iniquity was found in thee" (Ezek 28:15); "I will be like the most High. Yet thou shalt be brought down to hell" (Isa 14:14-15).

4. "He is a liar". This characterises his utterances, as being the opposite of truth. In all that he says, he speaks "from his own things" (*ek tōn idiōn*), namely from a reservoir of error. As "the father of it", he is the originator of all lying on the part of men.

45-47 Hence if men take sides with the devil, they cannot believe the truth as taught by the Lord. These form two incompatible attitudes. Their collaboration with the devil caused them to seek to find faults with the Lord, both with His doctrine and with His works. However, the Lord was the perfect embodiment of truth; none could ever point a finger at Him, since He was "without blemish and without spot" (1 Pet 1:19). They could see His perfection in works and character, even if they refused to own this openly. And His words would also match this character in truth, and hence they should own this also, even if His doctrine seemed new and unexpected. In v.46, the Lord asked questions relating to their state of unbelief, and He provided the answer in v.47. The difference between believers and unbelievers is that the former are "of God", while the latter are "not of God"; since there is no middle way, this means that these unbelievers were of the devil. The phrase "of God" that characterises believers occurs in John 1:13 and 1 John 3:9 in connection being born of God; such hear God's words through Christ, as being in intimate contact with Him. But for the Pharisees, He said "therefore"—their position was logical and inevitable.

5. *The Lord before Abraham* 8:48-59

v.48 "Then answered the Jews, and said unto him, Say we not well that thou art a Samaritan, and hast a devil?
v.49 Jesus answered, I have not a devil; but I honour my Father, and ye do dishonour me.
v.50 And I seek not mine own glory: there is one that seeketh and judgeth.
v.51 Verily, verily, I say unto you, If a man keep my saying, he shall never see death.
v.52 Then said the Jews unto him, Now we know that thou hast a devil. Abraham is dead, and the prophets; and thou sayest, If a man keep my saying, he shall never taste of death.
v.53 Art thou greater than our father Abraham, which is dead? and the prophets are dead: whom makest thou thyself?
v.54 Jesus answered, If I honour myself, my honour is nothing: it is my Father that honoureth me; of whom ye say, that he is your God:
v.55 Yet ye have not known him; but I know him: and if I should say, I know him not, I shall be a liar like unto you: but I know him, and keep his saying.
v.56 Your father Abraham rejoiced to see my day: and he saw *it*, and was glad.
v.57 Then said the Jews unto him, Thou art not yet fifty years old, and hast thou seen Abraham?
v.58 Jesus said unto them, Verily, verily, I say unto you, Before Abraham was, I am.
v.59 Then took they up stones to cast at him: but Jesus hid himself, and went out of the temple, going through the midst of them, and so passed by."

48 *The Jews speak.* The logic in the Lord's words struck the consciences of these Pharisees, and on logical grounds they could not answer. They adopted the usual refuge under such circumstances. Those proved wrong by one who is right seek to prove the one who is right to be wrong, often accusing the one who is right of being wrong on the same grounds as they have been proved wrong. Thus those who are terrorists often accuse those who oppose them of being terrorists also—this is an insidious process of self-justification. These Pharisees thought that the Lord was promoting a false approach to the law, and that He was a promoter of a perverted kind of worship, since His teaching did not correspond to their hardened thoughts. Because they considered the Samaritan religion to be false as pertaining to the law and worship, they were quite willing to accuse the Lord of being a Samaritan (knowing that He was a Jew according to the flesh, and having been brought up in Nazareth). As He had accused them of being of the devil, so they accused Him of having a demon. This is blasphemy, showing the kind of talk that the Lord had to listen to. They had used similar words in Matt 12:24, that He cast out demons "by Beelzebub the prince" of the demons; see John 7:20.

49-51 *The Lord speaks.* The Lord provided a simple answer, unlike the woes pronounced upon the Pharisees in Matt 23. "I have not a demon" corresponds with Matt 12:26, "If Satan cast out Satan", an impossibility. He then gave four facts concerning the special nature of His Person:

1. "I honour my Father". The One seated on the throne is worthy to receive honour (Rev 4:11).

2. "Ye do dishonour me". Hence they did not honour the Father (John 5:23).

3. "I seek not mine own glory". He did not set Himself up in a position of power; it is God who sets His King upon His holy hill of Zion (Ps 2:6); "Christ glorified not himself to be made an high priest" (Heb 5:5).

4. "There is one that seeketh and judgeth". Namely, the Father seeks the glory of the Son, whatever men may seek to do. As the Lord said, "Now is the Son of man glorified ... God shall also glorify him in himself" (John 13:31-32); "Father ... glorify thy Son" (17:1).

In v.51, to keep the sayings of the Lord is not identical with law-keeping. For the keeping of His sayings commences with the exercise of faith, and this in turn leads to the keeping of His will on the grounds of grace. Such a man "shall never see death"—not physical death, but the second death as the outcome of the judgment at the great white throne (Rev 20:14). This is in contrast with the Lord's previous statement, "ye shall die in your sins" (vv.21,24). As far as believers are concerned, they have eternal life as those who are born of God. This life is eternal because for each believer "his seed remaineth in him" (1 John 3:9). In such a seed and its growth, there is no pattern of decay as in life biologically.

To "see death" refers to the great white throne—that will never be the portion of a believer. But the corresponding expression to "taste of death" (Matt 16:28; Mark 9:1; Luke 9:27) refers, in the context of the transfiguration taking place shortly afterward, to physical death. (These expressions are also used in Luke 2:26 and Heb 2:9, though with different implications.)

52-53 *The Jews speak.* It is significant that they changed the Lord's word "see" in v.51 to "taste" in v.52. Clearly they misunderstood the implication of the word "see" as referring to the final judgment. They used the word "taste" to apply to physical death, and hence they accused the Lord once again of possessing a demon, because they assumed that the Lord's word suggested that Abraham and the prophets should never have died physically. Once again we can use 1 Cor 2:14 to describe the attitude of the Pharisees, "the natural man receiveth not the things of the Spirit of God".

The Jews held Abraham and the prophets in great esteem (though they really were the children of those who had killed the prophets, according to Matt 23:30-33). They had had authority from God, and yet they, apart from Elijah, had died. So to these Pharisees the Lord's teaching seemed even to conflict with common sense and with known OT history. Thus they accused the Lord of making Himself "greater than our father Abraham". This comparative "greater than" occurs five times in connection with the Lord; see the list that we have provided in our comments on 4:12.

This assertion that Abraham and the prophets are dead showed that these Pharisees had no idea whatever as to what happened afterwards. Abraham was seen in Luke 16:25-26, while Moses was seen again on the mount (Matt 17:2). In fact, "God is not the God of the dead, but of the living" (Matt 22:32).

Again, to claim that the Lord was able to make Himself greater then many OT worthies shows that the Pharisees had no idea as to His divine nature. Rather, many scriptures speak to believers that it is God who worked in the Person of the Son. Thus, "God hath made that same Jesus ... both Lord and Christ" (Acts 2:36); He was "made so much better than the angels" (Heb 1:4); He was "made like unto his brethren" (2:17); "Christ glorified not himself to be made an high priest; but he ..." (5:5); "the same is made the head of the corner" (1 Pet 2:7). Such verses as these show the divine word in the exaltation of the Son.

54-55 *The Lord speaks*. Three times in v.54 the verb and noun "honour" occur in the AV; strictly, the Greek words are *doxazō, doxa* meaning "glorify, glory". The Lord used this word to counteract the assertion by the Pharisees that He had made Himself something. His exalted status comes only from the Father. This is a contradiction of their own claim that "we have one Father, even God" (v.41). God cannot do two contrary things, firstly to exalt His Son, and then to be the Father of the Pharisees who had the devil as their father. For ourselves too, it is God who gives us blessings, status and gifts; neither we nor other men can give ourselves these things. Thus Paul "was made a minister, according to the gift of the grace of God given unto me" (Eph 3:7; Col 1:23; 1 Tim 1:12).

The contrast between the Lord and the Pharisees is great (v.55). He knows the Father; they do not know Him. His testimony could not be otherwise, else He would be a liar like them. Knowledge of the Father is not some automatic thesis of religion: as the Lord said in prayer, "neither knoweth any man the Father, save the Son, and he to whomsoever the Son will reveal him" (Matt 11:27; John 6:65). The Pharisees were liars because they claimed God as their Father, yet in reality the devil was their father. The reckoned without the insertion of "all liars" in the list in Rev 21:8 of those who would be found in the lake of fire.

56 The Lord would draw this conversation to an end; obviously the Pharisees would not accept the truth, and there was no further point in presenting truth to those who resisted it continuously. He returned to the subject of the one whom they claimed to be their father Abraham, who saw "my day" and "rejoiced . . . and was glad". Some expositors suggest that this "day" refers to the lifetime of the Lord here on earth, since Abraham was still alive as to his spirit (Matt 22:32). Yet the verbs in v.56 are in the past tense, and certainly the word "was" in v.58 implies the past. We can enumerate a number of instances when Abraham was in contact with Deity and with truth concerning Christ:

1. When "The God of glory" appeared to him (Acts 7:2).
2. When "the Lord appeared to him in the plains of Mamre" (Gen 18:1).
3. In connection with "thy seed, which is Christ" (Gal 3:16).
4. In connection with the offering of Isaac, and receiving Christ in resurrection in a figure (Heb 11:19).
5. In connection with the heavenly country (Heb 11:16).

57 *The Jews speak.* Note that they changed the Lord's words in their unbelieving amazement: "he saw" is changed to "hast thou seen?". The Pharisees demonstrated that they were entirely on natural and physical ground. They placed an upper limit on the Lord's age, to be on the safe side; it was supposed that He was about thirty years of age when He commenced His public ministry (Luke 3:23). Only if the Lord had been Deity could the Lord's statement have had any meaning, and this they refused to accept. So their question implied that they considered the Lord's assertion to be illogical and impossible.

58 *The Lord speaks.* Based on the natural rules of grammar that reflect upon the logical reasoning of the human mind, the assertion "Before Abraham was, I am" is impossible. It is only possible when the speaker is divine, and when the divine mind employs heavenly grammar. His eternal Person is implied, and hence His eternal pre-existence, eternally before Abraham. Not only does "I am" imply the eternal present for the Lord, but it is also an eternal title of His, *egō eimi*. This truth is brought out in verses such as 1:1; 17:5,24; it is found in His glorious declaration in Rev 1:18 literally "I am the living One (the eternal past), and became dead (His sacrifice in time); and behold, I am living for evermore (the present and the eternal future)". Again in Rev 1:8, He is described as "which is (the present-being One), and which was (the One ever being in the past), and which is to come (the One always approaching the eternal future)".

59 The deity of Christ is implied in v.58; the Pharisees realised this, and hence they sought to stone Him. In 8:7, the Pharisees counted themselves unworthy to cast a stone at a woman meriting death according to the law, but here they considered themselves very worthy to stone the Lord, with no conscience about the matter whatsoever. Yet angels protected Him, and so did the Lord Himself until His hour was come (Ps 91:11). He hid Himself (as in 12:36), and some suggest that He even became temporarily invisible. They sought to stone Him to death, as they had sought (and would seek) His life until His hour was come. We may quote the attempts in 5:16-18; 7:30; 10:31; 11:53.

Thus the Lord left the temple, effectively having been cast out. (The next time He is seen in the temple occurs in 10:23.) He did not always remain in situations that were hostile to Himself. Thus in the OT, God forsook the tabernacle of Shiloh (Ps 78:60) when the Philistines captured the ark (1 Sam 4:11,22), never to return to Moses' tabernacle. Again, He forsook the house in Jerusalem (Ezek 11:23), never to return to Solomon's temple. And so it was in the Lord's case; He left Herod's temple for the last time in Matt 24:1, having stated that that house was left desolate; He would never return there, and it was destroyed by the Romans after the end of Paul's life. So it can be with the congregations of Christendom which fail to appropriate and to practice the principles of church fellowship and service revealed in the NT.

As cast out, the Lord now on the outside would be ready to welcome others who would suffer a similar treatment. Thus the blind man whose sight was restored was cast out, and on the outside the Lord found him (9:35). The Good Shepherd and His flock remain on the outside, where heavenly fellowship and service are engaged in, with the flock never returning to the folds of men.

V. The Light of the World Rejected (9:1-41)

1. *The Sixth Sign: The Blind Man Healed*
9:1-7

v.1 "And as *Jesus* passed by, he saw a man which was blind from *his* birth.

v.2 And his disciples asked him, saying, Master, who did sin, this man, or his parents, that he was born blind?

v.3 Jesus answered, Neither hath this man sinned, nor his parents: but that the works of God should be made manifest in him.

v.4 I must work the works of him that sent me, while it is day: the night cometh, when no man can work.

v.5 As long as I am in the world, I am the light of the world.

v.6 When he had thus spoken, he spat on the ground, and made clay of the spittle, and he anointed the eyes of the blind man with the clay,

v.7 And said unto him, Go, wash in the pool of Siloam, (which is by interpretation, Sent). He went his way therefore, and washed, and came seeing."

This sign is going to lead to the Lord being revealed as the Light of the world, in just the same way as the feeding of the 5 000 in ch.6 led to the Lord being revealed as the Bread of life, and the raising of Lazarus in ch.11 led to Him being revealed as the Resurrection and the Life. It will also be illustrative of the gospel, as Paul wrote, "them that are lost: in whom the god of this world hath blinded the eyes of them which believe not, lest the light of the glorious gospel of Christ, who is the image of God, should shine unto them . . . For God, who commanded the light to shine out of darkness, hath shined in our hearts, to give the light of the knowledge of the glory of God in the face of Jesus Christ" (2 Cor 5:4-6). Moreover, in this sign there is a prophetic implication; for blindness has happened to Israel (Rom 11:25 AV), yet the prophet Isaiah shows that sight will be restored both to Israel and to the nations (Isa 29:18; 32:3; 33:17; 35:2; 40:5; 41:20; 52:10; 53:2; 66:18).

There are many cases of blind men being healed in the Gospels:

1. Two blind men in Galilee (Matt 9:27).

2. One blind man in Bethsaida (Mark 8:22).

3. Two blind men outside Jericho (Matt 20:30); one is named as Bartimaeus in Mark 10:46.

4. One blind man in Jerusalem (John 9:1).

In this connection, Matt 11:5 should be noted. "The blind receive their sight" is given as an answer to John the Baptist, who wanted to know whether the Son of God were the One who should come as promised in the OT. See also Matt 12:22, where a man "blind, and dumb" was healed, and the general statement in Luke 7:21, "unto many that were blind he gave sight". Finally, in the synagogue in Nazareth, the Lord quoted the OT, "recovering of sight to the blind" (Luke 4:18), though this aspect of His work is not in the Hebrew of Isa 61:1 (but it occurs in the Greek LXX from which the Lord quoted). However, it does occur in Isa 42:7, "to open the blind eyes".

After the miracle in vv.1-7, an inquisition commences that becomes more violent until the man is cast out. The Pharisees interviewed both the man and his parents, until the Lord found the man on the outside. The man's knowledge of the Lord increased from "Jesus" (v.11), "a prophet" (v.17), "of God" (v.33), to "the Son of God" (vv.35-38).

1 The Lord was now on the outside of the temple courts, and was confronted with human need and affliction everywhere. This blind man who was "blind from his birth" should be compared with the man in Acts 3:2, who was "lame from his mother's womb", and who was placed at a gate to the temple courts every day. Such affliction from birth that some have to suffer confirms the meaning of the Lord's words, "That which is born of the flesh is flesh" (John 3:6). The ravages of sin in nature tend to produce things that are not perfect.

The only exception was the body of the Lord Jesus, "for that which is conceived . . . is of the Holy Spirit" (Matt 1:20), and therein lay the complete difference. The Person of the Son of God had to reside in the holy temple of His body, which could not see malformation, disease, infirmity or corruption.

2 *The disciples speak.* To these men, there were only two possible explanations of this blindness from birth—their insinuations merely followed the traditions of the day.

1. Sinful parents can transmit physical defects to their offspring. This may be so, as far as drugs, tobacco, alcoholic beverages, and chemical methods of contraception are concerned, things that are foreign to the biochemical structure and reactions of the body.

2. That infants could sin before their birth. A strange notion indeed, that renders topsy-turvy all concepts of cause and effect, of past and future. Rom 9:11 states the proper point of view, "the children being not yet born, neither having done any good or evil".

3. Great calamities can, of course, be the results of great sin, such as Luke 13:1-5; 1 Cor 11:30. Even the heathen on Melita thought that Paul was a criminal because of the viper that fastened itself on his hand.

3-5 *The Lord speaks.* The Lord rejected outright the strange notions of the disciples. Of course, the man and his parents were not sin-free; rather the blindness was not the result of a direct action of God's judgment upon the man. (The two deaths in Acts 5:5,10 are the result of God's direct intervention in judgment.) Quite the reverse: the man had suffered over the years so that God's works should be manifest at the appropriate moment. Note that the word "works" is in the plural; not only physical sight but also spiritual insight were to be granted to the man.

The Lord had works given Him to do while He was here on earth; these must be done, since after His return to the Father, His ministry on earth would be complete. By the word "day", the Lord referred to the years of His ministry on earth; by "night", He referred to the state of the world after His departure. There is a time to every purpose, and the Lord knew how this applied to Him (Eccl 3:1-8). As far as we are concerned, this "night is far spent, the day is at hand" (Rom 13:12), a future day as far as the Lord's people are concerned. Yet we can work for the Lord now, since although night-conditions surround us, nevertheless we are "children of light . . . of the day . . . not of the night, nor of darkness" (1 Thess 5:5).

The Lord was "the light of the world" as long as He was here on earth; this turned the world's long night into day because His light was as the sun, casting the warmth of divine truth, love and compassion around Him. He also announced Himself as "the light of the world" in 8:12, with similar thoughts in 12:35,36,46. He did not state that He is the Light of the world during His absence: rather in the sermon of the mount He stated of His disciples, "Ye are the light of the world" (Matt 5:14). Although it is night and darkness morally all around us, we can be a little oasis of light in this darkness, and there in that little day we can work for the Lord. In the midst of "a crooked and perverse nation", we must "shine as lights in the world" (Phil 2:15).

6 This is a remarkable sign and miracle, since the Lord did not use His word only, nor did He just touch the man; rather, He used what appears to be a sign within a sign. There had been occasions before when spittle had been used by the Lord (Mark 7:33; 8:23); no explanation is given why this should have been so. In the present case, however, it was on the sabbath day that this miracle was performed (John 9:14), and this suggests a reason for the Lord's action. For the Pharisees thought that spittle had a beneficial use in medical work, but according to them its use was not permitted on the sabbath day. Consequently the Lord was showing that He could overrule the Pharisees' legal approach to the sabbath, demonstrating His divine authority when goodness and mercy are to be manifested on the sabbath day. Moreover, the use of spittle would be a symbol that divine power emanated from Him. Again, the use of clay on the man's blind eyes rendered him doubly blind—and internal and an external blindness.

7 *The Lord speaks*. The Lord asked no question, as in Matt 20:32, "What will ye that I shall do unto you?". He only issued an instruction, "Go, wash in the pool of Siloam". The man had to have simple faith formed in his heart to obey such a strange instruction. Two kinds of blindness were removed, with a parabolic meaning attached. The removal of the clay would speak of a physical healing, while the removal of blindness from his eyes would speak of spiritual healing (that this is implied in the event is seen by vv.39-41). "Siloam" means "Sent", as John explained; the man was sent by the One who had been sent from the Father, a thought that occurs nearly forty times in this Gospel. Without the Lord having been sent, and without the man having been sent, this miracle would not have been performed. The man had no hesitation; he "washed, and came seeing". Outward and inward healing took place at the same time (see this duality in the miracle in Matt 9:1-8). On the other hand, Naaman had to wash seven times in Jordan; at first he refused to go, but later he went and was healed (2 Kings 5:10-14). Today, the Lord's servants are sent into the harvest field, preaching that unsaved men should be sent to the Saviour for spiritual healing. Those who go find cleansing through His sacrifice.

2. *The Neighbours Question the Man* 9:8-12

v.8 "The neighbours therefore, and they which before had seen him that he was blind, said, Is not this he that sat and begged?

v.9 Some said, This is he: others *said*, He is like him: *but* he said, I am *he*.
v.10 Therefore said they unto him, How were thine eyes opened?
v.11 He answered and said, A man that is called Jesus made clay, and anointed mine eyes, and said unto me, Go to the pool of Siloam, and wash: and I went and washed, and I received sight.
v.12 Then said they unto him, Where is he? He said, I know not."

8-10 *The neighbours speak*. The man did not return to the Lord Jesus; that was impossible, since he would not recognise Him and did not know where to find Him. Contact with Him would only be possible when the Lord found him (v.35). He must have made his way home. He was like the healed man in 5:13, who "wist not who it was", and like the man in Mark 5:19 who went home to testify to his friends.

If men are divided about the Person of Christ, then they will be divided on almost everything else. Hence some thought that this was the man, while others thought that he was only similar. Their division persisted until they heard the man's personal identification. Their attention was drawn to the man because they noticed a great difference in him. This should be so with converts today. Thus in Paul's case, the Jews in the synagogue in Damascus asked, "Is not this he?", when they saw the complete difference in Paul's life; see Gal 1:23.

It should be pointed out that the Greek word for "blind" in v.8 is changed to "beggar" in many MSS, so this is the translation that appears in JND and the RV. (That is, the word *tuphlos* in the TR is changed to *prosaitēs*.)

The man speaks. The man's testimony was simple and according to the facts. First he announced his identity, and then his description of what happened (v.11). Note that the man's statement of identity was *egō eimi*, the same as that used by the Lord several times in ch.8.

The neighbours speak (v.10). In all the four interrogations, the word "how" was used, introducing questions of unbelief:

1. "How were thine eyes opened?" (v.10).

2. "How he had received his sight" (v.15).

3. "How then doth he now see?" (v.19).

4. "How opened he thine eyes?" (v.26).

11-12 *The man speaks*. Personal testimony should keep to the facts, and this characterised the man's words. He, of course, did not use the same words, but conveyed identical information and stress as in v.7 where the Lord gave him instructions. Thus in Paul's personal testimonies in Acts 22:1-21 and 26:2-23 there was no exaggeration nor embellishment; the presentation of truth needs neither. The only name he could give the Lord was "a man named Jesus"; he could not go beyond what had been revealed to him (vv.35-38).

The neighbours speak. Whether they had heard of this "man named Jesus"; we do not know. At least they asked "Where is he?", evidently in a hostile attitude of mind. They did not ask, "Who is He?" Note the two "Where" and "Who" questions asked in unbelief in 8:19,25.

The man speaks. By saying "I know not", the man was not afraid to confess his ignorance, particularly when this was a legitimate ignorance. Ignorance is not legitimate when there is no intention or desire to find out even when the opportunity is available.

It is interesting to note that the man's understanding of the Person of Christ corresponds in a measure to the four coverings of Moses' tabernacle (Exod 26:1-14). The Lord is seen as dwelling, or tabernacling, amongst men in John 1:14, so it is not surprising if features of tabernacle and temple arise in John's record.

1. "A *man named Jesus*" (v.11), corresponding to the outermost badger skins—His natural appearance as seen by men who saw no beauty in Him (Isa 53:2).

2. "A *worshipper of God*" (v.31), corresponding to the rams' skins dyed red. They speak of consecration (Lev 8:22), because of the preparation of Aaron and his sons for their priestly function of worship.

3. "A *prophet*" (v.17), corresponding to the curtains of goats' hair. Rough garments distinguished a prophet (Zech 13:4), enabling even a false prophet to deceive his fellows if he so wished. John the Baptist, the greatest of the prophets, was clothed with a raiment of camel's hair (Matt 3:4).

4. "*The Son of God*" (vv.35-38). Here are the interior coloured curtains of fine twined linen, Christ known in the presence of God.

3. *The Pharisees Question the Man* 9:13-17

v.13 "They brought to the Pharisees him that aforetime was blind.
v.14 And it was the sabbath day when Jesus made the clay, and opened his eyes.
v.15 Then again the Pharisees also asked him how he had received his sight. He said unto them, He put clay upon mine eyes, and I washed, and do see.
v.16 Therefore said some of the Pharisees, This man is not of God, because he keepeth not the sabbath day. Others said, How can a man that is a sinner do such miracles? And there was a division among them.
v.17 They say unto the blind man again, What sayest thou of him, that he hath opened thine eyes? He said, He is a prophet."

13-14 Whether the neighbours had known anything about the Lord Jesus is not clear, though here they seem ill-disposed towards Him, because they brought the man to their religious leaders. The reason was that this healing had taken place on the sabbath day; if their leaders objected to this practice, then they also would have their thinking directed by their leaders, so they would likewise object. The Lord had previously laid down many reasons why work was legitimate on the sabbath day (see the list we have provided in our comments on 5:17). If the leaders paid no attention to the Lord's words, then the people who were under their thumb would do likewise. It is the same in many religious circles today; congregations listen to their leaders rather than searching out the Scriptures, and are often completely duped and deceived. In the present event, the Lord provided no explanation as to why He had healed on the sabbath day. His previous explanations had fallen on deaf ears, so He ceased to provide explanations when men had lost their chance to hear.

15 *The Pharisees speak*. These men were not so much concerned with Who? and When?, but with How? No doubt they knew who it was, and when it had been done. But such a remarkable miracle would cause the Pharisees to want to know how it had been done. (This desire to know "how" occurs in all four interrogative paragraphs in this chapter.)

The man speaks. His answer is more abbreviated than that in v.11 spoken to his neighbours. The man omitted the reference to being sent. Whether this was deliberate on his part, we cannot say; at least, the Lord as the Sent One was not implied by his answer to the Pharisees.

16-17 *The Pharisees speak*. These men then expressed their discernment of the Person of Christ and His character, based on a hard-hearted practice of ritual without mercy and love, with the refusal to recognise power that must be divine in its origin. However, their remarks display disunity of thought.

1. Some insinuated that He was "not of God", although previously He had stated that they were "not of God" (8:47). This is a case of darkness calling light darkness. The man believed that He was "of God" (9:33).

2. "Others" (*alloi*, meaning others of the same kind) stresses the fact that they were similar Pharisees, even if their thoughts were somewhat milder. They asked a question rather than expressing a statement. They recognised that sinners could not have such miraculous capabilities. But they were not prepared to recognise the logic behind the question—one not a sinner would be divine (Matt 19:17).

This division (see 7:12,43; 10:19) would persist until all were finally united with a common voice against the Lord. A man like Nicodemus was more and more distanced from them, until he was absolutely separated from them.

In v.17 they asked the man another question—no longer how the miracle was performed, but what the man thought of the One who opened his eyes. This was a subtle question, trying to force the man to testify of his thoughts concerning the Lord, so that they could deal with the man in their own usual way.

The man speaks. Under interrogation and experience, the man grew in his understanding of the Lord. By saying "He is a prophet", he did not refer to the promised Prophet (Deut 18:15,18; John 6:14); rather he made a general declaration, as did the apostles in Matt 16:14, "one of the prophets". The Pharisees had said "not of God"; the man contradicted them, since a prophet was the only kind of man that he would know as "of God", based on a limited knowledge of the OT prophets such as Elijah and Elisha who performed miracles. Most of the prophets did no miracles, not even John the Baptist (John 10:41).

4. *The Pharisees (Jews) Question the Parents* 9:18-23

v.18 "But the Jews did not believe concerning him, that he had been blind, and received his sight, until they called the parents of him that had received his sight.
v.19 And they asked them, saying, Is this your son, who ye say was born blind? how then doth he now see?
v.20 His parents answered them and said, We know that this is our son, and that he was born blind:
v.21 But by what means he now seeth, we know not; or who hath opened his eyes, we know not: he is of age; ask him: he shall speak for himself.
v.22 These *words* spake his parents, because they feared the Jews: for the Jews had agreed already, that if any man did confess that he was Christ, he should be put out of the synagogue.
v.23 Therefore said his parents, He is of age; ask him."

18 These Pharisees (Jews) would believe neither the neighbours who had brought the man to them nor the man himself. Strictly they already had a duplicated witness, the man and the neighbours, and they should accept the tenet of their law that "the testimony of two men is true" (8:17). They would do this when it pleased them, as at the Lord's trial (Matt 26:59-61). Here, however, they wanted a triple witness, including that of the man's parents. They apparently still hoped that the whole affair was a trick, a substitute man with good eyesight being paraded in the blind man's place. To prove this (even falsely) would relieve them of the necessary conclusion that the "man called Jesus" was divine. In other words, they concocted lies because they were of an obstinate and bigoted party.

19 *The Pharisees speak*. Their question to the parents was a loaded one. In the statement "who ye say was born blind", there is a flavour of contradiction as if the blindness had not been real, just a parental lie. By the word "how", the parents had to explain how a physically impossible action had been achieved. The parents could only answer what they knew, not what they did not know.

20-21 *The parents speak.* The first part of their answer concerned factual family matters (v.20); no harm could come to them from the Pharisees by a truthful answer. On the other hand, we wonder whether v.21 is wholly true. If "by what means" refers solely to the clay and the washing in Siloam, then they must have known this from their son's own testimony. But if it refers to the healing and reformation of the man's optical system, then they could not know how God worked to achieve such a miraculous change. As the Lord said in another context, "he knoweth not how" (Mark 4:27). Moreover, "who hath opened his eyes, we know not" sounds untrue. Their son must have told them that it was "a man . . . called Jesus"; the fear of man often brings out untruths, particularly in the unsaved. So they put the onus entirely on their son; the Pharisees could listen to his testimony rather than to anything that they might say. They would keep on the safe side, regardless of what would happen to their son who was of age to answer for himself. How unlike the Lord when He finally appeared before the Sanhedrin; He threw the burden of testimony on no one except Himself. If Peter denied Him, what would the others have done in similar circumstances? He knew their weaknesses prior to the giving of the Spirit of God, so He requested that His disciples should be allowed to go away unmolested (18:8), so that He would stand alone. How gracious of the Lord to think of the safety of others, yet their own appreciation of this grace was to forsake Him and flee (Matt 26:56).

22-23 John the apostle has given this verse 22 as an explanation as to why the parents had said, "He is of age; ask him". They feared the consequences of the Pharisees thinking that they took the Lord's side even in the smallest way. Here it was "if any man should confess that he was Christ". They were not doing that, but they feared that even the mention of the name of Jesus might be regarded as a confession of Christ. Men were so under the domination of the religious leaders, and so infatuated by the synagogue ritual and service practised by the Pharisees, that the synagogue was a Christless place; the Lord Himself had been led out (Luke 4:29), and Paul left the synagogue in Corinth because of the unbelieving attitude of the people (Acts 18:6). Today, Christless religious buildings and congregations are no place for the people of God.

Excommunication could take various forms. The privileges of the synagogue could be withheld from a man for thirty days. A more severe form could involve flogging and the denial of all social contact except within the family; this could be ordered only by the Sanhedrin. All this was a manifestation of self-righteous bigotry, but there is a form of excommunication in a local church that has the stamp of divine authority upon it: "to deliver such an one unto Satan . . . put away from among yourselves that wicked person" (1 Cor 5:6,13); see 1 Tim 1:20.

5. *The Pharisees Question the Man* 9:24-34

v.24 "Then again called they the man that was blind, and said unto him, Give God the praise: we know that this man is a sinner.
v.25 He answered and said, Whether he be a sinner *or no*, I know not: one thing I know, that, whereas I was blind, now I see.
v.26 Then said they to him again, What did he to thee? how opened he thine eyes?
v.27 He answered them, I have told you already, and ye did not hear: wherefore would ye hear *it* again? will ye also be his disciples?
v.28 Then they reviled him, and said, Thou art his disciple; but we are Moses' disciples.
v.29 We know that God spake unto Moses: *as for* this *fellow*, we know not from whence he is.
v.30 The man answered and said unto them, Why, herein is a marvellous thing, that ye know not from whence he is, and *yet* he hath opened mine eyes.
v.31 Now we know that God heareth not sinners: but if any man be a worshipper of God, and doeth his will, him he heareth.
v.32 Since the world began was it not heard that any man opened the eyes of one that was born blind.
v.33 If this man were not of God, he could do nothing.
v.34 They answered and said unto him, Thou wast altogether born is sins, and dost thou teach us? And they cast him out."

24 In this paragraph we find the natural wisdom of the Pharisees, those who were the guardians of their own processes of religion. The man, in his simplicity and growing faith, could not understand the apparent difficulties of the Pharisaical learning and arguments.

The Pharisees speak. If a miracle had been done, it must have been done by God and not by "this man" they argued, so they attempted to turn the man's mind towards God to give praise to Him, and away from "this man" by claiming that He was a sinner, in which case He could not have done a miracle. Their so-called knowledge fixed upon the Lord's words implying that He was divine and that He did miracles on the sabbath day, concepts that they abhorred.

In the statement "Give God the praise", the last word is *doxa*, namely "glory", so a literal rendering is, "Give glory to God". The thought is that the man should justify God by owning his own personal sin, in that he spoke of Jesus and claimed that He was a prophet. Such an interpretation is found in the OT:

1. "Give, I pray thee, glory to the Lord God of Israel, and make confession unto him" said Joshua to Achan (Josh 7:19).

2. "Give glory to the God of Israel" said the Philistine priests (1 Sam 6:5).

3. "Give glory to the Lord your God" said Jeremiah (Jer 13:16).

4. "If ye will not lay it to heart, to give glory unto my name" said Malachi to the priests (Mal 2:2).

25 *The man speaks*. Here we find the thoughts of a new convert who, as yet, did not know Jesus as the Son of God. But he quickly learnt this truth, as did Paul after his conversion in Acts 9:20. The man knew that he could now see, just as converts today know the blessings that they receive upon conversion. His knowledge of the "man . . . called Jesus" was clearly deficient; he had had no opportunity to receive teaching or revelation. His claim to ignorance about the sinlessness or otherwise of this Man did not last long. The very interrogation led him to give quite a different answer in v.31, "God heareth not sinners". The perfection of the Lord quickly dawned upon him. Today, this knowledge of the Lord's Person does not appear to be appreciated by some believers; they claim that Christ could sin, although He did not do so. In other words, they claim that the root was there but not the flower. The consequences of such a doctrine are awful, for in Matt 4:7 the Lord said to Satan, "Thou shalt not tempt the Lord thy God", so if Christ could sin then God could also. This savours of blasphemy, and should be eradicated from the minds of all believers.

26 *The Pharisees speak*. This is the fourth time that this question was asked—twice by the Pharisees in their interrogation of the man. They were not satisfied with his previous answer, since it had led to a division amongst them.

27 *The man speaks*. The man could provide no more information than that given in v.15. As far as he could judge, the Pharisees wanted to hear the story again because they were becoming interested. One learns to value something by repetition, and stimulated interest leads to discipleship.

28-29 *The Pharisees speak*. Unbelievers revile their fellows when they realise that their position is untenable by rational argument. When the Lord was reviled He reviled not again (1 Pet 2:23), and neither would the man revile the Pharisees. Rather, by saying "Thou art his disciple", they admitted the clear-cut testimony of the man not fully emancipated from his ignorance. They had not learnt the lesson of Abraham in 8:40, "this did not Abraham". We can also add, "this did not Moses" since they were claiming to be "Moses' disciples". Their boast was in their interpretation of the Mosaic law, failing to realise that Moses wrote of the Lord Jesus (5:45-47). Moses in effect accused them, rather than recognise that they were his disciples! These Pharisees were no more Moses' disciples than were Korah, Dathan, Abiram and On (Num 16:1). True discipleship would involve faithfulness to the word of God given through Moses.

The Pharisees' claim, "God spake unto Moses", was merely formal knowledge according to the letter. Any unbeliever, upon reading the OT, could make that claim; it is there for all to see. Since they did not believe the writings of Moses (5:46-47), they did not really believe that God had spoken through him. Their statement was an untruth, as was their further statement, "we know not from whence he is". For in 7:28, the Lord had said, "Ye both know me, and ye know whence I am". His signs demonstrated His Person and the fact that He must have come down from heaven. They did not want to believe, since this would upset all their traditional and cherished theology.

30 *The man answers*. The man was amazed by the blindness of the Pharisees in the face of facts and legitimate deductions therefrom. No other man ever spoke to the Pharisees like that in the Gospels. The reason was that he knew that he had been healed. But how often a divine work can remain unrecognised by men! Thus "The heavens declare the glory of God" (Ps 19:1), but men refuse to recognise this fact, their foolish and darkened hearts sinking into idolatry (Rom 1:21). In Acts 4:14, the Sanhedrin saw the healed man standing with the apostles, and could say nothing against it; yet they were unmoved spiritually, and remained in unbelief. The Pharisees asked for more powerful signs, but the Lord would never grant such a request, since signs of that character do not lead to faith.

31 The man's theology was improving. The assertion that God does not hear sinners contrasts with his statements in v.25. No doubt this was a general observation based on the OT:

1. "The Lord will not hear you in that day" because of the king that they had chosen (1 Sam 8:18).

2. "If I regard iniquity in my heart, the Lord will not hear me" said the psalmist (Ps 66:18).

3. "When ye make many prayers, I will not hear: your hands are full of blood" (Isa 1:15); see Ezek 8:18.

The opposite to a sinner is a "worshipper of God", for this implies obedience to God in the mode of worship; that is why so many of the OT sacrifices were not acceptable to God (Isa 1:10-11).

32-33 Throughout OT history, there is no record that any "man" had ever done a miracle such as this, demonstrating the man's knowledge of OT facts. There had been promises such as "in that day . . . the eyes of the blind shall see out of obscurity, and out of darkness" (Isa 29:18; 42:7), but this did not refer particularly to physical blindness but to spiritual blindness. So the "man . . . called Jesus", a prophet, was unique. Put negatively in v.33, this one Man was "of God". This was the man's final conclusion until further revelation from the Lord in v.37. This conclusion and the further revelation had been the object of the sign.

34 *The Pharisees speak.* This verse represents the final conclusion of the Pharisees. They could no longer argue against the simplicity of the man's logic. So they reviled his integrity, claiming he was "born in sins", not perhaps in the sense implied by the disciples in v.2, but either in the sense of having been "born of fornication" (8:41) or as David said, "in sin did my mother conceive me" (Ps 51:5). These were unfounded suggestions to hurl at a new disciple of the Lord, these being a product of hate. Similarly with their question, "dost thou teach us?". They were the teachers, and could not bear to entertain the thought that a humble soul knew more than they. The man, like the Lord afterwards, had reduced the religious leaders to silence (Matt 22:34). It reminds us of the smug superiority of unevangelical clergy over the laity who sit at their feet. Unbelieving teachers display an unspiritual arrogance to justify their theories. Yet the position of a young convert faced by an unsaved teacher should be, "I have more understanding than all my teachers" (Ps 119:99).

As cast out, the man followed in the steps of the Lord (8:59), who would now find him on the outside. The Good Shepherd on the outside forms His flock also on the outside of men's organised religion. At least the Lord will not cast out His own people (6:37).

6. *The Son Questions the Man*
9:35-38

v.35 "Jesus heard that they had cast him out; and when he had found him, he said unto him, Dost thou believe on the Son of God?
v.36 He answered and said, Who is he, Lord, that I might believe on him?
v.37 And Jesus said unto him, Thou hast both seen him, and it is he that talketh with thee.
v.38 And he said, Lord, I believe. And he worshipped him."

35 *The Lord speaks.* Hearing, finding, asking—here are aspects of the Lord's work, which were to fulfil His promise that "whosoever hath, to him shall be given, and he shall have more abundance" (Matt 13:12). The title "the Son of God" upon the lips of the Saviour is quite rare; usually He used the title "Son of man", even in John's Gospel. In the discourses in chs.6,8, men were led away from Him, but here a man is led to Him. The question, "Dost thou believe on the Son of God?" was a challenge to the man; no make-believe answer was possible, neither could it be accepted.

Instead of "Son of God" (*huios tou theou*), a minority of manuscripts have "Son of man" (*huios tou anthrōpou*). The RV and JND both have "Son of God", and rightly so, though for some reason the NEB has "Son of man".

36 *The man answers.* He used the title *kurie* which, as we have pointed out before, means either "Lord" or "Sir" according to the context. The AV, RV and JND all use "Lord", but the NEB uses "Sir". Did the man immediately recognise who the Lord was before the revelation in v.36? If so, the title "Lord" is correct. But if not, then "Sir" is more appropriate. Certainly in v.38, "Lord" is now the appropriate translation, and the NEB uses this title in this verse, implying an immediate recognition of the Lord on the part of the man. But in v.36, the confession of ignorance is not a sin. It is the prelude to further knowledge. How gracious is the Lord!

37 *The Lord speaks.* In just the same way as the Lord revealed Himself as the Christ to the woman at the well by saying "*ho lalōn*", namely, "I that speak" (4:26), so here He revealed Himself as the Son of God by saying "*ho lalōn*", namely, "he that talketh". In both cases, the present participle of the same verb is used. In Peter's case, the knowledge of the Son of God came by revelation from the Father (Matt 16:16-17). The united divine testimony therefore makes the Son known to His people. The knowledge of the Son formed the pivot of Paul's understanding of spiritual things (Acts 9:20; 1 Cor 1:9; Gal 2:20; 1 Thess 1:10).

38 *The man speaks.* By stating "Lord, I believe", and then worshipping Him, the man reached an apex of the "work of faith" (1 Thess 1:3). Faith responds to the Lord as the Son, and then the man responds to faith by worshipping. Similarly in Matt 28:17, those who had responded to His resurrection, when they saw Him in Galilee, "worshipped him". This is more particularly seen in verses such as Rev 5:9,12,13, where many companies are seen in adoration of the Lamb. Verses such as these dispel the theory expressed by some that worship should not be directed more particularly to the Lord. See also Matt 2:2,11; 14:33; 28:9; Luke 24:52.

7. *The Lord Speaks to the Pharisees*
9:39-41

v.39 "And Jesus said, For judgment I am come into this world, that they which see not might see; and that they which see might be made blind.

v.40 And *some* of the Pharisees which were with him heard these words, and said unto him, Are we blind also?

v.41 Jesus said unto them, If ye were blind, ye should have no sin: but now ye say, We see; therefore your sin remaineth."

39 *The Lord speaks.* This was a general statement, one great object of the Lord's coming into the world. In effect, this is the same miracle in reverse, though considered spiritually. The idea of religious self-satisfied people, claiming to be able to see, yet being made blind, is obnoxious to such people. Yet this is "judgment", the Lord presenting Himself to men so as to reverse the knowledge that they think that they possess. Sight becomes blindness if men will not accept His Person as the Son of God. He will not always strive with unbelief; in the case of some men, this becomes hardened and fixed. Cherished tradition becomes like a cable of steel from which men cannot extricate themselves.

40 *The Pharisees speak.* These men were stung to the heart—"they perceived that he spake of them" (Matt 21:45). "Are we blind also?" was their question to confirm this perception.

41 *The Lord speaks.* Though the discourse continues into ch.10, yet these words terminate the immediate subject. It is all a question of sin. Blindness leads to recognition of sin, and hence to confession, faith and forgiveness. But sight implies self-justification, and hence no forgiveness. The difference is seen in the parable of the Pharisee and the publican (Luke 18:9-14). The former could see so remained blind; the latter was blind, so was granted sight unto justification. God abases or exalts those who exalt or abase themselves.

VI. The Good Shepherd Rejected (10:1-42)

1. *The First Parable*
10:1-6

v.1 "Verily, verily, I say unto you, He that entereth not by the door into the sheepfold, but climbeth up some other way, the same is a thief and a robber.
v.2 But he that entereth in by the door is the shepherd of the sheep.
v.3 To him the porter openeth; and the sheep hear his voice: and he calleth his own sheep by name, and leadeth them out.
v.4 And when he putteth forth his own sheep, he goeth before them, and the sheep follow him: for they know his voice.
v.5 And a stranger will they not follow, but will flee from him: for they know not the voice of strangers.
v.6 This parable spake Jesus unto them: but they understood not what things they were which he spake unto them."

We may well ask, How many men today know the Lord as Shepherd? And this in spite of the searching popularity of Ps 23 and the many hymns based on it. Pious utterances do not remove spiritual ignorance. In Gen 46:34 every shepherd was an abomination to the Egyptians, and this is what the Lord is to many in the unsaved world. Of the dozens of references in the OT to shepherds, only a small number refer to the Lord; we select a number of quotations:

1. "The Lord is my shepherd; I shall not want" (Ps 23:1);

2. "O Shepherd of Israel . . . thou that dwellest between the cherubim, shine forth" (Ps 80:1);

3. "He shall feed his flock like a shepherd" (Isa 40:11);

4. "I, even I, will both search my sheep, and seek them out" (Ezek 34:11);

5. "I will set up one shepherd over them . . . even my servant David; he shall feed them, and he shall be their shepherd" (Ezek 34:23);

6. "Awake, O sword, against my shepherd . . . smite the shepherd" (Zech 13:7).

These references are reflected in three great NT verses speaking of Christ:

1. The Good Shepherd (John 10:14): this is *past*, for the giving of His life brings us into the house. There is no rival in salvation.

2. The Great Shepherd (Heb 13:20): this is *present*, for He makes us perfect to do His will. There is no rival in sanctification.

3. The Chief Shepherd (1 Pet 5:4): this is *future*, for there are rewards when He comes. There can be no rival to spiritual service.

In John 10 there are two distinct parables, the first being in vv.1-5, and the second in vv.7-18.

1 Strictly this is a continuation of ch.9, and we can visualise both the man and the Pharisees being present. And yet the group of chapters 7-10, forming a consecutive narrative, span the period between the feast of tabernacles (7:2) and the "feast of dedication" (10:22), and we shall not attempt to suggest where a period of time can be inserted, nor whether the Lord left Jerusalem in the intervening period between October and December. This latter feast had been instituted two hundred years before when the temple had been rededicated after its pollution by Antiochus Epiphanes.

The Lord speaks. The "sheepfold" was an enclosure so as to contain several flocks of sheep. At night, the one entrance was guarded by a porter. The trend of thought in the parable enables us to determine the nature of the flocks. There were two:

1. The Jewish nation in unbelief, forming the majority. Gentile believers are not seen until v.16; they are "other sheep" in the second parable.

2. The Lord's disciples taken from the Jewish nation, those whom He called a "little flock" (Luke 12:32), those who would be as "lambs amongst wolves" (10:3).

The thief and the robber correspond to the Jewish leaders who sought to gain all the sheep as their own followers, regardless of the flock to which they belonged.

In the context, the Lord is referring to the Pharisees. Such men sought to gain the minds of others, to subjugate them to the legal demands of their own religion. Satan originated this procedure of attempting to captivate the minds of men in the beginning. The Lord warned against false prophets in sheep's clothing (Matt 7:15). Through Ezekiel God warned against the shepherds of Israel who fed themselves rather than feeding the flock (Ezek 34:2); such shepherds allowed the flock to become a prey since there was no true shepherd (v.8). In Matt 23:13 the Lord condemned the Pharisees for refusing to allow men to enter the kingdom of heaven, because they sought all men to be their proselytes. In a different context, even in a local church or assembly there can be grievous wolves (false leaders or elders) seeking to enter in to damage the flock (Acts 20:29).

2 On the other hand, there was one unique shepherd entering by the one unique way. In the second parable, the Lord identified Himself as the Good Shepherd (v.11), but here in the first parable no interpretation is given. The reason lies in v.6; there was to be understanding of the parable. The same happened in Matt 13:10-17, where the Lord gave reasons why He often spoke in parables, namely to hide the truth from men, unless He expounded the meaning to His disciples. Looking back, of course, believers today can understand the parables, even if no explanation is recorded. Thus in our v.2, the Lord is the Shepherd of the sheep. He enters to find His own sheep, an activity that commenced in ch.1. The thought follows on from 9:35, "when he had found him".

3 We believe that every element of a parable is susceptible to interpretation, although some expositors suggest that "the porter" is just an accessory. Others suggest Moses, or the Holy Spirit. But in the light of 1:6-7, that John the Baptist "came for a witness . . . that all men through him might believe", we feel that the Lord referred to John the Baptist, as He often did throughout His teaching. He opened the way for the Lord to enter upon His ministry, and to claim His own people. Certainly He did this in 1:29,36, declaring that the Lord was "the Lamb of God", thereby attracting the initial disciples to Himself.

We must distinguish between "the sheep" and "his own sheep" in this verse. All the sheep, of whatever flock, within the fold either heard or had the opportunity of hearing the voice of the Shepherd. Much of the Lord's teaching in John's Gospel had been to the Jews who remained in unbelief, while others who heard either were or quickly became believers. The object of the Shepherd's voice was to separate the sheep—to call His own sheep out of the religious environment of the fold. There was no question of going "in and out" as in the second parable in v.9; here it was "out" only. We have plenty of examples of this throughout the Gospels and in the Acts, such as the apostles, Nicodemus, the woman at the well, and the man granted eyesight. Calling "his own sheep by name" was an identification process; of the others the Lord would say, "I never knew you" (Matt 7:23). As examples, He named Simon (John 1:42), Lazarus (11:43), Philip (14:9), Mary (20:16), Thomas (20:27), Saul (Acts 9:4), all under differing conditions. Paul gave the general statement, "The Lord knoweth them that are his" (2 Tim 2:19), while in heaven above, not only are our names written there, but the Lord Himself promised to confess the overcomer's name before His Father (Rev 3:5).

4 As putting forth His own sheep, the Shepherd was engaging in a separating process. To lead them out and put them forth, He Himself went before them, after which "the sheep", namely "his own sheep", followed Him. No doubt the events of the preceding two chapters initiated this parable, for the Lord had been cast out of the temple (8:59), and as having gone before He found the man also cast out (9:34). Together, the Shepherd and the sheep remained on the outside; a profession of the Son of God ensured that the man would not be welcomed back into the general fold of Jewish religion. The Lord expressed this separation process in His prayer in 17:19, "for their sakes I sanctify myself, that they also might be sanctified through the truth". Namely, He was the first, and then He expected His own people to be second. He has delivered us from this present evil age (Gal 1:4), in just the same way as He "made his own people to go forth like sheep" (Ps 78:52).

5 Here we have the ideal—the stranger and his voice are foreign to the true sheep. Of course, in that day the Lord was referring to the Pharisees and their voices who were determined if possible to keep men under their own jurisdiction. But their doctrine was foreign to the Lord's disciples, for their teaching was merely "the commandments of men" (Matt 15:9). Thus the man with restored eyesight did not listen to them, and refused to be convinced by their arguments (9:82-30). This is the principle stated in Luke 8:18, "Take heed therefore how ye hear". Alas that there should ever have been failure on the part of the Lord's people, as sometimes there has been; they have delighted in the voice of the false shepherds; for example, "Beware lest any man spoil you through philosophy and vain deceit, after the tradition of men . . . and not after Christ" (Col 2:8). With many voices in the religious world today, the Lord's people need to flee from the stranger, but to follow the Good Shepherd.

6 With the parable concluded, we have the important observation by John that the Jews "understood not what things they were which he spake unto them". The actual meaning of many parables was hidden from the wise and prudent, but revealed unto babes. This was why many parables were given, and why the Lord would not provide an open interpretation; "to them it is not given" (Matt 13:11). Thus it was just to His disciples that the Lord explained the parable of the sower (vv.13,18). After the parable of the tares, He sent the multitude away, and in the house He explained it only to His disciples (v.36). He would not cast pearls before swine, yet how graciously He dealt with His own disciples who often failed to understand; to the slow in heart to believe He "expounded unto them in all the scriptures the things concerning himself" (Luke 24:26-27). Similarly for the apostles, "Then opened he their understanding, that they might understand the scriptures" (v.45).

2. *The Second Parable*
10:7-18

v.7 "Then said Jesus unto them again, Verily, verily, I say unto you, I am the door of the sheep.
v.8 All that ever came before me are thieves and robbers: but the sheep did not hear them.
v.9 I am the door: by me if any man enter in, he shall be saved, and shall go in and out, and find pasture.
v.10 The thief cometh not but for to steal, and to kill, and to destroy: I am come that they might have life, and that they might have *it* more abundantly.
v.11 I am the good shepherd: the good shepherd giveth his life for the sheep.
v.12 But he that is an hireling, and not the shepherd, whose own the sheep are not, seeth the wolf coming, and leaveth the sheep, and fleeth: and the wolf catcheth them, and scattereth the sheep.
v.13 The hireling fleeth, because he is an hireling, and careth not for the sheep.
v.14 I am the good shepherd, and know my *sheep*, and am known of mine.
v.15 As the Father knoweth me, even so know I the Father: and I lay down my life for the sheep.
v.16 And other sheep I have, which are not of this fold: them also I must bring, and they shall hear my voice; and there shall be one fold, *and* one shepherd.
v.17 Therefore doth my Father love me, because I lay down my life, that I might take it again.
v.18 No man taketh it from me, but I lay it down of myself. I have power to lay it down, and I have power to take it again. This commandment have I received of my Father."

7 *The Lord speaks*. The repeated "verily" (*amen*) is characteristic of John's Gospel. In the three Synoptic Gospels, it is always "Verily I say unto you", but in John's Gospel "Verily, verily, I say unto you (thee)" occurs 25 times. In the epistles and Revelation the single word is always translated "Amen", usually at the end of a prayer or doxology.

The point of view changes in this second parable. No longer does the fold consist of Jewish believers and unbelievers, with the Shepherd separating the one from the other. Rather, the fold now consists of Jewish believers; it is not a place to be separated from. Gentile believers later would occupy another fold, but the Lord would make one flock out of both. The Lord presented Himself as "the door", explained in v.19. Twice He announced Himself as "the door" and twice as the Good Shepherd. In connection with "the door", we have the conditions inside the fold (vv.7-10), while in connection with the Good

Shepherd we have conditions outside the fold (vv.11-18).

The fold is now a place of protection and rest, similar to the protection and rest under His wings, to quote another metaphor (Matt 23:37). There is no danger inside the fold, since no unauthorised person can enter through the door, which is Christ. Whether the fold is open or closed to us depends on our relationship to a Person; He later likens this safety to being firmly in His hand (v.28), from which none can pluck a believer.

8 In these verses the Lord differentiated between the inside and the outside of the fold. The "thieves and robbers" were on the outside; their intentions are given in v.10. The Lord provided safety, whether the sheep were inside or outside. In the immediate context, the Lord referred to the Pharisees, who placed heavy and grievous burdens upon men, who refused to let men enter the kingdom of heaven, who devoured widows' houses, searching sea and land to make proselytes (Matt 23:4,13-15). In "all... before me", no doubt He included all the false prophets in the OT who sought to intrude into the minds and lives of God's people. This practice extends into the church age, for which both Paul, Peter and John issued strong warnings (1 Tim 4:1-3; 2 Pet 2:1; 1 John 2:18-19). The object of the great whore of all false religion will be to trade in "the souls of men" (Rev 18:13). In spite of all this, the strength of the door is found in verses such as Heb 11:33-37, where faith is seen as that which cannot be overturned regardless of the insidious pressures exerted by men.

9 By "in", the Lord implied the security of salvation, security from the dangers existing on the outside. By "out" He referred to a place of pasture, of spiritual food, where nevertheless dangers existed. Saul, after his conversion, was joined to the church in Jerusalem after Barnabas had convinced the saints that this conversion was genuine; "he was with them coming in and going out at Jerusalem" (Acts 9:26-28). He came in for fellowship and service with the believers, and he went out for evangelistic service amongst the Jews, but not for long (Acts 22:18). The Lord Himself went "in and out" amongst His apostles during His years of ministry on earth—out to preach to the people, in to be alone with His own disciples as in John 13-16.

10 The intentions of the thief are stated here. Such a man is a religious soul-stealer; his method is to propagate heresy and false doctrine, even to deny the Lord Jesus Christ or to denigrate His Person. Men of this character may even be with the Lord's people, though they cannot be of them, as John wrote, "that they might be made manifest that they are not all of us" (1 John 2:19); such is the spirit of antichrist in the present day. However, since there was (and is) but one door, the Lord Himself, then these men cannot enter by that way. If the flock on the inside were vigilant enough, there would be no entrance whatsoever. Yet these men do enough damage, as Paul warned of the entrance of grievous wolves (Acts 20:29). For such men can break down another part of the surrounding wall and enter that way, if believers are not wholly dependent upon the Lord. That is why Paul had to face so much trouble in many of the churches he had founded, mainly due to Pharisaical influences to draw the believers back to the Law.

The object of such men is to undo the work of Christ, to render His people useless in their service. But the work of Christ is to organise fully the life that He has given each believer. A living plant is organised in its detailed structure; it is not just a heap of chemicals mixed together. A seed may appear small and insignificant, though it has life, and the potential to produce a plant and flowers—things of beauty, usefulness and productivity. This is life more abundant. A garden of weeds certainly possesses life, but certainly not life more abundant. Similarly with a believer; he has life at his conversion, but this must grow into maturity, and not be marred by allowing a thief to disturb and destroy that life's usefulness. Similarly a human body is a marvel of structure and organisation, else it could not function as it does; this symbol is used in 1 Cor 12 to describe a local church. The Corinthians possessed gifts, but these could not be described as more abundant. A spiritual church possesses gifts more abundant, but a carnal one does not. Growth into maturity implies that its service has beauty, usefulness and productivity clearly stamped upon it.

11 We now come to the outside of the fold. With the Lord as the door, the flock is safe on the inside, provided the foolish sheep do not start knocking down walls. But there is danger on the outside; the Lord as the Good Shepherd grants protection there. The blind man with his restored eyesight needed something more than a door; He needed the Good Shepherd on the outside, since during the rest of his life the man would be surrounded by Jewish enemies. As Isa 40:11 puts it, "He shall feed his flock like a shepherd: he shall gather the lambs with his arms, and carry them in his bosom, and shall gently lead those that are with young". In the parable, protection from the enemy demanded that the Good Shepherd should give His life. He gave Himself only once, so as to remove the evil influences and powers around the people of God. Also He gave Himself that He might remove us from these evil influences: He "gave himself for our sins, that he might deliver us from this present evil world (age)" (Gal 2:4).

12-13 The word "hireling" (*misthōtos*) in these two verses means a hired servant (Mark 1:20), and in particular a man who has no interest in his duties, and no sense of responsibility towards his employer, a man whose thoughts are towards his gain and who refuses to face difficulties when they arise. In the context, the hireling stands for the Pharisees whose declared policy was to cast out any who believed on the Lord (John 9:22; 12:42). The picture depicts what would happen if there were no Good Shepherd to intervene, if it were possible for some men to have faith and for there to be no faithful Lord to protect them in the midst of wolves. Satan would be rampant if One greater than he were not active in protection, for he is described as "the god of this world" (2 Cor 4:4), "a roaring lion" (1 Pet 5:8), and as "transformed into an angel of light" (2 Cor 11:14). The Pharisees would have no desire to resist him, so they would leave any sheep unprotected, which would then be wounded and scattered. There would be no shepherd to bring them back (Luke 15:4).

There can, of course, be hirelings today, though not in the sense implied in this parabolic picture. Since the Lord is the Good Shepherd, and since He has given His life already for the sheep, the dangers visualised in v.12 are hardly applicable. But there are many who seek gain from religion, such as men who take the oversight "for filthy lucre" (1 Pet 5:2), and men like Diotrephes who love "the preeminence" (3 John 9). Men of this character, whether saved or unsaved, quickly scatter the sheep, though now these still remain under the protection of the Good Shepherd. As the Lord said in Matt 6:2,5,16, these men, like the Pharisees, have their reward now, but there is no treasure laid up in heaven.

14-15 The meaning of these two verses can better be assessed by following the RV and JND, in which the sentence does not terminate at the end of v.14, but continues into v.15. The RV additionally inserts the word "even", so that v.15 commences "even as the Father knoweth me . . . ". There is a mutual Shepherd-sheep relationship even as there is a Father-Son relationship; both are in the realm of mutual knowledge. He knows His sheep because He has called and chosen them; they know Him either because He has revealed Himself to them (9:37) or because the Father has revealed Him (Matt 16:17). In the case of the Father-Son relationship, there was never, of course, a time when it did not exist. It is a knowledge from eternity that never had to be formed or developed; this knowledge implies intimacy; the prayer in ch.17 could never have been spoken apart from divine intimacy existing from "before the world was" (v.5). It gives confidence to the sheep to realise that similarly they know the Shepherd and He knows them. This same confidence enables them to live in the reality of the fact that the Shepherd had given His life for the sheep. (The thought of resurrection appears in v.17.)

16 Finally, the Lord spoke of "other sheep", a truth that even His Jewish disciples at that time were not able to understand. The word for "other" is *allos*, namely others of the same kind. Here were embraced believers from amongst the Gentiles. They would be taken out from the wide expanses of the Gentile fold, so as to join with the Jewish believers; all would be separated from the Jewish and Gentile folds of unbelief: as Paul wrote, "to the Jew first, and also to the Greek" (Rom 1:26), so that all "with one mind and one mouth" may glorify God (15:6). This truth is spelt out by Paul in Eph 2:13-18, in phrases such as "who hath made both one"; "that he might reconcile both unto God in one body"; "we both have access by one Spirit unto the Father".

The AV rendering "there shall be one fold" is very curious, since the word is properly flock, "there shall be one flock" (*poimnē*, not *aulē*). The Lord was speaking of the sheep, of His own people gathered in one. And of course, "one shepherd". This shows the uniqueness of the Lord as Head of His church, and the uniqueness of the church as the body of Christ. Men may introduce many churches with denominational names, and many heads of these churches, but all are contrary to the Lord's teaching in this verse. This oneness of the flock also appears in 11:52, "that also he should gather together in one the children of God that were scattered abroad". "One body . . . one Lord" is how Paul expressed it in Eph 4:4-5, whereas Peter stated that "God is no respecter of persons" at the time when the Gentiles were first brought in (Acts 10:34).

17-18 Finally in this second parable, the Lord introduced the subject of resurrection, for if the sheep have eternal life, then the Shepherd too would not remain in death after having saved them. The Father was vitally concerned with the fact that the Shepherd would lay down His life. Here was the Son as the burnt offering, with the Father's love placed upon Him. The fact that He would lay down His life was not, of course, the sole reason for this divine love upon Him. Both the love and the divine counsel that He should die were rooted in eternity past. For further remarks on this divine love for the Son see our comments on 3:16,35.

It is important to see the connection between the works of men, and the work of the Father and the Son. The work of the Father and the Son cannot be divided. As far as His death was concerned, there was an *outward* aspect to it, and an *inward* aspect. Outwardly, men were allowed to crucify Him, as He said to Pilate, "except it were given thee from above" (19:11). Several times the Lord spoke of His death as an act accomplished by men, "Destroy this temple" (2:19); "they shall . . . put him to death" (Luke 18:33). The Romans had put many criminals to death by crucifixion, but in the Lord's case the soldiers crucified Him, but they could not take away His life. Rather, "he gave up the ghost" at the appropriate moment (Luke 23:46). For the inward aspect of His death is seen in a verse such as "Christ . . . through the eternal Spirit offered himself without spot to God" (Heb 9:14).

Between His death and His resurrection, the Lord's body lay in the tomb, the seal protecting it from men, but we believe that Michael the archangel had something to do with its protection from the powers of darkness. The Pharisees may refute the fact of His resurrection, and the Sadducees may deny altogether the possibility of resurrection, but to the believer this fact is central and sure. Both the Father and the Son were involved in this work of resurrection:

1. *The work of the Son.* "In three days I will raise it up" (John 2:19); "I have power to take it again", where the word for "power" is *exousia*, namely, authority.

2. *The work of the Father.* "This same Jesus hath God raised up" (Acts 2:32); "God raised him from the dead" (13:30); "his mighty power, which he wrought in Christ, when he raised him from the dead" (Eph 1:19-20).

Both death and resurrection were regarded as "a commandment" by the Son in submission to the Father's will: see also 12:49; 14:31.

3. *The Effects of the Two Parables* 10:19-30

v.19 "There was a division therefore again among the Jews for these sayings.
v.20 And many of them said, He hath a devil, and is mad; why hear ye him?
v.21 Others said, These are not the words of him that hath a devil. Can a devil open the eyes of the blind?
v.22 And it was at Jerusalem the feast of the dedication, and it was winter.
v.23 And Jesus walked in the temple in Solomon's porch.
v.24 Then came the Jews round about him, and said unto him, How long dost thou make us to doubt? If thou be the Christ, tell us plainly.
v.25 Jesus answered them, I told you, and ye believed not: the works that I do in my Father's name, they bear witness of me.
v.26 But ye believe not, because ye are not of my sheep, as I said unto you.
v.27 My sheep hear my voice, and I know them, and they follow me:
v.28 And I give unto them eternal life; and they shall never perish, neither shall any *man* pluck them out of my hand.
v.29 My Father, which gave *them* me, is greater than all; and no *man* is able to pluck *them* out of my Father's hand.
v.30 I and *my* Father are one."

19-21 John has traced the growth of division amongst the people as a result of the Lord's presentation of the truth. We have noted this in 7:12,40-43; 9:16, the word "others" being used on each occasion, implying a division of thought. As Paul quoted, "they stumbled at that stumbling stone" (Rom 9:32).

Many of the Jews speak. The accusation, "He hath a devil", amounts to blasphemy, the word *diamonion* being properly translated "demon". This accusation is also found in 7:20; 8:48, as well as in the Synoptic Gospels in different contexts (Matt 9:34; 12:24; Mark 3:22; Luke 11:15). The Jews also accused John the Baptist of having a demon (Luke 7:33). The second accusation "He . . . is mad" is really a verb, *mainomai*, occurring five times in the NT, once of the Lord, once of Rhoda by those engaged in rather unbelieving prayer (Acts 12:15), and once of Paul (26:24-25). In Mark 3:21 another accusation (*existēmi*) is translated "He is beside himself". Intense dislike of a person, incapable of being expressed rationally, lends itself to such irrational accusations.

Others speak. No doubt these were not disciples, but those with more tender hearts, perhaps later to become the sheep of the Good Shepherd. They realised that demons could not do works of goodness, only of darkness. How true—"by their fruits ye shall know them" (Matt 7:20).

22 The "feast of dedication" was an artificial feast, in memory of the event when the temple had been rededicated after its pollution by Antiochus Epiphanes. Two months had elapsed since the previous feast of tabernacles, and as we have said before we cannot pinpoint the break in the continuous passage from 7:2. It may be that the break took place at this verse 22, with two months having passed since v.21. The Lord may have been out of Jerusalem during these months, and upon His return, the Jews brought up the previous miracle and subject, while the Lord returned to the theme of His sheep.

Note how John stressed the times and the seasons in his narrative: "it was winter"; "it was night" (13:30); "it was early" (18:28); "it was yet dark" (20:1). There are spiritual lessons here for the reader to consider.

23-24 The Lord was walking as the separated Good Shepherd, just as in 1:36 He walked as the Lamb of God. In this latter case, disciples were attracted to the Lamb, and these mostly became the apostles; in the former case, enmity grew so the Lord had to withdraw from the Jews for a season.

The Jews speak. It was a wicked insinuation to suggest that the Lord was deliberately withholding information about His Person, and that He held them "in suspense" (RV); a literal translation is, "Until when holdest thou our soul in suspense?". Strictly, they knew what the Lord was teaching, but they did not want to believe it. It was only when men were arrogantly blind that the Lord finally withheld information (John 9:41), for there comes a time when some men cannot believe. The Jews' faithless supposition "If thou be the Christ" was echoed by the rulers, "If he be Christ" (Luke 23:35), and by one malefactor, "If thou be Christ" (v.39). The chief priests asked the question, "Art thou the Christ?" (Luke 22:67). Peter made the true profession, "The Christ of God" (Luke 9:20), while God also made similar testimony, "Mine anointed (lit. my Christ)" (Ps 132:17).

25-26 *The Lord speaks*. He had already spoken about His names and titles, either directly to the Pharisees, or to others but overheard by them. For example, the great "I am" titles in ch.8, and the many witnesses to His Person in ch.5; additionally, His mention of "the Father" or "my Father" implied His Sonship. So these religious leaders were without excuse; nothing more could be added, either by direct testimony or by spectacular signs that they so much desired. Even if they failed to understand His direct testimony, then His works—the signs recorded in John's Gospel—should have been sufficient to identify Him. After all, a record of His works was the means that the Lord used to convince John the Baptist when he asked concerning His Person (Matt 11:4-6). But the Lord's testimony to the Pharisees was drawing to an end, since at that stage "they could not believe" (12:39). In fact, the Lord now appeared as their Judge, rather than as a Shepherd seeking the lost. "Ye are not of my sheep" was sufficient to indicate that they were outside the sphere of blessing.

27-28 In these two verses, the character of the sheep is described, so that the Pharisees could see easily that they were not participants. Finally, in vv.29-30, the character of the Father is described.

There is a complete distinction between "my sheep" and those who are "not of my sheep". The distinction between belief and unbelief is so marked that the darkest form of unbelief cannot but fail to understand its true position. So a declaration of this distinction can lead either to deep spiritual concern or to self-satisfied arrogance. In particular, the Lord drew attention to the following features of His sheep:

1. They hear His voice (as vv.3-5). The opposite is therefore implied; they do not know the voice of strangers—the Pharisees.

2. He knows them. Of the rest, the Lord said, "I never knew you" (Matt 7:23).

3. They follow Him. But they will not follow a stranger (8:12; 10:5).

4. They possess eternal life: "life" and "more abundantly" is how this is described in v.10. Such truth pervades John's Gospel (20:31).

5. They shall never perish. Such life has nothing of the old Adam about it.

6. There is lasting security. No power can remove a sheep from His hands. This shows the uselessness of the excommunication process carried out by the Pharisees. The man had been cast out (9:34), but on the outside the Lord met him, revealing Himself and protecting him as one of His sheep newly found.

29-30 This security also rests in the Father's power and Person—the sheep are thus doubly secure. Those attempting to do the plucking are essentially religious leaders energised by Satan, who loathe seeing believers following the Lord as the Good Shepherd. For example, there were "certain men" from Judaea, who taught that it was necessary to "be circumcised after the manner of Moses" for salvation (Acts 15:1); there were "certain men" who crept in unawares, denying the Lord Jesus Christ (Jude 4).

However, the Father is "greater than all", namely, in the context, greater than all the enemies who would seek to open the Father's hand so as to extricate the sheep. Their intentions would receive divine frustration. Thus Jethro said, "I know that the Lord is greater than all gods" (Exod 18:11); see also 2 Chron 2:5;

Ps 135:5. In 1 John 4:1-4, the apostle John wrote a similar thing: "greater is he that is in you, than he that is in the world", referring to "the Spirit of God" in believers and the "spirit of antichrist" in many false prophets who had gone out into the world with their false doctrine.

"My hand" and "the Father's hand" lead to the fundamental statement, "I and the Father are one" (RV, JND); the AV "my" before "Father" does not occur in the Greek text. Today, some deny that this implies oneness in Person, and minimise its import, while others exploit the verse to the full. Certainly the Jews understood what the Lord meant, for they sought to stone Him because of this claim to deity. John's Gospel as a whole supports the doctrine of oneness in Person, will, words, and in absolute deity.

4. *The Deity of the Son*
10:31-42

v.31 "Then the Jews took up stones again to stone him.
v.32 Jesus answered them, Many good works have I shewed you from my Father; for which of those works do ye stone me?
v.33 The Jews answered him, saying, For a good work we stone thee not, but for blasphemy; and because that thou, being a man, makest thsyelf God.
v.34 Jesus answered them, Is it not written in your law, I said, Ye are gods?
v.35 If he called them gods, unto whom the word of God came, and the scripture cannot be broken:
v.36 Say ye of him, whom the Father hath sanctified, and sent into the world, Thou blasphemest; because I said, I am the Son of God?
v.37 If I do not the works of my Father, believe me not.
v.38 But if I do, though ye believe not me, believe the works: that ye may know, and believe, that the Father *is* in me, and I in him.
v.39 Therefore they sought again to take him: but he escaped out of their hand,
v.40 And went away again beyond Jordan into the place where John at first baptized; and there he abode.
v.41 And many resorted unto him, and said, John did no miracle: but all things that John spake of this man were true.
v.42 And many believed on him there."

31 Here we have the reaction of the Jews. The word "again" stems from 8:59 (see 11:8); they sought to kill Him merely because of emotional instincts, unjustly without affording Him the opportunity of a fair trial. They thus went even beyond the Roman law, for at that time the Jews were not allowed to put a man to death by their own methods (18:31). Unconverted Saul exhibited similar base emotions when confronted with the testimony of the early believers; he was "exceedingly mad against them" (Acts 26:11).

32 *The Lord speaks.* The Lord knew that there was no point in referring to His Person, though He would constantly refer to "my Father" whatever the reaction of the Jews. He therefore mentioned His works, for these were such that men could believe in them to lead to higher knowledge (v.36). Previously He had said that His works bore witness of Himself (5:36), so men were without excuse. Even the man with restored eyesight drew proper conclusions from the Lord's miracle (9:30-33).

33 *The Jews speak.* The Jews recognised the fact that good works had been done, though they could not explain their origin. So illogically, they accused the Lord of blasphemy, rather than recognise the power of God. Their accusation goes back to 5:17 when the Lord said, "My Father worketh hitherto, and I work", from which they concluded that the Lord made Himself God. That statement was the cause of most of the opposition and hatred against the Lord subsequently. Thus they were content to own only that the Lord was "a man", and at His trial before Pilate they brought out this same accusation, "by our law he ought to die, because he made himself the Son of God" (19:7). However, the reality behind the situation was that, whereas they accused Him of blasphemy (see Matt 9:3 for another example of this, when the Lord was forgiving sins), they themselves were the ones really guilty of this offence (John 10:20; Matt 12:24).

34-36 *The Lord speaks.* Here we find a very unusual OT justification of the Sonship of Christ. The quotation in "your law" is taken from Ps 82, "God . . . judgeth among the gods . . . I have said, Ye are gods; and all of you are children of the most High. But ye shall die like men" (vv.1,6,7). It is remarkable that certain men are called "gods" (*elohim*), usually referring to idols, but on a few occasions the word is translated "judges" (Exod 21:6; 22:8-9). This word *elohim* is, of course, also the OT name of God, occurring well over two thousand times. Similarly, "Thou shalt not revile the gods (marg. judges)" (Exod 22:28) is quoted by Paul as "Thou shalt not speak evil of the ruler of thy people" (Acts 23:5). In Ps 82, having planted these judges among men, God as the supreme Judge examined how this His plan was working through these judges. All He found was that these judges were unjust, afflicting the poor, although they were "children (sons, LXX) of the most High", and so they would die like men when God the true Judge judged the earth.

The Lord interpreted this in a literal manner, stating that "the scripture cannot be broken". Taking the word "gods" as a divine title applying to Himself as Judge, being "sanctified" or set apart for this work, there was nothing wrong with the conclusion that He was the Son of God. Ps 82:6 is eminently fulfilled in Christ, as if He were saying, "Thou art God, the Son of the Father".

37-38 The Lord concluded His remarks in these verses. The only valid grounds for unbelief would be if He were not doing the works of the Father, but this was impossible. At the end of His life He said in prayer, "I have finished the work that thou gavest me to do" (17:4)—nothing more and nothing less. And although the knowledge of His works should lead to a knowledge of His Person, yet the Lord stated that even if the Jews did not believe His Person, yet they should believe His works, for faith in the latter would lead to faith in the former, if men were honest with their convictions. The ultimate of faith is to know that "the Father is in me, and I in him". Even on logical grounds, if X contains all of Y and Y contains all of X, then X and Y are equal. But the educated Pharisees were not educated in the obvious!

39 All the implications of the Lord's words were not accepted: the Lord's works, their OT Scriptures, and God-given logic, were all discarded. So they resorted to violence, namely the last resource of those who are thoroughly beaten verbally. John, in recording this conversation, had been leading up to this end. In 7:32, they had sent "officers" to take Him, but here the Pharisees tried to take Him directly. Since His hour was not yet come, He escaped. Similarly, Paul escaped many times until the hour of his departure arrived (Acts 9:25; 14:19; 16:26-39; 17:10; 23:14; 27:44; 2 Tim 4:17).

40-42 The Lord left Jerusalem completely, Bethabara being the place where John baptised at first (1:28). By "there he abode" it is not clear whether He remained there until ch.11 opens. Those who prepare "harmonies" of the Gospels, or maps of the Lord's itineraries, have differing ideas as to the events between 10:42 and 11:1. We can mention two very distinct schemes:

1. No recorded events took place between 10:42 and 11:1, but *after* 11:54, Luke 13:1 to 19:28; Matt 19-20 and Mark 10 should be inserted.
2. By contrast, *between* these two verses there should be placed Luke 13:23 to 18:30 with the corresponding passages in Matthew and Mark.

Many beyond Jordan speak. These people recalled the ministry of John the Baptist several years before, and contrasted him with the Lord. John did no miracle, but the Lord was performing miracles. Yet they realised that John's testimony concerning the forthcoming Christ was completely true. Miracles (or signs) were not necessary to produce faith; rather preaching, repentance, baptism and a testimony concerning Christ were essential.

The fact that many believed is something that often occurred; see 7:31; 8:30; 11:45; 12:11,42. Whether this was a faith in His Person, or just a non-rejection (rather than an acceptance) is difficult to assess; no doubt each case is different, and the Lord knows those who are His (2 Tim 2:19).

VII. The Resurrection and the Life Rejected (11:1-57)

1. *Before the Lord Came to Bethany* 11:1-16

v.1 "Now a certain *man* was sick, *named* Lazarus, of Bethany, the town of Mary and her sister Martha.

v.2 (It was *that* Mary which anointed the Lord with ointment, and wiped his feet with her hair, whose brother Lazarus was sick.)
v.3 Therefore his sisters sent unto him, saying, Lord, behold, he whom thou lovest is sick.
v.4 When Jesus heard *that*, he said, This sickness is not unto death, but for the glory of God, that the Son of God might be glorified thereby.
v.5 Now Jesus loved Martha, and her sister, and Lazarus.
v.6 When he had heard therefore that he was sick, he abode two days still in the same place where he was.
v.7 Then after that saith he to *his* disciples, Let us go into Judaea again.
v.8 *His* disciples say unto him, Master, the Jews of late sought to stone thee; and goest thou thither again?
v.9 Jesus answered, Are there not twelve hours in the day? If any man walk in the day, he stumbleth not, because he seeth the light of this world.
v.10 But if a man walk in the night, he stumbleth, because there is no light in him.
v.11 These things said he: and after that he saith unto them, Our friend Lazarus sleepeth; but I go, that I may awake him out of sleep.
v.12 Then said his disciples, Lord, if he sleep, he shall do well.
v.13 Howbeit Jesus spake of his death: but they thought that he had spoken of taking of rest in sleep.
v.14 Then said Jesus unto them plainly, Lazarus is dead.
v.15 And I am glad for your sakes that I was not there, to the intent ye may believe; nevertheless let us go unto him.
v.16 Then said Thomas, which is called Didymus, unto his fellow-disciples, Let us also go, that we may die with him."

1-2 We note that chs.5-21 of John's Gospel can be subdivided: "Conflict (chs.5-12); Communion (chs.13-17); Completion (chs.18-21)". So conflict continues.

The object of the seventh sign in this chapter was to present the next "I am" title (v.25), to develop faith (v.15), to glorify the Son of God (v.4), and to enable men to see the glory of God (v.40). It might seem that by means of death, Satan had plucked Lazarus out of the hand of the Good Shepherd; the miracle shows that death has no power over one of the Lord's sheep—there is safety in His hand. Moreover, the raising of Lazarus prefigures His own resurrection, though with many differences later to be described.

A summary of the chapter is as follows: The message sent to the Lord (vv.1-6); The Lord proposed to go to Jerusalem (vv.7-16); The meeting of Martha with the Lord (vv.17-27); The meeting of Mary with the Lord (vv.28-32); The Lord's grief at the grief of others (vv.33-38); The miracle of life (vv.39-44); The division amongst the onlookers (vv.45-46); The plot to take the Lord (vv.47-57).

Readers of the Synoptic Gospels would know of Bethany (Matt 21:17), a village on the eastern slopes of the mount of Olives. They would also know of Mary and Martha (Luke 10:38-42), but they would not know of Lazarus. So here John provided the necessary details for an overall understanding of the event. In v.1, the identity of Lazarus is given, both personally (his family association) and geographically (his own village); in v.2, his spiritual identity is given. In other words, of each sheep the Lord knows the answer to the questions, Who? Where? What? He was the brother of Mary, whose deed of love made such an impression (12:3). This deed of love was quite distinct from that of another woman recorded in Luke 7:37-50; we also believe that it was distinct from the similar event recorded in Matt 26:6-13; Mark 14:3-9, because of the difference in time, although there is much in common between the two events.

This description of the spiritual act of Mary is given so as to avoid confusion with the Mary of 20:11, namely with Mary Magdalene. Mary of Bethany looked forward to His burial, but Mary Magdalene was associated with events after His burial. Compare (i) the identification tag of betrayal always given to Judas to distinguish him from the other Judas; (ii) the identification "the disciple whom Jesus loved" that John often attached to himself; (iii) "the man who made Israel to sin" usually attached to Jeroboam in the OT.

3 *The sisters speak.* From their sending to the Lord, it is evident that the sisters knew where He dwelt beyond Jordan. This contrasts with 1:38 where Andrew and another had to ask Him, "where dwellest thou?". There is a lesson here for believers today: either they do know or they do not know where the Lord is to be found amongst those who gather in His Name (Matt 18:20). Mary and Martha did not use the name Lazarus, rather, "He whom thou lovest is sick". Thus the Lord loved Lazarus in his life (v.5), in his sickness (v.3), and in his death (v.36). Truly, "neither death, nor life ... nor things present ... shall be able to separate us from the love of God, which is in Christ Jesus our Lord" (Rom 8:37-38).

4 *The Lord speaks.* He immediately places the whole set of events upon a higher plane. He implied that this sickness was not designed to terminate in death but rather that it should lead to the extended glory of God and of the Son of God by means of a work of triumphal power. Glory was predominant in the signs and works of the Lord here below: the first sign showed forth His glory (2:11); answered prayer glorifies the Father in the Son (14:13); the Son would be glorified by reason of the offering of Himself (17:1,5). As far as death was concerned, this was but a transition, leading to life again:

1. In relation to the Lord, He lay down His life that He might take it again (10:17). We also read of "the sufferings of Christ, and the glory that should follow" (1 Pet 1:11).

2. In relation to the church, those "which sleep in Jesus ... the dead in Christ shall rise first" (1 Thess 4:14,16).

3. In relation to Israel, "the casting away of them ... life from the dead" (Rom 11:15). See also Ezek 37:1-14; Dan 12:2.

5 In this statement of the divine love for the family, Mary's name is omitted, no doubt to show that her particular devotion (v.2) did not exclude love for the other two in the family. Moreover, the statement of this love would remove doubt in the readers' minds that there was any lack of love for Lazarus on account of the Lord remaining where He was for two days after having heard the news, rather than doing anything outwardly and immediately.

6 In fact, by remaining a further two days beyond Jordan, the Lord would allow fallen nature to do its worst and Lazarus would die. This was necessary so as to allow Himself to be seen as the Resurrection and the Life, and not only as "the Lord that healeth thee" (Exod 15:26). In fact the four days mentioned in v.39 would even allow the decomposition process to commence, something that did not happen to the Lord's body in death, for this body did not see corruption (Ps 16:10; Acts 2:31; 13:35-37).

7-8 *The Lord speaks.* In the region beyond Jordan, it was the Lord who initiated the conversation after two days; He made the proposal to return to Judaea, where Jerusalem was the centre of opposition against Him. Although He had escaped in 10:19, men had no power against Him until His hour had come. He had not escaped on account of fear, but to prevent men's hatred from reaching its apex until His hour. This was quite unlike several men in the OT who fled for different motives, such as Moses (Exod 2:15), David (1 Sam 19:12) and Elijah (1 Kings 19:3).

The disciples speak. By addressing the Lord as "Master", they used the word "Rabbi", not the word for Teacher. They did not appreciate the Lord's motives, and could only visualise danger. What the Jews had done recently (10:31), they could as easily do again, perhaps with disastrous results, as they thought. They reckoned without the "determinate counsel and foreknowledge of God" (Acts 2:23).

9-10 *The Lord speaks.* The Lord provided a little parable, involving daytime, nighttime and stumbling. Two interpretations can be suggested:

1. The twelve hours of work correspond to the years of His ministry when on earth; during that time He could not stumble in the sense that men had no power over Him. There can be no danger until the end of the day. V.10 would not apply to Him, implying that it was impossible for any disaster to fall upon Him.

2. "The light of this world" can apply to the Lord, who used this title several times (9:5). The day corresponds to the period when men could look

upon Him with love and understanding. The night corresponds to the time of His absence, when the hearts of men are even more full of unbelief. The light, as an open divine testimony on earth, would cease when the day turned into night; men would stumble when they crucified Him.

11 With this little parable ended, the Lord spoke directly, or perhaps metaphorically, using the verb "sleep". Apart from "my friends", in Luke 12:4, only John used the word "friend" (*philos*) as seen from the divine point of view. We have "our friend" (11:11), "his friends" (15:13), "my friends" (15:14), "friends" (15:15), so distinct from being "a friend of the world" (James 4:4).

There are two verbs in the NT used for "sleep":

1. *Koimaomai*, used in v.11 in the perfect tense *kekoimētai*, indicating an act of having fallen asleep, with the results still present. This word is always used of physical death, except in Matt 28:13; Luke 22:45; John 11:12 (misunderstood by the disciples); Acts 12:6. This word is used in the two resurrection chapters (1 Cor 15:18,20,51; 1 Thess 4:13,14,15), "we shall not all sleep", "them also which sleep in Jesus".

2. *Katheudō*, used of physical sleep, except in connection with the damsel (Matt 9:24; Mark 5:39; Luke 8:52), and metaphorically in contrast to watchfulness (Mark 13:36; Eph 5:14; 1 Thess 5:6,7,10). Note that the two different words are used in 1 Thess 4 and 1 Thess 5 respectively. Only the former passage refers to the rapture.

When the Lord expressed His intention to "awake him out of sleep", the word "sleep" does not occur in the Greek text; only one word appears "to rouse" (*exupnizō*), occurring only here in the NT. The accomplishment of a sign or miracle was implied.

12-13 *The disciples speak.* No doubt Peter as spokesman voiced this opinion, and the other apostles acquiesced. By saying, "if he sleep, he shall do well", they used the same perfect tense of the verb for "sleep" as did the Lord. The word for "he shall do well" is *sōthēsetai*, namely "he shall be saved" (see RV and Newberry margins). They recognised the therapeutic value of rest and sleep, but failed to understand the meaning of the Lord's words. To associate a literal meaning with a metaphorical statement can manifest lack of faith. This usual misunderstanding on the part of the disciples pervades all the Gospels. In John's Gospel, various kinds of misunderstandings are found in verses such as 4:31-32; 6:7; 9:2; 13:8-9.

In v.13, the apostle John corrects their (and his) misunderstanding and spells out their (and his) error and supposition, by inserting this sentence many years later when he wrote his Gospel. For the maintenance of the truth and for the exact record of historical facts, such self-criticism is necessary on occasions even on the part of an apostle. No doubt experience is necessary in order to show how to interpret metaphorical statements correctly, as in the cases of the temple (2:21-22), of the living water (4:11-15), of food (4:31-33), and of the expression "a little while" (16:17).

14-15 *The Lord speaks.* Realising that His disciples failed to understand the meaning of "sleep", the Lord said "Lazarus is dead". The record states that this is "plainly". Similarly in 16:29, the apostles said, "now speakest thou plainly", using the same word *parresia* for "plainly", adding that the Lord now no longer used an allegory (or proverb). No doubt this is an example of those who require milk and not strong meat (Heb 5:12).

The fact that the Lord was glad that He had not been in Bethany when Lazarus was ill and when he died implies that otherwise He would have healed Lazarus, and the present miracle would not have taken place. This would have been a loss to those who already had faith, for the sign was intended to increase their faith. As they said elsewhere, "Lord, increase our faith" (Luke 17:5). Paul, like the Lord, was glad that he could write of the Thessalonians, "your faith groweth exceedingly" (2 Thess 1:3). The Lord arranges circumstances in life, so that faith may grow, and that His people can see His glory through these circumstances. The Lord's remark, "let us go" reminds us of 14:31, "let us go hence", the former to raise Lazarus, the latter to His own death and resurrection.

16 *Thomas speaks.* Apart from references in John's Gospel, this apostle appears only in four lists of the apostles' names (Matt 10:3; Mark 3:18; Luke 6:15; Acts 1:13). John has used the additional description "called Didymus" (namely, twin) on three occasions (11:16; 20:24; 21:2), evidently to distinguish him from another apostle, though which one is not stated. He manifested fatalism (11:16), ignorance (14:5), doubt (20:24-29), and worldly occupation (21:2). All these weaknesses were transformed by the Lord on each occasion.

The concept of "fellowdisciples" is important, suggesting that they had common objectives and interests, with lives lived for their Lord. Paul likewise made mention of fellowworker, fellowsoldier, fellowprisoner. However, Thomas' suggestion to go with the Lord to Judaea, "that we may die with him", savours of the fatalistic. He would be bold when there was no danger, but when danger threatened, they all "forsook him, and fled" (Matt 26:56). They wanted to preserve their lives for as long as possible, in spite of the Lord's teaching in Matt 16:25. In fact, they would act like the hireling in 10:12-13.

2. *Martha and Mary Meet the Lord*
11:17-37

v.17 "Then when Jesus came, he found that he had *lain* in the grave four days already.

v.18 Now Bethany was nigh unto Jerusalem, about fifteen furlongs off;

v.19 And many of the Jews came to Martha and Mary, to comfort them concerning their brother.
v.20 Then Martha, as soon as she heard that Jesus was coming, went and met him: but Mary sat *still* in the house.
v.21 Then said Martha unto Jesus, Lord, if thou hadst been here, my brother had not died.
v.22 But I know, that even now, whatsoever thou wilt ask of God, God will give *it* thee.
v.23 Jesus saith unto her, Thy broher shall rise again.
v.24 Martha saith unto him, I know that he shall rise again in the resurrection at the last day.
v.25 Jesus said unto her, I am the resurrection, and the life: he that believeth in me, though he were dead, yet shall he live:
v.26 And whosoever liveth and believeth in me shall never die. Believest thou this?
v.27 She saith unto him, Yea, Lord: I believe that thou art the Christ, the Son of God, which should come into the world.
v.28 And when she had so said, she went her way, and called Mary her sister secretly, saying, The Master is come, and calleth for thee.
v.29 As soon as she heard *that*, she arose quickly, and came unto him.
v.30 Now Jesus was not yet come into the town, but was in that place where Martha met him.
v.31 The Jews then which were with her in the house, and comforted her, when they saw Mary, that she rose up hastily and went out, followed her, saying, She goeth unto the grave to weep there.
v.32 Then when Mary was come where Jesus was, and saw him, she fell down at his feet, saying unto him, Lord, if thou hadst been here, my brother had not died.
v.33 When Jesus therefore saw her weeping, and the Jews also weeping which came with her, he groaned in the spirit, and was troubled,
v.34 And said, Where have ye laid him? They said unto him, Lord, come and see.
v.35 Jesus wept.
v.36 Then said the Jews, Behold how he loved him!
v.37 And some of them said, Could not his man, which opened the eyes of the blind, have caused that even this man should not have died?"

17-19 The fact that the record states that the Lord found that Lazarus had lain in the tomb for four days does not mean that the Lord did not know of this previously. Rather, the four days are mentioned to show the greatness of the following sign or miracle. Many miracles present the worst possible state prior to the miracle being performed, such as no wine, no food, an infirmity for thirty-eight years, and here a man dead for four days. Such signs show to faithful hearts "the exceeding greatness of his power" (Eph 1:19), but modern unbelief seeks to explain away every miracle in spite of the strongest evidence.

This tomb must have been a private one near Bethany, on account of the stone placed at its entrance. By stating that Bethany was "fifteen furlongs" (about two miles) from Jerusalem, John intended to convey to his readers the nearness of the Pharisaical danger, and from whence many of the Jews had come. Bethany was the village where the Lord would pass the night seasons during His last week before His crucifixion (Matt 21:17; Luke 21:37), and the place of His ascension (Luke 24:50; Acts 1:12). It is good that there should have been earthly comfort for the Lord in Bethany during those nights, no doubt in the home of Mary and Martha, but this is no substitute for divine comfort and the presence of the Father.

Clearly the family had many acquaintances in Jerusalem, and these came out to Bethany to offer comfort in the time of distress. These Jews are seen in the house (v.31), at the tomb (v.36), and exercising faith afterwards (v.45), but some were more disposed towards the Pharisees than towards the Lord (v.46). Grief is a natural reaction that cannot be stifled, though artificiality is hypocritical (Matt 9:23); thus lamentation was made over Stephen after his death (Acts 8:2) and over Dorcas (9:39). By contrast, king Jehoram "departed without being desired" (2 Chron 21:20).

20 Clearly Martha knew the way that the Lord would take to Bethany, and knew that He was near, for news travelled before Him. Thus she was able to meet Him. Similarly, the Lord's people will rise to meet the Lord in the air at His coming (1 Thess 4:15-17), a hope that brings comfort now. But Mary "sat still in the house", perhaps a sign of her continued grief, yet showing that she was the passive sister while Martha was the active one. Thus in Luke 10:39, Mary sat at His feet and heard His word, while Martha was occupied with details of the hospitality. It is a question of priorities, and no one should criticise from a personal point of view a fellowbeliever, whether he be active or passive. We are all different, but the Lord desires faithfulness and sincerity. To do something out of keeping with our character merely because of others is nothing but hypocrisy.

21-22 *Martha speaks.* She addressed Him as "Lord" (*kurie*), rightly translated thus, for she knew Him in a deeper way than implied by a mere "Sir". By saying, "if thou hadst been here, my brother had not died", she was thinking back to the past, to his illness, that the Lord would have healed him. She had no open thought of a present miracle; perhaps she had no knowledge of the Lord's other miracles when He had raised persons from the dead (Matt 11:5). Note that her statement is identical with that of Mary later in v.32; evidently they had discussed the matter at home and found that they had identical trust and knowledge. Consistency at home led to consistency away from home in the Lord's presence. But this should be contrasted with the event in Acts 5:1-11, where consistency at home also led to consistency in the apostles' presence, in this case lying to the Holy Spirit.

And yet she would leave her thoughts of the past, and in v.22 would express a vague hope—perhaps present, perhaps future. She did not rise to the height of confessing the Deity of Christ; she thought that His request would be made to, and answered by, God, thereby bypassing His divine power and Person. However, there was progress in her faith, as in the case of the man in ch.9.

23 *The Lord speaks.* In the great promise "Thy brother shall rise again", the verb *anistēmi* appears, largely used of the physical act of standing upright, but often for resurrection, either with or without the added word "again" (thus the word "again" is not used in Mark 9:9,31; 12:23,25 etc.). By this statement, the Lord appears to have been testing Martha, using an all-embracive statement to test what Martha really believed, since by "rise" one can understand either the forthcoming miracle or the resurrection of a future day (as understood then by the Jews, lacking a fuller revelation of the truth).

24 *Martha speaks.* In her confession, Martha made no reference to an immediate miracle. Her ideas about resurrection would derive from the OT, such as Job's declaration, "though after my skin worms destroy this body, yet in my flesh shall I see God" (Job 19:26), the psalmist's statement "I shall not die but live, and declare the works of the Lord" (Ps 118:17), and as the prophet's words, "many of them that sleep in the dust of the earth shall awake, some to everlasting life . . . " (Dan 12:2); also from the Pharisees' doctrine (Acts 23:8), and the Lord's own teaching about eternal life (John 3:16; 5:28-29). But Martha's mention of the "last day" shows that she had no idea about the distinction between various types of resurrection, namely that at the rapture and that at the commencement of the millennium. In non-evangelical circles today, it is usual to consider one resurrection day only, without distinguishing between differences taught in the NT.

25-26 *The Lord speaks.* The Lord graciously intervened in her state of grief. He showed her His Person, that He too would pass that way (though without seeing corruption). This is another of the great "I am" titles, *hē anastasis kai hē zōē*, namely, "the resurrection and the life". Because He is this, therefore He grants this to others. This title corresponds to Rev 1:18 (lit.) "I am the living one, and became dead; and behold, I am living for evermore". This is an important matter for faith, since if a believer doubts his own resurrection, then he also doubts the Lord's resurrection (1 Cor 15:16). Truly, the Lord gave Himself this name "resurrection", but the men of Athens were so ignorant that they thought that "Jesus, and the resurrection" were two deities (Acts 17:18).

V.25 implies that physical death in a man of faith will lead to resurrection, but v.26 implies that a man of faith, now living, will never partake of spiritual death. This latter truth is seen in verses such as, "If a man keep my saying, he shall never see death" (8:51), and "God is not the God of the dead, but of the living" (Matt 22:32).

27-28 *Martha speaks.* Her confession, "Yea, Lord", to the Lord's question, "Believest thou this?", shows that she believed the Lord's words (though not, we feel, with complete understanding). Nothing that the Lord had said really referred to the miracle that He was about to perform. His remarks apply to all believers, and were not intended to refer to one particular man, Lazarus.

Martha's great confession, "thou art the Christ, the Son of God, which should come into the world" goes beyond the answer expected to the Lord's question. Her knowledge of doctrine was perhaps somewhat vague, but under these circumstances it is better to know His Person. She believed that He was the expected Christ, an expectation known from the OT; clearly her faith and knowledge went beyond that of John the Baptist, who asked from prison whether the Lord were "he that should come" (Matt 11:3). But her knowledge of "the Son of God" must have been based on revelation and not on mere hearsay or rumour. Note the various confessions recorded in the Gospels:

1. His Power: "Of a truth thou art the Son of God" (Matt 14:33).
2. His Preaching: "we believe . . . that thou art . . . the Son of the living God" (6:69).
3. His Promise: "I believe that thou art . . . the Son of God" (11:27).
4. His Person: "Thou art . . . the Son of the living God" (Matt 16:16).

Leaving the Lord after having made so great a confession was no disrespect on Martha's part—rather it was a matter of urgent testimony and seeking, as in 1:40 when Andrew left the Lamb of God to find his brother Peter. She found her sister secretly to inform her of the Lord's nearness and of His desire to see her. This was reserved for Mary only—a close meeting of a believer with the Lord, with worldly comforters kept at a distance. The sanctuary is reserved for the Lord's people, when even the testimony of the gospel to others is out of place. The Lord calls us to go forth unto Him (Heb 13:13), though when He was here below many "would not" (Matt 23:37).

29-31 Mary made no delay in coming to the Lord, unlike the excuses that men made in Luke 9:59-61 when they should follow Him. One man even wanted to bury his father, failing to see that the true Life was calling him. A delay means to turn back, and then one is "not fit for the kingdom of God". Thus even Abraham delayed in following God's commandment to get out of his country, to go "into the land which I shall show thee" (Acts 7:3). He came halfway to Charran, where he delayed until his father was dead (v.4).

Yet the Lord deliberately delayed entering Bethany, allowing time for Martha to return home and for Mary to come out to meet Him in the same place. The Lord waits for us, but we should not keep the Lord waiting, though it is often popular practice for believers to arrive late for meetings, thereby keeping those who have gathered, and the Lord Himself, waiting for the meeting to begin! The Lord would wish for contact to be made by His own people coming to Him rather than by Him coming to them.

The Jews speak. The Jews who were attempting to comfort Mary watched her leave the house, and immediately came to the wrong conclusion, and sought to follow her to the grave. Worldly acquaintances can so often misunderstand the action of believers, particularly if these are spiritual actions. But they saw where she went, to Life and not to death, though only Mary was privileged to share in the most holy conversation with the Lord. His was the true comfort, unlike that of the Jews. (Note how the apostles often misunderstood the action of the Lord in their midst: v.16; 13:6-9,29.)

32 Mary came, saw, fell and spoke. Here was affection, reverence and need. In Luke 10:39, she "sat at Jesus' feet, and heard his word". Here was fellowship and learning of Him. In Song of Songs 2:3, the loved one said, "I sat down under his shadow with great delight". In Mark 14:18, John (with others) sat with the Lord, but on the isle of Patmos, he "fell at his feet as dead" (Rev 1:17), while later the four living creatures and the twenty-four elders fell down before the Lamb (5:8). The circumstances of the time dictate the suitable posture before the Lord—reverence is essential at all times, even if one sits or kneels before Him in prayer (1 Chron 17:16; Acts 20:36; 21:5). Even the blessed Saviour could fall down upon His face in the garden of Gethsemane (Matt 26:39); "he . . . fell on the ground" (Mark 14:35); "he . . . kneeled down, and prayed" (Luke 22:41).

Mary speaks. In our v.32, Mary spoke the same words as Martha had done in v.21. Like her sister, she thought only of what the Lord could have done had Lazarus been alive. As we have pointed out before, these identical statements must have arisen through the sisters having discussed the matter previously in their home.

33-34 The Lord had tested Martha's understanding, and had revealed Himself to her as the Resurrection and the Life. But the simplicity of Mary's weeping before Him caused the Lord to treat Mary differently—works and not words were necessary in this case. The Jews were also weeping, and He saw them. They would remain respectfully a little way apart, so that Mary alone should approach to her Lord; the sanctuary was for her alone.

The statement, "he groaned in spirit, and was troubled", reflects upon the true humanity of the Lord, as does v.35, "Jesus wept". This word "groan" (*embrimaomai*) appears only five times in the NT; its root is *brimē* meaning strength. It can be translated to be painfully moved, to express indignation, to rebuke sternly and to charge strictly (Matt 9:30; Mark 1:43; 14:5). The verb "was troubled" (lit., "he troubled himself", *tarassō*) occurs seventeen times in the NT: of the Lord (12:27; 13:21) in relation to His forthcoming hour and to the fact that there was one who would betray Him; of Zacharias (Luke 1:12); of Herod (Matt 2:3); of the apostles (Matt 14:26; Luke 24:38); of the water at the pool of Bethesda (5:4,7); of believers negatively (14:1,27), and of trouble-makers inside and outside a local church (Acts 15:24; Gal 1:7; 5:10). This wealth of usage will help the reader to assess the inner experience of the Lord as He contemplated both the ravages of sin, and the burden sustained by Mary and Martha. He wept in sympathy with those who were truly weeping, as Paul wrote later, "weep with them that weep" (Rom 12:15). We note, however, that the Lord did not desire that people should weep for Him (Luke 23:27-28).

The Lord speaks. He asked a simple question in love, "Where have ye laid him?", not that He needed this information. But such questions brought out the hearts of those addressed, such as "Whence shall we buy bread?" (6:5-6); "have ye any meat?" (21:5). In all cases, the Lord personally knew.

Mary and Martha speak. Their simple reply, "Lord, come and see", betrays the fact that their hearts were too full for words. It is interesting to trace the word "come" in this record:

1. When Jesus first came to the vicinity of Bethany (v.17).
2. The Jews came to Mary and Martha (v.19).
3. Martha heard that Jesus was coming (v.20).
4. The Christ who should come into the world (v.27).
5. Martha's words, "The Master is come" (v.28).
6. Mary came to the Lord (v.29).
7. Jesus was not yet come to Bethany (v.30).
8. When Mary was come to the Lord (v.32).
9. The Jews which came with Mary (v.33).
10. "Lord, come and see" (v.34).
11. The Lord came to the grave (v.38).
12. Lazarus came forth (v.44).
13. Many of the Jews who came to Mary (v.45).

However, not all these occurrences of "come" and its derivatives are represented by the same Greek verb; the interested reader should consult a concordance to ascertain the differences. The same may be said about the word "go" and its derivatives. There was a lot of movement, but in reverence and quietness.

35 This shortest verse in the Bible, "Jesus wept", is aptly descriptive of the tender humanity of the Lord. He wept on account of the grief of the sisters, not because Lazarus was dead, for only He knew exactly what was implied by his death, and the fact that he was about to regain his life. The other record in the Gospels of the Lord weeping is found in Luke 19:41, "he beheld the city, and wept over it" at the realisation that the enemies of Jerusalem (the Roman's) would destroy the city, so that not one stone would be left on another—because the citizens knew not the time of their visitation. The references to weeping in the OT are too numerous to mention, though a concordance would show the many matters that caused men of God to weep, matters about which today the people of God would not shed even one tear.

In the NT, Paul was the apostle of weeping:

1. He was working with tears (Acts 20:19).

2. He was warning with tears (Acts 20:31).

3. He was writing with tears (2 Cor 22:4).

4. He was walking with tears (Phil 3:18).

36 *The Jews speak.* Their statement "Behold how he loved him" is perfectly correct, but it really represents another misapprehension on their part. Their first misunderstanding occurred in v.31 as to why Mary left the house; now they misunderstand the Lord's tears as referring to Lazarus, whereas His weeping related to the two sisters and their grief.

37 *Some of the Jews speak.* They now demonstrate a third misunderstanding. What Martha and Mary had said explicitly in vv.21,32, is now expressed as a question; the fact that the opening of the blind man's eyes is mentioned shows that that miracle was still outstanding news. But a question is not a manifestation of faith, for these Jews knew nothing of the divine purpose in allowing Lazarus to die without prior divine intervention. The people would rejoice in the fact that there was power to open a blind man's eyes, but they themselves were blind to the fact that their religious leaders, the Pharisees, remained blind, a fact repeated five times later when the Lord condemned these Pharisees (Matt 23:16,17,19,24,26).

3. *The Seventh Sign: Life from the Grave* 11:38-46

v.38 "Jesus therefore again groaning in himself cometh to the grave. It was a cave, and a stone lay upon it.

v.39 Jesus said, Take ye away the stone. Martha, the sister of him that was dead, saith unto him, Lord, by this time he stinketh: for he hath been *dead* four days.

v.40 Jesus saith unto her, Said I not unto thee, that, if thou wouldest believe, thou shouldest see the glory of God?

v.41 Then they took away the stone *from the place* where the dead was laid. And Jesus lifted up *his* eyes, and said, Father, I thank thee that thou hast heard me.

v.42 And I knew that thou hearest me always: but because of the people which stand by I said *it*, that they may believe that thou hast sent me.

v.43 And when he thus had spoken, he cried with a loud voice, Lazarus, come forth.

v.44 And he that was dead came forth, bound hand and foot with graveclothes: and his face was bound about with a napkin. Jesus saith unto them, Loose him, and let him go.

v.45 Then many of the Jews which came to Mary, and had seen the things which Jesus did, believed on him.

v.46 But some of them went their ways to the Pharisees, and told them what things Jesus had done."

38 The Lord still feeling the intense grief in Himself, no doubt allowed the two sisters to lead the way to the grave, which was a cave with a stone. This indicated that the family was not poor, but possessed a cave of their own for burial purposes. In the Lord's case, He was poor as far as worldly possessions were concerned, yet "made his grave . . . with the rich in his death" (Isa 53:9) on account of loving hands having placed His body in a borrowed sepulchre.

There are many contrasts between the death and raising of Lazarus on the one hand, and the death and resurrection of the Lord on the other. Thus the miracle would not detract from the power of His own resurrection. We may tabulate these differences as follows:

	The Case of Lazarus	*The Case of the Lord*
1.	He died because he was ill.	He died voluntarily.
2.	He would not have died.	He must die.
3.	In the grave four days.	Raised on the third day.
4.	His body saw corruption.	He saw no corruption.
5.	It was a family grave.	It was a borrowed sepulchre.
6.	It was a cave.	It had been hewn out of the rock.
7.	Men took the stone away.	The angel rolled back the stone.
8.	Lazarus emerged bound.	The clothes remained in place.
9.	Some went to tell the Pharisees.	Some went to show the priests.
10.	The priests wanted to kill him again (this was a plot).	His disciples stole Him away (this was a lie).
11.	Many curious to see him.	No unbelievers saw Him as raised.
12.	He saw death again naturally.	Death had no more dominion over Him.
13.	An ordinary body again.	Glorified; passing through material things.

The Lord speaks. Knowing that His command would lead to consternation, the Lord said, "Take ye away the stone". This would be done, neither miraculously nor by an angel, when men could do it for themselves. We must do what we can in the service of God, but not step into the direct province of His own working.

Martha speaks. By stating "he stinketh", she still looked at the present unfavourable situation without faith, having no idea that a miracle was about to be performed. This verb *ozō*, to emit an offensive odour, shows that the normal corruption process had set in. This suggests that the body had not been embalmed with spices. These had been bought and kept in the house unused; Mary would use the ointment of spikenard in 12:3 as a token of the day of his burial, indicating a faith of quite a different nature.

40 *The Lord speaks.* He gave Martha a quiet word of rebuke (note He said "unto thee", to Martha alone, as if Mary did not share in her sentiments). In v.4, the Lord had told His disciples that Lazarus' sickness was "for the glory of God" and for His own glory as Son of God; He must have said a similar thing to Martha in the conversation in vv.23-26. This would not be His outward personal glory as on the mount of transfiguration, but glory seen in and through the sign about to be performed. Evidently faith leads to seeing; the converse is recorded in Deut 1:32,35, where lack of faith meant that the people would not see the promised land.

41-42 As we have pointed out, "they" took the stone away from the cave's entrance, unlike the resurrection of the Lord, when an angel rolled the stone back to demonstrate that the sepulchre was empty after having been sealed when the Lord's body had been placed there.

The Lord speaks. Although we read that the Lord "continued all night in prayer to God" (Luke 6:12), and that at other times He engaged in prayer (Luke 9:18,28; 11:1), we are not often privileged to hear His actual words. He gave thanks on several occasions (6:11; Luke 22:17,19), but again His actual words are not stated. His actual words in prayer are given in Matt 11:25, when He used the title, "O Father, Lord of heaven and earth"; in the garden of Gethsemane, when He said, "O my Father" (Matt 26:39); in John 12:27 when He said "Father"; and in ch.17 when He said "Father . . . O Father . . . Holy Father . . . O righteous Father" (vv.1,5,11,25). Here in 11:41, He said "Father". The use of a reverent scriptural title is essential today for prayer to be spiritual. The Lord also "lifted up his eyes", as He did in 17:1. Paul wrote of "lifting up holy hands" (1 Tim 2:8). There were those who could not lift up their eyes, such as the publican (Luke 18:13) and Ezra (Ezra 9:6).

The object of this brief prayer of the Lord was not to gain God's ear or His power—these were always available. In fact, the Son thanked the Father for hearing Him, even though He had not asked for the sign to be performed. Here was an aspect of His humanity that was always in unity with the will of the Father. Yet here were brief words spoken to the Father, with the intention that the people around should hear Him. This was unusual, for mostly prayer is in secret (Matt 6:6). Certainly it contrasts with His prayer in John 17, where only His own disciples must have heard Him, and with His prayer in the garden where no man heard Him. In fact, by this means, the Jews would know that it was the Father who was associated with this miracle, and not Beelzebub, as had been the accusation of the Pharisees before (Matt 12:24).

43 *The Lord speaks.* Here was the Lord's cry of a personal name, Lazarus, so that he only would come forth from the cave; certainly He calls His own sheep by name, not only now, but also in resurrection. As He said in 5:25, "the dead shall hear the voice of the Son of God". As far as the resurrection of believers at the rapture is concerned, "the trumpet shall sound" (1 Cor 15:52); moreover, "the Lord himself shall descend from heaven with a shout . . . with the trump of God" (1 Thess 4:16), and we would feel that this trump will be the voice of the Lord, for John heard His voice "as of a trumpet" on Patmos (Rev 1:10; 4:1).

44 We have already drawn attention to the differences between the raising of Lazarus and the resurrection of the Lord. Lazarus was bound with the graveclothes, for what the people could do the Lord would not do. In the Lord's case, His actual resurrection was unseen by His disciples; they could not have given Him garments suitable for resurrection, and so the linen clothes remained in the sepulchre. Lazarus came back to an ordinary life again, so his body could not have passed through the graveclothes, neither through the walls of the cave had the stone not been taken away. But the Lord returned in resurrection life on the other side of death; hence His holy body could pass through the linen clothes, and through the sides of the sealed sepulchre.

The Lord speaks. It was because Lazarus was impotent to help himself (except to walk out of the tomb) that the Lord commanded, "Loose him, and let him go". Others loosed him, suggesting the work of the evangelist helping a soul to pass from death unto life by means of faith, and commencing the walk of the christian pathway.

45-46 Here was the inevitable division that such an extraordinary sign would cause. This has also been the experience of evangelists throughout the ages; when Paul in prison in Rome expounded to the Jews the truth from the OT Scriptures, the effect was, "some believed the things which were spoken, and some believed not" (Acts 28:24). In our present verse 45, we have one of the few signs that stimulated the exercise of faith. It seems that other Jews had used the occasion to spy for the Pharisees, so they went into Jerusalem to report to their masters. The chief priests and scribes "sent forth spies, which should feign themselves just men, that they might take hold of his words" (Luke 20:20).

4. *The Sanhedrin Plots against the Lord* 11:47-57

v.47 "Then gathered the chief priests and the Pharisees a council, and said, What do we? for this man doeth many miracles.
v.48 If we let him thus alone, all *men* will believe on him: and the Romans will come and take away both our place and nation.

v.49 And one of them, *named* Caiaphas, being the high priest that same year, said unto them, Ye know nothing at all,
v.50 Nor consider that it is expedient for us, that one man should die for the people, and that the whole nation perish not.
v.51 And this spake he not of himself: but being high priest that year, he prophesied that Jesus should die for that nation;
v.52 And not for that nation only, but that also he should gather together in one the children of God that were scattered abroad.
v.53 Then from that day forth they took counsel together for to put him to death.
v.54 Jesus therefore walked no more openly among the Jews; but went thence unto a country near to the wilderness, into a city called Ephraim, and there continued with his disciples.
v.55 And the Jews' passover was nigh at hand: and many went out of the country up to Jerusalem before the passover, to purify themselves.
v.56 Then sought they for Jesus, and spake among themselves, as they stood in the temple, What think ye, that he will not come to the feast?
v.57 Now both the chief priests and the Pharisees had given a commandment, that, if any man knew where he were, he should shew *it*, that they might take him."

47-48 *The chief priests and the Pharisees speak.* The chief priest and the Pharisees gathered "a council", namely the Sanhedrin (*sunedrion*). Although the Romans as the occupying power had the ultimate authority, yet this Jewish council possessed religious, judicial and administrative powers. Membership consisted of the high priest and men who had previously been high priests, Pharisees and Sadducees, and legal experts known as scribes or lawyers (Acts 4:1,4,5). Their religious convictions determined how they would react to matters under investigation (Acts 23:7-10). The president of the Sanhedrin was the high priest (5:17; 7:1; 9:1; 22:5; 23:2; 24:1). If they passed the death sentence, this had to be confirmed by the Roman procurator.

The high priests were chosen by Pilate, in opposition to the true Aaronic high priests who were chosen by God. Annas had been deposed by Pilate, being replaced by Caiaphas, but the Jews regarded both as high priests (Luke 3:2), and both took part in the Lord's trial before the Sanhedrin (18:13,24). This recalls the time during David's reign when there were two high priests, Abiathar and Zadok, the former being deposed by Solomon (1 Kings 2:27). Paul had the proper attitude towards the high priest of man's choosing, "I wist not, brethren, that he was the high priest" (Acts 23:5), which we understand literally, and not a mere lack of recognition because of bad eyesight.

They were forced by evidence to recognise that the Lord was doing many signs, and that He was gaining many disciples. They feared the Romans who were occupying their country, for they would not allow a popular Jewish leader to rise who, to them, was leading a takeover movement. Not that the Jews liked the Romans, but in such an event they feared that there would be a complete

Roman takeover, with the Sanhedrin losing its powers. When it pleased them, the Jews could appear to acquiesce in submitting to the Roman authority, by saying, "whosoever maketh himself a king speaketh against Caesar" (19:12), and "We have no king but Caesar" (v.15). However, the Lord took no part in Jewish or Roman politics, saying, "Render therefore unto Caesar the things which are Caesar's" (Matt 22:21).

49-50 *Caiaphas speaks.* This man claimed to have the solution to the problem, and boasted that the others were not clever enough to concoct a solution. This man made an entirely natural and evil statement, a man who showed no compassion as a priest (Heb 5:2). The fact that there was a spiritual prophecy wrought by God in his words was unusual, and quite unknown to him. (This reminds us of Balaam, who loved the wages of unrighteousness in his error, 2 Pet 2:15; Jude 11, and who in spite of himself expressed a prophetic blessing upon Israel, Num 24:16-19). By saying "that one man should die for the people, and that the whole nation perish not", he implied that the Lord was to be put to death, thereby removing the threat that He was causing (as they thought) to the existing relationship between them and the Romans. They reckoned without the promises in their own OT Scriptures, such as "the Redeemer shall come to Zion" (Isa 59:20); the nation may perish for a time, but not for ever.

The priest used the expression "one man". In a spiritual sense, Peter spoke on "no other name . . . whereby we must be saved" (Acts 4:12), while Paul wrote of "one man, Jesus Christ" (Rom 5:15,17,18,19), showing the Lord uniquely in contrast to Adam.

51-52 Caiaphas spake "not of himself", but "from himself" (*aph' heautou*), namely not out of his own heart. The evil intentions came from his own heart, of course, but the second meaning behind his words came from God Himself. God would use the evil heart of men to testify of Him under unusual and unexpected circumstances, no doubt a preview of that great day when "every tongue should confess that Jesus Christ is Lord, to the glory of God the Father" (Phil 2:11).

The spiritual meaning behind his words deals with the death of Christ for the Jewish nation, but in addition, this death would be the only unifying force amongst the nations—and yet not amongst the nations at large, but only for "the children of God that were scattered abroad". All the efforts of men and politicians can never introduce unity and harmony amongst the nations; this will be a millennial blessing brought about by the Lord when He rules with a rod of iron. This concept of unity amongst the people of God was prominent in John's mind as he opened his record. Thus he wrote "not of blood . . . but of God" (1:13) in a national sense; the Lamb who takes away "the sin of the world" (v.29); "God so loved the world" (3:16); he gave the story of the Samaritan woman who found Christ (4:7,26); he recorded the "other sheep" of the Gentile fold to be brought into the one flock (10:16). To fulfil the commandment that the gospel should go to "the uttermost part of the earth" (Acts 1:8), there was given to Peter the vision of the beasts in the sheet: what God had cleansed was not common or unclean, referring to the Gentiles being brought in (10:11-16,28). Paul's doctrine is taken up with this unity: what was far off has been made nigh by the blood of Christ; He has reconciled "both unto God in one body by the cross" (Eph 2:13,16; Gal 3:26-28).

Particularly the Jews have been scattered abroad, yet there is no difference between Jew and Gentile, in the matter of sin (Rom 3:9), in the matter of salvation (1:16; 10:12); in the matter of baptism (Gal 3:27-28), and in the matter of the local church (1 Cor 10:32).

53-54 There had been other attempts to kill the Lord Jesus (5:18), but this present attempt was the first serious attempt to eliminate Him from their midst. This united attempt is called "counsel", recalling "the counsel of the ungodly" (Ps 1:1), and "the rulers take counsel together, against the Lord, and against his anointed" (2:1-2). Thus we read briefly in v.54 of the final stages of the Lord's ministry outside Jerusalem. John mentioned only "a city called Ephraim", about fourteen miles north of Jerusalem and twelve miles north-west of Jericho, the story of Zacchaeus then taking place (Luke 18:1-10). All the four Gospel-writers record the Lord's next triumphant entry into Jerusalem at the beginning of the last week (12:12), though first He came to Bethany.

55-57 The last Passover was quickly approaching, so many Jews went up to Jerusalem. All males were under a legal obligation to go up at this feast (Exod 34:18,22-23); three times annually they had to go up at the dominant spring and autumn feasts, with Pentecost in between. On this occasion, they did not realise that this would be the last Passover that God would recognise; "Christ our passover" (1 Cor 5:7) has been substituted, so He is the Passover for the people of God today.

The object of these men in going early to Jerusalem was not because they were glad that it was said, "Let us go into the house of the Lord" (Ps 122:1), but to engage in a purification process. Examples of such purification processes and the need for them are given in Num 19:11,12; 31:19. In Hezekiah's day, there were many who had not purified or sanctified themselves (2 Chron 30:17-18), so the Levites instead had to kill the passover lambs; otherwise, the king prayed, "The good Lord pardon every one". Today, verses such as 1 Cor 11:28; 2 Cor 7:1 apply, where we read, "let a man examine himself, and so let him eat of that bread, and drink of that cup", and "let us cleanse ourselves from all filthiness of the flesh and spirit, perfecting holiness in the fear of God". But this has nothing to do with the ritual in which the Jews engaged. As far as the leaders were concerned, the purification process was nothing but hypocrisy. They avoided entering in before Pilate, a Roman, "lest they should be defiled; but that they might eat the passover" (18:28). At the same time, they willingly concocted false witness against the Lord, and falsely were seeking His death, thereby defiling themselves a thousand times over with the guilt associated with the blood of the Son of God, and yet they were finicky about being seen with the Gentiles. The purification was not moral, but ritualistic.

Being satisfied with their purified state (as they thought), the people now sought for the Lord, no doubt spying around Jerusalem and its environs. Earlier, at the feast of tabernacles, the Jews had done the same thing, asking "Where is he?" (7:11). To discuss the possible movements of the Lord as they stood in the temple courts shows that they had nothing better to do with their time, and this reminds us of the men of Athens, who spent their time "in nothing else, but either to tell, or to hear some new thing" (Acts 17:21). In fact, the character of Herod's temple was determined by the occupations of the men who habituated its courts; it was "a den of thieves" on account of the financial irregularities that took place there in the cause of religion (Luke 19:46). These Jews thus reduced the temple courts to a place of gossip and supposition, whereas during the last week the Lord used these courts as a place for teaching those people who desired to listen to Him without criticism (Luke 21:37-38).

In fact, the people were under the thumb of the chief priests and Pharisees, who used their authority and mastery over the thoughts of men to issue a command that anyone knowing where the Lord was to be found was to let them know so that they could take Him. Their previous attempts to take Him had failed (7:45; 8:59; 10:39), though later they would seek to take Him in the absence of the multitude (Luke 22:6).

Alas, Judas, one of the twelve, fell for this command issued by the religious leaders. Apart from him, this plot to take the Lord failed in its objectives. Luke had recorded the pact that Judas made with "the chief priests and captains" (Luke 22:4-6). He communed with these leaders how he might betray the Lord to them, and they were glad and promised him money so as to achieve their purpose. For the people of God, "all things work together for good to them that love God" (Rom 8:28), but in the present event, all things in the background were working together for badness, leading to the final crucifixion of the Lord of life and glory.

VIII. The Corn of Wheat Rejected (12:1-50)

1. *The Supper in Bethany*

12:1-11

v.1 "Then Jesus six days before the passover came to Bethany, where Lazarus was which had been dead, whom he raised from the dead.

v.2 There they made him a supper; and Martha served: but Lazarus was one of them that sat at the table with him.

v.3 Then took Mary a pound of ointment of spikenard, very costly, and anointed the feet of Jesus, and wiped his feet with her hair: and the house was filled with the odour of the ointment.

v.4 Then saith one of his disciples, Judas Iscariot, Simon's *son*, which should betray him,

v.5 Why was not this ointment sold for three hundred pence, and given to the poor?

v.6 This he said, not that he cared for the poor; but because he was a thief, and had the bag, and bare what was put therein.
v.7 Then said Jesus, Let her alone: against the day of my burying hath she kept this.
v.8 For the poor always ye have with you; but me ye have not always.
v.9 Much people of the Jews therefore knew that he was there: and they came not for Jesus' sake only, but that they might see Lazarus also, whom he had raised from the dead.
v.10 But the chief priests consulted that they might put Lazarus also to death;
v.11 Because that by reason of him many of the Jews went away, and believed on Jesus."

We may sectionalise the chapter as follows:

1. Fragance in His death (vv.1-11).

2. Glory to be attained through His death (vv.12-19).

3. Fruitfulness through His death (vv.20-36).

4. Rejection leading to His death (vv.37-50).

We also note the subdivision of subject matter (suggestive or actual) in keeping with 1 Cor 10:32:

1. The church and its worship (vv.1-11).

2. The Jews and their King (vv.12-19).

3. The Gentiles (vv.20-22).

In Luke's Gospel, the following three events form a connected whole:

1. The story of Zacchaeus (Luke 19:1-10).

2. Immediately there follows the parable of the ten pounds (vv.12-27).

3. The Lord's triumphant entry into Jerusalem (vv.28-48).

1-2 Between events 2 and 3, the Lord came to Bethany six days before the Passover, event 3 taking place "on the next day" (12:12). In spite of the similarity between the descriptions, we believe that the event in the house of Simon the leper in Bethany two days before the Passover (Matt 26:2,6-13) was a separate occasion, the woman copying the devotions of Mary previously.

This being so, we believe that this supper took place in the home of Mary,

Martha and Lazarus, not in the home of Simon the leper. The order is the same as in Luke 10:38-42, where Martha served and Mary sat at His feet. Note that Mary was always at His feet: hearing (Luke 10:39); falling (John 11:32), and here anointing (12:3). Lazarus had a place of honour, "at the table with him", a living witness to the power of resurrection. In fact, we see in this story: witness (Lazarus), work (Martha), and worship (Mary).

3 Mary sensed by faith that the end was near, but the apostles' knowledge of the Lord's impending death was nil, in spite of His repeated statements about the subject; in Luke 18:34 we read that "they understood none of these things: and this saying was hid from them, neither knew they the things which were spoken". The pound of ointment of spikenard had been imported in a sealed alabaster box so as to preserve its fragrant properties. It was very costly, and hence it was suitable for anointing the Lord. Compare the costly gifts that the wise men brought from the east to the Child in Matt 2:11, forming part of their worship. Like David before her, Mary would not offer that which had cost her nothing (2 Sam 24:24). David had offered of his "own proper good" to the Lord (1 Chron 29:3), and though this was material in abundance, it can be compared with the sincerity in the widow's heart when she offered two mites (Mark 12:42-44).

V.7 shows that Mary had "kept" this ointment for this purpose, implying that it had not been used on the body of Lazarus previously in death. The fact that she used her hair to wipe the Lord's feet shows that she used what was a glory to her; this was properly used in the service of Christ (1 Cor 11:15). For the psalmist, what he described as "my glory" was his voice in song and praise (Ps 16:9; 57:8; 108:1). Thus the house was filled with the fragrance of the ointment, as had been the tabernacle and temple with the glory of God (Exod 40:35; 1 Kings 8:10) and with the fragrance of the holy anointing oil (Exod 30:23-33).

4-6 This man Judas is named eight times in John's Gospel. He is very carefully distinguished from anyone else of the same name, such as "Judas . . . not Iscariot" (14:22). He is often described as the one "which betrayed him" (18:2), being called a disciple, and also "one of the twelve" (Matt 26:14; John 6:71). The verb for "betray" is *paradidōmi*, usually translated to deliver, but the context must determine whether "betray" is the better and more appropriate rendering. In John's Gospel, up to 18:5 the verb is always translated "betray", but from 18:30 to 19:16 the verb is translated "deliver" (not referring to Judas). In our verse 4, the translation by JND uses "to deliver up" rather than "betray", a translation that does not carry the meaning of involved treachery. "Which should betray him" contains the verb *mello*, to be about to, so a suitable translation is "who was about to deliver him up".

Thus Judas was identified by his then future sin, though this was past when the Gospels were written. We may consider Jeroboam in the OT, usually identified as the man who made Israel to sin, and the man to whom all the bad OT kings of Israel were compared. The number eight (the number of times the name of Judas is mentioned in John's Gospel) recalls the eight men in 2 Timothy who were named as failures.

Judas speaks. Unbelief twists the true ways of faith; see 2 Tim 4:16. This is what Hophni and Phinehas did in 1 Sam 2:12-17 as they twisted the ritual of the sin offering into the gain of a carnal appetite. Judas was thinking of money. Had this spikenard been sold, then Judas might have been able to get his hands on the proceeds under the pretext that it would have been used for the Lord. His motive was that of a thief, and thus it was that he carried the bag containing the little money necessary for daily provisions. This bag appears again in 13:29, when the other apostles thought that he was leaving the upper room to buy some necessary provision or to give something to the poor. But Judas wanted financial gain rather than the fragrance of Christ. The proper way of giving to the poor is found in Paul's Epistles, and is a personal and local church matter. Thus we read, "we should remember the poor; the same which I was forward to do" (Gal 2:10); "a certain contribution for the poor saints" (Rom 15:26); as the Lord said, the poor were always present, and this fact could not be eradicated.

The temple authorities allowed financial greed to be practised in the temple courts (2:14), while the matter of finance entered into the first weaknesses and failures in the early church and its evangelistic outreach (Acts 6:1-11; 8:18-21).

7-8 *The Lord speaks.* He would not allow such criticism against one so faithful. Note that the Lord addressed Judas only in v.7, but all the disciples in v.8. By "against the day of my burying hath she kept this" and "me ye have not always", He was implying His forthcoming death in a very clear way—both to Mary in her faith, and to Judas in his unbelief ready to initiate that death. The fragrance poured out upon the Lord would remain upon His body even up to the cross and beyond into the sepulchre; Mary was the first to recognise this by faith. After His death, two faithful men used myrrh and aloes (19:39-40), while the additional spices and the ointments prepared by the women were of no use after His resurrection (Luke 23:56; 24:1); Mary of Bethany was not amongst them, for she had done her work of devotion beforehand.

In fact, Mary took advantage of showing her devotion Godward first. She loved the Lord first with all her heart, and then her neighbour in second place; she loved the Lord even more than she loved her brother Lazarus. And believers today should have the same priorities: thus the Lord's supper in 1 Cor 11:23-26 comes before the service of the local church in chs.12-14.

In Matt 26:7, ointment was poured on the Lord's head—speaking of His Godhead, while here in ch.12 ointment was poured on His feet—speaking of His Manhood. He was the Lamb and Son of God (relating to His Godhead), but John the Baptist beheld Him as He walked (relating to His Manhood). Clearly the fragrance was also left on Mary's head afterwards; she had indeed put on Christ.

9 The Jews showed divided interests, and indeed some showed mere curiosity: they wanted to see Jesus who had performed the miracle of raising Lazarus, and also Lazarus himself as if he were some wonderful animal in a zoo. Curiosity certainly does not demonstrate spirituality, and indeed shows up base instincts as in the case of Herod a few days later (Luke 23:8). Such aspirations debase the value of the Lord's miracles, as in 6:26.

10-11 In 15:18,20, the Lord told His disciples, "If the world hate you, ye know that it hated me before it hated you", and "If they have persecuted me, they will persecute you". This is now seen in our v.10, for they had first consulted to put the Lord Jesus to death (11:53), and now they consult to put Lazarus to death, since he was a focus of attention, leading to the Lord being a greater focus of attention. Anything that detracted from their own leadership was anathema to them. For many of the Jews (not the spies in 11:46) believed on the Lord Jesus. How deep this faith was we cannot assess; we have noted this faith in various verses before (see 11:45).

2. *The Lord's Triumphant Entry into Jerusalem* 12:12-19

v.12 "On the next day much people that were come to the feast, when they heard that Jesus was coming to Jerusalem,
v.13 Took branches of palm trees, and went forth to meet him, and cried, Hosanna: Blessed is the King of Israel that cometh in the name of the Lord.
v.14 And Jesus, when he had found a young ass, sat thereon; as it is written,
v.15 Fear not, daughter of Sion: behold, thy King cometh, sitting on an ass's colt.
v.16 These things understood not his disciples at the first: but when Jesus was glorified, then remembered they that these things were written of him, and *that* they had done these things unto him.
v.17 The people therefore that were with him when he called Lazarus out of his grave, and raised him from the dead, bare record.
v.18 For this cause the people also met him, for that they heard that he had done this miracle.
v.19 The Pharisees therefore said among themselves, Perceive ye how ye prevail nothing? behold, the world is gone after him."

12-13 The preview of the Lord's millennial triumph was seen by the three apostles when the Son appeared in glory on the mount of transfiguration (recorded only by Matthew, Mark, Luke and Peter in 2 Pet 1:16-18). The preview of this millennial triumph was seen by the Jews (visitors to, and inhabitants of, Jerusalem) quite openly, as the King rode gloriously into His own city from the mount of Olives (recorded by all four Gospel-writers). Thus the Father would ensure that His Son was vindicated even before His crucifixion:

1. He was welcomed in the home (the local church) (vv.1-8).

2. He was welcomed nationally—by His own nation (vv.12-16).

3. He was welcomed internationally—by the Greeks (vv.20-22).

This triumphant entry can be seen in the event when the ark of the covenant was brought up mount Zion by David (1 Chron 15:25-28). Many previews of the coming glory of His kingdom are seen in verses such as "the Redeemer shall come to Zion" (Isa 59:20); "he . . . shall suddenly come to his temple . . . he shall come . . . who may abide the day of his coming?" (Mal 3:1-2); "they shall see the Son of man coming in the clouds of heaven with power and great glory" (Matt 24:30); "I saw heaven opened, and behold a white horse; and he that sat upon him was called Faithful and True" (Rev 19:11).

The news that the Lord was actually coming into Jerusalem from Bethany went before Him; many of the people were prepared. The palm trees had large fanlike leaves suitable for processions, showing how the Lord fulfilled the verses, "the righteous shall flourish like the palm tree" (Ps 92:12), and "he carved all the walls of the house round about with cherubim and palm trees" (1 Kings 6:29). This was typical of One who would flourish in His own house. Matthew has recorded that they placed garments on the animals; the fact that the Lord sat on them demonstrated submission to His authority (Matt 21:7; Ps 110:3). (Thus in 2 Kings 9:13 men placed garments under Jehu when he was owned as king; this was an eastern custom for showing honour.)

The people cry. When the people cried, "Hosanna: Blessed is the King of Israel that cometh in the name of the Lord", they were quoting Ps 118:26. Psalms 113-118 were often quoted at the Passover. In particular, unwittingly the people take up this verse of praise from Ps 118, failing to realise that the Psalm was speaking of the sufferings of Christ and the glory that should follow, together with the response that people of faith would make to those events. The subject matter of the Psalm is as follows:

1. The Lord's rehearsal of His death (vv.1-13).

2. The Lord's rehearsal of His resurrection (vv.14-21).

3. The Stone, the Lord's doing, the day, all reflect the people's response (vv.22-24).

4. The Lord's reply: save now, send prosperity (v.25).

5. The people's reply: the Lord be blessed; blessing upon the people, light and sacrifice (vv.26-27).

6. The Lord's praise to God in resurrection (v.28).

7. A general (and common) ascription of praise (v.29).

The multitude's cry was, of course, traditional, but it expressed their aspirations. For their use of the title "the King" was not millennial in character, but rather political. They loathed the Roman occupying power, and for a long time had been looking for a deliverer (Luke 2:38; 24:21). They evidently thought that the nature of the procession descending from Olivet to Jerusalem indicated that the Lord was taking upon Himself Kingship and so to assume power over the Romans. They little thought that, far from taking a kingly throne, He was to take the cross as His throne. Only later, would God ensure that His Son was raised from the dead, and that He ultimately would sit upon His throne of millennial glory.

The Lord was not moved by such temporary rejoicing with its wrong motives. He accepted the praise, else the very stones on Olivet would cry out (Luke 19:40). In fact, upon seeing Jerusalem from the slopes of Olivet over the Kidron valley, He wept while the people rejoiced. He knew what was reserved for them, when the occupying power (far from being defeated) would destroy the city (vv.41-44). Their aspirations would come to nothing; He would not further their political objectives, knowing that His throne would be the cross, being then replaced by resurrection and being lifted up to His Father's throne on high.

14 Whereas John has mentioned only "a young ass", yet in Matt 21:2 we read of both an ass and a colt. There were two animals—the word "them" in Matt 21:3 makes this clear. The Lord Himself sat upon the colt, the mother ass following. Such an animal was ridden by kings and judges in times of peace, but horses were ridden in times of war.

15 The author John has given an OT quotation that describes this great event. The full quotation from Zech 9:9-10 is, "Rejoice greatly, O daughter of Zion; shout, O daughter of Jerusalem: behold thy King cometh unto thee: he is just, and having salvation; lowly, and riding upon an ass, and upon a colt the foal of an ass. And I will cut off the chariot from Ephraim, and the battle bow shall be cut off: and he shall speak peace unto the heathen: and his dominion shall be from sea even to sea, and from the river even to the ends of the earth". Most of this is omitted in John's quotation as being unsuitable for the occasion. For the prophet Zechariah was speaking of the introduction of the millennium kingdom, with no more warfare and peace reigning over all the earth. "Just, and having salvation" is omitted, since a manifestation of justice would have implied judgment, and salvation was not being brought to Jerusalem—rather the Lord was coming to work salvation out on the cross. This is an example where a more restricted form of prophecy is linked on to a far distant view of prophecy; other examples of this form of prophecy are Matt 24:3; Isa 61:1-3 (Luke 4:18-19).

16 During the event when the Lord was riding into His city in triumph, the disciples failed to connect the event with the verse in Zech 9. It was only after He was glorified—after His ascension and the giving of the Spirit to lead into all truth—that the disciples realised that part of these two verses in Zech 9 was being fulfilled. No longer were they ignorant of their own OT Scriptures when the Spirit came upon them. A similar confession was made by John when he recorded the incident of the cleansing of the temple (2:22). There is no excuse today for believers to display such ignorance, for they have every opportunity to learn the implications of the prophetic Scriptures.

17-18 In 11:45, many of the Jews believed on the Lord as a result of the raising of Lazarus; these now "bare record", the verb being the imperfect tense of *martureō*, to bear witness. This testimony added glory to the Lord Jesus, for it was spoken about Him in spite of the people knowing of the danger surrounding anyone who spoke up for the Lord. In the Acts, the testimony concerned the Lord's own resurrection, not that of Lazarus.

In v.18, "the people" who came out from Jerusalem had not seen the miracle, but had only heard the witness of others; v.12 shows that they were visitors to Jerusalem. In v.9, the people came out to see Lazarus, but here they came out to meet the Lord with the praises recorded in v.13. The unbelieving Jews are not mentioned in these verses.

19 *The Pharisees speak.* This verse follows on from vv.10-11. In these verses the priests were concerned that the inhabitants of Jerusalem went out to see the Lord. But in v.19, the Pharisees were concerned that visiting Jews went out to see and to praise Him. That is what "the world" means in this verse—Jewish visitors from every part of the world, namely from all the countries listed in Acts 2:9-11. Even the Greeks in v.20 would be included in "the world". The Pharisees confessed that up to now they had been unable to do anything to stop the growing popularity of the Lord. But this impotence would not last much longer, for the heading up of all evil was nearing its climax.

3. *The Lord's Answer to the Greeks' Desire to See Him* 12:20-36

v.20 "And there were certain Greeks among them that came up to worship at the feast;
v.21 The same came therefore to Philip, which was of Bethsaida of Galilee, and desired him, saying, Sir, we would see Jesus.
v.22 Philip cometh and telleth Andrew: and again Andrew and Philip tell Jesus.
v.23 And Jesus answered them, saying, The hour is come, that the Son of man should be glorified.
v.24 Verily, verily, I say unto you, Except a corn of wheat fall into the ground and die, it abideth alone: but if it die, it bringeth forth much fruit.
v.25 He that loveth his life shall lose it; and he that hateth his life in this world shall keep it unto life eternal.
v.26 If any man serve me, let him follow me; and where I am, there shall

also my servant be: if any man serve me, him will *my* Father honour.
v.27 Now is my soul troubled; and what shall I say? Father, save me from this hour: but for this cause came I unto this hour.
v.28 Father, glorify thy name. Then came there a voice from heaven, *saying*, I have both glorified *it*, and will glorify *it* again.
v.29 The people therefore, that stood by, and heard *it*, said that it thundered: others said, An angel spake to him.
v.30 Jesus answered and said, This voice came not because of me, but for your sakes.
v.31 Now is the judgment of this world: now shall the prince of this world be cast out.
v.32 And I, if I be lifted up from the earth, will draw all *men* unto me.
v.33 This he said, signifying what death he should die.
v.34 The people answered him, We have heard out of the law that Christ abideth for ever: and how sayest thou, The Son of man must be lifted up? who is this Son of man?
v.35 Then Jesus said unto them, Yet a little while is the light with you. Walk while ye have the light, lest darkness come upon you: for he that walketh in darkness knoweth not whither he goeth.
v.36 While ye have light, believe in the light, that ye may be the children of light. These things spake Jesus, and departed, and did hide himself from them."

20-22 These Greeks (*hellēnes*) were Gentiles, translated as such in 7:35. They must be distinguished from the Greek-speaking Jews in Acts 6:1 (*hellēnistēs*). The former word appears 24 times in Paul's Epistles, usually translated Greek or Greeks, but sometimes Gentiles. Thus Timothy's father was "a Greek" (Acts 16:1). Usually Paul employed the word in contrast to the Jews (Acts 18:4; Rom 1:16; 1 Cor 1:24; Gal 3:28; Col 3:11 being representative verses).

These Greeks were proselytes, having come to Jerusalem for the Passover. They were men who had embraced the Jewish religion. The concept stretches back to the original Passover in Exod 12:48, where "a stranger . . . shall be as one born in the land", circumcision being a necessity for such a recognition. See also Exod 20:10; Lev 19:34. We find these proselytes mentioned in the list of men who came up to Jerusalem at Pentecost (Acts 2:10). In the church, of course, there is neither Jew, Gentile nor proselyte, such distinctions being obliterated.

The Greeks speak. By saying "Sir (*kurie*), we would see Jesus", they joined the ranks of the curious (12:9), having heard the news of the Lord's power. But there would be no full revelation to the Gentiles until after the Lord was glorified, since vv.37-41 present still a picture of unbelief, applying to Jew and Gentile alike.

No doubt a certain deference caused them to ask the apostle Philip first. And we can then understand Philip's uncertainty about leading these Greeks directly to the Lord Jesus. He knew the Lord's teaching, "I am not sent but unto the lost sheep of the house of Israel" (Matt 15:24), and "Go not into the way of the Gentiles" (10:5), not knowing that the "other sheep" embraced the Gentiles (10:16). Hence Philip consulted first with another apostle Andrew. In 1:35-41,

Andrew had found "the Messias ... the Christ" through John the Baptist's testimony, but in vv.43-45, the Lord found Philip who in turn found Nathanael. Thus these two apostles had been together right from the beginning of the Lord's ministry. They appear last in the list in Acts 1:13. (The apostle Philip is not to be confused with the Philip who was one of the seven, Acts 6:5; 8:5-40; 21:8).

So both these two apostles "tell Jesus". The Lord did not display Himself; rather He spoke of His death and its results. Yet in His answer, there were hidden references to the Gentiles that only the initiated could perceive: the "much fruit" would involve the Gentiles (v.24); "all men" would also include the Gentiles (v.32), as do the words "whosoever" and "the world" (vv.46,47).

As others have pointed out, the rest of chs.12-17 suggest the OT tabernacle, at which we need not be surprised since John had already written that the Word tabernacled among them, with His glory being seen (1:14). Thus we have:

1. The rest of ch.12 shows the Lord as the burnt offering.

2. Ch.13 presents the laver.

3. Chs.14-16 deal with the holy place, and light therein.

4. Ch.17 takes us reverently into the Holy of Holies.

23 *The Lord speaks*. This discourse was heard not only by His disciples, but also by "the people" (vv.29,34), which may include the Gentile proselytes. After His long years of anticipation throughout His ministry, His hour had arrived, namely at the end of this last week. The Lord knew that He would be glorified as a result of passing through this hour. Later the Lord would say "Now is the Son of man glorified" (13:31) as a result of Judas leaving the upper room, but in our v.23 He appears to refer to His glory in resurrection and ascension. We may tabulate the references to His hour and time:

1. In Cana, "mine hour is not yet come" (2:4).

2. At the feast of tabernacles in Jerusalem, "My time is not yet come" (7:6,8); "his hour was not yet come" (v.30).

3. In the treasury, "his hour was not yet come" (8:20).

4. In Jerusalem prior to the last Passover, "The hour is come" (12:23); "Father, save me from this hour: but for this cause came I unto this hour" (v.27).

5. "When Jesus knew that his hour was come that he should depart out of this world unto the Father" (13:1).

6. The Lord's prayer: "Father, the hour is come" (17:1).

7. In Gethsemane, "he . . . prayed that, if it were possible, the hour might pass from him" (Mark 14:35).

8. In Gethsemane, "the hour is at hand, and the Son of man is betrayed into the hands of sinners" (Matt 26:45; Mark 14:41).

24 It is useful to gather together all the parables and word-pictures spoken by the Lord that refer to seed, growth, fruit and harvest. It is true that He took up the ideas behind the common occupations around Him, yet in brief words He moulded these ideas to describe deep spiritual realities.

In v.24 the Lord presented Himself in divine isolation until the climax and the turning point in divine history. For the OT sacrifices could never reintroduce fellowship with God that had been lost in Adam. The peace offering pointed the way forward to Christ, but in itself could achieve nothing lasting and spiritual. The word-picture of the corn of wheat dying could not by itself fully represent what the Lord passed through. For naturally a seed decays as it yields a new plant; the seed plays no more part in the development process. No doubt this can best be seen in a potato; when new potatoes are dug up, the old potato can usually be found as a dead mass of slime. That dead mass can never be revived, the fruit only remains. But in the Lord's case, He rose again, taking His life once more eternally, as well as having brought forth "much fruit". We should contrast this with 1 Cor 15:42, where the bodies of believers are "sown in corruption" whereas in the Lord's case He "saw no corruption" (Acts 13:37). The "much fruit" brought forth is described in Isa 53:11, "He shall see of the travail of his soul, and shall be satisfied", and in Heb 2:12-13, "my brethren . . . the children".

Thou wast alone, till like the precious grain,
  In death Thou layest, but did'st rise again;
And in Thy risen life, a countless host
  Are "all of one" with Thee, Thy joy and boast.

25-26 The Lord's service was a divinely-consecrated service, as implied in the previous verse. Here, He has unfolded principles of service that anyone who is called "my servant" should carefully note. We shall comment on believers as the Lord's possession in various aspects when we arrive at 13:1; here we would note servants and service involve (i) the will of God (2 Tim 1:1), (ii) the purpose of God (2 Tim 1:9), (iii) the appointment of God (2 Tim 1:11), and (iv) the gift of God (2 Tim 1:6).

A man who loves his life is one who puts the occupations of this world in a category far above spiritual things. His business, his pleasures, his meals, his friends, his house and his bed all come first, and if there is any time left over, then this can be devoted to prayer, to the Scriptures, to fellowship and service, but this is not continuing "stedfastly in the apostles' doctrine and fellowship, and in breaking of bread, and in prayers" (Acts 2:42). But a man who "hateth his life" is one who places the things of God first. Paul dealt with this in Phil 2, where the example of the Lord was followed by Paul, Timothy and Epaphroditus who for the work of Christ was "nigh unto death" (v.30). Men of opposite motivation were Demas (2 Tim 4:10) and Diotrephes (3 John 9).

Blessings are promised by the Lord to those who serve Him faithfully.

1. Life apparently lost will nevertheless lead to "life eternal".

2. Such a man will be following the Lord.

3. Such a man will be where the Lord is (14:3; 17:24).

4. The Father will honour such a servant.

The status and character of true "ministers of God" are detailed by Paul in 2 Cor 6:3-10. Many of these 28 features represent contrasts between those who hate their life and those who love it, such as "by evil report and good report", "as dying, and, behold, we live".

27-28 As the Lord was the true Servant, the circumstances through which He would pass were to be far worse than any through which His own servants would pass. In the sentence "Now is my soul troubled", the verb *tarassō* is used in the perfect tense, showing that this had been a past experience leading up to the present. In John's Gospel, the verb is used of the moving of the water (5:4,7), of the Lord Himself under three different circumstances (11:33; 12:27; 13:21), and of the apostles (14:1,27). On other occasions, the disciples were troubled when they saw the Lord under entirely new and unexpected circumstances (Matt 14:26; Luke 24:38). As far as the Lord was concerned, this trouble depicts Him as the meal offering baken in a pan or oven (Lev 2:4-5). An ordinary man would have asked to be delivered absolutely and completely from such anticipated trouble that this hour would bring, but the Lord spoke to His Father that He had come to this hour so as to pass through the ultimate of His trouble. In the divine counsel, He would pass through it, as He said in Gethsemane, "nevertheless not as I will, but as thou wilt" (Matt 26:39). He would not call upon the twelve legions of angels to save Him (Matt 26:53), nor would He listen to the taunts of the rulers, "let him save himself, if he be Christ" (Luke 23:35). He had come to do the will of God (Heb 10:7), and by His work, the Name of the Father would be glorified. Note that glory through these events was prominent in the record of these last days (12:16; 13:31-32; 17:1,5,24).

The Father speaks. It goes without saying that the Father was listening to every word from the Son. The Father had glorified His Name during the lifetime of service of His Son, and He would glorify it again through the cross and resurrection.

29 *The people speak.* Here is an example of people hearing a prominent sound, but not being able to discern either words, or even whether it was a voice. In Luke 3:22, John the Baptist heard the Father's voice from heaven, as did the three apostles on the mount of transfiguration (2 Pet 1:17-18). In the case of Paul's conversion, he himself heard the voice of the Lord from heaven, and knew the words that were spoken, but the people with him heard a sound but could not detect the words (Acts 9:7; 22:9). Similarly here, to the people the sound was either thunder (Rev 6:1; 14:2), or the undiscerned words of an angel (Acts 23:9). Unexplained circumstances cause men rapidly to turn to speculation!

It was not God's will that the people should hear the actual words that were spoken from heaven. The people really were putting themselves under the law (v.34), when once they had openly stated that they did not want to hear the voice of God from heaven (Exod 20:19; Deut 5:25; Heb 12:19).

30-32 *The Lord speaks.* The words *themselves* were spoken for the sake of the Lord—He alone heard them, and there was no need for physical sound when the Father spoke to the Son. However, the people heard the sound by divine choice, and this was "for your sakes". (Compare this with 11:42, where the Lord's words spoken in prayer were "because of the people which stand by".) No doubt the manifestation of sound to the people was to demonstrate that heaven owned the Person of the Lord Jesus, whatever man may do in unbelief.

The reference to "the judgment of this world" in the immediate context of His death on the cross may seem surprising to non-evangelicals, who seem to think that divine love is available at all times, with judgment a subject that is politely discarded as a medieval anachronism. But the Lord taught judgment as much as He taught divine love, for example, in 3:16-18. For His death and resurrection caused men to take sides, even more than they did when He was present amongst them. And this division brought about either divine love unto salvation or the prospect of divine judgment. At the same time, the work of Christ had a profound effect on Satan as "the prince of this world". This word *archōn* refers to Satan as "the prince of the devils" (Matt 12:24), "the prince of this world" (12:31; 14:30; 16:11), and "the prince of the power of the air" (Eph 2:2). Only once is this word used of the Lord Jesus Christ, "the prince of the kings of the earth" (Rev 1:5).

As far as Satan is concerned, we understand his movements to be as follows:

1. As Lucifer, he wanted to ascend into heaven, to exalt his throne, and to be like the most High (Isa 14:12-14). That time was implied by the Lord when He said, "I saw Satan as lightning fall from heaven" (Luke 10:18), from the third to the second heaven, and still having contact conversationally with God (Job 1:7).

2. With the work of Christ on the cross complete, Satan was "cast out" into the first heavens, namely the air. Then He destroyed "him that had the

power of death" (Heb 2:14), namely Satan had no more absolute power over the souls of God's people, and they were secure with eternal life. Satan is now "the prince of the power of the air" (Eph 2:2), acting as a roaring lion, walking about seeking those whom he may devour (1 Pet 5:8).

4. After the rapture, when Michael and his angels fight against "the great dragon, the old serpent, called the Devil, and Satan" (Rev 12:9), he is "cast out into the earth" to deceive the nations, to gather them together against Christ at the final battle of Armageddon (Rev 16:16).

5. Satan is then bound for a thousand years in "the bottomless pit" (Rev 20:1-3).

6. He is then cast into "the lake of fire" with the beast and false prophet (Rev 20:10). Thus these movements are always downwards.

In v.32, the Lord spoke of being "lifted up", and drawing "all men" unto Himself. Various aspects may be perceived in this all-embracive drawing power.

1. All believers are drawn to Him as Saviour. Both the Father and the Son are seen in this act of drawing (6:44). See Song of Songs 1:4.

2. In the establishment of His glorious kingdom, His elect will be gathered to Him in Jerusalem the city of the great King (Matt 24:31).

3. The word for "draw" (*helkuō*) is also used for drawing a net along without violence (21:6,11), suggesting the divine drawing of sinners to the judgment of the coming day.

33 The word "lifted up" implied His forthcoming death by crucifixion, and the people understood this (v.34). Note the various ways in which the word "up" appears in the AV translation:

1. "Delivered up" (Acts 3:13; Rom 8:32).

2. "Lifted up" (John 3:14; 8:28; 12:32,34).

3. "Raised up" (Acts 2:24,32; etc.).

4. "Taken up" (Acts 1:2,9,11,22).

5. "Carried up" (Luke 24:51).

Thus would be fulfilled the Scripture that the Lord had to die by hanging on a tree (Deut 21:23; Gal 3:13). This death could not be by the usual Jewish method of stoning.

34 *The people speak.* The title "Son of man" appears twice in this verse. On all other occasions in the Gospels, it is the Lord who used this title, speaking of Himself in the third person, except in Matt 16:13 where He identified Himself as the Son of man. But here is the exception—it is men who use the title. (The only other exception occurs in the closing words of Stephen in Acts 7:56.) The title represents the Lord in Manhood, in the glory of heaven ready to judge, and in the glory of His millennial kingdom.

Clearly the people did not identify the title with the Lord, who did not use this title in ch.12. In fact, their response shows that they were completely confused, changing the "I" in "if I be lifted up" into a question, "Who is this Son of man?" apparently not relating to the Lord. They could see no connection between the title and the fact that the Lord had just ridden in triumph into Jerusalem. They were also confused about the implications from their law. Their Messiah would dwell eternally, and hence there could be no possibility of His being crucified; see such verses as Ps 89:4,29,36-37; 110:4. The Lord's words were thus an enigma to them, because they failed to see that Christ had first to suffer before entering into His glory.

35-36 *The Lord speaks.* Here was the last opportunity for the people to hear Him. These words, together with those in vv.44-50, represent the last public teaching of the Lord in John's Gospel, while in Matthew His last teaching is found in chs.24-25 to His disciples. The teaching in John 13-16 is, of course, of a private nature to the apostles.

"Yet a little while" (*eti mikron chronon*) represents the last opportunity to behold the Lord amongst them, and to listen to His teaching (no doubt including the days of teaching recorded in Luke 21:37-38). In 16:16, the "little while" represents the time between His death and resurrection, a period that had meaning only to His disciples.

He was the guiding Light amongst them—the people should walk in that light, should believe in it, and should be children of it. The Lord had come into the world, and "lighteth every man" that came within the reach of His testimony (1:9). After His coming, He was the Light as long as He was in the world (9:5), but now believers are the light of the world in the sense that their testimony is all that is seen by men in the world (Matt 5:14; Phil 2:15). Our position is that of being "children of light", a phrase that also appears in Luke 16:8; Eph 5:8; 1 Thess 5:5, namely children whose place is in the light and who reflect the light of Christ from their life and character.

The contrast is great. Darkness would come upon unbelieving men when the true Light would be taken away from them. A man walking in darkness does not know "whither he goeth", either in this world or in the next. His destiny is quite unknown to him, for the day of the Lord would overtake such a man as a thief in the night (1 Thess 5:2), for which he would be unprepared.

Thus the Lord departed and hid Himself from them. Previously He had done this to prevent men from taking Him before His hour. But this does not seem to be the case in our v.36. It seems to have been a parabolic action (sometimes used in John's Gospel, 8:6; 9:6; 13:26; 20:22) to illustrate the unbelief that would exist in the darkness of His absence.

4. *Unbelief Illustrated from the Prophecy of Isaiah* 12:37-43

v.37 "But though he had done so many miracles before them, yet they believed not on him:
v.38 That the saying of Esaias the prophet might be fulfilled, which he spake, Lord, who hath believed our report? and to whom hath the arm of the Lord been revealed?
v.39 Therefore they could not believe, because that Esaias said again,
v.40 He hath blinded their eyes, and hardened their heart; that they should not see with *their* eyes, nor understand with *their* heart, and be converted, and I should heal them.
v.41 These things said Esaias, when he saw his glory, and spake of him.
v.42 Nevertheless among the chief rulers also many believed on him; but because of the Pharisees they did not confess *him*, lest they should be put out of the synagogue:
v.43 For they loved the praise of men more than the praise of God."

37-38 Previously the Lord had said, "though ye believe not me, believe the works" (10:38). Yet in our v.37, we find that this commandment is refused; the verse returns to miracles performed by the Lord "before" the Jews. Yet no faith had been formed in these men. Similarly in Matt 11:20, mighty works did not lead to repentance in many cities of Galilee. In 4:48, as a challenge to the man whose son was dying, the Lord had presented the matter the other way round: "Except ye see signs and wonders, ye will not believe". The difference can be traced to the attitude of heart in those who saw the works. Ultimately, after the apostolic age, the perpetuation of miracles led to weakness of faith, so the so-called sign-gifts were withdrawn, leaving those spiritual gifts of ministry to the heart to edify the Lord's people.

As far as John was concerned by the Holy Spirit, this lack of faith fulfilled the OT prophecy in Isa 53:1, "Who hath believed our report? and to whom is the arm of the Lord revealed?", speaking of the divine words and works. The very existence of this question proved that not all had believed and that not all had appreciated the works of the arm of the Lord. This is amplified in vv.2-3, where we find in men's hearts that there was no desire to see His beauty, where He was rejected by men who despised Him and esteemed Him not. Paul also quoted Isa 53:1 in Rom 10:16, "they have not all obeyed the gospel. For Esaias saith, Lord, who hath believed our report?". Note that Paul did not quote "the arm of the Lord", since in the context he was only dealing with faith that comes by hearing the word of God.

39-40 Thus John argued that "they could not believe". This only applies to certain men, not to everyone, else there would be no point in preaching the gospel to gain converts. John visualised a permanent blockage in some who had been given up by God, for whom the opportunity to repent had been withdrawn. God will not always strive with men, and examples of such men are found in the apostates described in 2 Pet 2-3 and Jude, for whom the opportunity of salvation had passed. Moreover, John then quoted a second passage from Isaiah that is even clearer in its implications. We may quote the actual words from the OT passage: "Hear ye indeed, but understand not; and see ye indeed, but perceive not. Make the heart of this people fat, and make their ears heavy, and shut their eyes; lest they see with their eyes, and hear with their ears, and understand with their heart, and convert, and be healed" (Isa 6:9-10).

In the OT passage, it is the voice of God that Isaiah heard. In John 12, the apostle had presented the Lord Jesus as saying this, for in v.41, John stated that he was speaking of "him", namely Christ. When Paul was imprisoned in his own hired house, he preached to the Jews who came to listen. Because of the unbelief of some, the apostle quoted Isa 6:9-10, stating that the Holy Spirit spoke to the fathers by Isaiah the prophet.

Eyes, ears and heart are all concerned. In Isa 6:9-10, the command is both to the people and to Isaiah by his preaching to render the faculties of men impotent to grasp the message. In John 12:40, the quotation is presented to demonstrate that is was God Himself who hardened the hearts of men. In Acts 28:27, the unbelief is brought about by men. So men cannot blame God for their predicament. God works after men have worked, and then the door is closed. As Ps 81:12 puts it, "I gave them up to the hardness of their hearts: and they walked in their own counsels" (AV marg). Paul wrote a similar thing, "even as they did not like to retain God in their knowledge, God gave them over to a reprobate mind" (Rom 1:28). "To them it is not given", said the Lord, quoting Isa 6:9-10 to show that from those who have not shall be taken away even that which they have (Matt 13:11-16).

41 Just as John has written "we beheld his glory" (1:14), so here he wrote about Isaiah, "he saw his glory". Hence this is the NT interpretation of Isaiah's vision, "I saw also the Lord sitting upon a throne, high and lifted up" (Isa 6:1); this took place "in the house" in Jerusalem (v.4). This therefore demonstrates that whenever the glory of God was manifested in the OT, this was the glory of Christ prior to His incarnation. This glory was manifested when the tabernacle was dedicated (Exod 40:34) and also when the temple was dedicated by Solomon (1 Kings 8:11). No man has seen God at any time, even in OT days, but the Son revealed Him in every manifestation of glory.

42-43 It is remarkable that amongst the chief rulers of the Jews in Jerusalem "many believed on him". Certainly by this time the faith of Nicodemus had grown, but John has not told us how he knew of the "many", for they were secret believers. This should be taken in conjunction with Acts 6:7, where "a great company of the priests were obedient to the faith", though this did not imply a secret faith.

In our verse, we cannot decide whether this belief was genuine faith in weakness, or whether it was a mere consent to the facts of the Lord's works. For John sometimes has used the idea of belief as relating to the mind knowing facts rather than to the heart knowing the Person of Christ. Certainly here the flesh dominated in these men, for their minds were held by the synagogue and also by the glory of men. (The word "praise" in v.43 should twice be "glory", *doxa.*) They were more interested in their own glory rather than in the glory of Christ (v.41). Moreover, the power of outward observation attracted them, for in Matt 6:1-8 the Lord showed that there was a desire for outward show in the matter of alms, prayer and fasting.

Their fear was that they would be cut off from the synagogue and its service that they loved. The true confession of Christ should bring about a complete separation from all forms of religion that are contrary to God's word. Young believers do not find that step easy today, any more than it was easy in the Lord's day. Today, of course, the separation occurs as an exercise on the part of the convert; but then, it would take place by the religious leaders excommunicating those whose contact with Christ they loathed; see 9:22. Such excommunication might be for a prescribed period, or by being cut off permanently with a curse. More positively, Moses was glad to be separated from the treasures in Egypt (Heb 11:24-26), as was Paul from his past Pharisaical profession, for as a believer he had no confidence in the flesh (Phil 3:4-7).

5. *Summary of the Lord's Teaching in John's Gospel*
12:44-50

v.44 "Jesus cried and said, He that believeth on me, believeth not on me, but on him that sent me.
v.45 And he that seeth me seeth him that sent me.
v.46 I am come a light into the world, that whosoever believeth on me should not abide in darkness.
v.47 And if any man hear my words, and believe not, I judge him not: for I came not to judge the world, but to save the world.
v.48 He that rejecteth me, and receiveth not my words, hath one that judgeth him: the word that I have spoken, the same shall judge him in the last day.
v.49 For I have not spoken of myself; but the Father which sent me, he gave me a commandment, what I should say, and what I should speak.
v.50 And I know that his commandment is life everlasting: whatsoever I speak therefore, even as the Father said unto me, so I speak."

44-50 *The Lord speaks.* These verses represent the Lord's final teaching to the people, on one of the days of His last week. No further public utterances are given in John's Gospel. The message in these verses should be contrasted with the Lord's last words to the people before His crucifixion, as recorded in Luke's

Gospel (Luke 22:28-31). He concluded with: "if they do these things in a green tree, what shall be done in the dry?", referring to the destruction of Jerusalem by the Romans in AD 70.

The message in our verses appears to be a final summary of the Lord's essential teaching to men. It may have been a short version of much more extensive teaching, abbreviated by John under the control of the Holy Spirit so that it should appear as a summary of the Lord's teaching that John by that time knew so well.

Against each verse, we can give other verses in the Gospel that contain a similar meaning. Many more references can be added.

1. V.44: Believing on the Father that sent Him, 5:24.

2. V.45:	Those who see Him,	6:40; 10:30; 14:7,9.
	Sent Me,	4:34; 5:23,24,30.
3. V.46:	Light,	1:4,9; 8:12; 9:5; 12:36.
	In darkness,	8:12; 12:35.
4. V.47:	Not judgment,	3:17; 8:15.
	To save,	3:17; 5:34; 10:9.
5. V.48:	Receive not,	3:32; 5:43.
	Last day,	5:28,29; 6:39,40,44; (11:24).
6. V.49:	Spoken from the Father,	5:19; 7:16; 8:26,28,38; 14:10.
7. V.50:	Life everlasting (eternal),	3:15; 4:36; 5:39; 6:54.

V.50 contains an important implication, "I know that his commandment is life everlasting (eternal): whatsoever I speak therefore, even as the Father said unto me, so I speak". We suggest that this provides an explanation of that difficult verse "of that day and that hour knoweth no man . . . neither the Son, but the Father" (Mark 13:32). This verse must not be interpreted so as to deny in any way the omniscience of the Son. Our suggestion is that the Lord was referring to information that He knew in absolute Deity, but that He had descended from on high with the commandment that this day was not to be revealed to men. The commandment indicated all that He was to teach to men; this the Son "knew". He knew everything else as well, but this was not to be taught (as, for example, the mystery of the church as the Body of Christ continued to be hidden when the Lord was here, a truth known to the Lord but only later revealed through the apostle Paul in Eph 3:3-6). In giving this suggested explanation, in no way do we seek to divide "the Son as God" and "the Son as Man", which are unscriptural expressions; the explanation only touches on what the Lord had to teach and make known in the purpose of God.

CHAPTERS 13-17
THE SON—HIS RECEPTION

I. The Upper Room: The Son's Activity (13:1-38)

1. *The Son–to be Called Lord*
13:1-17

v.1 "Now before the feast of the passover, when Jesus knew that his hour was come that he should depart out of this world unto the Father, having loved his own which were in the world, he loved them unto the end.
v.2 And supper being ended, the devil having now put into the heart of Judas Iscariot, Simon's *son*, to betray him;
v.3 Jesus knowing that the Father had given all things into his hands, and that he was come from God, and went to God;
v.4 He riseth from supper, and laid aside his garments; and took a towel, and girded himself.
v.5 After that he poureth water into a bason, and began to wash the disciples' feet, and to wipe *them* with the towel wherewith he was girded.
v.6 Then cometh he to Simon Peter: and Peter saith unto him, Lord, dost thou wash my feet?
v.7 Jesus answered and said unto him, What I do thou knowest not now; but thou shalt know hereafter.
v.8 Peter saith unto him, Thou shalt never wash my feet. Jesus answered him, If I wash thee not, thou hast no part with me.
v.9 Simon Peter saith unto him, Lord, not my feet only, but also *my* hands and *my* head.
v.10 Jesus saith to him, He that is washed needeth not save to wash *his* feet, but is clean every whit: and ye are clean, but not all.
v.11 For he knew who should betray him; therefore said he, Ye are not all clean.
v.12 So after he had washed their feet, and had taken his garments, and was set down again, he said unto them, Know ye what I have done to you?
v.13 Ye call me Master and Lord: and ye say well; for so I am.
v.14 If I then, *your* Lord and Master, have washed your feet; ye also ought to wash one another's feet.
v.15 For I have given you an example, that ye should do as I have done to you.
v.16 Verily, verily, I say unto you, The servant is not greater than his lord; neither he that is sent greater than he that sent him.
v.17 If ye know these things, happy are ye if ye do them."

As far as John's record is concerned, 12:44-50 is the Lord's last discourse to the world; chs.13-16 give the Lord's last discourse to His own disciples, while ch.17 gives the Lord's last prayer to the Father while in liberty. In tabernacle language, 12:24 shows the altar; 13:4-17 shows the laver; chs.14-16 take us into the holy place, while ch.17 takes us into the Holiest of all.

We may divide ch.13 into the following paragraphs:

1. The introduction to the upper room ministry, stressing the Lord's knowledge (vv.1-3).

2. The Lord, washing His disciples' feet, is misunderstood (vv.4-17).

3. The Lord predicts, and then identifies, the betrayer Judas (vv.18-30).

4. Alone with His true disciples, the Lord is glorified (vv.31-35).

5. A further prediction, Peter would deny Him (vv.36-38).

1 The words for "feast" (*heortē*) and "supper" (*deipnon*) are different. The former refers to a Jewish feast, here the Passover, while the latter refers to the chief meal of the day taken during the evening. It must be stressed that expositors find a difficulty here; in the three Synoptic Gospels, the Passover meal is described as taking place in this upper room prior to the introduction of the breaking of bread (Matt 26:17-19; Luke 22:13-15), but John mentions neither, implying that the Passover was the actual day the Lord was crucified. Many suggestions have been made as to how to resolve this matter, and interested readers must refer to more technical works.

Often in this Gospel the Lord referred to His "hour"; now it was about to come, and this the Lord knew, and would prepare His disciples for their lives and testimony afterwards. For this statement of His divine omniscience, see also 13:3,11; 18:4; 19:28.

Once again, the divine love (so characteristic of John's Gospel), is mentioned. The various circles of divine love have already been explained in our comments on 3:16. But in our verse, this love is centred on "his own" who were to be left in the world after He had departed from it. The Lord identifies His own in various passages:

1. "My servant" in relation to Him as Lord (12:26; 18:36).

2. "My disciples" in relation to Him as Master (15:8).

3. "My sheep" in relation to Him as Shepherd (10:4,14,15,26,27).

4. "My friends" in relation to Him as Man (15:14).

5. "My brethren" in relation to Him as Son (20:17; Matt 12:48).

He loved His own "unto the end" (*telos*), meaning the limit of a series of events. In the context, this refers to the upper room ministry the evening before He died; what is stressed is the fact that the Lord did not leave His own during His last hours. His love prepared them by various means for their testimony after His departure, unlike their love for Him when one would deny Him and all would forsake Him to flee to safety.

2-3 This supper took place in the "upper room" (Luke 22:12), a room that we believe was used for many other purposes, deliberately arranged by the Lord for the well-being of His disciples after His decease:

1. It was the place of the Lord's presence (Matt 26:20; Luke 22:14).
2. It was the place where the last Passover was celebrated (Luke 22:15).
3. Here the Lord's Supper was instituted (Matt 26:26).
4. Here the local church was prepared in practice (John 13).
5. Here a Bible Reading took place with the Lord leading (John 14).
6. Here was the only place where the disciples could resort after they had forsaken Him and fled (Matt 26:56).
7. Here Peter must have wept bitterly after his denial (Matt 26:75).
8. Here John must have taken the mother of Jesus from the scene of the cross (John 19:27).
9. Here the disciples must have assembled after the Lord's crucifixion (see Matt 28:7-8,10; Mark 16:10; Luke 24:9,33).
10. Here the Lord appeared twice to His disciples (John 20:19,26).
11. Here (we feel) were spoken the Lord's last words of instruction prior to His ascension (Acts 1:4).
12. Here the disciples gathered afterwards for prayer, fellowship and the understanding of the OT (Acts 2:13-16); note, "*the* upper room" (v.13).
13. Here in the "one place" the Spirit came upon them (Acts 2:1-4).
14. We cannot say when this room ceased to be used, but Acts 4:23; 5:1-10 may have been enacted there.

The devil must have appeared as an angel of light to Judas, for had he appeared as a roaring lion he would have taken evasive action. "Having now put" is a verb in the perfect tense (*beblēkotos*), implying that this had taken place previously, but that its effects—its germination—lasted to the present. For example, in Matt 26:15-16 we find that the conspiracy between Judas and the chief priests had already been arranged, so Judas, even in the upper room, was awaiting his time. But the Lord's actions were determined by the will of God and by the appointed hour; the time of Judas' betrayal was thus determined for him and strictly was beyond his capacity to arrange. The "all things" given into the Lord's hands by the Father were part of the joy that was placed before Him, enabling Him to endure the forthcoming sufferings. Some of the "all things" are mentioned by the Lord in His prayer in John 17 (the Father's words, and His disciples); again, He went to receive a kingdom (Luke 19:12); the authority to rule and judge had been received of the Father (Rev 2:27); the Headship over all things to the church had been given Him (Eph 1:22).

The Lord's movements from and to the Father (v.3) are distinct from men's experience today. His birth and His exodus were unique; the latter was now upon Him. He said, "I proceeded forth and came from God" (John 8:42; 16:27-28), a truth finally owned by His disciples (16:30). His movement back to the Father was before His mind several times in this last evening (14:12,28; 16:5; 17:11).

4-5 The washing of feet was an age-old custom, the washing being either of one's own feet or those of others (Gen 18:4; 24:32; 43:24; Jud 19:21; 1 Sam 25:41; 2 Sam 11:8; 1 Tim 5:10). Simon did not provide water in Luke 7:44, but the woman provided a suitable supply with her tears. Washing was also a ceremonial feature in the OT tabernacle and temple service (Exod 29:4). In the present passage, no doubt the water used by the Lord was that which had been brought to the house by the man with the pitcher (Luke 22:10). The Lord took up the simple act of a servant, Himself taking the servant's part.

In vv.4-5, the Lord did everything; the disciples were passive recipients. It was symbolical of His work for us in God's presence. Judicially, sin has been dealt with once and for all, but He now deals with the present effects of sin and with its prevention. Rom chs.3-5 are concerned with the former, while chs.6-8 with the latter. This washing is part of the ministerial work of Christ now, as a result of redemption accomplished. Certainly the passage declares the Lord's humility, so that the last shall be first, whereas the disciples afterwards sought the greatest position without the necessity of humbling themselves (Luke 22:24-27). In fact, seven movements of the Lord are described in vv.4-5, reminding us of the seven downward movements of the Lord in Phil 2:6-8 prior to His exaltation. Moreover, by saying "I am among you as he that serveth" (Luke 22:27), the Lord implied that none of His disciples would engage in this work; He Himself would do the work done by a slave.

The washing of the feet indicates that the believer's pathway must be sanctified by the Word. As far as the church is concerned, it was Christ who has sanctified and cleansed it "with the washing of water by the word" (Eph 5:26). The use that the Lord makes of the Word is seen in 2 Tim 3:16, Scripture being profitable "for reproof, for correction, for instruction in righteousness".

6-7 *Peter speaks.* As usual, Peter used the title "Lord" (*kurie*)—not the mere polite form of address when "Sir" would be appropriate, but the deep recognition of divine authority. This was the usual title by which the Lord was addressed by His disciples. The use of the name "Jesus" as a form of direct address was absolutely minimal (compare Luke 18:38 with Matt 20:30). Peter's remark shows his ignorance as to why the Lord humbled Himself, an ignorance that he manifested on many occasions (Matt 16:22; 17:24-25).

The Lord speaks. The Lord gave no rebuke, but recognised that Peter's ignorance in divine matters was inevitable, and this explains his further strange remarks in vv.8-9. This was characteristic of the period prior to the giving of the Holy Spirit. For example, during this period, "These things understood not his disciples at the first" (12:16). But Peter would "know hereafter", namely when the Spirit was given, for the Spirit would teach them all things (14:26), embracing the Person of Christ (15:26), and leading to "all truth" (16:13). Peter would then be a different man! He would know that humility leads to exaltation (1 Pet 5:6).

8-9 *Peter speaks.* By saying "Thou shalt never wash my feet", Peter went to the extreme of contradiction in one direction. The literal translation of the word "never" (*eis ton aiōna*) is "for ever" negated by *ou mē*, "in no wise". But the Lord dealt in grace with this one who refused a physical washing, since there was a spiritual meaning behind His action. Alas that Peter and the others often attempted to negate what the Lord said or did (Matt 16:22; 19:13).

The Lord speaks. This washing was essential. It is too awful to contemplate having no part with the Lord in the daily experience of the christian life. Redemption through His blood is not in question (one's standing is secure), but one's state is very much in question. Without washing, one would sink into practical darkness, in which case there would be no fellowship with Him (1 John 1:6).

Peter speaks. His third remark (there are several examples of triplication in Peter's statements; see 13:38; 21:17) was an exaggeration in the opposite direction—his hands and head were also to be included in the washing process. In other words, one wrong statement can lead to further wrong statements; progress in wrong doctrine is downwards, but progress in true doctrine is upwards. Peter manifested that he failed to see the difference between absolute cleansing (once and for all) and the daily washing of practical life.

10-11 *The Lord speaks.* The two words "wash" in v.10 are quite distinct in the Greek text. To make the difference, JND translates the first word as "washed all over", while the RV uses the word "bathed". The two Greek words are:

1. "He that is washed" (*louō*), a verb occurring only a few times in the NT, such as when the body of Dorcas was washed (Acts 9:37), when the stripes of Paul and Barnabas were washed (16:33), and metaphorically in Heb 10:22. It means "to bathe, to wash the body". In our verse, the verb is in the perfect tense (*leloumenos*), implying a washing in the past but whose effects last to the present. The spiritual meaning of the Lord's words implies a cleansing from sin once and for all.

2. "To wash his feet" (*niptō*), occurring mainly in John's Gospel thirteen times (all in chs.9 and 13), implies the washing of part of the body, such as the eyes (9:7), the face (Matt 6:17) and the hands (Matt 15:2). The washing of hands and feet deals with defilement by the way, ceremonially for the Pharisees, but morally by the Lord.

"Clean every whit" implies the present position of the believer brought about by the once-and-for-all cleansing granted by the Lord. This recalls the cleansing of the leper described in Lev 14:1-32. First there was washing in water (vv.7,8), and then the blood of the trespass offering was placed on the leper's right ear, thumb and great toe, and oil was then placed upon them (vv.14,17). The final result was "he shall be clean" (v.20).

Yet the Lord added that not all the disciples were cleansed in this absolute sense: "but not all". He knew the state of every heart, from the worst to the best. So Judas the betrayer was excluded from this blessing; the one who would deliver Him up was known to Him beforehand. Of the Pharisees, the Lord said, "God knoweth your hearts" (Luke 16:15), while to each of the seven churches the Lord said, "I know thy works" (Rev 2:2).

12 The subject of the divine garments, whether physical or spiritual, forms a profitable study. For example, in Isa 6:1, "his train (the hem of his garments) filled the temple"; as a babe He was "wrapped in swaddling clothes" (Luke 2:12); "his raiment was white and glistering" on the mount of transfiguration (Luke 9:29); the soldiers put upon Him "a purple robe" (John 19:2); His coat was without seam (19:23); on Patmos, He "was clothed with a garment down to the foot" (Rev 1:13); while at the future manifestation of His triumph and judgment, His vesture will be "dipped in blood" (Rev 19:13).

The Lord speaks. He asked the question, "Know ye what I have done to you?", the perfect tense "have done" being used to denote the spiritual results of the feet-washing as outlined in the next verse. He gave the disciples no opportunity to answer the question; He provided the answer Himself.

13 The Lord was setting a practical example for His disciples, since they so much needed it. He commenced by noting their recognition of His authority as "Master and Lord", the word for "Master" really being "Teacher". In other words, they recognised both His words and His works—the doctrine of the Teacher, and the deeds of the Lord.

We have already pointed out the dominant role played by the title "Lord" in the Gospels. But the title "Master" also appears frequently, and translates six different Greek words, all carrying different meanings:

1. *Didaskalos* (as here) appears many times in the Gospels. The title means "teacher", and is always translated "master" in the Gospels except when Nicodemus said "we know that thou art a teacher come from God" (3:2). This is also the word for "doctors" in Luke 2:46. In Paul's epistles, the word is always translated "teacher(s)" (1 Cor 12:28; Eph 4:11). The word is closely associated with "doctrine" (*didaskalia*).

2. *Epistatēs*, occurring six times in Luke only, means a commander or overseer. The disciples used this title of the Lord in connection with His authority.

3. *Rabbi* or *Rabbei*, was a polite form of address to teachers. The Lord was addressed by this title several times (1:38,49; 3:2,26; 4:31; 6:25; 9:2; 11:8). Judas used this title in duplicated form when he betrayed Him (Mark 14:45), where it is translated "Master, master".

4. *Kathēgētēs*, occurring twice in Matt 23:10, once as referring to the Lord as "Master", means a guide.

5. *Despotēs* implies a gracious despot when used of Deity. It is used five times of the master of slaves; four times of God (but translated "Lord" in Luke 2:29; Acts 4:24), and once of the Lord Jesus, "meet for the master's use" (2 Tim 2:21). In history, have there ever been gracious dictators?

6. *Kurios*, the title "Lord", but translated "master" a few times when denoting human relationships amongst men. It is used of the Lord in Eph 6:9, "knowing that your Master also is in heaven".

In our v.13, by quoting these two titles employed by the disciples, the Lord implied that they were being properly used by those who owned His authority.

14-15 Here the Lord acknowledged that He was giving them a demonstration, an example, in order that His disciples should follow Him; He knew that they were sadly lacking in this respect. Other examples are: "Christ also suffered . . . that ye should follow his steps" (1 Pet 2:21); the believer should walk "even as he walked" (1 John 2:6); "Be ye followers (imitators) of me, even as I also am of Christ" (1 Cor 11:1).

16-17 The vital principle that the Lord was demonstrating is contained in the words, "The servant (*doulos*, bondservant) is not greater than his lord". Again, "he that is sent" is the word "apostle" (*apostolos*). In each of these two contrasts, the disciples (servants, apostles) are in status far below the Lord Jesus as the One who sent them. This shows the nothingness of the spiritual man; we must not think highly of ourselves (Rom 12:3), taking the lowest position as did Paul (1 Cor 15:9). At the time, the apostles did not learn the lesson, for later they were still arguing as to who should be the greatest (Luke 22:24-30).

If the disciples did these things, the Lord announced that they were "blessed" (*makarios*, happy). Lowliness and obedience bring their rewards. But after their later failure, He restated the principle in other words, "ye shall not be so: but he that is greatest among you, let him be as the younger; and he that is chief, as he that doth serve" (Luke 22:26).

2. *The Son–to be Betrayed* 13:18-30

v.18 "I speak not of you all: I know whom I have chosen: but that the scripture may be fulfilled, He that eateth bread with me hath lifted up his heel against me.

v.19 Now I tell you before it come, that, when it is come to pass, ye may believe that I am *he*.

v.20 Verily, verily, I say unto you, He that receiveth whomsoever I send receiveth me; and he that receiveth me receiveth him that sent me.

v.21 When Jesus had thus said, he was troubled in spirit, and testified, and said, Verily, verily, I say unto you, that one of you shall betray me.

v.22 Then the disciples looked one on another, doubting of whom he spake.

v.23 Now there was leaning on Jesus' bosom one of his disciples, whom Jesus loved.

v.24 Simon Peter therefore beckoned to him, that he should ask who it should be of whom he spake.

v.25 He then lying on Jesus' breast saith unto him, Lord, who is it?

v.26 Jesus answered, He it is, to whom I shall give a sop, when I have dipped *it*. And when he had dipped the sop, he gave *it* to Judas Iscariot, *the son* of Simon.

v.27 And after the sop Satan entered into him. Then said Jesus unto him, That thou doest, do quickly.

v.28 Now no man at the table knew for what intent he spake this unto him.

v.29 For some *of them* thought, because Judas had the bag, that Jesus had said unto him, Buy *those things* that we have need of against the feast; or, that he should give something to the poor.

v.30 He then having received the sop went immediately out: and it was night."

18-20 *The Lord speaks*. There was one exception, however. There was one bad out of the twelve, unlike the sons of Jacob, where, apart from Benjamin, Joseph was the only one who was good (Gen 37). In John 6:70, the Lord had chosen twelve, but here in our v.18 He implied that only eleven had been chosen. Twelve had been chosen officially, but only eleven spiritually. This act of Judas was on his own initiative, though originating from Satan; the OT Scriptures were fulfilled—not in a fatalistic sense. They were inspired by the Holy Spirit through the prophets, since He knew all things future from the beginning.

Ps 41:9 is quoted, "which did eat of my bread, hath lifted up his heel against me". In this Psalm, the enemies of the Lord were not really triumphing, in spite of outward circumstances (vv.5,7,8). This refers to David's counsellor Ahithophel (2 Sam 15:12), who in David's great need turned traitor against him. Read also 2 Sam 16:21; 17:1,14,23, and note the similarities with Judas' case, particularly that Ahithophel went "and hanged himself". The lifted-up heel suggests an attempt to lift up the basest of man's natural aspirations above the exalted Person of Christ; this is the opposite of John 13:16.

The Lord made this fact known "before it come" so that they "may believe that I am" when the event actually took place. It was another proof that He was the great promised Prophet, in spite of going into death, for an accomplished prophecy validated the prophet who uttered the prophecy. This is in keeping with Deut 18:22 that answers the question "How shall we know?" in the negative, namely, if the prophecy was not fulfilled, then the prophet had not been sent from the Lord. Note that the Lord again used the title of His eternal existence, "I am (he)" (*egō eimi*).

V.20 enhances the apostolic position from which Judas fell, for this verse demonstrates the reception of Deity. If a man receives a divinely-sent apostle, then he also receives Christ, and hence he also receives the Father. If an apostle or his teaching is rejected, then Deity is also rejected. See 1 John 2:23; John 15:23. Thus the unspiritual who reject Paul's teaching cannot be believers (1 Cor 14:37), since they are rejecting Christ.

21 Between here and v.30, a company is cleansed, but throughout the passage the disciples did not understand. The cleansing of a company reminds us of:

1. Ananias and Sapphira (Acts 5:1-11).
2. The man in Corinth who was delivered unto Satan (1 Cor 5:1-13).
3. Hymenaeus and Alexander (1 Tim 1:19-20).
4. Nadab and Abihu (Lev 10:1-2).
5. Achan (Josh 7:1-26).
6. The cases of Adonijah, Joab, Abiathar, Shimei (1 Kings 2:13-46).
7. The tares amongst the wheat (Matt 13:33-43).

The verb "troubled" (*tarassō*) has a variety of meanings, both physical and involving a state of mind. Thus the water was troubled in 5:7. Men were troubled because of fear (Matt 2:3; 14:26). The Lord exhorted His disciples that their hearts should not be troubled (14:1,27). The verb is also used of Himself in John's Gospel (11:33; 12:27; 13:21). It indicates His deep sensitivity of soul; He was moved inwardly as He contemplated tragedy—here the fact that the betrayer would be "one of you".

The Lord speaks. In Matt 17:22, His betrayal was spoken of in the passive—not referring to any particular person. But in John's Gospel the identity of this person was narrowed down. Thus in 6:70 it was to be "one of you". In other words, the field was narrowed down to a company. This phrase "one of you" is thus employed a second time; see also Matt 26:21, and v.47 where Judas is described as "one of the twelve". Shortly afterwards, Judas was identified directly. This reminds us of Achan, when the narrowing process embraced Judah, the family, the household, and finally Achan (Josh 7:16-18). Conversely, any member of a local church should be known as "one of you", as was Onesimus and Epaphras (Col 4:9,12).

22-23 The doubt expressed by the disciples shows that they doubted even their own hearts. In Matt 26:22, everyone of them said, "Lord, is it I?"; Judas was included, although he knew that he had already arranged for the betrayal to take place. By joining with the rest, he sought to throw suspicion away from himself. A similar join-in-a-crowd attitude may be adopted today in a local church by someone intending to drop out; he may carry on as usual, until suddenly he disappears! But it is essential for any believer to know his own heart before the Lord. So many evils are described in the NT; thus each believer should take heed lest he fall. Each should know his own heart that he would not do this or that, without asking, "Lord, is it I?".

But the narrative switches from the worst to the best—to the apostle John, "whom Jesus loved"; not that the Lord loved John more than He loved the others, but John appreciated this love more than the others. This love was appreciated in spite of the question, "Lord, is it I?". This divine love was manifested at the cross (19:26); in the resurrection (20:2); in a time of weakness (21:7), and in expectation (21:20).

24-25 Simon Peter rapidly recovered from his doubt about himself, and immediately sought to find out who it would be. A very personal question would have to be put to the Lord, yet Peter was too far from Him around the table. But John was nearest to the Lord, and in the position best to ask Him who it would be. In v.23 John was "leaning" (*anakeimai*) upon the Lord; the RV has "reclining", on account of the position adopted at the meal. They would be reclining on cushions around the table, with John in front of the Lord. To ask the question, John gets even nearer; the AV has "lying" (*epipiptō*), but the RV uses the Greek word *anapiptō*, translated as "leaning back", showing clearly the idea of a slight movement rather than a mere static position.

John speaks. Strictly speaking, John's position was the most spiritual, and he could be assured of an answer to his question, "Lord, who is it?".

26 To us, as we read the Lord's statement and action, it is obvious that He thereby identified Judas as the betrayer. But it would appear that only John heard the Lord's reply, and hence knew the meaning of His action. The others did not hear, and did not know; moreover they did not know why Judas went out (v.29). Peter gave John a sign, and the Lord gave John a sign, but in both cases only John knew what was implied by the signs.

The Lord speaks. The giving of the sop to an individual was not the same sign as that which appears in Matt 26:23, "He that dippeth his hand with me in the dish". This refers to Ps 41:9, "which did eat of my bread". This act denoted that one of the twelve having fellowship with Him at the meal would be responsible. But in our v.26, the Lord Himself took the sop (a piece of bread dipped in the broth used at the feast). If the others (except John) had not heard what the Lord said, then Judas had not heard either; but by giving the sop to Judas the Lord thereby showed that He had identified the betrayer.

27 So Satan was active in one heart in the upper room. Over a year before, Judas was a demon (6:70), one of Satan's servants. In 13:2, the devil had placed the deed in Judas' heart; lust was conceiving ready to bring forth sin and death (Jas 1:15). But now Satan took possession of Judas in readiness for the deed to be done. This entering in of Satan is quite the opposite to the Spirit entering the hearts of believers at their conversion.

The Lord speaks. When He said, "What thou doest, do quickly", He spoke more loudly so that Judas and all the others could hear. This man knew that he had been identified. Matthew records another part of this brief conversation: Judas asked, "Master, is it I?", to which the Lord replied, "Thou hast said" (Matt 26:25). Knowing that he was identified, Judas might have wished to lie low for some time, but the Lord had to die on the morrow in keeping with the fact that His hour had come in the divine timetable, so Judas had to act quickly, even that night to accomplish his deed.

28-29 Only John now knew the inner character of Judas, at the same time knowing the divine ability of the Lord to pierce the motives in the hearts of men. All things were "naked and opened" to His eyes (Heb 4:13). The others heard the Lord's statement, but misconstrued it completely. The lesson for us is obvious: do not make deductions about a verse of Scripture if that verse is not understood. It is the natural mind rather than the spiritual mind that seeks to guess by carnal reasoning. The disciples ("some of them", but not John) had thought that the Lord had spoken other things to Judas, and that the statement "That thou doest, do quickly" was but the last of these statements, a command to action. Since Judas "had the bag", he must have been the sole treasurer of the few funds available to the Lord and His disciples, unlike Acts 6 where seven were appointed; (note in 2 Cor 8-9, responsibility for funds always belonged to a plurality and not to an individual). Hence the apostles could guess two possible reasons for Judas' departure, both of which were wrong:

1. To buy for the feast—not just for the Passover, but for the whole week of unleavened bread (Lev 23:6).

2. It was the Lord's custom in mercy to give to the poor who were always present. See 12:6, where Judas is identified as a thief, not caring for the poor, but holding the contents of the bag. During the church age, there was exercise financially towards the poor saints (Rom 15:26). See also Gal 2:10; 1 Cor 15:3 where love is essential.

30 Thus Judas went out, knowing that shortly it would be in the garden of Gethsemane that the betrayal would take place. The fact that "it was night" reflects on the moral conditions on the outside. Paul recalled this when he wrote "the same night in which he was betrayed" (1 Cor 11:23). Outside the sanctuary of the upper room, there was the greatest darkness amongst men, through whom the Lord moved to the cross. It is interesting to note the five occasions in Judas' experience when it is recorded that he "went":

1. He "went unto the chief priests" (Matt 26:14).

2. He "went immediately out" (John 13:30).

3. He "went before them, and drew near to Jesus to kiss him" (Luke 22:47).

4. He (and they) "went backward, and fell to the ground" (Luke 18:6).

5. He "went and hanged himself" (Matt 27:5).

3. *The Son–to be Glorified*
13:31-35

v.31 "Therefore, when he was gone out, Jesus said, Now is the Son of man glorified, and God is glorified in him.
v.32 If God be glorified in him, God shall also glorify him in himself, and shall straightway glorify him.
v.33 Little children, yet a little while I am with you. Ye shall seek me: and as I said unto the Jews, Whither I go, ye cannot come; so now I say to you.
v.34 A new commandment I give unto you, That ye love one another; as I have loved you, that ye also love one another.
v.35 By this shall all *men* know that ye are my disciples, if ye have love one to another."

31-32 *The Lord speaks.* The darkness having been expelled from the upper room, divine glory can be manifested. This is similar to 1 Kings 2:19-46, where four unpleasant characters of darkness had to be removed from the kingdom before the temple could be built and the glory of God manifested (8:10-11). Similarly, Elisha's place expanded after Gehazi "went out from his presence" (2 Kings 5:27; 6:1-2).

Though the darkness of the cross still lay before the Lord, with the departure of Judas the true Light could shine in the upper room. Man's unbelief had concealed His glory. For the Son to be glorified, and for God to be glorified in Him, a mountain-top experience was necessary, far removed from this world. In v.31 this glory is seen as accomplished, but in v.32 it is seen as yet to be, after the cross and resurrection. But the glory is mutual. Since God is glorified in the Son, then the Son will be glorified by God the Father "in himself", that is, the glory will be seen as one within the Godhead. The Son's glory and that of the Father is also seen in the prayer in 17:1,4,5.

33 Vv.31-32 had looked to heaven, but the disciples still had to live on earth; in these chapters, the Lord was greatly mindful of this fact. This is the only time it is recorded that the Lord called the apostles "Little children" (*teknion*), implying that the Lord viewed them as alone in weakness, as sheep amongst wolves. In the mature years of old age, John later described the readers of his first epistle as "little children" (1 John 2:1,12,28; 3:7,18; 4:4; 5:21), while Paul addressed the Galatians once in this style (Gal 4:19). Thus John later saw through Christ's eyes, perceiving younger converts in weakness and innocence. The "little while" in which the Lord would be with them refers to the brief while before His trial and crucifixion. The Lord was going into death, and then He would return to the Father. To neither place could they come, immediately at any rate. They might seek His body (20:2-9), and might seek Him by looking up to heaven (Acts 1:11), but He could not be found by such means. The Lord said similar things to the religious Pharisees in the temple (7:34; 8:21), but in unbelief they would never be able to make the heavenward journey. Similarly it was no use seeking for Elijah's body (2 Kings 2:16-18), "Ye shall not send".

34-35 The disciples would indeed rise in resurrection so as to be for ever with the Lord, but in the meanwhile He would give them a new commandment of love, based on His own example. This love of Christ was seen in humility meeting the needs of His disciples (v.1); it was also a sacrificial love leading to His death (Gal 2:20; Eph 5:2). The example of Christ is seen in the word "as". This word "as" is also seen in Eph 4:32 (dealing with forgiveness); Eph 5:2 (dealing with walk), and in 1 John 2:6 (also dealing with walk).

Moreover, this commandment was "new". The commandments of the law had also been in love (Lev 19:18), "thou shalt love thy neighbour as thyself", quoted by the Lord in His teaching (Matt 19:19; 22:39). But when grace supplanted law, the old love had to be transformed according to grace; the old had passed away. For example, as well as loving one's neighbour, one's enemy also had to be loved. The character of christian love is spelt out in 1 Cor 13, but this love may appear to be strange to an unbeliever in the world, not only when shown to them, but also when shown from believer to believer. In v.35, the world would know that this love originated from Himself, and could lead to salvation (17:21).

4. *The Son–to be Denied*
13:36-38

v.36 "Simon Peter said unto him, Lord, whither goest thou? Jesus answered him, Whither I go, thou canst not follow me now; but thou shalt follow me afterwards.
v.37 Peter said unto him, Lord, why cannot I follow thee now? I will lay down my life for thy sake.
v.38 Jesus answered him, Wilt thou lay down thy life for my sake? Verily, verily, I say unto thee, The cock shall not crow, till thou hast denied me thrice."

36 *Peter speaks*. In this brief paragraph, Peter breaks almost every characteristic of love detailed in 1 Cor 13:4-7. In fact, he bypassed the subject of love taken up in John 13:34-35, and in his question "Lord, whither goest thou?", he reverts to the Lord's statement "Whither I go" in v.33. It would seem that Peter had no idea that the time of the Lord's exodus had arrived.

The Lord speaks. By saying "thou canst not follow me now", He implied that His exodus and ascent back to His Father would be unique. Yet Peter would follow afterwards, in the sense that he also would be crucified in keeping with the Lord's words in 21:18-19 when He added "Follow me"; the apostle recalled this in 2 Pet 1:14, "shortly I must put off this my tabernacle, even as our Lord Jesus Christ hath showed me". Tradition tells us that Peter was crucified upside-down when he parted this life. By this death he would "glorify God" (21:19), so as to enter "an inheritance incorruptible, and undefiled, and that fadeth not away, reserved in heaven" (1 Pet 1:4).

37 *Peter speaks*. Once again, Peter mildly contradicted the Lord for such a statement (see Matt 16:22). In the upper room, Peter was full of courage; the enemies were on the outside. He thought that an ordinary sacrificial life was involved, and that he was equal to any eventuality. He did not realise that the giving up of the Lord's life was unique, and that no man could follow Him in being made a sacrifice for sin. Self-confidence can be the herald of an approaching fall—he did not take heed lest he should fall. In Luke 22:31, the Lord declared that Satan desired to have Peter—to obtain the chaff and not the wheat. But the Lord prayed for Peter's ultimate restoration, though he might be willing (in word but not in deed) to go to prison or to death (v.33).

38 *The Lord speaks*. He repeated Peter's assertion as a question, since He knew

Peter's heart and how he would fail. He predicted Peter's three-fold denial, a prediction that is also found in all three Synoptic Gospels (Matt 26:34; Mark 14:30; Luke 22:34). The mention of the cock (its two-fold crow is given only in Mark 14:30) showed that the time was short. Even though there was apparent safety in the upper room, this denial would take place before the night was over, before the first crow that would announce the coming morn.

Yet Peter and the others contradicted the Lord's prediction. In Mark 14:31 they all said that they would "die with" the Lord rather than deny Him. Inadvertently they were placing the Lord amongst the false prophets who predicted a thing, its non-fulfilment showing that God had not sent such a prophet (Deut 18:21-22). Had they realised the implications of their contradiction, they would have humbled themselves because the Lord knew that the denial would take place.

II. The Upper Room: The Son's Teaching about the Comforter (14:1-31)

1. *The Father's House on High*
14:1-4

v.1 "Let not your heart be troubled: ye believe in God, believe also in me.
v.2 In my Father's house are many mansions: if *it were* not *so*, I would have told you. I go to prepare a place for you.
v.3 And if I go and prepare a place for you, I will come again, and receive you unto myself; that where I am, *there* ye may be also.
v.4 And whither I go ye know, and the way ye know."

The Lord now gives an extended discourse, the subject matter of which is intended to prepare His disciples for His forthcoming absence. We have the subjects of Preparation (vv.1-4); His Person (vv.5-12); Prayer (vv.13-15); Promise (vv.16-26), and Peace (vv.27-31). The promise of the giving of the Spirit and His work is found essentially in John's Gospel. He would testify of the things that the Lord had said (v.26), of the Lord Himself (15:26), and of all truth and things to come (16:30).

Strictly, the chapter appears to be in the form of what we call a Bible Reading; the Lord rightly takes the dominant role, but His discourse is interspersed by three questions and comments by Thomas (v.5), Philip (v.8), and by Judas not Iscariot (v.22). The discourse takes place in the upper room.

1 *The Lord speaks*. This follows on from the previous chapter; the disciples might well have been discouraged, in not understanding the feet-washing performed by the Lord, in seeking to be the greatest, in the disciples not being certain of their own hearts, in John knowing that Judas would betray Him, and in the prediction of Peter's denial. Their hearts were not to be troubled by such weaknesses, since divine help was to be forthcoming. This verb "troubled" is the same as applied to water being agitated (5:7); it is used of mental agitation at false doctrine (Gal 1:7) and on account of fear (1 Pet 3:14). The word is used of the Lord in John 11:33; 12:27; 13:21, though obviously not in the sense of mental agitation so common amongst men.

To counteract their troubles, the Lord asserted that they believe in God, and hence that they also believe in Him in spite of betrayal, weaknesses and denials. Thus the soul rises above the trouble. The RV and JND both have "believe in me" in the imperative, but the Greek verbal form *pisteuete* can also be translated "ye believe" as a fact rather than as a command. To have instructed the disciples to believe would have made matters worse; they would not have known what to think, knowing that they believed in Him already! Rather, the Lord implied that their faith in Him rises above the weaknesses.

2 The Lord then took their hearts to their heavenly inheritance, to the Father's house (*oikia*) where there were "many mansions" (*monē*). He had spoken of His "Father's house" in 2:16 where the similar word *oikos* is used. Vine states that the original distinction between the two words was largely lost in NT times, so we suspect that the two distinct words in John's Gospel are used to show that one was on earth and one was in heaven. The Father's house on high is the eternal dwelling place of the Son and of believers. But the word for "mansions" (used only here and in v.23 in the NT) is more difficult to explain.

We do not believe that heaven is separated into compartments, rooms being provided for all. The Lord used the typical language and concepts from the OT. In Solomon's temple, three rows of "chambers" were built alongside the side walls of the temple (1 Kings 6:6), with winding stairs connecting the three levels (v.8). In the rebuilt temple after the captivity, there were likewise these chambers for storage (Neh 12:44), and similarly in Ezekiel's vision temple (Ezek 40:7; 41:6; 42:1-13), this last v.13 showing that they were to be used for the sacrificial service of the priests. Herod's temple likewise had such series of chambers according to profane history, though the NT does not mention them. We believe that by "mansions" the Lord referred to the availability of, and opportunities for, faithful service on high. The Lord has entered in to appear in the presence of God for us (Heb 6:20; 9:24). He did not go to prepare the mansions, rather to prepare a place, namely the entering in freely by believers, since under the earthly temple systems, all entry was barred by the veil. As those who enter in, "his servants shall serve him" (Rev 22:3).

3-4 Here the Lord promised that He would come again for His own people, a coming to be distinguished from His coming in power and glory (Matt 24:30). This does not refer to His reappearing in resurrection after His death, nor does it refer to the intermediate state after death, prior to the rapture. Rather, it is the truth made known to Paul "by the word of the Lord". This truth was that "the Lord himself shall descend from heaven . . . and the dead in Christ shall rise first: then we which are alive and remain shall be caught up together with them in the clouds, to meet the Lord in the air: and so shall we ever be with the Lord" (1

Thess 4:14-18). The object is eternal unity with Him—to be where He is. The past may seem gloomy, but there should be no trouble of mind, since the infinitely better future lies before at His return. When He will "receive" us unto Himself, He will present to Himself "a glorious church" (Eph 5:27), at the same time presenting us to God, saying "Behold I and the children which God hath given me" (Heb 2:13).

Moreover, the disciples should know both the pathway and the ultimate destination, since such aspects of truth had not been lacking from His teaching. Yet this remark showed up the continued ignorance of the apostles—an ignorance that persisted until after His resurrection and the giving of the Spirit, in spite of the clarity of the Lord's remarks in this chapter.

2. *The Question of Thomas*
14:5-7

v.5 "Thomas saith unto him, Lord, we know not whither thou goest; and how can we know the way?

v.6 Jesus saith unto him, I am the way, the truth, and the life: no man cometh unto the Father, but by me.

v.7 If ye had known me, ye should have known my Father also: and from henceforth ye know him, and have seen him."

5 *Thomas speaks.* It is remarkable that Thomas always appeared to misunderstand. In 11:16, he suggested that they should go to Jerusalem to die with Him; here in 14:5 he failed to understand what was implied by "the way"; in 20:25 he failed to believe that the others had seen the Lord; in 21:2 he failed to perceive the necessity of true consecration. Thus in our verse he contradicted the Lord's statement "ye know", as if he did not know the pathway and the destination. We would expect this ignorance from an unbeliever, but not from one who had been listening to the Lord's teaching for three years. After three years of listening to Paul's teaching, the Ephesians were mature in faith and knowledge.

6 *The Lord speaks.* He presented Himself as the way and the destination. As the way, He is the mediator between God and men, the "new and living way" (Heb 10:20), and "the forerunner" (6:20), the One who leads His people as the Good Shepherd. This way should be contrasted with the broad way that leads many to destruction.

Once a believer is on this way, then he can learn the truth that makes him free. No doubt the title "the truth" anticipates Pilate's question, "What is truth?" (18:38). Certainly this character of the Lord contrasts with "the lie" (the man of sin) whom men will believe in the future (2 Thess 2:11).

Again, only a believer can know the Lord as "the life", for "In him was life". Life is active, and in Christ a believer grows, manifesting that life, for it should be made "manifest in our mortal flesh" (2 Cor 4:11). This essential character of the Lord is in contrast with the man of sin, the anti-Christ, who will be consumed and will be destroyed (2 Thess 2:8).

Only by the Lord thus manifested can a man come to the Father and remain with the Father. Only thieves and robbers attempt other methods, of which religious men without Christ make so much. But the Lord knows those who are His.

These three great designations of the Lord can be contrasted with three OT characters (Jude 11):

1. The way: "they have gone in the way of Cain".

2. The truth: "the error of Balaam".

3. The life: "perished in the gainsaying of Core".

7 This verse should be contrasted with 8:19 spoken to the Pharisees. They did not know Him, and they did not know the Father. Yet the character and works of the Son certainly showed forth the Father, for He spoke and did all things received from His Father. The apostles may have been vague in the past, but they were not to be like the Pharisees in the future: "from henceforth" they would know the Father, and would have seen Him in the Son. Not that He could be seen absolutely, as Exod 33:20; John 1:18; 1 Tim 6:16 make plain. The Spirit reveals the Father now to believers in the Son; such truth is spiritually discerned, and cannot be attained by philosophy and natural reasonings (1 Cor 2:11-13).

3. *The Statement of Philip*
14:8-21

v.8 "Philip saith unto him, Lord, shew us the Father, and it sufficeth us.
v.9 Jesus saith unto him, Have I been so long time with you, and yet hast thou not known me, Philip? he that hath seen me hath seen the Father; and how sayest thou *then*, Shew us the Father?
v.10 Believest thou not that I am in the Father, and the Father in me? the words that I speak unto you I speak not of myself: but the Father that dwelleth in me, he doeth the works.
v.11 Believe me that I *am* in the Father, and the Father in me: or else believe me for the very works' sake.
v.12 Verily, verily, I say unto you, He that believeth on me, the works that I do shall he do also; and greater *works* than these shall he do; because I go unto my Father.
v.13 And whatsoever ye shall ask in my name, that will I do, that the Father may be glorified in the Son.
v.14 If ye shall ask any thing in my name, I will do *it*.
v.15 If ye love me, keep my commandments.
v.16 And I will pray the Father, and he shall give you another Comforter, that he may abide with you for ever;
v.17 *Even* the Spirit of truth; whom the world cannot receive, because it

seeth him not, neither knoweth him: but ye know him; for he dwelleth with you, and shall be in you.
v.18 I will not leave you comfortless: I will come to you.
v.19 Yet a little while, and the world seeth me no more; but ye see me: because I live, ye shall live also.
v.20 At that day ye shall know that I *am* in my Father, and ye in me, and I in you.
v.21 He that hath my commandments, and keepeth them, he it is that loveth me: and he that loveth me shall be loved of my Father, and I will love him, and will manifest myself to him."

8 *Philip speaks.* In John's record, this man was the first to whom the Lord said, "Follow me" (1:43). Philip then requested Nathanael to "Come and see". Later, the Lord proved him by asking where bread could be obtained (6:5); the apostle's answer showed that he was not expecting a miraculous event. Again, at the feast, certain Greeks told Philip that "we would see Jesus" (12:21). Twice, therefore, the possibility of others seeing the Lord arose in Philip's experience.

This was the apostle who broke into the Lord's discourse, not with a question, but with a request that they might be shown the Father. No doubt he would recall certain OT events when God had been seen, such as "they saw the God of Israel" (Exod 24:10), and "I saw also the Lord sitting upon a throne" (Isa 6:1), though evidently in restricted vision form. He would think that such could be repeated, since the Lord spoke so often of the Father. Philip would then be satisfied, "it sufficeth us". But a request made in weakness could never be satisfied, however great the response might be. On the other hand, God can provide satisfaction, as when He spoke to Paul, "My grace is sufficient for thee" (2 Cor 12:9), and so it turned out to be in his experience.

9 *The Lord speaks.* Note that the word "you" is changed to "thou", while in v.10 "thou" is changed to "you". The change from singular to plural, and vice versa, is prominent in Scripture (see, for example, 3:7), though the so-called modern translations obliterate the distinction, so cannot be assessed as suitable for detailed Bible study.

The truth is that "he that hath seen me hath seen the Father", and in connection with this the Lord asked three questions in vv.9-10. To a natural mind looking only on the outward appearance, this would seem impossible, but the spiritual mind must be taught by revelation so as to appreciate the Lord's remarks. No doubt mere words in either Greek or English cannot provide a full explanation of the Lord's statement, for human words are a poor vehicle through which to express the deep things of the Godhead. In fact, vv.10-11 form guidelines provided by the Lord as a means of educating faith in this matter. It is interesting to note that in 15:24 the world of unbelieving men had also seen "both me and my Father", but this had led to hatred and sin.

10-11 The Son in the Father and the Father in the Son expresses divine equality; faith must grasp the infinite within the infinite (see also 10:38; 17:21).

This should be distinguished from "ye in me, and I in you" (14:20); this does *not* imply equality, since we are but finite while He is infinite.

To stress the equality, the Lord mentioned "words" not "from himself" (*ap' emautou*), and also "the works", the result of the Father dwelling in Him. We have noted this duplication of divine activity before, in the matter of words, works, will and witness (see 5:30,36; 8:18,38; 10:37). This is the outward manifestation of the infinite within the infinite. The Lord invites us to believe this in v.11 (the imperative "believe" is plural), staggering not through unbelief, but being fully persuaded (Rom 4:20-21). But if faith lacks understanding, He substituted something more tangible, "believe me for the very works' sake". By this exercise of sight, a soul would perceive unity in purpose, and in time he would perceive by faith unity in Person.

12 The development of thought in these verses goes beyond the original request of Philip; the Father's works lead on to the apostles' works. They had already been granted the ability to do many of the wondrous works that the Lord did: "Heal the sick, cleanse the lepers, raise the dead, cast out devils (demons): freely ye have received, freely give" (Matt 10:8). This was, however, conditional upon faith (Matt 17:19-20). And this was perpetuated after His ascension, lasting for as long as it pleased God to give such gifts to men (Mark 16:18). Note that the Lord did not say "all the works" that He did; for example, the calming of the sea was never within the apostles' competence. By "greater works than these", we understand the Lord to refer, not to the totality of His works, but to the works that the disciples had been granted to do. They would do greater things, because His forthcoming presence in heaven with the Father would enable (i) prayer to be offered in His Name, and (ii) the giving of the Spirit of God. Their spiritual works in the Acts would then be greater than the physical works in the Gospels, because their sphere of ministry would be changed and enhanced.

13-15 The subject of prayer comes before the subject of the giving of the Holy Spirit. To ask in His Name was to be something new (see 16:24). To ask in His Name means that their prayer had to be as if the Lord Himself had prayed that prayer. For the Son had received answers from the Father; similarly He would ensure that answers were given to spiritual prayers after His ascension. The ultimate objective of answered prayer is that "the Father may be glorified in the Son". He had glorified the Father when he was on earth (17:4); now the Father will be glorified after the Son's return to heaven.

There are many conditions laid down in the NT for prayers to be answered: For example, a good thing asked (Matt 7:11); two or three agreeing (18:19); not to doubt (21:21); to believe that the things asked would be received (Mark 11:22-24); to have faith as a grain of mustard seed (Luke 17:6); to ask in His Name (that is, as if He were asking) with the objective "that the Father may be glorified in the Son" (John 14:13-14); to abide in Him, and His words in us

(15:7); to bring forth lasting fruit (v.16); not to ask amiss (James 4:3); the one praying must be "a righteous man" (5:16); to keep His commandments, and to "do those things that are pleasing in his sight" (1 John 3:22); to ask "according to his will" (5:14), an impressive list, for all to take heed in their prayer life.

There is a certain reciprocity in these verses: in v.14, the Lord will do what we ask; in v.15, He wants us to do what He asks. Keeping His commandments is based on love to Him. This is similar to 13:34; the commandment itself was that believers love each other, as He had loved them. And this mutual love was not in words, but in deed and in truth (1 John 3:18). Moreover, this love is not based on the law that regulated mutual activity between men, but is based on grace, as Paul wrote, the "labour of love" (1 Thess 1:3), against which there is no law.

16 The Holy Spirit is now brought before us in chs.14-16. There are described His character, reception and work in a soul. The giving of the Spirit would be the great divine provision made for believers following the Lord's exodus from this scene. This verse contains the three Persons of the Trinity: the Son prays to the Father who gives the Spirit. This prayer does not form the plan to give the Spirit, but it is a placing of His mediatorship before the Father so that the plan could be effected after He ascended back to heaven.

This verse and also v.26, where the Father sends the Spirit, are not inconsistent with 15:26; 16:7 where the Son is seen as sending the Spirit. For it is only by the Spirit that believers can be in contact with the Father. Thus the order must be: the Father provides for men; the Son receives the Spirit from the Father (Acts 2:33); the Son actually sends the Spirit to believers ("he hath shed forth this", Acts 2:33), thereby bringing men into contact with the Father, enabling them to address Him as "Abba, Father".

The word "other" is *allos*, meaning another of the same kind, namely divine. The name "Comforter" (*paraklētos*) implies One who has been brought alongside to help, showing the abiding presence of the Spirit. This name is the same as the title "advocate" (1 John 2:1), namely "Jesus Christ the righteous". He is our Advocate when we sin; the Spirit is the Comforter (Paraclete) as helping our infirmities (Rom 8:26), and this involves keeping us from sinning.

17 The title "Spirit of truth" differentiates the Holy Spirit absolutely from "the spirit of error" (1 John 4:6). This spirit of error is described as working in the "false prophets" who are gone out into the world (v.1); it is the spirit of anti-Christ that denies that Jesus Christ is come in the flesh (v.3). This spirit of error works in the false teachers who deny the Lord (2 Pet 2:1), and causes men to call "Jesus accursed", while the Spirit of God enables believers to confess Him as Lord (1 Cor 12:2-3).

The Spirit of truth is entirely foreign to the world; men who are occupied with the world-system of religion, politics, entertainment, social excesses, and immorality cannot see Him and cannot know Him; He (as well as the truth He brings) is spiritually discerned. These ideals and occupations of men are independent of faith and the heavenly realm. Such men cannot receive the Spirit, just as they did not receive the Lord Jesus (1:11). Nor can they receive the things of the Spirit of God (1 Cor 2:14).

But for believers, the Spirit dwells with them, and in them. Note carefully:

1. The Spirit "on" is an OT concept; see Num 11:29; Isa 61:1, though for the purpose of inspiration the Spirit was "in" the prophets (1 Pet 1:11).

2. The Spirit "in" is a NT concept for all believers, promised by the Lord in 14:17; 1 Cor 6:19; 1 John 3:24.

3. "In" the Spirit is a NT concept, baptism in the Spirit having taken place in Acts 2:2, when the disciples were sitting in the house that was filled by the rushing wind.

18-19 To the apostles at that moment, the Lord's words must have seemed somewhat mysterious, with the Lord going and the Spirit coming. They could not conceive what it would be like without the Lord being with them. He had called them "Little children" (13:33), and if He were no longer with them, they would feel like orphans. The Lord anticipated this feeling, so He stated that He would not leave them "comfortless", an unfortunate AV choice of word, since it tends to be confused with the title "the Comforter". The word used *orphanos* means children with no parents or father. In James 1:27, the word is translated "fatherless"; the RV uses "desolate" in John 14:18. Hence the Lord promised, "I will come to you". This is quite distinct from His promise in v.3; in the light of v.19, it must refer to His resurrection manifestations, such as coming to them in the upper room. Indeed the world would not see Him again after His holy body had been taken down from the cross, "but ye see me", an indication of His resurrection when He showed Himself to them as alive from the dead. Many infallible proofs would be supplied to them, so that they would become witnesses of His resurrection. His resurrection life would prove that they had life also; if He were not risen, all believers would still be in their sins, ultimately perishing (1 Cor 15:16-19). Our life derives from, and depends on, His life.

It should be pointed out that other expositors interpret the words "I will come to you" differently. Some suggest that it refers to the whole period between His ascension and the rapture; that is true (Eph 3:17; Matt 28:20), though to the present author this truth does not fit into the context. In fact, this is the truth announced in v.23 of our chapter.

20 Those expositors would explain "that day" as the day of Pentecost onwards, as if the truth of the Son being in the Father, of believers being in the Son, and of the Son being in believers, were a truth only revealed by the Spirit. But the Lord was expressing this truth there and then in this discourse (14:11): His resurrection would serve to enhance the truth.

21 The relationship between love and His commandments is rather different here. In v.15, love is a condition for keeping His commandments; here, keeping His commandments is a condition for love to be shown. A whole series of results follows from the believer's love for Christ. Firstly, he shall be loved of the Father. This is evidently not the evangelical love of God that provides for the salvation of a repentant sinner; rather it is the manifestation of divine satisfaction with a believer on account of his new life in Christ. Secondly, this believer will be loved by the Son. This is not the evangelical love of Christ, as expressed by Paul, "the Son of God, who loved me, and gave himself for me" (Gal 2:20). Rather it is the continued subsequent love, "the love of Christ, which passeth knowledge" (Eph 3:19). Thirdly, the Son "will manifest" Himself to such a believer. This is not a resurrection manifestation of the Son, since it is personal to every individual believer. Rather, it is a permanent manifestation throughout a believer's life. It is through the Holy Spirit who sheds His love abroad in our hearts (Rom 5:5).

It is true that we love Him because He first loved us (1 John 4:19); this is the love of Christ in the gospel unto salvation—a love that came first. But in our verse the Lord taught the reverse—when we love Him, we shall be loved by the Father and the Son. This refers to the subsequent christian life that brings forth the divine love in satisfaction of a soul that is already saved.

4. *The Question of Judas (not Iscariot)* 14:22-31

v.22 "Judas saith unto him, not Iscariot, Lord, how is it that thou wilt manifest thyself unto us, and not unto the world?

v.23 Jesus answered and said unto him, If a man love me, he will keep my words: and my Father will love him, and we will come unto him, and make our abode with him.

v.24 He that loveth me not keepeth not my sayings: and the word which ye hear is not mine, but the Father's which sent me.

v.25 These things have I spoken unto you, being *yet* present with you.

v.26 But the Comforter, *which is* the Holy Ghost, whom the Father will send in my name, he shall teach you all things, and bring all things to your remembrance, whatsoever I have said unto you.

v.27 Peace I leave with you, my peace I give unto you: not as the world giveth, give I unto you. Let not your heart be troubled, neither let it be afraid.

v.28 Ye have heard how I said unto you, I go away, and come *again* unto you. If ye loved me, ye would rejoice, because I said, I go unto the Father: for my Father is greater than I.

v.29 And now I have told you before it come to pass, that, when it is come to pass, ye might believe.

v.30 Hereafter I will not talk much with you: for the prince of this world cometh, and hath nothing in me.

v.31 But that the world may know that I love the Father; and as the Father gave me commandment, even so I do. Arise, let us go hence."

22 In Matt 10:3 we read of an apostle "Lebbaeus, whose surname was Thaddaeus", while in Mark 3:18, we read of "Thaddaeus" only. But in the corresponding list of apostles in Luke 6:16, there only appears "Judas the brother of James", implying the identity of these three names. Luke repeats this name in Acts 1:13. In all lists in the Gospels, Judas Iscariot appears last. In our v.22, John distinguishes very carefully between the two men with the names Judas, by using the additional description "not Iscariot". Of all the activities and discourses of the apostles, this verse is the only one that informs us of any statement by this Judas—he was evidently a man of few words, and yet his question brought forth further truth by the Lord in His discourse.

Judas speaks. Clearly Judas did not appreciate the meaning of the word "manifest". He associated the word with manifestation as from one man to any other, as in 7:4, "show thyself to the world", where a word *emphanizō* with the same root as in *phaneroō* is used. The fact that Judas asked about manifestation to the world shows that he had no spiritual thought, either of resurrection or of the permanent dwelling of the Lord with His people after His ascension. It was a natural question only, or it may have been connected with the Lord's manifestation in glory when every eye shall see Him, in which case he could not understand why the world should be excluded.

23-24 *The Lord speaks*. In this verse, the conditions for His manifestation are revealed, showing clearly why the world cannot partake in this blessing. It is a matter of loving Him and keeping His words, effectively repeating v.21 that caused Judas to interrupt. The manifestation is then described as "we will come unto him, and make our abode with him". So both the Father and the Son will make their abode with the believer, as well as the Holy Spirit, implying that the three Persons of the Godhead take up their residence in the temple-body of the believer. The word "abode" (*monē*) is the same as that in v.2, though the context refers to a different implication.

Note that there are three comings in this chapter (as we perceive their explanations):

1. In the future, when the Lord comes for all believers (v.3).

2. His resurrection manifestations prior to His ascension (v.18).

3. His coming throughout the believer's life (v.23).

In v.24, the Lord presented the negative, thereby excluding the world, thus dealing with the two sides of Judas' question. An unbeliever's lack of love for the Lord, and his disobedience to His sayings (that is, His words, *logos*), have their only possible consequences—the Lord cannot come and manifest Himself to a man who hates Him (15:18,23-25). Note that the Lord again stressed that His word was really the Father's word; hence there is a double disobedience involved in unbelievers. Previously, He had called such men "foolish" when they built their houses on sand; these are the men who hear but do not (Matt 7:26-27).

25-26 No doubt the apostles would think that their responsibility to keep His words was great, particularly when their memories concerning these words were failing in many important matters (Luke 18:34), and over the years the Lord had taught them so much. When He was present, His many sayings were verbal, not recorded in written form as in the OT; hence much could be overlooked in ignorance after His exodus. How, for example, would John and Matthew (who had been with Him in the days of His flesh) be able to record in detail the various long discourses of the Lord? So He introduced one of the great works of the forthcoming Holy Spirit in His capacity of helping. Two aspects of this are stated here:

1. He will teach "all things", showing the origin of all subsequent new doctrine and revelation (1 Cor 11:23; 1 Thess 4:15).

2. The new doctrine that the Lord had introduced in His teaching would also not be forgotten; it would be revived in their minds by the indwelling Spirit. The proper meaning of the OT would also be revealed, enabling Peter to quote so much from the OT about the resurrection in Acts 2, and enabling Paul (as Saul) to "prove" that Jesus is the Christ from the OT so soon after his conversion (Acts 9:20,22).

27 The Lord now repeated the same exhortation as in v.1, "Let not your heart be troubled". With the upper room discourse nearly over, He would still provide comfort for His disciples when they would be alone. In vv.1-3, the comfort related to the possession of a hope for the future—when He would come again. But here in v.27 the comfort would be that of present peace during His absence. The giving of peace was a common greeting amongst the Jews, just as we say "Good morning" whether the morning is good or not. Recently the Lord had spoken of wars in the world (Matt 24:6), but this should not lead to anxiety. Most men desire peace, but nations often engage in war to achieve an advantage. Men say, "Peace and safety", but sudden destruction comes (1 Thess 5:3), for there is no peace to the wicked. The world's peace always has war just around the corner. But the Lord's peace is different; it is not how the world gives. Rather, it is heavenly, and independent of outward circumstances. His peace passes all understanding and can keep the heart (Phil 4:7); it is God who fills the believer with joy and peace (Rom 15:13). With this peace, there should be no anxiety about things in this world, since He has overcome.

28 This repeated statement "I go away, and come again unto you" refers to v.3, so the Lord was placing both present peace and a present hope of the future before the disciples. The Lord's leaving them should not engender any sense of sadness, particularly after His resurrection when His sufferings would be over. The two on the Emmaus road were sad until their hearts burned with joy (Luke 24:17,32); the apostles would experience the same emotions (John 16:22). Thus in our v.28, love should lead to rejoicing because the ultimate destiny of the Lord was not to be death but to return to the Father. Then He added "for my Father is greater than I". We are not allowed to interpret this as implying inequality in Person or works (as Paul did for himself in 1 Cor 15:9). In the context when the Lord was speaking, He was on earth with His infinite divine glory hidden from natural eyes, while the glory of the Father was shining throughout heaven. We believe that this is the sense in which the words lesser and greater can be used. See Phil 2:5-9; Heb 2:9. Note the RV of Ps 8:5, "thou hast made him but little lower than God", which again refers to His form when on earth, and not to His divine Person itself.

29 In the statement "before it come to pass", the word "it" refers to His return to the Father. This actually took place when He was carried up into heaven (Luke 24:51), when "a cloud received him out of their sight" (Acts 1:9). The disciples did not see His actual reuniting with the Father, for the cloud hid this triumphant event from human eyes. But they would believe that the event fulfilled His words, and this would enhance their faith in Him. Thus Peter afterwards could say that He had been "by the right hand of God exalted" (Acts 2:33), quoting Ps 110:1 to prove it.

30-31 To terminate this upper room discourse, the Lord said "Hereafter", namely, referring to the following events before His cross on the next day. This discourse (and chs.15-17) would mark the end of the disciples' open association with the Lord in the days of His flesh. Up to now, He had dominated in the circumstances through which He had moved. But now it would appear that Satan as "the prince of this world" would dominate circumstances, commencing with his work in Judas and the betrayal. As the Lord later said to the priests and captains of the temple who came to arrest Him, "this is your hour, and the power of darkness" (Luke 22:53). The power of the unseen world took control of men, and even Peter temporarily (Luke 22:31), and thus the Lord was crucified. But there was nothing whatsoever in the Lord to respond adversely to anything that Satan might hurl against Him; see, for example, Matt 27:40-43. There was perfection at the beginning of His ministry, and perfection at the end. Satan still works in the same guise; unbelievers walk "according to the prince of the power of the air" (Eph 2:2), but believers have been delivered "from the power of darkness" (Col 1:13).

The Lord was going to the sufferings of the cross because of His love to the Father. The world of unbelievers would never understand or know that, as long as men remain in unbelief. But if some are converted, then they will know. And in the future, when He comes in power and great glory, then all will know,

though then it will be too late to exercise faith. He will say, "I never knew you".
The commandment led Him to the cross, as He said prophetically, "I come . . . to do thy will, O God" (Heb 10:7). It was therefore time to leave the upper room, to leave Jerusalem, to cross the brook Kidron, and to enter the garden of Gethsemane, thereby preparing the way for the betrayal. Truly He knew all things that were shortly to come upon Him. "Arise, let us go hence" shows the perfection of obedience, to leave the sanctuary and safety of the upper room that He would not see again until after His resurrection (20:19). Judas had left the room before for his mission; the Lord was now leaving for His mission. Judas went "to his own place" (Acts 1:25); and the Lord ultimately went to His rightful place, the right hand of the Father on high.

III. The Way to Gethsemane: The Son's Teaching about Fruitfulness (15:1-27)

1. *The True Vine: its Branches and its Fruit*
15:1-8

v.1 "I am the true vine, and my Father is the husbandman.
v.2 Every branch in me that beareth not fruit he taketh away: and every *branch* that beareth fruit, he purgeth it, that it may bring forth more fruit.
v.3 Now ye are clean through the word which I have spoken unto you.
v.4 Abide in me, and I in you. As the branch cannot bear fruit of itself, except it abide in the vine; no more can ye, except ye abide in me.
v.5 I am the vine, ye *are* the branches: he that abideth in me, and I in him the same bringeth forth much fruit: for without me ye can do nothing.
v.6 If a man abide not in me, he is cast forth as a branch, and is withered; and men gather them, and cast *them* into the fire, and they are burned.
v.7 If ye abide in me, and my words abide in you, ye shall ask what ye will, and it shall be done unto you.
v.8 Herein is my Father glorified, that ye bear much fruit; so shall ye be my disciples."

1 This discourse took place along the way from the upper room, through Jerusalem, and across the Kidron valley. It must have taken place before Matt 26:36, and within Luke 22:39. Ch.15 is remarkable in the sense that it is the only chapter in John's Gospel (apart from ch.17) where a conversation does not take place. The apostles made no interruption—no questions and no statements.

Chs.15-16 are concerned with the new life of the believer lived in the world. There is fruitbearing before the Father (vv.1-16); persecution in the world (v.17 to 16:4); the Spirit's work in the believer and in the world (vv.5-15), and the Lord's final words on His death and resurrection (vv.16-33).

The idea of a vine is an OT concept. Ps 80:8-11 shows that Israel was a prosperous vine out of Egypt. From v.12, this vine is seen as broken and burnt, though there would be a strong branch (Judah's line) leading to Christ. Again, in

Isa 5:1-7 Judah and Israel are likened to a vine, though in Isaiah's time it was bringing forth wild grapes. However, in the Lord Jesus, Israel as a vine would be replaced by One who would bring forth fruit for God. Ch.15 does not deal with the fruit that He has brought forth personally, such as "the travail of his soul" (Isa 53:11), and the "much fruit" (John 12:24). Rather, His teaching deals with the method by which He brings forth fruit in and through His people. His object is to enable a branch to produce even more fruit. Different explanations have been given for v.2, where a branch is "taken away". This verb *airō*, among other meanings, has the sense of taking or lifting up thirty six times in the NT. A vine has long weak branches which sink to the ground, taking root, becoming earthbound and fruitless. Thus men called "lifters" are employed to raise the branches. An interpretation is therefore given that the Father causes the branches to be lifted up away from the influence of the world, so that more fruit can be produced.

The Lord speaks. The Lord introduced Himself as the new and true Vine. His Father is the One in control, seeking fruit not from the Jewish nation as in the parable in Matt 21:34, but from the Lord's disciples. This control over fruitbearing is within the province of the Godhead. The Father controls as in 1 Cor 3:6-8; the Son conveys and channels life; the Spirit is the current flowing through the branches to the fruitbearing twigs.

2 No believer (except perhaps apostles like John and Paul) can produce maximum fruit. Two kinds of believers are considered as to their responsibility in fruitbearing.

1. Those branches that have become earthbound, He lifts up, for contact with the world interferes with effective service. Thus in 1 Cor 3:3, there were those in Corinth who walked "as men", with but little to distinguish them from unbelievers. In Gal 3:1, there were many who had been "bewitched" by religionists around. There may be an unsanctified preoccupation with the literature and sport of this world. Such believers need to be lifted up by exhortation, that they should mortify their members upon the earth so as to rise to spiritual heights (Col 3:1-4), that they should separate themselves from degrading moral and religious influences (2 Cor 6:14-16).

2. Those branches producing fruit are purged so as to produce more. Here is pruning so as to render believers even more spiritual, separated and practically holy. In v.3, these are already "clean", referring to the apostles who were with Him. This cannot refer to the original cleansing from sin upon one's conversion; rather to the daily cleansing by the word, as in 13:10. This would lead to further hearing the word, understanding it, and to the production of fruit, even one hundredfold (Matt 13:23), where a different metaphor is used (seed and not the vine).

3 Certainly the agent of cleansing is the word of God in its many aspects, for it is profitable "for doctrine, for reproof, for correction, for instruction in righteousness" (2 Tim 3:16). By this means, the branches receive every possible help, as was Paul's exercise when he wrote, "we do all things, dearly beloved, for your edifying" (2 Cor 12:19).

4-5 Note that these two verses contain truth in reverse orders. In v.4, we first have a spiritual statement, and then a botanical metaphor. But in v.5, we first have a botanical metaphor, and then a spiritual statement. What is being described is a series of pipes connected to a central reservoir. All plants, trees and flowers are like that—a series of tubes connecting all parts of the living organism to the source of sap, thus maintaining life, growth and fruitfulness. A good example of this is found in Zech 4:2-3,11, where tubes lead oil from the two olive trees to a central bowl, to which are connected seven further pipes leading oil down to seven lamps. In our day no doubt we could use the metaphor of wires, cables and the grid system connecting every electrical appliance in house, street, office, factory and railway to the electrical generators, but this metaphor lacks the underlying truth of the transmission of life. Note that the Lord implies that the branch by itself cannot bear fruit; neither can a believer. He must abide in the vine—he must be attached by an undisturbed faith to the Lord, so life can flow from Head to the body. This is a different metaphor, but the whole body is fitly joined, member to member, but ultimately growing up in Christ who is the Head (Eph 4:15-16). Such an attachment is permanent, undeflected by the various winds of doctrine.

6 We agree with those expositors who assert that believers are not in view in this verse. It is not a question of a christian, once being a branch, through weakness being cut off and destroyed. Rather the person is a mere religious professor, not possessing the life of Christ. A believer could *never* sever living links with Christ, since as a sheep he is *always* in the hands of the Good Shepherd (10:28-29). Rather, here are the Pharisees and priests, false prophets, servants and builders, followers of the Jewish system. No doubt the original priests, Aaron and his two faithful sons, could be described as branches, but later men in this office such as Annas and Caiaphas were but spurious branches. Their ultimate destination was to be gathered as the tares and burnt (Matt 13:40-42). (This must be distinguished from 1 Cor 3:13-15, where works are burned by fire, though the carnal christians producing them would be saved.) "Withered" means that such men are spiritually dead. Indeed, dead wood is used to make all sorts of attractive things, including idols, yet whatever the final product, the wood is dead. But the wood of the vine is useful for nothing (Ezek 15:1-5); it can only be cast as fuel into the fire. As one writer has expressed it, "There is first the spiritual death—the withering; then the eternal death—the burning".

7-8 Abiding in Christ, and its reciprocal, His word abiding in believers, had other consequences. The will of the believer is moulded by the divine will, and hence prayers are according to His will and will be answered. This, in itself, is an example of fruitbearing. This is one way in which the Father is glorified, for the Lord stated that this amounts to the production of "much fruit". Note that vv.2,5 contain an increase in the volume of production, "fruit", "more fruit" and "much fruit", the latter being when the believer's will is in perfect subjection to the Father's will, with prayer being answered. Again, note that Paul's prayer in Col 1:3 is associated with "bringeth forth fruit" in the Colossians (v.6).

Fruitfulness (or otherwise) is a familiar subject in the NT. Alas, there was no fruit in Matt 21:19,37; Luke 13:16. But in believers, there is an abundant scope for fruitfulness, as found in Rom 7:4; 2 Cor 9:10; Gal 5:22-23; Phil 1:11; Col 1:10. Fruitfulness arises from learning of the Lord—this is the basis of true discipleship. In connection with "my disciples", we have already commented on the possessions of the Lord under the theme of "his own" (13:1).

2. *Love, the First Fruit of the Spirit in the Believer* 15:9-16

v.9 "As the Father hath loved me, so have I loved you: continue ye in my love.
v.10 If ye keep my commandments, ye shall abide in my love: even as I have kept my Father's commandments, and abide in his love.
v.11 These things have I spoken unto you, that my joy might remain in you, and *that* your joy might be full.
v.12 This is my commandment, That ye love one another, as I have loved you.
v.13 Greater love hath no man than this, that a man lay down his life for his friends.
v.14 Ye are my friends, if ye do whatsoever I command you.
v.15 Henceforth I call you not servants; for the servant knoweth not what his lord doeth: but I have called you friends; for all things that I have heard of my Father I have made known unto you.
v.16 Ye have not chosen me, but I have chosen you, and ordained you, that ye should go and bring forth fruit, and *that* your fruit should remain: that whatsoever ye shall ask of the Father in my name, he may give it you."

Vv.9-16 deal largely with love, stated by Paul in Gal 5:22 to be the first manifestation of the fruit of the Spirit. By contrast, vv.17-27 deal largely with the subject of hate, a prevalent fruit amongst unbelievers (the seventh in Paul's list of the fruit of the flesh in Gal 5:20).

9-10 *The Lord speaks.* The words "abide" (v.7), "continue" (v.9) and "remain" (v.11) are one and the same Greek word *menō* (though in v.11 the RV and JND follow other Greek texts and merely have the word "be" in place of "remain"). V.9 contains what we may term the transmission of love—from the

Father, to the Son, to believers, who continue in His love by manifesting it to others. Love receives and love gives, since abiding in His love is not passive, it is active. For the example of the Son is given—He abides in the Father's love, so must we abide; He keeps His Father's commandments, so must we keep His commandments. These commandments are not the commandments of the law; rather there is a definition of the commandment in v.12, "That ye love one another, as I have loved you". Love itself is not defined in Scripture, but its manifestations are to be seen wherever believers are to be found.

11 In 14:27, the Lord referred to "my peace"; in 15:10 to "my love", and in our v.11 to "my joy". These are the first three manifestations of the fruit of the Spirit given in Gal 5:22. Thus the Lord's joy is transferred to "your joy" as another example of the fruit produced by the vine. The Lord's joy is seen in Luke 10:21, when He rejoiced in spirit that what had been revealed to babes had been hidden from the wise and prudent. The joy in the presence of the angels can but be His own joy over one sinner that repents (Luke 15:10). The joy that was set before Him as He endured the cross was that by means of suffering He would be able to introduce many sons to glory (Heb 12:2). Such joy is far removed from the natural joy of the world. The believer's joy is never filled up with the fleeting joys of the unsaved. True joy was announced by the angel at the birth of the Lord, "I bring you good tidings of great joy" (Luke 2:10). Paul's joy was composed of the saints, "Fulfil ye my joy" (Phil 2:2); "my brethren dearly beloved . . . my joy and crown" (4:1).

12 This verse expands on v.10; there, the keeping of His commandments implied that His disciples would abide in His love; here the commandment itself was to love one another as He loved them. The order is: we love Him because He first loved us—His was a sacrificial love, seeking the good of others at the expense of Himself, as stated in Eph 5:2, "walk in love, as Christ also hath loved us, and hath given himself for us an offering and a sacrifice to God for a sweetsmelling savour".

13-14 Yet there was a difference. The greatest love amongst believers is that such a man can lay down his life for his friends. In the boasting and self-certainty of the minute, Peter may claim to be willing to lay down his life for the Lord (13:37), but sacrificial love was absent when he denied the Lord. But in His case, the divine love went further, "God commendeth his love towards us, in that while we were yet sinners, Christ died for us" (Rom 5:8). This love took place when we were far from loving Him, as John wrote, "not that we loved God, but that he loved us, and sent His Son to be the propititiation for our sins" (1 John 4:10). Hence John concluded, "we ought also to love one another" (v.11). Such love amongst believers is found in Phil 2:17-30, where the apostle listed himself, Timothy and Epaphroditus as being exponents of the act of seeking the good of others, the latter being "nigh unto death" (v.30) for the work of Christ committed to him in Rome.

The Lord loved us while we were yet sinners, but here His love is shown to His friends. Only in John's Gospel do we find friends owned by One divine. In 3:29, there is the Bridegroom's friend, while in 11:11 the Lord called Lazarus "Our friend"; here the Lord said "Ye are my friends", the word *philos* meaning one who is loved. The contrast is found in James 4:4, where "the friendship of the world" leads to one who is the "friend of the world" being "the enemy of God".

15 In this verse we must distinguish between "servants . . . lord . . . friends". The word for servant is *doulos*, a bondservant. Of course, a believer is both a friend and a servant; Simeon called himself by this designation (Luke 2:29), as did the apostles (Acts 4:29), and Paul (Rom 1:1, and many other references); Epaphras, James, Peter and Jude also had this designation. In our v.15, the idea behind the designation servant is that of social distance, ignorance and lack of intimacy. But a friend is stated to involve nearness, having a knowledge of the purpose and mind of Christ. This discourse was effectively changing the apostles from being servants only, to the blessed experience of also being friends of the Lord. In Gal 4:1-7, the change is from being a servant to being a son, with the privilege of approaching the Father. Yet all believers must realise that intimacy does not eliminate the servant's position; in service we are the latter, but in communion we are the former.

The existence of this friendship is to explain why the Lord was making known to them "all things" that He had received from the Father. This "all" cannot imply all the counsels of the Godhead; rather, the Son had received much to transmit to His people on earth, and all of this had been transmitted. These were the truths that they were able to bear there and then (John 16:12) prior to the giving of the Spirit. No doubt "all the counsel of God" that Paul declared in Ephesus went further than the Lord's teaching, since by then the Holy Spirit was operative in believers' hearts (Acts 20:27).

16 To prevent Paul from boasting, he was given a thorn in the flesh that would not be removed (2 Cor 12:7). So in this v.16, the Lord gave a safeguard against boasting on the part of the apostles. For the Jews were well capable of boasting (Rom 2:17-23). Thus the status of the apostles was not of their own making, just as the power to become sons of God was solely derived from the will of God (1:12-13). Thus the Lord stated that He had chosen them (*eklegō*) and had ordained them (*tithēmi*). The divine choice of men out of the world for Himself is very important, and is a well-established doctrine in the NT. Thus Paul was a "chosen vessel" (Acts 9:15), who in turn taught this great truth that "he hath chosen us in him" (Eph 1:4). The Lord expressed this truth four times in John's Gospel (6:70; 13:18; 15:16,19). In the case of the apostles, He chose them when He first met them, as for example in Matthew's case, but later He "chose twelve, whom also he named apostles" (Luke 6:13). In other words, choice is involved first when a believer finds the Lord Jesus unto salvation, and then a second time when he is called to specific service.

The word "ordained" has no theological connotation here, nor in other places where the word translates different Greek words. The very common word "to lay" is used, and can be translated "appoint". Examples with a spiritual meaning are: "the Holy Spirit *hath made* you overseers" (Acts 20:28); "God *hath set* some in the church" (1 Cor 12:28); He "*hath committed* unto us the word of reconciliation" (2 Cor 5:19); "*putting* me into the ministry" (1 Tim 1:12); "I *am ordained* a preacher" (1 Tim 2:7; 2 Tim 1:11). All these refer to service.

Thus in our v.16, the production of fruit derives (i) from our character as saved by grace, and (ii) from our service rendered in His Name. The effects are twofold: firstly that this fruit remains as the "gold, silver, precious stones", withstanding all inspection at the future judgment seat of Christ (1 Cor 3:12-14), and secondly that such fruit declares that the believer is moving in the current of the divine will, and hence prayer will be answered.

3. *Hate, the Fruit of the Flesh in the Unbeliever* 15:17-27

v.17 "These things I command you, that ye love one another.
v.18 If the world hate you, ye know that it hated me before *it hated* you.
v.19 If ye were of the world, the world would love his own: but because ye are not of the world, but I have chosen you out of the world, therefore the world hateth you.
v.20 Remember the word that I said unto you, The servant is not greater than his lord. If they have persecuted me, they will also persecute you; if they have kept my saying, they will keep yours also.
v.21 But all these things will they do unto you for my name's sake, because they know not him that sent me.
v.22 If I had not come and spoken unto them, they had not had sin: but now they have no cloak for their sin.
v.23 He that hateth me hateth my Father also.
v.24 If I had not done among them the works which none other man did, they had not had sin: but now have they both seen and hated both me and my Father.
v.25 But *this cometh to pass*, that the word might be fulfilled that is written in their law, They hated me without a cause.
v.26 But when the Comforter is come, whom I will send unto you from the Father, *even* the Spirit of truth, which proceedeth from the Father, he shall testify of me.
v.27 And ye also shall bear witness, because ye have been with me from the beginning."

17-18 *The Lord speaks.* A summary of the Lord's teaching here is as follows:

1. Why believers are persecuted (vv.17-20).

2. Why the Lord was persecuted (vv.21-25).

3. The testimony of believers in a world of hatred (vv.26-27).

4. Warnings concerning religious persecution (16:1-4).

Vv.17-18 present a contrast; believers love one another on the one hand, and they are hated by the world on the other. This is the same contrast as presented by John many years later in his first epistle: "In this the children of God are manifest, and the children of the devil . . . that ye should love one another. Not as Cain . . . Marvel not, my brethren, if the world hate you" (1 John 3:10-13). John wrote through experience, since between the Lord's words and the writing of this epistle, he had suffered many years of persecution. In vv.18-20, two reasons are given why believers are persecuted. The first reason is that the world hated Christ before it hated His disciples. This attitude of hatred is permanent. Since men could no longer persecute Him after His cross and exodus from this earth, their attention was turned immediately to His people (Acts 4:1-3). There are several "firsts" in these chapters, applied to the Lord before being applied to His people: His love for us came first (13:34; 15:12), and men's hatred for Him came first.

By "the world", the Lord referred both to men apart from Himself, and to all that they stand for. When the interests of men centre upon traditional values that are an abomination in the sight of God; when they value the activity of the four beasts of Dan 7 (Rome being the beast when the Lord was here); when they adhere to formal religion that the Lord hates (Rev 2:6,15) whether in deed or in doctrine; when they are lovers of pleasure more than lovers of God (2 Tim 3:4); when they are seekers after irresponsible or illegal financial gain (Luke 12:15-21; 15:13; 19:2); when they engage in the detestable sins described by Paul in Rom 1:20-32; this is the world that hates the Lord and hates His people.

19-20 The second reason is because believers are so different from other men. Men "think it strange that ye run not with them to the same excess of riot, speaking evil of you" (1 Pet 4:4), wrote Peter, perhaps thinking of the Lord's words "If ye were of the world, the world would love his own". Believers are different because the Lord has chosen them out of the world, although they are still in it physically and temporarily (17:14-16). The world would love believers to walk with them and to follow them. The Corinthians were walking as men (1 Cor 3:3), and consequently they were immune from persecution (in 1 Cor 4:8-16 Paul described his own sufferings, but these were absent from the Corinthians' experience). In the epistle to the Galatians, submission to circumcision would immediately have stopped persecution (Gal 6:13). Hence believers should beware of any false attachment to the world, as John wrote, "Love not the world, neither the things that are in the world" (1 John 2:16). Similarly James wrote that believers should keep themselves "unspotted from the world" (James 1:27). Our companionship is not with the world, but with those who fear God and keep His precepts (Ps 119:63).

Thus believers must always keep the word of the Lord before them, in particular, "The servant is not greater than his lord" (13:16), meaning that what happens to Him will also happen to His people, whether in the matter of persecution or in the matter of hearing His word spoken by His disciples.

21-22 Persecution of a believer would be on account of the Lord's "name's sake", as He later said about the new convert Paul, "I will show him how great things he must suffer for my name's sake" (Acts 9:16). That is to say, men would know that they were really seeking to continue the persecution of Christ, using His people as a channel to reach Him; "why persecutest thou me?" was spoken to Saul when he was persecuting the church.

The ultimate cause of this persecution complex in unbelievers is traced by the Lord to their ignorance of the Father, for had they known the Father, they would have known Him. Moreover, it was because the Lord had come down from on high that this persecution complex towards Him was formed—note the double negative used in v.22 to express this fact. His presence brought out the worst in men, as well as the best in His disciples. The worst attitude of men was expressed in a parable, "let us kill him" because the Son had been sent (Matt 21:38). If He had not come down, then they would not be seeking His life, though they often treated the prophets like that (Matt 23:30-35). The idea of a "cloke" (*prophasis*) strictly involves a pretence or an excuse. There was no excuse for the hatred shown to the Lord, though in the judgment day men may try to make excuses (Matt 7:22).

23 Moreover, this hatred towards the Son is not confined to Him; because of the unity of the Godhead, this hatred is also shown to the Father. This shows the uselessness of the attitude of many religious leaders and their followers who apparently seem to accept God, but discount Christ; this was the ground of the Pharisees. It is similar to 5:23, honouring not the Son means that the Father also is not honoured; and to 1 John 2:23 where a denial of the Son means that the Father is also denied.

24 This verse is similar to v.22. There, it is a question of what the Lord said; here it is a question of what He did. The Lord was stressing the uniqueness of His works, using a double negative to express this. No doubt because this comes in John's Gospel, we must interpret "the works", not as miracles, but as signs. Men were willing to rejoice in miracles, since these brought blessings and healing. But as signs, they had a message implying His deity. If these works had not been done, men would not have sinned as they did. But since the works had been accomplished, and since the truth that those who had seen Him had also seen the Father (14:9) could also be applied to unbelievers (though they knew it not), then the hatred shown to the Lord was also being shown to the Father. This conclusion also appears in v.23 in connection with His words. Hence today, if men profess to be christians, and yet reject all or parts of the words and works of the Lord, then they are in effect showing hatred to the Father. Men tend to cherish the thought of the universal Fatherhood of God, but this is just a vain hope when taken with this proven hatred shown to the Father.

25 This verse is the conclusion of the matter. In both the AV and the RV, the words "this cometh to pass" appear in italics, showing that the words have been added to the Greek text to complete the sense. The object was to form a proper sentence apart from the quotation "They hated me without a cause". But strictly, this quotation forms part of the sentence, as in JND's translation, "But that the word written in their law might be fulfilled, They hated me without a cause". (The verb "hated" is thus the principal verb in the sentence.) The fulfilment of Ps 35:11-21 (v.19 in particular) is seen in all this continual hatred shown to the Lord. There could be no righteous cause for their hatred, though men invented many unrighteous reasons. As Ps 69:4 expresses the matter, "they that would destroy me, being mine enemies wrongfully, are mighty". Again, "they dealt perversely with me without a cause" (Ps 119:78). With no righteous reason to justify their actions, in the judgment day men will be "without excuse" (Rom 1:20), when "every mouth may be stopped" (3:19), for men will be struck dumb before the terror of the great white throne, when they finally recognise their sin and error, when it will be too late to repent. A lesson for believers is that they give unbelievers no righteous cause for complaint against them, else the testimony would be damaged (1 Pet 2:20; 3:17-18).

26-27 As surrounded by a hostile world that hates the Lord and hates His people, how can a believer live and witness for Him? The answer to this continues into the next chapter, up to v.15. Since true testimony is entirely from and about another world, far removed from the present world here below, the Lord stressed twice that the Spirit of truth comes from the Father—He will be sent from the Father, and He proceeds from the Father. The object of the Spirit's testimony is twofold, namely "of truth" and "of me". This contrasts with the religion of this world, where men speak of themselves rather than of the Lord. Most men want their own things, and not the things of the Lord Jesus. Men will receive one coming in his own name, but not One who comes in His Father's Name (5:43).

Believers must be able to distinguish between the Spirit of truth and the spirit of error (1 John 4:6); the latter confesses not that Jesus Christ is come in the flesh, working through the many false prophets that are gone out into the world (v.1). But the Spirit of truth confesses that Jesus Christ is come in the flesh; His gracious activity is to testify of Christ.

Note the direction of testimony. The Spirit testifies to believers, and believers testify to the world. As Peter said in Acts 5:32, "we are his witnesses of these things; and so is also the Holy Spirit". This ladder of testimony arises because "ye have been with me from the beginning". The Spirit has known the Son from eternity past; the apostles knew the Lord from the beginning (from the beginning of the Lord's ministry when He called them; see Acts 1:22), but men in the world do not know the Son at all (16:3). Consequently, those who have the knowledge have the responsibility to pass it on to those who have not. But in those early days, this led to severe trouble, as the opening verses of ch.16 indicate.

IV. The Way to Gethsemane: The Son's Teaching about His Departure (16:1-33)

1. *Aspects of Persecution*
16:1-4

v.1 "These things have I spoken unto you, that ye should not be offended.
v.2 They shall put you out of the synagogues: yea, the time cometh, that whosoever killeth you will think that he doeth God service.
v.3 And these things will they do unto you, because they have not known the Father, nor me.
v.4 But these things have I told you, that when the time shall come, ye may remember that I told you of them. And these things I said not unto you at the beginning, because I was with you."

1 *The Lord speaks*. By "These things", evidently are meant the Lord's previous statements about the Holy Spirit, about persecution, and about the believers' testimony. As Paul wrote later, one who was born after the flesh would persecute one born after the Spirit (Gal 4:29). The Lord would not allow His disciples to enter upon this persecution without warning them beforehand, for He was sending them forth "as lambs among wolves" (Luke 10:3). His warning was designed to prevent them being "offended", or "stumbled" as the word *skandalizō* means, since they would have been stumbled had they not received any prior explanation.

2 Religious men would engage in several methods to damage or prevent the disciples' testimony. Firstly, they would be put "out of the synagogues". The word used for "put out" is not the same as in 9:22; 12:42, where excommunication is implied (*aposunagōgos ginomai* is used). Membership was suspended, something dreadful to contemplate for an orthodox Jew. But in our v.2 the word used is *aposunagōgous poieō*, and we feel that this means to be physically turned out of the synagogue, as in the Lord's case (Luke 4:29), or to have his teaching rejected as in Paul's case (Acts 13:45). This could lead to scourging in the synagogues (Matt 10:17), and ultimately to the second method stated by the Lord, even to death itself. This division process was brought about by the Jewish leaders so as to maintain the traditional, formal, barren and state-recognised religion, as contrasted with the apparently small, unorganised, ignorant with no formal training, downtrodden little flock of the Lord's disciples. Religious persecution has often led to christian martyrs, giving their lives for the cause of Christ, yet with their murderers boasting that they were doing their deeds in God's name. Satan appears to them as an angel of light whereas his followers behave as roaring lions. Satan's agents will claim that they have worked and taught in the Lord's name (Matt 7:22), but a tree is known by its fruit.

There may be a sense in which the word "synagogues" is not used as meaning a Jewish meeting place. After all, the apostles and converts would have come out of such establishments upon their conversion. The word carries the roots: a leading together. In these days, it is common in religious circles to designate a building for gatherings by "church", but this has no scriptural authority whatsoever, and should be avoided. We may call a building by the name "hall" or "Gospel hall", but even the word "chapel" has unpleasant undertones associated with it. In those early days believers used to meet in houses (Rom 16:5; 1 Cor 16:19; Col 4:15), but when they met in other premises, what word would they use? It appears that James answers this question (2:2), "if there come unto your assembly a man". The word for "assembly" is *sunagōge*, a remarkable fact, clearly not referring to a Jewish synagogue. Both the RV and JND translate this word "assembly" by "synagogue"; the NEB uses "place of worship"; Weymouth uses "one of your meetings"; JND's French translation has "votre synagogue"; Segond's French translation has "votre assemblée", while Luther's German translation has "Versammlung". The reader can therefore see that translators have no common word with which to designate a "christian synagogue" as distinct from a "Jewish synagogue". It may be that the Lord visualised a christian meeting place, into which enemies would come so as to scatter the flock out from it. We suspect that Paul used the word in this sense in Acts 22:19; 26:11.

3-4 The reason why men will do such evil things to God's people is because of their complete ignorance of the Father and the Son. Ignorance of divine Persons is equivalent to blindness caused and maintained by Satan (2 Cor 4:4). The Lord said that Satan was their father, and his deeds they would do (8:44). This ignorance leads to every kind of evil, the worst deed being that accomplished by the murderers of the Son of God.

These things had been spoken by the Lord in advance of their fulfilment after His ascension. When He was present, men persecuted Him alone; when He was absent men would turn their attention to His people instead, until the beginning of the battle of Armageddon, when men will think initially that they have the opportunity to "make war with the Lamb" (Rev 17:14). In fact, shortly after this warning issued by the Lord, He protected the apostles from the power of the enemy when He said, "let these go their way" (18:8)—the time of their persecution had not yet arrived (it rose in a crescendo in the book of Acts). The Lord left it to the last to present these warnings; He had not said these things at the beginning of His ministry, for His very presence was preserving them during the three years of His ministry.

It should be pointed out that the word for "time" is really "hour"; also that some Greek texts (followed by the RV and JND) contain "their hour" rather than "the hour". The word "their" applies either to the hour of persecution after His ascension, or to the hour of evil men. When He said, "This is your hour, and the power of darkness" (Luke 22:53), "your hour" referred to the hour of His trial and crucifixion. But "their hour" in our verse refers to the subsequent trials of the apostles after His return to the Father.

2. *The Work of the Holy Spirit*
16:5-15

v.5 "But now I go my way to him that sent me; and none of you asketh me, Whither goest thou?
v.6 But because I have said these things unto you, sorrow hath filled your heart.
v.7 Nevertheless I tell you the truth; It is expedient for you that I go away: for if I go not away, the Comforter will not come unto you; but if I depart, I will send him unto you.
v.8 And when he is come, he will reprove the world of sin, and of righteousness, and of judgment:
v.9 Of sin, because they believe not on me;
v.10 Of righteousness, because I go to my Father, and ye see me no more;
v.11 Of judgment, because the prince of this world is judged.
v.12 I have yet many things to say unto you, but ye cannot bear them now.
v.13 Howbeit when he, the Spirit of truth, is come, he will guide you into all truth: for he shall not speak of himself; but whatsoever he shall hear, *that* shall he speak: and he will shew you things to come.
v.14 He shall glorify me: for he shall receive of mine, and shall shew *it* unto you.
v.15 All things that the Father hath are mine: therefore said I, that he shall take of mine, and shall shew it unto you."

In this section, we have the following paragraphs:

1. The Lord, in going away, would send the Comforter (vv.5-7).

2. The Spirit's work in relation to unbelievers (vv.8-11).

3. The Spirit's work in relation to believers (vv.12-15).

5-6 *The Lord speaks.* The Lord had always stressed throughout this Gospel that He had come forth from the Father; had they not been told this, His apostles could not otherwise have known these mysteries of heaven. Again, once more He was telling them that He had to return to the same place, the final enactment taking place in Acts 1:9. Yet the apostles remained silent when the Lord said this. In 13:36, Peter had asked, "Lord, whither goest thou?", and Thomas had effectively asked the same question in 14:5. On neither occasion had the Lord answered directly. So in our verse, by "none of you asketh" (a verb in the present tense, so it does not refer to their previous questions), He meant that they did not interrupt Him there and then to seek an interpretation of His words. In fact, they were thinking only of His going, not of His destination, nor of His work to be accomplished when in heaven. Natural sorrow would fill their hearts, unlike the rejoicing that would fill the minds of men in the world (16:20) when they had removed the Lord from their midst. This sorrow is seen in the women who "bewailed and lamented him" (Luke 23:27), and in Mary Magdalene who stood at the sepulchre weeping (20:11-13).

7 Yet the presence of the Spirit would do more than the presence of Christ, for the Spirit's ministrations would be based upon the sacrifice of Christ as an accomplished reality. This was the divine plan—for the Lord worked on bodies needing healing, but the Spirit would work in hearts and souls. Both divine Persons would not work at the same time on earth: One would go and the Other would come. It was therefore "expedient" that the Lord go away, so that the Comforter could come after His ascension. The word for "expedient" is strictly a verb *sumpherō*, meaning to be profitable, namely there would be ood results flowing from His exodus, even though present circumstances must have seemed dark and fearful to the apostles. His going would not only accomplish salvation, but hearts would be cleansed so that believers could become temples of the Holy Spirit. The Spirit would not be sent into hearts that the apostles possessed there and then; One divine could not dwell in a sanctuary that was not cleansed by precious blood, in just the same way as God's glory could not remain for ever in tabernacle and temple filled with sin in the OT.

8 Although the world of men could not be indwelt by the Holy Spirit on account of their sin, yet He would exercise a divine ministry, without which there would be no conversions. Evangelists may be used as channels, but ultimately the power of conviction and faith-formation lies with the Spirit. The AV word "reprove" (*elenchō*) has been given a large number of differing renderings in different contexts. In his *Commentary on the Gospel of John*, William Hendriksen has given a series of lists giving renderings in the AV, ARV and RSV; the words are "tell him his fault, show him his fault, reprove, expose, convince, convict, confute, punish". No doubt it is the exposure of sin that is implied by the Lord, for apart from the Spirit, men would not want their sins to be reproved or discovered (3:20). See Eph 5:13. Of course the world can refuse to hear the divine voice, as quoted in Heb 3:7, "To day if ye will hear his voice, harden not your hearts".

9-11 The three aspects of exposure (of what is in men or outside them) are given in these three verses.

1. "Of sin, because they believe not on me". Nothing else can be appreciated unless first of all there is an appreciation of the sinfulness of the human heart and life. Whether men realise it or not, sin in men is the opposite of righteousness in God—a righteousness that will be manifest in judgment. Unforgiven sin and the lack of faith join hand-in-hand; they go together, "for whatsoever is not of faith is sin" (Rom 14:23). If a Pharisee thinks he can see without faith in Christ, then his sin remains (9:41). An example of this exposure of sin leading to faith is found in Acts 2:37-40; men "were pricked in their heart", leading to repentance, faith, forgiveness and baptism, as well as the reception of the gift of the Holy Spirit.

2. "Of righteousness, because I go to my Father, and ye see me no more". This is not righteousness in men, neither imputed righteousness, but the righteousness of Christ personally. Because of this, He could go to the cross, and then return to the Father. The centurion recognised this righteousness (Luke 23:47), and certainly the apostles knew that He was the "just" One (Acts 4:14). And the righteous One manifests righteousness in all that He does or will do; for example, "he will judge the world in righteousness by that man whom he hath ordained" (Acts 17:31).

3 "Of judgment, because the prince of this world is judged". Certainly Satan suffered defeat when the Lord died, "that through death he might destroy him that had the power of death, that is, the devil" (Heb 2:14). And what happened (and will happen) to this prince will also happen to unbelievers in that coming day. The Spirit thus issues a warning regarding the consequences of remaining in sin, in spite of its exposure. Thus in Acts 24:25, when Paul reasoned with Felix, the subjects were "righteousness, temperance, and judgment to come"; Felix trembled, showing the power of the Spirit, but he put the matter off until "a convenient season", which we can but assume never arrived (though we would not judge harshly), since he merely desired bribes so as to release Paul. The desire to remain in sin refuses the convicting grace of the Holy Spirit.

12 The Lord now proceeded to show the apostles one great effect of the giving of the Spirit of truth, an effect reserved only for believers. The Lord admitted that His teaching had been deliberately restricted, because of their state. They could not "bear" further truth, since they did not as yet possess the Holy Spirit. Even after the Lord's resurrection, the apostles gained further truth as He opened "their understanding, that they might understand the scriptures" (Luke 24:45). Again, after His resurrection the apostles "remembered... and believed the scripture"; until then they did not know what the zeal of the Father's house really was. Under those new circumstances, they could bear further truth.

13-15 But when the Spirit of truth came, there was a divine power on the inside. The words "because they believe not on me" relating to unbelievers stand in contrast to "he will guide you into all truth" for believers. The words "ye see me no more" relating to unbelievers and natural sight stand in contrast to "he will show you things to come" relating to believers. The words "the prince of this world is judged" stand in contrast to "the Spirit of truth".

The order of transmission of truth is as follows:

1. "All things that the Father hath are mine". Here is a joint possession within the Godhead. Thus in the prayer in ch.17, the Lord spoke of many things (including the disciples) that the Father had given to the Son, evidently consequential upon His becoming Man.

2. In a way which is not explained, the Spirit then took of these things (v.15); He received of these things (v.14); He heard of these things (v.13). By this means, He does not speak "of himself" (*aph' heautou*), being properly translated "from himself"; namely He was not the Source.

3. Then comes His testimony to the Lord's people. "He will guide you into all truth"; "that shall he speak". Moreover prophetical matters concerning the ultimate glory of Christ would also be within His sphere of testimony, "he will show you things to come". The things that He will show are "of mine" (v.15), showing that His testimony will essentially be of the Son; by this means "He shall glorify me". All this testimony would be direct revelation to the apostles, prophets, and the writers of the NT Scriptures. To us now His testimony comes through the written word of God, "not in the words which man's wisdom teacheth, but which the Holy Spirit teacheth" (1 Cor 2:13), enabling us to know the things that are freely given to us by God.

4. Lastly comes the testimony of the Lord's people, "ye shall bear witness" (15:27). As Paul wrote, "Which things we also speak" (1 Cor 2:13), although the natural man cannot know them until he responds to the inward strivings and conviction of the Holy Spirit. It was only by being filled with the Holy Spirit that the apostles were able to speak "the word of God with boldness" (Acts 4:31).

5. And what the apostles preached, all believers can pass on in their measure, "knowing of whom thou hast learned them" (2 Tim 3:14). Thus Timothy heard from Paul (2 Tim 2:2); he committed them to other faithful men, who in turn taught others also.

3. *The Lord's Statements Regarding His Death and Resurrection* 16:16-22

v.16 "A little while, and ye shall not see me: and again, a little while, and ye shall see me, because I go to the Father.
v.17 Then said *some* of his disciples among themselves, What is this that he saith unto us, A little while, and ye shall not see me: and again, a little while, and ye shall see me: and, Because I go to the Father?
v.18 They said therefore, What is this that he saith, A little while? we cannot tell what he saith.
v.19 Now Jesus knew that they were desirous to ask him, and said unto them, Do ye enquire among yourselves of that I said, A little while, and ye shall not see me: and again, a little while, and ye shall see me?
v.20 Verily, verily, I say unto you, That ye shall weep and lament, but the world shall rejoice: and ye shall be sorrowful, but your sorrow shall be turned into joy.
v.21 A woman when she is in travail hath sorrow, because her hour is come: but as soon as she is delivered of the child, she remembereth no more the anguish, for joy that a man is born into the world.
v.22 And ye now therefore have sorrow: but I will see you again, and your heart shall rejoice, and your joy no man taketh from you."

In these last verses 16-33, we have the Lord's final words by which He taught His disciples. In Matthew, Mark and Luke, the Olivet discourse (that took place earlier) forms the last recorded teaching of any length. Vv.16-33 contain the following subjects:

1. The Lord's statement concerning the "little while" (v.16).

2. The disciples' question about the "little while" (vv.17-19).

3. The Lord's proverbial answer (vv.20-22).

4. The subject of prayer to the Father (vv.23-28).

5. The apostles' final confession of understanding (vv.29-30).

6. The apostles' failure before and triumph after the "little while" (vv.31-33).

16 *The Lord speaks.* The word *mikron* (a little while) appears seven times in vv.16-19 (also in 13:33; 14:19). It refers to a short period of time, but in Matt 26:39, "he went a little further", it refers to a short distance. In our v.16, there are two short periods of time involved. Some expositors believe that the Lord refers to the (long) period prior to His coming again for His people, but to the present author the whole passage in its context seems to be associated with His death and resurrection. The two periods are:

1. The period when "ye shall not see me". We believe that this refers to the period between the Lord's death and His resurrection. This was the only prolonged period during which the disciples had not seen Him. It had been previously defined: "so shall the Son of man be three days and three nights in the heart of the earth" (Matt 12:40); "and be raised again the third day" (Matt 16:21); "the third day he shall rise again" (Matt 20:19); "in three days I will raise it up" (John 2:19). During this little while, the apostles were still in uncertainty, failing to expect His resurrection.

2. The period when "ye shall see me". This would be the forty days leading to His ascension, "being seen of them forty days" (Acts 1:3). The Lord had not spoken much of His ascension; He had often spoken about returning to the Father who had sent Him (7:33; 14:28), without saying anything about the actual events by which this would be achieved.

17-18 *Some of the disciples speak.* Throughout the Lord's ministry, the disciples betrayed a regrettable ignorance concerning His death and resurrection. As they walked together along the road leading from Jerusalem to the lower slopes of the mount of Olives, it is therefore not surprising that they discussed the Lord's words privately and quietly amongst themselves—they did not ask the Lord directly; perhaps as in Mark 9:32, they "were afraid to ask him". For verses showing this continued ignorance, see Matt 16:22; 17:23; Mark 9:9-10,31-32; Luke 9:44-45; 18:34. No wonder the Lord had to say, "O fools, and slow of heart to believe all that the prophets have spoken" (Luke 24:25). Thus in our v.18, they confessed amongst themselves their complete ignorance as to the meaning of the Lord's words. Today there is no excuse for the Lord's people to remain in ignorance concerning any truth relating to the Son of God.

19-20 *The Lord speaks.* The Lord's question here is very pointed, repeating what He had just said to them, and which they in turn had repeated amongst themselves. When the text says that "Jesus knew", this was either because He had heard audibly what they were trying to keep to themselves, or because of His divine knowledge of all hearts, thoughts and conversations. Thus concerning the Pharisees and their blasphemous ideas, Matt 12:25 says, "Jesus knew their thoughts"; the same is said of the Pharisees in Luke 6:8. John wrote that "he knew what was in man" (2:25), in keeping with Heb 4:13, "all things are naked and opened unto the eyes of him with whom we have to do".

V.20 forms a direct statement, though only clear to readers after the event; v.21 is a metaphor relating to the same subject. The weeping and lamenting of the Lord's disciples would contrast with the rejoicing of the world, for they were to be overjoyed at the apparent success of their venture. This is what Zophar said in Job 20:5, "the triumphing of the wicked is short, and the joy of the hypocrite but for a moment". Weeping is satisfactory under the right circumstances, though in our present verse it would be a case of weeping without the assurance of the Lord's resurrection on the third day. Thus Paul's weeping denoted a sincere sensitivity of heart, and was justified (Acts 20:19,31; 2 Cor 2:4; Phil 3:18).

For the Lord, His sufferings were replaced by glory; for the disciples, sorrow was replaced by joy, "Then were the disciples glad, when they saw the Lord" (20:20). As Ps 30:5 expresses it, "weeping may endure for a night, but joy cometh in the morning". After the Holy Spirit was given, "the kingdom of God is . . . joy in the Holy Spirit" (Rom 14:17).

21 This verse consists of a metaphor, or "proverb" as stated in vv.25,29. The word *paroimia*, a byword or maxim, is distinct from the usual word for parable. The Lord was not referring to His own pain and sorrow that would precede His entrance into glory, as in Isa 53:11, when He would see of the travail of His soul and be satisfied. Rather, in the context the Lord was referring to the sorrow of the apostles that would be turned into joy. Sorrow is forgotten when it is replaced by a lasting joy. The metaphor of childbirth is often used in Scripture, not always with a happy ending, as in Jer 4:31; 6:24; 1 Thess 5:3. In Gal 4:19 Paul used this picture in anticipation of a happier outcome.

22 Truly the Lord knew the circumstances of the near future. By "now", He evidently referred to the present time on the road to Gethsemane, to the next day and the sufferings of the cross, and to the following short period when His body would be in the tomb. After that, He would appear in resurrection, and their joy would be permanent; no one could remove that joy, since He would be living in the power of an endless life. Any trial of faith would have as its fruit a rejoicing "with joy unspeakable" (1 Pet 1:6-8). Thus Paul and Silas could sing praise to God while in prison (Acts 16:25). This joy is permanent because no one can separate us from the love of God in Christ Jesus our Lord (Rom 8:38-39).

4. *Prayer in His Name to the Father* 16:23-33

v.23 "And in that day ye shall ask me nothing. Verily, verily, I say unto you, Whatsoever ye shall ask the Father in my name, he will give *it* you.
v.24 Hitherto have ye asked nothing in my name: ask, and ye shall receive, that your joy may be full.
v.25 These things have I spoken unto you in proverbs: but the time cometh, when I shall no more speak unto you in proverbs, but I shall shew you plainly of the Father.
v.26 At that day ye shall ask in my name: and I say not unto you, that I will pray the Father for you:
v.27 For the Father himself loveth you, because ye have loved me, and have believed that I came out from God.
v.28 I came forth from the Father, and am come into the world: again, I leave the world, and go to the Father.

v.29 His disciples said unto him, Lo, now speakest thou plainly, and speakest no proverb.
v.30 Now are we sure that thou knowest all things, and needest not that any man should ask thee: by this we believe that thou camest forth from God.
v.31 Jesus answered them, Do ye now believe?
v.32 Behold, the hour cometh, yea, is now come, that ye shall be scattered, every man to his own, and shall leave me alone: and yet I am not alone, because the Father is with me.
v.33 These things I have spoken unto you, that in me ye might have peace. In the world ye shall have tribulation: but be of good cheer; I have overcome the world."

23-24 *The Lord speaks.* This verse contains the last "Verily, verily" prior to the Lord's crucifixion; it appears once again after His resurrection (21:18).

The Lord introduced here something new—the new privilege arising from His forthcoming ascension to the Father, which would make possible for the first time an approach by believers to the Father. Previously when on earth, only the Lord had approached the Father; but in that day believers would be able to approach in His Name (as good as if He were approaching, using their prayers and petitions). The Lord provided here one condition for prayer to be answered; we have already considered other conditions in our comments on 14:13-15. It should be pointed out that some Greek texts offer an alternative wording of v.23; thus the RV differs from the AV, with the translation, "If ye shall ask anything of the Father, he will give it you in my name". But in v.24 the text remains unaltered—asking is in His Name.

The English word "ask" occurs five times in these vv.23-24,26, but two different Greek words are used. The first occurrence of "ask" in v.23 ("ye shall ask me nothing") and also the word for "pray" in v.26 ("that I will pray the Father for you") translate *erōtaō*, while the other occurrences in vv.23-24 and that in v.26 ("ye shall ask in my name") translate *aiteō*. (A phenomenon such as this, where one English word translates two different Greek words in the same context, is not uncommon in John's Gospel.) The difference is important, and a very full explanation is given by Vine in his *Expository Dictionary of New Testament Words*. Thus *aiteō* is never used by the Lord in addressing the Father. Thus *aiteō* often implies the act of asking by a lesser to a greater, while *erōtaō* often implies equality or familiarity between the two parties. Since both words occur many times in the NT, the interested reader should consult a concordance where full lists of both words can be found.

By "Hitherto", the Lord distinguished the past from what was soon to take place. Here was a blessing to be able to approach before the throne of grace; the previous tabernacle and temple had presented a barrier to a man's approach to God with the priests only having access into these structures. This is perpetuated today with the clergy apparently being able to approach God in a way barred to the laity. But the Lord's words here show how unscriptural is this practice of the Nicolaitanes.

25 As already pointed out, the word for "proverb" (*paroimia*) denotes a simile or comparison, something that can even be obscure when contrasted with "plainly" in vv.25,29. The word was often used as a common saying such as could be heard on the highways and streets (for the word *oimos* meant "a way"). The word is therefore very suitable in the context (though deprived of any common element about it, since the word was used by the Lord), because the Lord was speaking on the way from Jerusalem to the mount of Olives.

The Lord was not speaking *everything* in proverbs, as we can easily recognise. No doubt, the proverb appears in v.21, where He used the everyday event of a woman in travail. But the Lord promised the time when His teaching need not be expressed in such terms—He would show them "plainly of the Father". This would be during the time of His resurrection manifestations. According to the Gospel records (and no doubt these are limited in their references), He spoke of the Father in Matt 28:19 where baptism would be "in the name of the Father, and of the Son, and of the Holy Spirit"; in Luke 24:49 where the promise of the Father would be sent; and in John 20:17 where the Father of the Son would become the Father of believers.

26 This repeats v.23 in a different way. In v.23, believers will not ask the Lord in their prayers; rather in v.26 they will ask the Father directly in His Name. He negates the thought that He would continue to ask the Father for them; that would not be necessary any more. Certainly He had prayed for Peter in Luke 22:32, "I have prayed for thee", and in the greater part of the prayer in John 17. The disciples were to have no fear that prayers addressed to the Father would be inferior in any way, for they would not be left alone in a barren wilderness of unanswered prayer out of contact with God.

27 The Father was greatly concerned and interested in the disciples, for there was a new relationship with the Father to be formed by the Spirit through the work of Christ. This was proved by the Father's love for the believers—the love in 3:16 was the commencement, and this love continues throughout life. Moreover, this divine love towards the disciples had already been stated in 14:23; the reality of it is known because a disciple has loved Christ, and because the disciple has believed that He "came out from God" (17:8). Note that the Lord referred only to their faith in a great past event—the fact that He had come "out from God"; He did not mention their faith in connection with a forthcoming future event, when He would ascend into the Father's presence.

28 Regardless of this, the Lord here presented the complete truth—His entry into the world from heaven, and His return to heaven from the earth. In both these movements, the Father is involved: He came from the Father, and He would return to the Father. The former truth is stressed many times in John's Gospel: "the Word was made flesh, and dwelt among us" (1:14); "He that cometh from above" (3:31); "my Father giveth you the true bread from heaven ... which cometh down from heaven" (6:32-33,58); "I proceeded forth and came from God" (8:42). The latter truth of His leaving this world does not appear in as many verses: "I go unto my Father" (14:12); "I go my way to him that sent me" (16:5). These two movements mark the two extremities of His tabernacling upon earth. They can be used to distinguish between the two often-used names of the Lord, "Christ Jesus" and "Jesus Christ". The former takes our thoughts from heaven to earth—His descent; the latter takes our thoughts from earth to heaven—His ascension.

29-30 *The disciples speak.* Their recognition that He was now speaking "plainly" does not mean that previously they had thought that He always spoke in proverbs. Rather, they were distinguishing between the metaphor in v.21 and the details of His forthcoming movements in v.28. At the end of v.30, they confessed their faith, "we believe that thou camest forth from God". This is remarkable, since it is still limited to the past; their faith still could not appropriate the truth of the Lord's ascension in the near future. Perhaps it was a mental blockage to faith; how gracious of the Lord that they were enabled to witness this ascension into the clouds (Acts 1:9). So their subsequent faith in His resurrection and ascension rested upon their being eyewitnesses, and not only upon His words. In v.30, the disciples expressed two reactions:

1. "We are sure that thou knowest all things", namely the circumstances surrounding His entry into this scene (for ordinary men have no direct knowledge about their birth into this scene), and the then future circumstances attending His ascension (apart from faith, ordinary men have no idea what will happen to them after death).

2. "Thou ... needest not that any man should ask thee". This is taken to refer back to v.19, where they were desirous to ask Him about various statements He was making. But at that stage, there was no need to ask any more; the Lord anticipated their questions, and answered directly without being prompted. Some expositors view this as a reference to v.23.

31-32 *The Lord speaks.* By the question, "Do ye now believe?", the Lord was showing the shallowness of their limited faith prior to the giving of the Spirit. It was easy to say "we believe", but did their works correspond with their faith? Was something missing in both faith and works?

The Lord's statement in v.32 shows that something was amiss. The hour of crisis was not only coming, but it had now arrived; see 13:1; 17:1. In spite of the Lord's warnings to His disciples, they were not really aware that the crisis was at hand. How ill-prepared they were in courage to stand by the Lord at His moment of need. They would be scattered, an event that took place immediately after 18:12, "Then all the disciples forsook him, and fled" (Matt 26:56). Previously, as they left the upper room, the Lord in Matt 26:31 quoted Zech

13:7, "it is written, I will smite the shepherd, and the sheep of the flock shall be scattered abroad". We believe that there was only one place in Jerusalem where they could go, that is, to the upper room that they had left a few hours previously. Naturally, they would thus leave the Lord alone, yet the Father was always with Him, a fact demonstrated by His prayer when being nailed to the cross, "Father, forgive them" (Luke 23:34). When on the cross and when He confessed to being forsaken by God (Ps 22:1; Matt 27:46), it was in His capacity as Judge that God was addressed, and not in the filial relationship as between Father and Son.

33 The whole of this discourse was designed to offer peace to the disciples—a peace of heart that transcended the perplexities and difficulties of those days. This peace had been offered at the beginning of this discourse, "Let not your heart be troubled" and "Peace I leave with you" (14:1,27). The world was a place of tribulation, but the peace of Christ was far greater than that. This tribulation (*thlipsis*, elsewhere translated affliction, anguish, persecution, trouble) does not refer to the "great tribulation" in a prophetical sense (Matt 24:21,29), but to general tribulation endured by some of the Lord's people because of their testimony. The Lord could offer them His comfort, "be of good cheer", because He had trodden that pathway before. We are conquerors in a time of tribulation, distress or persecution (Rom 8:35,37), because He has overcome the world. As He stated in the conclusion of the letter to Laodicea, "even as I also overcame, and am set down with my Father in his throne" (Rev 3:21). Truly, if we suffer with Him, we shall reign with Him (2 Tim 2:12). Who is now an overcomer? John answers, "whatsoever is born of God" and "he that believeth that Jesus is the Son of God" (1 John 5:4-5).

V. The Way to Gethsemane: The Son in the Sanctuary (17:1-26)

1. *The Son's Eternal Relationship with the Father* 17:1-5

v.1 "These words spake Jesus, and lifted up his eyes to heaven, and said, Father, the hour is come; glorify thy Son, that thy Son also may glorify thee:
v.2 As thou hast given him power over all flesh, that he should give eternal life to as many as thou hast given him.
v.3 And this is life eternal, that they might know thee the only true God, and Jesus Christ, whom thou hast sent.
v.4 I have glorified thee on the earth: I have finished the work which thou gavest me to do.
v.5 And now, O Father, glorify thou me with thine own self with the glory which I had with thee before the world was."

The Lord and His eleven disciples were now approaching the western bank of the brook Kidron that flowed in the valley between the steep eastern slopes of Jerusalem and the western slopes of the mount of Olives. They would cross this brook afterwards in 18:1, to enter the garden of Gethsemane where the Son would engage in a further session of prayer recorded in the Synoptic Gospels (Matt 26:36-46). John 17 is concerned with the *work* of the Father; Matt 26:36-46 with the *will* of the Father. The former looked beyond the sufferings, while the latter looked at the sufferings themselves.

No doubt this prayer in John 17 is one of the most difficult passages to comment upon, for the prayer is something altogether out of this world, although its subject matter concerns His own still in the world. Here we have the inner thoughts of Christ in intimate communion with the Father, so it is a very solemn task to seek to explain the very thoughts and utterances expressed by the Son in the sanctuary. A shorter prayer of the Son is recorded in Matt 11:25-27, and other short prayers can also be found dispersed throughout the Gospels.

This prayer does not reveal the divine mind through the medium of *teaching*, rather through the medium of *prayer*, yet expressed so that the apostles—John at least—could hear. It should move us more than the event described in Isa 6:1-4, when Isaiah saw the glory of God in the holy place. For John 17 took place in the Holiest of all, to use tabernacle language. The prayer is a "structured" prayer with a definite trend of thought throughout, unlike some "scattered" prayers that we may hear today. The prayer contains three main sections:

1. The Son's eternal relationship with the Father (vv.1-5); here we have the mutual divine glory of the Father and the Son.

2. A prayer on behalf of the disciples who would be left (vv.6-19); here we find the subject of the sanctification of believers while in the world.

3. A prayer on behalf of all subsequent converts (vv.20-26); here we have the unity of all believers.

By means of this prayer, the Lord showed that He loved His disciples unto the end (13:1). He demonstrated that He was not looking on His own things, but also on the things of others (Phil 2:4).

1 *The Lord speaks*. To engage in prayer, He lifted up His eyes to heaven—whether He had stopped by the bank of the brook, or whether He was still walking towards the brook we are not told. The posture in prayer is evidently important. Clearly, the Lord's posture was determined by the subject matter of the prayer. Here, He lifted His eyes upwards, answering to "the glory that should follow" (1 Pet 1:11); but in the garden of Gethsemane, He kneeled down and then "fell on his face" (Luke 22:41; Matt 26:39), implying a gaze downwards, answering to "the sufferings of Christ" (1 Pet 1:11). In the case of men, a self-satisfied sinner could stand and pray "with himself" for all to see (Luke 18:11), while a repentant publican "would not lift up so much as his eyes unto heaven". For believers, it is quite in order to lift up holy hands (1 Tim 2:8), and to kneel down for corporate prayer (Acts 20:36; 21:5), though on one occasion David the king sat before the Lord in prayer (1 Chron 17:16).

The Lord commenced by saying "Father". Later He used the titles "Holy Father" (v.11) and "righteous Father" (v.25), the former being on account of the world being mentioned. Here was no use of divine names in a haphazard fashion; spiritual intelligence should mark our use of divine names in prayer, rather than an apparent vain repetition of names in almost every sentence, sometimes the names having no Scriptural justification at all.

In 13:1 the Lord knew that His hour was come to depart out of this world; here, He expressed this fact to the Father, while in Matt 26:45 He used the fact when addressing His disciples. The prayer that the Father should "glorify thy Son" (and in v.5) is the only personal request in ch.17. Yet this glory was mutual, since the Son would also glorify the Father (see 13:31). The Son would be glorified in resurrection, and then in ascension on the Father's throne (7:39); then the Son would glorify the Father in heaven, as He had glorified Him on the earth (v.4).

2-3 One means whereby the Son had glorified the Father was to grant eternal life to all those whom the Father had given Him. He had authority over all flesh (the word for "power" is *exousia*, meaning authority), and He exercised this authority by giving eternal life to certain men, but not to all. Thus in the future, He will manifest authority (power) over the nations, at the same time granting this power to the overcomers (Rev 2:26-27).

This prayer is full of the thought of giving, since giving is a manifestation of the existence of love. (We have pointed out this character of love in our remarks on 3:16.) The following have been given: eternal life (v.2); the manifestation of the Father's Name (v.6); the Father's words—specific words (v.8); the Father's Word—generally (v.14); glory (v.22). Conversely, the prayer is full of the thought that believers have been given to the Son by the Father (vv.2,6(twice),9,11,12,24).

The eternal life that has been given is defined in v.3. This life possesses the ability to know the true God, and the sent One, Jesus Christ. This is not the only characteristic of eternal life. The words "eternal life" (*aiōnios zōē*, or reversed in order) occur seventeen times in John's Gospel—sometimes the translation is "everlasting life"; the first occurrence is in 3:15, and the last is here in 17:3. Clearly the knowledge of divine Persons forms the basis of the possession of eternal life; without this knowledge no life could be possessed. Such a knowledge is unique. Indeed, there are "gods many, and lords many", but for the Lord's people there is but "one God, the Father . . . and one Lord Jesus Christ" (1 Cor 8:5-6). Again, Paul wrote, "One Lord . . . one God and Father" (Eph 4:5-6). To a believer, both names appearing together is a demonstration of unity in Deity, though this is rejected by those who seek to deny the Deity of Christ. The juxtaposition of both Persons is found in verses such as 5:23; 10:30; 15:23; 1 John 2:23.

4 Here the Son reviewed His life on earth prior to the cross. In all His words and deeds, He glorified the Father. No word and no deed was accomplished that did not glorify the Father. At the end of Dan 5:23, Daniel, in interpreting the writing on the wall to king Belshazzar in Babylon, said, "the God in whose hand thy breath is, and whose are all thy ways, hast thou not glorified"; what a contrast to the Son of God! Secondly in our verse, the Son said, "I have finished the work which thou gavest me to do". Some suggest that this refers in anticipation to the work of the Lord on the cross, but this does not seem probable in the context. We cannot see that this refers to the work on the cross before it actually took place (see 19:30 when He could say "It is finished"). As a review of His life of ministry, the things given Him to do relate to what He did for His own; nothing remained undone at this last stage. He mentioned several things in this prayer: He manifested the Father's Name (v.6); He gave them the words from the Father (v.8; 12:49); He had kept His own (v.12); He had sent them (v.18); He had given them glory (v.22); He had declared the Father's Name (v.26).

5 This completed work meant that the time had come for His departure. In a lesser measure, Paul knew when the time of his departure had arrived; reviewing his life's service, he could write, "I have . . . finished my course, I have kept the faith" (2 Tim 4:7), leading to a crown of righteousness. In the Son's case, He would take up in glory the position that He had occupied in the eternal past; this would be "with (*para*)" the Father, or as JND translates it, "along with thyself". The pre-incarnate glory of the Son is here linked with His ascension glory—His Manhood on earth, His sacrifice and death coming in between. There are many references to His eternal existence in the past: 17:24; Heb 7:3; 1 Pet 1:20; Rev 1:18. In our case, our eternal life stretches to the future, but does not extend from the past, except as promised by God in verses such as 2 Tim 1:9; Titus 1:2.

2. *Prayer on Behalf of His Disciples Who Would be Left* 17:6-19

v.6 "I have manifested thy name unto the men which thou gavest me out of the world: thine they were, and thou gavest them me; and they have kept thy word.

v.7 Now they have known that all things whatsoever thou hast given me are of thee.

v.8 For I have given unto them the words which thou gavest me; and they have received *them*, and have known surely that I came out from thee, and they have believed that thou didst send me.

v.9 I pray for them: I pray not for the world, but for them which thou hast given me; for they are thine.

v.10 And all mine are thine, and thine are mine; and I am glorified in them.

v.11 And now I am no more in the world, but these are in the world, and I come to thee. Holy Father, keep through thine own name those whom thou hast given me, that they may be one, as we *are*.

v.12 While I was with them in the world, I kept them in thy name: those that thou gavest me I have kept, and none of them is lost, but the son of perdition; that the scripture might be fulfilled.
v.13 And now come I to thee; and these things I speak in the world, that they might have my joy fulfilled in themselves.
v.14 I have given them thy word; and the world hath hated them, because they are not of the world, even as I am not of the world.
v.15 I pray not that thou shouldest take them out of the world, but that thou shouldest keep them from the evil.
v.16 They are not of the world, even as I am not of the world.
v.17 Sanctify them through thy truth: thy word is truth.
v.18 As thou hast sent me into the world, even so have I also sent them into the world.
v.19 And for their sakes I sanctify myself, that they also might be sanctified through the truth."

6 *The Lord speaks.* The Son now gives a detailed and prayerful consideration of His disciples who would be left after His departure. Not only does He pray for them, but He also makes positive statements of truth about them.

He had manifested the Father's Name—His Person and character—to the men given Him out of the world. This had been the essential work of Christ; by words and deeds He had made the Father known, as later the Spirit would make the Son known. For example "neither knoweth any man the Father, save the Son, and he to whomsoever the Son will reveal him" (Matt 11:27). The status of these disciples was "out of the world". The selection process was therefore a separating process; morally and spiritually a believer has been called out from the immorality and unspirituality of the world system. A believer should not be in two places at the same time. Thus the children of Israel had been brought out of Egypt, and seekers after the Lord were found "without the camp" (Exod 33:7; Heb 13:13); practically speaking, the exhortation is for believers to come out from the circles and fellowships of unregenerate Christendom (2 Cor 6:14-18).

Believers are separated because they belong to the Father who had given them to the Son. During His lifetime here below, His people were kept safe (v.12; 10:28-29). And His prayer was that the Father would keep them after His departure (v.11). Moreover, His people had "kept thy word"—this was their response to His teaching, and He graciously made no reference to their failures. Note "thy" denoting divine possession of the word. Thus He also said, "I have given them *thy* word" (v.14); "*thy* word is truth" (v.17). Paul wrote, "not as the word of men, but as it is in truth, the word of God" (1 Thess 2:13).

7-8 Here there is reference to the faith and knowledge of the disciples—the divine perception of their hearts in spite of weaknesses. Their faith and knowledge related only to the past, not to the future, as we have noticed elsewhere (16:30). Thus they knew the origin of the Son's possessions—"whatsoever thou hast given me are of thee", namely His authority (v.2) and

His words (v.8), for He had said before, "My doctrine is not mine, but his that sent me" (7:16).

The Son acknowledged that His disciples had "received" the words. The Jews had rejected His teaching, as in chs.6,8, but the disciples were receptive, in spite of many weaknesses caused by lack of understanding—for example, when Peter contradicted the Lord in Matt 16:22. Certainly they knew and believed that the Son "came out from thee", not referring of course to any supposed origin, since He existed absolutely and eternally without beginning, but to the place of the Father's presence from whence He came forth to earth at His birth. The fact that they believed is a result of divine revelation (Matt 16:17).

9 The Son was then praying for them—He identified those for whom He was praying. By saying "I pray not for the world", the Son was making a solemn distinction—here was the world without God, without hope, and without a prayer on its behalf, for the world lies under the authority of the wicked one. This should be contrasted with evangelistic prayers of believers today, when they pray for the salvation of the unsaved, and with Paul's words, "my heart's desire and prayer to God for Israel is, that they might be saved" (Rom 10:1). The Lord's prayers for His disciples are found in vv.11,15,17: that the Father should keep them, and that He should sanctify them. Alas that some believers should attempt to place themselves outside the scope of this prayer, by loving the pleasures and religion of this world as if they had not been sanctified.

10 We have here the reason for the prayer—because of the mutual possessions within Deity. Believers belong to the Father, and to the Son. As Paul wrote in 1 Cor 3:22-23, "all are yours: and ye are Christ's; and Christ is God's". Again, "ye are not your own", and "ye are bought with a price: therefore glorify God in your body, and in your spirit, which are God's" (6:19-20). This leads us to note the mutual ownership of property in the early church in Jerusalem, "neither said any of them that ought of the things which he possessed was his own; but they had all things common" (Acts 2:44-45; 4:32-37). This state of affairs could not last, since their finance came to an end, when they had to be nourished by members of Gentile churches who possessed homes and finance (Rom 15:25-27).

In the OT, the possessions of God were often designated, as "my people", "my jewels", "his vineyard", though sometimes there was a reversal; "my" was changed to "thy", when the people arrogated to themselves the holy things, defiling them with material pride and advantage (Ezek 16:14-22).

The Son recognised that He was glorified in His disciples. Thus He was seen in His people; God has shined in our hearts, and there is found the "light of the knowledge of the glory of God" (2 Cor 4:6). This reminds us of Moses whose skin shone both inside and outside the tabernacle (Exod 34:29-35). This was the divine glory, and Moses was charged with it temporarily. In the case of believers, this glory of Christ possessed inwardly comes about because the

Godhead dwells within (14:23), and because our bodies are the temple of the Holy Spirit (1 Cor 6:19).

11 By "now", the Son referred to the forthcoming time when He would ascend to the Father. This would mean a physical separation of His own from Himself. The Son felt very keenly that, as He had suffered at the hands of men, so would His disciples in their measure. They suffered nothing while He was present, but He knew what was coming afterwards (16:33). Hence He prayed for their safety—that the "Holy Father"—would keep them. It is easy to trace this keeping power through the Acts, from imprisonments, shipwrecks and even death. As examples, Paul wrote of his experiences in 1 Cor 4:11-13; 2 Cor 6:5-10; 11:23-33. Yet he could always say, "the Lord shall deliver me from every evil work, and will preserve me unto his heavenly kingdom" (2 Tim 4:18).

The object of this keeping power was "that they may be one, as we are". This does not refer to unity in Deity; rather there was a unity of will for the pathway, however dark and difficult it might be. May the disciples be kept from deflection, possessing one common outlook. Paul expressed the same desire for the Philippians, to stand fast in "one spirit", not being terrified by their adversaries (Phil 1:27-28). The same aspirations are found in Heb 10:32-36.

12 The Father would keep the disciples in future, whereas the Son had kept them during His sojourn on the earth. He had done this "in thy name", namely He acted as the Father would have acted.

It should be noticed that the twice-repeated verb "keep" in this verse represents two different Greek words. The first verb is *tēreō* (in the imperfect tense showing the continuity of the Son's keeping love and power), meaning to preserve, watch over. But the second verb is *phulassō*, translated "guarded" in the RV, as an act of protection (as "a strong man armed keepeth his palace" in Luke 11:21).

This preserving and protecting power kept the disciples from being deflected back to the religious world of the Jews; none was lost, for it had been the Father's will that none should be lost, but raised at the last day (6:39). The Son's assertion that none was lost is seen in action in 18:9, where He would not allow His disciples to be taken captive along with Himself.

And yet there is the apparent exception, "the son of perdition; that the scripture might be fulfilled". There is disagreement amongst expositors as to whether Judas had first been a believer, and then had been lost because of his great sin. We hardly think that such was the case, since he was a thief and had a demon. 6:71 shows clearly that the Lord knew whom He had chosen—chosen not to blessing as in the case of the eleven, but chosen so that the Scripture might be fulfilled. Ps 41:9; 109:8-9 refer to Judas in the OT, so the Lord chose this man in Matt 10:1 so as to place him in the right position where he could accomplish his intended deed. He was chosen, not as a disciple, but as a man to further his evil work. As the "son of perdition", he was fit for destruction, as a "child of hell" (Matt 23:15). After hanging himself, he went "to his own place". Some expositors identify Judas with the coming "son of perdition" in 2 Thess 2:3, suggesting that he will return to become the second beast of Rev 13, the anti-Christ. However, this is merely a suggestion, and cannot be proved; we are not therefore committed to this idea.

13 In spite of this darkness of the human heart, the Son desired that His resurrection-joy—"my joy"—should be fulfilled in His disciples. The joy of the world would have no part in the joy of their souls. He had already spoken of this joy in 16:20,22,24, a joy that none could remove from them. This joy would be "full" (v.24), since its origin would be divine.

14 The word can ultimately come from no other source, except One divine bringing it down from above. Today, we may have teachers and ministers of the word, but their teaching is not self-manufactured, not borrowed from others; to be effective it must come from above by the Holy Spirit. Anything to the contrary must be judged for what it is worth, the word of man. But the possession of the word in any believer makes a complete difference, and the world perceives a consecrated life devoted to the word of God. The world cannot bear a sincere believer who loves the word and the Lord revealed in that word; he is therefore hated. The word has a separating influence upon those who are attached to it. As in the OT where God said, "ye shall be holy unto me: for I the Lord am holy, and have severed you from other people, that ye should be mine" (Lev 20:26), so the Son's disciples "are not of the world". It is shocking when christians are of the world, in its pleasures, interests, dress and activity; rather they should not be "conformed to this world", but "transformed" (Rom 12:2). Note:

1. The Lord said, "I am not of this world" (8:23; 17:16), in contrast to Satan, the prince of this world.

2. "They are not of the world" (17:14), in contrast to the Pharisees who were "from beneath", "ye are of this world" (8:23).

3. "My kingdom is not of this world" (18:6), in contrast to the principles of the kingdom of Rome occupying Jerusalem at that time.

15 It was not the divine will that the disciples should be taken out of the world at the same time as the exodus of the Son. The divine intention was to leave the testimony in their hands. This intention had already been stated openly, "I send you forth as sheep in the midst of wolves" (Matt 10:16); "I send unto you prophets, and wise men, and scribes" (23:34). This was translated into practice in Matt 28:19; Mark 16:20; Luke 24:48; Acts 1:8.

The powers of darkness would surround them in their testimony, so the prayer of the Son was that the Father should "keep (preserve) them from the evil". We believe that *ek tou ponērou* implies both Satan and his powers working in unbelievers—not from tribulation causd by men, for in the world the disciples would have tribulation (16:33), but from spiritual wickedness and from falling into false doctrine. The dispensation of law had failed as soon as it had commenced, so the Son was determined that the dispensation of grace would not fail as soon as He left this world. The preservation of truth in Acts 15 is a good example of an answer to this prayer, else Christianity would have been reduced to a sect of Judaism. However, a prayer like this is effective as long as christian teachers desire to live in the light of divine truth. A blanket preservation is not placed upon teachers who are determined to teach falsely.

16 The disciples would be on the same ground as the Son—they and He were "not of the world". Thus they would testify that the works of the world were evil (7:7), and they would not physically fight for His kingdom on earth (18:36). There was to be a complete separation from the moral and spiritual rottenness in the world—in its religious, commercial, political, financial, personal, unrighteous, entertainment and sporting aspects.

17 While v.16 is absolute, yet v.17 is practical. To be a useful servant sent forth as in v.18, sanctification is necessary. Daniel was sanctified in his youth, refusing to be defiled with the king of Babylon's sustenance (Dan 1:8); hence he became such a power of good throughout a long life. Thus the word of truth sets men apart when they act upon it—doers and not hearers only (James 1:22). The OT sets a man apart under law, morally and ceremonially; the NT sets a man apart under grace under "the royal law"—the law of the kingdom of God (Jas 2:8). This is the principle of laver-washing, to use tabernacle language. As the Son had said earlier that night, His disciples were clean through the word spoken to them (15:3); a young man would cleanse his way by taking heed "according to thy word" (Ps 119:9).

18 So these sanctified men are sent into the world from which they are separated. For heavenly-minded men, the world is an unnatural environment. These disciples, like Paul, were to be ambassadors from heaven, representing the heavenly court in a world of men dominated by Satan. The Son was the first divine Ambassador sent forth from heaven, and the disciples would follow His steps. It is not profitable to be a servant in this world with a high and heavenly calling, and yet seeking to be unsanctified practically. Neither is it profitable to go here and there in the world without having been sent.

19 The Son went before. His own sanctification was an object lesson. He lived out His own holy character: He was described as holy in Isa 6:3; the One to be born of Mary would be "that holy thing" (Luke 1:35); in His lifetime, He is described as "holy, harmless, undefiled, separate from sinners" (Heb 7:26).

This was not only in words, but in deeds, so the Gospel records show us the Son as separated from every foreign deed and thought of men. His disciples had to follow in this pathway, "come out from among them, and be ye separate... touch not the unclean thing... perfecting holiness in the fear of God" (2 Cor 6:17; 7:1).

3. *Prayer on Behalf of All Subsequent Converts* 17:20-26

v.20 "Neither pray I for these alone, but for them also which shall believe on me through their word;
v.21 That they all may be one; as thou, Father, *art* in me, and I in thee, that they also may be one in us: that the world may believe that thou hast sent me.
v.22 And the glory which thou gavest me I have given them; that they may be one, even as we are one:
v.23 I in them, and thou in me, that they may be made perfect in one; and that the world may know that thou hast sent me, and hast loved them, as thou hast loved me.
v.24 Father, I will that they also, whom thou hast given me, be with me where I am; that they may behold my glory, which thou hast given me: for thou lovedst me before the foundation of the world.
v.25 O righteous Father, the world hath not known thee: but I have known thee, and these have known that thou hast sent me.
v.26 And I have declared unto them thy name, and will declare *it*: that the love wherewith thou hast loved me may be in them, and I in them."

20-21 *The Lord speaks.* The Son now prays for the effects of the expansion of the testimony after His departure. His prayer was not restricted to the eleven apostles; it was for other believers also. "Through their word" is the essential means whereby propagation takes place, as seeds are scattered from a seed-pod of a flower. The NT knows of no other method, certainly not the methods of modern entertainment and the flesh. Paul spelt out this in 2 Tim 2:2, the truth spreading forth from himself, to Timothy, to "faithful men" and to "others also". See also Joel 1:3. Paul's case was different, since he received a direct vision from heaven. Thus in His prayer the Son could foresee all converts, their faith being the basic ingredient of their status in Christ. The essential request in the prayer was for unity, "that they all may be one". The oneness between Father and Son is used as a similitude for the oneness between believers, though the essential Oneness of Deity can hardly be the point here. Rather there is oneness of thought and purpose in divine things. Another aspect of oneness is found in Heb 2:11-13, "all of one... I and the children". (Unity within the Godhead is seen in verses such as 1:1-3; Heb 1:8, but this is not applicable here even as a pattern for all believers.)

The world takes notice of such a testimony; some may believe, but not all, and faith would be centred upon the One who had been sent. Of the men in Jerusalem, Acts 5:13 shows the effect on them, "of the rest durst no man join himself to them", when they were together as a united company; but believers were "the more added to the Lord".

22 Vv.21-23 constitute a prayer for the Lord's people here, while v.24 is a prayer relating to blessing above. The glory given to the Son, and which is passed on to believers, should promote unity and harmony. Certainly this glory is not the outward glory of the tabernacle and temple of old. That ministration of death was glorious (2 Cor 3:7); how much more is the ministration of the Spirit glorious, and not fading (vv.8-11,18), as believers are changed from the outward to the inward, from the old to the new, from death to life, from the law to Christ. This glory of Christ is not that which is His eternally as One in Deity, but the glory consequential upon His becoming Man, and returning with added glory. This glory is in our hearts, and shows itself in our profession and testimony; disunity shows that some hearts are void and empty.

23 Another aspect of this unity is that of maturity. The Son in us is seen in verses such as, "that Christ may dwell in your hearts by faith" (Eph 3:17), and "Christ in you, the hope of glory" (Col 1:27). He is present in us through the vehicle of the Spirit possessed inwardly. This maturity provoked by His presence is concerned with having the mind of Christ, allowing His ruling influence to dominate. This maturity leads to non-natural manifestations of unity. Politics, sport, and any sort of rivalry, all bring in disunity. The world knows that the Son has brought down the love of the Father, thereby establishing this unity in His people, namely the "one accord" in Acts 2:1. But men will resist it and mock at it, so that they with their deeds of evil can remain outside the sanctifying and unifying sphere of the love of God in Christ Jesus.

24 This is the last occasion in this prayer in which "whom thou hast given me" occurs. Nevertheless, it is the only time that this occurs in this paragraph when the Lord's thoughts had turned to converts in general. It is no longer "I in them" as in v.23 (in this present life), but believers "with me where I am" (in the future life above). In other words, the promise "where I am" (14:3) did not apply to the apostles only, but to all converts. Thus Paul's words are in keeping with this truth, "so shall we ever be with the Lord" (1 Thess 4:17). The glory on high is spoken of in several verses, such as "when his glory shall be revealed" (1 Pet 4:13), and "the presence of his glory" (Jude 24). To gaze upon His glory (given as in v.22, and yet a glory possessed from the eternal past in v.5) will be our eternal privilege. Of course, He will have also a glory displayed in His coming kingdom, a preview having been granted to three of the apostles on the mount of transfiguration (Matt 16:28 to 17:9; 2 Pet 1:16-18). Moreover, the apostles had seen both His moral glory and His glory through His miracles during His life on earth (1:14; 2;11). Note how the glory of the Lord was to appear to the consecrated priests in the OT (Lev 9:4,6,23).

In the statement "thou lovedst me *before* the foundation of the world", we must note carefully the word "before", implying the period before the creation, and relating to the past eternal state. Thus the Lamb was "foreordained *before* the foundation of the world" (1 Pet 1:20), and we have been chosen "in him *before* the foundation of the world" (Eph 1:4). The salvation of members of the church therefore rests in the eternal counsels of God. But the blessings of the coming kingdom are viewed as more attached to the creation below, when the preposition "from" and not "before" is used, "the kingdom prepared for you *from* the foundation of the world" (Matt 25:34).

25-26 The word "these" suggests that the main thought now returns to the eleven apostles. No doubt the title "righteous Father" is used so as to present a contrast with the world in its ignorance and unbelief, and hence in its unrighteousness. Several different kinds of knowledge appear in these two verses:

1. "I have known thee"—the eternal and ever-present knowledge of the Father by the Son, a knowledge passed on to men by revelation (Matt 11:27).

2. "The world hath not known thee"; in fact, any "natural" knowledge that men may have of God tends to degrade downwards to idolatry (Rom 1:20-23).

3. The apostles knew the Father's Name since the Son had declared it, and they also knew that the Son had been sent by the Father. The declaration would also be made in the future; no doubt 20:17 was in mind.

The object of such knowledge was that divine love should be in the apostles, and that the Son should be in them. The relationship of love between divine Persons is not something hidden in heaven; it should be seen as reflected in His people.

These last words of the Son in prayer must have riveted themselves upon the heart of John, the apostle whom Jesus loved. For divine love, together with love in His people, have a prominent place in John's first epistle (1 John 4:7-21). "If God so loved us, we ought also to love one another" (v.11).

I. The Betrayal by Judas and the Denial by Peter (18:1-27)

1. *The Betrayal of the Lord by Judas*
18:1-11

v.1 "When Jesus had spoken these words, he went forth with his disciples over the brook Cedron, where was a garden, into the which he entered, and his disciples.

v.2 And Judas also, which betrayed him, knew the place: for Jesus ofttimes resorted thither with his disciples.

v.3 Judas then, having received a band *of men* and officers from the chief priests and Pharisees, cometh thither with lanterns and torches and weapons.

v.4 Jesus therefore, knowing all things that should come upon him, went forth, and said unto them, Whom seek ye?

v.5 They answered him, Jesus of Nazareth. Jesus saith unto them. I am *he*. And Judas also, which betrayed him, stood with them.

v.6 As soon then as he had said unto them, I am *he*, they went backward, and fell to the ground.

v.7 Then asked he them again, Whom seek ye? And they said, Jesus of Nazareth.

v.8 Jesus answered, I have told you that I am *he*: if therefore ye seek me, let these go their way:

v.9 That the saying might be fulfilled which he spake, Of them which thou gavest me have I lost none.

v.10 Then Simon Peter having a sword drew it, and smote the high priest's servant, and cut off his right ear. The servant's name was Malchus.

v.11 Then said Jesus unto Peter, Put up thy sword into the sheath: the cup which my Father hath given me, shall I not drink it?"

There were four stages in the Lord's trial at the hands of men:

1. The taking of the Lord in the garden of Gethsemane.

2. The Lord's trial by the Jewish Sanhedrin.

3. The Lord's trial by Pilate, representing the Roman occupying authority.

4. The Lord's appearance before Herod (only in Luke 23:6-12).

1 The Lord's prayer on the western bank of the brook Kidron can be divided into three parts (see our commentary on ch.17); His prayer on the eastern side also consisted of three parts. This is not recorded in John's Gospel, but is found in the three Synoptic Gospels (Matt 26:36-46; Mark 14:32-42; Luke 22:39-46). This brook is spelt Kidron in the OT; it was the brook at which king David was rejected (2 Sam 15:23), where Asa destroyed his mother's idol (1 Kings 15:13), and where Josiah destroyed the idolatrous refuse that had accumulated in the temple in Jerusalem (2 Kings 23:6,12). John did not record the name of the garden at the foot of the mount of Olives, but this was the garden of Gethsemane into which the Lord and His disciples entered. Matt 26:36-37 provides further details; as they entered, the Lord was "with them", but the three chosen apostles He took "with him". There were thus circles of nearness: there were eight left at the entrance to the garden, three were taken further in, while One went "a little further". In tabernacle language, no doubt these positions correspond to the court, the holy place, and the Holiest of all.

2 Judas knew the place, and he knew that the Lord often visited the garden evidently to be quietly away from the multitudes. This was why Judas chose this place to accomplish his deed of treachery—"in the absence of the multitude" (Luke 22:6) (or "without tumult" AV and RV marg). Thus in the Holiest of all the dark deed would be done (far worse than the slaying of Joab in the court of the tabernacle in 1 Kings 2:28,34). This choice of venue by Judas would correspond to Ps 79:1, "the heathen are come into thine inheritance; thy holy temple have they defiled".

The mount of Olives played an important part in the Lord's experience. The western slope contained the place of prayer, but the eastern slope contained Bethany, where the Lord often lodged, no doubt in the home of Mary, Martha and Lazarus (Matt 21:17). The top of the mount had been the commencement of His triumphant ride into Jerusalem a few days before. "Ofttimes" the Lord resorted there—this divine consistency sometimes contrasts with the unseemly attitude of some believers who treat a gathering for prayer as irrelevant and unnecessary. But this occasion was the last visit of the Lord to this sacred spot. Having finished His prayer, He waited for the arrival of Judas, watching over the sleeping apostles until Judas drew near, when He said "Rise" (Matt 26:46).

3 Judas headed a band of men from the religious leaders—the chief priests and the Pharisees, men of the temple and synagogue stock respectively. This band of men were the servants of the Jewish council, the Sanhedrin. The priests represented the ceremony of the law, while the Pharisees represented the doctrine of the law, all according to men. No doubt these Jewish leaders were "the people . . . the rulers" in Ps 2:1-2, while "the heathen . . . the kings" refer essentially to the Gentile power of Rome.

It had been night when Judas departed from the upper room, so now "lanterns and torches" were necessary. In other words, mere natural light intruded into the Holiest of all. Today, spiritual things can be marred by natural intrusions, for the natural or carnal man uses natural or carnal means in his religion.

4 *The Lord speaks.* In v.2, Judas knew; here, the Lord knew, but what a difference! In these chapters, John stressed the divine knowledge possessed by the Lord, that His hour was come and that He went to God (12:23; 13:1,3; 17:1). The Lord took the initiative; He anticipated them by asking the question "Whom seek ye?", before the men had a chance to speak themselves. He took this direct action so that there might be the opportunity for the full effect of the radiancy from His divine Person to be seen, and to isolate Himself from His disciples so as to preserve them in safety. It would appear that the Lord stood between His disciples and the approaching band of men.

5 *The men and officers speak.* By answering "Jesus of Nazareth", they used not only a popular name that was circulating among men, but also so as to distinguish Him from other men who might have had the same name. Nazareth implied the town where He had been brought up in Galilee, but to their minds the name of the place also denoted a town that was despised, and they desired that this description should pass over to the Lord Himself. Others, however used the Name in a more reverent fashion, particularly as it was also used by the Lord Himself, as the following list shows. (Three slightly different Greek words for the translation "Nazareth" occur in the text of the Greek NT: *Nazareth* (or *Nazaret*), *Nazarēnos*, *Nazōraios*, as a Greek concordance will demonstrate.)

By Philip (John 1:45).

By the multitude (Matt 21:11).

By the man with the unclean spirit (Mark 1:24; Luke 4:24).

By blind Bartimaeus (Mark 10:47; Luke 18:37).

By the men and officers who came to arrest the Lord (John 18:5,7).

By the maid at Peter's denial (Matt 26:71; Mark 14:67).

By Pilate in the title affixed to the cross (John 19:19).

By the angel at the resurrection (Mark 16:6).

By the two men on the Emmaus road (Luke 24:19).

By Peter (Acts 2:22; 3:6; 4:10; 10:38).

By men of various synagogues disputing with Stephen (Acts 6:14).

By the Lord Himself on the Damascus road (Acts 22:8).

By Paul in recalling his unconverted days (Acts 26:9).

The Lord speaks. The simple, yet profound answer "I am he" (*egō eimi*) is strictly "I am", declaring the eternally existing Person of the Son. We have noted that He used this title before when speaking to the Pharisees in John 8:24,28,58, recalling God's Name in Exod 3:14.

The writer John was watching, so he carefully noted the presence of Judas standing with these men, one whom he had last seen earlier in the upper room. Previously, Judas had stood with the apostles, but now the Lord stood between the eleven and Judas.

6 The effect of the declaration "I am" was profound. The eternal power of the Son was exercised before He submitted Himself to the evil hands of men. An irresistible force radiated forwards from Him, and the men "went backward, and fell to the ground". As Ps 40:14 (a Messianic Psalm) puts it, "Let them be ashamed and confounded together that seek after my soul to destroy it; let them be driven backward and put to shame that wish me evil". This contrasts with the effect of the glorious Person of Christ upon John on the isle of Patmos, "when I saw him, I fell at his feet as dead" (Rev 1:17), to be revived by the Lord's right hand and by His words. As Augustine wrote:

> "What will He do, when He comes to judge, who did such things when taken to be judged? What will He inflict from the throne, who had this power when about to die?"

7 *The Lord speaks.* He asked the question again, so as to extract from them a double confession of His Name. Moreover, this was to focus their attention upon Himself alone, thereby protecting His eleven disciples behind Him.

The men and officers speak. They repeated their first answer, "Jesus of Nazareth"; their attention was not diverted to the disciples until after the ascension, when their power and testimony in His Name could not be overlooked. Men would do then to the disciples what they had done first to the Lord.

8-9 *The Lord speaks.* This repetition of His Name "I am" did not produce any further confusion amongst the band of men. The Lord had made His point on the first occasion with divine power; after that it was man's hour and the power of darkness (Luke 22:53). By saying "let these go their way", the Lord was providing safety for His disciples. He had kept them throughout His ministry (17:12), and they would always be kept in safety, for believers "are kept by the power of God through faith unto salvation" (1 Pet 1:5), and "let them that suffer according to the will of God commit the keeping of their souls to him in well doing" (4:19). The Lord knew that He would suffer alone, and that the hatred of man would fall first of all upon Him only.

10 The natural man was immediately aroused in Peter; the existence of two swords had been mentioned previously in Luke 22:38. This natural character in Peter had been manifested before; for example in Matt 16:22. There it was in connection with the Lord's words about His sufferings, but here it is in connection with the beginning of the fulfilment of the Scriptures. Peter, in effect, was attempting to prevent the fulfilment of the Scriptures and also of the Lord's own words. But the Lord would not resist in any way; He would not seek the twelve legions of angels to protect Him from the puny hands of evil men. No doubt Peter's blow with the sword was but an initial warning of his intentions, so only an ear was cut off the high priest's servant. Only Luke's Gospel informs us that the Lord "touched his ear, and healed him" (Luke 22:51), while only John's Gospel informs us of the servant's name, Malchus. (It is John's style to identify men, such as Annas in 18:13, this being the only place in the crucifixion story where this man's name appears.)

11 *The Lord speaks.* The Lord would allow no natural protection to be afforded Him; there would be no fighting by His servants, since His kingdom was not of the world (18:36). It was not a case of man's sword being raised in His defence, but a case of the sword in Zech 13:7 being in operation, "Awake, O sword, against my shepherd ... smite the shepherd, and the sheep shall be scattered". Thus He would submit "himself to him that judgeth righteously" (1 Pet 2:23). It was the Lord's will that He should drink of the cup that had been given Him. The Lord's cup and baptism would indeed be shared in one sense (Matt 20:23), but the cup about which He spoke in prayer in Gethsemane's garden would not be taken from Him—it was His alone. Thus His lifetime's work had been given to Him (John 17:4)—this work had now been finished. But the cup given to Him would be drunk completely on the cross, "It is finished". There are other cups in the NT, such as the cup of blessing for believers (1 Cor 10:16), and the cup of judgment for idolaters (Rev 14:10).

2. *The Lord Taken, and Peter's First Denial* 18:12-18

v.12 "Then the band and the captain and officers of the Jews took Jesus, and bound him,

v.13 And led him away to Annas first; for he was father-in-law to Caiaphas, which was the high priest that same year.

v.14 Now Caiaphas was he, which gave counsel to the Jews, that it was expedient that one man should die for the people.

v.15 And Simon Peter followed Jesus, and *so did* another disciple: that disciple was known unto the high priest, and went in with Jesus into the palace of the high priest.

v.16 But Peter stood at the door without. Then went out that other disciple, which was known unto the high priest, and spake unto her that kept the door, and brought in Peter.

v.17 Then saith the damsel that kept the door unto Peter, Art not thou also *one* of this man's disciples? He saith, I am not.

v.18 And the servants and officers stood there, who had made a fire of coals; for it was cold: and they warmed themselves: and Peter stood with them, and warmed himself."

12-13 The fact that there was a "captain" present is not stated in v.3. The three classes of men who took the Lord and bound Him are:

1. "The band" (*speira*), meaning a body of men-at-arms. This answers to "a great multitude with swords and staves" (Matt 26:47). In Matt 26:55 the Lord questioned why they needed swords and staves to take, not a thief, but One who had taught daily in the temple courts. In Acts 10:1; 21:31; 27:1 the word refers to a Roman cohort consisting of about 600 men.

2. "The captain" (*chiliarchos*), or "chief captain", was the commander of a Roman cohort. It is interesting that the Jews had sought the presence of a Roman military authority at that stage of their proceedings (prior to the Lord being brought to Pilate). The word "chief captain(s)" is used eighteen times in Acts 21-25 in connection with Paul's imprisonment.

3. The "officers" (*hupēretēs*) were servants of the Jewish Sanhedrin (used eight times in John's Gospel of such men). The word was also used in a spiritual sense: "*ministers* of the word" (Luke 1:2); "then would my *servants* fight" (John 18:36); "to make thee a *minister*" (Acts 26:16), and "the *ministers* of Christ" (1 Cor 4:1). It is also used in a practical sense in Acts 13:5, "they had also John to their *minister*".

Annas had originally been high priest, but had been deposed by the Romans, who then had made Caiaphas the high priest. Neither had any divine authority to be high priest, as Aaron had originally. But the Jews still regarded the senior man Annas as high priest (also mentioned in Luke 3:2; Acts 4:6). This reminds us of the two high priests Zadok and Abiathar who were high priests at the same time in the OT (2 Sam 8:17; 20:25), though in this case Zadok was God's choice in the proper Aaronic line. Political choice in religious matters is not uncommon in the present day.

Only John has recorded this preliminary visit to Annas. Although in v.24 we read that Annas had sent the Lord bound to Caiaphas, yet this must have taken place before Peter's first denial in v.15 (see Matt 26:57,70).

14 Here John recalled that this man Caiaphas had previously made a remarkable prophecy (11:50) that "one man should die for the people". God had forced an evil man to say something true when he had meant it to be something evil. There are two entirely different meanings associated with his words. In an evil sense, the Lord had to be killed so that the Romans would not destroy the Jewish nation; in a spiritual sense, He would die sacrificially for all His people. Indeed the wrath of man shall praise God (Ps 76:10).

15-16 Before this verse took place, we must insert Matt 26:56, "all the disciples forsook him, and fled", and then Matthew's record states that "Peter followed him afar off" (v.58). John also must have fled initially, but clearly he also followed the Lord afterwards. "Another disciple: that disciple was known unto the high priest" is an oblique way that John used to refer to himself. Apparently this acquaintance enabled John to be present without severe repercussions. Was he perhaps obliquely showing that he did not deny the Lord?

John went deliberately with greater boldness; Peter went with lesser courage, and failed when he denied the Lord. What a difference the indwelling Spirit of God would make later, for both Peter and John possessed the same boldness when appearing before the Sanhedrin (Acts 4:13).

There was a doorkeeper for "the palace of the high priest", as v.17 intimates. In this case, it was a woman (and it would appear that it was a woman keeping the door of Mary's house in Acts 12:14). In the OT temple, the doorkeepers were Levites (2 Chron 23:19; Ps 84:10).

The word "palace" (*aulē*), also used in Matt 26:3,58,69; Luke 22:55 (hall), properly means a courtyard, as in the OT tabernacle and temple. Neither Peter nor John went into an actual building where the Sanhedrin was sitting in judgment upon the Lord in their midst; in fact, Mark 14:66 shows that the court was on a lower level than the building, for "Peter was beneath" in the court (not "palace" AV). Later, the place where Pilate conducted the interrogation of the Lord is called "the hall of judgment" or "Praetorium" (18:28), though the Jews remained on the outside; (the RV translates this as "palace").

So Peter stood at the door leading into the court, and evidently he made no attempt to enter until invited in, although the Lord had promised him safety.

17 *The damsel speaks.* The woman appeared to challenge Peter immediately, "Art not thou also one of this man's disciples?". If the accounts of Peter's denial as recorded in all four Gospels are collated, remarkable differences will be found. The author has listed these differences in detail on pages 378-379 of his commentary on Matthew's Gospel in this series of NT Commentaries, so he will not reproduce these details again. The differences arise because Peter was surrounded by many hostile people, and several were accusing him at the same time; the differences in his answers on each occasion arise because he was seeking to deny his connection with the Lord to all the various speakers. He was known to be a disciple; he was known to have been in the garden and responsible for the cutting off of the man's ear; he had a Galilaean dialect; all these considerations weighed on Peter's mind, leading to his rapid denials.

Peter speaks. By saying "I am not" (*ouk eimi*—not I am), he took a low natural position, contrasting with the elevated eternal Name that the Lord confessed in v.5, "I am he" (*egō eimi*—I am). In v.25, Peter repeated his denial "I am not". It is interesting to note that only Luke has recorded the fact that the Lord, after Peter's third denial, looked on the apostle, who then went out and wept bitterly (Luke 22:61-62).

18 The "servants" (*doulos*) would be the domestic servants of the building where the Sanhedrin was meeting, while the "officers" were the servants of the Sanhedrin itself, some of whom guarded the temple. Peter, who originally had followed "afar off", was now standing very near, not to the Lord but to the world. The verb "warmed" is in the imperfect tense, showing that Peter was engaged continuously in the process, enjoying the physical comforts that these men were enjoying, while the Lord on the outside was being accused by the high priest. There is always a danger when believers seek to "walk as men", being carnal and not spiritual (1 Cor 3:1-3).

Fires in Scripture often brought about sinful deeds. Thus there was a man gathering sticks for a fire on the sabbath day, contrary to the commandment (Num 15:32-36); again, when Jehudi read Baruch's roll of Jeremiah's written words, king Jehoiakim cut the roll with a knife and cast it into the fire burning before him in his winterhouse, thus destroying part of the written word of God (which was, however, written again, Jer 36:21-26). Yet a fire was also the occasion of the working of a miracle (Acts 28:1-6).

3. *The Lord before the High Priest, and Peter's Further Denials* 18:19-27

v.19 "The high priest then asked Jesus of his disciples, and of his doctrine.
v.20 Jesus answered him, I spake openly to the world; I ever taught in the synagogue, and in the temple, whither the Jews always resort; and in secret have I said nothing.
v.21 Why askest thou me? ask them which heard me, what I have said unto them: behold, they know what I said.
v.22 And when he had thus spoken, one of the officers which stood by struck Jesus with the palm of his hand, saying, Answerest thou the high priest so?
v.23 Jesus answered him, If I have spoken evil, bear witness of the evil: but if well, why smitest thou me?
v.24 Now Annas had sent him bound unto Caiaphas the high priest.
v.25 And Simon Peter stood and warmed himself. They said therefore unto him, Art not thou also *one* of his disciples? He denied *it*, and said, I am not.
v.26 One of the servants of the high priest, being *his* kinsman whose ear Peter cut off, saith, Did not I see thee in the garden with him?
v.27 Peter then denied again: and immediately the cock crew."

19 *The high priest speaks.* This high priest must have been Caiaphas, not Annas, since the Lord had been sent bound by Annas to Caiaphas (v.24). Caiaphas was recognised by the Romans, so it had to be he who would send the Lord to Pilate. Two features marked a leader, according to the questions posed by Caiaphas:

1. The kind of men whom he has as his followers.

2. The teaching that he holds and by which he gains his followers.

20-21 *The Lord speaks.* In His answer, the Lord did not mention His disciples—this was a part of His safety policy, by which He would stand alone, without bringing His disciples into the matter at all. Consequently, He introduced only matters relating to His public teaching in the world (not His private teaching to His disciples, as in Matt 13:11,34-36; John 13-16), namely the world (morally), the Jews (nationally), the synagogue (for religious services), and the temple (for religious ceremonies). The Lord had taught in the synagogues when invited, and as long as His teaching was listened to (Matt 4:23; Luke 4:15-28). In Jerusalem, He taught in the temple courts (Luke 21:37-38) where the Jews congregated and heard Him gladly. No little synagogue or temple cliques had been formed, where the Lord might teach secretly; all had been public, and all the people, if honest, could testify as to the subject matter of His teaching. Thus in v.21, He invited the Sanhedrin to bring in other witnesses (quite distinct from the two false witnesses mentioned in Matt 26:59-62), so as to bear witness of His teaching. It was no use their asking Him directly, since they would not believe Him. But He would seek to bring in others so as to keep out His disciples. The sheer numbers of the common people would be an adequate testimony to His teaching, while it would be an encouragement to the multitude to testify of their knowledge before a hostile Jewish leadership. But the Sanhedrin had no intention of involving the common people in the issue.

22 *One of the officers speaks.* The venom and brutality in men's hearts is here manifested—the beginning of the cruelty that would be inflicted upon the Lord. He had invited further witnesses in v.21; the consciences of His accusers were pricked, and they resorted to cruelty to justify themselves (Luke 16:15). If a man cannot defend his own actions, then he will seek to reduce to silence the One speaking the truth by striking Him with a savage blow, justifying his action merely by a question, "Answerest thou the high priest so?". When Paul later stood before the Sanhedrin, his first words of testimony caused the high priest to command that he should be smitten on the mouth to silence him (Acts 23:1-2). All this was contrary to their law, which had stated that judges should "justify the righteous", yet not to exceed forty stripes on those who were guilty (Deut 25:1-3), an unjust punishment that Paul suffered five times (2 Cor 11:24).

23-24 *The Lord speaks.* With quiet and effective logic, the Lord presented two unique alternatives each demanding an answer:

1. If He had spoken evil, then His judges should show in what way He was wrong—this they could not do.

2. If He had spoken well, then they should explain why they had smitten Him—this they would not do, else they would have exposed the evil of their actions.

Note that the Lord was silent when they brought false witnesses against Himself (Matt 26:63); truly, "when he was reviled, (he) reviled not again" (1 Pet 2:23). But in our v.23, He was not silent. Neither was Paul silent when he was smitten on the mouth, but he approached the matter in quite a different way, by saying "thou whited wall", also stating, "I wist not, brethren, that he was the high priest", because this man was *not* God's high priest—he was just a usurper of the office (Acts 23:3-5).

We have already observed that John inserted v.24 to show why the Lord was now appearing before Caiaphas, when He had first been led to Annas.

25 The other Gospels provide other events that took place before the Sanhedrin. Here, John returned quickly to the subject of the series of denials by Peter. The apostle has shown that this series took place in two stages. Between the first and the second denial, there was "a little while" (Luke 22:58), and between the second and the third, there was "about the space of one hour" (v.59). Meanwhile, Peter was still warming himself with the world before the fire.

The bystanders speak. The second set of accusations against Peter was made by "another maid" (Matt 26:71), "another" (Luke 22:58), "they" (John 18:25). Leading to the third denial, the accusers were "they that stood by" (Matt 26:73), "another" (Luke 22:59), "one of the servants of the high priest" (John 18:26).

Peter speaks. To the question, "Art not thou also one of his disciples?", Peter gave the same answer as before, "I am not". Peter was a stranger amongst them, and his presence may therefore have kindled suspicion. One cannot hide in a crowd; either one fails or one stands for the Lord.

26 *One of the servants of the high priest speaks*. The incident of the sword in the garden now drew attention to Peter; a swift unpremeditated action may have all sorts of consequences that are not anticipated at the time. In a more rational frame of mind, Peter would have realised that someone who had been in the garden would recognise him in the courtyard. A relationship according to the flesh with Malchus caused this kinsman to take advantage of Peter's previous denials (which he knew to be false), so as to taunt him again. These interrogators were "natural", while Peter was "carnal".

27 Peter denied a third time, and in keeping with the Lord's prediction the cock crew. The cock was a sort of alarm clock for the morning, but in Peter's case it was used to cause him suddenly to remember the Lord's words. The Lord's prediction was that it would be that particular morning and not another—Peter would deny the Lord in the same night as that in which Judas would betray Him. Here were works of darkness—either in a sinner or in a saint. Peter could "cast off the works of darkness" (Rom 13:12), but Judas could not. Peter was later in the upper room, while Judas had gone to his own place (Acts 1:13,25). We believe that it was to this upper room that Peter went so as to weep bitterly. Later there was a new Peter; he could write, "be not afraid of their terror . . . be ready always to give an answer to every man that asketh you" (1 Pet 3:14-15).

II. The Lord before Pilate (18:28-19:16)

1. *Pilate out to the Jews* 18:28-32

v.28 "Then led they Jesus from Caiaphas unto the hall of judgment: and it was early; and they themselves went not into the judgment hall, lest they should be defiled; but that they might eat the passover.
v.29 Pilate then went out unto them, and said, What accusation bring ye against this man?
v.30 They answered and said unto him, If he were not a malefactor, we would not have delivered him up unto thee.
v.31 Then said Pilate unto them, Take ye him, and judge him according to your law. The Jews therefore said unto him, It is not lawful for us to put any man to death:
v.32 That the saying of Jesus might be fulfilled which he spake, signifying what death he should die."

28 Here is religion at its worst. The Jewish leadership knew that they were plotting the Lord's death without a cause, and yet at the same time they feared ceremonial defilement. They had to remain "clean" for the Passover by not going into a Gentile house. They would keep the ritual of the deliverance of the Passover, yet they had no idea that the true Passover Lamb was standing before them. It was a case of reading and acting on the OT without Christ. Today, many men have the NT without Christ, yet they keep the ritual of the Breaking of Bread. In the present event, the Lord had already celebrated the last legitimate Passover, so the one being celebrated so hypocritically by the Jews was not valid. OT ceremony, so often copied in ecclesiastical circles today, had its end on the cross. As a preparation for Hezekiah's great Passover, all forms of religious evil in Jerusalem were cast into the brook Kidron, when the people sanctified themselves for the feast (2 Chron 30:13-20). But here, when the Jews did not want to be defiled, their evil intentions remained in their hearts as they forced the issue of the Lord's crucifixion. When evil claims to be good, then men are trying to call black white.

29 *Pilate speaks*. So as to please the Jews, Pilate went out from "the hall of judgment" (the Praetorium) in the which he was confronting the Lord. The judge went out to them, instead of the Jewish leaders coming in to him. On ceremonial grounds, they did not want to enter, and John in his record has traced this coming and going on Pilate's part (as we demonstrate by our paragraph titles). This strange phenomenon does not appear in the Synoptic Gospels, but John was an eyewitness, and Pilate's strange behaviour evidently caught John's eye. How different were the comings and goings of the Lord and of Paul (Acts 1:21; 9:28). Pilate asked the Jewish leaders about their accusation against the Lord. They could not advance any religious complaints, so they had to change their ground and make political allegations that Christ was a king, forbidding to give tribute to Caesar (Luke 23:2; Matt 27:11); note how their subtle accusations were complete lies, a twisted version of the Lord's actual remarks (Luke 20:21-26).

30 *The Jewish leaders speak.* Their answer "If he were not a malefactor" adds nothing to their accusations. In this answer, we see the poverty of their case, and that they used the importance of their office to seek to gain an evil end, which otherwise they would not achieve.

31 *Pilate speaks.* Even at this stage, Pilate saw that he was heading for a confrontation with the Jews. He wanted to avoid his responsibility to enact Roman judgment by offering the responsibility back to the Jews to enact Jewish judgment according to "your law".

The Jewish leaders speak. They wanted the Lord's death, but at that time this was not possible, since the Romans had taken away the Jews' right to execute their own criminals. Thus they depended solely on Pilate's decision and authority. So they had to admit that it was not lawful (that is, according to Roman jurisdiction) for them to put a man to death—they would have been humiliated by the necessity of making such a confession.

32 John provided an explanation of the situation. The Lord had to die by the Roman method of crucifixion, and not by the Jewish method of stoning. He had to be "lifted up" (3:14; 12:32) in keeping with the OT Scriptures, and with the direct teaching of the Lord Himself (Matt 20:19). Only then would be fulfilled "Cursed is every one that hangeth on a tree" (Gal 3:13; Deut 21:23). Later, the Jewish right to stone men was restored to them (Acts 7:58-59).

2. *Pilate into the Judgment Hall*
18:33-38

v.33 "Then Pilate entered into the judgment hall again, and called Jesus, and said unto him, Art thou the King of the Jews?

v.34 Jesus answered him, Sayest thou this thing of thyself, or did others tell it thee of me?

v.35 Pilate answered, Am I a Jew? Thine own nation and the chief priests have delivered thee unto me: what hast thou done?

v.36 Jesus answered, My kingdom is not of this world: if my kingdom were of this world, then would my servants fight, that I should not be delivered to the Jews: but now is my kingdom not from hence.

v.37 Pilate therefore said unto him, Art thou a king then? Jesus answered, Thou sayest that I am a king. To this end was I born, and for this cause came I into the world, that I should bear witness unto the truth. Every one that is of the truth heareth my voice.

v.38 Pilate saith unto him, What is truth?"

33 *Pilate speaks.* Note that Pilate entered into the judgment hall "again", a word that occurs also in v.38; 19:4,9, showing how John took note of what he witnessed, and recorded it. The question "Art thou the King of the Jews?" is Pilate's first recorded question in John's Gospel, as also in Matt 27:11. But Pilate's question must have derived from the Jew's accusation previously, that the Lord claimed to be "Christ a King" (Luke 23:2-3), a rival authority to Caesar. The Lord was finally crucified under this accusation, as is witnessed by the inscription attached to the cross. However, even though He was the Messiah, He never took a throne while here on earth, and refused to be made a king by force (6:15). It will be God Himself who will establish His King upon His holy hill of Zion (Ps 2:6).

34 *The Lord speaks.* This double question was intended to show Pilate the source of his question in the previous verse. Either Pilate as governor had experienced a rival King in Jerusalem; or he had been deceived by others. He must have known the position quite clearly; he knew that the accusations were baseless (Luke 23:14), realising that the Jews had delivered the Lord "for envy" (Matt 27:18).

35 *Pilate speaks.* "Am I a Jew?" was spoken in contempt; Pilate was outside the political squabbling of the Jews. Yet he confessed that it was "Thine own nation and the chief priests" who had delivered Him, and consequently had accused Him. He had listened to the Jews, and now wanted to know how He had set Himself up against Caesar, since Pilate had no information that this Rival to Caesar had been in Jerusalem attempting such a revolution. This would not have been an easy business with Roman soldiers occupying the city; in the OT things had been easier and more open when Adonijah said "I will be king" (1 Kings 1:5).

36 *The Lord speaks.* This is one of the great verses that separates the people of God from political affiliations. The kingdom of God is quite distinct from all the national and political organisations of men. The Lord recognised them, and was even subject to them (Matt 17:27), as indeed all believers should be (Rom 13:1), but He played no part in such organisations. A divine and heavenly Ambassador retains the status and characteristics of His own heavenly kingdom, and not of the country (the world) to which He is accredited. If believers recognised this, they would be happy to remain separated from the politics of the nations. But there was to be no fighting, since He was subject to the Sanhedrin, even though their judgment was so unjust. (Modern political electioneering may be the present-day counterpart to His servants fighting, if christians engage in this.) Certainly there is no justification for christians engaging in physical fighting in seeking to achieve some spiritual objective.

The Lord made it quite clear that His kingdom was "not of this world", in the same way as the Lord Himself was "not of this world" (8:23; 17:14,16), and His disciples were "not of the world" (17:14,16). The Scriptures show very clearly that the kingdoms of men were completely distinct from the kingdom of God, both in its present and its future aspects. Thus we have already pointed out that in 6:15 men would seek by force to make the Lord King, but this was not possible, since God Himself would set His King on His holy hill of Zion. It will be the God of heaven who will set up His kingdom that will stand for ever, in complete contrast to the kingdoms of men that will be broken in pieces (Dan 2:44). On a spiritual plane, we have been delivered from the power of darkness, and translated "into the kingdom of his dear Son" (Col 1:13). Admittedly, in the OT God maintained by warfare the kingdom of Judah, but His ways are different now. Any fighting for christian rights is outside the teaching of the NT. In fact, our warfare is not carnal (2 Cor 10:4-5).

37 *Pilate speaks.* This is the second time that Pilate asked the question, "Art thou a king then?" (v.33). The Lord's words "my kingdom" led Pilate to the assumption that there must be a king. This was correct, but the Lord would have to suffer and to enter into His glory long before He would be manifested as King of kings and Lord of lords (Rev 19:16). But Scripture does not always associate a king with a kingdom. Today, members of the church are part of the kingdom of God (Rom 14:17), but Christ is the Head of the church, not its King, in spite of the many popular hymns that use the title King frequently, often to rhyme with "sing".

The Lord speaks. He did not answer the question directly; had He said "I am", the power of this Name would have driven Pilate backwards (as in v.6). But His hour had come, and this could not happen to Pilate and his entourage; outwardly they had the upper hand, though allowed by God. Instead the Lord stated that these were Pilate's words, not His words. Rather, the Lord explained the reason for His coming into the world. There were two aspects:

1. "To this end was I born", namely from a physical point of view. The conception had been miraculous, but His birth was normal (Luke 2:7).

2. "For this cause came I into the world", namely from a spiritual point of view—His descent from the Father stressed so often in John's Gospel.

As "the truth", He bore witness to the truth. His voice was heard by those who were "of the truth". John, writing many years later, explained that to be "of the truth" one had not only to be occupied with doctrine but that one's love had to be "in deed and in truth" (1 John 3:18-19). By saying "Every one", the Lord sorted men into two groups—those who heard His voice, and those who would not listen to it, such as the priests and Pilate, the Pharisees and the politicians.

38 *Pilate speaks.* His question, "What is truth?", has gone down into the annals of history as being characteristic of Pilate. Yet it is really typical of men of a philosophical disposition today. Pilate was seeking to justify himself by a philosophical question that showed up his own ignorance of a definition of truth, particularly when the One who was "the truth" was standing before him. There are also other profound questions in Scripture, such as "What is man?" (Ps 8:4), and "What hast thou done?" (Gen 4:10). Such questions require spiritual answers; any other answers bring the exhortation, "Beware lest any man spoil you through philosophy... after the tradition of men... and not after Christ" (Col 2:8).

3. *Pilate out to the Jews* 18:38-40

v.38 "And when he had said this, he went out again unto the Jews, and saith unto them, I find in him no fault *at all*.
v.39 But ye have a custom, that I should release unto you one at the passover: will ye therefore that I release unto you the King of the Jews?
v.40 Then cried they all again, saying, Not this man, but Barabbas. Now Barabbas was a robber."

38 *Pilate speaks*. Since the Jews would not enter into the judgment hall, Pilate once again had to accede to their hypocritical legal niceties. He came out to them, stating that He found no fault at all in the Lord. In other words, the Jewish leaders had not proved their point, as Paul said later, "neither can they prove the things whereof they now accuse me" (Acts 24:13). At least the unjust judge was honest at that stage, and he would repeat his conclusion two further times in 19:4,6. Yet he condemned himself, by later not releasing the Lord. Evidently it was to please the Jews, in spite of his mocking them somewhat at certain points of the proceedings. Felix and Festus acted similarly in relation to Paul: Felix "willing to show the Jews a pleasure, left Paul bound", and Festus offered to let Paul go to Jerusalem to be tried (Acts 24:27; 25:9). In all these cases, it was a case of judgment without justice.

39-40 The word "custom" (*sunētheia*) occurs only twice in the NT, here and in 1 Cor 11:16, "we have no such custom" to be contentious about Paul's presentation of truth. Jewish customs are scattered throughout the Gospels, such as in the washing of hands, cups and pots (Mark 7:3-4), and the stepping into the pool of Bethesda for healing (John 5:7). This custom of the Jews to expect Pilate to release a prisoner at the Passover occurs in all the four Gospels, only in the account of this trial. To the Jewish mind, it would symbolise their release from bondage in Egypt, but their choice of Barabbas (quite unlike their moral state in Egypt before their deliverance) shows how deep was their hatred of the Lord. For Barabbas "was a robber", a man who lay "bound with them that had made insurrection" (Mark 15:7), a man who "for a certain sedition made in the city, and for murder, was cast into prison" (Luke 23:19). Pilate knew about this man, that he was a menace to society, and he would have preferred to have released the Lord, knowing that He was faultless, and of no menace to society or to the Roman authorities.

But this custom was allowed by God so as to bring out the venom in the Jews' hearts towards His Son, for Peter later said of Barabbas, "ye denied the Holy One and the Just, and desired a murderer to be granted to you" (Acts 3:14). This shows the type of man that people desire when Christ is rejected. Sometimes today, this is the type of man that people desire in the name of their politics and religion. Certainly it is the type of man that people desire to satisfy their craving for entertainment, for they "not only do the same, but have pleasure in them that do them" (Rom 1:32).

The name "Barabbas" is very revealing, for he stands in complete contrast to the Lord.

1. The Lord Jesus was the Son of the Father, standing condemned by the Jewish Sanhedrin; He had been born holy, and remained holy throughout life.

2. The meaning of the name "Barabbas" is also "son of his father". The prefix *Bar* means "son of", as in the two examples of Peter who was *Bar-Iōna* namely "son of Jonah" (Matt 16:17 RV), and *Bartimaios*, namely "blind Bartimaeus, the son of Timaeus" (Mark 10:46). Moreover, *abbas* means "father", otherwise appearing in the holy Name of the Father, "Abba" (Mark 14:36; Rom 8:15; Gal 4:6). The implication is that Barabbas derived all his unholy characteristics from his father, a derivation that stemmed ultimately from Adam himself. But the matter is deeper than that, for the Lord said, "Ye are of your father the devil . . . and the lusts of your father ye will do. He was a murderer from the beginning, and abode not in the truth" (John 8:44). Thus the contrast between the Lord and Barabbas is complete; yet men desired the murderer rather than the Prince of life.

4. *Pilate into the Judgment Hall*
19:1-3

v.1 "Then Pilate therefore took Jesus, and scourged *him*.
v.2 And the soldiers plaited a crown of thorns, and put *it* on his head, and they put on him a purple robe,
v.3 And said, Hail, King of the Jews! And they smote him with their hands."

1 Although John has not recorded the fact, Pilate must have entered the judgment hall again, since in this verse he confronted the Lord with an act of cruelty. At some stage prior to this, the Lord must have been sent to Herod (Luke 23:7-12) whose men had mocked Him by dressing Him in a gorgeous kingly robe. But now Pilate "scourged him", an act normally carried out after the sentence had been passed. In Paul's case (Acts 22:24) the chief captain intended that the apostle should be "examined by scourging", so that he might ascertain the facts behind the uproar in Jerusalem. In fact, Paul had already suffered this cruelty five times (2 Cor 11:24) during his missionary journeys. In the Lord's case, Pilate intended this to be the prelude to the Lord's release (Luke 23:16,22) even after the people had clamoured for the release of Barabbas. It would appear that Pilate hoped to move the Jews to pity at the sight of the sufferings of Christ under the chastisement, so that they would consider that this form of punishment was sufficient. In fact, Pilate offered to chastise Him, although he confessed with the same breath that there was no fault in Him that merited death (Luke 23:22).

It would appear from Matt 27:26-27 that scourging took place in the open so that the Jews could witness the act, but John has not recorded this. The Roman method was to tie the victim bent to a post, or to stretch the victim on a frame. The scourge was made of leather thongs with sharp projections of bone and metal, a contraption that tore the flesh from the back and breast wherever it fell by the cruel lashes. As one looks at a picture of such a Roman device, we are amazed that the Son of God should submit Himself to this torture prior to His crucifixion. This would have involved injurious humiliation and pain, and some men died under such torture. Rome was well represented as a nation by the description of the fourth beast: "dreadful and terrible, and strong exceedingly; and it had great iron teeth: it devoured and break in pieces" (Dan 7:7).

2-3 So not only the soldiers of Herod, but also the Roman soldiers engaged in a form of royal mockery, for the crown of thorns and the purple robe were intended to mimic His kingly character. Pilate connived at the activity of his soldiers—he would mock both the Lord and the Jews by this deed.

The soldiers speak. It appears that the court proceedings were interrupted by this deed of the soldiers, and by their cry of mockery "Hail, King of the Jews". A man already suffering brings out further the worst in some men, and so it was here. If the scourging was not enough, these soldiers smote the Lord with their hands. At this stage, Pilate was unable to control his own men and the Jewish leadership; he had abdicated himself into their hands and desires. Mark 15:19 shows further indignities that men heaped upon the Lord, and false worship is included, "bowing their knees, (they) worshipped him". In the future day of the Lord's triumph and victory, when He will be revealed as "King of kings, and Lord of lords" (Rev 19:16), He will have "many crowns" on His head (v.12); He will be clothed in "a vesture dipped in blood", namely He will appear as a Judge-King; instead of men using a reed with which to smite Him, He will use a sharp sword out of His mouth to smite men (v.15). As the King-Priest, He shall "strike through kings in the day of his wrath" (Ps 110:5). Moreover, every knee shall bow before Him at His Name, and every tongue will confess that He is Lord in that day (Phil 2:10-11)—there will be no mock worship then. The roles will be reversed in the day of His power.

Throughout this cruelty, there was the fulfilment of the OT prophecies: "He was bruised for our iniquities: the chastisement of our peace was upon him; and with his stripes we are healed" (Isa 53:5); "He was oppressed, and he was afflicted, yet he opened not his mouth" (v.7). The Saviour had taught, "resist not evil . . . but whosoever shall smite thee on thy right cheek, turn to him the other also" (Matt 5:39). Peter has described this in his first epistle, "Who, when he was reviled, reviled not again; when he suffered, he threatened not" (1 Pet 2:23). Truly, in His approach to sufferings, there was no man like this Man.

5. *Pilate out to the Jews*
19:4-7

v.4 "Pilate therefore went forth again, and saith unto them, Behold, I bring him forth to you, that ye may know that I find no fault in him.
v.5 Then came Jesus forth, wearing the crown of thorns, and the purple robe. And *Pilate* saith unto them, Behold the man!
v.6 When the chief priests therefore and officers saw him, they cried out, saying, Crucify *him*, crucify *him*. Pilate saith unto them, Take ye him, and crucify *him*: for I find no fault in him.
v.7 The Jews answered him, We have a law, and by our law he ought to die, because he made himself the Son of God."

4 *Pilate speaks.* The Roman governor would now display the Lord's state openly—both His sufferings due to the scourging, and also His outward manifestation of mock Kingship. This was the worst that Pilate could do in seeking to gain the Lord's release by appealing to Jewish sympathy. Whatever happened, he wanted the Jews to know that their case had not been proved, and that he still found no fault in Him even after the scourging.

5 What a contrast this scene presented! The Lord came forth dressed in the mock regalia of kingship on the one hand; on the other hand, a few days previously He had entered Jerusalem from the mount of Olives on an ass's colt as the coming King, being acclaimed by the people with the words "Blessed is the King of Israel that cometh in the name of the Lord" (12:12-16), while in the future He will come as King of kings in the glory of His kingdom and in the power of cleansing judgment (Rev 19:11-16).

Pilate speaks. Pilate's great declaration "Behold the man" should move the heart of every believer, though Pilate spoke as an unbeliever. In the Scripture, we have four declarations concerning the Lord that correspond to the four Gospels:

1. "Behold your God!" (Isa 40:9), corresponding to John's Gospel.

2. "Behold my servant" (Isa 42:1; Matt 12:18), corresponding to Mark's Gospel.

3. "Behold the man!" (John 19:5), corresponding to Luke's Gospel.

4. "Behold your King!" (John 19:14), corresponding to Matthew's Gospel.

Two of these are the words of Pilate, one of God, and one of the Spirit of prophecy. As far as the declarations of Pilate are concerned, that in v.5 refers to the Lord personally, while that in v.14 refers to the Lord officially. There are other declarations introduced by "Behold" that we may mention:

1. "Behold the Lamb of God" (John 1:29,36), spoken by John the Baptist.

2. "Behold, thy King cometh unto thee" (Zech 9:9).

3. "Behold the man whose name is The Branch" (Zech 6:12).

6 *The chief priests and officers speak.* The sight of the sufferings of Christ brought out the venomous worst in the hearts of these leaders. Nothing would change the intended course of the chief priests. The suggestion that the Lord should be crucified came towards the end of His trial before Pilate (Matt 27:22; Mark 15:13; Luke 23:21; John 19:6), though the leaders knew from the beginning that this was what they wanted to persuade Pilate to do.

Pilate speaks. This man representing Rome capitulated to the leaders over whom he had jurisdiction. Knowing that the Victim was guiltless, he suggested that the Jews should crucify Him themselves. Yet he knew that this was strictly impossible; only the Romans at that time could put a man to death, and in any case crucifixion was not the Jewish method of capital punishment. Later in v.16 he finally delivered the Lord to the priests to be crucified, though the Roman soldiers would carry out the deed.

7 *The Jews speak.* The Jewish leaders recognised that they had failed to persuade Pilate with their political charges, so they finally changed their ground and resorted to religious charges. After all, Pilate had some knowledge of their religious activity even if he lacked knowledge of their doctrinal attitudes. Thus Pilate was the one who appointed the high priests, although in the OT only men who were "called of God" could be a high priest (Heb 5:4), and Pilate also had the ultimate responsibility for the temple funds.

So they reverted to the law that they possessed. Their mention of "our" law is changed in the RV to "that law", following an amendment to the Greek text. The Jews knew that the Lord's references to Sonship implied Deity (5:18). In this, they were correct, but unfortunately they asserted that the Lord "made himself" to be the the Son of God, refusing to believe that this status was personally His from eternity past. They were repeating what they had said to Him directly in 10:33, "For a good work we stone thee not; but for blasphemy; and because thou, being a man, makest thyself God". The wrong in their accusation was the word "maketh". They knew that the commandment had stated, "Thou shalt have no other gods before me" (Exod 20:3); they knew what the law said about blasphemy, "he shall surely be put to death, and all the congregation shall certainly stone him". Similarly in 19:12, they asserted to Pilate that the Lord "maketh himself a king". But believers know differently; for example, "unto the Son he saith, Thy throne, O God, is for ever and ever" (Heb 1:8), and "Christ glorified not himself to be made an high priest; but he that said unto him, Thou art my Son, to day have I begotten thee" (Heb 5:5). These two quotations are taken from the Jews' OT Scriptures (Ps 45:6; 2:7), so clearly their knowledge of the law was restricted to the commandments and not to the Psalms. But hatred and deliberate unbelief is the father of invention when it comes to interpreting and understanding the Scriptures.

6. *Pilate into the Judgment Hall* 19:8-12

v.8 "When Pilate therefore heard that saying, he was the more afraid;
v.9 And went again into the judgment hall, and saith unto Jesus, Whence art thou? But Jesus gave him no answer.
v.10 Then saith Pilate unto him, Speakest thou not unto me? knowest thou not that I have power to crucify thee, and have power to release thee?
v.11 Jesus answered, Thou couldest have no power *at all* against me, except it were given thee from above: therefore he that delivered me unto thee hath the greater sin.
v.12 And from thenceforth Pilate sought to release him: but the Jews cried out, saying, If thou let this man go, thou art not Caesar's friend: whosoever maketh himself a king speaketh against Caesar."

8 If Pilate had been afraid when the Jewish charge concerned kingship, now he "was the more afraid" when the charge concerned Sonship. He did not understand the theology of the Jewish point of view, but no doubt he thought of the many Roman mythological gods, so feared lest he should disturb his Roman gods by admitting that there existed one more!

9 *Pilate speaks*. To satisfy himself about this new Jewish assertion, Pilate went in again to interrogate the Lord. He did not ask, "Who art thou?", but "Whence art thou?". He did not ask about His Person, but about His origin. To a believer, the Son had no origin; rather the eternally-existent One descended from heaven. Clearly Pilate did not know what to think, and the Lord would not satisfy his curiousity—He had not satisfied Herod's when He had appeared before him (Luke 23:9). In fact, the Lord would not cast pearls before swine, nor would He give what was holy to the dogs (Matt 7:6). Hence "Jesus gave him no answer". Such silence is found often in Scripture. Thus: "I was as a dumb man that openeth not his mouth" (Ps 38:13); "I was dumb, I opened not my mouth; because thou didst it" (Ps 39:9); "yet he opened not his mouth" (Isa 53:7). But there is a contrast. In that coming day of judgment, man's mouth shall be stopped, with no possibility of making false excuses to cover a sin-stained life on earth: "that every mouth may be stopped" (Rom 3:19); "kings shall shut their mouths at him" (Isa 52:15).

10 *Pilate speaks.* Here is a man whose natural thought boasted in power that he wielded over an occupied nation. The word "power" (*exousia*) appearing three times in vv.10-11 properly means "authority". Of course his authority derived from Rome far away, but in Jerusalem he sensed that he had almost unlimited power, and he was glad to exercise it. Both David and Solomon recognised that their positions and possessions derived from God, but Pilate had his counterpart in Nebuchadnezzar, who boasted, "Is not this great Babylon, that I have built for the house of the kingdom by the might of my power, and for the honour of my majesty?" (Dan 4:30); see also Eccles 2:4-10. Pilate failed to see what Nebuchadnezzar was forced to see, that "the most High ruleth in the kingdom of men, and giveth it to whomsoever he will" (Dan 4:32). Thus Pharaoh was raised up, so that God's power might be shown in him (Rom 9:17). The powers that be are ordained by God (Rom 13:1), but the evil that they often accomplish is their own responsibility, though God may allow it for a season, as in Pilate's case. The overall authority is exercised by God Himself; thus the Lord claimed that all authority had been given to Him in heaven and on earth (Matt 28:18); all angels and authorities and powers are subject unto Him (1 Pet 3:22). But here before Pilate, the Lord appeared as the subject One, with judgment withholden from falling on Pilate for a season, on account of his base and unjust treatment of the Son of God.

11 *The Lord speaks.* The Lord corrected Pilate openly, although He had been silent in v.9. Pilate had authority against his Victim only because his authority had been given to him "from above". Yet his misuse of this authority was his own business. Thus the several evil kings over Judah in the OT had their status granted by God, as being in the royal line from David leading to Messiah, but their misuse of their authority was their own responsibility, and led to divine judgment on them on occasions. The order of misused responsibility was fourfold, namely in order: Judas, the priests, Pilate, and the people.

1. Judas. This man had responsibility as treasurer of the small funds possessed by the Lord and His apostles, yet he was a thief, and manifested greed as the son of perdition. By betraying the Lord, he commenced the process whereby the Lord was delivered to be crucified.

2. The priests. It was "for envy" (Matt 27:18) that they had delivered the Lord to Pilate.

3. Pilate. In unrighteousness as the unjust judge, and in weakness, he delivered the Lord to the priests to be crucified (John 19:16).

4. The people. They had been persuaded by the chief priests and the elders (Matt 27:20), though Peter later claimed that it was "through ignorance" that the Jews had done so great a deed (Acts 3:17).

The Lord could see degrees of responsibility when He said, "he that delivered me unto thee hath the greater sin". No doubt in the immediate context this refers to Caiaphas the high priest, rather than to Judas. The sin of Judas was the worst of all, because he had a demon and was the son of perdition, having betrayed innocent blood.

12 Here, Pilate appeared to be completely satisfied with the Lord's answers, and sought to release Him. Yet the Jewish leaders could sense that Pilate was very concerned about himself and with his standing before his superiors in Rome. Pilate must have been outside in the court to hear the Jews' masterstroke, though it is only in v.13 that we read of Pilate coming out. He valued his reputation, and was bound by national considerations rather than by the desire to exercise righteous judgment.

The Jews speak. In Matt 27:22-23, they appear to have worn down Pilate by constantly crying, "Let him be crucified". In Mark 15:15, Pilate is seen as "willing to content the people". In Luke 23:23, the loud voices of the chief priests prevailed. But here in our verse the Jews touched upon the friendship between Pilate and Caesar in Rome. To them, a false King, who had "made himself a king", was a revolutionary against Caesar, and if Pilate released such a Man, then this proved that Pilate had no regard for the ultimate authority in Rome. How logical indeed, but based upon the false premise that the Lord had made Himself King. For Pilate, however, this was the last straw, and now to preserve his position he was prepared to pronounce judgment upon the Lord.

7 *Pilate out to the Jews*
19:13-16

v.13 "When Pilate therefore heard that saying, he brought Jesus forth, and sat down in the judgment seat in a place that is called the Pavement, but in the Hebrew, Gabbatha.

v.14 And it was the preparation of the passover, and about the sixth hour: and he saith unto the Jews, Behold your King!

v.15 But they cried out, Away with *him*, away with *him*, crucify him. Pilate saith unto them, Shall I crucify your King? The chief priests answered, We have no king but Caesar.

v.16 Then delivered he him therefore unto them to be crucified. And they took Jesus, and led *him* away."

13 Pilate emerged with the Lord for the last time, and sat down "in the judgment seat" ready to pronounce judgment. The word for "judgment seat" is *bēma*, denoting the tribunal of a Roman magistrate. This word is used:

1. in Matt 27:19—the tribunal in the court of the Praetorium in Jerusalem;

2. in Acts 12:21—the throne of Herod in Caesarea;

3. in Acts 18:12,16-17—the judgment seat in Corinth of the deputy Gallio;

4. in Acts 25:6,17—the judgment seat of Festus in Ceasarea;

5. in Acts 25:10—the judgment seat of Caesar—not in Rome, but this still refers to the judgment seat of the procurator in Caesarea, a representative of Caesar's authority. Paul distinguished this from the bar of the Jewish Sanhedrin in Jerusalem;

6. in Rom 14:10; 2 Cor 5:10—this ordinary word was pressed into use to describe the heavenly tribunal before which believers will have to stand in that coming day (Rom 14:10; 2 Cor 5:10).

The word "Pavement" (*lithostrōtos*) was the name given to an area paved with stones; its Hebrew name Gabbatha implied a raised area.

14 John carefully noted the day and the time—"the preparation of the passover" and "about the sixth hour". By "the preparation" was meant the period when all leaven was removed, in keeping the original Passover and the deliverance from Egypt, when the people were instructed to "put away leaven out of your houses" (Exod 12:15). The moral implications—"the leaven of the Pharisees and of the Sadducees" (Matt 16:6); the purging out "of the old leaven . . . the leaven of malice and wickedness" (1 Cor 5:7-8)—were quite outside the understanding of Jewish leadership, as they engaged in the most wicked deed of all time.

The period between sunrise and sunset was divided into twelve hours. These were rough subdivisions, and usually only the third, sixth and ninth hours are mentioned in an approximate sense. Thus a time half way between the third and sixth hour could be denoted either as the third hour or the sixth hour, according to mental taste. Hence in Mark 15:25, Mark denoted the time of the crucifixion as "the third hour", but John stated that it was "about the sixth hour". There is no discrepancy, for they did not have watches in those days to tell the time exactly. By the use of the word "about", the Spirit of inspiration did not record the time any more accurately than ordinary witnesses would have conceived it. (Thus note the word "about" in "about three thousand souls" (Acts 2:41) and "about five thousand" (4:4).)

Pilate speaks. "Behold your King!" forms with "Behold the man!" that great couplet of mockery originated by Pilate. He did not believe it, but he used it as a lever against the Jews, since he felt trapped by their insistence that the Lord should be crucified. And yet how true a statement this was that issued from unclean unsanctified lips—here was the King, humiliated in order to be glorified.

15 *The Jews speak*. Here they cried "Away with him" twice, and "crucify him" once; by contrast, in Luke 23:18,21, they cried "Away with this man" once, and "Crucify him" twice. Here was an overt and public rejection of their King: it reminds us of the parable of the vineyard, where they cried concerning the Son, "This is the heir; come, let us kill him" (Matt 21:38). The apostle Paul later suffered the same threats, "Away with him . . . Away with such a fellow from the earth: for it is not fit that he should live" (Acts 21:36; 22:22).

Pilate speaks. His question, "Shall I crucify your King?", shows that he was still keeping up his pretence in presenting the Lord to the Jews as their King, a fact that they flatly denied.

The chief priests speak. "We have no king but Caesar" represents their final rejection of God's King in favour of a Gentile monster. This was contrary to the words of Gideon, "the Lord shall rule over you", not a man (Jud 8:23). As they desired a man to rule over them, God spoke to Samuel, "they have rejected me, that I should not reign over them" (1 Sam 8:7). These Jewish leaders had forgotten the message of the four beasts in Dan 7; they had unwillingly been under the dominion of the first beast as of a lion, representing the Babylonian empire with Nebuchadnezzar as king (Dan 7:4). But now they willingly placed themselves under the dominion of the fourth beast, the worst beast of all, a beast that men will worship in a future day (Rev 13:8). So by their claim to have no king but Caesar, the leaders were rejecting all divine moral and doctrinal authority. There were those who were looking for redemption from the Roman yoke, but these priests were not among them (Luke 2:38; 24:21).

16 So the Roman governor delivered the Lord into the hands of the Jewish priests to be crucified: these priests would do everything except the final act of crucifixion itself, the physical act of cruelly driving the nails into the Lord's hands and feet. (Compare how Pashur, priest and governor of the house of the Lord, smote Jeremiah in Jer 20:1-2.) This act was the last collusion of Jew and Gentile before the Lord died (Ps 2:1-2); the Jews were the bulls and the Gentiles were the dogs in Ps 22:12,16. The Lord died, however, to effect union between Jews and Gentiles through faith (Eph 2:14-18).

These priests led the Lord to Golgotha; they brought Him "as a lamb to the slaughter" (Isa 53:7). There must have been a huge crowd, with the Lord in the midst. Moreover, there were many women who lamented Him (Luke 23:27). Then follow in vv.28-32 the most solemn words spoken by the Lord—His last words spoken to men publicly, "what shall be done in the dry?", referring to the calamity that would befall the nation because of its sin.

III. The Crucifixion of the Lord and His Death (19:17-42)

1. *Pilate, the Soldiers and the Cross* 19:17-24

v.17 "And he bearing his cross went forth into a place called *the place* of a skull, which is called in the Hebrew Golgotha:

v.18 Where they crucified him, and two other with him, on either side one, and Jesus in the midst.
v.19 And Pilate wrote a title, and put *it* on the cross. And the writing was, JESUS OF NAZARETH THE KING OF THE JEWS.
v.20 This title then read many of the Jews: for the place where Jesus was crucified was nigh to the city: and it was written in Hebrew, *and* Greek, *and* Latin.
v.21 Then said the chief priests of the Jews to Pilate, Write not, The King of the Jews; but that he said, I am King of the Jews.
v.22 Pilate answered, What I have written I have written.
v.23 Then the soldiers, when they had crucified Jesus, took his garments, and made four parts, to every soldier a part; and also *his* coat: now the coat was without seam, woven from the top throughout.
v.24 They said therefore among themselves, Let us not rend it, but cast lots for it, whose it shall be: that the scripture might be fulfilled, which saith, They parted my raiment among them, and for my vesture they did cast lots. These things therefore the soldiers did."

17 John has recorded that the Lord was bearing His cross, but Matthew has provided further information. A man of Cyrene, Simon by name, and arriving from a distance in Jerusalem for the feast, was compelled to carry the cross (Matt 27:32); physical weakness after the cruel scourging meant that the Lord could not carry it far; He had heavier things to bear when on the cross. This man was "the father of Alexander and Rufus" (Mark 15:21); this son Rufus may be the man named by Paul, whose mother evidently had offered hospitality to Paul on one occasion (Rom 16:13). Luke 23:26 informs us that Simon bore the cross after the Lord. To be a disciple of the Lord, a believer must carry his own cross. This hardly refers to bearing patiently the common ills of daily life, but to the cost of giving up one's life by way of sacrifice so as to serve the Lord.

The place of crucifixion was "the place of a skull" (*kranion* in Greek, *calvaria* in the Latin Vulgate translation, and Golgotha in Hebrew as John has informed us). This name "of a skull" appears in all four Gospels (Matt 27:33; Mark 15:22; Luke 23:33 RV; John 19:17). The remarkable thing is that the holy and well-known name "Calvary" occurs nowhere in the NT. In the AV it appears in Luke 23:33 though the margin properly gives "The place of a skull". The translators used the Latin equivalent in Luke 23:33, though not in the other three Gospels; we do not know why. Suggestions have been made as to why the place had the name "skull": because skulls were found there; because it was a common place of Roman executions; because the place was shaped like a skull. Morally, the name reflected on the state of mind of those responsible for crucifying the Lord—they were spiritually dead, and their heads were merely skulls, empty of sympathy and understanding.

18 The cruel act of crucifixion is described in the minimum of words, "Where they crucified him" (three words in Greek). Two men were also crucified with the Lord, one on each side. The descriptions of these two in Luke and John are quite distinct. In Luke 23:32, we read, "there were also two other, malefactors"; the word for "other" is *heteros* meaning "of a different kind"—Luke therefore had distinguished the Lord morally from the malefactors. But in John 19:18, we read, "and two other with him"; the word for "other" is *allos* meaning "of the same kind"—not morally but physically; they were all treated the same.

The existence of these two malefactors fulfils the OT, as Mark 15:28 quotes from Isa 53:12, "he was numbered with the transgressors". This was also quoted by the Lord just before entering the garden of Gethsemane (Luke 22:37). Thus men would identify the Lord with criminals, but God would identify our sin in His holy body. These two men demonstrated two entirely different reactions when suffering near the Lord; Luke 23:39-43 provides the story of the repentance of one man, addressing the Lord with the words, "Lord, remember me when thou comest into thy kingdom"; evidently he had drawn a truthful conclusion from Pilate's mocking superscription that the Lord was "the King of the Jews".

19 Each of the four evangelists has focussed attention on part of the title; all-in-all, the complete title was, "This is Jesus of Nazareth the King of the Jews". Once again, John has drawn attention to the Hebrew by placing this first in his observation; Luke placed Greek first, since he was writing for Greeks. Evidently Pilate sought to mock and annoy the Jews by using this title.

20 Crucifixion was a common spectacle in Roman days; many of the Jews went out of the city to the place of a skull, especially to see the crucifixion of the One who had done many miracles among them, and who had engaged in so much teaching in the temple courts. In verses such as Acts 2:23; 3:13-15 Peter did not distinguish between those who were physically responsible for the crucifixion and those who were only spectators; all were guilty. So Pilate's words were available to all classes of spectators: to the world of religion, to the world of wisdom, and to the world of politics. They came out of the city Jerusalem. Morally, this extended beyond the physical city itself, as Rev 11:8 puts it, "the great city, which spiritually is called Sodom and Egypt, where also our Lord was crucified". The Lord suffered without the gate, according to Heb 13:12; we must be exactly the opposite to these spectators, for we must go forth to the Lord "without the camp", taking our stand with the Lord in spite of the many spectators who daily behold our lives and our witness.

21 *The chief priests speak*. These men had thwarted Pilate three times when he had wanted to release the Lord (18:38; 19:4-6,12), so by writing "the King" in three languages, Pilate annoyed the Jews by making them read the title three times. Pilate was correct in what he wrote, but he did not know the truth behind his words. Consequently, the priests wanted the words changed to reflect their point of view—not that the Lord was King, but that He merely claimed to be

King. Note that the Lord never spoke such outspoken words as "I am King", quite unlike Adonijah who said easily, "I will be king" (1 Kings 1:5); the Lord exalted not Himself. But in front of the general population the priests would have been embarrassed by the admission of kingship; hence their dislike of the words.

22 *Pilate speaks.* He refused to bow to the demands of the priests—he had listened too much already to their demands. Now that the Lord was crucified, Pilate had control of the situation once again. His answer contained a double Greek perfect tense, *ho gegrapha gegrapha*—in other words, the past act of writing the words remained, and would not be altered.

23-24 This act of the four soldiers in dividing amongst themselves four of the Lord's garments adds certainty to the prophetic word, for Ps 22:18 had prophesied, "They part my garments among them, and cast lots upon my vesture". Here was man's final inhuman attempt to strip dignity from the Lord. No doubt the articles of clothing were the headdress, the shoes, the outer garment, the girdle, and the inner garment. The soldiers would not rend the inner garment (*chitōn*) because it was woven in one piece from the top.

The soldiers speak. By saying, "Let us not rend it", they had no intention of damaging something made of material fabric only, but they had no hesitation in damaging the body of the Son of God. By casting lots, they adopted a familiar method, a method that the apostles used in Acts 1:24-26 when choosing a replacement apostle, though the outcome was subject to prayer. Such a method was not used again by the apostles after the giving of the Holy Spirit. We are not told how long these four soldiers kept these items of clothing, but believers today have nothing to do with the so-called relics that are supposed to be in existence, and that tend, like the serpent that Moses made, to be the subject of idolatrous veneration.

Thus these soldiers unknowingly fulfilled Ps 22:18. All four Gospel writers have recorded this event, but only Matthew's and John's accounts contain the direct reference to Ps 22:18. These soldiers thus reduced the Lord to the position described by Paul in 1 Tim 6:7, "we brought nothing into the world, and it is certain we can carry nothing out"—except that He gained His redeemed as His own, and these He will take to be with Him in the coming day.

2. *The Women, and the Lord's Death* 19:25-30

v.25 "Now there stood by the cross of Jesus his mother, and his mother's sister, Mary the *wife* of Cleophas, and Mary Magdalene.

v.26 When Jesus therefore saw his mother, and the disciple standing by, whom he loved, he saith unto his mother, Woman behold thy son!

v.27 Then saith he to the disciple, Behold thy mother! And from that hour that disciple took her unto his own *home*.

v.28 After this, Jesus knowing that all things were now accomplished, that the scripture might be fulfilled, saith, I thirst.
v.29 Now there was set a vessel full of vinegar: and they filled a sponge with vinegar, and put *it* upon hyssop, and put *it* to his mouth.
v.30 When Jesus therefore had received the vinegar, he said, It is finished: and he bowed his head, and gave up the ghost."

25 Here there are three named women standing by the cross, (i) The Lord's mother, (ii) His mother's sister, Mary the wife of Cleophas (properly, Clophas), (iii) Mary Magdalene. (Some expositors assert that there are four women implied here.) According to Mark 15:40 there was a fourth woman, Salome. In John's account they are seen as standing quite close to the cross, but in Mark 15:40, they are seen as "looking on afar off". Evidently, before the Lord died they had quietly left the near vicinity of the cross, perhaps at the same time as the Lord's mother left the scene with John. There were also other women standing afar off, those who had followed Him from Galilee to Jerusalem, ministering unto Him. The four named women seem to be a spiritual counterpart to the four soldiers who divided His garments.

26 The Saviour manifested affection for those who remained loyal to Him, in spite of the sinbearing that the Lord sustained on the cross. It is not possible to be sure whether this event took place before or after the hours of darkness; we suspect the former, since John had time to take the Lord's mother away, and then to return to the cross to witness the end. It may appear strange that John and the women had such nearness of access to the cross; the Lord could see them as those who loved Him, unlike the unbelieving multitudes who appeared to Him to be like bees compassing Him about (Ps 118:11-12).

The Lord speaks. Obliquely, John referred to himself as "the disciple . . . whom he loved". Seeing him, the Lord spoke to His mother, "Woman, behold thy son". He did not direct her attention to her sons of natural conception, who as far as we know were unbelieving until His resurrection (Matt 12:46; John 2:12; 7:3-5; Acts 1:14; 1 Cor 15:7; Gal 1:19). Rather, He would direct her attention to the apostle John.

27 *The Lord speaks.* He then addressed the apostle, "Behold thy mother". The implication was clear; John would have the responsibility of caring for His mother. John received this commission only because he was near to the Lord. No doubt commissions come the way of the Lord's people when their hearts are quiet to hear His voice, but it may be that some commissions are not even heard, because a believer may be more attuned to the world.

John took her "unto his own home". It is good to have a home open to the Lord's people in need; thus Paul found a lodging in the home of Aquila and Priscilla when he was a stranger in Corinth (Acts 18:2). But this need not be the meaning of the words *eis ta idia* (to his own). John's roots were in Galilee miles to the north; we never read that he had a home in Jerusalem. As pointed out before, and in keeping with what took place after the resurrection, we believe that it was to the upper room (left the previous evening) that John took the Lord's mother, for the apostles and many others were there between the resurrection and the day of Pentecost when the Spirit was given.

28-29 We have already stressed the Lord's divine knowledge mentioned several times in this Gospel. Here, He knew the deepest things—that all things had been fulfilled in His life and sufferings on the cross, so the time had come for Him to yield up His life. In other words, He was not on the cross for one minute longer than necessary (neither was He in the tomb awaiting resurrection one minute longer than necessary). The apostle John perceived that the OT Scriptures gave many details relating to the Lord on the cross:

1. "that the scripture might be fulfilled" concerning the Lord's garments (v.24; Ps 22:18);

2. "that the scripture might be fulfilled" concerning His thirst (v.28; Ps 69:21);

3. "that the scripture should be fulfilled" concerning the Lord's legs not being broken (v.36; Exod 12:46; Num 9:12; Ps 34:20).

4. "again another scripture saith" concerning the piercing of His side (v.37; Zech 12:10).

The details in the OT show how the Spirit of prophecy was moving in the writers to speak of the sufferings of Christ.

The Lord speaks. He knew that His words "I thirst" would fulfil the OT Scripture, but the soldiers in v.24 had no idea that they were fulfilling Scripture. The word for "accomplished" is the Greek perfect *tetelestai*, exactly the same word as in v.30, "It is finished". Nothing was left undone. Crucifixion gave rise to a deep-seated thirst, showing that the Lord had not been immune from these sufferings (as some have asserted). He had not drawn attention to this thirst until the end—certainly not during the hours of darkness. But Ps 69:21, "They gave me also gall for my meat; and in my thirst they gave me vinegar to drink", had to be fulfilled. The gall had been offered at the beginning, so as to alleviate pain, yet He would not partake of that (Matt 27:34). But this "vinegar" (*oxos*) was offered at the end; this was a sour wine drunk by workmen and soldiers, and was therefore available to the Roman soldiers and others standing there, in keeping with Ps 69:12, "I was the song of the drinkers of strong drink" (marg).

30 All the relevant Scriptures had been fulfilled, as had the work of redemption achieved only on the cross; the Lord therefore gave expression to

His last words. They should be taken with the seven utterances recorded as proceeding from His lips when on the cross:

1. "Father, forgive them; for they know not what they do" (Luke 23:34).

2. "Verily I say unto thee, To day shalt thou be with me in paradise" (Luke 23:43).

3. "Woman, behold thy son! . . . Behold thy mother!" (John 19:26-27).

4. "My God, my God, why hast thou forsaken me?" (Matt 27:46).

5. "I thirst" (John 19:28).

6. "It is finished" (John 19:30).

7. "Father, into thy hands I commend my spirit" (Luke 23:46).

The Lord speaks. His triumphant statement "It is finished" implies that all that which had been written of Him concerning His death, all the types and shadows that had prefigured His death, all God's purpose in His death, all was complete, and from then onwards blessings would flow to men from this finished work. There would be no repetition of a finished work, though idolatry may seek to crucify the Lord afresh. The Jewish day of atonement had been enacted "every year" (Heb 10:3); other sacrifices had been offered "daily" (v.11), but the Lord "offered one sacrifice" that avails for ever (vv.12-14). The law was finished with when the Lord died, else "Christ is dead in vain" (Gal 2:21).

Thus the Lord "gave up the ghost" (*pneuma*, properly "spirit"). This was in keeping with His declaration, "I lay down my life . . . No man taketh it from me, but I lay it down of myself" (10:17-18). This was the final act in His voluntary sacrifice: the fact that He could yield up His spirit shows that He was different from all other men. The Lord needed no physical means by which spirit could be separated from body (therefore quite unlike Judas who committed suicide in Matt 27:5; Acts 1:18). Death by crucifixion lasted much longer for ordinary men; sometimes days would be necessary as the victims sought relief by successively taking the strain on the hands and then on the feet. But not so in the Lord's case: He had died quickly so that Pilate marvelled (Mark 15:44). The fact that He "gave Himself" is a truth recorded six times in the NT: Gal 1:4; 2:20; Eph 5:2,25; 1 Tim 2:6; Titus 2:14.

3. *The Lord's Body Laid in a Sepulchre* 19:31-42

v.31 "The Jews therefore, because it was the preparation, that the bodies should not remain upon the cross on the sabbath day, (for

that sabbath day was a high day,) besought Pilate that their legs might be broken, and *that* they might be taken away.
v.32 Then came the soldiers, and brake the legs of the first, and of the other which was crucified with him.
v.33 But when they came to Jesus, and saw that he was dead already, they brake not his legs:
v.34 But one of the soldiers with a spear pierced his side, and forthwith came there out blood and water.
v.35 And he that saw *it* bare record, and his record is true: and he knoweth that he saith true, that ye might believe.
v.36 For these things were done, that the scripture should be fulfilled, A bone of him shall not be broken.
v.37 And again another scripture saith, They shall look on him whom they pierced.
v.38 And after this Joseph of Arimathaea, being a disciple of Jesus, but secretly for fear of the Jews, besought Pilate that he might take away the body of Jesus: and Pilate gave *him* leave. He came therefore, and took the body of Jesus.
v.39 And there came also Nicodemus, which at the first came to Jesus by night, and brought a mixture of myrrh and aloes, about an hundred pound *weight*.
v.40 Then took they the body of Jesus, and wound it in linen clothes with the spices, as the manner of the Jews is to bury.
v.41 Now in the place where he was crucified there was a garden; and in the garden a new sepulchre, wherein was never man yet laid.
v.42 There laid they Jesus therefore because of the Jews' preparation *day*; for the sepulchre was nigh at hand."

31 According to Lev 23:6-7, the day following the Passover was the beginning of the feast of unleavened bread; "no servile work" was to be done on that day, regardless of whether it was a formal sabbath day or not. The Passover day was therefore the "preparation", the day in which all leaven was to be removed from the houses. (Strictly, according to Exod 12:18, no leaven was to be eaten on the Passover day, so the Jews' day of preparation appears to have been rather misplaced by one day.) It was a Jewish rule not to allow a victim to remain on the cross on the sabbath, called by John a "high day". Some authors have explained this to mean that two sabbaths fell upon the same day—(i) the actual sabbath, and (ii) the day beginning the feast of unleavened bread when no work was to be done. Others have explained this "high day" as the Friday prior to the actual sabbath, thus asserting that the Lord died on a Thursday, with two sabbaths between His death and the resurrection.

The Jews speak. To observe their own rules, the leaders requested that the victims' deaths should be hastened so as to take place on the day of preparation rather than leaving them suffering on their crosses until the following day. The evil of murder was of no consequence compared with adherence to their own rules. In fact, Roman cruelty was requested by the Jews.

32 The breaking of the victim's legs was the method employed to hasten death, however barbarous it may sound to our ears. The soldiers did this to the two malefactors first of all; John used the description "the other" (*allos*) to indicate the second man. As we have said before, this word "other" means another of the same kind. Here obviously John referred to both men being of the criminal community. Their end was independent of the fact that one had repented, having addressed the King as "Lord", and possessing the promise to be with the Lord after death (Luke 23:40-43). Today, if a man becomes a christian after having committed a crime punishable by a court of law, the law takes its course; he does not become immune from man's laws merely because he has become a christian.

33 But the Lord was dead already: this was obvious to the Roman soldiers. He died first, so as to prepare the way for all men of faith afterwards—including the repentant thief on the next cross. Hence the soldiers realised that there was no need to break the Lord's legs, unwittingly following the necessary prediction of the OT that John was to quote shortly in v.36.

34 But the pent-up venom in the soldiers' hearts knew no bounds. The Lord's quiet divine dignity when suffering on the cross, taken with His seven utterances that they must have heard, coupled with the mocking from Pilate and from one malefactor, as well as the hatred shown by the chief priests, all brought out hatred that caused one soldier to pierce the Lord's side with his spear.

To John, the blood and the water were a manifestation that the Lord really had died. Some today propound the theory that the Lord did not really die, that He merely became unconscious, and that He revived sufficiently to meet His disciples again, after which He left them, so as to travel into a far country to die many years later. In those early days, heretics taught that the Lord's body was not truly physical. John particularly wrote to counter such heresy. Thus "the Word was made flesh" (1:14); "which we have heard . . . and our hands have handled" (1 John 1:1); "Every spirit that confesseth that Jesus Christ is come in the flesh is of God: and every spirit that confesseth not that Jesus Christ is come in the flesh is not of God" (4:1-3). Knowing of this false teaching, John stressed the reality of the physical body of the Lord, and the absolute fact of His death when he wrote his Gospel. Anyone who suggests otherwise is an anti-Christ. Additionally, in his epistle John stressed the cleansing power of "the blood of Jesus Christ his Son" (1 John 1:7).

35 So John stressed that he was an eyewitness, and that both his written record and verbal testimony were true. If these facts be denied, then the whole Gospel can be denied. If Christ did not really die, or if His resurrection was only illusory and not physical, then all preaching and all faith is vain, and believers are still in their sins (1 Cor 15:13-19). The apostle stressed the truthfulness of his testimony again in 21:24. If any one seemed to be vague or doubtful about these truths, then the object of John's Gospel was to lead such men to believe that the Lord Jesus is the Christ, the Son of God (20:31).

36-37 Not only did John claim that his testimony was true, but he had the OT Scriptures on his side as well.

1. "A bone of him shall not be broken" (Exod 12:46; Num 9:12; Ps 34:20). The original passsover lamb had to be made in type like the Lord (not vice versa). The marks of the cross would be on the Lord's body after His resurrection (20:20), but it would be unthinkable for His bones to appear broken in resurrection. Needless to say, the bodily infirmities of the Lord's people will not enter through their resurrection, for they will be changed and glorified.

2. "They shall look on him whom they pierced" (Zech 12:10; Rev 1:7), that is, as His body was taken down from the cross; after His resurrection (20:20); and at His coming again in glory and judgment. It is God's purpose that man's worst act shall lead to man's humiliation at His manifestation.

38 We read about this man Joseph of Arimathaea in all four Gospels. Taken together, we have the following facts.

1. He was "a rich man" (Matt 27:57), being linked in thought with Isa 53:9, "with the rich in his death".

2. He came from Arimathaea, "a city of the Jews" (Luke 23:51), thought by ancient writers to be Ramah where Samuel was born.

3. He was "Jesus' disciple" (Matt 27:57), although we do not read of him before in the gospel narrative. This was "secretly for fear of the Jews" (John 19:38), clearly above the character of those in John 12:42-43 who loved the praise of men.

4. He was "an honourable counsellor" (Mark 15:43), namely, a member of the Jewish Sanhedrin. Yet he had not consented to the "counsel and deed" of the Sanhedrin in condemning the Lord to death (Luke 23:51).

5. He "waited for the kingdom of God" (Mark 15:43), that is, for the kingdom of glory promised in the OT, and that would replace the Roman kingdom under which the Jews were suffering. As a disciple, he may have heard the Lord speaking about this in His teaching.

6. He was "a good man, and a just" (Luke 23:50), this being a suitable commendation for the work he was now going to do for the Lord.

7. No doubt he witnessed the crucifixion, being quite separated from the

other members of the Sanhedrin who were pleased with the outcome of their evil policies toward the Lord.

8. He "went in boldly unto Pilate" (Mark 15:43). In other words, the Lord's death now gave him courage, whereas previously he had lived in fear of the Jews, although mixing with their leadership.

9. He "besought" Pilate (or "craved" as in Mark 15:43) the body of the Lord.

10. He had holy initiative, so as to prevent the holy body being taken away with the two malefactors. God used two men to ensure that the body of His Son was properly treated until the resurrection day, else the body would have been thrown out as refuse.

39 Nicodemus, also a member of the Sanhedrin, joined with Joseph in this deed. John in his record has taken the minds of his readers back to 3:2, when Nicodemus came to the Lord by night—he did not want to be seen openly then. In 7:50, he is again referred to as "he that came to Jesus by night"; here he partially stood up for the Lord on legal grounds, without appearing to be a disciple. But after the Lord's death, he appears openly as he assisted Joseph in taking down the body from the cross. This verse tells us that Nicodemus provided the myrrh and aloes, while Mark 15:46 shows that Joseph had bought and provided the linen cloth for the burial. Both were rich men, and they used their resources for this holy purpose, quite unlike those in Matt 6:2; Mark 12:41 who gave an abundance of alms especially to be seen of men for self-glory.

Nicodemus brought a mixture—"an hundred pound weight" of "myrrh and aloes". The "pound" (*litra*) consisted of about twelve ounces, so 100 pounds really amounted to about 75 UK pounds weight, an amazingly large quantity. Myrrh was an aromatic resin derived from the trunk and branches of a small thorny tree. Aloes derived from wood from the aloe tree reduced to powder.

40 To take the Lord's body from the cross, thereby undoing physically what the Roman soldiers had done, would have been a deed of love coloured with reverence, holiness and tenderness that we cannot imagine or describe. Rembrandt's painting "The descent from the cross" may display imagination for detail, and shows a strange mixture of sorrow and helplessness, but their deed goes far beyond what words can possibly describe.

The spices were inserted between the wrappings of the linen, and no doubt this was done speedily since the evening (the beginning of the sabbath) was drawing nigh. Normally, this procedure was to prevent corruption setting in; this was a display of love, but with ignorance of the OT Scripture that this Holy One would not see corruption (Ps 16:10; Acts 2:27). A full embalming would have to wait until after the sabbath when more time would be available. But God would allow no permanence in this embalming, since His Son would rise from the dead before further steps could be taken. But at least the burial was according to Jewish custom, and not Gentile custom. Thus Jacob was embalmed by the Egyptian physicians leading to forty days mourning. There is a lesson here: a christian burial should be as unlike a burial of an unbeliever as possible.

41-42 Near this place of a skull was a garden. This word *kepos* (garden) occurs only in Luke 13:19 in a parable; in John 18:1,26 referring to Gethsemane, and here in 19:41 referring to the place of the tomb. After sin entered, Adam and Eve were driven out from a garden; now that sin had been put away, the Lord's body was placed in a garden tomb. This sepulchre is called "new"—it was the new tomb hewn out of a rock, and it belonged to Joseph (Matt 27:60). Thus when the Lord was born, it was as Mary's firstborn—her womb had been a new vessel for the growth of the body of the Son of God. When the Lord rode into Jerusalem, it had been on "a colt . . . whereon yet never man sat" (Luke 19:30). Now the Lord's body was placed in a new tomb that had never been occupied by death, and He would soon be the firstborn from among the dead (quite unlike, for example, the body of Jacob which was placed in a cave already occupied by death, Gen 49:30-32; 50:13).

This deed had to be done on the Jews' preparation day, for such activity could not take place on the following sabbath day. They laid the body there, anticipating that they would see it again after the sabbath. Certainly it was laid in a place of safety; God would ensure that it was safe in any case, for no doubt Satan would have attempted to have eliminated the body. Perhaps Michael the archangel was also connected with the safety of the body until the resurrection day, as he had been occupied with the body of Moses in Jude 9.

CHAPTERS 20-21
THE SON—HIS RECEPTION

I. Resurrection Manifestations in Jerusalem (20:1-31)

1. *Mary, Peter and John at the Sepulchre*
20:1-10

v.1 "The first *day* of the week cometh Mary Magdalene early, when it was yet dark, unto the sepulchre, and seeth the stone taken away from the sepulchre.

v.2 Then she runneth, and cometh to Simon Peter, and to the other disciple, whom Jesus loved, and saith unto them, They have taken away the Lord out of the sepulchre, and we know not where they have laid him.

v.3 Peter therefore went forth, and that other disciple, and came to the sepulchre.

v.4 So they ran both together: and the other disciple did outrun Peter, and came first to the sepulchre.

v.5 And he stooping down, *and looking in*, saw the linen clothes lying; yet went he not in.

v.6 Then cometh Simon Peter following him, and went into the sepulchre, and seeth the linen clothes lie,
v.7 And the napkin, that was about his head, not lying with the linen clothes, but wrapped together in a place by itself.
v.8 Then went in also that other disciple, which came first to the sepulchre, and he saw, and believed.
v.9 For as yet they knew not the scripture, that he must rise again from the dead.
v.10 Then the disciples went away again unto their own home."

All four Gospels provide many details about the resurrection manifestations of the Lord Jesus; it may not be completely clear how all these details fit together so as to form a continuous narrative. More complete theological works must be consulted if a picture is desired that embraces all details. There is also a difficulty as to how the words "The first day of the week" arise from the Greek text, which contains the words "*tōn sabbatōn*" (of the sabbaths). We have discussed this on page 407 of our commentary on Matthew's Gospel in this series of commentaries; we will not repeat what we have written there.

The contents of ch.20 are as follows:

1. Uncertainty regarding the fact of the empty tomb; uncertainty leads to certainty (vv.1-10).

2. The misunderstanding of Mary leads to understanding at the Lord's revelation of Himself (vv.11-18).

3. Fear leads to gladness at the Lord's revelation of Himself to the ten apostles (vv.19-23).

4. Unbelief leads to faith at the Lord's revelation of Himself to Thomas and the ten apostles (vv.24-29).

5. Faith enhanced through reading this Gospel (vv.30-31).

1 There was a long vigil at the tomb before anything happened. Originally there were two Marys watching over against the sepulchre, as well as the watch set by the Jewish leaders (Matt 27:61,66). The time is mentioned by all four evangelists: "as it began to dawn toward the first day of the week" (Matt 28:1); "very early in the morning . . . at the rising of the sun" (Mark 16:2); "very early in the morning" (Luke 24:1); "when it was yet dark" (John 20:1). These all describe the same time, namely at the dawn. The first day of the week had begun after sunset on the previous evening. We believe that the Lord rose then, but a night passed before the manifestations of His resurrection commenced. There is a vigil for believers today, for "The night is far spent, the day is at hand" (Rom 13:12). We know what we wait for, but Mary did not know what she was waiting for, though the disciples should have known (Luke 24:25). Mary

Magdalene (previously seen in 19:25 and Matt 27:61) found the stone had been rolled away from the opening to the tomb. (This stone was not mentioned in 19:42, though it appears in Matt 27:60,66). The rolling away of the stone had been miraculous, associated with the angel of the Lord and an earthquake (Matt 28:2).

2 For Mary, this was a matter of urgency—nothing was left till later that should be done immediately. The apostle John once again did not mention himself by name personally, only the oblique reference "the other (*allos*, of the same kind) disciple, whom Jesus loved". As far as discipleship was concerned, both Peter and John were on the same footing. This statement does not mean that the Lord loved John more than the others, but that John appreciated this love more than the others.

Mary Magdalene speaks. At this stage, she had not heard any message from the heavenly messengers regarding the resurrection. She used the title "the Lord", rather than "my Lord" as in v.13. Her devotion was mingled with natural reasoning. Her only explanation was that "they" had taken the body away to a place unknown (the pronoun "they" does not appear explicitly in the Greek text). In this verse, ignorance of the facts led to a natural assumption. In v.9, ignorance of the Scripture led to natural reasoning. In v.15, ignorance of the resurrection led to a natural assumption. Who the "they" were is not stated; certainly not the Jews since they wanted to keep the body safe—so either the guards or the Roman authorities, though why they should want to take the Lord's body away Mary no doubt could not explain.

3-4 The only way to verify the story of Mary Magdalene was to come and see (though this savoured of unbelief, as in Mark 16:11,13). The detail in these two verses is that which only a direct participant would provide. When they arrived, any other women who might have been at the site had already left. Both Peter and John ran together (in Acts 3:1 they were together again when going up to the temple courts). John described himself three times as the "other disciple" (vv.3,4,8); clearly John was the better runner, and arrived first, but he let Peter enter the sepulchre first. John was still the apostle of the ardent affection, while Peter was still the apostle of weeping and repentance, until the Lord treated him differently (Mark 16:7; Luke 24:34; John 21:15-19; 1 Cor 15:5). Both therefore were running the race set before them (Heb 12:1).

5-7 John looked in, and waited for Peter to arrive, allowing him to enter in first. There was always a difference of temperament, personality and forwardness, though in the church both were "pillars" according to Paul (Gal 2:9). From the outside, John saw only the "linen clothes lying", but it was necessary to enter in to see the napkin lying separately. The position of these items of linen was extraordinary if "men" had taken the Lord's body away, giving every impression of resurrection. Thus these finer details were seen by

Peter by going a little further. Recall that the Lord "went a little further" in the garden of Gethsemane (Matt 26:36); it is the little further that counts—into the sanctuary, into the realm of faith, and into the sphere of service. To hesitate or to withdraw is to disappoint the Lord.

8 Thus John also entered the sepulchre, so as to gain a firsthand knowledge of the facts. However, we must note that this did not lead immediately to faith in the Lord's resurrection. In Luke 24:12, Peter merely "wondered in himself at that which was come to pass"; he did not know the reality of the resurrection until the Lord showed Himself to him at a special manifestation (v.34). When it says in our verse 8 that John "believed", this does not mean faith in the Lord's resurrection, but that he now believed Mary's words that the Lord's body was no longer in the tomb, that the body had been taken away. This was only a mental and natural belief in physical facts, not a spiritual faith in the resurrection.

9 This verse proves the correctness of what we have just said. Neither Peter nor John had any realisation that the OT Scriptures had to be fulfilled in the resurrection of Christ. There are four important necessities for us to grasp:

1. "Even so must the Son of man be lifted up" (3:14).
2. "He must rise again from the dead" (20:9).
3. "Whom the heaven must receive" (Acts 3:21).
4. "He must reign" (1 Cor 15:25).

This knowledge would come later, in spite of the evidence of the empty tomb. Their first real knowledge of the Scriptures is found in Luke 24:44-46, when the Lord in resurrection power explained to them from the OT that He had "to rise from the dead the third day". Shortly afterwards, Peter was a changed man as he handled the OT in a way that had not been possible before. Thus

1. In Acts 1:20 he quoted Ps 69:25; 109:8.
2. In Acts 2:25-28 he quoted Ps 16:8-11.
3. In Acts 2:30 he quoted Ps 132:11.
4. In Acts 2:34 he quoted Ps 110:1.
5. In Acts 3:22 he quoted Deut 18:15,19.
6. In Acts 3:25 he quoted Gen 12:3; 22:18.

7. In Acts 4:11 he quoted Ps 118:22.

What a change was effected by the Lord opening the Scriptures, and by the indwelling of the Holy Spirit received at Pentecost.

10 The place to which they returned was "their own home", namely the place where they were staying, the upper room. They were in a dreadfully ignorant state, not knowing the Scriptures, nor knowing the promise of the Lord, nor the fact that the Lord had been raised. Contrast this ignorant state with the state of David when he returned to bless his house (1 Chron 16:43), a good state to be in when returning home, unlike the people generally who merely "departed every man to his house". No doubt this latter state of mind characterised those men in 7:53, "every man went unto his own house", while the Lord went to the mount of Olives, perhaps to the home of Mary and Martha on the eastern slopes.

2. *The Lord with Mary in the Garden*
20:11-18

v.11 "But Mary stood without at the sepulchre weeping: and as she wept, she stooped down, *and looked* into the sepulchre,
v.12 And seeth two angels in white sitting, the one at the head, and the other at the feet, where the body of Jesus had lain.
v.13 And they say unto her, Woman, why weepest thou? She saith unto them, Because they have taken away my Lord, and I know not where they have laid him.
v.14 And when she had thus said, she turned herself back, and saw Jesus standing, and knew not that it was Jesus.
v.15 Jesus saith unto her, Woman, why weepest thou? whom seekest thou? She, supposing him to be the gardener, saith unto thim, Sir, if thou have borne him hence, tell me where thou hast laid him, and I will take him away.
v.16 Jesus saith unto her, Mary. She turned herself, and saith unto him, Rabboni, which is to say, Master.
v.17 Jesus saith unto her, Touch me not; for I am not yet ascended to my Father: but go to my brethren, and say unto them, I ascend unto my Father, and your Father; and to my God, and your God.
v.18 Mary Magdalene came and told the disciples that she had seen the Lord, and *that* he had spoken these things unto her."

11 Back at the sepulchre, Mary was weeping (16:20); she had no certain knowledge of the OT promises, she had as yet not seen the risen Lord, she had as yet no message from the heavenly messengers, and she still thought that the Lord's body had been taken away by men. Her state was as described by Paul in 1 Cor 15:19, "we are of all men most miserable". Of course it is right to weep at the appropriate time and under appropriate circumstances: thus Paul wept while working (Acts 20:19), warning (v.31), writing (2 Cor 2:4), walking (Phil 3:18).

12 Although faithful men had done their best to ensure the safety of the Lord's body, when the powers of darkness are abroad the power of heaven was necessary to provide complete safety. No doubt there had been heavenly messengers responsible for the safety of the body—in a different context we read, "he shall give his angels charge over thee, to keep thee in all thy ways" (Ps 91:11). We recall that angels were operative at the birth and at the temptation of the Lord Jesus.

13 *The two angels speak*. How thankful we can be that angels always talked in the language of the people, whatever may have been the language of heaven. The "tongues ... of angels" (1 Cor 13:1) were always everyday languages as far as the Scriptures are concerned. Otherwise their question "Woman, why weepest thou?" would not have been understood. This question, as so many others in the Scriptures, was designed to bring forth a sincere and honest answer.

Mary Madalene speaks. She still engaged only in natural reasoning, based on what appeared to be physically obvious. However, in divine things, what is obvious disregards the miraculous. But Mary's statement is now more personal. In v.2, she had said "the Lord" and "we"; now, however, she used "my Lord" and "I". Note the five occurrences of "my Lord".

1. Prior to the birth of the Lord, spoken by Elizabeth (Luke 1:43).

2. Spoken by Mary Magdalene at the sepulchre, thinking only of the body of "my Lord", with no thought of His resurrection (20:13).

3. Spoken by Thomas in the upper room (20:28).

4. Spoken by the psalmist David (Ps 110:1), quoted in Matt 22:44.

5. Written by Paul when in the Roman prison (Phil 3:8).

14 Mary was still facing the entrance to the tomb; something attracted her attention behind her, perhaps an unrecorded word spoken by the Lord. One has to turn away from the place of death to face the opposite direction in order to perceive life. She saw the Lord, but failed immediately to discern Him as her Lord. There will always be ignorance as to His Person prior to revelation which is granted to a sincere soul. Thus in Luke 24:16 the two on the Emmaus road did not recognise Him; in v.37 the apostles did not recognise Him; in John 21:4 some of the apostles did not recognise Him standing on the shore.

Note that in 1:26 the Lord was standing, but was not known. It was the same in 20:14 and 21:4; He was standing, but was not recognised. Yet in Acts 7:56 and Rev 5:6 He was standing, and was fully recognised.

Compare this with the apostle John on Patmos. He also turned round to see the One talking and standing, but he saw One whom he recognised as the Son of man, who immediately announced Himself as "I am the first and the last: I am he that liveth, and was dead; and, behold, I am alive for evermore" (Rev 1:12-13,17-18).

15 *The Lord speaks.* He asked the same question as the two angels, but added the further question, "whom seekest thou?". This second question was to turn her heart from sorrow to His Person. Certainly true seeking will find. Thus in 1:38 He asked Andrew and another disciple, "What seek ye?", for they were seeking the Lamb of God, and claimed to have found the Messiah. Shortly afterwards Philip also claimed to have found the One promised in the OT (v.45).

Mary Magdalene speaks. The word "Sir" translates *Kurie,* the word for "Lord". Not that she recognised Him as her Lord, but this was a polite form of address. By thinking that He was "the gardener" (a word occurring only here in the NT), she manifested the ignorance of grief; perhaps her tears did not allow her to see clearly. Evidently she thought that she was still the custodian of his body, and that this body had been taken away—even by a gardener. Of course God would ensure that no unholy hands would ever touch the body of the Lord between His death and His rising again.

Elsewhere, men had strange thoughts concerning the Lord. The ignorance of formal religion thought that He was John the Baptist, Elijah, or Jeremiah (Matt 16:14). The ignorance of blasphemy thought that He was associated with the prince of the devils (Matt 12:24). To none of these was a revelation of His Person given, but to Mary He revealed Himself immediately.

16 *The Lord speaks.* If Mary had not known who the Lord was, there was no possibility of the Lord not knowing who Mary was; He calls His own sheep by name (10:3). Thus He addressed this weeping woman (who had not recognised Him by His voice in v.15) as "Mary". It is a good exercise to list all the men and women whom the Lord addressed by their names once, and the smaller list whom He addressed by their names twice as Simon (Luke 22:31) and Saul (Acts 9:4).

Mary Magdalene speaks. In v.14 it may be that she turned just her head, while here she turned her whole body in wonder and amazement at the recognition of the risen Lord. No longer "Sir", but "Rabboni", this being more respectful than "Rabbi" (applied to the Lord several times). John interpreted the meaning, by writing "Master", namely *didaskalos,* a teacher. Of all the Lord's attributes and works, Mary formulated just one in her surprise, namely that of Teacher, but a very great Teacher.

17 *The Lord speaks.* "Touch me not" (*haptomai*) is a common word in the NT, and has given rise to much speculation as to the Lord's meaning, from a manifestation of little faith to a manifestation of great faith. The verb can mean "to cling to, to lay hold of", and the Lord's meaning appears to be that Mary's contact with Him must be by faith after His resurrection, else she might attempt to preserve His presence physically by force of her hands, so great was her relief at seeing her Lord again. He could read Mary's intention and desire to restrain Him from disappearing, so that He could be with her as previously prior to His crucifixion. This could not be so, for His presence spiritually after His ascension would be a greater blessing; then she could touch Him by faith. Certainly by saying "not yet", the Lord discounted a later theory that He had ascended to His Father between His death and resurrection.

If Mary had said "my Lord", then He said "my brethren"; in our comments on 13:1 we have listed the names that He used to describe His own: "my disciple, servant, sheep, friend, and brethren". Mary must not stop, but take the good news to the other disciples.

By calling them "my brethren" He was putting them in relationship with the Father as sons. Their recent failures did not cause this relationship to diminish in spiritual intensity. How deep was that eternal relationship, "my Father ... my God". This had existed from eternity. Yet now after His resurrection, this relationship was also the portion of His disciples. Note that previously in John's Gospel there had always occurred "the Father", "my Father", but never "your Father". Indeed in the Synoptic Gospels we find "your Father" providentially many times, but here in John's Gospel by "your Father" spiritual affection, relationship and nearness are implied, made possible only through the sacrifice and resurrection of the Lord. The Father as "your God" and the Lord Jesus as "my God" (v.28) imply the Deity of Christ.

18 *Mary Magdalene speaks*. Love led to obedience; Mary did not detain the Lord, but she perceived the necessity of immediate testimony. Initially, the disciples did not believe her (Mark 16:11), neither did they believe the testimony of the two on the Emmaus road (v.13).

3. *The Lord with the Apostles in the Upper Room* 20:19-31

v.19 "Then the same day at evening, being the first *day* of the week, when the doors were shut where the disciples were assembled for fear of the Jews, came Jesus and stood in the midst, and saith unto them, Peace *be* unto you.
v.20 And when he had so said, he shewed unto them *his* hands and his side. Then were the disciples glad, when they saw the Lord.
v.21 Then said Jesus to them again, Peace *be* unto you: as *my* Father hath sent me, even so send I you.
v.22 And when he had said this, he breathed on *them*, and saith unto them, Receive ye the Holy Ghost:
v.23 Whose soever sins ye remit, they are remitted unto them; *and* whose soever *sins* ye retain, they are retained.
v.24 But Thomas, one of the twelve, called Didymus, was not with them when Jesus came.
v.25 The other disciples therefore said unto him, We have seen the Lord. But he said unto them, Except I shall see in his hands the print of

the nails, and put my finger into the print of the nails, and thrust my hand into his side, I will not believe.
v.26 And after eight days again his disciples were within, and Thomas with them: *then* came Jesus, the doors being shut, and stood in the midst, and said, Peace *be* unto you.
v.27 Then saith he to Thomas, Reach hither thy finger, and behold my hands; and reach hither thy hand, and thrust *it* into my side: and be not faithless, but believing.
v.28 And Thomas answered and said unto him, My Lord and my God.
v.29 Jesus saith unto him, Thomas, because thou hast seen me, thou hast believed: blessed *are* they that have not seen, and *yet* have believed.
v.30 And many other signs truly did Jesus in the presence of his disciples, which are not written in this book.
v.31 But these are written, that ye might believe that Jesus is the Christ, the Son of God; and that believing ye might have life through his name."

19 John has omitted certain features that are included in the other Gospels. Mark 16:11-14 informs us twice that the apostles did not believe the testimony of others, and that the risen Lord upbraided them for the fact that they did not believe those who had already seen Him as risen. Luke 24:37 shows that the apostles were "terrified and affrighted" when He first appeared to them. Matthew and John, who were present, omitted these features that reflected badly upon themselves, while Mark and Luke, who were not present, had no hesitation in recording these weaknesses.

The first day of the week was drawing to its close when these events occurred. The room that they occupied was, we believe, the same upper room that the Lord had selected in the evening before He died. Fear filled their hearts because of the hostility of the Jews without. The doors were shut (a Greek perfect participle, showing that they had been closed and were still closed) so as to prevent any intrusion by the Jews. The Lord's entrance was therefore a miracle, just as had been His exit from the sepulchre, and as His previous vanishing from the room where the two men on the Emmaus road were staying (Luke 24:31); closed walls were no barrier to the risen Lord. The ten apostles were assembled in the room, thereby forming the first nucleus of a local assembly or church; the Lord would come where they were assembled, and this answers to Matt 26:20, "he sat down with the twelve", namely, He presented Himself where they were.

The Lord speaks. He knew their fear of the Jews, and the fear that they experienced when they thought that he was "a spirit" (Luke 24:37). Consequently He said, "Peace be unto you". This would remove fear experienced at an unexpected miraculous manifestation of Himself (as in Acts 9:3-9; Rev 1:17). Later in Acts 2, they had no fear, while in Acts 4:29-31 they prayed for boldness and then preached with boldness. The Lord's peace was therefore quite distinct from any peace that the world might be able to give (14:27).

20 *The Lord speaks.* By showing them His hands and His side, the Lord invited identification. His wounded side proved that He could not possibly be either of the two men crucified with Him, and His wounds proved that He had been dead. The reality of His resurrection was proved by the sight of His wounded body, though in Luke 24:39 there was the opportunity to touch Him also. This touch is quite distinct from the touch that Mary had wanted to engage in (John 20:19); the former was a touch of proof, while the latter was a touch of restraint. After His resurrection the Lord always bore in His body the marks of His sufferings and death: in Rev 5:6 the Lamb is seen "as it had been slain".

Fear gave place to gladness, in keeping with the Lord's words, "your sorrow shall be turned into joy . . . your heart shall rejoice, and your joy no man taketh from you" (16:20-22). God would have His people rejoice, and David recognised that the opportunity to be glad came from God and not from men, "Thou hast put gladness in my heart, more than in the time that their corn and their wine increased" (Ps 4:7).

21 *The Lord speaks.* By repeating "Peace be unto you", He gave them a twofold peace in this upper room. The first related to the peace that comes through the reality of His presence, while the second related to the peace necessary for the outworking of the commission He was about to give them. We may quote Isa 26:3: "Thou wilt keep him in perfect peace" (the literal Hebrew is "peace peace"; see Newberry marg). This double hope is the aspiration of unbelievers until the day of destruction, for they will cry "Peace and safety" (1 Thess 5:3). In the OT, many prophets and servants of God had been sent, but in the NT the Lord sent His servants because He had been sent by the Father; they follow in His steps.

Originally, His disciples had been sent only to the lost sheep of the house of Israel (Matt 10:5-6), but at the end of His life He would send them "into the world" (John 17:18). Thus Paul was sent "far hence unto the Gentiles" (Acts 22:21). After His resurrection, in all four Gospels it is recorded that the Lord gave this commission: "Go ye therefore" (Matt 28:19); "Go ye into all the world" (Mark 16:15); "that repentance and remission of sins should be preached . . . among all nations . . . ye are witnesses" (Luke 24:47-48); "even so send I you" (John 20:21).

22-23 This was a simple act indeed, to breathe upon them. In the OT, the divine breath was often a symbol of judgment (Ps 18:15; Isa 11:4) where the word also means *wind*. But here in our verse a different word is used (*emphusaō*), unique in the NT, perhaps to differentiate it from "wind" in 3:8. No doubt it stands in contrast with Gen 2:7 where the biological creation of man is in question, and Ezek 37:9,14 where the rebirth of a nation is implied. Expositors differ in their understanding of "Receive ye the Holy Spirit". Some see the actual reception of the Spirit there and then in the gentle act of the Lord; others see the words as a precursor and a promise of that which would take place at

Pentecost. Certainly in the latter there was "a rushing mighty wind", though sent from the Lord (Acts 2:2,33). In Elijah's case, the wind gave place to the still small voice (1 Kings 19:11-12), but here the quiet breathing gave place to the mighty wind. In any case, v.23 links the proclamation of the Gospel with this reception of the Spirit, so we would believe that the Lord referred to the promise that the Spirit would shortly be given from on high.

In v.23, the statement "Whose soever sins ye remit, they are remitted unto them; and whose soever sins ye retain, they are retained" has given rise to much speculation and arrogant assumption. (The word for "remit", *aphiēmi*, is the usual word for "forgive".) Evangelicals know where they stand in the matter, but false assumptions are claimed by ecclesiastical arrogancy. For some men claim to have been granted the ability to forgive sins. Even the Pharisees knew better when they said "Who can forgive sins, but God alone?" (Luke 5:21), though they failed to recognise the Deity of Christ. This divine prerogative is recorded only twice in the Gospels (Luke 5:20; 7:48). In Acts, we do not find any preacher forgiving men of their sins. We forgive one another for personal wrongs (Eph 4:32), but that is another matter.

The only thing that preachers can do is to preach the gospel of the forgiveness of sins. Peter promised this in Acts 2:33; he declared it to Cornelius in Acts 10:43. Paul preached it in Antioch (Acts 13:38), and was a minister of the truth that "they may receive forgiveness of sins" (Acts 26:18), but he could not impart this; it was included in "redemption through his blood" (Eph 1:7).

The retention of sins was a very solemn matter, and suggests the apostolic ability to discern men who had placed themselves beyond the reach of the gospel message, at least for a season. For the Lord spoke of a man who "hath never forgiveness" (Mark 3:29). Paul, as filled with the Holy Spirit, seemed to have had this ability in Acts 13:10, when he called a man "O full of all subtilty and all mischief, thou child of the devil, thou enemy of all righteousness". This man was blind for a season, and forgiveness was impossible during that time. On the other hand, there was also the question of discipline in a local assembly. The assembly must be so in touch with the mind of God, in the name of the Lord Jesus with Him in the midst, that any binding that is done on earth can also be ratified in heaven. The assembly in Corinth, in the name of the Lord Jesus, and with Paul present "in spirit", also had to exercise discipline; the man's sin remained until the man was forgiven (1 Cor 5:1-5; 2 Cor 2:7,10).

24 In Mary's case, we have seen faith rekindled by His call; in the case of the apostles, faith was rekindled by sight. Now in the case of Thomas, the Lord gave the invitation to rekindle faith by natural proof (touch). The opening word "But" presents an important contrast. (In the resurrection chapters, note this word in Matt 28:17; Luke 24:37.) In the three Synoptic Gospels, Thomas appears only at the Lord's call of the twelve apostles (Matt 10:3; Mark 3:18; Luke 6:15). But the apostle John rescues him from being just a name! Four times he appears in John's Gospel as:

1. Fatalistic (11:16), "Let us also go, that we may die with him".

2. Factless (14:5), "how can we know the way?".

3. Faithless (20:25), "I will not believe".

4. Failing (21:2), since he followed Peter to go fishing.

Three times he is called "Didymus" (11:16; 20:25; 21:2) meaning a twin.

The immediate question that arises is, Why was he not with the other apostles in the upper room? Was fellowship of no importance to him? Or was his faith and devotion weak (as seen in the four points stated above), so that it did not matter where he was or what he was doing? In Acts 1:13-15 he was in the upper room with the hundred and twenty, but we may then ask where were the others, for over five hundred had seen the risen Lord at one time (1 Cor 15:6)? Again, in Num 24:7 Phinehas the priest had to do Eleazar's work, since he was absent for some reason. Such examples seem to savour of the desire to forsake the assembling of themselves together (Heb 10:25), and believers are warned against such an attitude.

25 *The ten apostles speak*. United in testimony, they asserted, "We have seen the Lord". It should be noted that they not only used the title "Lord" when speaking *to* Him directly (v.28; 21:15,20), but when speaking *about* Him (21:7), quite unlike much modern practice. Their immediate dissemination of the glorious news is similar to Acts 4:20, "we cannot but speak the things which we have seen".

Thomas speaks. As the other disciples had not believed prior witnesses of His resurrection (Mark 16:13), so also these other disciples were not now believed! Thomas' insistence on physical and bodily proof (seeing and feeling), together with his dogmatic assertion "I will not believe" would almost lead one to feel that he was an agnostic, had it not been known that he was an apostle. Even the sense of the eyes was not sufficient—he wanted the proof of touch as well. This shows that the marks were sufficient to demonstrate that death had taken place. Thomas was very quick with his tongue, before his mind had come to a conclusion. Faith and unbelief were both emerging from his tongue, of which phenomenon James has written "these things ought not so to be" (James 3:10).

26 Eight days would lead again to the first day of the week—the Lord's Day, the first weekly anniversary of the Lord's resurrection. This would be a new start for Thomas' faith. Under identical circumstances with the door closed, the Lord reappeared to the eleven apostles, and stood in their midst.

The Lord speaks. "Peace be unto you" repeats vv.19,21. Here it is peace associated with the discernment of faith. As the Lord revealed Himself to Thomas, we should note the kinds of men to whom the Lord revealed Himself, and those from whom a sign is withheld. Certainly no sign would be given to a wicked and adulterous generation (Matt 16:4); no truth would be revealed to those who remain "wise and prudent" (Matt 11:25); most of the wise, mighty and noble are not called (1 Cor 1:26). Rather the weak things of the world are susceptible to divine revelation and calling. Thus Thomas was weak in faith, but in effect the Lord would say to him, as He said unto Peter, "O thou of little faith, wherefore didst thou doubt?" (Matt 14:31). Yet to Thomas there was the same blessing, the same manifestation of His presence, as in v.19 to the other apostles.

27 In grace and mercy, the Lord offered His body to the senses of sight and touch. Thus many things would He grant to a soul in weakness, to draw him back to the realities of faith. In Thomas' case, sight only was sufficient after all. The Lord's words to Thomas were almost identical to the words of Thomas to the disciples (v.25), showing that He had heard every word that Thomas had uttered in unbelief, for "there is nothing covered, that shall not be revealed; and hid, that shall not be known" (Matt 10:26).

28 The Lord had promised that the disciples would see Him again after "a little while" (John 16:19). This was fulfilled, but for Thomas, the "little while" lasted for over a week.

Thomas speaks. This apostle offered no explanation for his previous absence; the Lord knew all about it in any case. He could but make the great confession, "My Lord and my God". In our remarks on 1:1; 5:17-18, we have explained at length the implications of this confession "my God"; it refutes heresy that argues that the Lord Jesus was not God, for in Greek, the definite article "the" stands before "God", namely "*the* God". The Lord accepted such a confession, for it was true, unlike Rev 19:10; 22:8-9 where angels immediately rejected worship being offered to themselves. Paul and Barnabas did the same in Acts 14:11-18.

In some modern translations of the NT, the Deity of Christ is minimised if not discarded; it is therefore important for believers to know those verses that openly imply the Deity of the Lord Jesus: John 1:1; 5:17-18; 10:30-33; Matt 1:23; Rom 9:5; 1 Tim 3:16; Titus 2:13; Heb 1:8; 1 John 5:20.

29 *The Lord speaks*. He directed the first part of His statement to Thomas (note the use of the word "they"). The Lord would desire that not even sight should be formative of faith, not that sight should lead to the deepening of faith, for the Lord knew that after His ascension, any case similar to that of Thomas could not be resolved by a direct appearance of Himself. Men would have to believe without the aid of sight; such men are called "blessed" (*makarios*). So the Lord laid down a programme that would mark the years of His physical absence. There were men in mockery who claimed that they would believe if they saw Him perform a great miracle (Matt 27:42), but belief formed under those circumstances would not be faith at all. The Lord wanted men's faith to be centred in the words of His servants, and in the written record given by the Holy Spirit. A supreme example is that of Abraham, who was not weak in faith, and "staggered not at the promise of God in unbelief; but was strong in faith" (Rom 4:19-22). At the time when he exercised this faith, there was nothing physically to see. As Paul wrote, "we walk by faith, not by sight" (2 Cor 5:7), although he himself had seen the Lord. The OT men of faith had only seen the promise afar off (Heb 11:13), but this was a reality and their faith did not waver.

30 With this blessed statement of the Lord, John concluded his record about the resurrection manifestations of the Lord in Jerusalem. But there were many other signs that could have been recorded. These "many other signs . . . in the presence of his disciples" appear to refer to the resurrection manifestations, rather than to the signs (or miracles) performed in His lifetime. For all other signs recorded in John's Gospel (except that in 6:19) were done in the presence of other people as well, so "in the presence of his disciples" suggests those signs done in the privacy of the presence of His disciples only, namely His post-resurrection signs. The "many things which Jesus did" in 21:25 refer to His acts throughout His lifetime on earth.

These "other signs" would be known to John, but clearly their record was not necessary for the purpose of the Holy Spirit to lead readers into a deeper knowledge of the Son. What is written will lead to faith; the lasting value of the "more sure word of prophecy" was more important than the physical sight of the Lord on the mount of transfiguration (2 Pet 1:17-19). For faith comes "by the word of God" (Rom 10:17). The value of the written word is stressed even in the OT: "he shall write him a copy of this law . . . it shall be with him, and he shall read therein . . . that he may learn" (Deut 17:18-20); "This book of the law shall not depart out of thy mouth; but thou shalt meditate therein . . . then thou shalt make thy way prosperous" (Josh 1:8).

31 Here is the objective before John as he wrote his Gospel: "that ye might believe". Certainly, the reading of this Gospel has led many to an initial faith in the Son of God. But we feel that this is not John's meaning here, since the statement derives from the example of Thomas. This man as an apostle had faith already, but his experience in the upper room deepened his faith in new directions. When a believer reads John's Gospel, his faith likewise is renewed and extended, primarily in the Person of the Son of God, and then in the possessed personal blessings of life. Such additions to a basic faith are prominent in a growth into spirituality. For the Lord Himself is the Author and Finisher of faith (Heb 12:2)— it commences and grows to completion, as "your faith groweth exceedingly" (2 Thess 1:3), while Peter records many features that are added to faith as faith grows (2 Pet 1:5). So all believers never have to regain that initial faith by which salvation and eternal life were originally possessed; but all need to grow, so as to transcend infinitely any false teaching about the Person of the Son that John had to counteract. To grow thus in faith is to possess life more abundantly.

II. Resurrection Manifestations in Galilee (21:1-25)

1. *The Eighth Sign: The Lord's Provision in Service* 21:1-14

v.1 "After these things Jesus shewed himself again to the disciples at the sea of Tiberias; and on this wise shewed he *himself*.
v.2 There were together Simon Peter, and Thomas called Didymus, and Nathanael of Cana in Galilee, and the *sons* of Zebedee, and two other of his disciples.
v.3 Simon Peter saith unto them, I go a fishing. They say unto him, We also go with thee. They went forth, and entered into a ship immediately; and that night they caught nothing.
v.4 But when the morning was now come, Jesus stood on the shore: but the disciples knew not that it was Jesus.
v.5 Then Jesus saith unto them, Children, have ye any meat? They answered him, No.
v.6 And he said unto them, Cast the net on the right side of the ship, and ye shall find. They cast therefore, and now they were not able to draw it for the multitude of fishes.
v.7 Therefore that disciple whom Jesus loved saith unto Peter, It is the Lord. Now when Simon Peter heard that it was the Lord, he girt *his* fisher's coat *unto him*, (for he was naked,) and did cast himself into the sea.
v.8 And the other disciples came in a little ship: (for they were not far from land, but as it were two hundred cubits,) dragging the net with fishes.
v.9 As soon then as they were come to land, they saw a fire of coals there, and fish laid thereon, and bread.
v.10 Jesus saith unto them, Bring of the fish which ye have now caught.
v.11 Simon Peter went up, and drew the net to land full of great fishes, an hundred and fifty and three: and for all there were so many, yet was not the net broken.
v.12 Jesus saith unto them, Come *and* dine. And none of the disciples durst ask him, Who art thou? knowing that it was the Lord.
v.13 Jesus then cometh, and taketh bread, and giveth them, and fish likewise.
v.14 This is now the third time that Jesus shewed himself to his disciples, after that he was risen from the dead."

We now have a connected series of events that led to the Lord's reference to John in v.22. The contents of the chapter are as follows:

1. John with others displaying spiritual weakness (he was one of the sons of Zebedee in v.1) (vv.1-6).

2. The recognition of the Lord (vv.7-14).

3. The verification of Peter's love (vv.15-17).

4. The latter end of Peter and John foretold (vv.18-23).

5. The truth of apostolic testimony (vv.24-25).

1 There is now a break in John's narrative, while the apostles journey up to Galilee. We are not surprised that they made this journey, although John has given no explanation for the move. Later, they were instructed not to depart from Jerusalem (Acts 1:4), but that instruction was given later. The night before the Lord died, He had informed them that He would "go before you into Galilee" after His resurrection (Matt 26:32). On the resurrection day, the women at the sepulchre were reminded of the Lord's words by the angel (28:7), and later the eleven apostles went to Galilee to "a mountain where Jesus had appointed them" (28:16). Galilee was the place where most of the Lord's mighty works had taken place, and no doubt other faithful souls who lived there had the opportunity of seeing Him alive again.

Tiberias was a city founded by Herod Antipas, and named after the Roman emperor. It was situated on the west side of the Sea of Galilee, and is mentioned as a city only once in the Gospels (6:23). The Sea of Galilee therefore took the name "sea of Tiberias", though John also used the title "sea of Galilee" once in 6:1.

2 Seven of the disciples were involved in this fishing expedition.

1. Peter, James and John (the two sons of Zebedee, Matt 4:18-22). Note that John did not mention himself by name explicitly. These three had been privileged to see the Lord on three special occasions (the raising of Jairus' daughter, the mount of transfiguration, and the garden of Gethsemane, none of which is found in John's Gospel). They had been former fishermen before being called to discipleship at the beginning of the Lord's ministry (Matt 4:19-22; Luke 5:4-7).

2. Thomas called Didymus. We have already commented on this apostle in 20:24.

3. Nathanael, a man who appeared last in 1:45-51. It is usually assumed that he was one of the twelve apostles, and he is identified with Bartholomew in particular, though this cannot be proved conclusively.

4. "Two other of his disciples". No doubt these were two who had not been named before in John's Gospel, so they are not named here either. (No complete list of the apostles appears in John's Gospel, unlike the other three Gospels: see Matt 10:2-4; Mark 3:16-19; Luke 6:14-16.) At least the

word for "other" is *allos*, meaning "of the same kind", so apostolic discipleship appears to be confirmed.

3 How quickly had these disciples forgotten the power of His resurrection, and the promise "he goeth before you into Galilee" (Matt 28:7). It would appear that the Lord's teaching, "No man, having put his hand to the plough, and looking back, is fit for the kingdom of God" (Luke 9:62), was forgotten.

Simon Peter speaks. Peter's declared intention "I go a fishing" represented the desire to take up again an occupation that he had abandoned when he was first called by the Lord. Almost as soon as He was no longer physically with them, they turned their back on the separated pathway of discipleship. They had followed the Lord (Matt 4:20,22), thus to become "fishers of men", but now the energy of the flesh was prompting the desires of the heart.

The other six disciples speak. Peter was always the leader, and his policy immediately became their policy, as they answered "We also go with thee". This was a case of a leader leading others astray, rather than the setting of a good spiritual example. Leaders in any walk of life have a status of responsibility, and this applies particularly to spiritual things. Thus in 2 Chron 1:3 Solomon led "all the congregation" to the arkless tabernacle in Gibeon, that God had forsaken years before, and it was only with difficulty that he could lead them back when he decided to return to Zion. On the other hand, Paul alone had the vision in Acts 16:9 to come to Macedonia; but afterwards, "we endeavoured" to follow—here was good leadership.

Today, this danger can be widespread, when there are blind leaders of the blind, when some elders in a local church may not provide good and sound leadership, and when younger believers easily follow them in a downward slide into unspiritual activity. This is a failure of the flesh, when the Lord is not brought into an intended enterprise to guide and superintend.

Peter had been this way before! He had been called in 1:40-42 and Matt 4:18-20, and had followed the Lord for a season. Yet in Luke 5:1-5 we find Peter back again at his occupation of fishing, with nothing caught all through the night. The teaching and the miracle brought Peter to his spiritual senses once again, and he thus confessed, "I am a sinful man, O Lord" (v.8). Hence twice the Lord said to him "thou shalt catch men", thereby bringing men to the Lord through faith.

The lesson behind this eighth sign is obvious. The picture was that of a man seeking to serve the Lord in his own strength. What can an evangelist do if he neglects the power and ability granted by the Lord? "Except the Lord build the house, they labour in vain that build it" (Ps 127:1). It is God that gives the increase, not the one who plants nor the one who waters (1 Cor 3:6-8). Service is barren if one's own energy displaces the energy of God.

4 The apostles waited until the morning before something happened: the same had happened in Luke 5:5. But there was a great difference. Here in 21:4, none of them "knew... that it was Jesus", but in Luke 5:5, Peter recognised Him and called Him "Master" (*epistatēs*), meaning "one who is set over", in the matter of teaching. So Peter, although having seen the Lord already in resurrection, joined the ranks of those whose eyes were temporarily closed. Some may explain this by suggesting that the morning mists had somewhat hidden the One standing on the shore, but we prefer to think that the reason lay in the state of heart of the apostles who had occupied themselves with fishing rather than with the things of the Lord. In spite of the Lord having breathed upon them in Jerusalem, here in Galilee they appear to have forgotten Him because of their toiling with natural things.

5 *The Lord speaks.* The word "children" (*paidion*) properly means "little children". Nine times in Matt 2 the Lord Himself is called a "young child". John used the word twice in his first epistle (1 John 2:13,18), distinguishing spiritual youthfulness from greater maturity. In the four Gospels, the Lord used the word only once as a form of direct address, though in Heb 2:13 He says, "Behold I and the children which God hath given me". No doubt this was a suitable title just after the Lord had said "my Father, and your Father" (John 20:17). Moreover, the word reflects upon their present childlike state—in ignorance they were fishing instead of serving.

The Lord's question "have ye any meat?" was designed to force them to confess their incapacity to accomplish their fishing effectively. The word for "meat" (*prosphagion*) occurs only here in the NT, and means a kind of fish relish. The Lord would, of course, provide something better.

The apostles speak. By saying "No", they confessed that they possessed nothing. This may have been the reason why they embarked upon a fishing expedition. Having caught no fish, they would be hungry. By way of spiritual interpretation, they were ministerially empty of spiritual food, and evangelically they were powerless to gain souls. Only the presence and the power of the Lord could effect a complete change.

6 *The Lord speaks.* By commanding them to cast their net on the right side of the ship, the Lord implied that He, being divine, knew where the fish were at that particular moment. For the sea, oftentimes gripped by storms, represents the nations of men in sin, often engulfed in turmoil; "the wicked are like the troubled sea, when it cannot rest, whose waters cast up mire and dirt. There is no peace, saith my God, to the wicked" (Isa 57:20-21). But amidst all the unbelief and wickedness of men, the Lord can see those who are to become His own by salvation. He will direct His evangelists there when they are dependent upon Himself. Thus He knew of Cornelius' devout state, and that he would respond to the message when preached; hence Peter was directed there (Acts 10). Philip was directed to Samaria because many would respond there (Acts 8:12). Again, Paul was directed to Corinth, because God had much people in that city (Acts 18:10). The command to cast so as to catch men for Christ could

either be a direct command or an indirect command; the evangelist must have a quiet heart so as to discern the Lord's will. To cast contrary to the Lord's will can only lead to barrenness. Generally, Paul received the direct command to go to the Gentiles, and he testified that he was not disobedient to the heavenly vision (Acts 26:17-20). Similarly, these disciples in the ship were not disobedient, but cast their net in the right place, and their evangelistic net was full to overflowing. This corresponds to the "much people" in Corinth (Acts 18:10), and to the large numbers saved in Jerusalem (Acts 2:41; 4:4). Not that faithful testimony will always net a great catch, for in Athens only a few were gained for Christ (Acts 17:34).

7 *John speaks*. Once again, as the author, the apostle referred to himself in an oblique way, "that disciple whom Jesus loved". His stronger affections enabled him to be the first one to recognise the Lord. Note that he used the title "the Lord" (*kurios*) rather than any other name or title. He recognised the Lord because of His power in this miracle; perhaps his mind went back to the former miracle in Luke 5:1-11, when Peter also called Him "Lord" (v.9). But here, Peter had neither the requisite affections nor the recognition of divine power to be able to recognise the Lord; he had to rely on the testimony of another. It is far better for the affections of a believer to recognise the Lord immediately, even before any demonstration of divine working in the service of such a believer.

But Peter's response was immediate, as soon as he heard that it was the Lord. Of course, he had to trust the apostle John, that his statement was correct. Statements made by believers immersed in unspiritual occupations can hardly be trustworthy, so we must be careful today as to whom we listen and trust.

No doubt Peter's action to cast his coat around him and to jump into the sea was because of a great desire to get to his Lord as soon as possible. But typically, Peter seems here to hide his Jewish self with the spiritual robes of an evangelist-fisherman, and thus he enters the nations as he makes progress to meet the Lord at the rapture. He did not now walk upon the sea (Matt 14:29) (that is, separated from the nations as in Matt 10:5, and walking above them), but he enters the sea so as to work in them, making his way to the Lord. This is what he did in Acts 10, though this was an exceptional ministry (Gal 2:7-9).

8 By translating "in a little ship" the AV gives the impression that there was more than one ship involved. But the RV (following the Greek text) uses the definite article, "in *the* little boat". In other words, there was only one boat, and the meaning is by way of contrast—Peter cast himself into the sea, but the other disciples remained in the ship, and made for the shore (about one hundred yards away). Each one took his place in the service of God, and all made their way to the Lord; a distance had to be covered, as in all cases of conversion.

The word "draw" (*helkuō*) in v.6 is different from the word "drag" (*surō*) in v.8. The first word occurs six times in the NT (five times in John's Gospel, 6:44; 12:32; 18:10: 21:6,11) and is the less energetic form. The latter word occurs five times in the NT (as in Acts 8:3; 14:19; 17:6, where a more violent forceful act on men and women is implied). Thus in v.6, the power of drawing could not move the net towards the ship, but in v.8 the net could be moved by a more powerful dragging act. No doubt these two ideas focus attention on the means whereby souls are saved. Some can be drawn, but some must be more forcefully attracted to the Lord. Souls that are saved have to be separated from their preconversion bondage and their attachment to many different forms of sin.

9 Arriving on the shore, the disciples found something that they had not been able to prepare before their fishing expedition—a fire, with fish laid on it, and bread. Note that these fish were not taken from those that they had just caught. This was a divine provision for the disciples, and it was quite distinct from any natural catch of fish, even though miraculous. In the midst of evangelistic service, food of the Lord's providing must be recognised and spiritually eaten. This food may come directly from Himself, or by way of ministerial provision by teachers in the churches. But the fire would speak of sacrifice (as seen in 6:53 in a different context), and sacrifice is also necessary on the part of teachers who give up so much time and energy to serve the Lord's people. Thus Paul would spend and be spent sacrificially in his service (2 Cor 12:15).

10-11 *The Lord speaks*. When He asked for the fish to be brought, they had not as yet been brought ashore—just to the shore. This bringing is the work of an evangelist; converts must be brought out of fellowship with the unsaved, and brought specifically and positively to the Lord. Any half-way stage is not visualised in the meaning of the sign. "Come out from among them", wrote Paul (2 Cor 6:17). Peter put this into effect by exhorting, "Save yourselves from this untoward generation" (Acts 2:40), thereby following the Lord's words that His disciples had been given to Him "out of the world" (John 17:6).

Physically speaking, Peter being out of the ship was the first one to land, and could therefore make the final effort to get the net and fish onto the shore. Clearly one or more of them had counted the number of fish at some stage, since the exact number, one hundred and fifty three, is given. This is unlike the round numbers found in the Acts when large multitudes trusted the Lord (Acts 2:41; 4:4). Thus there is scope sometimes for an exact evaluation of the results of evangelistic endeavour, and at other times for an approximate estimation. Boasting by evangelists is excluded. We are unable to read any symbolical meaning into the number 153, though those with a powerful imagination may be able to make suggestions. Exact counting is usually the counting of heaven, for not one is lost (6:39; 17:12). It may be of interest to mention that the number of strangers in Israel who were engaged on the building of the temple amounted to 153 600 (2 Chron 2:17), and in the counting of God one is equivalent to a thousand (2 Pet 3:8). The few at the beginning develop into the many at the end. This shows that strangers who are converted are then engaged on construction work in God's building, the local church.

At least the net was not broken, showing the fact that God preserves the means that He has introduced by which souls can be saved. If the preaching of the gospel were found to be powerless and broken, then there would be justified the many other methods which have been used in recent years, some involving the practice of entertainment. But God's method was all that was used throughout the Acts, in spite of every attempt by the enemy to break the net.

12 *The Lord speaks.* "Come and dine" was His gracious invitation to His own disciples on account of their physical and spiritual needs. Others may eat and drink until the flood (Matt 24:38), saying "let us eat and drink; for to morrow we die" (1 Cor 15:32). But the provision of the Lord leads to life, whether it be the manna come down from heaven, or the fish and bread in the present event. Elsewhere, the Lord issued other invitations, such as "Come unto me" (Matt 11:28); "Come and see" (John 1:39); "Come up hither" (Rev 4:1). On the other hand, there are invitations that lead to death and judgment, such as "Come and gather yourselves together unto the supper of the great God" (Rev 19:17); "come ye, assemble all the beasts of the field, come to devour" (Jer 12:9); "Assemble yourselves, and come" (Ezek 39:17).

Not one of the disciples dared say "Who art thou?", since they knew that it was the Lord. It is remarkable that John should conceive the necessity of asking this question, since he also stated that they all knew that it was the Lord. But his remark shows that there was a deep lack of apostolic confidence in the Lord, even when they knew Him. This was also manifested in Mark 9:32 when the apostles "were afraid to ask him" concerning His remarks on His forthcoming death and resurrection.

13 When they landed on the shore, the Lord approached them, rather than letting them come up to Him. This had happened already several times in ch.20. In the OT, men approached God as dwelling in His tabernacle or temple. But in the NT, He approaches His people when they gather together in His Name. The Lord giving the bread and the fish to them reminds us of other occasions when He gave bread, such as Matt 14:19; 15:36; 26:26; Luke 24:30.

Note that the bread and the fish were what He provided—not the fish that the disciples had caught. This contrasts with 4:31-34, where the disciples had provided for the Lord, food which He refused to eat since He had more important meat, namely to do the will of the Father.

By this simple act, the Lord took the position of a Servant, as in 13:4-17; Luke 22:27. Elsewhere, others served Him at meals (Luke 10:40; John 12:2).

14 How do we understand "the third time"? Not that the Lord had manifested Himself only on three occasions, for more are recorded even in John's Gospel, including that to Mary. Rather, John is summarising the Lord's manifestations that he has recorded in this Gospel, such manifestations being to groups of the disciples—to the ten in 20:19; to the eleven in 20:26; and to the seven in the present event. This does not rule out the possibility that He revealed Himself to the disciples on further unrecorded occasions. See 4:54 as another example of this writing technique; by "the second miracle" he did not mean that this was the second miracle overall, but just the second miracle accomplished in Cana of Galilee. The fact that John mentioned the number three suggests that he had the subsequent event in mind, when the Lord would question Peter three times.

2. *Peter's Love*
21:15-17

v.15 "So when they had dined, Jesus saith to Simon Peter, Simon, *son* of Jonas, lovest thou me more than these? He saith unto him, Yea, Lord; thou knowest that I love thee. He saith unto him, Feed my lambs.

v.16 He saith to him again the second time, Simon, *son* of Jonas, lovest thou me? He saith unto him, Yea, Lord; thou knowest that I love thee. He saith unto him, Feed my sheep.

v.17 He saith unto him the third time, Simon, *son* of Jonas, lovest thou me? Peter was grieved because he said unto him the third time, Lovest thou me? And he said unto him, Lord, thou knowest all things; thou knowest that I love thee. Jesus saith unto him, Feed my sheep."

This three-fold conversation must be taken in conjunction with the three-fold denial of the Lord by Peter, and with the recorded three-fold manifestation of the Lord to His disciples (though He appeared separately to Peter (Luke 24:34), as Paul has also informed us in 1 Cor 15:5).

14-17 Before looking in detail at this conversation, basing our remarks mainly on the meanings of certain pairs of distinct words, let us note the conversational simplicity of this personal contact between the Lord and Peter.

The Lord speaks. "Lovest thou me more than these?".
Peter speaks. "Yea, Lord; thou knowest that I love thee".
The Lord speaks. "Feed my lambs".
The Lord speaks. "Lovest thou me?".
Peter speaks. "Yea, Lord; thou knowest that I love thee".
The Lord speaks. "Feed my sheep".
The Lord speaks. "Lovest thou me?".
Peter speaks. "Lord, thou knowest all things; thou knowest that I love thee".
The Lord speaks. "Feed my sheep".

Different translations use different words, and for a proper understanding of the conversation it is essential to know why the differences arise. In the following table, we present the five words in question, together with the corresponding Greek words, and the equivalents as found in the AV, RV and JND. Readers possessing other translations can compare them with the table.

		"lovest" *by the Lord*	"love" *by Peter*	"knowest" *by Peter*	"feed" *by the Lord*	"sheep, lambs" *by the Lord*
	Gk	*agapaō*	*phileō*	*oida*	*boskō*	*arnion*
First	AV	lovest	love	knowest	feed	lambs
	RV	lovest	love	knowest	feed	lambs
	JND	lovest	am attached to	knowest[1]	feed	lambs
	Gk	*agapaō*	*phileō*	*oida*	*poimainō*	*probaton*
Second	AV	lovest	love	knowest	feed	sheep
	RV	lovest	love	knowest	tend	sheep
	JND	lovest	am attached to	knowest[1]	shepherd	sheep[4]
	Gk	*phileō*	*phileō*	(1) *oida*	*boskō*	*probaton*
Third	AV	lovest	love	knowest	feed	sheep
	RV	lovest	love	knowest	feed	sheep
	JND	art attached to	am attached to	knowest[1]	feed	sheep[4]
	Gk			(2) *ginōskō*		
	AV			knowest		
	RV			knowest[2]		
	JND			knowest[4]		

Margin, footnotes and Greek text:

[1]conscious knowledge;
[2]perceivest;
[3]objective knowledge;
[4]some Greek texts have *probaton*, a little sheep.

The conversation took place "when they had dined"—strictly this was an early morning meal. The physical needs were met before the deeply spiritual side could commence without distraction. Thus the feeding of the 5 000 took place before the subsequent spiritual teaching (6:5,26); again, supper was ended before the Lord commenced His final discourse in the upper room (13:2).

Vv.15-17 appear to be the restoration of the apostle Peter. Only John has recorded this interview with the Lord (v.20 suggests that the apostle whom Jesus loved was a witness to the conversation). The progress of thought in how the Lord treated Peter can be seen by the following distinctions extracted from the above table.

1. *Love.* Twice the Lord used the appropriate word for the response of love from a disciple. In his answers, Peter used a different word that did not come up to the Lord's expectations. The Lord understood Peter's difficulty, so on the third occasion, He lowered the tone of His question,

and used the word that Peter used. Peter knew why the Lord had done this, and hence he "grieved" that the Lord had to alter His question to suit Peter, and that he could only meet the Lord's remoulded question by his lower standard. The essential difference between the word *agapaō* used twice by the Lord and *phileō* used once by the Lord and three times by Peter can only be decided by consulting comprehensive dictionaries. Certainly *agapaō* is used far more times in John's Gospel than *phileō*. One remarkable fact is that in the expression "the disciple whom Jesus loved", *agapaō* is always used except in 20:2, where *phileō* is used. In his Dictionary Vine asserts that the two words "are never used indiscriminately in the same passage". Godet has compressed the difference in a nutshell: "Peter, with a humility inspired by the memory of his fall, first drops from his answer the last words: 'more than these': then for the term *agapan*, to love, in the sense of veneration, complete, profound, eternal love, he substitutes the word *philein*, to love, in the sense of cherishing friendship, simple personal attachment, devoted affection." One is deeply spiritual; the other in the context touches more the emotions. The Lord's first question contained a comparison, "more than these", that is, did Peter love the Lord more than the other disciples loved Him? for Peter had been guilty of an unspiritual and boasting superiority when he said, "Though all men shall be offended because of thee, yet will I never be offended" (Matt 26:33). Clearly, Peter learnt the lesson, for he wrote later, "whom having not seen, ye love (*agapaō*)" (1 Pet 1:8).

2. *Feed*. Two words are represented by the one. English word "feed" in v.15,16,17 (see the table). At the end of Peter's first and third answer, the Lord used the word *boskō*, to provide food as He had just done with the bread and fish. Of course a spiritual provision is implied (all other uses of the word in the NT are physical). But the word used after Peter's second answer is *poimainō* (similar to "shepherd" (*poimēn*) naturally and spiritually). The word refers to the work of a shepherd in tending to the sheep. Spiritually, the word occurs in Acts 20:28 "to *feed* the church of God" (meaning more than providing food), and in 1 Pet 5:2, "*Feed* the church of God". In other words, Peter had many pastoral reponsibilities given to him by the risen Lord. (The word is also translated "rule" in Rev 2:27; 12:5; 19:15, referring to the Lord's exercise of authority over the nations.)

3. *Lamb, sheep*. The word *arnion* (lamb) occurs only once in John's Gospel, but many times in the Revelation: twenty-eight times as the Lamb, and once (13:11) as describing the second beast. Although the Greek word is diminutive in form, Vine informs us that the word had lost this implication. As applied to the Lord, His sacrifice is seen as completed, yet in the case of believers, Peter was to view them as youthful and needing

provision. But the word *probaton* (sheep) is used twice (and many times in ch.10), evidently standing for believers of more maturity. All need feeding and tending, and the restored Peter was given this responsibility amongst the churches. No doubt the first word refers to his earlier work in the Acts, while the latter word refers to his later ministry in his two epistles. (Other Greek texts use the word *probation*, a diminutive form, carrying with it a sense of endearment to the Lord, since they belonged to Him.)

4. *Know*. There are two different words used by Peter. The former (*oida*) appears hundreds of times in the NT, often meaning "see". The latter, used once by Peter here (*ginōskō*) also appears many times in the NT. The former suggests a fulness, "thou knowest all things", applicable to the absolute knowledge of Deity. The latter suggests progress and perception; Peter was asking the Lord to recall that, throughout His years of ministry, he, Peter, had grown in grace and love in spite of several examples of weakness. Peter appealed to the Lord's knowledge, apparently gained through daily watching him, his life, service and his testimony.

5. *Saith, said*. Two tenses are used in these verses. These two tenses, present and past (aorist) are faithfully reproduced in the AV, RV and JND, but, for example, the NEB uses the past tense throughout the paragraph. (The past tense "said" occurs twice in the middle of v.17.) The frequent use of the present tense "he saith" (and other verbs), when strictly the action was in the past, is characteristic of NT Greek, a feature called by the grammarians "the historic present", and can be used for the sake of vividness. Certainly the reader of the AV will gain this impression, which is quite absent when the NEB is read. See, for example, 1:29, "John seeth Jesus coming unto him" (AV); "he saw Jesus coming towards him" (NEB). One sparkles with life; the other is blunt and dull.

17 By saying, "thou knoweth all things", Peter made a desperate confession of his realisation of the absolute knowledge of Deity, for all things are naked and opened unto Him (Heb 4:13). John has stressed this knowledge of the Lord in his Gospel, "Jesus knowing that the Father had given all things into his hands..." (13:3); "Now are we sure that thou knowest all things" (16:30); "knowing all things that should come upon him" (18:4); "knowing that all things were now accomplished" (19:28).

3. *The Apostles' Future Foretold*
21:18-25

v.18 "Verily, verily, I say unto thee, When thou wast young, thou girdedst thyself, and walkedst whither thou wouldest: but when thou shalt be old, thou shalt stretch forth thy hands, and another shall gird thee, and carry *thee* whither thou wouldest not.

v.19 This spake he, signifying by what death he should glorify God. And when he had spoken this, he saith unto him, Follow me.
v.20 Then Peter, turning about, seeth the disciple whom Jesus loved following; which also leaned on his breast at supper, and said, Lord, which is he that betrayeth thee?
v.21 Peter seeing him saith to Jesus, Lord, and what *shall* this man *do*?
v.22 Jesus saith unto him, If I will that he tarry till I come, what *is that* to thee? follow thou me.
v.23 Then went this saying abroad among the brethren, that that disciple should not die: yet Jesus said not unto him, He shall not die; but, If I will that he tarry till I come, what *is that* to thee?
v.24 This is the disciple which testifieth of these things, and wrote these things: and we know that his testimony is true.
v.25 And there are also many other things which Jesus did, the which, if they should be written every one, I suppose that even the world itself could not contain the books that should be written. Amen."

18 *The Lord speaks.* The Lord now exhibited His knowledge of the past and the future. His words form an indirect way of showing how Peter would finally redeem his denial, in spite of faithful service to be accomplished over many years. Three stages in Peter's life are implied in vv.18-19.

1. The past in Peter's experience—the liberty of youth, with his will dominant ("whither thou wouldest").

2. The present in Peter's experience, as a servant of Christ: "Follow me" (v.18). This recalls the first "Follow me" spoken to Peter in Matt 4:19.

3. The final future in Peter's experience—death by crucifixion. The words "old", "stretch forth thine hands", and "carry thee whither thou wouldest not" all imply crucifixion. The word "gird" refers to a loin cloth, which was all that was allowed for crucifixion. Towards the end of his life, the apostle recalled these words of the Lord, "Knowing that shortly I must put off this my tabernacle, even as our Lord Jesus Christ hath showed me" (2 Pet 1:14). He would thereby follow his Master even to the end.

The record of Peter's death is not given in the NT, neither is that of Paul though he anticipated it in 2 Tim 4:6. The apocryphal "Acts of Peter", written apparently by someone in Asia Minor about AD 200, contains an account of the martyrdom of Peter. This martyrdom account (preserved in Greek, Latin, Coptic, Slavonic, Syriac, Armenian, Arabic, Ethiopic), which certainly does not necessarily correspond to the actual facts, informs us that Peter was crucified upside down, after which he preached a lengthy sermon.

19 The apostle John here interpreted the Lord's words as applying to the death of Peter—the means whereby he would "*glorify* God". It was the same when the Lord gave His own life—"the hour is come . . . that thy Son may also *glorify* thee" (17:1). This explanation may have been written by John more than twenty years after Peter's death, but it is not obvious whether John knew the explanation prior to Peter's decease, or whether he realised the meaning afterwards. Peter, at least, seemed to know the meaning by the words in v.21.

The Lord speaks. This crucifixion of the apostle was the supreme reversal of his denial. Thus the words "Follow me" applied not only to the service of Peter in his subsequent life, but also to his death in following the Lord as to the method of death. Peter had claimed in 13:37 that he would follow the Lord even to the laying down of his life. The Lord stated that Peter would indeed follow Him afterwards, but not "now". Words spoken in haste had to be fulfilled afterwards. A boasting "I will" may yield its painful penalty later.

20 Peter understood, but was immediately curious about the others, particularly about the apostle John. No doubt he chose John because he was opposite in character to Peter. The latter had denied the Lord with lack of courage, but John had been the boldest at the Lord's trial, and had stood by the Lord's cross. Would John have to suffer like Peter, or would he escape? Again, note John's method of self-identification in the verse; he used three personal features to identify himself:

1. "The disciple whom Jesus loved".

2. The one who "leaned on his breast at supper".

3. The one who said, "Lord, which is he that betrayeth thee?".

This showed his special affection and his special nearness to the Lord, facts that the apostle must have cherished to the end of his life.

21 *Peter speaks.* Peter looked at John, but spoke to the Lord. The AV translation "what shall this man do?" arises from the Greek *houtos de ti*, namely, "but what this one?"; the RV follows the AV, but JND gives "and what (of) this (man)?". There is no thought of John "doing" anything, but rather of what would happen to John.

22 *The Lord speaks.* Commentators differ in their interpretation of the Lord's words, "If I will that he tarry till I come, what is that to thee? follow *thou* me", depending on how they view the doctrine of the Lord's return. At least the Lord implies that the matter was between Himself and John, and not between Himself and Peter. His responsibility was to follow the Lord, and this command is stressed over and above that contained in v.19, with the word "thou" being added. Some commentators state that the Lord meant that John was not to have a violent death like Peter. Others suggest that John was not to die until after 70 AD when Jerusalem was destroyed. Others assert that the coming referred to was that to John on the isle of Patmos (Rev 1:10-20). We feel that the Lord intended Peter and John to realise that it was not the divine will for men to know the circumstances of their death long beforehand, but instead to have the hope of the near return of the Lord to be prominently in their thoughts and aspirations. If John were to pass through 1 000 generations, and if 1 000 disciples were to die like Peter, then John's decease was of no concern to Peter. Each had to follow as He leads. There are other verses relating to the time until the Lord comes:

1. 1 Cor 11:36, remembrance: "ye do show the Lord's death till he come".

2. Luke 19:13, service: "Occupy till I come".

3. Rev 2:25, faithfulness: "hold fast till I come".

4. John 21:22, anticipation.

Note that the tarrying is on the part of John, not on the part of the Lord (Heb 10:37): "yet a little while, and he that shall come will come, and will not tarry". The phrase "if the Lord tarry" is hardly scriptural.

These words of the Lord form His last recorded words in this Gospel.

23 A misunderstanding then developed amongst "the brethren", something that happened now and again amongst the disciples during the Lord's lifetime. They still contemplated the future naturally, instead of spiritually. They could see in the Lord's words that John would not die, but John flatly contradicted this interpretation, for the Lord's words could not possibly have had this meaning. Rather, there was a spiritual meaning in the words—the Lord spoke of His promised coming again which should be prominently before the hope and aspirations of all believers. John maintained this blessed hope till old age, when he wrote, "we know that, when he shall appear, we shall be like him; for we shall see him as he is" (1 John 3:2). John wrote this Gospel in his old age, when he was still patiently waiting for the blessed hope. Effectively John closed the Gospel at this point. In Matthew, the Gospel closed with witnessing (Matt 28:19-20); in Mark with the Lord still working (Mark 16:19-20); in Luke with the disciples worshipping (Luke 24:52-53), and in John with the believers waiting.

24 By way of conclusion, John presented himself (namely, as "the disciple") as witnessing and writing. It is good personally to know when one's work is acceptable to God and beneficial to His people. Yet he added to his personal testimony, "*we* know that his testimony is true". This concluding "we" should be compared with the beginning "we", "*we* beheld his glory" (1:14), where it is obvious that the apostles are meant, and with 19:35 where John wrote that "*his* testimony is true"—in the singular and not the plural. What did John mean by "we"? Some suggest that the Gospel was written in Ephesus, and that the Ephesian elders added their own testimony to that of John; the original elders had been well taught by Paul (Acts 20:27). On the other hand, we feel that by "we" John sought to bring all his readers into the overall umbrella of accepting the truth of the Gospel record. It is the repercussion of 20:31; those who believe can then say that all John's testimony is true. This therefore refutes the validity of any critical comments on John's record.

25 In 20:30 the apostle wrote that the Lord did many other signs—this refers to His resurrection signs. But here in our verse 25, the "many other things" refer to the events in His lifetime. In Matt 1:1, we read of "The book"; in Luke 1:1 many books had been written, but here in our verse 25 there is an infinite number of books. The libraries of the world, past and present, contain millions and millions of books (duplicated in their thousands since the advent of printing), on a vast number of developing subjects. But the events in the Lord's life of ministry and teaching far exceed the knowledge and writings of men. We have all that is necessary for the formation and development of faith, but heaven contains the record of the totality of the Lord's life and works, a record that the world could not possibly contain. Certainly the temple could not contain Him (1 Kings 8:27). There was also "the volume of the book" in which the heart of the Lord was recorded, whereby He came to do the will of God even unto sacrifice (Heb 10:7). And we are not left out of the record in heaven. For the lives of God's people are in "thy book" (Ps 56:8); "a book of remembrance was written" before the Lord concerning those who feared Him (Mal 3:16); the names of the saints are "in the book of life" (Phil 4:3); while the divine purpose in judgment on unregenerate men is contained in the book sealed with seven seals (Rev 5:1). Many other references exist concerning records on high, some applying to believers and others not, but as we are occupied with the Gospel records of the Lord Jesus, our faith is strengthened and our worship is deepened.